CSI:
CRIME SCENE INVESTIGATION™

MORTAL WOUNDS

Original novels in the CSI series:

CSI:

CRIME SCENE INVESTIGATION™

MORTAL WOUNDS

Max Allan Collins

Based on the hit television series
"CSI: CRIME SCENE INVESTIGATION" produced by
CBS Productions, a business unit of CBS Broadcasting, Inc.
in association with Jerry Bruckheimer Television

Executive Producers: Jerry Bruckheimer, Carol Mendelsohn,
Anthony E. Zuiker, Naren Shankar, Cynthia Chvatal,
William Petersen, Jonathan Littman

Series created by: Anthony E. Zuiker

POCKET BOOKS
New York London Toronto Sydney

Pocket Books
A Division of Simon & Schuster, Inc.
1230 Avenue of the Americas, New York, NY 10020

First Pocket Books trade paperback edition November 2007

POCKET and colophon are registered trademarks of Simon & Schuster, Inc.

For information about special discounts for bulk purchases,
please contact Simon & Schuster Special Sales at
1-800-456-6798 or business@simonandschuster.com.

Manufactured in the United States of America

10   9   8   7   6   5   4   3   2   1

Designed by Claudia Martinez

ISBN-13: 978-1-4391-4889-1
ISBN-10:   1-4391-4889-9

Table of Contents

DOUBLE DEALER

In memory of our friend
David R. Collins
author, teacher, mentor

M.A.C. and M.V.C.

"With a scientific third degree,
the master criminalist
makes the physical evidence talk,
wringing confessions from blood, guns, narcotics
hair, fibers, metal slivers,
tire marks, took marks, and bullets."

—JACK WEBB

1

The siren's squeal split the morning, the flashing blue-then-red-then-blue dashboard light reflecting off other cars as the black Chevy Tahoe weaved its way through rush-hour traffic on US 95. The sun was rising orange and bright, tinting the clouds pink, and the air conditioning within the SUV was already grappling with the July heat.

In the passenger seat sat Gil Grissom, graveyard-shift supervisor of the Las Vegas Criminalistics Bureau. In the driver's seat was Warrick Brown—rank CSI3, just one notch under Grissom—and in back was another member of their team, Sara Sidle, rank CSI2. Warrick sawed the steering wheel right and left as he dodged between cars, his expression impassive. He might have been watching paint dry.

Grissom's boyishly handsome features were slightly compromised by the gray encroaching on his brown hair, and crow's feet were sneaking up on the edges of his eyes, frown lines etching inroads at the corners of his mouth. The politics of this job had taken their toll on Grissom of late. As much as he loved the science of investigation, the constant jousting with day-shift supervisor Conrad Ecklie, the strain on his budget, and the pressures of management had started to age the perennially youthful Grissom. This reality was aided and abetted by the fact that, even though he had never needed much sleep, now he hardly got any at all.

The SUV hurtled toward a small Honda. Warrick slashed to the right, barely missed a FedEx truck, then bounced back left, coming within inches of a blue Lincoln stretch limo.

From the back, Sara yelled, "Geez, Warrick, he's not gonna get more dead. Slow down."

Warrick ignored her remark and jumped into the diamond lane to pass a cab, then hopped back into his own lane.

"Why didn't you let me drive?" Sara asked her boss as she bounced around, her seat belt straining. "Grissom, will you say something to him?"

Ignoring the exchange, Grissom turned his gaze toward the reddish sky. Quietly, without even realizing he was talking, Grissom said, "Red sky at night, sailor's delight—red sky at morning, sailor take warning."

Sara leaned forward. "What was that, Grissom?"

He shook his head as he studied the clouds. "Nothing."

"Please tell me that wasn't an aphorism," she said. "Please tell me you're not spouting quotes while this maniac is—"

"Sailors?" Warrick asked. "Gris, we're in the desert."

"Shut up," Sara snapped, "and keep your eyes on the road."

Warrick shot her a glance in the rearview mirror, twitched a half-smirk, and crossed all three lanes of traffic, jerking the wheel to the right as they turned onto Decatur Boulevard. Seconds later the SUV squealed to a halt in front of the Beachcomber Hotel and Casino.

"Six minutes, twenty-seven seconds," Warrick said as he threw open his door, bestowing on his boss a tiny self-satisfied smile. "How's that for response time?"

As the limber driver turned to jump out of the truck, Grissom gripped Warrick's shoulder, startling him a little. Grissom kept his voice quiet, even friendly, but firm. "From now on, unless I say otherwise, you obey the speed limit—okay, Mario?"

Warrick gave him a sheepish smile. "Yeah, Gris—sorry."

In the backseat, Sara shook her head in disgust, her ID necklace swinging as she muttered a string of curses. As she climbed out, dragging a small black suitcase of equipment with her, she said, "Gonna get us all killed, then who's going to investigate our scene? I mean, we'll all be dead."

Grissom turned and looked over his sunglasses at her, through the open back door. She got the message and piped down.

Warrick grabbed his own black suitcase from the back of the vehicle and fell in next to Sara. Climbing down, Grissom—carrying his silver flight-case-style field kit—led the way. This early, the sidewalk was nearly empty in front of the hotel, the doormen outnumbering the guests. The little group was almost to the front door when Captain Jim Brass materialized to fall in step with Grissom.

Brass said, "The hotel manager wants to know how soon we're going to be out of there."

"Why?"

Brass blinked his sad eyes. "Why? So he can let the guests move in and out of their rooms on that floor."

Shaking his head, Grissom asked, "What'd you tell him?"

Brass shrugged. "As soon as we possibly can."

A rotund doorman stepped forward and opened the big glass front door for them. Sunglasses came off as they moved through the gaudy lobby—Grissom tuning out the sounds of spinning slots, rolling roulette balls, dealers calling cards, the typical dinging and ringing casino cacophony—and Brass led them to the right, toward a gleaming bank of elevators.

"Where's the vic?" Warrick asked.

"Fourth floor," Brass said. "Right there in the hall, outside his hotel room door, shot twice in the head, small caliber, a .22 or a .25 maybe. Looks like a mob hit, might be a robbery got outa hand."

"We'll see," Grissom said, never interested in theories so early. "Is there videotape?"

Most of the resort hotels on the Strip had video cameras in every hall, but not all the ones off the Strip, like the Beachcomber, had caught up.

Brass nodded. "It's set up in the main security room—waiting for you, whenever you're ready."

When they were safely alone in the elevator, away from guests and staff, Grissom turned to Brass. "You tell the manager we'll be done when we're done. I don't care if he has to use a cherry picker to get these people out of their rooms, they're not going to disturb my crime scene. The hotel gets it back when my people have finished with it."

Brass held up his hands in surrender. "Okay, okay, I'll tell him. I just wanted to save the guy for you to alienate."

Taking a deep breath, Grissom let his head drop a little as he exhaled. "Tell him we'll work as fast as we can, but this is not fast work."

The elevator dinged, the door slid open, and it began. Stepping out, Grissom looked to his left where Detective Erin Conroy, stood interviewing a twenty-something young man who wore a white shirt, black bow tie and black slacks—a waiter.

The CSI group paused to snap on their latex gloves.

"Guy's a spitting image for David Copperfield," Warrick said softly, behind Grissom.

"The waiter," Sara said, amused. "Yeah—spot on."

Grissom turned to them. "Who?"

Sara's eyebrows climbed. "Grissom—you live in Vegas and you don't know who David Copperfield is?"

"A Dickens character," Grissom said. "Is this pertinent?"

Sara and Warrick, silenced, exchanged glances.

Moving forward, Brass on his left, Warrick and Sara behind him, Grissom stopped in front of a uniformed officer on watch at the near end of the crime scene. Beyond the officer, Grissom saw the body slumped in a doorway alcove; a large, circular, silver tray lay on the carpet across the hall; and spaghetti, meat sauce, and the components of a tossed green salad lay scattered everywhere. A white carnation, spilled out of its vase, lay at the corpse's feet like an impromptu funeral offering.

"Anyone been through here since you arrived?" Grissom asked.

Garcia shook his head. He pointed to a rangy officer at the other end of the hall. "My partner, Patterson, had the manager let him up the fire stairs down there."

"Good work."

"Thank you, sir."

Turning to Brass, Grissom asked, "Any idea who our victim is?"

"Sure—'John Smith.' "

Grissom raised an eyebrow.

Brass shrugged elaborately. "That's how he registered. Paid for everything in cash too."

"Right. You check for a wallet?"

Brass shook his head. "Waiting for you to clear the scene. I used to have your job, remember?"

Brass had indeed been the CSI supervisor until not so long ago; he'd been something of a prick, in fact, but had mellowed since returning to Homicide.

Grissom asked, "Your people canvassing the guests?"

"They're on it now—they started at either end, so they don't disturb the scene."

"Good call. And?"

"Nobody saw anything, nobody heard anything."

Stepping in carefully, Grissom bent over the body.

Lying on his stomach, head just slightly to one side, his brown eyes open, glazed, staring at nothing, John Smith looked surprised more than anything else. Cautiously, Grissom changed position to better see the wound. Clean, double tap, small caliber; Brass was probably right—a .25. The odd thing was the placement. Two small holes formed a colon in the center back of John Smith's skull, and—if Grissom didn't miss his bet—almost exactly one inch between them.

Grissom felt gingerly for a wallet, found nothing, gave up and rose; then he turned to his CSIs. "Footprints first, you know the drill. If this guy wasn't Peter Pan, he left his mark."

Warrick nodded, alertness in the seemingly sleepy eyes. "All comes down to shoe prints."

"Yep," Sara said.

Grissom stepped aside so Warrick and Sara and their field kits could pass. "Sara, you do the fingerprints. Warrick the photos."

"Good thing I skipped breakfast," Sara said.

"Least there's no bugs yet," Warrick said to her. Bugs and larva were about the only thing that threw the strong-spined Sidle.

"I wouldn't bet on that," Grissom said. "This hotel might not like it, but our little friends are here."

Sara and Warrick began by scouring the entire crime scene for footprints. This would take a while, so Grissom followed Brass over to where policewoman Conroy stood with the waiter.

Flicking the badge on his breast pocket, Brass said to the waiter, "I'm Captain Brass and this is CSI Supervisor Grissom."

The skinny dark-haired waiter nodded to them.

Conroy, her voice flat, said, "This is Robert LaFay. . . ."

"Bobby," the man interjected.

She went on as if he hadn't spoken. ". . . a room-service waiter. He was taking an order to room . . ." She checked her notes. ". . . four-twenty, but he never made it. Ran into the killer."

Turning sharply to the waiter, Grissom asked, "Mr. LaFay . . . Bobby—you *saw* the killer?"

LaFay shrugged his narrow shoulders. "Sort of . . . not really. He was standing over the body, his back to me. Jesus, the guy was already down and he shot him again, right in the back of the head! Then he heard me and turned around, and blocked his face with his arm—you know, like Dracula with his cape?"

"Bobby, did you get any kind of look at his face?"

"No. Not really."

"Was he a big man, small man, average?"

"Mostly what I saw was the gun. It seemed so big and it was the second gun I'd seen tonight."

Grissom and Brass exchanged glances, and the former said, "Second gun?"

The waiter nodded. "Up in eight-thirteen. Big guy, had a cannon on his nightstand. He said he was FBI, but . . ."

"FBI?" Brass said, incredulously.

"You didn't believe him?" Grissom asked.

"Nope."

Grissom gave Brass another quick look, then returned his attention to LaFay. "So, you saw the killer here—and then?"

His eyes widened. "Then I took the hell off toward the elevator and I guess he went the other way."

"Down the hall?"

"Yeah. Anyway, he didn't shoot at me that I know of."

Brass said, "Bobby, wouldn't you know if you were shot at?"

"I'm not sure. That gun wasn't very loud."

Eyebrows up, Brass asked, "No?"

"No. Loud enough to scare the crap outa me, though."

Brass grunted a laugh, but Grissom was thinking he'd have to tell Warrick to dust that stairwell. "Can you tell us *anything* about the killer?"

"I didn't see him good at all."

"Think, Bobby. Close your eyes and visualize."

LaFay did as he was told, his brow furrowing. "White guy."

"Good. What else do you see, Bobby?"

"Older guy."

"Older?"

"Forty maybe, maybe even older."

Feeling suddenly ancient, Grissom nodded his encouragement. "Anything else? Scars? Tattoos?"

The waiter shook his head. "Nope."

"What was he wearing? Shut your eyes, Bobby. Visualize."

". . . Jacket—a suit coat." His eyes popped open and he grinned. "I remember that! 'cause afterward, when I had time to think about it, I wondered why anybody would wear a suit coat in Vegas in July."

"Good, good—anything else?"

"Nope. Mr. Grissom, I can close my eyes till tomorrow this time, and I won't see anything else."

Grissom granted the waiter a smile, touched his arm encouragingly. "Mr. LaFay, do you think you could identify the killer?"

The waiter thought for a moment, looked at Grissom and shook his head slowly. "No. . . . That good I can't visualize."

Grissom and Brass thanked him, then rejoined Warrick and Sara. They found Warrick kneeling over something on the floor as, nearby, Sara carefully bagged a piece of tomato.

"Got anything?" Grissom asked.

"I've got a footprint in the blood," Warrick said, "but it's smeared, like the guy slipped trying to take off."

Carefully stepping around Sara, Grissom moved in next to Warrick and followed Warrick's gaze.

Warrick was right: the footprint was useless. Turning on his haunches and lowering his head, Grissom carefully studied the hallway. "Look," he said pointing another three feet down the hall, behind Warrick. "Another one."

Warrick got to it, checked it, then turned back to Grissom. "Smeared too."

His head still bent down near the floor, Grissom said, "Go another yard."

"I don't see anything."

"Ever use Leuco Crystal Violet?"

Warrick shrugged. "Yeah, sure, but it's been a while."

Grissom grinned. "Now's your chance to get back in practice."

Brass walked up as Warrick withdrew a spray bottle from his black field-kit bag. "What's that?"

"See the spot on the carpeting?" Grissom asked.

The detective shrugged. "All I see is a dirty carpet."

"There's a bloody footprint there."

"Really."

"Yes—we just can't see it."

Brass frowned. "A bloody footprint we can't see?"

"The red cells have all been rubbed off the shoe, but the hemoglobin and white cells remain."

Warrick carefully sprayed an area of the rug and picked up the lecture. "This is Leuco Crystal Violet—a powder. But here today on the Home Shopping Network, we've added it to a solution of sulfosalicylic acid, sodium acetate, and hydrogen peroxide."

With a small chuckle, Brass asked, "If it's going to explode, you mind giving me a heads up?"

As the solution began to work, Grissom jumped back in. "It's going to work like a dye and bring out the footprint in that dirty carpet."

"No way."

"Way," Grissom said as the spot on the floor turned purple, showing the outline of a running shoe.

"About a size eleven, I'd say," Warrick said. "Now we photograph it."

Brass asked, "Can you match that to anything?"

Grissom nodded. "Once we get it back to the lab, we'll tell you exactly what kind of shoe that print belongs to. After the database tells *us*, that is. Then, when we get a suspect, we'll be able to compare this to a shoe of his and give you an exact match."

"Hey, Grissom," Sara called. "All I'm finding is pasta and a salad. And let me tell you, the buffet at Caesar's is better."

"Keep digging, anyway. And, Warrick?"

Warrick's head bobbed up. "Yeah, Gris?"

"Make sure you do the stairwell—that's the way Elvis left the building."

Warrick nodded.

"So—mob hit?" Brass asked.

Grissom led Brass back up the hall toward the elevators. "Too soon to tell."

"Robbery gone wrong?"

Grissom ignored the question. "Let's go see the videotape."

"Go ahead," Brass said. "I'll join you after I head upstairs and talk to that guy first."

Grissom's eyes tightened. "Our FBI man with the cannon?"

"Precisely."

"The tape can wait. I'll come with you."

"Fine. You interface so well with the FBI, after all."

Upstairs, Brass led the way out of the elevator. Grissom slid in next to him as they moved down the hall toward room 813. Pulling his service revolver from its holster, Brass signaled for Grissom to hang back out of the alcove.

Frowning, Grissom stopped short of the doorway as Brass moved into the alcove and knocked on the door with his left hand.

"Just a sec," said a muffled voice beyond the door.

His feet set, Brass leveled his .38 at the door, which thankfully had no peephole. Peeking around the corner, Grissom watched as the door cracked slowly open. He saw the big man in boxer shorts—and the monstrous automatic in his beefy hand.

And Grissom said, "Gun!"

Brass ducked out of the alcove, plastered himself to the wall, away from the door, and yelled, "Police! Put that gun down, and open the door, and put your hands up—high!"

Silence.

"Do it now!" Brass said.

The door opened and the big man—hands way up—stepped back. His expression was one of alarm, and he was nodding toward the nearby bed, on which the pistol had been tossed.

"I'm unarmed!" he said. "Unarmed . . ."

Brass forced the big man up against a wall.

"Spread 'em."

He did as he was told and Grissom eased into the room behind the pair as Brass frisked the man.

"Why the gun, sir?" Grissom asked, his voice cool.

Over his shoulder, the big man said, "I deliver jewelry. It's for protection."

Brass jumped in. "Did you know a murder was committed downstairs this morning?"

The man looked thunderstruck. "No! Hell no! You don't . . . you don't think *I* did it?"

Grissom moved forward. "Let's slow down for a moment. What's your name, sir?"

"Ron Orrie."

"ID?" Brass asked.

Orrie nodded toward the nightstand. "My wallet's right there."

"Do you have a permit for the pistol?"

"In the wallet, too."

Grissom studied the gun for a moment, a .45. "Is this your only handgun?"

Looking nervous, Orrie nodded. "Only one I have with me."

Glancing toward Brass, Grissom shook his head. "Wrong weapon. Too big. John Smith was killed with something smaller."

Brass didn't seem so eager to let Orrie off the hook. "Why did you tell the waiter you were with the FBI?"

Orrie shrugged. "I didn't want to explain my business. The more people that know what I do, the better chance I'll get knocked over. It was my own damn fault. Normally, I wouldn't have left the gun laying out. But I'd ordered breakfast from room service and he showed up before I was completely dressed and had it holstered."

The detective looked skeptical.

Grissom thumbed through the wallet, finding a New Jersey driver's license and concealed weapons permits from both Jersey and New York. "You are in fact Ronald Eugene Orrie," Grissom said as he compared the photo on the license to the man, "and you have up-to-date concealed weapons permits."

"I know."

"With your permission, I'd like to have your hands checked for residue."

"What . . . what kind of residue?"

"The kind a gun leaves when you fire it."

"I haven't fired a gun in months!"

"Good. Any objection?"

"No . . . no."

"Thank you. Someone from criminalistics will come to see you, within the hour."

The man winced. "But can you make me stay in this room? I don't mean to be uncooperative, but . . ."

A frown seemed to involve Brass's whole body, not just his mouth. His whole demeanor said, *I knew it couldn't be this easy,* and Grissom's eyes replied, *They never are.*

Brass said, "Mr. Orrie, do you have a concealed weapons permit from the state of Nevada?"

Orrie shook his head.

"Then you know you can't leave this room with that gun, correct?"
The man nodded.

"If I catch you on the street with it, I'm going to bust you."

"Yes, sir."

"And don't tell anyone else you're with the FBI."

"No, sir . . . I mean, yes, sir."

"And wait here until somebody from the crime lab comes to see you."

"Yes, sir."

"And if we decide to search your hotel room, will you require us to get a warrant?"

"No, sir."

"Are we done here?" Grissom asked.

Brass still seemed to want to hang on to the only suspect he had. Finally, he said, "Yeah, we're done."

Grissom said, "Let's go look at the tapes."

2

Nick Stokes, at the wheel of the crime lab's twin black Chevy Tahoe, threw a smile and a glance out his window, as if someone on the sidelines of his life might be able to make sense of it—a ref, maybe. "Can you believe this shit?" Nick asked, as he drove up the Strip in medium traffic. "Only fifteen minutes before the end of shift!"

In the passenger seat, Catherine Willows's reddish-blonde hair bounced as she shushed him, her cell phone in hand. Catherine tapped numbers into the phone and punched SEND, then waited impatiently.

The phone was picked up on the third ring. "Hello."

"Mrs. Goodwin?" Catherine asked.

"Yes?"

"It's Catherine. We caught a case. Can you get Lindsey off to school?"

The woman's voice was warm, even through the cell phone. "Sure, no problem."

"How is she?"

"Sleeping like an angel."

Catherine felt a heaviness in her chest and a burning behind her eyes. "Thanks, Mrs. Goodwin. I owe you."

"Don't be silly," Mrs. Goodwin said, "we'll be fine," and hung up.

She'd no sooner pressed the END button on her phone than Nick started again on his litany of woe.

"Do you know who was going to meet me for breakfast after shift?"

"Surprise me."

"A cheerleader."

"Really."

"Yeah, a beautiful UNLV cheerleader."

"As opposed to one of those homely UNLV cheerleaders."

"Now I gotta miss breakfast. This girl was getting out of bed for me."

Despite her anxiety over Lindsey, Catherine couldn't help but laugh. "No comment."

A chagrined smile flickered across Nick's well-chiseled features.

Catherine liked the idea that Nick finally seemed to be coming out of his shell; though the demands of the job kept her—and Nick—from thinking about their own problems, giving them focus, she knew that crime scene investigation was also the kind of work from which you should have at least an occasional break. She'd finally learned as much, and she hoped that now Nick would too.

She asked him, "What do we know about this call?"

Shaking his head, Nick said, "Some construction workers got an early start today, trying to beat the heat. They found a body under a junky old trailer."

"New body, or junky old body?"

"That's all I know, Cath."

They passed the Mandalay Bay, crossed Russell Road, and turned into the construction site for the new Romanov Hotel and Casino. Supposedly the Strip's next great resort, Romanov would play thematically on the opulence of Czarist Russia, the main building modeled after Nicholas and Alexandra's palace in St. Petersburg, featuring rooms based on those of the actual palace. And if Catherine knew anything about Vegas, the joint would also have dancing Rasputins and Anastasias.

Right now, however, a construction crew had been engaged to clear away debris from the years the lot had stood vacant and become something of a dumping ground. The sun glinted off metallic garbage and presented a rocky, rubble-strewn landscape more suited for Mad Max than Russian royalty. A line of pickups on the far side told her that a pretty good-sized crew was working at the site.

She spotted a semicircle of construction workers standing around the remnants of an old mobile home trailer, staring at something on the ground. Behind them a few feet sat an idling hydraulic excavator, its bucket still hanging over the back of a dump truck where it had been left by its operator. Off to one side, maybe twenty yards away, sat two black-and-whites, the patrolmen leaning against them, sipping coffee, shooting the breeze. Beyond that squatted the unmarked Ford of an LVPD detective.

Nick braked the SUV to a stop near the yellow dump truck. Catherine threw open the door only to be met by a wall of heat that told her she'd be sorry for leaving the comfort of the air-conditioned truck. Nick piled out the other side, they grabbed their field kits, and Catherine led the way to the huddle of men.

Burly, crew-cut Sergeant O'Riley separated from the construction workers and met them halfway.

"Never seen anything like it," he said.

"What?" Nick asked.

"The guy's a damned mummy."

"A mummy," Catherine said.

O'Riley extended his arms, monster fashion. "You know. A mummy."

Nick shrugged at Catherine. "A mummy."

She smirked at him. "Come on, daddy-o. . . ."

The cluster of construction workers split and made room for them to pass.

The rusted hulk of the former trailer looked as though God had reached down and pulled out a fistful of its guts. Through the hole, beneath what was left of the floor, something vaguely human stared upward with dark eye sockets in what looked like a brown leather head.

"Anybody gone in there?" she asked.

The construction workers shook their heads; some stepped backward.

She set down her field kit and turned to O'Riley. Sweat ran down his face in long rivulets, his color starting to match that of his grotesque sports coat. "You wanna fill me in, Sergeant?"

"The crew came in at four-thirty. Trying to get ahead, work when it was cooler, so they could knock off at noon."

Catherine nodded. It was a common practice in a desert community where the afternoon heat index would probably top 130 degrees.

"They'd only been at it about an hour or so when they found the mummy," O'Riley said, waving toward the trailer.

"Okay, get a couple of uniforms to cordon off the area."

O'Riley nodded.

"We want to make sure that he's the only one."

Frowning, O'Riley said, "The only one?"

Pulling out her camera and checking it, Catherine said, "A lot of stuff's been dumped here over the years, Sarge. Let's make sure there's only been one body discarded."

Nick, at her side, said, "You think we got Gacy's backyard here?"

"Could be. Can't rule it out."

O'Riley called to the uniforms and they tossed their coffee cups into a barrel and plodded toward him.

"Oh," she said, lightly, "and you might as well send the construction workers home. We're going to be here most of the day."

Nodding, O'Riley spoke briefly to the uniforms, then talked to the foreman, and slowly the scene turned from a still life into a moving picture. The workers dispersed, their dusty pickups driving off in every direction as the patrolmen strung yellow crime-scene tape around the junk-infested lot.

"Times like this," Nick said, as the yellow-and-black boundary took form, "I wish I'd invested in the company that makes crime-scene tape."

"It's right in there with the smiley face," she agreed.

Catherine stepped into blue coveralls, from her suitcaselike field kit, and zipped them up; she was all for gathering evidence, just not on her clothes. She put on a yellow hard hat, the fitted band feeling cool around her head, for a few seconds anyway.

While Nick and the others searched the surrounding area, Catherine took photos of the trailer. She started with wide shots and slowly moved in closer and closer to the leathery corpse. By the time she was ready to move inside the wreck, with the body, Nick had returned and the cops were back to standing around.

"Anything?" she asked as she reloaded the camera and set it on the hood of the Tahoe.

"No," Nick said. "Our 'mummy' has the place to himself."

"Okay, I'm going in." She pulled on a pair of latex gloves and picked up her camera again.

"Careful."

Catherine tossed him a look.

"I'm just saying, Cath, it's rusty metal, unstable . . ."

"I've had my tetanus shot."

Entering through a huge bitelike hole in the trailer's skin, she picked her way through the rubble, slipped through the gash in the floor and slid down next to the body, half of it now exposed to the sunlight pouring in through the wide tear in the roof. The ground felt cooler in the pools of shadow beneath the trailer. She noticed hardly any smell from the cadaver and, judging from the condition of the skin, he'd been dead for quite a long time.

"White male," she said, snapping the first of half a dozen photos.

Outside, Nick repeated her words as he wrote them in his notebook.

Finishing the photos, she set the camera to one side. The body had been laid to rest on top of a piece of sheet metal, probably a slab of the trashed trailer's skin, and slid in under the dilapidated derelict. Though the killer had hidden the body well, he'd also managed to protect it so that instead of rotting, the corpse had mummified in the dry Nevada air.

They did indeed have a mummy of sorts.

Moving carefully, Catherine examined the body from skull to oxblood loafers. The eyes and soft tissue were gone, leaving empty sockets, and the skin had contracted around the bone, resembling discolored beef jerky. Shocks of salt-and-pepper hair remained and the teeth were still intact. *Good.*

The clothes had held up surprisingly well, though the narrow-lapeled suit had probably faded from popularity well before this poor guy ended up buried in it. She checked the victim's coat pockets as best she could and found nothing. She could tell, even through the clothes, that some of the man's organs had survived. Shrunk, but survived. It wasn't that unusual in a case like this. Moving down, she went through the corpse's pants pockets.

"No wallet," she called.

Nick repeated her words.

In the front left pocket she found a handful of change and counted it quickly. "Two-fifteen in change, the newest coin a nineteen-eighty-four quarter." She put the coins in an evidence bag, sealed it, and set it to one side.

Again, Nick repeated what she had said.

She looked at the victim's hands and said, "He'll never play the piano again."

"What?"

Shaking her head, she said, "The killer hacked off the victim's fingertips at the first knuckle."

"Trying to make it harder to ID the guy if anybody ever found the body," Nick said.

"Yeah, looks like he used pruning shears or something. Pretty clean amputations, but there's a gold ring that got left behind."

Picking up the camera, she snapped off several quick shots of the mummy's hands showing the shrunken, blackened stubs of the fingers, and the gold ring. She set down the camera and, lifting the mummy's right hand carefully, she easily slid the band off the ring finger.

"Gold ring," she repeated, "with an 'F' inlaid in diamonds."

"Interesting," Nick said, then he repeated her description.

"It would not seem to be a robbery, yes," Catherine said, as she pulled an evidence bag from her pocket, put the ring inside and sealed it.

"Cause of death?" Nick called.

"Not sure—nothing visible in the front."

Gingerly, she eased the corpse onto its left side and looked at the sheet metal underneath the body, but saw no sign of bugs or any other scavengers. That would disappoint Grissom, who did love his creepy crawlies. The suit seemed to be stained darker on the back and, moving slowly toward the head, Catherine found what she was looking for.

"Two entry wounds," she announced. "Base of the skull, looks like a pro."

"Firearm?"

"Firearm is my call."

"Anything else?"

She didn't want there to be anything else. The heat now pressed down on her from above. Any relief brought on by the cooler soil down here had evaporated and sweat rolled down her back, her arms, and her face.

But she forced herself to stay focused on the job at hand. Then, just to the left of the mummy's head, something caught her attention, something black poking out of the dirt. She at first thought it was one of Grissom's little friends, a bug; but closer inspection proved it to be metallic: a gun barrel, almost completely buried! Almost. . . .

She picked up the camera and clicked off several more shots.

"What have you got?" Nick asked.

"At least the barrel of a gun, maybe more."

Maneuvering around the body, Catherine pulled herself closer. Carefully, she dug around the black cylinder and left it completely exposed. Though the pistol was gone, the killer had figured he'd fool the firearms examiners by leaving the barrel with the victim.

More than one way to skin a cat, she thought, as she shot three more photos, then bagged the evidence. Catherine Willows knew lots of other ways to catch a murderer besides matching bullets.

She glanced back into the hole from which she had extracted the barrel, and saw nothing . . . or was that something? Pulling out her mini-flash, Catherine turned it on and stroked its beam over the shallow hole. A small bump, slightly lighter in color than the rest of the dirt around it, showed at one end of the hole.

Excavating with care, she uncovered the remnants of an old cigarette filter. Part of this murder case, she wondered, or the detritus of a field used as a garbage dump for the last quarter century? Better safe than sorry, she told herself, and snapped some pictures before bagging it.

"One last thing," she said.

"Yeah?" Nick said.

"Cigarette filter. I've bagged it."

Climbing out of the wrecked trailer, she handed the evidence bags to Nick.

"Small caliber," he said, holding up the clear bag, peering in at the gun barrel. "A twenty-five?"

She nodded as O'Riley came up to them.

"Any ID?" the detective asked.

Catherine said, "I didn't find a wallet or anything and his fingertips are gone."

O'Riley frowned. "No fingertips?"

"Don't worry, Sarge. We can still print him."

"It's like Roscoe Pitts," Nick said.

O'Riley looked confused. "Roscoe Pitts? I thought you said . . ."

"No," Catherine said. "Roscoe Pitts was a bad guy back in the forties. Had a doctor remove his fingerprints, then had skin grafted to his fingers from under his arms."

Nick picked up the story. "He walked around like this for weeks."

Nick crossed his arms, his hands flat against each armpit. "When he got them cut free," Nick said, wiggling his fingers, "smooth skin."

Getting it, O'Riley said, "No fingerprints."

Catherine grinned. "What Roscoe didn't understand was that, A, with smooth fingertips, he'd made himself stand out even more, and, B, you can get prints past the first knuckle."

"So he got busted?" O'Riley asked.

"Almost immediately."

"And that's how you're going to ID this guy?"

Nick nodded. "If our mummy's in the computer, we'll know who he is before the end of the day."

They turned when they heard one of the EMTs swearing.

"What's the matter?" Catherine asked.

The EMT, a big guy with a blond crewcut, held up one of the loafers with the foot still snugly inside. "I'm sorry. It just came off. It's like trying to pick up a potato chip."

Catherine said, "Nick, let's get the hands bagged first, then help these guys before they dismember the whole body."

With a grin, Nick said, "Sure—I always listen to my mummy."

Catherine tried not to smile, and failed.

Then, two small figures in the midst of a vast, crime-scene-taped lot, they got back to work.

3

The security room took up much of the second floor of the hotel, an anonymous blue-gray chamber where banks of VCRs covered one full wall, a security guard checking off a list on a clipboard whenever he changed tapes. The adjacent wall, constructed of one-way glass, overlooked the casino floor, the frantic universe of gamblers on silent display.

The east wall and most of the middle of the room were taken up by security guards sitting in front of computer screens. Some seemed to be watching one camera feed or another, while several more seemed to be monitoring gauges. One gauge, Grissom noticed, was the temperature inside the casino. A huge console inset with nine video monitors filled the south wall. In front of it sat a young Asian man, in attire similar to a desk clerk, tapping on a keyboard.

"Let's see," the computer tech said. "The fourth floor hall, between when?"

Behind him, Brass checked his notes. "Five-thirty and six o'clock this morning."

Grissom watched as the center video screen went black, then flipped to a grainy black-and-white shot of a vacant corridor, a time code in the bottom right-hand corner, the date in the left. "Can we speed it up until someone comes into sight?"

The guard said, "Sure. Probably not much traffic at that hour." He tapped some more and nothing seemed to happen in the hallway, but the time code was racing ahead. A man appeared and, as suddenly as the numbers had sped up, it slowed to normal.

"Mr. Smith Goes to Vegas," Brass said.

Picking up the narrative, Grissom said, "Heading for his room—practically running. Does he know his killer is coming for him?"

Starring in the documentary of his death, Smith ducked into an alcove about halfway down the hall on the right-hand side. In less than twenty seconds, a second man entered the corridor at the far end. This man stayed near the center of the hallway, glancing from side to side as he went, careful to keep his head lowered so his face never appeared on the video.

"Camera shy," Grissom said. "Stalking his victim—here! He ducks in after John Smith."

The videotape had no sound, so they didn't hear either gunshot. But when the killer stepped back into the hall, they saw the muzzle flash of the second shot. Bobby LaFay entered the hallway, the killer spun to face him, and the tray of food fell to the floor soundlessly as LaFay ran back toward the elevator. The killer turned back this way, head still lowered, slipped in Smith's blood, then ran headlong toward the camera, throwing up an arm to cover his face. He passed the camera and disappeared, presumably down the fire stairs to the first floor.

"Run it again," Grissom said.

Now that he knew what happened, he would be free to hone in on the details.

Again Smith scrambled down the hall wearing a dark suit, a look of fear etched on his face as he fumbled with his keycard until he ducked out of sight into the alcove. Next came the killer, a light-colored sports jacket over a light-colored shirt, dark slacks, possibly jeans, and dark shoes, maybe running shoes of some kind, the small pistol already in his right hand, his left hand also up in front of him, doing something. *What was that about?* Grissom asked himself.

"Run it back ten seconds," Grissom told the tech, adding, "and can you slow it down?"

The tech tapped the keys, the time code reversed ten seconds, and the tape ran forward again, this time crawling along in slow motion. The killer entered the corridor, his two hands up in front of his chest, his right holding a gun, his left . . .

"He's screwing on a noise suppresser," Grissom said.

"Mob hit," Brass said automatically.

"Too soon to say," Grissom said just as automatically.

With the silencer in place, the killer ducked into the alcove out of sight. Then Smith's feet appeared as he fell.

Grissom said, "Impact forced him face first into the door. He hit it, then slid down, his feet coming out into the hall."

Stepping back, the killer pointed the pistol at his fallen victim and fired a second shot, the muzzle flash a bright white light. And at that precise moment came Bobby LaFay carrying his tray. Once again the killer turned, raising the pistol toward the waiter, the tray of food spilled all over the floor, this time not only silently but in slow motion, and both men took off running in opposite directions. The killer sprinted by one more time, his arm still up, his face still hidden, no distinguishing marks, no rings on his fingers, no bracelet on his wrist, nothing.

Turning to Brass, Grissom said, "You're bringing in all the tapes from this morning, right?"

"Yeah."

"Then I'm going back upstairs."

Brass made some quick arrangements with the tech, then accompanied Grissom back to the fourth floor, where Warrick approached them, a plastic evidence bag in hand.

"What have you got for me?" Grissom asked.

Holding the bag up for inspection, Warrick said, "Five large— money clip in his front left pants pocket."

"Well, the tape didn't look like a robbery anyway," Grissom said.

Warrick asked, "Anything else good on the tape?"

"Looks like a pretty typical mob hit," Brass said.

Giving Brass a sideways look, Grissom said, "Let the evidence tell us what it was. Don't be so quick to judge."

Brass rolled his eyes.

Sara ambled up to join the group. "Found a shell casing under the body, but there's no sign of the second one."

Grissom nodded and led them back to the murder scene.

"I've gone over every square inch of this hallway, Grissom," Sara said somewhat peevishly. "There isn't a shell casing here anywhere."

Warrick nodded his agreement. "We've been over it twice, Gris— there's nothing."

Grissom's eyes moved over the hallway, took in the spilled tomato sauce and the trail of water from the vase that had held the carnation.

His eyes followed the trail of wet carpeting, his gaze finally settling on the door across the hall. "Can we get into that room?"

"Someone's in there," Brass said, pulling out a list from his pocket.

Careful where he placed his feet, Grissom moved into the opposite alcove and knocked on the door.

"Mr. and Mrs. Gary Curtis," Brass announced.

Grissom heard a shuffling of feet on the other side and the door slowly opened. He stood face to face with a fortyish man with a peppery goatee.

"Can I help you?" the man asked.

Looking down at the end of the trail of water in the corner of the doorjamb, Grissom saw the brass shell casing winking up at him. "You already have, Mr. Curtis, you already have."

Brass said to the guest, "We're conducting an investigation, Mr. Curtis."

"I know," Curtis said, mildly annoyed. "I was interviewed already. How much longer are my wife and I going to be confined to our room?"

Brass smiled meaninglessly. "Not long. Be a good citizen. Murder was committed on your doorstep."

Curtis frowned, shrugged.

Ignoring all this, Grissom had bent down to scoop the casing into a small plastic bag; now he was holding the bagged shell casing up to the light. "No such thing as a perfect crime."

Brass said, "That's all, Mr. Curtis," and the guest was shut back in his room.

Grissom pulled a keycard from his pocket. He glanced at Warrick and Sara. "Party in Mr. Smith's suite. Interested in going?"

Warrick asked, "Get that keycard from the manager?"

With a quick nod, Grissom said, "You bagged the victim's, right?"

"You know I did."

"Well, you can't use that one, 'cause it's evidence. But now you two can do the room."

Warrick accepted the keycard.

Sara asked her boss, "What about you?"

"I'll take the stairwell."

"We're on it," Warrick said, and they retreated across the hall.

The EMTs now loaded John Smith onto a gurney and wheeled him down the hall toward the elevator.

"You can let these people off this floor now," Grissom said to Brass. "Have them take all of their bags with them—the manager needs to get them new rooms."

"It's a busy time of year," Brass said. "Might not be rooms available. . . ."

"Then have 'em pitch tents in the lobby, I don't care. This is a crime scene, Jim."

"Yeah, I was just starting to gather that."

The sarcasm didn't register on Grissom. "Station some of your men in the hall, though, and keep them to this side." He pointed to his left. "We don't want them tromping through like a chorus line. Just get them on the elevator and get 'em out of here."

Brass nodded and got out his cell phone. Warrick and Sara disappeared into the victim's room while Brass and Grissom walked to the stairwell.

The first thing Grissom did was run a piece of duct tape across the door latch so they could get back into the fourth-floor corridor. The fire escape stairwell consisted of eight textured metal steps rising to a metal landing, then did a one-eighty down eight more stairs to the third floor. No point in working the textured stairs, but the landings made Grissom smile.

"Sit on these and you'll be okay," Grissom said, pointing to the flight up to the next floor.

"Swell," Brass said, and sat, and made his phone calls.

When the fourth-floor landing yielded nothing, Grissom moved down to the next one.

On his hands and knees, he used a rubber roller to flatten a Mylar sheet on the landing. Black on the downside and silver on the upside, the sheet would help him lift footprints out of the dust. With the sheet pressed flat, Grissom turned to the small gray box nearby. The box's front contained a switch, a red light, a voltmeter, and two electric leads, one ending in an alligator clip, the other ending in a stainless steel probe roughly a quarter-inch in diameter.

Brass, off the phone, asked, "How about footprints?"

"We'll know in a second."

Grissom fastened an alligator clip to one side of the Mylar sheet, then touched the probe to the other side of the sheet. When the meter on the front of the box spiked, he smiled and removed the probe. Turning off the box, he took off the alligator clip, then turned his attention to the Mylar sheet.

"Here we go," he said, rubbing his palms on his pants legs.

Carefully, he pulled back the Mylar sheet, revealing two distinct footprints, one going up, one going down.

"Wouldn't you know," Grissom said. "One of them stepped right on top of the killer's print."

"One of them?"

"Either your man Patterson or the manager. Judging from the print, probably the manager."

"What makes you think it's the killer's footprint?"

"Running shoe. Looks like the bloody one in the hall, but it might just be wishful thinking, and the manager is wearing something smooth with a rubber heel. Florsheim maybe."

Next, Grissom dusted the right-hand banister between the landing and the third floor. The railing on the same side between the fourth floor and the landing yielded dozens of prints. The odds of getting a useful one from the killer were maybe one in a thousand or so. Guests, hotel staff, both security and maintenance, fire marshals, and who knew who else had touched these railings since the last time they were cleaned.

Looking up through the railing at Brass, Grissom asked, "Can you find out who cleans this stairwell and how often?"

"No problem. Find anything?"

"Anything?" Grissom echoed, with a hollow laugh that made its own echo in the stairwell. "More like everything. It's a fingerprint convention."

Grissom spent the better part of an hour and a half finishing in the stairwell. He gathered scores of prints, but had very little confidence that any would prove helpful. The downside of public places, even one as seldom used as this stairwell, was that crime scene investigators could get buried under the sheer volume of information, most of which had no bearing at all on their case.

The hotel room looked like any other one in Vegas, with only a few differences. The bedspread lay askew, puddling near the bottom of the bed. A champagne bottle sat on the dresser with two glasses next to it. Clothes hung in the small closet and the victim's shaving kit was laid out neatly in the bathroom. A briefcase, a pile of papers, and a Palm Pilot lay arrayed on the round table in the corner.

"I'll take the table and the bathroom," Sara said to Warrick, "you get the dresser and the bed."

"I had the bed last time."

Shaking her head, she said, "It's all the same, Warrick."

He gave her a slow look. "Like hell it is."

She threw her hands up. "Okay, you take the bathroom. I'll take the bed."

Glad he didn't have to enter the DNA cesspool that he knew existed on those sheets, Warrick entered the bathroom. On the right, the sink was clean. Next to it, on the counter, the signs of an exceptionally neat man. A washcloth had been laid out, a razor, toothbrush, toothpaste, and a comb lay on top of it, each one approximately an inch apart. Behind them stood deodorant, shaving cream, mouthwash, and after-shave, each with the label facing front, each item about one inch from its neighbor, soldiers at attention. Warrick took quick photos of the bathroom, then passed the camera to Sara, who did the other room.

Lifting the wastebasket onto the counter, Warrick peered inside, thinking how his job seemed at times two parts scientist, three parts janitor. All he found was the tamper-proof shrink wrap from the mouthwash bottle and some wadded-up tissues . . . but one of the tissues had a lipstick smear.

"He had a woman here," Sara called from the other room.

Warrick looked quizzically at the tissue, then into the mirror, finally out into the other room to make sure Sara wasn't just messing with him, but she was nowhere in sight. He said, "I've got a tissue with some lipstick in here, says the same thing."

"Lipstick on one of the glasses and a cigarette butt with a lipstick stain in the ashtray. I'm betting our victim didn't smoke Capris."

Exiting the bathroom, Warrick studied the skinny cigarette in the bag in Sara's hand. "Not exactly a macho cigarette, is it?"

"Unless John Smith wore lipstick, it's not his brand."

Warrick almost smiled, and Sara put the evidence bag inside her kit, then moved to another, smaller, black briefcase. Opening it, she pulled out what looked like a telephoto lens with a pistol grip on it.

"I see our friend RUVIS made the trip," Warrick said.

"Yep," Sara said, flipping the switch on the gadget—Reflective Ultra-Violet Imaging System. "If John Smith and his lady friend had sexual congress in this bed, RUVIS will show us."

"You make it sound so political."

The machine had been on for less than ten seconds when Sara let out a long sigh.

Warrick asked, "What's wrong? Didn't you find anything?"

Sara rolled her eyes. "What didn't I find? These sheets are covered with stains."

She handed the RUVIS to Warrick. He turned toward the bed and looked through the lens. With only the UV illumination, the bed looked like a giant camouflage blanket as the stains shown up like large white flowers in half a dozen different spots. "Busy guy if those are all his."

"You think they are?"

"Nope. Remember when Mike Tyson got busted?"

"Sure," Sara said. "Indianapolis."

"Right. The criminalist who investigated spoke at a seminar I went to. He said the suite went for eight bills a night. And the hotel was less than a year old."

"Yeah?"

Warrick turned off the RUVIS and set it back in its case. "How many semen stains do you suppose he found?"

Sara shrugged.

"One hundred fifty-three."

Her eyes widened. "A hundred and fifty-three?"

"Yep . . . and none of them were Tyson's."

Making a face, Sara said, "I may never stay in a hotel again."

"I heard that," Warrick said, and went back to work in the bathroom. He pulled some hairs from the shower drain, but found nothing else. Within minutes, he rejoined Sara in the other room. While she continued to take samples from the bed, he bagged the Palm Pilot, the papers, the champagne bottle, and glasses.

"You know," Warrick said, in the bathroom doorway, "Grissom never once mentioned anything to me, about, you know . . . me working an investigation in a casino."

Still hard at it, Sara said, "Well, that's Grissom."

"Yeah. I just wasn't sure he would ever trust me again."

Studying him now, Sara asked, "Warrick?"

"Yeah."

"Is it tough for you?"

"What?"

"Being around it. A casino, I mean."

He looked at her for a very long time. "No harder than a recovering alcoholic working a crime scene in a liquor store."

Her gaze met his. "That hard?"

A slow nod. "That hard."

Awkwardly, she said, "Look, uh . . . if I can help . . ."

"If anybody could help," he said, "we wouldn't be having this conversation."

They continued working the scene, silently.

4

The Las Vegas Criminalistics Department—housed in a modern, rambling one-story building tucked between lush pine trees—was a rabbit warren of offices, conference rooms, and especially labs, with a lounge and locker room thrown in for the hell of it. This washed-out world of vertical blinds, fingerprint analysis, glass-and-wood walls and evidence lockers was strangely soothing to Catherine Willows—her home away from home.

Catherine had managed to pick up her daughter Lindsey from school, have a quality-time dinner, and even catch a couple hours of sleep before coming into work a little after nine in the evening.

Now, a few minutes after ten, her eyes already burned from the strain of studying the computer monitor. Buried in the minutiae of an unsolved missing persons case—this one a fifty-two-year-old white man named Frank Mayfield who had disappeared thirteen years ago—she sensed someone standing in the doorway to her left.

She turned to see Grissom there, briefcase in one hand, the other holding a stack of file folders and a precariously balanced cup of coffee. In a black short-sleeve sportshirt and gray slacks, he managed to look casual and professional at once. He held the door open with a foot.

"You're in early," he said.

"Trying to figure out who our mummy is."

His eyes tightened. "And you are . . . ?"

"Going through missing persons cases, back ten to twenty years ago. The preliminary report says Imhotep died about fifteen years ago."

He was at her side now, the coffee cup set down on the desk. "How many cases?"

"No more than grains of sand in the desert," Catherine said, stretching to release the tension in her spine. "You know, there's been over thirty-two-hundred missing persons calls in the last two years alone."

Grissom shook his head. "Any luck?"

"Not yet."

"Is this kind of fishing expedition productive?"

She smirked, shrugged. "I've got to do something. Can't use DNA or dental until we at least have some idea who our guy is."

He sat on the edge of the desk. "Got anything at all?"

"A ring with an 'F' in diamonds inlaid in it."

Grissom's eyebrows rose; he liked that. "First name or last name?"

Catherine shrugged again. "Your guess is as good as mine."

"Any other engraving? To so-and-so, from so-and-so? With love?"

"No. Just an effin' 'F.' "

Grissom raised an eyebrow. "Do we know how the victim died?"

"Shot in the head."

". . . Funny."

"Ha-ha?"

"The other kind—our hallway corpse was shot in the head."

Another smirk. "Well, nothing separating the corpses except maybe fifteen years."

Grissom pressed. "Have you fingerprinted him yet?"

"I was waiting for Nick to come in. Our mummy's in pretty bad shape. One foot already fell off when they were hauling him out from under the trailer."

"I hate when that happens."

"I figured it would be easier processing the prints with two of us."

Nodding, Grissom said, "Good call. But you're here now, and Nick isn't—how about I lend a hand?"

"Or a foot?" Her sigh turned into a yawn. "I appreciate the offer—I can use a change of scene. It's like searching for a needle in a hundred haystacks."

Grissom nodded, hefting the stack of files. "Let me put this stuff in my office and we'll get right on it."

Turning off the computer, she rose; he was already back to the door, but had left his coffee behind. Detail work on a crime scene was Grissom's strength; but in daily life he had a hint of the absent-minded professor.

Joining him at the doorway, she said, "Hey, thanks for the coffee, Grissom."

He frowned at her, as she seemed about to drink it. She handed him the cup. "I'm kidding. Come on."

In the hallway, between sips of coffee, Grissom said, "Sometimes I can be a little thoughtless."

"I wouldn't say that. Not just any guy would walk a girl to the morgue."

And soon that was where they stood, blue scrubs over their street clothes, John Doe #17 outstretched on a silver metal table in front of them, his hands still bagged at his sides.

"I can't believe we already have seventeen John Does this year," she said.

Putting on a pair of glasses, Grissom moved forward; he didn't seem to have heard her. Catherine stood back a little as he studied the corpse. She knew he loved this part of the job—he was much better with dead people than live ones. There was something almost innocent about Grissom, something pure in his love for investigation and the search for truth.

But even more, Grissom loved to learn. Each new body presented the opportunity for him to gain more knowledge to help not only this person, but other people in the future. Wherever his people skills lagged, the criminalist made up for it in a passion for serving the victims of crime, and compassion for the grieving survivors.

At first, he took in the whole body. Catherine got the impression that Grissom wasn't so much seeing the body as absorbing it. *Stay curious,* he always said. He circled the metal table, observing the mummy from every angle.

"Your killer did us a big favor hiding the body the way he did," Grissom said.

"You didn't crawl under a rotting trailer to get at him."

His eyes flicked to her. "You know if we lived anywhere but the desert, there wouldn't have been anything left but a few bones."

She nodded. "Your bugs got cheated out of their buffet."

He stepped in next to the body and pressed gingerly on the abdomen. "Feels like the organs might still be intact."

Grissom with a body reminded her of how Lindsey had been when Catherine had given her that glass tea set last Christmas, the little girl examining each item, careful not to damage or crack the tiny pieces as she inspected each one. The criminalist did the same thing with the mummy, poking here, prodding there, bringing the work light down to more closely examine a section of the chest.

"Okay," he said finally.

"You through?"

He looked at her sheepishly. "Sorry. This is your deal—where do you want to start?"

Before they could move, Dr. Robbins, the coroner, walked through the swinging doors, a set of X rays in one hand. "Oh, sorry— didn't know anybody was in here."

"Bad place to be startled, Doc," Catherine said with a half-smile.

Around sixty, bald with a neatly trimmed gray beard, the avuncular Robbins—like them, he was in scrubs—slid his arm out of the metal cuff of his crutch and leaned it against the wall.

"What have you got, Doc?" Grissom said.

"Cause of death." Robbins stuck the first X ray under a clip on the viewer and turned on the light. The fluorescent bulbs came to life, illuminating a side view of the skull of John Doe #17 with several dark spots readily apparent. The second X ray the coroner put up showed the back of the skull with only two dark spots. He pointed to that picture first. "These two dark spots are your entry wounds."

"Are you *sure?*" Grissom asked, eyes tight.

Robbins looked at Grissom the way a parent does a backward child. "Why wouldn't I be sure?"

"Have you got the right X rays?" Grissom was having a closer look—much closer. "Is this John Smith or John Doe #17?"

"The mummy, of course, John Doe #17," Robbins said, more confused than offended, now. "I don't even know who John Smith is."

"Victim from the Beachcomber," Grissom said. "Two entry wounds vertically placed almost precisely one inch apart. Just like this. . . ."

Catherine frowned, shook her head, arcs of reddish-blonde hair swinging. "The same pattern? You're kidding."

Grissom twitched half a frown back at her. "When do I kid?"

"Well," Robbins said, "there's no mistake, I haven't even seen the other corpse yet. Hell of a coincidence."

"I don't believe in coincidences," Catherine said. "There's always a way to explain them away."

Grissom shook his head slowly. "I don't deny the existence of coincidence—particularly when our corpses are separated by so many years."

Mind whirling, Catherine said, "Do we have two cases, or one case?"

Grissom's eyes almost closed; his mouth pursed. Then he said, "We have two victims. We work them as two cases. If the evidence turns them into one case, so be it. Until then . . . we live with this coincidence."

"But we keep our eyes open."

Grissom's eyes popped wide. "Always a good practice."

Pointing to the other X ray, Robbins indicated a dark spot on the right side of the forehead. "Here's a good place to start looking—there's one of your bullets. Embedded itself in the skull."

Grissom asked, "And the second one?"

"EMTs found it on the gurney when they brought him in. Little devil just rolled out."

"Where's the slug now?" Catherine asked.

"With the other evidence," Robbins said, picking up his crutch again. "Now, if you'll excuse me, I think I better go make the acquaintance of Mr. John Smith."

After the coroner left, Catherine and Grissom got down to work. They carefully unbagged the hands.

Grissom said, "Killer took the fingertips. Thinks he stole the victim's prints."

"I love it when we're smarter than the bad guys."

He raised a lecturing finger. "Not smarter—better informed."

"You think we should rehydrate the fingers?"

Studying the desiccated fingers, he finally said, "It might help raise the prints."

Catherine set out two large beakers, each a little more than half full of Formalin; behind her, Grissom was rustling in a drawer. When she turned back, Grissom stood next to the body with a huge pair of pruning shears.

Taking a deep breath and letting it out slowly through her mouth, Catherine moved into position next to the mummy.

"You okay?" he asked.

"Yeah." No matter how many times they did this, she never learned to accept it easily. At least this would probably be better than the times he had made her wear the skin stripped from dead hands as gloves, to provide fingerprinting pressure.

She held the leathery right hand still as Grissom stepped in and lopped it off. Catherine flinched a little, the sound echoing in her ears like the snapping of a pencil. She took the hand, slipped it into one of the beakers and they moved to the other side of the body and repeated the process with the left hand.

Setting the shears aside, Grissom said, "I can't get over the similarity of those wounds."

Slowly, Catherine turned the mummy's head so Grissom could see the bullet holes.

He stared at the wound. "You know what Elizabeth Kubler-Ross said?"

"About what?"

"Coincidence."

"Why don't you tell me."

He gave her an unblinking gaze, as innocent as a newborn babe, as wise as the ages. " 'There are no mistakes, no coincidences—all events are blessings given to us to learn from.' "

"I thought you didn't deny the existence of coincidence."

"I don't accept it, either."

"Identical wounds, over a decade apart. And from this we learn . . . ?"

He shook his head. "Just keep digging. It's two separate cases. We treat it as two separate cases."

Was he trying to convince her, she wondered, or himself?

Catherine examined the wounds. "It is funny."

Nodding, Grissom said, "But not ha-ha. Sooner you find out who this guy is, the sooner we can lay the coincidence issue to rest."

"Nick and I will be all over this."

Grissom granted her a tiny smile. "Keep me in the loop, Catherine."

She nodded and watched him leave. Something in his manner didn't seem right, but she couldn't quite put her finger on it; he seemed vaguely distracted, even for Grissom. She told herself to keep an eye on her boss.

In the meantime, she'd hunt up Nick and if he didn't have any ideas, she'd go back to digging in the computerized records. The hands would take about an hour to rehydrate.

Nick sat in the break room, sipping coffee, a forensics journal open in front of him.

"Hey," he said to her.

"Hey," she said.

She poured herself a cup of coffee and sat across the table from him. "Where have you been?"

He turned to the clock on the wall. "You mean since the shift started three minutes ago?"

Following his gaze, she looked at the clock. She grinned and shook her head. "Sorry. I came in early. Tired, I guess."

"I thought we were going to do the mummy's prints."

"Been there, done that. Grissom helped."

Nick frowned. "I wanted to lend a hand."

"So to speak." Catherine shrugged. "Grissom offered."

Nick was already over his disappointment. "Well, he's the best. Learn anything?"

"I've got the mummy's hands in the Formalin now—we can look at them later."

He grinned at her. "Isn't that an old movie?"

"What?"

"*The Mummy's Hands?*"

"His hands are only part of the show. We found one of the bullets in his skull. Popped up in the X ray."

"Just one?"

She nodded. "The other fell out on the gurney. We'll wait for Robbins to dig the one out of the skull, then take them both to the firearms examiner."

He sipped his coffee. "What do we do in the meantime?"

"Back to the computer for me. I've been going through missing persons cases that somehow involve the initial 'F.' "

"Seems worth doing. I think I'll go through the guy's effects— maybe I can find something."

They finished their coffee, sharing a little small talk, and exited the break room, moving off in opposite directions.

Nick went into the morgue to study John Doe #17's clothes more thoroughly. Though the suit had survived fairly well, it had now become part of the mummy; in essence, his second skin. Head wounds bleed a great deal, which was the reason for the dark stain on the back of the jacket.

The clothes gave the mummy a musty smell, not exactly the aroma Nick would have expected to find coming from a dead body. He took scrapings from the bottom of the mummy's shoes in hopes that Greg Sanders, their resident lab rat, could tell him something about where the man had been walking before his death. He picked lint out of the mummy's pockets and bagged that. Anything that might give them some kind of hint to who this long-dead murder victim was.

Next, he studied the two dollars and fifteen cents in change: six quarters, five dimes, two nickels and five pennies. The newest was a 1984 quarter, the oldest a 1957 nickel. The coins, except for the '57 nickel, were all pretty clean and Nick dusted them but lifted only two usable partials.

The ring yielded no prints, but did have a set of tiny initials carved into it—not an inscription. He knew enough about jewelry to recognize they probably belonged to the jeweler that crafted the piece and not the victim. Well, at least that gave him something to go on. It would still be a few hours before he'd be able to find any jewelers in their stores.

Finally, he looked at the bag with the cigarette filter remains. Not much left after fifteen years, but more than he would have expected. Filters never biodegraded—an environmentalist's nightmare, a CSI's dream. Taking the bag, he wandered back toward the lab to find Greg Sanders.

Nick found the skinny, spiky-haired guy, as usual, poring over his microscope. Though well into his twenties, Sanders always had the cheerfully gleeful expression of a kid with a new chemistry set.

"Studying the DNA of another prospective soulmate?" Nick asked.

Sanders looked up, eyes bright. "Dude—science can be used for better things than putting people in jail."

"Marriage and jail—I sense a connection there."

Sanders batted the air with a hand. "Some guys are boob men—some're leg men. Me, I'm an epithelial sort of guy."

Nick held out the bagged cigarette. "Swell—'cause I need DNA on this."

Picking it up, holding it to the light, Sanders said, "Ugh—grotty! How long has this baby been part of the ecosystem?"

With a shrug, Nick said, "I don't know. You tell me."

"Take a number. Got a backlog. Gonna be a while."

"What else isn't new?"

Sanders shot him a look. "Hey, I'm only one guy."

"I know, Greg, but who else is ready to loan you *Gran Turismo Three* on PlayStation Two?"

All business now, Sanders said, "You just hit the top of my list."

The files rolled by one after one, blurring into each other, the coffee growing more bitter with each cup, and still Catherine couldn't seem to find a lead.

Nick came through the door and plopped down on a plastic chair just inside her office. "Anything?"

"Well, I think I've eliminated about forty missing persons with either a first initial or a middle initial of 'F.' "

"And now?"

"Starting on the 'F' last names."

"How many are there?"

"From ten to twenty years ago, only another hundred or so that are still open."

"*If* our mummy's from Vegas."

A look came across Catherine's face. "Got a better idea?"

Nick checked his watch. "Time to try the prints."

Returning to the morgue, they lifted the hands out of the Formalin, and set them on an autopsy table to dry.

"Give them a while, then we'll print them," she said. "Let's get something to eat, then come back."

He nodded. "Sounds good."

She smirked, shook her head. "You think there's anything gross enough to spoil a CSI's appetite?"

"When something comes up," Nick said slyly, "I'll let you know."

Forty-five minutes later, after their deli sandwiches, they returned and printed both the palms and the second flange of the fingers below the amputations. They fed the prints into AFIS, got fifteen possible matches. It took the rest of the shift to go through them and, when they finished, they still had nothing.

Catherine stretched her aching muscles, looked at her watch and said, "I've got to get home to get Lindsey off."

Nick nodded. "I'm going to catch some breakfast."

"Food again."

"Then I might log a little overtime, try to run down the jeweler's initials on the ring. You wanna join in, after you get Lindsey to school?"

She shook her head. "I need some sleep. I put my overtime in on the front end of my shift. . . . Call me later, tell me what you find."

"You got it," he said, picking up the evidence-bagged ring.

In the parking lot, Catherine headed left toward her car and the trip home to her daughter while Nick went right, climbed into his own ride, and took off to find a bite to eat. When he had first moved from Dallas to Vegas, he frequently took advantage of the casinos' breakfast buffets. But now, after working off the pounds he had gained doing that, he was more careful about where and how much he ate.

He only knew one jeweler, personally, in the city—an older guy named Arnie Mattes, who a while back Nick had helped to prove innocent of robbing his own jewelry store in a suspected insurance scam. Mattes wouldn't be at his store for another hour at least; this gave Nick time for a leisurely breakfast at Jerry's Diner, and a chance to actually read the morning paper, instead of just glancing through it.

Though the *Las Vegas Sun* carried a front-page story about the discovery of the mummy at the construction site, the murder at the Beachcomber found itself relegated to a small story on page two of the Metro section. The mummy story was unusual, just a hint of sensationalism for morning reading; but the dead man in the hallway might have alarmed tourists, so that was played down. The city fathers, Nick knew, were sensitive to any scandal that might ruin the wholesome, family environment they'd been working so hard to cultivate.

He moved on to the sports section. Nick was a dyed-in-the-wool baseball fan—the Las Vegas 51's had shutout the Nashville Sounds last night—but because of his work attended few games and was forced to follow the team's progress in the paper when he got the chance.

After finishing his meal, Nick drove the short distance from the small café to Mattes's jewelry store, just off Charleston Boulevard. The CLOSED sign still hung in the door when Nick pulled up, but he spotted Mattes placing a necklace in the window, and parked the car in front. Walking briskly to the door, Nick knocked.

Mattes recognized the young criminalist at once, waved, and moved to the door to unlock it. "Nick Stokes, as I live and breathe. Welcome, welcome—come in, get out of the heat."

Smiling, Nick entered. "How are you doing, Mr. Mattes?"

"Fine, Nick, fine, fine." Pushing seventy, the jeweler stood maybe five-six and seemed almost like a child playing dress up, his skinny arms practically swallowed up by the baggy short sleeves of his white shirt. Black-rimmed glasses slid halfway down his nose, with a small magnifying glass, looking like a little crystal flag, waving from the left corner of the frames. "What about you, son?"

"I'm good, but I've got a problem I thought you might be able to help me with."

"Anything."

Pulling the evidence bag from his pocket, Nick held it up so Mattes could see the ring inside. "Can you tell me who made this?"

Mattes took the bag from Nick, held it up to the light. "May I remove it from the bag?"

"Please."

Carefully, the jeweler set the plastic bag on the glass counter, separated the seal, and almost religiously lifted the ring out. "Kind of gaudy, for my taste. Of course, that's typical in this town."

A crooked smile played at the corners of Nick's mouth. "What else can you tell me?"

Pulling his magnifying glass down over the left lens of his glasses, Mattes studied the ring for a long moment, turning it this way and that. "These initials," he said, pointing inside the gold band.

"J-R-B."

"Yes. The manufacturer of this particular item. The initials of J.R. Bennett."

"You know him?"

Mattes nodded. "An acquaintance from many years in the business. He runs a shop in the mall attached to the Aladdin. . . . Oh, what is it called?"

"Desert Passage?"

"That's it, son, Desert Passage. His store is called . . . something a little too precious . . . uh, yes. Omar's."

"Omar's?"

"Silly theme they have, there, desert bazaar. When you visit Mr. Bennett, give him my regards."

"I will, Mr. Mattes, and thanks."

"Stop by any time, Nick. Remember what I said—you find a girl, we'll find a ring for her."

Nick glanced to one side and grinned, then looking back at the jeweler said, "I'll keep that in mind, sir."

Supposedly fashioned on a Casablanca marketplace, the Desert Passage mall was the only place in Vegas that could be counted on for regular rainfall. Every quarter hour, in fact, the mall's indoor thunderstorm broke loose for five minutes; positioned over the lagoon, the manmade storm managed to rain a great deal and yet never get anything wet. The tourists seemed to love it, stopping to take pictures of the water gushing from hidden sprinklers in the ceiling, amazed by the white flashes of strobe lightning.

Nick had walked about a quarter of the way around the mall— thinking about his late girlfriend, Kristi, for whom he'd bought bath and body oil at a little kiosk here—when he spotted Omar's.

The jewelry store was small, but Nick could tell the good stuff when he saw it—and this was the good stuff. Only one U-shaped glass counter showed the various wares of the store, designed for lucky winners with new money to burn; but for the most part, this wasn't the place to buy off the rack: this was where the wealthy had jewelry designed for them.

Behind the counter stood a fiftyish man who had to be six-seven, at least. The tall man had short hair thinning on top, an angular face that gave away very little, and large brown eyes that revealed even less. He gave Nick what might have been a smile. "May I help you, sir?"

Showing the man his credentials, Nick asked, "Are you J.R. Bennett?"

"Yes."

Nick withdrew the evidence bag from his pocket, showed the jeweler the gold ring with the diamond "F." "Have you seen this ring before?"

"Most certainly," Bennett said. "I designed and crafted it."

"Can you tell me for who?"

"Whom," Bennett corrected.

Sighing, Nick turned back to the jeweler and said, patiently, "Can you tell me for whom you made this ring?"

"Malachy Fortunato."

That was a mouthful.

Nick frowned. "You don't have to check your records or . . ."

"Malachy Fortunato. I designed and crafted this ring exactly eighteen years ago at the order of Mr. Fortunato himself."

"One glance, and—"

"Look at it yourself. The ring has no elegance, no style. I remember most of the pieces I have created fondly. Not this one—but it was what the customer wanted."

"So," Nick said, "you're sure about the ring—but the timing? Eighteen years ago . . . ?"

"Yes, three years before he disappeared."

"Disappeared?"

The jeweler sighed; this apparently was an imposition. "Yes, I don't recall the details. It did make the newspapers, though. Does this ring mean that you've found him?"

"I don't know, Mr. Bennett. But you've been a big help. Thanks for your time, sir."

"My pleasure," he said, though it clearly hadn't been.

Nick was barely out of the shop before he was punching Catherine's number into his cell phone. He had a strong suspicion she would want to log some overtime on this one, too.

5

In the chem lab, Warrick checked the instruction sheet on the counter for the fourth time, then slowly stirred the fluid in the beaker. Sara appeared in the doorway just as he was finishing up. Her jeans and dark blue blouse looked crisp enough, but Sara herself looked about as tired as he felt.

"What witch's brew is that?" she asked.

Tapping the beaker with his glass stirring rod, Warrick said, "Smith's Solution."

"Whose solution?"

"Smith's."

She drifted in, leaned against the counter. "New to me."

"New to everybody. Just got printed up in the journals, couple months ago. I found the recipe in *The Journal of Forensic Identification*."

"Always a handy cookbook." Sara nodded toward the beaker. "What wonders does it work?"

"Fingerprints on shell casings come up nice and clean. . . . Intern named Karie Smith, working in Bettendorf, Iowa, came up with it."

"God bless the heartland," she said, flashing her distinctive gap-toothed smile. Her interest was clearly piqued. "No kidding—no more smears?"

"Thing of the past—buggy whips and celluloid collars." Using a forceps, Warrick picked up one of the hotel shell casings by the rim and dipped it into the solution. He left it there for only a few seconds, then pulled it out and ran some tap water over the casing. Holding it up to the light, he let out a slow chuckle. "Got it."

"Show me."

He turned the casing so Sara could eyeball the partial print near the base. Her smile turned wicked as she said, "Let's shoot this sucker, and get it into AFIS."

They both knew there was no way to successfully lift the print off the casing. All they could do was photograph it. But that would get the job done just fine. While Sara got the camera, Warrick set up the shot on the countertop. He placed the casing carefully on top of a black velvet pad, with the print facing up. She snapped off four quick shots.

"Where you been all night?" he asked.

"Running the prints from the room."

"Yeah? Come up with anything?"

She moved to a different angle and shot the shell casing four more times. "Not much—just the victim."

"Give!"

"A Chicago attorney—one Philip Dinglemann."

Warrick frowned at her. "Why do I know that name?"

"I don't know. Why do you?"

"Don't know . . . but I do. . . ." He sighed, frustrated at the rusty gears of his own thinking; long night. "What about the woman's prints?"

"A hooker."

"What a shock."

"Working girl's been busted three or four times in town, but mostly she works outside Clark County at the Stallion Ranch. You'll love this—her name's Connie Ho."

Warrick's sleepy expression woke up a little. "Ho?"

Sara lifted her hands palms up. "What're you going to do? She's from Hong Kong; is it her fault her name's a pun? Been in the States almost ten years. Became a citizen year before last."

"Long enough to know Ho is a bad idea for a hooker's last name."

"Maybe she considers it advertising."

Warrick smiled a little. "I can't wait for you to tell Grissom we need to go to the Stallion Ranch to interview a Connie Ho."

Sara gave him a wide smile; even Warrick had to admit that gap was cute. "We only work the evidence, remember? Isn't that what you always say?"

It was—but Warrick, like the rest of the CSIs, sometimes questioned suspects relative to evidence because, frankly, the detectives just didn't have the familiarity with crime scene findings to pull it off properly.

"Anyway," she was saying, "I already filled Grissom in. He called Brass and got him to go out to the ranch, so we could work the evidence."

"Great," Warrick said. "Much rather spend my time with prints and shell casings than go out to the Stallion Ranch."

Her grin turned mischievous. "I knew you wouldn't want to be bothered interviewing a bunch of silly half-naked women."

Actually, she was right, but he wouldn't give her the satisfaction.

"So," she said, their photography session completed, "what's next?"

"First, we put these prints into AFIS," he said, nodding to the camera, "then we go downstairs and see how Sadler did with that Palm Pilot. I asked him to rush it."

Before long they were in the minuscule basement cubicle of computer technician Terry Sadler. In his late twenties, with short brown hair and long narrow sideburns, Sadler had skin with the pale glow of someone who saw the sun far too infrequently.

"What's up, Terry," Warrick said. "Find anything on our Palm Pilot?"

Like a manic ferret on a double cappucino, Sadler sat hunkered over his work station with his fingers flying and his keyboard rattling. "Just the usual stuff," he said, his words as rapid as his actions. "A list of phone numbers, his schedule, couple of pieces of e-mail. I printed it all off for you."

"Where is it?"

Rooting around his desk with one hand, other hand hunt-and-pecking, Sadler finally held up a thin manila folder. "Here you go."

Sara was watching this with wide eyes.

"Thanks, Terry," Warrick said, as low-key as Sadler wasn't. "I owe you."

"That's right." The computer tech threw a glance at the criminalist. "The usual."

"Usual. . . . How's tomorrow night?"

"Just fine, Warrick. Just fine."

They headed back up the stairs, Warrick leafing through the papers in the file as they went.

"What's 'the usual'?" Sara asked.

"Once a week, I spring Chinese delivery for him and two of his cellmates down there."

"Jeez—that's gotta run fifty bucks."

He gave her a slow smile. "Sometimes the wheels of justice need a little grease."

Shaking her head, she asked, "So, what's in the file?"

Putting the e-mail file on top, he handed it to her.

Aloud, she read, " 'Phil, this is no time to get lost. Less than a week till showtime. We should be getting prepped. Where the fuck are you?' Touching missive—unsigned."

They moved into the break room; Sara sat while Warrick poured cups of coffee.

"We can trace the address of the sender, easy enough," Warrick said. "It's got to lead to somebody."

" 'Showtime,' " Sara said, re-reading the e-mail. "Was this guy an entertainment lawyer?"

Driving out to the Stallion Ranch was not how Homicide Detective Jim Brass really wanted to spend a July morning. The news radio voice had reported the temperature at 105° and he'd shut off the radio before any more good news could ruin his day further. The brothel was outside his jurisdiction, so Brass had taken the liberty of trading in his unmarked brown Ford Taurus for his personal vehicle, a blue Ford Taurus. Such small distinctions—brown car for blue—were the stuff of his life of late.

When he had been demoted to Homicide from heading up the Criminalistics Bureau, he'd been angry, then frustrated and of course bitter. But time—and not that much of it—had smoothed things out. Strangely, working as an equal with Gil Grissom and the quirky group that made up the crime lab unit was proving much easier—and more rewarding—than supervising them.

A desk was no place for Jim Brass. Now he was back in the field, doing what he did best—doggedly pursuing murderers, and the suspects, witnesses, and evidence that bagged them.

When Grissom had called him toward the end of night shift, Brass had been only a little surprised to learn that his victim had been a lawyer and not at all surprised to find the woman was a prostitute. But the hooker's name—Connie Ho—just had to be a put on.

The Stallion Ranch sat all alone in the scrubby desert landscape, just south of Enterprise, on the other side of the county line. The only other sign of life out here was a truck stop a half-mile down the road. The neon sign of a horse rearing was hard to miss even shut off in the morning sun. He swung into the short drive that led to the actual "ranch house," which was what they called it in the brochures, anyway. The structure looked more like a T-shaped concrete bunker with the top of the "T" facing the road. Only a few other cars, and two eighteen-wheelers parked off to one side, dotted the nearly deserted dirt parking lot.

A teasing breeze kicked up some dust around the car as he got out and ambled toward the building. On the trip out here, he had considered several ways to play this. Several scenarios had been rehearsed in the theater of his mind. Now, none seemed right, so he would play it straight.

Jim Brass always did.

He opened the door, the rush of cold air like a soothing slap. A tall, impressive redhead stepped forward to meet him in a reception room running to dark paneling, indoor-outdoor carpeting and gold-framed paintings of voluptuous nudes, none more voluptuous than the hostess approaching him, and her voice carried a soft southern lilt. "Hello, Handsome. I'm Madam Charlene—and how may we help you, today?"

She was probably fifty and looked forty—albeit a hard forty. She had been gorgeous once, and the memory lingered.

He flipped open the leather wallet and showed her his badge.

"Oh, shit," she said, the southern lilt absent now from a Jersey-tinged voice. "Now what the fuck?"

He said nothing, let her take another, closer look at the badge to see that he was from town.

She frowned. "You're not even in the right county, Sugar."

He twitched a nonsmile. "I'm looking for one of your girls."

Her hands went to her hips and her mood turned dark. "A lot of fellas are. For anything in particular?"

"For information. She was with a trick at the Beachcomber. That *is* my county."

The frown deepened, crinkling the makeup. "And you're going to bust her for that? What two adults do in the privacy of their own, uh, privacy?"

Brass shook his head. "This isn't a vice matter. The trick ended up dead—shot twice in the head."

Alarm widened the green eyes. "And you think one of my girls did it?"

He kept shaking his head. "I know she didn't. I just need to ask her a few questions. She was with the guy some time before he died—probably the last to see him alive, other than his killer."

She studied Brass. ". . . Just some questions and nothing more?"

"That's right. I don't want to be under foot any longer than necessary."

"Considerate of you. . . . Which girl?"

He gave her half a smile. "Uh, Connie Ho. That's not her real name, is it?"

Madam Charlene gave him the other half of the smile. "Sad, ain't it? I think she's come to wear that name as badge of honor."

"If you say so."

"Anyway, she's one of our best girls. Popular, personable. Trim little figure—but legal."

"Thanks for sharing."

"You can go on back." She pointed the way. "Room one twenty-four. Down the hall and to the right."

"Thank you, Charlene. We'll do our best not to make each other's lives miserable."

She gave him a smile that didn't seem at all professional. "For a cop, you have possibilities."

Brass made the turn, walked down more indoor-outdoor carpeting and finally came to room 124 almost near the bottom of the "T." He knocked, waited, knocked again.

"Coming," said a female voice through the door.

Very little accent, he noticed. "Ms. Ho?"

She opened the door. Connie Ho was Asian, yet very blonde—platinum, in fact. Maybe five-four and 110, she wore a tissue-thin lavender negligee and black pumps and nothing else.

"What can I do for you, Handsome?"

Brass had been called "Handsome" maybe four times in recent memory—two of them, this afternoon. He flashed the badge and her eyes and nostrils flared, as she tried to shut the door in his face. Wedging his foot inside, door-to-door-salesmen style, and bracing the door with both hands, he forced his way in.

She backed to the far wall and wrapped her arms around herself, as if she'd suddenly realized how nearly naked she was.

The room was small, just big enough for a double bed and a mirrored makeup table with a chair in front of it. The walls were pink brocade wallpaper, and the bedsheets were a matching pink, no blankets or spread. An overhead light made the room seem harsh, and the smell of cigarette smoke hung like a curtain.

"Who the hell do you think you are," she snarled, "barging into my room without a warrant!"

"The proprietor invited me in, Ms. Ho—I don't need a warrant."

"You know we work within the law out here. I'm a professional."

He held up a single hand of peace. "Ms. Ho, I just want to ask you a few questions."

"I've got nothing to say."

"How do you know, when I haven't raised a subject?"

"That was a Las Vegas badge. I don't have to talk to you."

"It's about the other night—at the Beachcomber?"

"Never heard of the place—never been there." She stalked over to the makeup table, where she plucked a cigarette out of a pack and lit it up. Suddenly she seemed much older.

"Maybe we got off on the wrong foot, Ms. Ho. Shall we make a fresh start?"

"Go to hell."

He just smiled at her. "I've got your fingerprints and lip prints on a wineglass, and I just bet if we check the stains on the bedspread, your DNA is going to turn up. And you're telling me you've never heard of the Beachcomber?"

"Never. I don't work Vegas. I work the ranch."

"Then it won't be much of an incentive to you, if I make it my life's work to bust you every time you come into the city to turn a trick?"

Her upper lip curling back over tiny white teeth, she gave him the finger. "Sit and spin."

Exasperated, he started for the door. Turning around, he said, "That john, at the hotel? Here's how serious this is: he got murdered, shortly after you left him."

Her face changed but she said nothing. She took a few little drags on the cigarette, like she was trying to make it last.

Brass said, "Hey, I know you didn't kill him. I just want to ask you about the time you spent with him."

"I don't know anything."

He started to turn away again, but her voice stopped him.

"Listen—he was nice to me. Seemed like a nice enough guy."

Brass went over to her—not rushing. He got out a small notebook and a pen. "Did you know him? Was he a regular?"

She shook her shimmering blonde head and plopped onto the chair in front of the mirror. "Charlene sent me. I'd never seen the guy before."

"What can you tell me about him?"

She shrugged. "He was clean and that's about as nice as tricks get."

"Anything else? Did he talk about his business or anything?"

She shook her head.

"Did he seem nervous or overwrought?"

Another head shake.

"Walk me through the night."

She sighed, thought back. "I went up about eight. We had some champagne. I gave him a blowjob, he came real fast. He'd paid for a full evening, so I helped him get it up again and we did it again. You're not gonna find any DNA, though."

"Oh?"

"We used rubbers both times."

How little they knew. "Go on," he said.

"He showered, got dressed, and said he was going out. He said I could stay in the room for a while, order room service, take a shower or a nap. He didn't care. He just said that I had to be out before he got back and he said that would be around five in the morning."

Brass jotted notes, then asked, "Can you think of anything else?"

"That's it. I kind of liked him. It's too bad."

"Yeah."

"Well, I gave him a good time before he went."

"Twice," Brass said, nodded at her, thanked her, and went out into the hall.

He found Madam Charlene inside a small wood-paneled office off the lobby. She sat at a metal desk with a telephone and several small piles of what looked like bills; Post-it's were all over the place. A computer on the desk symbolized how far prostitution had come.

Knocking on the doorjamb, still being polite, Brass asked, "Charlene—could I talk to you? Won't take long."

She stopped in the middle of writing a check and looked up at him with large green eyes. "Anything else I can do for you, Sugar?" she asked, the southern lilt back in her voice.

He mimicked the drawl back at her. "Why didn't you tell me you set up Connie's date at the Beachcomber—Sugar?"

Again the Southern lilt wilted. "I provide rides out here, for guys who wanna get laid."

"You don't provide an . . . out-reach service?"

"I don't risk it—I leave that to the escort services in Vegas. Not my gig."

"So Ms. Ho is lying—she booked this client herself, against your wishes."

She sighed, leaned forward. "Look—I just didn't think it was important. You said you wanted to talk to her. Have I cooperated?"

He nodded. "Yeah—and I do appreciate it. Now I'm asking you to cooperate a little more—what about setting up that date? You did set it up?"

"I did, but . . ." Madam Charlene gave him an elaborate shrug. "It was just another date."

Shaking his head, he said, "I don't think so. If it was a normal date, you would have told the guy to come out here. Let him find his way, or send your limo service. So why'd you send Connie into the city? You said it yourself: it's a risk; not your gig."

She shrugged again.

"Look, Charlene, I don't want to sit at the county line and bust any of your girls that enter Clark County, but I will."

". . . Close the door."

He did.

"If I tell you what I know, you'll leave me and my girls outa this?"

"If I possibly can."

"You promise?"

"Boy Scout oath."

She sighed heavily, found a pack of Camels on her desk, and lit up a cigarette.

Everybody in this joint must smoke, Brass thought. For about the millionth time, he wished he hadn't quit.

She took a long drag, then blew it out. "You know who the guy is?"

"Lawyer named Philip Dingelmann."

Her forehead frowned; her mouth smiled. "And that doesn't mean anything to you?"

Brass shrugged. "Such as?"

"Dingelmann is the lawyer for, among other illustrious clients, a fine citizen name of Charlie Stark."

That hit Brass like a punch. "As in Charlie 'The Tuna' Stark?"

Stark was high up in the Chicago outfit—a mobster with a rap sheet going back to the days of Giancana and Accardo. Sinatra had sung at Stark's daughter's prom.

"Maybe it's some other Charlie Stark," she said dryly. "And maybe I did this favor for Dingelmann 'cause he represents little old ladies in whiplash cases."

"A mobbed-up lawyer," Brass said to himself.

"You will keep me out of it?"

"Do my best," Brass said, "do my best."

And he stumbled out of the brothel into the sunshine, at first shellshocked, and then a smile began to form.

He had said, from first whiff, that this was a mob hit; and Grissom had, typically, pooh-poohed it. Evidence was Grissom's religion; but Brass had known that his twenty-two years in the field, as an investigator, counted for something.

Jim Brass headed back to Vegas.

6

After three-and-a-half hours' sleep, a shower, and some fresh clothes, Catherine found herself back in the office again. She grabbed a cup of the coffee from the break room and forced herself to drink some of it. Not so bad—a little like motor oil laced with rat poison. She found Nick in her office, camped in front of the computer monitor.

"I don't get out of bed in the middle of the day for just any man," she told him.

"Glad to hear it." He cast one of those dazzling smiles her way, and pointed to the screen. "Check this one out."

Catherine peered over his shoulder. "Fortunato, Malachy? How 'fortunate' was Malachy?"

"Not very," Nick said, referring to the file on screen. "Disappeared from his home fifteen years ago, leaving a bloodstain in the carport, on the gravel driveway—no sign of Malachy since. The original investigators let the case drop—a bloodstain does not a crime scene make."

"True."

"Plus, the detectives were convinced the married Mr. Fortunato ran off with his girlfriend, and that the blood stain was a dodge to throw the mob off the track."

"The mob?"

"Gamblers, anyway. The variety that breaks limbs when markers go unpaid."

"If Malachy's the mummy, I'd say his dodge didn't work." Looking over Nick's shoulder, she slowly scanned the file. "Small-time casino worker, big gambling debts, suspected of embezzling at work. Ouch— that might have gotten a contract put out on him."

"He worked at the Sandmound," Nick said, referring to a long-since demolished casino, which had dated back to the days when Vegas had been a syndicate stronghold. "Two bullets in the back of the head, that's a fairly typical expression of mob displeasure."

"Okay," Catherine said. "I'm liking this . . . but why do you think Malachy's our mummy?"

Nick's tight smile reflected pride. "I traced the ring you found on the body. Jeweler who made the bauble recognized it. Bada-bing."

"Please. . . . Okay, you did good. Let's print out this report so we can look at it a little closer."

Nick printed the file.

"There's a sample of the bloodstain from that carport and a cigarette butt from the backyard in Evidence," Catherine said, sitting, reading the hard copy. "We can pull them, and try to get a DNA match, to make sure this is our guy."

Nick flinched. "Damn—that's gonna take forever."

"Good things come to those who wait . . . and while we're waiting . . ." Her voice trailed off as she noted Fortunato's address, and reached for a phone book. "Says he lived with his wife Annie." Thumbing the white pages, Catherine found the FOR's, ran a finger down the column, and said, "And she still lives there."

Neither was too surprised; the real residents of Vegas put down roots, like anyone anywhere else.

Nick squinted in thought. "Does that mean we have a fifteen-year-old crime scene?"

"It means I'm going to track O'Riley down, and run out there." She waved the printout. "I want to meet the little woman whose husband ran off with his girlfriend . . . and have a look at what may be a *really* not-fresh crime scene."

Nick bobbed his head. "I'll get on the DNA."

"Good." Glancing through the file one more time, she noticed a note that said the police had returned Mr. Fortunato's personal effects to his wife. "What the hell?"

She handed the note to Nick, who read it and shrugged. "So?"

Catherine's half-smile was wry and skeptical. "If Malachy the mummy was missing, what personal stuff did they have of his?"

"There's no inventory?"

She shuffled through the papers one more time. "Nope."

Nick shrugged. "Could be anything."

"Could be something." She rose, went to the door and turned back to him. "Nice work, Nick. Really nice."

He gave her another dazzler, pleased with himself. "I'm not as dumb as I look."

"No one could be," she said with affection, and he laughed as she waved and went out.

O'Riley met Catherine in front of the Fortunato house and she filled him in. She liked working with the massive, crew-cut detective because the man knew his limitations, and wasn't offended when she broke protocol and took the lead in questioning. She did wonder where he'd come up with that brown-and-green-plaid sportshirt; maybe the same garage sale as the who-shot-the-couch sportcoat.

The one-story stucco ranch had an orange tile roof and a front yard where the sparse grass was like the scalp of a guy whose transplant wasn't taking. Heat shimmered up off the sidewalk, and from the asphalt drive that had, in the intervening years, replaced the gravel driveway of the file photos. The carport, at least, remained.

The detective knocked on the door and almost immediately it opened to reveal a thin, haggard, but not unattractive woman in her fifties, with a cigarette dangling between her lips.

"Mrs. Fortunato?" O'Riley asked, flashing his badge. He identified himself and Catherine.

"I used to be Mrs. Fortunato. But that's kind of old news—why?"

Catherine said, "You're still listed under that name in the phone book, Mrs.—"

"I'm still Annie Fortunato, I just don't use the 'Mrs.' It's a long boring story." She looked from face to face. "What's this about, anyway?"

Catherine held the evidence bag containing the ring out in front of her—the distinctive gold-and-diamond ring winked in the sunlight, the "F" staring at the woman, the woman staring back.

Taking the bag, a slight tremor in her hands, Mrs. Fortunato studied the gaudy ring. A tear trailed down her cheek and she wiped it absently. Another replaced it and another, and soon the woman shook violently and slipped down, puddling at O'Riley's feet even as he tried to catch her.

A burly man in a white T-shirt and black jeans bounded into the living room from the kitchen. "Hey, what the hell?" he yelled, moving forward toward the stricken woman.

O'Riley, surprised to see the guy, pulled his badge and tried to show it to the man who barreled toward them, his fist drawn back ready to punch O'Riley in the face. The badge slipped from O'Riley's grasp and his hand came back toward his hip.

In horror, Catherine realized the big cop, spooked and unnerved, was going for his gun. She grabbed O'Riley's gun hand, keeping him from drawing his pistol and, in the same fluid motion, stepped in front of the detective, ready to take the blow from the large man freight-training toward them.

Facing the oncoming potential attacker, she almost yelled, "It's all right, sir! We're with the police."

The punch looped toward her and Catherine flinched, but the blow never landed. Her words registered just in time, and the brute halted the punch just short of her face.

She gasped; but she would have done it again, because if she hadn't, O'Riley might well have been up before the shooting board for firing on an unarmed citizen. A lousy career move. And dead or wounded citizens were not helpful to an investigation.

"Police?" the big guy was asking, dumbfounded.

Behind her, on the stoop, O'Riley stumbled backward, regained his balance, and stood there staring at Catherine as the big guy helped Annie Fortunato to her feet. The apparent man of the house led the shaken woman inside, helping her to take a seat on the sofa. Finally, O'Riley followed.

"Who are you, sir?" Catherine asked, as she quickly took in the living room, an ode to the brass-and-glass movement of the eighties. After picking his badge up, O'Riley relegated himself to the background. The big detective was trembling, and embarrassed, and Catherine was only too happy to carry the ball.

Catherine repeated: "Sir, who are you, please?"

The T-shirted brute's attention was on the weeping woman, but he said, "Gerry Hoskins. I'm Annie's . . . uh . . . friend." Middle-aged, the powerfully built six-foot Hoskins wore his brown hair almost as short as O'Riley's; his oval face had a bulldog look, offset by deep blue eyes which Catherine supposed would look attractive when they weren't blazing with anger . . . as they were now.

"What did you do to her?" he demanded.

Fighting to regain control, Annie Fortunato handed Hoskins the evidence bag.

"They . . . they found Mal," the woman managed between sobs.

He looked at the initial on the ring. Then he stared at his agonized lady friend, and, finally, Hoskins seemed to get it. "Oh, God. You finally found him? You wouldn't be here, he wasn't dead, right?"

Catherine ignored this; and O'Riley was just another outmoded hunk of furniture. Crouching on her haunches so she could look the woman in the eye, Catherine said, "We think your husband is dead, Mrs. Fortunato . . . but we need to make sure. I know it's been many years . . . do you remember, did Malachy have a dentist he visited regularly?"

Not missing a beat, the woman said, "Dr. Roy McNeal."

"You're sure? It has been a long time—"

"He's still my dentist. And Mal was so busy, at work, I always made his appointments for him."

"Good. Good."

Clutching her boyfriend's hand, Mrs. Fortunato kept her eyes on Catherine. "You really think you've found Mal? I mean, after all these years?"

"A body discovered yesterday was wearing this ring—on the third finger of his right hand."

Annie Fortunato drew in a breath; then she nodded. "Yes, that's where he wore it. Where did you find him?"

"A vacant lot toward the end of the Strip."

Eyes tight, Mrs. Fortunato said, "I know that lot—the one with all the garbage?"

"Yes. A resort's going in. Romanov's."

"I read about that in the paper," Hoskins said, as he plucked a tissue from a box on an end table. He handed Mrs. Fortunato the tissue, and she managed a weak smile of thanks, dabbing at her eyes.

"A crew has started to clear the lot," Catherine said. "They found the man we believe to be your husband under an old abandoned trailer."

The woman seemed to have another question that she couldn't quite get out. Catherine leaned in, touched Mrs. Fortunato's arm. "Yes? What is it, Mrs. Fortunato?"

Shakily taking a cigarette from a pack on the glass end table next to her, the woman lit it, took a deep drag, let it out in a blue cloud, and finally turned her attention back to Catherine. "Was she with him?"

"She?"

"His whore," she snarled. "Was *she* with him?"

Woah . . .

Catherine said, "He was alone. We searched the lot thoroughly—no other body was present."

Patting Mrs. Fortunato's knee, Hoskins—his manner very different now—said to Catherine, "There was this dancer that some people thought Mal was sleeping with. You know—a stripper."

"I know about strippers," Catherine said.

"Slut disappeared the same night Annie's husband did. Annie had some trouble with some . . . uh . . . people Mal owed money, bad debts, you know. They told Annie that Mal had probably just run off with this woman, and they wanted her to give them the money Mal owed."

Something like a growl escaped Mrs. Fortunato's throat. "Like *I* had a goddamn penny to my name, back then. It wasn't until we got Mal declared legally dead after seven years that I got any peace from anybody."

"These people," Catherine said, "were they organized crime?"

"Yeah," Hoskins said. He shook his head. "It was different, back then. Mal worked for one of the old-school casinos, Chicago or Cleveland guys owned it . . . they claimed he was skimming. Anyway, some characters who make me look like a fashion model come around a few times, right after Mal . . ."

Struck by how vivid this recapitulation was, Catherine interrupted. "Excuse me, Mr. Hoskins, were you here, then?"

He shook his head. "No—but I heard Annie talk about it so much, it's like—"

"Then I need to hear this from Mrs. Fortunato, okay?"

The big guy looked sheepish. "Oh. Yeah. Sorry."

Mrs. Fortunato picked up right where he had left off. "They came around right after Mal . . . disappeared. They made a lot of noise, made me show them my damn bank book. Tax statements, too, they made me show 'em. Wanted to know what safe deposit boxes I had, God. Finally they saw I didn't have the money, and left me alone."

Catherine nodded. "They wanted to make sure you weren't in with your husband on the embezzlement."

Defensively, the woman said, "It was never proven that Mal stole their money."

"Mrs. Fortunato, your husband's death is a murder, and it looks like a mob assassination." Catherine let it go at that; she preferred not to share any details with the woman, not this early in the investigation, anyway.

Mrs. Fortunato took this in blankly, eyes not teary anymore—red, glazed, but not teary.

Catherine said, "If you're up to it, I'd like to ask you a few more questions."

"I suppose we should get this over with," Mrs. Fortunato said, and sighed. "What do you think, Gerry?"

"Yeah. I'll make us some coffee, okay?"

A tired smile crossed the woman's face. "Thanks."

Awkwardly, Hoskins looked from Catherine to the totem pole that was O'Riley. "Would you people like anything? Coffee? I got diet root beer."

Catherine said, "No thank you," and O'Riley shook his bucket head.

Hoskins swallowed, stood, and went over to O'Riley in his corner. He extended his hand. "Sorry, man. I shouldn'ta swung on you. It's just that it looked like . . ."

"Forget about it," O'Riley said, taking the guy's hand.

"Am I gonna get charged with anything? Swinging on a cop like that?"

O'Riley waved it off. "Simple misunderstanding."

"Sure you don't want any coffee?"

"I could use some," O'Riley admitted.

Wanting to keep Hoskins busy, Catherine said, "Me, too. Thanks."

Hoskins went into the kitchen and O'Riley melted back into the corner.

"Gerry's been good to me," Mrs. Fortunato said, her eyes following Hoskins into the kitchen. "These last years, he helped me survive."

Catherine pressed forward. "Mrs. Fortunato, tell me about the day Malachy disappeared."

Again, not missing a beat, the woman knew: "January twenty-seventh, nineteen eighty-five."

"Yes. What do you remember?"

"Everything," Mrs. Fortunato said, stubbing out one cigarette in the ashtray on the end table and immediately lighting up another. "Mal had been nervous—trouble at work, I figured. He never really told me much about things like that. He always got up early, around five-thirty, and by six-thirty, he was on his way to work. He was dedicated to his job, despite what those people said. Anyway, on that morning, I didn't hear him get up."

"Go on."

"I worked late nights, in those days. I was a cashier over on Fremont Street. Mal worked at the Sandmound, in the office, accounting."

"Excuse me—wasn't your husband a gambler?"

"Oh yes."

"I thought the casinos didn't hire gamblers for jobs of that nature."

"No one knew he was gambling . . . except me. He was doing it from phone booths. Calling bookies out east. By the time anyone found out what was going on, him and that dancer had disappeared." She drew on the cigarette; her eyes glittered. "I hope the bastards killed her too. She was the one turned him from a guy who liked a friendly bet into a gambler."

"How do you mean?"

"Well, it's obvious. If he hadn't tried to keep us both happy, he wouldn't have stolen that money. He wouldn't have been betting on games trying to make enough money to support two women."

Catherine frowned. "So, he really was embezzling? Whether it was proven or not?"

Another shrug—a fatalistic one. "Why would they lie to me about it? What could they get out of me? They weren't so bad, anyway, for a bunch of goddamn mobsters. I worked in casinos for years, myself."

Catherine hit from another side. "Could it have been the bookies he bet with out east that put out a contract on him? Not his bosses at the casino?"

"Your guess is as good as mine." Mrs. Fortunato snuffed out her latest cigarette. "You know, in my head, I always hoped he ran off. Then at least he'd be alive. But in my heart? I knew he was dead."

Steering her back, Catherine asked, "About that day?"

The woman stared into the past. "I got up about ten that morning.

Got the paper off the stoop. It didn't always come before Mal left for work. If it did, he brought it in. But that morning it was on the stoop. I picked it up, looked toward the carport, and Mal's car was gone, just like it ought to be. So, I went about my business. I read the paper, had some breakfast, called my mom—she was still alive back then—you know, stuff and things."

Catherine nodded.

"About four-thirty, I decided to go to the grocery store, get something nice for dinner. I hadn't talked to Mal all day, but I expected him home around six or so. It was my day off and he usually came right home on my day off, so we could spend the evening together." A wistful smile flickered; her eyes grew moist again.

Catherine knew what it was like, loving a louse. "You must have loved him a great deal."

Tears overflowing again, she nodded.

Catherine moved up onto the couch and let the woman cry on her shoulder.

After several long moments, Mrs. Fortunato shuddered, then pulled away, mumbling her thanks. Then she spoke quickly: "I decided to go to the grocery, and went out the back door. We used the back door almost exclusively. I went out and saw this dark red blotch on the gravel of the carport. This was before we paved the driveway. Goddamn asphalt. It's for shit in this heat. But the contractor said it was cheap and I didn't know any better."

Catherine tried not to rush the woman, but she could see O'Riley getting antsy in the corner.

Hoskins returned, carrying a tray with four cups and sugar and cream.

The woman said to him, "I was just telling them about the asphalt."

"Contractor was a goddamn crook," he said and went back into the kitchen for the coffee.

"You saw the dark red blotch," Catherine prompted.

"Yeah, yeah, and I just knew. I looked at it close and I just knew it was drying blood. I came right back in the house and called the police."

Hoskins brought in the coffee. They each took a cup and he poured. Mrs. Fortunato used lots of sugar and some cream, Hoskins only the cream, while O'Riley and Catherine drank theirs black. Much better than the break-room swill.

Catherine thanked Hoskins, as did O'Riley—she noticed a tiny tremor in the cop's big hand. She turned back to Mrs. Fortunato. "So, you called the police."

"Yes. They came, took a sample of the blood, and were never able to tell me anything. They never even found Mal's car."

"The report said that the police returned your husband's personal effects."

The woman nodded.

"There was no inventory in the report—I was curious what they had of his."

"Gerry, could you get the box? You know where it is."

Hoskins left the room again.

"When the cops brought back the box," the woman said, "I barely opened it. Mostly it was junk from Mal's desk at work." An edge was creeping into her voice. "One of the things they found, though, was a letter to him from his whore. That's what made them think he ran away with her."

Hoskins came back in carrying a plain brown cardboard box and handed it to Catherine.

"May I take this with me?" she asked.

The woman scowled. "Be my guest. And do me a favor—this time, don't bring it back. There's nothing in that box I ever want to see again. That was the property of a different man—not my Mal."

Accepting the box, Catherine asked, "By the way, did Malachy smoke?"

"No, not ever. He thought it was a filthy habit." She glanced at the cigarette in her hand. "Ironic, huh? I'd quit smoking 'cause of him . . . then when he disappeared, started in again. Nerves."

"I'm sorry, Mrs. Fortunato, but I have to ask you one more question."

"Yes?"

"Can you tell me the name of the dancer your husband was involved with?"

Mrs. Fortunato's jaw set, her lips whitened. She stabbed out the cigarette, repeatedly jabbing it into the ashtray, sending up a small shower of sparks.

Hoskins said, "Joy Starr."

"Why do you need her name?" Mrs. Fortunato asked.

"We'd like to talk to her," Catherine said. "But first we'll have to find out what became of her."

Hoskins offered, "Annie never knew if that was her real name, or just a stage name. . . . But she worked at a place called Swingers. It's still there—way down south on Paradise Road."

Catherine knew the place. "Okay, Mr. Hoskins—thanks." She turned to the woman. "Thank you, Mrs. Fortunato, for your time and patience. I know this has been difficult. We'll be looking into your husband's murder, now, so we may have more questions later."

Catherine held out her hand and the woman grasped it, warmth in her grip. The stoniness in Mrs. Fortunato's face seemed to melt away.

"Somehow," the woman said, "I feel . . . better. Thank you."

When the cop and the criminalist got outside into the July heat, O'Riley stopped Catherine, near her car.

"Thanks for doin' my job in there. And, uh . . . well, just thanks."

She gave him a look.

The crew-cut head shook, and he blew out wind. "I was ready to draw down on the S.O.B."

"Forget it, Sarge. Could have happened to anyone."

Catherine noticed a slight shudder in O'Riley's hands as the detective got into his car. After placing the box of Malachy Fortunato's effects in the backseat, she climbed into the Tahoe and phoned Nick.

"Nicky, Malachy's our mummy. Get the address of a dentist named Roy McNeal and get back to me. I want to pick up Fortunato's dental records before I come back to the office."

"Cool," Nick said. "Get right back to you."

She sat in the SUV and studied the house as she waited for Nick's call. So Malachy didn't smoke, and at the time of his disappearance, his wife wasn't a smoker, either. A cigarette butt in the backyard could mean somebody waited for Malachy Fortunato to leave the house, that morning fifteen years ago. . . .

He lit the cigarette, clicked the Zippo closed, and leaned against the house as he took a long drag. Dew still clung to the new sod. Grass probably wouldn't last long here, but they always seemed to make the effort when they put up one of these new homes. The house he stood behind had been built within the last six months and only inhabited for the last two. The mark inside, some guy named Fortunato, had pissed off the wrong people.

Houses on either side held families that still slept peacefully. Behind the house, where he now stood puffing away on his Marlboro, the backyard butted up against one from the next block. Those homes, however, had not been completed, and the construction crews hadn't yet arrived to begin the day's work. So he had the neighborhood to himself. . . .

Fortunato's schedule seemed etched in stone. For the week the hitter had been watching him, the mark had left the house within a two-minute window, every morning. The hitter loved a clockwork guy. Same time, same path, every day, an invitation for someone to cap a poor, sad son of a bitch.

He took another drag, let the smoke settle in his lungs, then slowly blew it out through his nose. Glancing at his watch, he smiled. Plenty of time to enjoy this cigarette, no reason to rush. Finish the smoke, put on his gloves, then go to work.

Taking one last drag, the hitter held it in for a long time before blowing the smoke out and stubbing the butt into the yard with his foot. He pulled the gloves from his pocket and slipped them on. Rotating his head, he felt the bones in his neck crack as he loosened up; then he checked his watch one last time.

Time to punch the clock.

He withdrew his automatic from its holster, checked the clip, then screwed on the silencer. He shifted slightly so he could see around the corner. No target yet. Ducking back, he slowed his breathing, waited. . . .

The mark walked out of the door, closed it, then the screen, and turned to his car. The hitter came up behind Fortunato, squeezed the trigger and felt the small pistol buck in his hand. A tiny flower of red blossomed from the back of the mark's head. Didn't even have time to yell, simply folded in on himself and dropped.

Going down with him, the killer put another shot one inch above the first—an insurance policy and a signature. Then the killer pulled the car keys from the dead man's hand, peered over the fender of the car to make sure no one had seen the action. Satisfied the neighbors still slept, he jumped up, opened the trunk, picked up the body and *dumped it in, slammed the lid, then got in the front, behind the wheel, and turned the key.*

The engine turned over, rumbling to life and, not rushing, the hitter backed the car out of the driveway and eased down the street, just another middle-class joe on his way to work.

There was no one around when he arrived at the vacant lot off Russell Road. None of the passing motorists paid any attention to a guy driving into the lot to dump his trash, like so many others had before him. It took only a moment to find what he sought. To his left, shielded from the road, was the abandoned house trailer he'd spotted earlier. The hulk had already begun to rust, and he figured no one would be nosing around it for some time. Several sheets of its aluminum skin had slipped off. Some hung precariously from the side, others lay scattered like molted scales.

He pulled the body from the trunk, careful to avoid the bleeding skull, and dragged the meat by its feet to the trailer. He shoved the body onto a sheet of aluminum, then pushed the sled of metal underneath the trailer. As a parting gift, he unscrewed the silencer, which he dropped in a pocket; then removed the barrel from the automatic and tossed it under the trailer with the corpse. With more strips of trailer skin, some wood and rubble, he blocked the opening. Then, using his foot, he covered over the blood trail with dirt, wiping out most of the footprints (among so many footprints already), and casually drove off. He would ditch the car elsewhere.

The cell phone rang and shook Catherine from her reverie-cum-reconstruction.

"Write down this address," Nick said, and he gave it to her, and she did. "Dr. McNeal's nurse'll have Malachy Fortunato's file waiting for you."

Within an hour an energized Catherine Willows was driving back to headquarters with the dental records in hand, certain she was about to establish the identity of their mummy.

Finding him had only been yesterday; today, with the victim identified, the search would shift to his killer.

7

As if hypnotized by a fascinating work of cinematic art, Grissom watched the gray grainy picture crawling across the monitor; this was yet another Beachcomber video, one of scores he'd examined over the past twenty-four hours. Right now he was taking a second pass through the stack of tapes that represented the morning of the shooting. Occasionally he would remove his glasses and rub his eyes, and now and then he would stand and do stretching exercises, to relieve the low back pain all this sitting was engendering.

But mostly he sat and watched the grainy, often indistinct images. A normal person might have gone mad by now, viewing this cavalcade of monotony; but Grissom remained alert, interested. Each tape was, after all, a fresh piece of evidence, or at least potential evidence. Right now, in an angle on the casino, the time code read 5:40 A.M.

The ceiling-mounted camera's view—about half-way back one of the casino's main aisles, looking toward the front—included a blurry picture of the path from the lobby to the elevators. At this time of morning, casino play was relatively sparse. Notably apparent in frame were a man sitting at a video poker machine, on the end of a row near the front, and a woman standing at a slot two rows closer to the camera, this one facing it. For endless minutes, nothing happened—the handful of gamblers gambling, the occasional waitress wandering through with a drink tray; then Grissom noticed a figure in the distance—between the lobby and the elevator.

Sitting a little straighter, forcing his eyes to focus, Grissom felt reasonably certain the blurry figure in the background was their victim from upstairs. He hunched closer to the screen, eyes narrowed, watching—yes!—John Smith as he took a few steps, and then glanced casually in the direction of the man at the video poker machine. Almost as if Grissom had hit PAUSE, John Smith froze.

Smith was too far in the background for the security camera to accurately record his expression; but Grissom had no trouble making out Smith as he abruptly took off toward the elevator. Nor did Grissom have any trouble seeing the poker player start after him, get stopped by something attaching him to the machine, which he pulled out, and then followed Smith to the elevator.

As the man on the monitor screen moved away from the poker machine, Grissom was able to note the same clothes he'd seen on the fleeing killer on the videotape from upstairs, right down to the black running shoes.

Damn—how had he missed this first time around? Grissom shook his head—it had all happened quickly, in the time it might have taken him to rub his eyes from fatigue.

Grissom stopped the tape, replayed it, replayed it again. As with the hallway tape, the killer never looked at the camera. *Had he knowingly positioned himself with his back to the security camera? Was he a hit man stalking his prey?*

He watched the tape several more times, concentrating now on the hesitation in the killer's pursuit. Finally he noticed the flashing light on top of the machine. The killer had hit a winner just as he took off after the victim! Was that what had stopped him?

No. Something else.

Grissom halted the tape. He knew who could read this properly. He knew *just* the man. . . .

He stood in the doorway and called down the corridor: "Warrick!"

When this got no immediate response, Grissom moved down the hallway, a man with a mission, going room to room. He stuck his head inside the DNA lab, prompting the young lab tech to jump halfway out of his skin.

"I didn't do it, Grissom," Greg Sanders said. "It's not my fault!"

This stopped Grissom just long enough for him to twitch a tiny smile. "I'm sure you didn't do it, Greg—whatever it is. Have you seen Warrick?"

"Last I saw him, he and Sara were working on AFIS . . . but maybe that was yesterday. . . ."

At that, Grissom frowned. "Precision, Greg. Precision."

Back in the hallway, he moved on in his search, and almost bumped into the lanky Warrick, stepping around the corner, typically loose-limbed in a brown untucked short-sleeved shirt and lighter chinos.

"You rang, Gris?"

Grissom was on the move again. "Come with me—I want to show you something."

Back in his office, Grissom played Warrick the tape—twice.

"Well?" Grissom asked.

There was never any rushing Warrick; his eyes were half-hooded as he played the tape for himself one more time.

Then Warrick said, "Looks to me like he's pulling a casino card from the machine."

Grissom smiled. "And we know what that does for us."

"Oh yeah. Casino can track the card. They can give us the *name* on the card." Warrick frowned in thought. "You don't suppose the killer's local?"

"I don't suppose anything," Grissom said. "But that possibility hasn't been ruled out. . . . What are you working on?"

Warrick jerked a thumb toward the door. "Sara and me, we were working on tracing the sender of a piece of e-mail on Dingelmann's Palm Pilot."

Grissom frowned. "Dingelmann?"

Warrick gave him a look. "That's the victim's name—Philip Dingelmann."

"Were you waiting for Christmas to give it to me?"

"Didn't you see Brass's report—it's on your desk."

Grissom nodded toward the monitor. "I've been in here a while."

"You were in here yesterday when shift ended. This is a *new* shift, Gris. You oughta get some sleep, maybe even consider eating a meal now and—"

"Dingelmann! Chicago. The mob lawyer?"

Warrick, now wearing his trademark humorless smirk, just nodded.

Grissom put a hand on Warrick's shoulder. "Okay, let Sara work the e-mail; she's the computer whiz—you're my resident gambling expert."

"Is that a compliment?"

"I don't care what it is—I want you back at that casino, now. Check that machine for prints, and find out whatever you can from the slot host."

"Should I page Brass, and call in a detective?"

"When the time comes."

Already moving, Warrick said, "I'm on it," as Grissom assured him, "I'll tell Sara what's up."

Grissom walked back down the hall to the office where Sara worked at a keyboard. "Any luck?" he asked.

"Sure—all lousy," she said. "This guy covered his tracks pretty well. This e-mail must have been laundered through every freakin' ISP in the world."

"Okay, relax." Grissom sat on the edge of the desk, smiled at her; he'd hand-picked the Harvard grad for his unit—she'd been a seminar student of his, and he valued her tech skills, dedication, and tenacity. "There are other things to be done, right?"

"Always. Where's Warrick?"

"I sent him back to the Beachcomber."

Her brow tightened. "Without me?"

"Yes."

"Think that's a good idea? Sending him to a casino all by his lonesome?"

Grissom shrugged a little. "I trust him."

A sigh, a smirk. "You're the boss."

"Nice of you to notice," Grissom said. "Anyway, I need you."

She looked at him, eyebrows up, not quite sure how to take that.

"We have a date in the morgue."

They both wore blue scrubs and latex gloves, and stood between the two autopsy tables. In front of them lay Philip Dinglemann, behind them Catherine and Nick's mummy.

"So, what are we doing here?" Sara asked.

"Read this," he said, handing her the autopsy report for John Doe #17.

She scanned it quickly, stopped, read part of it more slowly. "What's this, a screw-up? Robbins got the bodies backward?"

Grissom shook his head. "The pattern's the same, to within an eighth of an inch."

"That can't be right. . . ."

"The evidence says it's right, it's right. But you and I are going to measure them again just to be sure."

"It's a heck of a coincidence."

"Is it?"

"Grissom, why didn't you tell Warrick and me about this?"

"Keeping the cases separate. No assumptions that we have one case, here, until or unless the evidence tells us so."

Nodding, she said, "Which one first?"

"Age before beauty," Grissom said, turning to the mummy.

Warrick parked in the vast lot behind the Beachcomber, entering through the casino, a smaller version of his field kit in hand, including fingerprinting gear. He knew (as Grissom surely did) that this was probably a pointless exercise, all this time after the killer had left the machine behind; but you never knew.

Grissom had sent him here alone, even making the questionable call of not inviting a detective along for any questioning that might come up. Either Grissom finally trusted him completely, Warrick figured, or this was a test. The whirrings of slots, the calling out of dealers, the dinging, the ringing, made for a seductive madhouse through which he walked, somehow staying focused on the job at hand.

Soon he found himself standing under the camera that had captured the videotape images Grissom had shared with him. He ignored the bells and whistles, the smoke-filled air, the expressions on faces—defeat, joy, frustration, boredom—and just did his job. He strode to the video poker machine where, less than twenty-four hours ago, the killer had sat.

The patron sitting there now, bald, bespectacled, in his mid-thirties, wore a navy Polo shirt, tan Dockers, and sandals with socks. Warrick watched as the man kept a pair of tens, drew a wild deuce and two nothing cards. Three of a kind broke even, returning a quarter for the quarter bet. Big spender, Warrick thought, as the man kept a four, six, seven, and eight, a mix of clubs and diamonds.

Sucker bet, Warrick thought; trying to fill an inside straight, what a joke. The guy drew an eight of spades—another loser. Mr. Sandals-with-socks quickly lost four more hands before he turned to Warrick, standing peering over his shoulder.

Irritation edged the guy's voice. "Something?"

Warrick flashed his badge. "I'm with the Las Vegas Criminalistics Bureau. Need to dust this machine for fingerprints."

The gambler flared with indignation. "I been sitting here since Jesus was a baby! I'm not giving up this machine."

Nodding, Warrick bent down closer. "A killer sat at this very machine yesterday morning."

The man didn't move; but he also didn't return his attention to the poker machine.

Warrick gestured with his head. "You see that camera over my shoulder?"

Looking up at the black bulb sticking out of the ceiling, the guy nodded.

"From a videotape shot by that camera," Warrick said calmly, "I viewed the killer sitting right here. Now, I'm going to call over someone from the staff and we're going to dust this machine, so I can find out who that guy was."

"What about me? What about my rights?"

"Do you want to cash out now, or you wanna wait in the bar till I'm done? That way you can get your machine back . . . protect your investment."

The guy gave him a sour look. "I'll be in the bar. Send a waitress over when you're finished."

"Thank you," Warrick said. "Be advised I may decide to print you, as well, sir—so I can eliminate your prints."

Grumbling about his right to privacy, the guy hauled away his plastic bucket (with several unopened rolls of quarters in it) and walked toward the bar, padding away in his socks and sandals. Right then a casino security officer came gliding up to Warrick.

"May I help you, sir?" he asked, his voice mingling solicitude and suspicion.

The guard was black and Warrick's height, more or less, but carried an extra forty pounds—apparently of muscle—on a broad-shouldered frame. That much was evident even through the guy's snug-fitting green sports coat with its BEACHCOMBER patch stitched over the pocket. The walkie-talkie he carried in a big hand looked like a candy bar.

Again, Warrick flashed his badge and explained the situation. "I need to see the slot host."

"I'll have to call my supervisor," the guard said.

"Okay."

The guard spoke into the walkie-talkie and, in less than two minutes, Warrick found himself surrounded by half a dozen of the crisply jacketed security guards, a green sea that parted for a California-ish guy in a double-breasted navy blue suit. Though he was the youngest of them, this one seemed to be the boss—six-one, blond, good-looking.

"I'm Todd Oswalt, the slot host," he said, extending his hand. He smiled, displaying the straight white teeth and practiced sincerity of a TV evangelist.

"Warrick Brown," the criminalist said, shaking with the guy, "crime lab following up on the murder, yesterday."

Oswalt's smile disappeared, his eyes darting around to see if any of the customers had heard Warrick. "Mr. Brown, we'll be happy to help you if you'll please, please just keep your voice down."

Now Warrick smiled. "Gladly, Mr. Oswalt. There was a man sitting here around five-thirty yesterday morning. I need to know everything about him that you can tell me."

"Based on what? We have a lot of patrons at the Beachcomber, Mr. Brown."

"This one used a slot card on this machine at 5:42 A.M yesterday."

Oswalt's eyes were wide; he nodded. "I'll get right on that."

"And while you're doing that," Warrick said, easily, "I'll need to fingerprint this machine."

Oswalt frowned, glanced around again. "Right now?"

"I could do it after business hours."

"We never close."

"Neither do we—so is there a better time than right now? Since I gotta be here anyway, while you're checking out that slot card?"

"Uh . . . your point is well taken. Go right ahead, Mr. Brown."

The slot host instructed two guards to stay nearby, then he and the other of his green-jacketed merry men disappeared. Warrick spent about an hour on the machine, at the end of which time he had dozens of prints and doubted that any of them would be of any use. There was just no telling how many people had tried this machine since the killer left.

Gesturing that burly guard over, Warrick said, "You can tell your boss I'm done."

The guard pulled out a walkie-talkie and talked into it. He listened, then turned back to Warrick. "We're supposed to escort you to the security office."

"Fine. And I need to have this machine held for a guy in the bar—can you send a cocktail waitress after him?"

"Sure thing. How will I know him?"

"He'll be the only bald guy with glasses wearing socks and sandals."

"All right. Man, you're certainly thoughtful."

"Hey, gamblers got it hard enough already."

The other guard was called over to escort Warrick, and the blond Oswalt was waiting for them at the security-office door. "We've got your information, Mr. Brown. The man's name is Peter Randall."

Warrick got out his notepad and pencil. "Address?"

"P.O. Box L-57, 1365 East Horizon in Henderson."

Warrick felt a sinking feeling in his gut. He jotted the address down, knowing it would wind up being one of those damn rent-a-mailbox places. "Anything else, Mr. Oswalt?"

"Not really."

Warrick put the notepad away. "We're going to need to go back a few days, maybe a few weeks, to look for this guy some more—the tapes we have so far don't give us a look at his face."

"He could be a regular customer," Oswalt admitted.

"Right. How long to round up those tapes?"

"I'm short staff, and those tapes are stored—"

"How long, sir?"

Oswalt thought about it. "Tomorrow morning?"

"Can I look at them here?"

"We'd prefer it if you did."

Warrick nodded. "Thanks. I'll be back."

From the car, Warrick called Grissom and told him the name and address. Again Grissom approved him going alone—a killer was on the loose, and trails could go quickly cold.

The drive to Henderson—a community of stucco-laden homes aligned like green *Monopoly* houses, many of them behind walls and/or gates—took twenty minutes on the expressway. Just as he thought, the address belonged to a strip mall rent-a-box storefront.

The mailboxes ran down one wall, a long counter along the opposite one. The girl behind the counter might have been eighteen, her blue smock covering a slipknot T-shirt and faded jeans. Her hair was dishwater blonde and she had a silver stud through her left nostril.

"Can I help you?" she asked with no enthusiasm.

"Is the manager here?"

"No."

"Will he be back soon?"

"She," the girl corrected. "She just went to lunch."

"Do you know where?"

"Yeah, the Dairy Queen around the corner."

"Thanks," Warrick said. "Can you tell me her name?"

"Laurie."

This was like pulling teeth. "Last name?"

The girl thought for a moment. It seemed to cause her pain. "I dunno."

"You don't know?"

"Never came up."

"Yeah. Well. Thanks again." Meaning it, he said, "You've been a big help."

With the pep of a zombie, she said, "Come back any time."

Warrick walked to the Dairy Queen around the corner, spotted the woman who must be Laurie sitting at a table alone, picking at an order of chicken strips and fries. She wore the same blue smock as the girl back at the store; her brown hair, cut at shoulder length, matched her brown eyes in a narrow, pretty face, and she appeared to be about six months pregnant. He went straight to her. "Laurie?"

She looked up and, guardedly, asked, "Do I know you?"

"No, ma'am. My name is Warrick Brown. I'm with the Las Vegas Criminalistics Bureau." He showed her his badge. "May I sit and talk to you for a moment?"

"Well . . ."

"It'll just take a few moments."

"I suppose. Can you tell me what this is about?"

Pulling out one of the plastic-and-metal chairs, Warrick joined her at the small square table. "I need to talk to you about one of your clients."

Laurie shook her head. "You know I can't talk to you about my clients without a warrant. Their privacy is at stake."

"This man is a killer and we can't waste time."

That impressed her, but still she shook her head again. "I'm sorry. I just can't . . ."

Warrick interrupted her. "His name is Peter Randall."

Her eyes tightened.

"What is it, Laurie?"

"Funny you should ask about Mr. Randall. He closed out his account just yesterday."

"Can you talk to me, off-the-record, while we're waiting for a warrant to arrive?"

Again she looked as if she didn't know what to do.

Warrick pulled out his phone, called Grissom, and explained the situation.

"Sara will be there with a warrant within the hour," Grissom said. "And I'll alert Brass."

While they waited, Laurie finished her lunch and they returned to the storefront. The nose-stud girl seemed as bored as ever, paying little attention to them as they came to the counter, Warrick staying on the customer side, Laurie going behind it. The woman had decided to cooperate—she asked him several times, "He's a murderer, right?"—and she pulled Randall's record right away.

"His home address?" Warrick asked.

Laurie looked at the file. "Forty-six fifteen Johnson, here in Henderson."

Warrick made a quick call on his cell to dispatch, for directions.

Moments later, he said, "Damn."

"What's the matter?"

"No Johnson Street or avenue or anything like it in Henderson. That's a fake address."

"Oh. I mean, we don't check these kind of things. We take our customers at their word."

Warrick went to Box L-57. "I know you can't open this for me, until the warrant arrives. But can you say whether or not Mr. Randall has cleared it out?"

"I'm afraid he has," Laurie said. "There's nothing in it—Mr. Randall emptied it when he closed his account."

"Shit."

"I'm sorry," Laurie said.

"You're just doing what I'm doing."

"Huh?"

He smiled at her. "Our jobs."

She smiled back, and the nose-stud girl rolled her eyes.

Five minutes later, Sara—accompanied by Detective Erin Conroy—turned up with the warrant; he filled them both in on the situation.

Sara smirked and shook her head. "So, there's nothing?"

Warrick shrugged. "We can print the mailbox door, but that's about it. Looks like a dead end."

Conroy said, "I'll question her . . . what's her name?"

"Laurie," Warrick said.

"Last name?"

Embarrassed, he shrugged again. "Never came up."

Conroy just looked at him; then she went over to question the woman and put on the record the things that had been told to Warrick, off.

Sara sighed and said, "I gave up running prints for this?"

"You were tired of doing that, anyway."

She tried not to smile, but finally it broke through. "Yeah, I was."

"Well, you're gonna love it when I give you the dozens of prints I got off that slot machine."

"More prints. You find anything good?"

"Yeah." He leaned in conspiratorially, as Conroy's questioning echoed in the hollow storefront. "A Dairy Queen, around the corner. Lunch. You buy."

She clearly liked the sound of that; but as they were exiting, Sara nudged him in the ribs, saying, "Buy your own damn lunch."

Two hours later, back in the office, Warrick had already struck out with "Peter Randall"—an alias, of course—and Sara had run the prints from the casino, which had also proved worthless. And the guy's mailbox door had failed to yield a single usable print.

Laurie Miller, the manager, had waited on "Randall" both times he'd been in the store, and her description of him to Detective Conroy was painfully generic: dark glasses, dark baseball cap was all that got added to what the hotel tapes had already told them. A witness sketch would be worked up, but not much hope was held for it.

Backing up, Warrick decided to see what they could get on the footprints from the hallway.

Sara used a database that identified the running-shoe design as the probable product of a company called Racers; the match was not exact, due to the imperfect nature of the crime-scene footprint. So Warrick went online and found the number for the corporate office in Oregon.

"Racers Shoes and Athletic Apparel," said a perky female voice. "How may I direct your call?"

"My name is Warrick Brown. I'm with the Las Vegas Criminalistics Bureau. I need to talk to someone about sales of different product lines of your shoes."

There was a silence at the other end.

Finally, Warrick said, "Hello?"

"I'm sorry, sir," the voice said. "I had to ask my supervisor how to route your call. I'm going to transfer you to Ms. Kotsay in sales."

"Thank you."

He heard a phone ring twice, then another female voice—somewhat older, more professional—said, "Sondra Kotsay—how may I help you?"

Warrick explained the situation.

"This is a most unusual request, Mr. Brown. We manufacture many lines of shoes."

"I know. And we have a tentative match from a database, already. But I could really use your expert confirmation."

"Am I going to have to testify?"

He smiled to himself. "Probably not. I'd just like to fax you a footprint."

"Oh," she said, "well, that would be fine," and gave him the number.

He chose not to send her the bloody print he'd highlighted with the Leuco Crystal Violet and instead sent her one from the landing that Grissom had obtained with the electrostatic print lifter.

A few minutes later, he was asking the woman, "Did you get that?"

There was a moment of silence on the line, then Sondra came back on the phone. "Came through fine," she announced. "Give me a little time. I'll call you back when I've got something."

How tired he was just dawning on him, Warrick wandered down to the break room and got himself some pineapple juice out of the fridge. He went to see Sara, at her computer, but she wasn't there. He tracked her down—in all places, at the morgue, standing over Dinglemann's corpse.

"You okay?" he asked.

"Yes," she said. "No . . . I don't know."

"What?"

"Why are we working so hard to find out who killed this guy? Why am I busting my butt to find his killer?" She pointed at the body. "I mean, mob lawyer, getting the scum of the earth off, scot free . . ."

"Better not let Gris hear you talking like that."

She threw her gaze at him, and it was almost a glare. "I'm not talking to Grissom. I'm talking to you."

"You know it's not for us to decide." Warrick moved a little closer, so that Dinglemann lay between them. "This guy, he's past all that now. Good, evil—doesn't matter. He's been murdered. That puts him in the next world, if there is one—but his body's in our world."

She thought about that, then she shrugged. "Maybe it is that simple. I don't know. It's just . . . hard for me."

"Well, if you can't divorce yourself from the good and bad, think of the guy who did this. Somebody who takes money to take lives. That bad enough for you?"

She smiled, just a little. "Yeah. Yeah, that'll do it."

His cell phone rang and they both jumped. He almost dropped it in his haste to answer. "Warrick Brown."

"Sondra Kotsay, Mr. Brown. I think I can help you."

Waving at Sara that he had to take this call, Warrick went back down the hall to his office, grabbed a pad and plopped into his chair.

The professional voice said, "The print that you faxed us is for our X-15 running shoe."

"Okay."

"It's a line that, I'm sorry to say, has not done very well for us."

Warrick knew that the smaller the production run, the better his chances. "How many have been produced?"

"Before production stopped, just under one million pair."

His heart dropping to his stomach, his head drooping, he said, "A million?"

"I know that sounds daunting, Mr. Brown. But it's not that bad—at least not for you."

"Uh huh."

"Over half were never sold."

That helped—sort of. As she gave him her report, he scribbled the information on the pad.

"And of the remaining half-million," she said, "only about one hundred pair were sold in the greater Las Vegas area."

He was liking the sound of this more and more.

"The particular size that you gave us, men's size eleven, sold less than two dozen pair in the Vegas area."

The smile split his face nearly in half. "Thank you, Ms. Kotsay. Great work."

"Would you like the names and addresses of the retailers that sold them?"

Would you like to marry me? he thought. "Thank you, Ms. Kotsay—that would be incredibly helpful."

She faxed him the list.

And then Warrick Brown went looking for Grissom.

8

As Catherine looked on, Dr. Robbins matched Malachy Fortunato's dental records against the teeth of the mummy. Both criminalist and coroner were in scrubs, but underneath his, Robbins was in a pinstriped shirt and diagonally striped tie with charcoal slacks; he'd had a court appearance today.

It was a little before seven P.M.—Catherine in early again, shift not officially beginning till eleven.

The coroner would study the dental X ray, then bend over the mummy, then straighten to check the X ray, a dance Robbins repeated half a dozen times before waving her over. "Catherine Willows, meet Malachy Fortunato."

She smiled. "At long last?"

Nodding, he said, "At long last—trust me, this is indeed the elusive Mr. Fortunato. We have a textbook dentalwork match."

"Well, well," she said, looking down at the mummy, her hands pressed together as if she were contemplating a fine meal. "Mr. Fortunato, it's nice to finally meet you. . . . Now that we know who you are, we'll see if we can't find your murderer."

The leathery mummy had no reply.

"Nice work, Doc," she said, and waved at Robbins on her way through the door.

"That's what I do," he said to the swinging door.

Out of her scrubs, Catherine ran into Nick, coming out of the lab.

"Hey," she said. "You're in early, too, I see."

"Hey," he said. But he looked a little glum. "DNA's going to take another week—they're completely backed up in there."

"Doesn't matter," she said with a grin. "Dr. Robbins just matched the dental records to our mummy—Malachy Fortunato."

"All right!"

"You did good with that ring, Nick."

"Thanks."

They headed into the break room for coffee. Nick poured, asking, "When was the last time this office solved a mob hit?"

"A week ago never. Surprisingly little of that in Vegas."

"Like they say, you don't defecate where you dine."

"I always try not to." She sipped her coffee, feeling almost giddy. "We're on a roll, Nick. Let's get this guy."

"Sure—what's fifteen years between friends?"

She half-frowned, half-smiled. "You tryin' to rain on my parade?"

"No way. No statute of limitations on murder. What do you need from me?"

She headed out of the break room, coffee cup in hand. "We'll get to that. First, let's go tell Grissom what we've got."

After Warrick explained what they'd turned up at the casino and at the storefront in Henderson, Grissom said, "This still doesn't prove he's local."

Grissom was behind his desk, jumbles of papers, a pile of binders seemingly about to topple, and an unfinished glass of iced tea cluttering the desk, as well as assorted displayed insect specimens, dead and alive. Warrick sat in one of the two chairs opposite his boss, and Sara leaned against a file cabinet in the corner.

Sara said, "But the maildrop—"

Grissom shook his head. "Our man could just be using the maildrop. And who knows how many slot cards he has in how many names, and in how many casinos . . . in how many towns."

"What about the shoe?" Warrick asked.

Grissom said, "That will help, particularly in ascertaining whether he's local. But half a million pair were sold nationally, you said."

Warrick nodded, unhappily.

Grissom continued: "For that shoe to be of any real benefit, we've got to find the foot that goes in it."

Sara smirked. "The guy attached to the foot would also be nice."

Warrick sighed and said, "Tomorrow morning, I can start watching the older tapes at the casino. If our man is local, that's a good place to look."

"It is," Grissom said, nodding. "No luck with the prints? Anything on 'Peter Randall'?"

"No and no," Sara said.

Warrick shook his head. "Gris, you really think we're going to track this guy down? I mean a mob hit . . ." He shrugged helplessly.

"You're thinking of that guy at the Sphere," Grissom said, "aren't you?"

Not so long ago, Warrick had worked the murder, still unsolved, of a bad debtor who had been shot to death in a glass elevator at the Sphere Hotel—that M.O., though different, also reeked mob.

"Maybe," Warrick said. "What makes this different?"

"Among other things," Grissom said, "the evidence."

Before Grissom could amplify, Brass came into his office from one direction, quickly followed by Catherine and Nick from the other. Brass, a stack of files tucked under an arm, gave Grissom a quick nod.

"We've got a positive ID from the dental records," Nick said, dropping into the chair next to Warrick. "Our mummy is Malachy Fortunato, a local who disappeared fifteen years ago, owing the mobbed-up casino bosses a whole lot of money. The mummy's a mob hit."

Warrick—who'd been kept in the dark about the similarity of the wounds on the two murder victims—sat forward, alert.

"The mummy seems to be," Grissom said. "I'm still not sure about Philip Dingelmann. But I do believe they were both shot by the same man."

With the exception of the blank-faced Brass, mouths dropped open all around the room.

The homicide detective stepped up and tossed the stack of files on Grissom's desk. "We're pretty sure both crimes are the work of an assassin the FBI has monikered, of course, 'The Deuce.' He is apparently responsible for at least forty contract killings across the length and breadth of our fine country, over a period approaching twenty years."

Perched in the doorway, Catherine asked, "How do you know?"

"By the signature," said Brass. "Two vertically placed small caliber wounds approximately an inch apart."

"'Deuce,' " Warrick said dryly.

"But we're going to need more than just the signature," Grissom said, "to prove we're right that these murders share a murderer."

A brief discussion ensued, as those who knew about the similarities between the corpses skirmished with those who hadn't been in the know.

Finally Grissom notched up his voice. "We may have a legitimate coincidence in the discovery of these bodies," he said.

"The timing, you mean," Catherine said.

"Yes—Dingelmann was killed prior to the discovery of Fortunato's remains, but basically they were simultaneous, unconnected events . . . a murder going down just about the same time as a long-dead victim of the same killer is unearthed. And nothing here indicates the two murders have anything to do with each other. Nothing yet, anyway."

Nodding, Catherine said, "But the signature suggests the victims share a killer."

"Now that's a coincidence I *can't* accept," Grissom said. "That two different murderers, connected to two different mob-related murders, would have the same M.O."

Warrick said, "Two bullets in the back of the head, Gris, that's a sign of mob displeasure that goes *way* back."

"This is more specific—vertically placed shots in this exact same location, an inch apart. That struck me from the start, not as a coincidence, but as the signature we now know it is."

"*How* do we know?" Nick asked.

Grissom sat forward. "After I examined your mummy, Nick . . . Catherine . . . I told Jim my theory, and he got his people digging in the national computers."

Brass tapped the stack of files on Grissom's desk—twice. "This guy is not tied to any one organized crime family, in any one part of the country. He is apparently a freelancer with a shared client base—no one knows what he looks like and, as far as we can ascertain, no one's ever seen him in action . . . and lived to tell."

"We already knew we had a contract assassin who did mob hits," Sara pointed out. "We now believe two murders, fifteen years apart, were the work of the same assassin. Other than that . . . how does this help us?"

"It's more than we had," Grissom said. "We have context, now—we have direction."

"Swell," Catherine said. "What do we do different?"

"Nothing." His gaze met hers, then swept around the room including them all. "We still operate as if it's two separate cases . . . but now we keep everybody informed about what we learn. Catherine, you and Nick keep working on the mummy. Like Brass says, we need corroborating evidence. Find it."

"You want us to prove this is the same hitter," Nick said.

Catherine, an eyebrow arched, stared at Grissom.

He looked back at her for a second. "No," he said to Nick, but holding her gaze. "Follow the evidence—it's still possible we might have two murderers."

Catherine smiled.

"What about the farm team?" Sara asked.

Grissom turned to Warrick. "Watch those hotel tapes till your eyes bleed. . . . Sara, I want you to find out everything that's known about this killer. Study the files, but dig deeper. Look for linkages. Maybe other investigators missed something."

She nodded.

"Nicky," Grissom said, "get the bullets from both cases to the firearms examiners for ballistics tests."

"Sure thing," Nick said. "But, uh . . ."

"But what?"

Nick shrugged. "We already know the riflings on the bullets match the gun barrel found half-buried next to Mr. Fortunato."

Grissom nodded. "The killer ditched the barrel, yes, but maybe he didn't ditch the gun. We've still got bullets with a matching caliber on these two murders. We've got to cover all the bases."

Warrick had been studying his boss, and his voice conveyed confusion as he said, "I don't get it, Gris. Why do you think Dingelmann may not have been a mob hit?"

"Just staying objective."

"I'm the subjective asshole," Brass said, pointing a thumb to himself. "Philip Dingelmann was getting ready to represent Charlie 'The Tuna' Stark in the biggest mob trial since Gotti—why kill him? He's a golden mouthpiece, who'd already gotten Frischotti off, and Vinci, and the two Cleveland guys, Tucker and Myers."

"What was he doing in Vegas?" Warrick wondered aloud.

Brass shrugged. "This was probably his last chance to blow off steam, 'fore going into the tunnel of the trial."

Nodding, Warrick said, "Yeah, yeah . . . but why kill him?"

No one had an answer for that.

"Let Jim here worry about motive," Grissom told his unit. "Concentrate on the only witnesses who never lie: the evidence."

Nods and smiles, all around—they'd heard it before.

Brass said, "We've done a lot over the years to get the mob influence out of this city. We need to catch this son of a bitch to remind these scumbags this is not their turf anymore—it's never going to be like the old days again."

The homicide detective told Grissom the files were copies for the unit, reminded the others to stay in touch, and slipped out.

"Personally," Grissom said, now that Brass was gone, "I think we owe less to the city fathers, and more to our two victims. Time doesn't lessen the injustice done to Malachy Fortunato—and an unsavory client list doesn't justify what was done to Philip Dingelmann."

Warrick and Sara exchanged glances.

"So," Grissom said, cheerfully. "Let's go to work."

Outside the office, Catherine stopped Nick with a hand on his elbow. "After you get those bullets dropped off, can you check something for me?"

"Sure—what?"

"Mrs. Fortunato mentioned a dancer her husband was involved with at the time of his disappearance. She said the dancer . . . a stripper . . . disappeared the same day as her husband."

"Do we have a name?" Nick asked.

"Joy Starr. It may be a stage name. . . ."

"You think?"

"Either way, Nicky, we need to find her if she's out there somewhere. Preferably, alive."

"You mean she could be another corpse, hidden away someplace?"

"Definite possibility."

Nick sighed. "Know anything else about her?"

"Not much. She worked at Swingers—that dive out on Paradise

Road. When she was dancing, it would have been a little nicer than now."

"And?"

"And what?"

"She worked in a strip club before disappearing fifteen years ago? That's it?"

"That's it. Maybe you can round up one of Brass's people and go out there—though this many years later . . . Check the newspaper websites first. Check missing-persons records—she apparently dropped out of sight when Fortunato did."

He shot her one of his dazzlers. "Hey, if you want me to hang out at a strip club, I guess I can make the sacrifice."

"First, check the records. That club, at this late date, is a real long shot."

"Okay. What about you?"

Catherine was on the move already. "I'm going back to the house. Back when Malachy wasn't a mummy yet, this was a missing persons case. Now it's the scene of a murder."

"A crime scene," Nick said, understanding.

Catherine wheeled the Tahoe out of the lot and pointed it toward the Fortunato home. She was considering calling in O'Riley, but decided against it. This was an evidential fishing expedition, and didn't involve interrogation; not a lot of point in him wasting time, too.

On her way, on her cell phone, she called the Fortunato home, got Gerry Hoskins, and asked if it would be all right to come around at this time of evening.

When she arrived, Catherine told Mr. Hoskins what she would be doing and got his okay. Annie was lying down, he said, and he wanted her to try and rest, after the stress of today's news.

Understandable.

While Catherine prepared, Hoskins moved their two cars out of the driveway and onto the street. The scene had been done once, fifteen years ago, and now she hoped to turn up something those guys had missed. Although massive changes had occurred in the science of investigation since then, sometimes you just had to fall back on the old stuff.

Hauling the metal detector from the back of the Tahoe, Catherine pulled the headphones on, cranked the machine up, and started at the end of the driveway nearest the street. Moving slowly back and forth, Catherine combed the driveway. In the original Fortunato file, there had been nothing about shell casings; of course, blood on the gravel drive or not, the detectives hadn't known they were searching a murder scene.

And the file said nothing about the discovery of shell casings.

Even though the sun had long since started its descent, the fiery orange ball seemed in no hurry to drop behind the mountains, the heat still hunkered down on the city, settling in for the long haul. If she weren't at a crime scene, she wouldn't have minded one of those refreshing if rare summer rains, though that would bring the danger of flash flooding.

She made it all the way to the far end of the carport and nothing had registered on the metal detector. Her shoulders ached, her eyes burned, and she seemed to be sweating from every pore in her body. She'd been working crazy hours, even for her. Taking the headphones off, she ran a hand through her matted hair and pulled a paper towel out of her pocket to mop her forehead.

"Brutal, huh?"

Mildly startled, Catherine turned to see Annie Fortunato standing there, holding two large glasses of lemonade, a smoke draped from her lip. The woman of the house handed one of the moisture-beaded glasses to Catherine.

"Why, thank you, Mrs. Fortunato."

"Would you stop that? Call me Annie."

"Sure. Thanks, Annie." Catherine took a long gulp from the icy glass. "You're saving my life."

The woman shrugged. "It's just powdered . . . but this hot, even that junk'll hit the spot."

Smiling, Catherine nodded and pressed the cool glass against her forehead.

Mrs. Fortunato removed her cigarette long enough to gesture with it toward the metal detector. "What're you lookin' for out here, with that thing?"

"Frankly," Catherine said, seeing no reason to withhold the information, "I was hoping to find the shell casings from the bullets that killed your husband."

She frowned in alarm. "You think he was shot . . . *here*?"

"Blood was found."

"Yes, but . . . I didn't hear any shots, and I was a light sleeper. Hell, I still am."

"The killer could have used a noise suppresser—a silencer. . . . Are you okay with me being so blunt?"

"Hell yes. I had my cry. Go on."

"Anyway, the gun barrel we found with your husband's body belonged to an automatic. That means shell casings, which had to go somewhere."

Mrs. Fortunato nodded, apparently seeing the logic of that. "Well—you havin' any luck?"

Catherine sighed. "No, not really—and it would have been a lucky break if we had." She took another big drink of the lemonade. "I'm going over it one more time, before I hang it up."

Mrs. Fortunato was studying Catherine. "You know, I want to thank you for what you've done."

Catherine didn't know how to react. "You're welcome, Mrs. Fortunato . . . but I haven't really done anything yet."

The woman sipped at her lemonade, then puffed on her everpresent cigarette, and a tear trickled down her cheek. "Yes, you did. I know Malachy wasn't perfect, but he was . . ." The tears overtook her. She stubbed out the cigarette on the ground.

Catherine put her arm around the woman.

"Shit, I had my cry."

"It's all right," Catherine said, "it's all right."

"Don't get me wrong—I love Gerry!"

"I know. It shows."

Something wistful, even youthful touched the woman's wellgrooved face. "But, Mal, he was the love of my life. You only have one—and sometimes they're even sonuvabitches . . . you know what I mean?"

Catherine smiled a little. "I'm afraid so."

"When you brought me his ring out here today, well, I finally knew what happened to him. No more wondering, weaving possibilities in the middle of the night . . . that's why I say, 'thank you.' "

Squeezing the woman to her, Catherine said, "In that case, Annie, you're very welcome."

Catherine walked her over to the stoop and they sat on the

cement, where they finished their lemonade in silence, the sun finally touching the horizon, the sky turning shades of violet and orange and red.

Finally Mrs. Fortunato said, "I better get back inside. I need a cigarette. You want to join me?"

"No, thanks." Catherine rose. "I better get going, if I'm going to get this done before it's too dark to see."

"I'll turn on the outside lights." Picking up the empty glasses, the woman said, "If you want some more lemonade, holler."

"I will," Catherine answered, and returned to the metal detector as Mrs. Fortunato disappeared back into the house. Again Catherine slipped on the headphones.

"High tech," she said to herself wryly.

Starting at the back end of the carport, Catherine swept back and forth holding the three-foot handle, the disk-shaped detector barely two inches off the black asphalt. The machine always made her back hurt from the slightly stooped posture she assumed working it. Halfway back through the carport, on the side nearest the house, she got a tiny hit.

It was so small, at first she thought her ears were playing tricks on her. Over and back, over and back, the same spot, each time—the small sound echoing in her head.

Might be a shell casing, might be a screw, could be anything. One thing for sure, though: it was definitely something, something metallic. She pulled out her cell phone and punched Grissom's number on speed dial.

"Grissom."

"I think I've got something here," Catherine said.

"What?"

She explained the situation. "Any ideas?"

"Maybe. Give me half an hour. How's your relationship with the homeowners?"

"They love me."

"Good. Get permission to dig a hole."

". . . In their asphalt driveway?"

"Not in their flower bed."

"Oh-kay, Gil, I'll be waiting." She pressed END, slipped the phone away as she walked to the front door, where she knocked.

Gerry Hoskins, still in T-shirt and jeans, opened the screen.

"I think I may have found something," Catherine said.

Mrs. Fortunato had apparently filled him in already, as he did not hesitate. "I'll get Annie."

By the time Grissom showed up, the three of them stood in the yard, waiting. Catherine met Grissom at the Tahoe. "Are you going to do what I think you're going to do?"

"No—*we* are. And it's going to be slow and it's probably going to be messy."

He and Catherine put on coveralls and carried the equipment to the spot she'd marked on the asphalt. She handed him the headphones so he could hear the faint tone.

"All right," he said. "Let's get started."

Catherine watched as he picked up a small propane torch and lit it. She asked him, "Is this going to work?"

"It's the only way I could think of that would give us a decent chance of preserving the evidence. If that's what it is."

The torch glowed orange-blue in the darkness.

"I hope so," she said, worried. "This is a lot of trouble to go through if I just located some kid's lunch money."

Grissom smiled. "Then we'll turn the treasure over to these good citizens, with our thanks."

On their hands and knees, with only the porch light to aid them, they hovered over the area as Grissom held the torch to the spot she had marked. As the asphalt softened from the heat, Catherine carefully dug the material out with a garden trowel. The closer they got to the bottom, the slower they went. Grissom held the torch farther away, heating smaller and smaller sections of the carport at a more measured pace. Catherine now used a tablespoon to scrape away the heated asphalt, and a miniflash to light the area as she scoured it for the bit of metal that had pinged her detector.

Finally, after nearly two hours of this tedious labor, her knees killing her from kneeling, and with bits of the old gravel visible at the bottom of their short trench, Catherine saw something that looked out of place.

"Hold it," she said.

Grissom pulled back even further. "You see something?"

She said, "I think so," and moved forward, shining the light down at the hole. Setting the spoon aside, she pulled on a pair of latex gloves and carefully picked at the edge of the hole. Her gloves were no match for the hot asphalt and she had to be careful. She poked and prodded at the spot until finally the thing popped loose.

Grissom turned off the torch and took her flashlight, so she could use both hands.

Scooping up the small dark object, she juggled it from palm to palm, blowing on it as it cooled. He shone the light on the thing in her hand. Small, about the size of a fingertip and about a third the diameter, the object was obviously metal but covered with the sticky black mess.

"When we get back to the lab and clean all this goop off," she said, holding the object up to the light, "I think we'll find we have a twenty-five-caliber shell casing."

Grissom said nothing, but his eyes were as bright as the torch, right before he shut it off.

9

For nearly two hours Sara immersed herself in the files Brass had provided, learning several significant facts the rumpled homicide detective had failed to mention.

While the killer's career covered nearly twenty years, only a handful of thumb prints from shell casings linked a single suspect to any of the murders. The two vertical bullet holes approximately one inch apart, his signature, had shown up in forty-two murders (prior to this week's discoveries) in twenty-one states. Interestingly, the signature seemed to have dropped off the planet just under five years ago. Their very new murder—the dead mob attorney in the Beachcomber hallway—was the only known exception.

Nick popped in. "Any luck?"

"Predicatably, Brass missed a few things," Sara said.

File folder in hand, he took a seat beside her.

She filled him in quickly, concluding, "I'm not sure any of this is stop-the-presses stuff. How about you?"

"Tests are going to take a while," Nick said.

Her chin rested in her palm, elbow propped against the desk. "There is one other little item Brass overlooked."

"Yeah?"

"None of the investigators seem to have made it an issue, but . . ."

"Give."

"The bodies of victims are found . . . although who knows how many other vics, like your mummy, remain hidden away . . . but their cars? Never."

"I'm not sure I'm following you."

"Okay, I'll give you the large print version. Take Malachy Fortunato—did the police ever find his car? Both he and his wheels were missing from that driveway, remember."

Nick, thinking that over, said, "I'd have to check the file for sure, but you know . . . I think you're right."

"Of course I'm right." She leaned toward him. "Hey, trust me—nobody's seen that car since it pulled outa the driveway that morning . . . with Mr. Fortu-nato most likely riding in the trunk."

"And a pretty darn docile passenger, I'd bet," Nick said. "But what about Dingelmann?"

"That, I grant you, doesn't fit the pattern," she said. "But then, Dingelmann didn't have a car. Took the shuttle from the airport."

"No rental?"

"No rental. Doorman saw Dingelmann taking cabs a couple of times."

Nick was interested. "All the victims' cars disappeared?"

"If they had cars, yeah. Also, victims tended to disappear from home, from work, or some other familiar haunt—and the bodies turned up elsewhere."

Nick was nodding. "Dumped, here and there."

"That would seem a reasonable assumption . . . of course you know how Grissom feels about assumptions."

Nick gestured to the stack of file folders. "Anything else in there we can use?"

"Well," she said, shrugging, "there is one thing I can't quite get a handle on."

"Which is?"

Sara went back into full analytical mode. "For some reason this prolific, professional assassin disappears almost five years ago. Why does he show up now? Especially if Grissom's on to something, and Dingelmann wasn't a mob hit . . . in which case, what the hell is this guy doing in Vegas, getting proactive again, all of a sudden?"

With a shrug, Nick said, "Maybe he was hired by somebody else."

"Like who?"

"Dingelmann's ex-wife, a disgruntled business partner, who knows? Just because no bodies have turned up with that distinctive 'Deuce' signature doesn't mean our man hasn't been active."

"Yeah, yeah, possible, possible—and we know at least one instance when he hid a body. So what do you think?"

Nick threw his hands palms up.

"You suppose Grissom wants to hear . . ." She mimicked his gesture.

"Okay," he said, rising, throwing a grin off to the sidelines, "I get it—more digging."

Sara gave him a mock sweet smile. "Well, don't go away mad—what have you dug up, thus far? I showed you mine, you show me yours."

His smile in return was almost embarrassed, and he laughed, and leaned against the doorjamb and said, "I went to the website for the *Las Vegas Sun,* and plowed through all the old newspaper coverage on Fortunato and his disappearance, him and this dancer he was involved with . . . as well as going over the original file for the dancer's disappearance. She was also officially a missing person, it turns out."

Sara frowned in interest. "Dancer?"

"Exotic type. A stripper. Innocent child like you wouldn't know about such things."

"Catherine would."

Nick grinned. "Yeah—that's where I heard about 'Joy Starr'—stripper having an affair with casino employee Fortunato . . . a stripper who disappeared on the same *day* as casino employee Fortunato."

Sara was grinning; she made a yummy sound. "This is getting good."

"Seems 'Joy Starr' was a stage name for a Monica Petty. I'm going to turn the name over to Brass, see what he can do with it."

"But you might just ride along to the strip club with him."

"I might. . . . She was a doll, in her day."

"Joy whatever?"

"Starr." Nick pulled a photo from the file folder, handed it to Sara. "Next on the bill, ladies and germs—the exotic dance stylings of Joy Starr."

"Cue the ZZ Top," Sara said, looking at an 8-inch by 10-inch head shot of a pretty, dark-eyed, dark-haired woman of maybe twenty-one, with that overteased '80s-style hair. "That's some mall hair."

"What?"

She laughed a little. "That's what we used to call it, my girlfriends and me—mall hair."

"You ever have hair like that?" he asked, puckishly. "Middle school maybe?"

"I was a heartbreaker then," she said, "and I'm a heartbreaker now. Run before you get hurt, Nicky."

"Ouch," he said, glanced again at the photo, then tucked it back in the folder, and went back to his work.

Once she and Grissom had returned, Catherine went directly into the lab and spent the next hour painstakingly cleaning the asphalt off the casing, dabbing it with acetone, doing everything within her power to make sure she did not damage it. Preserving fingerprints was a hopeless cause, but the casing itself could have other tales to tell.

She found the firearms examiner, a friendly twenty-eight-year veteran named Bill Harper, already examining the bullets that Nick had brought in earlier.

Harper's longish curly gray hair looked typically uncombed and he apparently hadn't missed a meal at least since the Nixon administration; but Catherine knew there was no better firearms examiner in the state.

"Anything?" she asked him.

"Not much," he replied.

"Nothing?"

"Something, but . . ." He shrugged and stepped away from the microscope, gesturing for her to look. She stepped up and looked down at two different shells. Obviously they had not come from the same barrel.

"Rifling's completely different," he said. "Of the four shells, each pair matches, but the two pairs don't match. The pair from the mummy matches the barrel found with the body. These other two slugs are strangers. The only commonality between pairs is they're all the same caliber."

Nodding, Catherine pulled back from the microscope and held up three evidence bags. "You want to take a crack at the shell casings?"

Harper's brow creased in interest. "What have you got?"

"Number one is from our mummy, two and three here are from the shooting at the Beachcomber."

"Sure," Harper said. "Understand, this could take a while."

"I'll wait," she said, sitting down at Harper's desk in the corner, allowing herself to lean back.

Watching him work, she counted the hours since she had last slept. Somewhere around twenty-four, she nodded off.

Greg Sanders found Nick at a computer, and presented him with the DNA match for Malachy Fortunato.

"Thanks, Greg. Matched the dental already though."

"*Gran Turismo* is still a deal, right?"

"I don't renege on a man who controls so much of my destiny."

"Smart move." Sanders shrugged. "Not much off the guy's shoes, either. He'd been on some sort of loose rock. Driveway maybe. That make any sense to you?"

"Yes it does," Nick said. "What about the cigarette filter?"

Sanders smirked. "That piece of crud was about fifteen years old—barely anything left."

"Way it goes."

Now Sanders grinned; the demented gleam in his eyes meant he was proud of himself. "Got some DNA off it though."

Nick sat up. "You're kidding."

"Not workable, though."

This guy was a walking good news/bad news joke. "Thanks, dude," Nick said wearily. "I'll bring that game in tomorrow."

"Yes!" Eyes dancing with joy-stick mania, Sanders departed.

Nick Stokes spent two hours trying to find Brass and had no luck; the detective was not answering his page, so finally Nick decided he'd make the first run out to Swingers himself. At least the change of pace might help him stay awake. Figuring he'd be a nice guy about it, he went hunting for Warrick, to give his fellow CSI a chance to tag along.

He found Warrick in a darkened lab, his head on a counter, snoring. With the hours they'd all been working, this made a whole lot of sense to Nick; and, instead of waking his co-worker, Nick retreated and closed the door.

Grissom's door, usually open, was shut now, lights off. The boss had kept pretty much to himself since returning with Catherine, and Nick wondered whether to bother him. On the other hand, if he didn't check with him, Grissom might be pissed—and Nick hated that.

He knocked on the door.

"Yeah," came the tired voice from the other side.

Nick opened the door and stuck his head into the darkened office. "Boss—hey, I don't mean to disturb you."

"Get the switch, will you?"

Nick did, bathing the room in fluorescent light.

Grissom, catching a nap on the couch, sat up; his graying hair was mussed, black clothes rumpled.

"You look like hell."

"Thanks," Grissom said, getting to his feet, stretching, "you too." Grissom met Nick at the doorway. "What?"

"Did Catherine tell you about the dancer that disappeared, same night as Fortunato?"

Little nod. "Yeah."

"Well, she used to work at this place called Swingers."

"On Paradise Road," Grissom said. He rubbed his eyes, yawned a little. "Sorry."

"Even you get to be human."

"No I don't. And don't let me catch you at it, either."

Nick couldn't tell if Grissom was joking or not; drove him crazy.

"That place still open?" Grissom asked, meaning Swingers.

"Should be," Nick said, with a thumb-over-his-shoulder gesture. "I thought I'd go out there, see if anybody remembered her."

"That's Brass's responsibility."

Nick shrugged. "Can't find him."

"O'Riley?"

Nick shook his head. "Off duty."

"Conroy?"

"The same."

Grissom considered the possibilities. "Take Warrick with you."

"He's snoring in a lab," Nick said. "I don't think he's slept in, I dunno, twenty-four hours."

"Okay," Grissom said casually, "then let's go."

Nick reacted as if a glass of cold water had been thrown in his face. "What—you and me?"

Cocking his head, Grissom gave Nick a look. "Something wrong with that?"

Hurriedly, Nick said, "No, no, it's fine. You want to drive?"

"That's okay. You drive . . . but this isn't official, understand. We're just taking a break."

"Right."

"Give me a second to brush my teeth."

"Sure, boss."

"And, uh—brush yours, too. There'll be ladies present."

Shaking his head, Nick went to quickly freshen up. Every conversation with Grissom was always a new experience.

The clapboard barn-looking building housing Swingers squatted on Paradise Road, a couple of miles southeast of McCarren Airport. Fifty years ago, before the tide of the city rolled out here to engulf it, the place had been a particularly prosperous brothel. Now, with the paint peeling and the gutters sagging, the structure looked like a hooker who'd stayed a little too long in the trade.

Even though Vegas was a twenty-four-hour town, the strip joint closed at three A.M., though the red neon SWINGERS sign remained on, with its pulsing electric outline of a dancing woman. Nick eased the Tahoe into a parking place with only about five minutes to spare. Perhaps half a dozen cars dotted the parking lot, with only a battered Honda parked near the Tahoe and the front door.

"Slow night," Nick said.

"Experience?" Grissom asked.

"I mean, looks like," Nick said. "Looks like a slow night. I wouldn't really know."

Skepticism touched Grissom's smile.

A shaved-bald, short-goateed bouncer met them at the door; he wore a bursting black muscle T-shirt and black jeans. "We're closing," he growled. Maybe six-four, the guy had no discernible neck, cold dark eyes, and a rottweiler snarl.

Nick said, "We're . . ."

"*We're* closed," the bouncer repeated. "We look forward to fillin' your entertainment needs some other night."

Nick keep trying. "We're from the Las Vegas . . ."

The bouncer's eyes bulged, his upper lip formed half a sneer. "Are you deaf, dipshit?"

Grissom stepped between the two men, showed the bouncer his badge. "Las Vegas Criminalistics Bureau."

The bouncer didn't move. "So?"

"We'd just like to speak with the owner."

"About what?"

Giving the big man a friendly smile, Grissom said, "Well, that would be between us and him."

The bouncer's eyebrows lifted; he remained unimpressed. "Well, then, you girls must have a warrant."

Nick's patience snapped. "Just to talk, we don't need a warrant!"

The bouncer glared and took one ominous step forward.

"Forgive my co-worker's youthful enthusiasm," Grissom said, moving between them again, getting in close to the guy, keeping his voice low.

The soft-sell caught the bodyguard off-balance—Grissom had the guy's attention.

With an angelic smile, Grissom said, "You'd like us to get a warrant? Fine, I'll make a call and we'll do just that. I can have it here in ten minutes. . . . Of course, in the meantime no one leaves the premises, and when it gets here we'll come in and find every gram, every ounce, every grain of any illegal drug here. Of course we'll do background checks on all the girls working here, to make sure they're of legal age. After that comes the fire marshal and the building inspector." He flipped his phone open. "I'm ready if you are."

Suddenly smiling, the bouncer patted the air in front of him. "Whoa, whoa. The owner? I think he's back in the office. Just a minute. You can wait at the bar." He pointed inside. "Anything you want, on the house."

They strolled into the smoky room, where southern rock music blared, neon beer signs burning through the haze, the walls rough, gray barnwood that never met primer let alone paint. A dozen men were present. The bouncer was disappearing toward the back.

"Nice work," Nick said.

Not surprisingly, the bar smelled of stale beer, cigarettes, urine and testosterone—not the most attractive joint in town, but low maintenance. Green-and-white plastic tables and chairs—lawn furniture—were scattered around the room. They faced a stage that ran most of the length of the far wall, chairs lining it for the front-row patrons; the only show-biz accouterments were cheap colored lights and two fireman's poles, one at either end of the stage.

A skinny blonde was sliding down one of the poles, half a dozen customers watching. Wadded-up dollars were scattered about the hardwood floor of the stage like so much green refuse.

To the left edge of the stage a doorway said DANCERS ONLY—this was where the bouncer had gone, and was clearly the pathway to the dressing room and the owner's office. Nick and Grissom stood at the right end of a U-shaped oak bar. Behind it, a tired-looking blonde woman of at least forty, wearing only a skimpy bikini, gave Nick the eye as she washed glasses in one sink and rinsed them in the next one.

"We just had last call, fellas," she said over the blare of southern rock, the flirtation heavy in her voice. "But if you want somethin', who knows? I been known to make exceptions."

She might be too old to strip, but she remained attractive enough to hustle.

"We're fine," Grissom said.

Frowning now, but still eyeing Nick, the woman resumed washing glasses, pumping them up and down on the brushes. The action was not lost on Nick and he turned away before allowing himself a little chuckle. Grissom either didn't notice, or was pretending as much.

The bouncer came out of the DANCERS ONLY door, holding it open for a thin young man who looked like a high school kid in his low-slung jeans and UNLV T-shirt; neither one, Nick knew, was a "dancer" he would pay to see perform. The young guy had curly blond hair, a scruffy goatee and a gun-metal gray barbell stud through his left eyebrow.

"Wanna talk to me?" he asked, in a voice not far removed from puberty.

Nick couldn't help himself. "You're the owner?"

"I'm the manager." The kid looked from Grissom to Nick. "You boys got a problem with that?"

Both criminalists shook their heads.

The kid gestured. "You mind if we step outside? I don't want to bother the customers—few we got left, tonight."

They moved into the parking lot, where a desert breeze stirred weeds surrounding the driveway. The flush of red neon bathed them as their conversation ensued, during which an occasional customer or two would exit to their cars.

Forehead tensed, Grissom asked, "How old are you?"

Neon buzzed, shorting out, like a bug zapper.

"Twenty-three," the kid said. "I'm workin' on my MBA at UNLV. This place is paying for it. My uncle owns it. Hey, I'm a business major—works out swell for both us."

"What's your name?"

"John Pressley."

"Like Elvis?" Grissom asked.

"Like Elvis but with two *s*'s."

Nick had his notepad out, and was jotting that down, as he asked, "How long has your uncle owned this business?"

"Not very—couple years. It was an investment property."

"I see. Can you tell us anything about the previous owner?"

Pressley gave him a dubious look. "Why?"

"We're trying to find a woman who danced here fifteen years ago. Way before your time."

Pulling a crumpled pack of cigarettes from his jeans pocket, Pressley lit up; he looked at Nick, then at Grissom, as if taking their measure.

"Marge," he finally said. "Great old broad. She owned this dump forever."

That piece of information was a nice break, Nick thought, and asked, "What was her last name, do you remember?"

"Sure. Kostichek. Marge Kostichek." He spelled it for Nick, who wrote the name down.

"Address?"

The kid puffed on the cigarette. "I got no idea—you're gonna have to work harder than that, guys."

Grissom smiled the angelic smile again. "How hard, Mr. Pressley?"

"Oh, she's still around. You could probably find her in the phone book. Let your fingers do the walkin'."

"Thanks," Nick said.

The kid raised his studded eyebrow. "You gonna hassle us anymore?"

Grissom stepped forward. "Is Marge Kostichek the straight skinny, or are you blowing smoke?"

Keeping his eyes on Grissom, Pressley snorted a laugh and said, "She's so real I can't believe you never heard of her. She's a legend in this business, man."

"She pans out," Grissom said, "no hassles."

"Yeah . . . for how long?"

"Till next time," Grissom said, pleasantly, and led the way as they walked toward the Tahoe.

Outside, Grissom said, "Let's go back to the office. We'll find an address for Marge Kostichek, and you can round up Conroy or Brass to go with you."

"Yeah," Nick said. "Uh, Grissom."

"Yeah?"

" 'Straight skinny'?"

Grissom just smiled, and Nick laughed.

They climbed back into the Tahoe and Nick started the engine. They were passing the airport when Grissom finally spoke again. "I guess you've picked up on my being hesitant to let you out on your own."

Nick said nothing.

"You don't like that much, do you?"

Turning, Nick met Grissom's eyes, but he said nothing.

"You know why that is, don't you?"

Nick shrugged. "You don't think I'm ready." A traffic light turned red and Nick braked to a stop.

"I *know* you're not ready."

Nick turned to his boss and even he could hear the earnestness in his voice. "You're wrong, Grissom. I'm ready. I'm so ready."

Grissom shook his head.

The light turned green and Nick fought the urge to stomp on the gas. He slid ahead slowly.

"That bouncer," Grissom.

Embarrassed, Nick said, "Yeah, yeah . . ."

"If I hadn't stepped in, you'd have wound up in a fight with a citizen. Which would have led to suspension for you, and a black eye for our unit."

"I just . . ." Nick stopped. He knew Grissom was right and somehow that made him even angrier. He looked down at the steering wheel, his knuckles white.

"You forgot why you were there," Grissom said, "and let it turn into some kind of . . . macho foolishness. The case is the thing, Nick. It's the only thing."

Nick hung his head. "You're right. I know."

"Don't beat yourself up—fix it."

"Yeah, I will. Thanks, Grissom."

"Anyway, this is a good example of why we let Brass and his guys handle the people. We're better at evidence."

"Hey," Nick said, pulling into the Criminalistics parking lot, "we didn't do so bad, end of the day, did we?"

"Not so bad," Grissom admitted.

"Of course I'm not so sure we needed to brush our teeth."

In the firearms lab, Bill Harper laid a hand on Catherine's shoulder and she jumped.

"Sorry," he said, jumping back himself.

"No! No, I'm sorry. I must have . . ."

"Slept for hours?" he offered.

"Oh, no, I couldn't have. . . ."

He pointed at the clock on the lab wall.

"Oh, my God," she said, flushed with embarrassment. "I'm really sorry, Bill."

His smile told her it was okay. "Hey, it was all right—you seemed to need it. You really looked bushed."

"Do I look any better?"

"Catherine, few look any better, at their worst. . . . Go wash up, and then we'll talk."

With a reluctant smile, she took his advice.

Ten minutes later she returned from the locker room to the lab, face washed, hair combed. She hated to admit her own human frailty, but she felt worlds better after the nap. "Okay, Bill, what have you got?"

"Have a look at the monitor."

She looked at the computer screen on Harper's work table and saw the butt ends of two casings next to each other.

"What do you see, Catherine?"

Studying the two images, she said, "Twenty-five caliber, one Remington, one Winchester."

He pointed to the primers.

"They've both been struck," she added.

"They've both been struck—*identically.*" Reaching over, he

clicked the mouse and the two primers suddenly filled the screen. He pointed out three different bumps. They were correspondingly placed on each primer.

She could feel her whole face light up as she smiled. "The same firing pin?"

He nodded. "Helluva thing, ain't it? Fifteen years apart—two different crimes . . . same firing pin."

Catherine took a step back.

Harper clicked again and the picture zoomed back out to show the ends of the casings. "And look here," he said, pointing to tiny barely visible indentations at four points on the end of the cartridge, "this is where each one hit the breech wall."

She felt almost giddy. "You're going to tell me they're identical, too, aren't you?"

"Yes, ma'am—and that ain't all. . . . The scratches from the extractor, when the shell was ejected?"

She nodded her understanding.

Harper grinned. "They match too."

Catherine let out a long breath, shaking her head, amazed and delighted at the findings. "He's using the same gun . . . and thinks he's fooling ballistics, changing out the barrels. Grissom was right—Malachy Fortunato and Philip Dingelmann were killed by the same gun, presumably the same killer, fifteen years apart."

Harper said, "That's what the evidence says."

"And that's what Grissom likes to hear," Catherine said, on her way out. "Thanks, Harper—I needed this as much as that nap. More!"

Grissom sat behind his desk, munching a turkey-and-Swiss sandwich. He sipped his glass of iced tea, and looked up to see a figure pause in his open doorway—a man maybe six-one in a well-tailored light blue suit, muscularly trim, with blond hair combed slickly back from a high forehead, and a strong, sharp nose, narrow blue eyes . . . and a smile of cobra warmth.

"Special Agent Rick Culpepper," Grissom said, setting his iced tea carefully back on his desk. "Up late, or early?"

"How do you stand these hours?" The FBI agent smiled his oily smile. "With all the people you encounter, I'm complimented you remember me."

"How could I forget?" Grissom gave the agent a smile that had little to do with the usual reasons for smiling. "You're the man who tried to get one of my CSIs killed, using her as bait."

Strolling uninvited into the office, Culpepper said, "My God, you're still upset about that? Sara Sidle volunteered, and everything came out fine—let it go, Grissom. Get past it."

"I have trouble getting past you using . . . misusing . . . my people, Culpepper. We're busy here. What do you want?"

"You're takin' a lunch break," Culpepper said, nodding to the half-eaten sandwich Grissom had put down. "I won't eat up any of your precious crime-solving time. . . . Relax, buddy. Ever think I might be here to help?"

Bullshit, Grissom thought; but he said nothing. He would let the FBI agent do all the work.

Sitting, Culpepper said, "Your people ran a print from a shell casing through AFIS."

"We do that a lot."

"Yes, and your federal government is glad to be of service."

"Do you have a specific print in mind?"

Culpepper nodded. "Related to a recent shooting at a resort hotel—the Beachcomber."

"We got no match from that."

"That's right. That's because a little flag went up—AFIS wasn't allowed to make that match—classified information."

"Is that the federal cooperation you mentioned?"

"The man who belongs to that print is a contract assassin. No one knows what he looks like, or who he is . . . but we've been looking for him ourselves, for a long, long time. And that's why I'm here—to share information."

"Well thank you," Grissom said. "Let me think—when was the last time the FBI shared anything? Blame excluded."

Leaning forward, wearing a disingenuous grin, Culpepper said, "I know we've had our differences in the past, Grissom—but this is a crucial matter. It relates to a plethora of organized crime matters. Consider this a heads up, if nothing else—this guy is bad people."

Grissom remained cautious, skeptical. "Which is why you're going to help us catch him?"

"Yes, oh yes—he needs to be stopped . . . and your unit, and

Detective Brass and his fine contingent of investigators, seem to have the best shot at finally doing it."

". . . Right."

"In fact," Culpepper said, "I've already forwarded our files to Detective Brass—everything we have on the Deuce."

"That *is* cooperative," Grissom said. He didn't tell Culpepper that he and Brass were already on the trail.

Culpepper beamed. "Now, you want to tell me what you have?"

"Anything to cooperate," Grissom said.

He didn't want to give up anything, but Gil Grissom knew how to play the game. He gave Culpepper the basics of the Beachcomber shooting—information he was pretty sure the FBI agent already had. He left out, among other things, the videotape evidence; and said nothing about the mummy at all. When he finally finished, he looked at Culpepper's insincere grin and said, "Now what?"

"Nothing in particular," Culpepper said, rising. "Just nice to know we can work together like this."

And he gave Grissom his hand, which Grissom accepted—the agent's flesh cool, clammy—and when Culpepper had gone, Grissom sat there for a while, looking at his own palm, as if thinking of running it through the lab.

10

These linked murder investigations represented just the sort of case Jim Brass needed—not that he'd ever admit it to anyone, himself included.

Since his unceremonious return trip to Homicide, after the Holly Gribbs debacle, many of his colleagues avoided him as if he were a terminal case. Sheriff Brian Mobley spoke to Brass only when necessary. In recent months, Brass had, whenever possible, avoided Mobley, and would have ducked out fifteen minutes ago if the sheriff hadn't ordered him to come in and provide an update.

With no enthusiasm, Brass knocked on the wooden door with Mobley's name and rank inscribed in raised white letters. After losing command of the Criminalistics Bureau, Brass had been reduced to a plastic nameplate on an anonymous metal desk in the bullpen.

"Come in," came the muffled response.

Bright sunshine from the huge window behind Mobley's desk infused the office with a white light that Brass supposed was meant to give the sheriff the aura of God. Unfortunately, it seemed to be working.

Despite a well-tailored brown suit and crisp yellow tie, attire worthy of the chairman of the board of a small company, the redheaded, freckle-faced Mobley looked not so much youthful as adolescent, a boy playing cops and robbers . . . and the top law enforcement officer of a city of over one million souls.

"Have a seat, Jim."

The politeness made Brass even more uneasy, but he did as instructed. The wall next to the office door was lined with shelves of law books; on the left wall, a twenty-one-inch television—tuned to CNN, at the moment, sound low—perched atop a credenza. A computer sat on a smaller table on the sheriff's left, while his desk—smaller than the Luxor—appeared, as always, neat and clutter-free. The detective in Brass wondered if the sheriff ever worked.

Brass had been under Mobley, some years before, when the latter had been captain of Homicide. In truth, the man was probably as conscientious and hardworking as anyone; but Mobley's job was more about politics, these days, than actual law enforcement.

In 1973, the Clark County Sheriff's Department and the Las Vegas Police Department merged into one entity, putting the Las Vegas Metropolitan Police Department under the command of the sheriff. Now, the office more closely resembled that of a corporate CEO. Mobley was the fourth man to hold the position since the unification; rumor had it Mobley had his sights on the mayoral office.

The sheriff used a remote to switch off the television. "Well, at least CNN hasn't picked up Dingelmann's murder yet."

Brass nodded. "Local press has stayed off it—mob stuff's bad for tourism."

"You got that right—but the national press will pick up on this, and soon. Dingelmann's too high-profile for some national stringer not to connect the dots."

"I know."

"It's bad enough that the newspapers and the local TV picked up on this 'mummy' business. Now that's everywhere. Is it true it was our CSIs who dubbed the corpse that way?"

"I don't know."

"Well, the press sure loved that baloney." Sighing, the Sheriff loosened his tie. "Tell me where we're at, Jim."

The detective filled him in.

Mobley closed his eyes, bowed his head, and pinched the bridge of his nose between two fingers. "Do we really think the same asshole killed two people, fifteen years apart?"

"The CSIs are working to prove it now."

"And?"

"Who knows?"

Mobley shook his head, scowled. "Stay on top of this, Jim. There's a lot riding on it."

"Sir?"

"We can look like champs if we catch this killer, or chumps if this guy gets away—bottom line'll be, *we* can't protect our city."

"Yes, sir," Brass said.

"And let's *handle* the FBI."

"Sir?"

A tiny sneer curled the baby upper lip. "Take all the help they want to give . . . but if the FBI makes the arrest, they get all the glory. Now, if we make the arrest before them . . ."

"Yes, sir."

"Okay, go get him."

Brass left the office, searching the halls for Grissom, wanting to tell him about Mobley's challenge, in particular the avoidance of the FBI, which put him in rare agreement with the sheriff. Instead Brass met Warrick Brown coming down the hall in the opposite direction.

"What are you still doing here?" Brass asked.

Warrick looked at his watch and laughed once and grinned. "Overtime, I guess. I was working on stuff, lost track. I've got something I need you to do."

Skeptical, Brass asked, "What?"

The CSI explained about the running shoes and the different retailers.

"All right, I'll look into it. You going home?"

Shaking his head, Warrick said, "No. I'm going to the Beachcomber to look at some more tapes."

"Cheaper than Blockbuster. Grissom still here?"

Warrick nodded back down the hall. "Yeah, we're all still here. Somethin' about these cases, you know, intertwined like they are—it's like a bug we all caught. Can't shake it."

Warrick disappeared one way down the hall, Brass continued the other. He finally caught up with Grissom in the break room. They sat on opposite sides of the table.

Grissom took off his glasses, rubbed his eyes and looked at Brass. "So—tell me about our friend Brian."

Brass gave him the whole story, concluding, "The sheriff's hot to trot to close this case—these cases. Show the tourists we're on top of it. Show the citizens he's a great man."

Grissom's half-smirk was humorless. "We'd like to solve it too, Jim. We're all working double shifts, what more—"

"Whoa, whoa," Brass interrupted, holding up a palm. "Remember me? I'm on your side."

Shaking his head, Grissom said, "Sorry. Stress. We're all feeling the pressure on this one."

"Warrick said it was like a sickness."

"The flu you can get over," Grissom said. "Search for the truth has no cure."

"Who said that?"

Grissom blinked. "Me."

Looking surprisingly fresh in a blue silk blouse and black slacks, Catherine strolled in, a devious smile making her lovely face even lovelier.

"I was wondering who committed the crime," Grissom said.

"What crime?" she asked.

"So you're the one that ate the canary."

Her smile widened, eyes sparkled.

Brass looked at her, then Grissom, then back at Catherine. "What?"

"She knows something," Grissom said, his own smile forming.

Pouring herself a cup of coffee, she said, "I know a lot of things."

"For instance?"

"For instance . . . I know that the same gun killed both Philip Dingelmann and Malachy Fortunato."

Brass said, "I don't know whether to laugh or cry. The same killer responsible for two murders, fifteen years apart?"

Grissom remained skeptical. "We can't say that yet, can we?"

"No," Catherine said, sitting down with them. "Not quite yet. But I can prove that both men were shot with the same gun."

Astonished, Brass said, "I thought you found a discarded gun barrel with the mummy."

She said, "We did. Riflings matched the bullets we found in Mr. Fortunato's head, too."

Brass struggled to follow. "But the bullets didn't match Dingelmann, right?"

"No match, that's right."

"So," the detective asked, "how can you say they were shot with the same gun?"

Grissom—arms folded, sitting back—just watched her work.

"Wait," Brass said, thinking back, "I've got it. This is just like Brad Kendall, the coffee shop guy."

"Not quite," Catherine said. "Even though Kendall had changed out the barrel, we proved he used bullets from a box in his possession, matching the manufacturer's imprint. We can't do that here— these bullets not only didn't come from the same box, they didn't come from the same manufacturer. Doubtful our man would be using bullets from the same box of ammo, fifteen years later, anyway, right?"

"Right, right, of course," Brass said, bewildered.

Grissom just smiled.

Catherine continued, "When a bullet is fired from an automatic what happens?"

Brass sighed. "The firing pin strikes the primer, the bullet fires through the barrel, the casing gets ejected."

"Bravo," Grissom said.

"Shut up," Brass said.

"There are," Catherine said, "three distinct marks on any shell casing fired from an automatic. Like you said, the firing pin strikes the primer. The extractor scratches the casing as it grabs it, and the casing gets slammed into the breech wall before it's sent sailing out of the pistol. Each of those strikes leaves its own individual mark that, like fingerprints, is different for every weapon."

Eyes narrowed, Brass said, "And you're saying . . ."

"The shell casings from the Beachcomber and the casing we pulled from Mr. Fortunato's driveway are from the same weapon."

Brass allowed a smile to form. "Can we use that in court?"

"There's no way of arguing against it," Grissom said.

"But couldn't they say this evidence is tainted, because one of the casings was buried under asphalt for years?"

Catherine said, "The defense can *say* that, but saying it's tainted won't make it so, and the argument won't fly."

"Why?"

"You familiar with these guys that collect guns from the Old West?"

Brass shrugged. "What about them?"

"Lately they've been using these same marks to verify the authenticity of pistols from Little Big Horn."

"Matching firing pins to shell casings?"

"Yeah," she said. "They've dug up shell casings from the battlefield and matched them to firing pins from pistols used by Custer's men. Those casings have been in the ground for over a hundred years. Our casing was protected from the environment between the gravel and the asphalt, and for only fifteen years."

"Science and history meeting," Grissom said, loving it.

Brass could only ask, "And this will work?"

"Yeah," Grissom said. "It will work fine."

"But we don't have the gun?"

"Not yet," Catherine said. "But now we do know we're only looking for one gun, and the chances are if this guy hasn't gotten rid of it in the last fifteen years, he won't get rid of it now."

Now Brass had something to offer: "It is amazing how some of these guys have a sentimental attachment to a damn weapon. It's put a bunch of them away."

Sara joined the group. Grabbing a soda out of the fridge, she plopped into the chair next to Brass. She looked at Catherine, but her question was for all of them. "Why would a hit man . . . gee, somehow that's fun to say . . . why would a hit man *this* successful have a five-year hole in his career? Then, suddenly, resurface now?"

"A hole?" Grissom asked.

"Yeah," Sara said, nodding, sipping her soda, "no one's reported anything on this guy for just over five years. It's like he fell off the edge of the world."

"Or went to jail for something else," Brass offered.

Grissom shook his head. "No, there would have been a set of prints to match, then."

Brass said, "Yeah, right. Didn't think."

"Maybe he was sick," Catherine tried.

"For five years?" Sara asked.

"Or retired," Grissom said.

They all paused to look at him.

"Anything's possible," he said. "No more guessing—keep digging."

"Well, fine," Sara said, "but where do you look on the Internet for retired hit men?" And she rose and headed back to work, her soda in her hand.

Brass blew air out and said, "I better get going, too. I've got to hit the retailers that sold those running shoes." He got up, looked at Grissom and shrugged. "I guess we do what the man says."

Grissom nodded. "The part about keeping the FBI at bay, I got no problem with."

The detective departed leaving Catherine staring at Grissom. "And what was that about?"

He tried to shrug it off, but she was having none of it.

"C'mon, tell me."

"Politics. Mobley wants to let Culpepper 'help' us, then he wants us to make the bust and cut the FBI out of it."

"Kind of a dodgy game."

"Yes, it is."

She smiled. "But then, Culpepper is a real son of a bitch."

Grissom managed to keep a straight face. "Yes, he is."

In a nicely padded desk-type chair, Warrick sat next to a security guard in front of the wall of Beachcomber monitors. The guard, a short Hispanic guy in his early twenties, had just loaded the tape that Warrick brought in, showing Peter Randall's back at the poker machine, and Philip Dingelmann's reaction to seeing Randall. Then Dingelmann disappeared around the corner, Randall got dragged back to the machine, pulled his card, then followed, disappearing around the corner as well.

They reran the tape and Warrick pointed at Randall. "I want to see anything else you might have with this guy in it."

The guard nodded. "He's here nearly every Monday and Wednesday."

Warrick's pulse skipped. "What was your name again?"

"Ricky."

"Hey, Ricky. I'm Warrick."

Pleased, the guard said, "Hey, Warrick."

"Tell me more about this guy, this regular."

"Well, he didn't come this Wednesday, but he's a guy who likes the kind of off-times. Even a big place like this, you get to spot the regulars—particularly when studying these monitors for hours and hours."

Dingelmann had been murdered Monday morning; and "Peter Randall" had missed his usual Wednesday round of poker-machine playing.

"This guy, Peter Randall, he's a regular?"

"I mean, I don't know the guy's name, but he's been around a lot—but just Mondays and Wednesday, early hours, like I said, off-times, slow times. Some people don't like a crowded casino."

Warrick had never had a preference, as long as the dice were rolling. "Ricky, can you show me some more tapes of Mondays and Wednesdays?"

"Warrick, don't get too excited. I don't wanna get your hopes up, man. You're not going to see his face on camera any other day either."

"Why not?"

Nodding again, the guard said, "I noticed him, all right? But he's pretty careful."

"If you never saw his face, how do you recognize him?"

"I don't know, man—watch these monitors long enough, you get a feel for it. I mean, the back of him always looks the same, right?"

"Oh-kay," Warrick said.

"I mean his height, shape of his head, haircut, even the style of clothes . . . you just start to read people. Know 'em."

"Ricky, you ever get tired of this job, come see me where I work. I may have somethin' for you."

Warrick and his new best friend looked at a tape from the previous Wednesday, about the same time. Again, Randall sat at the poker machine, his back to the camera, obviously wearing a different sports coat. He never turned toward the camera and when they tried other cameras in the casino, he managed to avoid those too.

"How does a man come in here every day and never get his face on a camera?"

Ricky shrugged. "Beats me."

Warrick rolled his eyes. The guard had been right though, Randall came in every Monday and Wednesday; and his hair, frame, style of dress, made it easy enough to spot him, when you knew what you were looking for. They watched tapes for the Monday before the murder, and of the week before that, loading multiple tape decks of multiple angles on the casino, and Randall always showed up.

He didn't always play the same poker machine, but he never went to the tables where he would have to interact with a live dealer. In fact, he usually stuck to the row of poker machines closer to the back door. Monday, Wednesday, week after week, he came. He played for about two hours, then he left. Sometimes he won, sometimes he lost. Either way, the next Wednesday, the next Monday, there he was again. And never once did the son of a bitch show his face on any camera.

Todd Oswalt, the slot manager, stuck his head in once to ask how it was going.

"We're still working," Warrick said. "Still looking. Ricky's a big help—Ricky's the man."

Ricky beamed, and Oswalt said, "Glad to hear it—was that address a help?"

"Everything's a help, sir. But the maildrop he already abandoned. And the address he gave those people was for a street that doesn't exist."

Blond Oswalt in his navy blue suit shook his head and tsk-tsked. "Well, best of luck, Detective Brown."

Warrick didn't correct him. "I'm about due for some luck, sir."

Oswalt ducked back out.

They were five weeks back in the tapes now and Warrick wondered how many of these he should watch before he gave up. In truth, he wondered how many more of these he could take. It was like watching this bastard's boring life in reverse. On Wednesday of that week, Randall got up from his machine and disappeared off the screen. Warrick looked at the camera pointing up the main aisle—no Randall.

"Whoa, whoa! Where'd he go?"

Ricky shook his head as if he had been daydreaming. He swiftly scanned all the screens, finally spotting their man in the frame in the lower right hand corner.

"He's over there," Ricky said, pointing. "Just using the ATM, is all."

"Stop the tape," Warrick said quietly.

The guard was back in his own world and didn't hear.

Warrick said it again, louder. "Stop the tape, Ricky. Run it back."

Ricky did as told.

"That's it. We got him. Run it back."

Sitting up a little straighter, the guard again ran the tape back. Then, in slow-motion, ran it forward. They watched as Randall—back to the camera—used the ATM again.

"Yeah," Warrick said. "Yeah! What bank owns that ATM?"

Ricky shrugged. "I don't use the ATM here. I'm sure Mr. Oswalt would know."

"Get him. Please."

It took the slot host almost ten minutes to return to the security room, but Warrick didn't care—he had a clue.

Finally, Oswalt trudged in. "Yes, Detective Brown, what is it?"

"What bank owns this ATM?" Warrick asked, pointing at the frame.

"Uh, Wells Fargo. Why?"

"Mr. Oswalt, thanks." Warrick patted the guard on the shoulder. "Ricky, *muchas gracias* for your help, man. And you can take that to the bank."

"Hey, I remember that show," Ricky said, with a grin.

But Warrick was already gone.

11

Nick leaned over to open the door for Sergeant O'Riley, who hopped into the Tahoe for the ride to Marge Kostichek's. As they rolled across town, O'Riley made a point of studying the features of the SUV. "Nice ride," he said at last.

Nick nodded.

O'Riley shifted his beefy frame in the seat. "Lot better than those for-shit Tauruses they make us drive."

Stokes refused to rise to the bait. Though the crime lab unit had helped Homicide solve numerous cases, O'Riley and many of his brethren referred to the CSIs as "the nerd squad" behind their backs. Harboring a feeling that down deep O'Riley longed for the good old days when a detective's best friend was a length of rubber hose, Nick asked, businesslike, "What was that address again?"

Pointing up ahead, O'Riley said, "Two more houses—there on the left."

Pulling up in front of a tiny bungalow with peeling pale yellow paint and two brown dead bushes that needed removing, Nick parked the Tahoe facing the wrong way. The whole neighborhood looked as though it could use a coat of paint and some TLC. The scraggly grass was almost as brown as the bushes, and as they got closer Nick could make out where the stoop had started to draw away from the house, as if making a break for it. With O'Riley in the lead, they walked up the cracked-and-broken sidewalk and the two crumbly concrete stairs, the detective ringing the bell, then knocking on the door.

They waited—no answer.

O'Riley rang again, knocked again, with the same lack of success. O'Riley turned to Nick, shrugged elaborately, and just as they were turning away, a voice blared from behind them.

"Well, you don't *look* like Mormons!"

They turned, Nick saw a squat woman in a hot pink bathrobe and curlers.

"We're with the police, ma'am," O'Riley said, holding up his badge in its leather wallet. "We'd like to talk to you."

Waving an arm she announced, as if to the whole neighborhood, "Better get your asses in here then, 'cause I'm not staying outside in this goddamn heat!"

With arched eyebrows, Nick looked at O'Riley and O'Riley looked at Nick; whatever unspoken animosity might been between the cop and the CSI melted in the blast-furnace of this woman's abrasive personality. Nick followed O'Riley back up to the house and through the front door, glad to let the cop take the lead.

Little eyes squinted at them; her curlers formed a grotesque Medusa. "Don't just stand there! Close the damn door. Do I look like I can afford to air-condition the whole goddamn city?"

"No, ma'am," O'Riley said, the idea of a rhetorical question apparently lost on him.

Closing the door, Nick moved into the pint-sized living room next to the king-sized detective. Looking around, he couldn't help but feel he had just stepped into an antique mart—and a cluttered one at that. A maroon velvet chaise longue stood under the lace-curtained front window. Next to it, a fern stretched toward the ceiling, threatening to outgrow its pot. The room also contained two tall cherry end tables with doilies on them, a nineteen-inch TV on a metal stand, and the oversized Barcalounger tucked in a corner. In the opposite corner was a writing desk, and everywhere were stacks of things—*TV Guides*, women's magazines, antiquing newsletters, newspapers, mail.

O'Riley, rocking on his feet, said, "Are you Marge Kostichek?"

"That's the name on the mailbox, isn't it? Aren't you a detective?"

"I'm Detective O'Riley," he said, either ignoring or not recognizing the sarcasm, "and this is CSI Nick Stokes."

"Cee ess what?"

Nick amplified: "Crime Scene Investigator."

"Why, is it a crime to be a goddamn slob, all of a sudden?"

"No, ma'am," O'Riley said, flummoxed. "What I mean is, ma'am—"

"Let me see that goddamn badge again. You can't be a real detective."

Flustered, O'Riley was reaching for the badge when the woman grabbed his arm.

"I'm just pulling your pud, pardner." She laughed and various chins wiggled. "A big dumb boy like you couldn't be anything *but* a cop."

Nick had to grin. In spite of himself, he was starting to like this cranky old woman, at least when she wasn't on his ass.

"We'd like to ask you some questions," O'Riley said.

"I didn't figure you stopped by to read the meter."

Listening, Nick began to prowl the room—just looking around, stopping at this pile of magazines and mail and that, snooping. It was his job.

O'Riley was saying, "We'd like to ask you about Swingers."

"Oh, Jesus Christ on roller skates," she said, plopping into the Barcalounger. "I've been outa the skin racket for years now. I figured this was about that damned dog, two doors down! Goddamned thing won't shut the hell up. Bark, bark, bark, all the time, yapp, yapp, yapp. Isn't there a law against that crap?"

"Well . . . " O'Riley said.

"Actually," Nick said, back by the writing desk, "we're here about a girl who used to dance at your club."

"Just make yourself at home, good-looking. You gotta pee or something?"

"No, ma'am."

"Are you nervous? Why don't you light in one place?"

"Yes, ma'am. About that girl, at Swingers . . ."

She waved a small pudgy hand. "Been a lot of them over the years. Hundreds. Hell, maybe thousands. They don't keep their looks long, y'know—small window, for them to work."

From the file folded in half in his sport-coat pocket, O'Riley pulled out the photo of Joy Starr and handed it to the woman.

Nick noticed her lip twitch, but she gave no other outward sign that she might have recognized the girl.

"Joy Starr," O'Riley prompted.

Ms. Kostichek shook her head. "Don't remember this one."

Interesting, Nick thought: suddenly no wise-ass remark.

O'Riley pressed. "About sixteen years ago."

She shook her head some more.

"Her real name was Monica Petty. She disappeared . . ."

Marge Kostichek cut him off. "A lot of them disappeared. Here one night, gone the next. Met some guy, did some drug, had a baby, overdosed, here a sad story, there a happy ending, they all had one or the other. So many little girls with nothing but a body and face to get 'em somewhere, hell—how could I remember 'em all?"

Nick, still poised at the writing stand, said, "But you do remember this girl."

The old woman looked at Nick and suddenly her face froze, the dark eyes like buttons. "Why don't you come closer, Handsome? Where I can hear you better?"

The better to see you with?

Something about this "granny" struck Nick funny—and something told him he was standing right where he needed to be. . . .

"I'm okay here, ma'am," Nick said. "The detective asks the questions."

The eyes tightened; something was different in that face now. "I musta been dreamin', then, babycakes, when you asked me that shit?"

O'Riley said, "Please take another look at the picture, Ms. Kostichek."

Giving it only a cursory glance, she said, "Don't know her, I said. Said I didn't, and I don't—if she worked for me fifteen, sixteen years ago, why the hell are you askin' about her now?"

Nick, without turning, glanced down at the writing desk. Numerous piles of opened letters, back in their envelopes, were stacked here and there, overlapping, haphazard. Private correspondence, bills, even junk mail . . .

The woman thrust the photo out for O'Riley to take; he did. "Why are you digging up ancient history, anyway?" she asked. Almost demanded.

Nick didn't handle a thing—but his eyes touched the envelopes on the desk.

O'Riley said, "Her name has come up in the investigation of another case."

A cloud crossed the old woman's features and disappeared. But if she wondered what that case was, she didn't ask.

O'Riley cleared his throat. "Well, thank you for your time, Ms. Kostichek."

On the far side of the desk, barely within his eyes' reach, he saw it: a letter postmarked in Los Angeles, the name on the return address . . .

. . . *Joy Petty.*

Nick froze, only for an instant, then turned back to the frumpy, feisty woman. "Yes, thank you, ma'am."

"Don't let the door hit you on the ass on the way out, fellas," she said.

He followed O'Riley, as they let themselves out, O'Riley pulling the door shut behind them. Inside the Tahoe, Nick put the key in the ignition, but made no move to start the vehicle.

"Something on your mind, Nick?"

He turned to the detective. "She's lying."

With a shrug, O'Riley smirked, said, "You think? That old broad wouldn't give a straight answer to a *Jeopardy!* question."

"I don't *think,* Sarge—I know."

The creased face under the trim crew cut tightened with interest. "How?"

"Her mail. You see all those piles here and there and everywhere?"

"She's a pack rat—so what?"

"So back on that writing table, on top of one of those piles, was a letter from a 'Joy Petty.' What do you suppose the odds are that she knows a Joy Petty who isn't also the Joy Starr whose real name is Monica Petty?"

O'Riley's eyebrows had climbed. "I think the odds are we're goin' right back up there, right now."

"Can we do that?"

"Was the letter out in plain sight?"

"Oh yeah."

"Then watch and learn, bucko."

O'Riley was out of the SUV and going back up the sidewalk before Nick could pull the keys from the ignition. The CSI trotted to catch up, the pissed-off detective already ringing the bell, then throwing open the screen door and knocking on the inside door before Nick even got to his side. Just then, Marge Kostichek jerked the door open.

"What now?" she bellowed. "We already gave!"

"That's what you think, lady." Getting right in her face, O'Riley bellowed back, "Why the hell did you lie to us?"

She backed up, inadvertently making room for both men to reenter the house.

O'Riley glared at her, saying to Nick. "Show me."

Pulling on a latex glove even as he moved, Nick went to the writing desk and picked up the top letter on the stack of mail.

"Hey," she shouted, "you can't do that! That's private property! Where's your warrant?"

"Evidence in plain sight, ma'am," O'Riley said. "We don't need a warrant."

Nick came over to the hair-curled harridan and held up the letter from Joy Petty for her to see. "You want to explain this to us?"

The old woman took a step back, then stumbled over to her Barcalounger and sat heavily down, with an inadvertent whoopee-cushion effect. It might have been funny if she hadn't been crying.

Sara Sidle and ponytailed Detective Erin Conroy caught up with Warrick in the lobby of the Wells Fargo branch on South Nellis Boulevard. The air conditioning seemed to be set just below freezing; even though it was July in the desert, the tellers all wore sweaters.

"I've got another shot at getting our guy," Warrick said.

Professional in a white pants suit, Conroy lifted an eyebrow. "Is this going to be like the mailbox place?"

He looked for evidence of sarcasm in her voice and didn't find any. "I hope not, but who knows."

"Nice piece of work, Warrick," Sara said, meaning the ATM machine.

"Thanks. I haven't been this lucky in a casino in a long time."

A plumpish woman of forty sat behind the receptionist's desk talking on the phone. When they approached, she held up a finger: she'd be with them momentarily. . . . At least that's what Sara hoped she meant. In her lightweight short-sleeve top, Sara felt like she was standing in a meat locker.

Finally, the receptionist hung up the phone and turned to Warrick as if the two women weren't even there.

But it was Erin Conroy who held up her badge, and said, "We need to speak to whoever is in charge of ATM transactions."

The woman checked a list on the pullout shelf of her desk. "That would be Ms. Washington." She picked up the phone, pressed four numbers and said, "Ms. Washington, there are three police officers here to speak to you." She listened for a moment, hung up, and said to Warrick, "She'll be right with you."

Sara was seething but she didn't bother to correct the receptionist's description of all three of them as police officers.

They'd waited less than a minute before Sara heard the staccato rhythm of high heels on the tile floor to her right and behind her. Turning, she saw a woman in a conservative black suit approaching— with expertly coifed black hair, jade eyes, and a narrow, porcelain face. The woman held out her hand to Conroy and offered all three a wide smile. "Good morning—I'm Carrie Washington. May I help you, Officers?"

Conroy showed her credentials and shook the woman's hand. "I'm from Homicide, and Warrick Brown and Sara Sidle, here, are from the Las Vegas Criminalistics Bureau. We need to talk to you about one of your ATM customers."

"Fine. Quite a crowd of you, for one customer."

"Overlapping interests in our investigation," Conroy said.

Ms. Washington clearly didn't understand a word of that—Sara barely did herself—but the woman, crisply cooperative, said, "Won't you follow me to my office?"

In the smallish suite at the far end of a wide hallway off the lobby, Carrie Washington offered them seats in the three chairs that faced her large oak desk. A computer sat on the credenza next to it, a potted plant perched in the corner, and two picture frames were placed at the edge of her neat desk, facing away from them.

"Now," she said, steepling her fingers. "How may I help you?"

Conroy nodded to Warrick to take the lead. He did: "We need to know the name of one of your ATM customers."

Ms. Washington's expression conveyed her discomfort. "I'm afraid that would be—"

"It's quite legal," the homicide detective said, and withdrew the document from her shoulder-slung purse, and tossed the warrant onto the desk. "Judge Galvin has already authorized the action."

The woman put on a pair of half-glasses, read the warrant. "Tell me what you need."

"The ATM at the Beachcomber," Warrick said, "that's yours?"

Ms. Washington frowned thoughtfully. "I can find out—but I assume you already know as much, or you wouldn't be here in such an impressive array."

"It is your ATM," Conroy said.

"Five weeks ago," Warrick said, reading her the date from his notes, "your machine was accessed at five thirty-nine A.M. Can you tell me who did that?"

Typing the information into her computer, Ms. Washington said, "You're quite sure about the time?"

Warrick nodded. "Yes, ma'am."

"This is going to take a few minutes."

Conroy said, "That's fine. We'll wait."

O'Riley sat across from Marge Kostichek at the plain wooden table in the center of the interrogation room. She was no longer a sarcastic handful, rather a morose, monosyllabic interrogation subject.

Also in the cubicle were two other chairs, one on each side of the table, a digital video camera trained on the woman and an audio tape for backup on the table. A large wall mirror—nobody was kidding anybody—was really a window with one-way glass, on the other side of which were Grissom, Catherine, and Nick, who had already filled his boss and co-worker in on why he and O'Riley thought it best to bring the former bar owner in for more questioning.

The room they were in was small with no furniture. They stood there watching the interview in the other room.

"He's not getting anywhere with her," Grissom said.

"Maybe there's nowhere to get to," Catherine offered.

"No way," Nick said. "She knows something. That letter can't be a coincidence."

"Please," Grissom said. "Not the 'c' word."

Catherine seemed lost in thought; then she asked Nick, "Where's that letter now?"

"On top of my desk—why?"

She arched an eyebrow toward Nick, and Grissom noted it as well, as she said, "Remember the box of her husband's personal effects Mrs. Fortunato turned over to us?"

130 MAX ALLAN COLLINS

"Of course," Nick said.

Grissom was smiling.

Catherine said, "One of the things in that box is a letter to her husband . . . from Joy Starr."

Pleased, Grissom said, "This was the letter that made the police assume Fortunato and Joy Starr ran off together?"

"Yes," Nick said. "Am I missing something?"

"It'll come to you," Catherine said, mildly amused, her eyes alive with a fresh lead. "Get me your letter, I'll get mine, and meet me in the parking lot."

Nick was lost. "The parking lot?"

A slight grin tugged at a corner of Grissom's mouth. "I see where you're going, Catherine . . . nice thinking. But even if you're right, that won't completely settle the issue. Nick, where did you say that letter was postmarked?"

"L.A. Within the past month."

"I'll contact the California DMV," Grissom said. "Let's see what we can find out about Joy Petty. Then I'll call Jenny Northam and tell her you're on your way."

"Jenny who?" Nick asked. "On our way where?"

"Jenny's a forensic document examiner," Grissom said. "A fine one—she'll tell us whether or not 'Joy Petty' wrote both letters."

"And if she didn't?" Nick asked.

"Then," Catherine said, "the fun begins—let's get going."

The bank air conditioner continued to work overtime and even the unflappable Warrick looked chilly after twenty minutes of waiting in Carrie Washington's office. The small talk had evaporated and the four of them sat in awkward silence.

At last, the phone rang. Everyone jumped a little, the shrill sound serving as a release for the tension that had filled the room. Now, with the second ring, anticipation elbowed its way into the office.

Carrie Washington picked up the phone. "Yes?" She listened, and scribbled notes. "Address? . . . Employment?" One last scribbled note, and she hung up.

"Do you have something?" Conroy asked.

"Yes. The customer in question is Barry Thomas Hyde. He lives in

Henderson, at fifty-three Fresh Pond Court. Owns and manages a video rental store—A-to-Z Video—in the Pecos Legacy Center. That's a strip mall at twenty-five sixty-two Wigwam Parkway."

Conroy wrote quick notes on the addresses; Warrick had them memorized already. He said, "Thank you, Ms. Washington."

"Will there be anything else?"

Conroy rose, and then so did Sara and Warrick. The homicide detective said, "I think we've got what we need."

"We do what we can," Ms. Washington said, and something that had clearly been working on the woman finally emerged: "You said you were with Homicide, Officer Conroy?"

"That's right."

"So this is a murder case."

"It is."

This seemed to impress the professional woman, and Warrick said, "That's why your help is so important. This involves a dangerous individual, still at large."

"Anything to help," the banker said. "Anything."

Anything with a warrant.

Sara fought the urge to sprint from this building, to stand in the sun and, with luck, regain some of the feeling in her feet.

"Holy shit," she said, once they were outside, "am I freezing."

Conroy laughed lightly. "Then it wasn't just me—my teeth were chattering!"

"That name and those addresses didn't warm you ladies up?" Warrick asked.

"If it's not another dead end," Sara said, "I'll be warm and toasty."

Warrick shrugged. "Let's go see."

As they walked to the Tahoe, which was parked nearby, Sara said, "I'll bring Grissom up to speed," pulling out her cell phone with gunfighter aplomb.

She got him at once, informed him they had a possible ID on the Deuce, filled him in on the details.

"We'll try the house first," Grissom said. "Meet me there ASAP—I'll have Brass with me."

"We already have Detective Conroy with us."

"Good. If this is our man, he's a dangerous suspect."

Sara said 'bye, hit END, and filled Warrick and Conroy in.

"Anybody know Henderson very well?" Conroy asked, looking at the address.

"Not really," Sara said.

"Can't say I do," Warrick admitted. "We've worked a few crime scenes there. . . ."

"Well, I don't really know where this address is," Conroy admitted, gesturing with her notepad.

The absurdity of it hit them, and they laughed: three investigators and none of them knew how to find an address.

Sara, giggling, said, "Maybe we better get some help from dispatch."

"Just don't tell anybody," Conroy said.

" 'Specially not Grissom," Warrick said.

12

Jenny Northam shook her head, her long dark hair bouncing gently, then she looked through the microscope one last time.

"Well?" Catherine asked.

"No fuckin' way," Jenny said, her voice deeper than would be expected for a woman her size—barely over five feet, weighing in at maybe a hundred pounds. "Shit, guys, this isn't even close."

Jenny's office nestled in the corner of the second floor of one of the oldest downtown buildings just off Fremont Street. Tiny and slightly seedy, the office boasted apparent secondhand office furniture and carpeting dating to when the Rat Pack ruled the Strip. The back room, where Catherine and Nick had an audience with the sweet-looking, salty-speaking handwriting expert, was exactly the opposite.

Cutting-edge equipment lined three walls with file cabinets and a drafting table butted against the other wall. Two huge tables topped with UV, fluorescent and incandescent lights stood in the middle of the room. Nick and Catherine sat on stools near the walls while Jenny Northam rode a wheeled stool, rolling from station to station around the room, like she was piloting a NASCAR stock car.

"You're sure," Catherine said.

"Is a bear Catholic? Does the Pope shit in the woods? Whoever wrote this letter . . ." She held up Joy Starr's vintage note to Malachy Fortunato. ". . . wasn't worried about being discovered. This can only loosely be termed a forgery—it's just some dumb shit signing this Joy Starr's name *to* the letter."

Catherine frowned. "That's the only possibility?"

"No—this letter . . ." The handwriting expert pointed to the letter taken at Marge Kostichek's house. ". . . could be the forgery. But any way you look at it, they weren't written by the same person."

The two CSIs watched as Jenny dipped the letter into a series of chemical baths, then set it to one side to dry. She did the same thing with the original note to Fortunato.

"While we're waiting," Jenny said, "let's compare the handwriting, using the two photocopies we made earlier."

Catherine sat on one side of the handwriting expert, and Nick on the other, as Jenny read slowly aloud the letter to Fortunato:

"My loving Mal,

Im so happy that were finally going to getaway just the 2 of us.

It will be great to be together forever. You are everything Ive always dreamed of. See you tonight.

Love you for ever
Joy"

The new letter from Joy Petty read:

"Dear Marge,

Thanks for the great birthday card. I don't know why you keep sending me money, you know I make plenty. But you're sweet to do it. I hope you've been thinking about our invitation to come over and stay with us for a few weeks. The guy I been living with, Doug, could even drive over and pick you up so you don't have to take the bus. It would be great fun.

Please come.
Love, Joy"

"She's older now," Nick said, "her handwriting may have changed."

"Not this much," Jenny said. "Just not possible. Over the years our handwriting changes, granted. To varying degrees. But somebody's signature? That's something that people do not drastically change."

Jenny displayed the two letters side by side on the table. "Look at the capital 'J' in 'Joy.' "

They moved closer.

"This new one, the Joy Petty letter, the 'J' is extremely cursive. She started at the line and made this huge fuckin' loop that goes over the top line, then the smaller bottom loop that's equally full of itself. See how it goes down, almost all the way to the next line? This is somebody who craves attention—wants to stand out in the crowd."

Catherine gestured to the older document. "Tell us about the person behind this other signature."

Jenny pointed. "This is a scrawl. Almost looks like a kid did it. Very straight, more like printing than script. No way this is the same person. I don't give a shit how many years you put between 'em."

She went on to point out the capital "M" in "Marge," which was round and smooth, "Demonstrating the same pressure all the way through." The "M" in "Mal," however, was pointed, extra pressure at the joints of the lines.

Jenny shook her head. "Definitely two different writers."

Catherine smiled at Nick; Nick smiled at Catherine.

"The documents should be dry now," Jenny said, heading back over to the original documents. "Let's have a look." The expert positioned herself on one side of the table, Nick on the other. Catherine studied the photocopies a few more seconds, then followed, joining Nick on his side of the table.

"You dipped this in Ninhydrin?" Nick asked pointing at the note.

Shaking her head, Jenny said, "Nope—that's the old mojo."

Catherine said, "I remember reading in the Fortunato file that the lab tried that, back in '85, when they first found the note . . . but came up empty."

"Yes," Jenny said. "Though it was good in its day, even then Ninhydrin wasn't always successful. It worked well on amino acids, left on paper by people who touched it. But this new stuff, physical developer, it's the shit—works on *salts* left behind."

Nick was nodding, remembering something from a forensics journal article he'd read a while back. "This is the stuff the British came up with, right?"

"Right," Jenny said.

"Oh yeah," Catherine said, "finds way more prints than Ninhydrin."

"We've got something," Jenny said. "Look here."

The expert held up the original note: a black print, the side of the author's palm presumably, and several fingerprints in various places, dotted the page.

Jenny grinned. "Looks like the writer tried to wipe the paper clean of prints. These shit-for-brains never seem to grasp fingerprints are ninety-nine-and-a-half percent water. They're *in* the document, not on it."

Fewer fingerprints showed up on the new letter, but there were some to play with.

"Your fingerprint tech'll tell you these two prints don't match," Jenny predicted. "The letters were written by different people, and the fingerprints will prove it, as well as the handwriting differences. Additionally, the writing style—the amount of schooling indicated— also suggests two authors; but that's a more subjective call."

Catherine looked at Nick. "So, now what are you thinking?"

"We already knew that Fortunato didn't run off with the stripper."

"Right."

"We also believe that she's still alive and well and living in L.A. as Joy Petty."

Nodding, Catherine said, "Yes, and we should know more about that when we get back and talk to Grissom."

Nick got up, pacing slowly. "So we have a forged note from Joy to our victim, right around the time of his murder . . . but why? Why was such a note written?"

"Whoever hired the killing planted it, obviously," Catherine said. "And it worked—Fortunato's disappearance was dismissed as just an-other guy with a seven-year itch that got scratched by running off with a younger woman."

Nick stopped pacing, spread his hands. "So—mob guys hire the killing, and plant the note . . . or have it planted."

Catherine shook her head. "Doesn't make any sense."

"Why not?"

"Okay, look at it from the mob end of the telescope. You don't want anybody to know you killed this guy—you don't even want it officially known the welsher is dead. You instruct your hired assassin to hide the body where it won't be found for years, if at all, then you write this let-ter to make it appear Fortunato left town with his girlfriend."

"Yeah, right," Nick said. "That all hangs together."

Catherine smiled. "Does it? If you do all that, why do you allow your assassin to sign the body? Give it the old trademark double tap?"

"Why not?"

"Because if the body is found, you know damn well it's going to look like a mob hit to the cops. What did it look like to us?"

"But the Deuce, he's a mob hitter . . ."

"No, Nicky," Catherine said. "He's a freelancer. His best customers are organized crime types; but they're not necessarily his only customers."

Nick was seeing it now, shaking his head, disappointed in himself. "Grissom always says, 'assume nothing,' and what did we do? Assumed it was the mob."

"If it wasn't," Catherine said, "it was a perfect set-up for anybody who wanted Fortunato dead, for personal reasons or business or any motive. Already owing bookies out east, Fortunato was a sure bet to have a contract put out on him, if the mobbed-up casino owners knew he was embezzling from the casino. Instant blame."

"If somebody else hired the Deuce—who was it?"

"Ever notice every time we answer one question on this case," Catherine said, "we end up asking ourselves another, brand-new one?" She turned to the document examiner. "Jenny, how much writing would you need to find a match on these two letters?"

Jenny's answer was automatic. "When you get a suspect, don't take a handwriting sample—that's for shit. Get me a sample they've already written, grocery list, anything."

"And if we can't?"

"Then, what the hell—get a new sample." The petite woman shrugged. "There are some things you can't disguise."

"How big a sample?" Catherine asked.

"Couple of sentences, at least. More is better."

"Usually is," Nick said.

"Thanks, Jenny," Catherine said. "You're the best."

"Not hardly," she said. "My father was."

Catherine nodded. "We'll be back when we've got something."

Jenny returned to some waiting work. "I'll be here till five, and you can page me after that—long as you don't need me tonight."

"What happened to your fabled 'twenty-four-hour service'?" Catherine kidded her.

"Don't break my balls," Jenny said. "I got choir practice."

Catherine guided the wide-eyed Nick out of the office, and, as they drove back down the Strip, Nicky behind the wheel, Catherine punched a speed-dial number on her cell phone. It only rang once.

"O'Riley," came the gruff voice.

"Is Marge Kostichek still with you?"

"Yep."

"No change in her story?"

"Nope."

"You gonna cut her loose?"

"Yep."

"She's in the room with you right now, isn't she?"

"Yep."

". . . Okay, we're going to get you a court order for nontestimonial identification."

"Say what?"

"A writing sample and fingerprints."

"Oh! All right."

Catherine heard Marge Kostichek's voice in the background. "Aren't you the gabby one?"

Catherine said, "I'll call Grissom—you should have the paper you need in less than an hour."

"I like the sound of this." He disconnected.

So did she; then she called Grissom, who said he'd take care of the court order and get it to O'Riley.

"Have either of you slept?" he asked.

"Earlier this year," she said, with a sigh. "Haven't eaten in recent memory, either."

"Well, stop and eat, at least. We're going to get sloppy if we don't watch ourselves. . . . I'll handle things here for a while."

"Thanks. We'll be back soon."

She hit END, leaned back in the seat; she wished Grissom hadn't reminded her how tired she was.

"What did he say?" Nick asked.

"That we should eat."

"Good. I haven't eaten since I got a bear claw out of the vending machine about twelve hours ago."

The Harley-Davidson Cafe looked like a cross between a fifties style diner, a pub, and a high-end heavy metal club. Though she'd been past it many times, Catherine had never eaten here before—she seldom stopped at tourist places like this. She made a decent living, but not enough to regularly afford eight-dollar hamburgers, and still raise a daughter.

An American flag made out of three-inch anchor chain filled one wall, all the way up to the thirty-foot ceiling, well above the open second-floor gameroom. A conveyer running through the restaurant, the bar, the gift shop out front and up to the second floor, carried twenty antique Harleys in a constant parade.

While waiting for Nick's lemonade and Catherine's iced tea, they talked the case.

"All right," Catherine said, "if the mob didn't kill Fortunato, who did?"

He thought about that. "How about the wife? Always the first place to look. And he was fooling around on her, after all."

"I don't know," Catherine said. "She seems pretty genuinely distraught, finally finding out he's dead . . . but her anger for Joy sure hasn't ebbed, over the passage of time."

"What about her boyfriend?"

The waitress set their drinks in front of them, took their order, and Catherine suffered through the req-uisite flirting ("Aikake" was a "beautiful name," according to Nick, and "Hawaiian," according to the waitress).

"You ready now?" Catherine asked as the waitress hip-swayed away.

"Sorry. The boyfriend?"

"Gerry Hoskins. Annie Fortunato claims he wasn't even in the picture when Malachy disappeared, but no one's checked the story."

"Someone should."

"That's why God made the likes of Jim Brass."

"I was wondering. Any other ideas?"

"How about Marge Kostichek?"

He shrugged. "She lied about knowing Joy, yeah—but what the hell motive could she have?"

Catherine sighed. "I don't know. How's that for an answer?"

Nick talked up over Steppenwolf. "What about Joy herself? She disappeared the same day—and until we found that letter we had no idea she was alive."

"But the letter from fifteen years ago probably isn't from Joy—why hire somebody killed, and then plant a forged letter that would've been more convincing had you written it yourself?"

"My head is starting to hurt."

Catherine was thinking. "I wonder if Grissom had any luck with the California DMV."

"Later," Nick said, gazing up hungrily.

Their food had arrived—whether it was the waitress or the cheeseburger that put that look on his face, Catherine didn't really care to know.

In less than a day they had gone from identifying the killer back to square one as they tried to figure out who paid for the Deuce to whack Malachy Fortunato. Perhaps, Nick did have the right idea. For now, maybe she should just eat her chicken sandwich and try to forget about the sudden multitude of suspects they had.

After lunch, Catherine dropped Nick off at HQ, so he could begin going through the evidence again. Such a reappraisal was always a necessary aspect of scientific criminal investigation, because new information and perspectives continually put the evidence in a different light. But if they were going to catch the person who hired the killer, that would likely depend upon matching the fingerprints on the documents, and Jenny Northam matching the handwriting.

Catherine wasn't far from Annie Fortunato's residence when her cell phone rang.

"Hey, it's Nick. Grissom had Joy Petty's driver's license photo waiting for me here when I got back."

"And?"

"It's her, all right. Older, not so cute, but it's her—Monica Petty or Joy Starr or Joy Petty or—"

"A rose by any name." Catherine's hand tightened on the wheel of the Tahoe. "Tell O'Riley or Brass—maybe one of them can go out to L.A. and interview her."

"Speaking of O'Riley," Nick said, "he got the fingerprints and writing sample from Marge Kostichek."

"Good—just pulling up in front of the Fortunato house," she said. "Be back in an hour."

"Later," he said, and disconnected.

Catherine parked the car and walked up to the door, the smaller version of her field kit in one hand. A single dim light shone through the living room curtains. Catherine knocked on the door.

After a moment, Annie Fortunato opened the door slowly. Though she was completely dressed, in a blue T-shirt and darker blue shorts, she looked a little disheveled; as usual, a glowing cigarette was affixed to thin white lips. "Hi, Miz Willows—come on in, come on in."

Catherine stepped inside.

Smiling, Mrs. Fortunato asked, "What can I do for you?"

A smell Catherine instantly recognized—Kraft macaroni and cheese—wafted through from the front room; it wasn't long after lunch.

"I apologize for not calling first . . ."

"Hey, no problem." She took a drag off the cigarette. "I know you're trying to help."

"I'm glad you understand that. I need to get a set of fingerprints from you."

Her eyes wide, Mrs. Fortunato said, "Pardon?"

"I need a set of your prints—I need them from Gerry, too."

"Why?" The warmth was gone from the woman's voice now.

"We found fingerprints on the Joy Starr note. In your husband's effects?"

"Why on earth . . ."

Hoskins's voice floated in from the back of the house. "What is it, Annie?"

Mrs. Fortunato turned and, in a loud hard voice, called, "Catherine Willows is here—she needs our *fingerprints!*" Then she turned back to Catherine and rage tightened the haggard features. "You think one of us did it? . . . hell, I didn't even know Gerry then. He didn't even live in this town."

The awkwardness of it lay heavy on the shoulders of the already-tired Catherine. "It's just a formality really, to make it easier . . . you know, to eliminate you from the others."

But the more Mrs. Fortunato thought about it, the more worked up she got. "You think I killed my own husband? I thought you were my friend."

"Mrs. Fortunato . . ."

Smoky spittle flew. "You bitch! How dare you come around here?"

Catherine held up her hands, tried to explain. "Honestly, Mrs. Fortunato, I'm not even considering the possibility that you killed your husband," she lied. At this point, she only knew she didn't want to leave without those prints. "But when we catch who did this terrible thing, their lawyer is going to be looking for any way to get his client off—including implicating either you or Gerry in the murder."

Mrs. Fortunato stood there frozen; she had been listening, at least. Catherine, with relief, watched as the woman's anger evaporated.

Hoskins came in from the bedroom, still pulling on a shirt, as he tried to zip his jeans with one hand. "You all right?" he asked.

Catherine wondered if she'd interrupted something—dessert, after the macaroni and cheese, maybe.

"She wants to take our fingerprints, yours and mine, she says."

"What shit is—"

"So that if they catch whoever killed Mal, their lawyer won't be able to implicate us."

They both looked at Catherine now—suspicion in their eyes.

Wearily, she leveled with them. "Look—it's my job to find out who murdered Malachy. And you're both going to be considered suspects, now that his body has finally been found."

"So you are just a bitch," the woman said.

"Listen to me—please."

Hoskins wrapped a protective arm around Mrs. Fortunato. "How in hell you could ever think . . ."

"I'm not your friend," Catherine snapped. "And I don't have an opinion one way or the other. I follow the evidence—that's my job. That's why I was digging in your driveway last night—that wasn't for fun. The more evidence I have, whether it convicts or exonerates, gets me closer to finding out who murdered Malachy Fortunato, and bringing that person or persons to justice. Not just the hired killer, but the person—or persons—who hired him . . . whether it was the mob, you, or someone else altogether."

Stunned, the pair just stared at her. Hoskins kept his arm around Mrs. Fortunato, but said, finally, "How can we help?"

Sighing, relieved but weary, she started over: "I need fingerprints from both of you."

The man nodded. "Can you do it here, or do we have to go to the station?"

From her field kit, Catherine removed a portable fingerprint kit. "We can do it here." She wanted to kick herself for botching this so badly. It shouldn't have gone like this; thank God Grissom wasn't around.

Mrs. Fortunato seemed embarrassed. "I'm sorry for calling you . . . for what I said."

Managing to summon up a gentle smile, Catherine said, "I'm sorry if I misled you in any way. I know this isn't how you thought things would go . . . but I have to investigate everything, every aspect—good or bad, comfortable or uncomfortable."

"I know, I know. It's just all been so . . . emotional. Gerry and I are both on edge. I'm sure you folks are too."

Every day, Grissom would remind them, *we meet people on the worst day of their lives.*

Catherine printed them quickly, now in a rush to get the hell out of there. She had just opened new wounds in this old affair, and she wanted to slip away as swiftly as possible.

As she finished and handed Hoskins a paper towel, to wipe off the ink, he said, "Thank you," and Catherine said, "No, thank you, Mr. Hoskins."

He walked her to the door. "Ms. Willows."

"Yes?"

"One favor?"

"Try."

He swallowed. "Catch the son of a bitch."

Her eyes met his and held. "Oh, Mr. Hoskins. I will. I will."

13

In Henderson, Warrick—with Conroy riding in front, Sara in back—guided the Tahoe down Fresh Pond Court, looking at street numbers; this was a walled (not gated) housing development, designed for, if not the rich, definitely the well-off. When the SUV pulled up at the house in question, Brass's Taurus was already parked in front, Grissom in the passenger seat. The two CSIs and the homicide detective got out and jogged up to the unmarked vehicle, Warrick taking the lead.

The stucco ranch was the color the local real estate agents called "desert cream," and sported the obligatory tile roof, with a two-car attached garage and a well-manicured lawn. Not many houses in the area could boast so richly green a lawn, or even grass for that matter; most front yards were either dirt or rock. This one rivaled a golf-course green, but instead of a flagged hole, a single sapling rose right in the middle. The rambling house had a quiet dignity that said "money"—no, Warrick thought, it whispered the word.

"Somebody made the American dream pay off," Warrick, leaning against the roof of the Taurus, said to his boss. "You been up to the door yet?"

His expression blank, Grissom still had his eyes on the place. He said, "When we got here. Nobody home. Where have you been?"

A sheepish half-grin tugged a corner of Warrick's mouth. "We kinda got lost."

"How many CSIs does it take to screw in a light bulb?" Brass asked, sitting behind the wheel.

"Two and a homicide detective, apparently," Sara said. "Conroy's with us."

"Hey, it's a new neighborhood," Warrick said. "Last time I was out this way, it was scrub brush and prairie dogs."

"Skip it," Grissom said. "Nobody home anyway."

Conroy had gone around the other side of the vehicle, to talk to Brass; she was asking him, "You want me to check around back?"

"We don't have a warrant," Brass said. "We're gonna step carefully on this—case like this, you don't want to risk a technicality."

"Almost looks deserted," Sara, sidling up next to Warrick, asked her seated boss. "Nobody home, or does maybe nobody live here?"

A dry wind rustled the leaves of the front yard sapling.

"Furniture visible through the front windows," Grissom said, "and the power company, water company, and county clerk all agree—this is the residence of one Barry Hyde."

"You don't let any grass grow," Warrick said.

"Except for occasionally getting lost, neither do you."

Warrick took that as the compliment it was.

"In fact, I think we've earned a break," Grissom said.

"Huh?" Sara said.

"I think we should go check out the new video rentals," Grissom said.

Warrick, pushing off from the roof of the Taurus, said, "Might be some interesting new releases, at that."

Conroy stayed with the Taurus, at the residence, while Brass piled into the Tahoe, in back with Sara, with Warrick and Grissom in front.

From the backseat Brass said, "If you'd like me to drive, I do know the way."

"I came up with this address," Warrick said, trying to keep the edge out of his voice. "I'll do the honors."

Barry Hyde's video store was close to his house, just a few turns away and onto Wigwam Parkway. Glad he had his sunglasses on, Warrick turned into the Pecos Legacy Center parking lot, where glass storefronts reflected bright afternoon sunlight. A-to-Z Video—a typical non-chain store of its kind with a neon sign in the window and movie poster after poster taped there—sat at the far end of the strip mall, a discount cigarette store its next-door neighbor.

Brass led the way into the video store, Grissom hanging back, in observer mode. To Warrick, it looked like every other non-chain video store he had ever been in—new releases around the outside wall, older movies in the middle. DVD rentals filled the section of the wall to the right of the cash register island, which was centered between the two IN and OUT doors. At the rear of the store was a door that presumably led to the storage area and the manager's office.

Behind the counter, in the cashier's island, stood the only person in the store, a petite American Indian woman of about twenty, a blue imitation Blockbuster uniform over slacks and T-shirt, her straight black hair worn short. Her name tag said SUE.

Fairly perky, and perhaps a trifle surprised to have customers, she asked, "Hi—welcome to A-to-Z Video. Are you looking for a particular title?"

"Sue, I'm looking for Barry Hyde," Brass said. He didn't get out his badge—this seemed to be a toe in the water.

The cashier smiled. "Mr. Hyde is out for the day. May I be of assistance?"

"When do you expect him back?"

"I'm sorry. He's not going to be available until after the weekend."

Now Brass displayed his badge in its leather wallet. "Could you tell me why he's not available?"

Seeing that badge, the cashier's cheerfulness turned to mild apprehension. "Oh, well—I'd like to help you, but I'm just . . . uh, maybe you should talk to Patrick."

Brass's melancholy face twitched a sort of smile. "And who is Patrick?"

"The assistant manager. He's in charge until Mr. Hyde gets back."

"I'd like to talk to Patrick. Is he around?"

"In the back," she said. She pressed an intercom button and said, "Patrick, someone to see you?"

The intercom said, "Who?"

"I think it's the police. . . . I mean, it *is* the police."

Patrick said, "Uh . . . uh, just a minute, uh . . . I'll be . . . uh . . . right . . . uh . . . out."

Four minutes later, more or less, Grissom was prowling the store like each video was potential evidence; but the others—Warrick included—were getting impatient.

Warrick realized that mid-afternoon wasn't a busy time for any video rental store; but this place seemed particularly dead. He noted the posted rental rates—they weren't bargains.

Brass leaned against the counter. "Sue—would you rattle Patrick's cage for me again?"

The cashier was about to touch the intercom button when the door in the back opened and ambling out came a zit-faced kid who seemed younger than the cashier. Bleached blond with a dark goatee and black mid-calf shorts, he had a sharp, short nose, small lips, and green eyes with pupils the size of pinheads; but for the blue polo shirt with A-to-Z stitched over the breast pocket, he looked like a guitar player in a metal band.

As the kid stepped by him, Warrick noticed Patrick (as his name tag confirmed) smelled like a combination of Tic Tacs and weed. Which explained their four-minute wait.

The assistant manager said, "Can I . . . uh . . . like, help you?"

Brass seemed to be repressing a laugh; they'd sent for a manager and got back Maynard G. Krebs. "Are you Patrick?"

He thought about it. Then, without having to refer to his name tag, he said, "Yeah. McKee. Is my last name."

"Patrick, we'd like to talk to you about your boss—Barry Hyde."

The kid's sense of relief was palpable in the room and Warrick turned away to keep from laughing out loud. He pretended to study the new DVD release wall so he could still listen to the conversation.

Patrick asked, "What about Mr. Hyde?"

"He's out of town?"

Nodding, Patrick said, "Until Monday."

"Is Mr. Hyde out of town a lot?"

The kid had to think about this question for a while, too. Finally, he managed, "Some."

"For how long? How often?"

"He's been doing it since I've been here." Shrug. "Uh . . . eight months."

Brass shook his head. "That's not what I meant, Patrick. I mean, how long a period of time is he generally away?"

"Sometimes a couple of days, sometimes a week."

Warrick pulled a DVD box off the shelf and pretended to read the back—*Real Time: Siege at Lucas Street Market.* He knew Hyde couldn't be gone for long stretches, because the man had rarely missed his regular Monday and Wednesday visits to the Beach-comber.

Patience thinning, Brass was asking, "Do you know where Mr. Hyde is now?"

Patrick thought about that one for a long time too. "No. I don't think he said."

"What if there's an emergency?"

The kid's face went blank. "Emergency?"

"Yeah, emergency. He's the boss. Don't you have a number to call if you get robbed or a customer has a heart attack in the store? Or maybe a valuable employee, like you, has a family crisis?"

"Oh, sure," Patrick said.

"Could you give us that number?"

"Yeah—nine-one-one."

Brass just looked at the kid. Then he blew out some air, and called back to Grissom, at the rear of the little group. "You want to take a crack at this?"

Grissom put his hands up in surrender.

Warrick put the DVD box back—*100% Multi-angle!!!*—turned, and stepped forward. "Why don't you guys wait outside. I'll talk to Patrick."

Sara's eyes met Warrick's—they were on the same wavelength. She said, "Yeah, guys—I'll stay with Warrick."

Grissom, sensing something from his CSIs, turned to look at Brass, shrugging. "Any objection, Jim?"

"All right," Brass said. He said to Grissom, "Why don't you run me over to the house."

His car and Detective Conroy were there, after all.

"Sure," Grissom said. Then to Warrick and Sara: "Pick you up in fifteen."

Once the homicide cop and Grissom had left, Warrick turned to the assistant manager. "Okay, Patrick, truth or dare—just how stoned are you?"

The eyes widened; however, the pupils remained pinpoints. "No way!"

Sara said, "Cut the crap, Patrick. Dragnet has left the building—this is the Mod Squad you're talking to. . . . We know there's stoned, and there's stoned."

Patrick seemed to have lost the ability to form words. He stood there with his mouth hanging open.

"Why don't the three of us," Warrick said, slipping his arm around the skinny kid, "go into the back office, and just chill a little."

"Not the back room. I mean . . . uh . . . it's . . . uh . . . private."

"That's why we're going to use it," Sara said. "Because it's private—customer comes in, we won't be in the way."

The beleaguered Patrick looked to the cashier for help, but she turned her back, suddenly very interested in sorting returned videos. "Uh . . . I guess so . . ."

"Cool," Warrick said. He led the way to the back and was the first one through the door. The cubicle reeked of weed, even though the kid had lit three sticks of incense before he'd come out front. The "office" consisted of a shabby metal desk, a cheap swivel chair, some two-by-four-and-plywood shelves piled with screener tapes, and walls decorated with video promo posters, mostly for XXX-rated tapes.

"Sorry," Patrick said, coming through the door next. "It's kind of . . . uh . . . grungy back here."

"And," Sara said, just behind him, "it smells like Cheech and Chong's van."

"On a Friday night," Warrick added.

Unable not to, the kid grinned at that.

She wide-eyed the porno posters. "You actually carry this trash?"

Patrick's silly grin disappeared and professionalism kicked in: he was the assistant manager of A-to-Z Video, after all. He said *"American Booty* and *The Boner Collector* are our top two adult rental titles. You have to reserve them a couple weeks in advance."

"I'll pass," Sara said.

"So, then," Warrick said, sitting on the edge of the desk, "store does a pretty brisk business, huh?"

Patrick snorted. "Yeah, right, whatever."

Sara asked, "Is it always like this—tumbleweed blowing through the place?"

"Lot of the time," Patrick admitted. "We do pretty good on the weekends sometimes, but there's a Blockbuster on the next block, and the supermarket, at the other end of the mall? They rent tapes, too."

"Does Mr. Hyde seem concerned about business?"

"What do you mean?"

"I mean, if it's slow, do you have meetings—pep talks, try to figure out strategy, lower your prices. . . ."

"No, not really. Barry's pretty cool for a boss. He's got a wicked sense of humor—really dark, man, I mean brutal."

I'll bet, Warrick thought.

Patrick was saying, "He doesn't give us a lot of shit . . ." He glanced at Sara. ". . . trouble about stuff."

"Does Hyde come in every day? When he's in town, I mean?"

"Yeah, yeah, he does. He doesn't stay very long, most days. He comes in, maybe orders some tapes, checks the books, goes and makes the deposit from the night before. Oh, and sometimes he brings in munchies like doughnuts and stuff."

"How many people work here?"

"Besides Mr. Hyde, four. Me, Sue—she's out front now—Sapphire, and Ronnie. Me and Sue are usually paired up, Sapphire and Ronnie, same. We trade off every other week working days and nights. This week we're on days, next week we'll work nights. We don't get bored that way, and then everybody can kind of, like, have a life, you know?"

"That does sound cool," Warrick said. "We just work the night shift."

"But it's day," Patrick said, shrewdly.

Sara said, "We like to think of it as flex hours. How much do you make, working here, Patrick?"

"Eight-fifty an hour. Me and Ronnie, I mean, 'cause we're both assistant managers. Sapphire and Sue are makin' seven-fifty an hour."

"Not bad pay," Sara said, "for sitting here getting stoned."

Patrick tried to parse that—nothing judgmental had been in Sara's tone, but she was with the cops—but finally he said, "I only do that if it's real dead."

"Which is a lot of the time."

Patrick's shrug was affirmative.

Warrick, feeling Sara was getting off track, asked, "Do you remember, exactly, when Mr. Hyde has been out of town?"

"Oh, hell—all his trips are marked on the calendar."

Warrick traded glances with Sara, then asked, "What calendar is that, Patrick?"

"This one," the kid said, pointing to the July Playmate, who loomed over the desk.

"Mind if I have a look?" Warrick asked.

"No, but . . . don't you need a warrant or something?"

Warrick's reply was casual. "Not if you don't mind."

"Oh, well. Sure. Go ahead."

Flipping the pages with a pen, Warrick read off the dates and Sara copied them down. When they finished, she used the little camera from her purse to take shots of the calendar, just in case.

Patrick became a tad nervous, when Sara started shooting the photos, and Warrick put an arm around the young man. "Patrick, I'm going to make you a deal."

"A deal?"

"Yeah, if you don't tell Mr. Hyde that we were here asking questions, I won't bust your ass."

"Bust my ass . . ."

"You know—for felony possession."

"Felony? I've only got half a . . ." Patrick froze as he realized what he was saying. His eyes looked pleadingly from Warrick to Sara. "I mean . . . I thought you guys were cool. . . ."

Warrick's voice went cold. "Patrick, have we got a deal?"

Reluctantly, Patrick nodded. "Yeah."

Outside in the sunshine, Warrick said to Sara, "There's something not right here."

"More than pot smoke smells in there," Sara agreed. "The manager's never around, doesn't worry about business, and lives in an expensive new house in an upscale neighborhood."

"And he's gone from time to time—just short hops."

"Like maybe the Deuce *isn't* retired, you mean?"

"That does come to mind. We better go do some research about Mr. Barry Hyde."

That was when Grissom swung in, in the Tahoe; and on the way back, Warrick driving, they told their supervisor what they'd learned— and what they thought.

"I want that list of dates," Grissom said, "when Hyde was out of town."

Other than that, however, Grissom said nothing.

Which always made Warrick very, very nervous.

Culpepper was waiting in Grissom's office, the FBI agent having helped himself to the chair behind the desk, his feet up on its corner. "Hey, buddy, how're you doing?"

Feeling his anger rising, Grissom breathed slowly and stayed calm. "Why, I'm just fine, Special Agent Culpepper—and how are you?"

Brass came into the office, saw the FBI agent, and said, "Our government tax dollars at work."

Culpepper's feet came off the desk and he sat up straight, but he said nothing for several endlessly long moments. At last, he said, "I hear you guys got something on the Deuce."

Grissom kept his face passive, though he wondered where Culpepper got his information. "You heard wrong."

"I've been waiting here for half an hour. Where were you, Grissom?"

"Lunch. I don't remember having an appointment with the FBI."

"I heard you were so dedicated, you don't even find time for lunch."

"Today he did," Brass said. "With me. We would have invited you, but you didn't let us know you were coming."

Grissom said, "Was there a purpose to your visit, Culpepper, or are you just fishing?"

The FBI agent's smile was almost a sneer; he straightened his tie while he stalled to come up with an answer. "I stopped by to tell you that we heard the Deuce has left the area."

Grissom allowed his skepticism to show through a little. "If you think he's gone, why are you still nosing around here?"

"Just covering all the bases, buddy. Like you, this is my turf— keeping my fellow law enforcement professionals informed. You should know that."

"Covering your what?" Brass asked.

Culpepper rose and came around the desk, stopping in the doorway. He beamed at Grissom. "Too bad you didn't come up with anything, buddy. I figured if anybody would catch this guy, it would be you. They say you're the number two crime lab in the country . . . not counting the FBI, of course."

"Yeah," Brass said, "your lab's got the reputation we're all longing for."

Culpepper made a tsk-tsk in his cheek. "Must be hard not being number one."

"We try harder," Grissom said.

The FBI agent nodded. "You'll need to. Good luck, gentlemen— keep the good thought."

And Culpepper was gone.

"Damnit," Brass said, leaning out into the hall, making sure the FBI agent wasn't lingering. "How did he know?"

"Maybe he doesn't."

"Maybe he does."

Grissom shrugged. "You talked to the county clerk, the utilities, and I don't know how many other agencies."

"He's not helping us, is he? He's watching us. Why?"

"Easier than solving the case himself maybe—steps in and takes the credit." Grissom shook his head, disgusted. "What a backward motivation for this line of work. . . . Until just now, I was tempted to give him the list of dates Warrick gave me."

"Of times Hyde's been out of town this year?"

"Yeah. See what unsolved murders or missing persons cases match up to those dates."

"Give me that list, and I'll do what I can."

Grissom did.

"You think the killer's still active?" Brass asked.

Grissom got back behind the desk, sitting. "We know he is—he shot Dingelmann. Maybe he stopped doing mob-related work and his contracts are with individuals now. That could be the reason he hasn't turned up on the FBI's radar in the last four years."

"Are you convinced Hyde is the Deuce?"

"No. Too early. Hell of a lead, though. Warrick gets the MVP of the day."

On cue, Warrick appeared in the office doorway, Sara just behind him; Grissom waved them in.

"The esteemed Agent Culpepper looks steamed," Warrick said.

"Good," said Brass.

"Saw him in the parking lot," Sara said. "What did you say to him?"

Eyes hooded, Brass said, "We just did our best to share as much with him as he shared with us."

Warrick said, "Bupkis, you mean."

"Oh, we didn't give him that much," Brass said.

Shifting gears, Warrick fell into a chair across from Grissom, saying, "Something stinks about that video store."

"Besides cannabis?" Grissom asked innocently.

Warrick and Sara smiled, avoiding their boss's eyes.

Brass picked up on the train of thought. "You're referring to that horde of customers we saw in there today."

"Even for an off time," Warrick said, "that was grim."

With a twinkle, Sara said, "And Patrick—who was very open, you know, to young people like us—admitted they don't ever do a lot of business."

"Yet the four kids that work there," Warrick said, "are pulling down decent money, and Barry Hyde doesn't seem to care about the lack of cash flow."

"Money laundry?" Brass asked.

Grissom ignored that, saying to the two CSIs, "Okay, let's take Barry Hyde to the proctologist. Sara, I want you to look into his personal life."

"If he has one, I'll find it."

"Photocopy these," Brass said, handing her his field notebook, indicating the pages, "and get that back to me. . . . This is what we do know about Hyde, from the phone calls I made around."

She scanned the notes quickly. "Not much, so far."

"It's a place to start," Grissom said. "Find out more. Warrick."

"Yeah?"

"Try coming at this through the business door."

"You got it."

Then Warrick and Sara went off on their respective missions, and Brass departed as well, leaving Grissom lost in thought, trying to figure out what the hell Culpepper was up to. For someone supposedly sharing information because both groups were looking to bring the same animal to justice, Culpepper hadn't contributed a thing to their investigation—just a vague, unsubstantiated notion that the Deuce was no longer in the area.

How long he'd been pondering this, Grissom didn't know; but he was pulled out of it by a knock on his open door. He looked up to see Sara standing there.

"You look confused," he said.

"I am confused." She came in, plopped down across from him.

"This Barry Hyde thing just keeps getting weirder and weirder."

"Weird how?"

She shifted, tucked a foot under her. "Let's take his college years, for example."

"Let's."

She flashed a mischievous smile. "You can get a lot of stuff off the Internet these days, Grissom."

"So I hear. Some of it's even legal."

"Legal enough—lots of records and stuff you can go through."

"Less how, more what," he said, sitting forward. "Did you find Barry Hyde's college records?"

"Sort of," she said, wrinkling her nose. "Barry Hyde has a degree in English from the University of Idaho."

"Our Barry Hyde?"

She nodded, going faster now, in her element. "Only thing is, I went to the University of Idaho website and they have no record of him."

"You mean they wouldn't give you his records?"

"No. I mean they have no record of his ever having been a student there."

"Maybe he didn't graduate."

"You don't have to graduate to get into the records, Grissom. He didn't matriculate."

"Anything else?"

"Oh yeah. Everything for the last five years is fine. Barry Hyde's a sterling citizen. Bank loans paid on time, credit cards paid up, member of the Rotary, the Henderson Chamber of Commerce, the guy even pays his traffic tickets."

"Good for him."

"But before that? Hyde's military record says he was stationed overseas, but I found a medical file where he claimed to have never been out of the country. The whole thing's nuts. Information either doesn't check out, or is contradicted somewhere else. This guy's past got dumped into a historical Cuisinart."

"Or maybe," Grissom said, eyes tightening, "it came out of one."

14

Exiting the break room with a cup of coffee, Catherine almost bumped into O'Riley, who was bounding up to her, a file folder in hand.

"Well, hello," she said.

Grinning, O'Riley said eagerly, "I've got a buddy in LAPD. Tavo Alverez."

"Good for you, Sergeant."

"Good for all of us—he tracked down Joy Petty."

"Great! Walk with me . . . I've got to catch up with Nick. . . ."

O'Riley did. "Tavo stopped by the Petty woman's place in Lakewood—she's unemployed right now, but I guess she's mostly a waitress. Unmarried, lives with a guy, a truck driver."

"Okay, she's alive and well—but is she Joy Starr?"

"Oh yeah, sure, she admitted that freely. Tavo said she seemed kinda proud of her days in 'show business,' once upon a time. Joy Starr, Monica Petty, Joy Petty—one gal."

Catherine stopped, their footsteps on the hard hallway floor like gunshots that trailed off. Her gaze locked with O'Riley's less-than-alert sagacious stare. "Now that we've confirmed that, we need to have Joy Petty interviewed in more depth."

He shrugged his massive shoulders. "I can work this through Tavo—he's a good guy."

"Can you fly over there, or even drive?"

"I think we're better off usin' Tavo. I mean, he's willing, and he's tops."

"Then get back in touch with him," Catherine said, walking again, heading toward the lab where Nicky worked. "We need Joy Petty interviewed in detail about her relationship with Marge Kostichek."

"Okay, but Tavo phoned me from the site of a homicide, to give me that much. I mean, it is L.A.—they do have a crime of their own go down, sometimes."

"Stay on him, Sarge."

"Will do. Here." He handed her the folder. "Background check on Gerry Hoskins."

"Good!"

Another shrug. "Seems to be a right guy, got his own contracting business—you know, remodeling and stuff."

"Thanks, O'Riley. Fine job."

He smiled and headed off. Catherine caught up with Nick in the lab where he was already poring over the fingerprints.

"What do we know?" she asked as she came up next to him.

"It's looking like Gerry Hoskins is in the clear." Nick sat on a stool before a computer monitor whose screen displayed two fingerprints, one from Joy Starr's note to Fortunato, the other from Hoskins's fingerprint card. "This is not his print."

Catherine nodded and held up the file folder. "O'Riley just gave me this. Hoskins's background check."

"What's it say?"

She opened the folder, gave its contents a quick scan, saying, "Carpenter, got his own business, lived in Scott's Bluff, Nebraska till, seven years ago. Got divorced, moved here, been relatively successful, moved in with Annie Fortunato . . ." She did the math. ". . . five and a half years ago."

"Okay," Nick said, "one down."

Catherine filled him in on what O'Riley had told her about Joy Petty.

"An in-depth interview with her could really fill in some blanks," Nick said.

"We won't know until O'Riley's guy gets back, and that could be hours. For now, we stay at it."

The next print he brought up belonged to Annie Fortunato.

"The wife's prints don't match the forged note, either," Nick said.

Silently, Catherine gave thanks; she had hoped that Annie Fortunato was innocent. Grissom could preach science, science, science all he wanted: these were still human beings they were dealing with.

And the CSIs were human, too—even Grissom. Probably.

"This print, though," Nick said, bringing up a third one, "is a very definite match. Textbook."

Catherine leaned in. "The former owner of the strip club?"

"Yeah—Marge Kostichek." Nick's smile was bittersweet; he shook his head. "I'm almost sorry—the salty old girl is a real character."

"Character or not," Catherine said, studying the screen, "she wrote that note to Malachy Fortunato."

Nick's eyes narrowed. "I don't think it really was written for Malachy to read, do you?"

"No. Our friend Mr. Fortunato was probably tucked away under that trailer, by then—a fresher corpse than when we found him, but a corpse."

"But why would Marge sign Joy Starr's name to a note like that? What motive would the old girl have for killing Fortunato?"

"*Having* him killed," Catherine reminded him. "Working strip clubs in a mobbed-up town like Vegas used to be, Marge might well have access to somebody like the Deuce."

Nick just sat there, absorbing it all; finally he said, "I think we need a search warrant."

"Oh yeah."

Hopping off his stool, Nick asked, "We better round up O'Riley—seen him lately?"

"Just," Catherine said. "He's probably back in the bullpen by now. . . . You get your field kit organized, and I'll go tell Grissom what we're up to—and see if he can't find a judge to get us that warrant."

Ten minutes later, Catherine and Nick were moving quickly into the detectives' bullpen. Two rows of desks lined the outer walls and another ran down the center, detectives in busted and battered swivel chairs behind gray metal desks about the color of Malachy Fortunato's desiccated flesh. The skells, miscreants, and marks that made up their clientele sat in hard straightback metal chairs bolted to the floor, to prevent their use as weapons.

O'Riley was nowhere to be seen; his desk—the third one from the back on the far wall—looked like an aircraft carrier. His in-out baskets served as the tower, his phone perched on the corner like a parked fighter, and the desk top was as clean as a deserted flight deck.

Nick ran a finger over the surface and said, "I wonder if he does windows?"

Catherine called to Sanchez, the detective at the desk behind O'Riley's. "Where's he hiding?"

Without looking up from his one-finger typing, Sanchez said, "Do I look like his mother?"

"Just around the eyes and when you smile."

The detective graced her with a sarcastic smirk and resumed his hunt-and-pecking.

"Leave him a note," Nick said to her. "And we'll page him from the car."

There wasn't so much as a Post-it on that spotless desk top. She turned to Sanchez. "You got a . . ."

A small pad came flying at her and she caught it.

"Thanks." She wrote the Post-it, stuck in right on the phone, then, without looking, tossed the pad over Sanchez's way, heading out of the bullpen with Nick on her heels. When driven by a sense of urgency like this, Catherine felt frustrated by the minutiae of daily existence.

They were halfway to the suspect's house when Catherine's cell phone rang. "Willows," she said.

"It's O'Riley. I got your page, and I got your note. I'm on my way. Somebody had to pick up the search warrant, y'know."

"Ah. You're leaving the courthouse?"

"Yeah, what am I . . . maybe five minutes behind you?"

"Yep. You want us to wait for you, Sarge?"

Nick stopped for a red light. "O'Riley?"

She nodded.

"Has he got the warrant?"

She nodded again.

"Tell him he better hurry if he wants to be there when we question her."

O'Riley's voice said in her ear, "I heard that. You tell him to wait till I get there."

And O'Riley clicked off.

Matter of factly, Catherine said to Nick, "He wants us to wait for him."

"Damn."

"It's procedure, Nick. His job—not ours."

"But it's our case. . . ."

As the light turned green and Nick eased the Tahoe into the intersection, he shook his head. Ahead of them the sun was just dipping below the horizon leaving behind a trail of purple and orange that danced against fluffy cumulus.

"He wants us to wait for him," Catherine repeated, not liking it any better than Nick, but accepting it.

Nick shrugged elaborately. "I don't see why. The old girl likes me. We'll just chat with her until O'Riley shows. Loosen her up."

Catherine said nothing.

Five minutes later, Nick pulled the Tahoe up in front of Marge Kostichek's tiny paint-peeling bungalow. Darkness had all but consumed dusk, but no lights shone in the windows. For some nameless reason, Catherine felt a strange twinge in the pit of her stomach.

Nick opened the door of the SUV and unbuckled his seatbelt.

"Let's wait for O'Riley," she said reasonably. "How long can it take him to get here?"

"Why wait?"

"We should wait for O'Riley. We don't have a warrant."

But then they were going up the walk, and were at the front door, where Nick knocked. He threw her one of those dazzlers. "It'll be fine."

This is wrong, Catherine thought; she was the senior investigator on the unit—she should put her foot down. But the truth was, she was as anxious as Nick to follow this lead; and she knew that once O'Riley got here, she herself would take the investigative lead, anyway.

So why this apprehension, these butterflies?

No answer to Nick's knock, so he tried again and called, "Ms. Kostichek? It's Nick from the crime lab!"

Through the curtained window, Catherine saw a figure move in the gloomy grayness, someone with something in his or her hand—*was that shape . . . a gun?*

She shoved Nick off the porch to the left, her momentum carrying her with him just as a bullet exploded through the door and sailed off into the night. Another round made its small awful thunder and a second shot drilled through the door, at a lower trajectory, and spanged off the sidewalk.

Catherine and Nick lay sprawled in the dead brown bushes to the left of the front door.

"You all right?" she asked.

Shaken, startled, Nick managed, "I think so. How did you . . ."

She rolled off the shrubbery, pistol in her hand—she didn't even remember drawing it—and she said to Nick, "Head for the truck—I got your back . . . stay low." She lay on the lawn, gun trained on the front door.

Nick, shaken, was clearly afraid, but concerned for her. "I'll cover you. Never mind the Tahoe—just get the hell out of here."

"Damnit, Nick—we don't leave, we contain the scene. Get behind the truck, and call this in. Now, *move!*"

This time Nick didn't argue—he rolled out of the bushes, got to his knees, then blasted off like a sprinter coming out of the blocks, keeping low as he raced across the front yard.

Another shot splintered through the door and Catherine wanted to return fire, but who would she be shooting at? She couldn't blindly shoot at the house.

"Put your weapon down!" she yelled, remaining on her stomach, on the grass, handgun aimed at the doorway. "Come out with your hands high, and empty!"

Nothing.

Nick was already behind the Tahoe, his own pistol in hand. A distant siren wailed and Catherine knew help was on the way. Some neighbor had called 911.

"Come on, Cath," Nick yelled. "I've got you . . ."

But a bullet cracked the night and shattered its way through the window and smashed the driver's side window of the Tahoe.

Nick ducked and Catherine took the opportunity to roll left, come up running, and plaster herself against the side of the house. Her heart pounding, gunshots echoing in her ringing ears, she glanced out front to make sure Nick was all right. She couldn't see him.

"Nicky—you okay?" she yelled.

"Peachy!"

The siren grew. Sliding along the clapboard side of the bungalow, she made her way toward the back. Only two windows were on this side of the house, the living room picture window, and one in what might be a back bedroom. She tried to see in the edge of the shattered picture window, around the border of the curtain, but it was just too damn dark. She was moving along the side of the house when she heard a car squeal to a halt in front—O'Riley.

"What the hell!" O'Riley was saying, and Nicky's voice, softer, the words not making their way to her. Then another three shots cracked from out front—O'Riley drawing fire now.

She took a hesitant step around the corner. If she could slip in through the back door, maybe she could get the drop on the old woman—if that was who'd been firing on them. Ducking down below a window, Catherine took a second step, then the back door flew open and she froze as a tall figure—male figure—in head-to-toe black bolted out the door and sprinted across the yard. Her pistol came up automatically, but she saw no weapon in the man's hands and did not fire.

She took off after him.

The perp ran with the easy grace of an athlete, but Catherine managed to keep pace with him for half a block before he vaulted a chain link fence, stopping for a split second on the other side, then speeding across the yard, jumping the fence on the other side before disappearing into the night.

"Damnit," she said, stopped at the first fence. She holstered the weapon, and walked back to the house, still trying to catch her breath.

When she got back out front, she found O'Riley pacing in the yard, talking to two uniformed officers, whose black-and-white at the curb, with its longbar, painted the night blue and red.

"Where's Nick?" she asked him.

O'Riley pointed. "Inside. . . . The woman's dead."

"What?"

He shook his head. "It's ugly in there, Catherine—double-tapped, just like Fortunato and Dingelmann."

She filled him in quickly, about the perp's escape, and he turned to the uniformed men, to start the search, and she went inside to help Nick process the scene.

Marge Kostichek lay facedown on the shabby living room rug, a large purple welt on her left cheek, her eyes mercifully closed. A gag made from a scarf encircled her head, blocking her mouth. A large crimson stain stood out where her mouth was. So much blood was on the floor, it was hard to find a place to stand without compromising the evidence.

"It's him," Nick said, his complexion a sickly white. "He got to Kostichek before we could. He even cut off her fingertips, like Fortunato. Two of them anyway—we must have interrupted him." He swallowed thickly. "Judging from the gag, I think she bit through her tongue."

They heard another vehicle squeal to a halt outside. Within seconds, Grissom—his black attire not unlike the perp's—stood in the doorway.

"What were you doing here without O'Riley?" he demanded.

"O'Riley was on his way with the search warrant," Catherine said, covering. "We had no way of knowing the Deuce would be here."

"Tell me," Grissom said, and Catherine filled him in, in detail.

Then Grissom took a deep breath. "All right," he said. "Let's do the scene and see if maybe we can find a way to get this guy."

Catherine pointed to the floor. "If he's still using the same gun, these shell casings will be a great start."

Expressing his agreement with a nod, he jerked his cell phone out and punched speed-dial. ". . . Jim, get over to Hyde's house, now. Someone just killed Marge Kostichek. . . . I know—maybe he's on his way home right now. . . . Not yet, we're doing that now." He hit END, then turned to Catherine and Nick. "Find us what we need."

Catherine was already bagging shell casings.

Grissom, clearly pissed, said, "I don't like murders on my watch."

At the front doorway, O'Riley—keeping out of the way of the crime scene investigation—called Catherine over. Grissom came along.

O'Riley said to them, "I got a little good news—my man Tavo in L.A. just interviewed Joy Petty."

Catherine and Grissom exchanged glances, the latter prompting, "And?"

"Seems the Kostichek woman took Joy in as a runaway, raised her like a daughter. Joy says her 'mom' considered Malachy Fortunato a 'bad influence'—you know, a married man, a degenerate gambler, with the mob nipping at his heels. After Malachy disappeared, Joy says she was afraid the mob had killed him, so she took off, to protect herself."

Grissom asked, "Where is Joy now?"

"Still there at the stationhouse with Tavo—my LAPD contact."

"Have him take another run at her—but this time tell her about Marge's murder."

Catherine glanced at Grissom quizzically.

"Yeah?" O'Riley said. "Why?"

But now Catherine had caught up with her boss, saying, "Because Joy might stop protecting her mom, if she knows her mom is dead . . . particularly if she knows *how* her mom died."

O'Riley looked from one of them to the other. "No details spared?"

"None," Grissom said. "The LAPD uses digital tape for their interviews, right?"

"I think so. I mean, we do."

"Good. Tell your man Tavo I'm gonna want this interview sent up to our server, toot sweet, so we can download it."

O'Riley nodded and ambled out.

Grissom pitched in with them, as they looked for footprints first. Nick used the electrostatic dust print lifter and pulled up a running-shoe print from the linoleum floor in the kitchen. Next they photographed the body, the living room, the kitchen, and an open drawer that Catherine found in a back bedroom.

With Grissom's help, they fingerprinted everything the killer might have touched. While Nick did the flat surfaces, Catherine used Mikrosil to print the doorknobs, but she had seen the killer wearing gloves when she chased him. She didn't expect to get much and they didn't. She bagged all of Marge's shoes so they could later prove that none of them matched the print they got from the kitchen. Catherine found nothing in her search of the backyard or the alley. Then, shining her mini-flash on the top of the chain link fence, she saw something glimmer.

Moving closer, she found a few strands of black fiber and a small patch of blood. She snapped some photos and then, using a pair of wire cutters, snipped two of the ends off the top of the fence and deposited them in evidence bags.

She shared this with Grissom, who had spent much of his time in the house supervising their work, but also snooping around on his own.

"Come with me," Grissom said, and in the kitchen he pointed out a knife almost out of its holder on the counter, and, on the floor, a few drops of blood and some strands of gray hair.

Then Catherine followed Grissom into the living room, where he pointed out a suspiciously clear area on the cluttered writing desk—had something been taken?

Now Grissom was staring, apparently at the wall.

"You think you know how this went down," Catherine said, knowing that look.

"Yes," he said.

The Deuce knew they would never let up now. All he could do was cover his tracks as much as possible. He'd seen the article in the Las Vegas Sun *and knew they had stumbled onto Fortunato's mummified body. If the cops had that, how long until they found the woman?*

The old woman didn't think he knew about the younger one, but he did. It was his business to know. The stripper had been sleeping with the mark, so damn right he knew about her. According to the phone book, the old woman, Kostichek, still lived where she always had. That made it easier. He had no idea where the stripper was, but he would find out. That was part of the reason for his visit to the old woman.

He parked a couple of blocks away in the parking lot of a grocery store, no point in getting careless now. Taking his time, he walked a block and a half before cutting up the alley behind her house. Even though the sun had started to set, it still beat down on him, his black clothes absorbing the heat like a sponge, and he felt the sweat beginning to pool at the small of his back, behind his knees, and under his arms. A lighter color would have been cooler, but he knew he'd be here past dark and he might want to leave without being seen, so he wore the black.

He came up behind the house, pulling on black leather gloves as he edged closer. Looking around carefully, he tried to make sure no one saw him as he took the silencer from his pocket and screwed it on the handgun. Then he knocked lightly on her back door, stepping to one side so she would have to open both the inside door and the screen to see him. Reaching around, he knocked again, louder this time.

"Jesus jones, I'm coming!" she yelled.

The woman opened the door, said, "Who's there?" and then opened the screen and saw him.

She tried to pull the door shut, but he was much stronger, and jammed himself into the frame. Ducking back inside, she tried to close the inner door in his face, but again he overpowered her. She fell back against the stove, turned, and reached for a knife from the block on the counter. He pressed the silenced snout of the automatic to her cheek and she froze.

Raising the noise-suppressed weapon, he cracked her across the face and she collapsed to the floor. Grabbing her by the hair, he dragged her, struggling, into the living room.

"Where is she?" he asked, crouching over her.

The old woman seemed confused. "Who?"

"The stripper—where is she?"

"Go to hell!"

Casually, he pulled a pair of garden clippers from his pocket. "I'm going to find out anyway. You can make this easy, or hard."

Her eyes filled with tears, but her jaw set and she said nothing.

"Hard it is," he said. Putting down the clippers, he picked up one of her scarves off the back of a chair. He gagged her with it, then picked up the clippers and closed them around the pinky of her left hand.

Tears running down her cheeks now, her sobs fighting to get out through the gag, she closed her eyes.

"This little piggy . . ." He tightened the clippers' grip on her finger, blood leaked out around the edges. "Are you sure it has to be this way?"

She said nothing, sobs still wracking her body.

". . . goes to market." The clippers closed with the angry crack of her fingertip snapping off.

Her scream was louder than he would have expected with the gag and she tried to crawl away, but he cuffed her alongside the head, grabbed a handful of hair and jerked her back. She wailed now, her right hand coming up to cup the left one as she watched blood stream down her hand.

Only risk was, he knew, she might pass out from pain and shock . . . but she was a tough old bird.

Batting away her good hand, he closed the clippers on her ring finger. "This little piggy stayed home . . . ready to tell me? Just nod."

She shook her head, defiant, but this time she screamed into the gag before he did it. That didn't stop him. He heard the same crack and watched the fingertip fall to the floor.

"Ready now?"

The old woman curled into a ball and tried to protect her hand, *but he jerked her hand up, closed the clippers around the middle finger. Her eyes went wide and wild, and, using her good hand, she pointed toward the desk.*

"What?" he asked.

She couldn't speak; the gag was bloody. She'd bit through her tongue, so taking the gag off would not aid clarity.

"You're telling me the information is in the desk?"

Weakly, she nodded.

He went to the desk and looked back at the old woman. He picked up piles of mail until lifting one rubber-banded stack of letters made the woman nod. Joy Petty, *the return address said. Sticking the stack inside his shirt, he returned to the woman. She tried to crawl away but couldn't. Right on top of her, he fired a shot into the back of her head, then one inch below it, a second.*

He had just removed the noise suppresser when a car door slammed outside and he saw a man and woman coming up the front stairs. They came to the front door and the man knocked. At first he did nothing. The man knocked again—and announced himself as the police!

Moving slightly to to his right, the killer fired through the door. Then a second shot. He moved back left, saw the woman aiming at the house and the man take off across the front yard. He fired once more at the running man, then the woman yelled—identifying them as police . . . big surprise.

He heard the man shout something from behind their black SUV. Firing through the front window now, he blew out the truck's driver's side window. An encroaching siren told him there was no point in hanging around here waiting for them to surround him. He pulled on his hood, got to the back door, opened it quietly, then taking a deep breath, took off at a sprint across the backyard.

He thought he heard footsteps advancing behind him, but he couldn't be sure. He vaulted a neighbor's chain link fence, the top of it cutting into his hand. The sudden pain stopped him, but only for a second. Seeing a silhouette running toward him, he turned and took off across the yard jumping the front fence, and then he was gone.

After two hours, they had worked the scene thoroughly, pausing only to watch as the EMTs loaded Marge Kostichek's body onto a gurney and wheeled her out.

Grissom, at the writing table, had found two more bundles of letters from Joy Petty, which Nick bagged, saying, "This guy is starting to piss me off."

"Nobody likes to get shot at, Nick," Grissom said.

"But it's like he's always one jump ahead of us."

Catherine said, "He just reads the *Sun*, is all."

But a cloud drifted across Grissom's face.

Catherine said, "What?"

"Nothing," he said. "Just a feeling."

She gave him a small wry smile. "I thought you didn't believe in feelings—just evidence."

"This feeling grows out some piece of evidence," he said, "or anyway, something I already know, that I just haven't given proper weight. But I will."

O'Riley bounded in. "My buddy Tavo called. He got a videotape statement of Joy Petty saying that Marge Kostichek hired the Deuce to kill Malachy Fortunato."

Grissom and Catherine exchanged wide-eyed glances.

"Just that simple?" Nick asked.

"It's not all good news," O'Riley said. "Joy Petty's in the wind."

"What?" Grissom snapped.

O'Riley shrugged. "She asked to use the john. She wasn't a suspect, she wasn't even a witness—just a citizen cooperating of her own free will. She smelled the danger. She's gone."

"Have they checked her house yet?"

"Yes. All her clothes were gone, she even took her cat. Like she'd been ready for this day for years."

She had been, Catherine thought.

Grissom asked, sharply, "Well, are they looking for her? She's an accessory after the fact."

"Oh, yeah. I mean, I don't know what kind of priority they put on this—it's not their case. This was just a favor Tavo was doing me."

"Get your friend on the phone now, Sergeant," Grissom said. "We're heading back to home base and in half an hour, I want to be able to download that interview. We need to see this for ourselves."

"I'll try."

"Don't try. Do it."

*   *   *

In just under forty-five minutes, Grissom had assembled Catherine, Nick, and O'Riley in his office.

On the computer screen was the image of an interrogation room.
Across the table from the camera sat a fortyish woman with shoulder-
length black hair, brown eyes, and a steeply angled face.

Though the interrogating officer wasn't in the picture, his voice
now came through the speaker. "State your name."

O'Riley whispered, "That's my buddy Tavo."

The woman on screen was already saying, "Joy Petty."

Grissom shushed O'Riley.

The off-camera Tavo asked, "Your address?"

She gave an address in Lakewood.

"You are here of your own volition without coercion?"

She nodded.

"Say yes or no, please."

"Yes, I'm sorry. Yes, I'm here of my own volition, without no coercion."

As they watched, the woman before them grew more agitated.
She took a pack of cigarettes from her purse.

Tavo must have been looking at his notes, because she had it
lighted before he said, "No smoking, please."

With a smirk, she stubbed the cigarette out in a black ashtray in
front of her.

"You've used other names during your life, correct?"

"Yes. Joy Starr, Joy Luck, and several more other stage names.
They called me Monica Leigh in the *Swank* layout; that's a magazine.
The name I was given at birth was Monica Petty."

Without even thinking about it, she lit another cigarette and took
a deep drag. Tavo said nothing. She took a second drag, blew it out
through her nose, and finally realized she was smoking where she
shouldn't be and blotted out the second butt in the ashtray.

Half-annoyed, half-curious, she asked, "Why is there a goddamn
ashtray if we're not allowed to smoke?"

"It's just always been there," Tavo told her.

For several minutes Tavo elicited from her the story of Marge
Kostichek taking in her in as a runaway, raising her like a daughter (albeit a daughter who worked in her strip club). Catherine wondered if

a sexual relationship might have developed between the women, but the officer didn't ask anything along those lines.

Finally, Tavo lowered the boom. "Ms. Petty, I'm afraid I have bad news for you."

"What? What is this about, anyway? What is this really about?"

"Marge Kostichek was murdered this evening."

"No . . . no, you're just saying that to . . ."

Tavo assured her he was telling the truth. "I'm afraid it was a brutal slaying, Ms. Petty."

Her lip was trembling. "Tell me. Tell me. . . . I have a right to know."

Tavo told her.

"Ms. Petty—do you know who killed Malachy Fortunato in Las Vegas in nineteen hundred eighty-five?"

"I . . . I know what they call him."

"And what is that?"

"The Deuce. Because of those two head wounds, like Marge got."

"The Deuce is a professional killer?"

"Yes. I don't know his name, otherwise."

"Do you know who hired him?"

". . . I . . . know who hired him, yes."

"Who?"

The woman seemed fine for a moment, then she collapsed, her head dropping to the table as long, angry sobs erupted from her. Tavo's hand came into the picture, touched her arm. The gesture seemed to give her strength and she wrestled to control her emotions.

"I've . . . I'm sorry." A sob halted her, but she composed herself again and said, "I loved him, but Malachy was not a strong man. He didn't have the strength to choose between his wife or me. And neither of us would give him up, either. He had a tender touch, Malachy. But he was selfish, and weak, too—that's what led him to embezzle from the Sandmound, you know . . . the casino where he worked."

Tavo said nothing, letting her tell it in her own time, in her own way.

"I stripped at a bar called Swingers. I'd been there since the owner, Marge Kostichek, took me in when I was fifteen. Marge knew that once the mob found out Mal was embezzling they'd kill him, and anybody who had anything to do with him. So, she beat them to the punch.

"She hired this guy who did these mob hits. I don't know how she knew about him, how to contact him; I heard Swingers was a money laundry for some mob guys . . . I just heard that, you know . . . so maybe that was how. Anyway, hiring this guy cost her most of the money she'd saved over the years. The rest she gave to me along with a bus ticket to L.A."

"Excuse me, Ms. Petty—I want to remind you that I did advise you of your rights."

"I know you did. See, I didn't know Marge did it, till years later. I thought . . . I thought the mobsters had Malachy killed. And Marge told me I was in danger, too, and put me on that bus. And I went willingly. I was scared shitless, believe me."

"So . . . you stayed in touch with Marge over the years?"

"Yes—we wrote to each other regularly. She even came out to visit a few times."

"Have you been back to Las Vegas?"

"I'm not that brave."

"So how did you come to find out the truth?"

"Maybe five years later, when she visited me. I was in Reseda at the time. We spent a long evening, drinking, reminiscing . . . and she spilled her guts. I think she felt guilty about it. I think she'd been carrying it around, and she told me how about, and cried and cried and begged me to forgive her."

"Did you?"

"Sure. She did it to save me, she thought—those mobsters mighta killed me, too, *and* Mal's wife . . . I mean, if they thought one of us was in on it, the embezzling?"

"I see."

"Do you? End of the day, I loved her a hell of a lot more than I did that candy ass Malachy. . . . Listen, Officer—I need to use the restroom."

And that was the end of the taped interview.

O'Riley covered for his pal Tavo in L.A. "Hey, she wasn't under arrest or anything. She came in voluntarily. He let his guard down. By the time he got a female officer to check the john, and hunted down his partner, they were fifteen minutes behind her, easy."

"Plenty of time," Nick said, "for Joy to pack up and get out of Dodge . . . but why? Why did she run?"

Grissom was staring at the blank screen.

"Running is all she knows how to do," Catherine said, with an open-handed gesture. "That's what she's done her whole life. It started at fifteen when she ran from her parents, and she's never stopped since."

"And Marge Kostichek was just trying to help the poor girl," Nick said, bleakly.

"You don't win Mother of the Year," Grissom said, "by hiring a hit-man to commit first-degree murder."

15

About the time O'Riley and Nick found Marge Kostichek's body, Warrick was hunkered over a computer monitor in the layout room at work. His eyes burned and his temples throbbed and his neck muscles ached. A while back Sara had stopped by to tell him about the bewildering background search on Barry Hyde's personal history, and Warrick had told her that Hyde's business life was proving equally messy and mysterious.

"No matter what I learn," he'd said to her, "something else suggests the opposite."

"I know the feeling," she'd said.

Now, an hour later at least, things were messier and more mysterious. Although the business spent money buying the latest video releases, A-to-Z did little advertising and had the worst rental rates around. Patrick the pot-smoking manager had copped to the store's light traffic, and yet every month Hyde paid what Warrick considered an exorbitant rent in addition to buying more and more movies. Where did the money come from?

He turned away from the monitor's glow, rubbing his eyes, wondering where he would search next.

That was when Brass stumbled in, exhausted and a little disheveled, looking for Grissom.

"Not sure where he is," Warrick said. "One minute he was here, then O'Riley called from Kostichek's house."

"What was it?"

"Frankly, sounded like your ballpark—I think Marge got sent to that big strip club in the sky."

Brass's well-pleated face managed to tighten with alarm. "You don't think it's the . . ."

"Deuce if I know," Warrick said.

Brass slipped into a chair next to Warrick, slumping. "The more we work on this, the more bizarre it gets."

With a slow nod, Warrick said, "Tell me about it. It's like that damn video store—hardly any business, you wouldn't think much cash flow, and yet Hyde seems to have plenty of dough."

The cop grunted a humorless laugh. "What do you make of Hyde traveling all the time?"

"If he's the Deuce, maybe he's got gigs all around this great land of ours."

Brass shrugged. "So we just trace where he went. And see who got murdered, or disappeared, there."

"I'm all over that—for what good it's doing. No record of Barry Thomas Hyde on any passenger manifest for any airline . . . ever."

"Some people hate to fly. Maybe he drives."

Warrick shook his head. "Last month, when he was traveling, his car was in a Henderson garage getting serviced."

"What about ren—"

"No rental records. And he doesn't have a second car—I mean, he's unmarried, no record of a divorce or kids, either."

"What are you telling me?"

"That the guy leaves town regularly. He doesn't fly, drive his own car to get there, or even rent a car."

"Bus? Train?"

"No records there, either. For a guy who gets around, there's no sign he ever left home."

Brass smirked. "Just that calendar and that pothead's word."

"Why would Hyde tell his video store staff he was gonna be out of town, if he wasn't?"

"Well, then he's got another identity."

"Our maildrop guy, Peter Randall, maybe? That's the only thing that makes sense—particularly if he's still taking assignments as the Deuce, despite the lack of bodies that've turned up in the past few years."

Brass stared into nothing; then he shook his head, as if to clear the cobwebs, and turned to Warrick and asked, "What about hotels?"

"Well, that's going to take forever to check in detail, you know, to try to see if he was registered anywhere . . . I mean, he never told Patrick where he was off to . . . but I can tell you this: Hyde never charged a hotel or motel room to any one of his three credit cards, and never wrote 'em a check either."

Brass sighed heavily—then he rose, stretched; bones popped. "Something very wrong here—very wrong . . . When Grissom gets back, have him page me."

"You got it."

Brass walked out of the office, got about four feet, and his cell phone rang. The conversation was a short one, Brass sticking his head back inside the layout room moments later, his expression suddenly alert.

"C'mon," Brass said, waving impatiently. "You're with me."

"All right," Warrick said, and in the corridor, falling in next to Brass, he asked, "What's up?"

Brass wore a foul expression. "Barry Hyde's number, I hope."

Sara awoke with a start. She had fallen asleep at her computer and evidently no one had noticed. She sat up, made a face, then rolled her neck and felt the tight stiffness that came when she slept wrong. Reaching back, she kneaded her neck muscles, applying more and more pressure as she went, but the pain showed little sign of dissipating. Standing up, her legs wobbly, she got her balance and went out into the hall to the water fountain. Then she wandered from room to room looking for the rest of the crew, but found no one.

At least not until she stepped into the DNA lab, where she discovered skinny, spiky-haired Greg Sanders, on the phone, a huge grin going, his eyes wide.

"You're going to do what?" he asked. "You . . . you're such a bad girl. . . ."

Clearing her throat, Sara smiled and, when he spun to face her, gave him a little wave.

The grin turned upside down, as he said, "Um, we'll continue this, later. I've got to go." He hung up without further comment.

"Serious, meaningful relationship?" she asked.

"Hey, it's not as kinky as you think."

"No, Greg, I'm pretty sure it is. Where is everybody?"

He shrugged. "Catherine and Nick are at a murder scene. I think Grissom went to join the party, and Warrick left with Brass, like, I dunno, ten minutes ago."

She felt very awake, suddenly. "Murder scene?"

He held up his hands. "I don't know the details."

She sat down on an empty stool. "What do you know?"

On his wheeled chair, he rolled over to another work station, saying, "I know the cigarette butt Catherine brought in, from the mummy site, is too decomposed, and too old, to give us any workable DNA after all that time."

"Okay. That's the bad news part—how about some good news?"

"If you insist. How about that other cigarette butt? The one they brought in from Evidence—it was old, too, but somebody bagged it years ago."

"What about it?"

"It doesn't match the mummy's blood . . . or the wife's DNA, either." Warming to the topic, Sanders grinned at her in his cheerful fashion and pulled a sheet of paper out of a folder. "Take a peek."

She rolled on her stool over next to him. "DNA test results," she said, reading, pleased. "So, the cigarette butt came from the killer?"

"Hey, I just work here. I don't know whose DNA it is—it just isn't the wife's or the mummy's."

"Does Grissom know about this? Anybody?"

"No." Sanders shook his head. "I haven't had a chance to tell them."

"I know," she said. "You were busy—had phone calls to make."

"Listen, I get break time like anybody—"

She leaned in and smiled her sweetest smile. "Greg—I'm just teasing you. From what I heard, sounded like you enjoy it. . . . Anyway, I'll pass the news along. You're going to be popular."

He shrugged and smiled. "Good. I like being popular."

"So I gathered."

And she left the lab.

Warrick sat in the darkened car next to Brass. The unmarked Taurus was parked at the intersection of Fresh Pond Court and Dockery Place, with a good view of Hyde's house and its putting-green front yard. The car windows were down, the evening nicely cool, the night a dark one, not much moon. Patrol cars were parked on Eastern

Avenue, South Pecos Road, and Canarsy Court, observing the sides and back of the house, to make sure Hyde didn't sneak in on foot.

The Hyde residence stood dark and silent, a ranch-style tomb. The neighbors' houses showed signs of normal life, the faint blue glow of televisions shining through wispy curtains in darkened rooms; others were well-lit with people occasionally crossing in front of windows, somewhere a stereo played too loud, and a couple of houses away from Hyde's, somebody had his garage door open, fine-tuning the engine of a Kawasaki motorcycle. At this hour the guy was pushing it—it was almost ten P.M.

"You think Hyde's really the Deuce?" Warrick asked.

Brass shrugged.

"If he is, you think he'd come back here, right after murdering somebody?"

Within the dark interior of the car, the detective gave Warrick a long appraising look. "You know, Brown, sometimes it's better not to think so much. Just wait for it and react. If he comes, he comes. Don't try to out-think these mutts. Leave it to them and they'll do it. That's when we pick them up."

Warrick knew Brass was right; but it frustrated him.

They sat in silence for a long time; how long, Warrick didn't know—he thought he might even have dozed off a couple of times. Stakeout work was boring, even when there was an undercurrent of danger, and it made Warrick glad he wasn't a cop. The neighbor with the motorcycle either got tired or somebody called to complain, because he stopped working on the machine and shut his garage door. One by one the lights in the windows around the court went out.

"Maybe he's made us," Warrick said, "or one of the squads."

Brass shrugged. "Wouldn't surprise me. He didn't stay alive in that business this long being careless. I doubt if he spotted us, though—there hasn't been a car on this street since we got here."

Just then a vehicle turned toward them off South Pecos Road. Its headlights practically blinded them and they slid down in their seats. Then the vehicle—a big black SUV—pulled to a stop almost even with them.

"Grissom," Brass said, sounding a little peeved.

The black Tahoe idled quietly next to them and Grissom rolled down his window. "So?"

"Nothing," Brass said. "House has been dark and quiet since we got here."

"All right. When you get back, Jim, you need to see an interview the LAPD sent over—Joy Petty confirming Marge Kostichek hired the Deuce."

Brass blew out air. "Jesus—so she was an old loose end getting newly tied off."

Grissom didn't respond to that, saying, "I'm going back to the lab. Warrick . . ."

Brass shushed him and pointed to Hyde's house where a light had just come on in the living room. Grissom eased the Tahoe over to the far curb, parked it and returned to the Taurus on foot, quietly slipping into the backseat.

The walkie seemed to jump into Brass's hand. "Light just came on in the house."

The reports came back quickly. No one had seen anything.

"Damnit," Brass said. He sighed. "All right—I'm going to go take a peek in the window. You two stay here."

"No way, Jim," Grissom said. "We're not going to let you go up there alone."

"Let's not completely blow our cover," Brass said. "It could just be a timer."

"And," Warrick added, "Hyde might be a professional killer who has already done one murder tonight, and forty-some others over the years—that we know about. You really want to go up there alone?"

Brass scowled at Warrick. "Are you trying to tell me how to do my job?"

Letting out a long tired sigh, Warrick said, "No, I just asked a question. Do you really want to go up there alone?"

Brass thought about it; finally he said, "All right—one of you."

Warrick opened the door and jumped out, beating Grissom to the punch. The pair made their way cautiously up the street, moving through yards and trying to avoid the circle of light thrown off by the only street light, back on the corner. Warrick stayed behind the much shorter Brass, keeping low. At the edge of Hyde's yard they ducked in next to the garage.

"You only go as far as that end of the garage," Brass whispered, pointing.

"What are you going to do?"

"I'm going around the back, and come up the other side, and try to see in the window."

Warrick nodded. "I'll follow you to the back of the garage. When you go up the far side, I'll move up to the front."

"Okay," Brass said, and pulled his revolver from his hip holster. He eased to the back of the garage and Warrick, his own pistol in hand, crept along in Brass's shadow. At the corner, in darkness out of the range of the street light, the detective gave Warrick a little wave and edged around the corner. Taking position, Warrick watched as Brass moved across the huge backyard. The detective was halfway across when a high-mounted motion light came on, putting Brass in the spotlight. . . .

Warrick dipped into shooter's stance, pistol leveled at the back door, centered above a wide octagonal deck. Initially, Brass froze; but the deer-in-headlights moment passed, and he dove to his right, rolled, and came up running toward the far side of the house, in darkness again.

Ready to shoot, Warrick searched for a target, finding none, and not unhappy about it. Brass, now on the far side of the house, would be making his way toward the front and expecting Warrick to be there to cover him.

Spinning, Warrick sprinted back to the front. He turned and, at the garage door, stayed close as he slithered to the far end. Peeking around the corner, Warrick saw nothing and wondered if something had happened to Brass. Fighting panic, he saw Brass's face slide out from behind a shrub at the corner of the house. Warrick's trip-hammer heartbeat slowed only slightly, as he watched the detective trying to see inside.

The CSI watched intently, as Brass crawled beneath the window, stopping to peer over the edge of the frame. Just when he thought they were going to pull this off without a hitch, Warrick felt a hand settle on his shoulder. He jumped and turned, bringing his pistol up as he went.

Grissom just looked at him. "Damnit, Gris," Warrick half-whispered, keeping his voice down at least, as the adrenaline spiked through his system. Turning back, he realized he couldn't see Brass now, and—panic rising again—wondered where the detective had gone. As he prepared to stick his head around the corner, Brass came the other way, suddenly appearing three inches in front of him, and Warrick jumped again. Damn!

"Hyde's not home," Brass said, his voice low, but no longer a whisper.

"Not home," Warrick echoed numbly—but as much as he wanted this son of a bitch, he couldn't help feeling relieved.

Brass was saying, "Those lights gotta be on a timer. No sign of him in the living room, and the lights are still off in the rest of the house."

Spinning back to Grissom, Warrick asked, "And just what the hell were you doing?"

"Neighbors called in a prowler," he said. "Henderson PD is coming—silent response."

The words were no sooner out of his mouth than three police cars rolled into the court, cherrytops making the night psychedelic, spotlights trained on the three of them. No sirens, though—that might disturb the neighborhood.

Officers piled out, using their doors for cover as they aimed their pistols at Brass and Warrick.

"Drop your guns," one of them ordered, and then another one or two yelled pretty much the same thing.

Carefully kneeling, Warrick and Brass set their guns on the ground in front of them.

"Is our cover blown yet?" Grissom asked.

As Brass explained the situation to the Henderson Police Department, Warrick and Grissom stood staring at the big, expensive, and apparently very empty house.

"He's making us look like fools," Warrick said.

Grissom didn't reply immediately; but then he said, "When we're done here, we'll swing by the video store."

"He could be there."

"Yes he could."

Brass returned, shaking his head. "They're a little pissed."

Warrick said, "I guess we coulda given 'em a heads up."

"It's not ideal interdepartmental relations," Brass admitted. He looked at the disgruntled uniforms, who were milling out by their black-and-whites, cherrytops shut off. "They also informed me that Barry Hyde has been a model citizen since moving to Henderson . . . and if in the future we want to do some police work in their fair city, they would like us first to ask their permission."

"They said that?" Grissom asked.

"I'm paraphrasing, but the message was the same. So—let's go home."

Warrick said, "Gris wants to drop by A-to-Z Video on the way back."

"Hell no," Brass said.

"Maybe I want to rent a movie," Grissom said.

Brass seemed to struggle for words. Finally he managed, "You know, Warrick, after your boss finishes this case, it's possible you and I are both going to be looking for work."

"Maybe they could use us in Henderson," Warrick suggested. "Looks like a nice town to work in. But till then, what do you say we go scope out the vids?"

Brass shook his head again. "Might as well. It'll give me something to look at while I'm on suspension."

16

About the time night shift actually started—after she had already put in over four hours that included getting shot at and working a particularly unpleasant crime scene—Catherine Willows nonetheless exuded vitality as she made a bee-line for the DNA lab. From behind her, Sara's voice called out: "Hey, wait up!"

She slowed, turning to see Sara hustle up, a report in hand. "If you're headed for DNA, I may have something for you."

As they walked, Sara handed her the report, saying, "I told Greg I'd give this to you. It's the DNA results from your Fortunato evidence."

Catherine took it, but asked, "What's the news?"

"Blood was the mummy's. Cigarette taken from the Fortunato backyard sixteen years ago contains DNA that doesn't match either the late husband or his living wife."

Catherine smiled wickedly. "Could be the Deuce's."

Sara flashed her cute gap-toothed grin. "Could be. But why are we still headed to the lab?"

" 'Cause this isn't what I was going there for."

Quickly Catherine filled Sara in, slightly out of order: telling her Marge Kostichek had been murdered, apparently by the Deuce, then about the tight scrape she and Nick had been in. And finally she brought Sara up to speed on Joy Petty and the Kostichek woman hiring the murder of the mummy.

Sara, clipping along beside her, said, "And here I thought sure Fortunato was a mob hit."

"We all did," Catherine said, with a sour smirk. "Grissom told us not to assume anything, yet we all bit. Maybe that's why this woman is dead now."

"And I take it you've already dropped off the Kostichek crime scene evidence to Greg. . . ."

"Yes, and maybe we'll match up that ancient cigarette DNA—when I chased the son of a bitch tonight, he cut himself on a chain link fence."

Sara, mimicking the milk ad, asked, "Got blood?"

"Oh yeah," Catherine said, and strode into the lab, Sara right behind her.

Sanders almost jumped off his stool. "God! Don't you guys ever knock?"

Catherine leaned on his counter. "That murder crime scene stuff I dropped off? You said you'd get to it ASAP."

"And I will."

She just looked at him. Then she said, "Maybe it's time to define 'ASAP.' "

The normally cheerful lab rat scowled at the two women. "Listen, I'm so far behind it'll be, like, Monday before I can get to it. I got overload from Days to deal with—day shift has, like, two murders, a rape and—"

"Days?" Catherine asked. "You're giving priority to dayshift?"

His brow lifted and half his mouth smirked. "You ever had Conrad Ecklie on your ass?"

"I'm not interested in your personal life, Greg."

He lowered himself over a microscope. "I'll laugh next week, when I have the time."

Leaning near the door, Sara said, "Speaking of time, Cath—while you're waiting for that DNA evidence, we could check the phone records around here . . . for personal calls."

Greg glanced up.

"You know," Sara continued, with a shrug, "as responsible public servants, we need to make sure the taxpayers are being well-served."

Sanders stroked his chin as if a beard were covering his baby face. "For two such dedicated public servants, I might be able to squeeze it in."

"Thanks, Greg—you're the best."

The Taurus and Tahoe pulled into the parking lot and glided side by side into stalls in front of the video store. Warrick climbed down from the driver's seat of the Tahoe, and Brass got out of the Taurus, where Grissom had ridden in the front passenger seat. The CSI supervisor—after taking a long, deep breath, letting it out the same way—followed, joining the two men on the sidewalk.

The normally cool Warrick seemed just a little nervous to Grissom; the lanky man was bobbing on his feet, as he looked in the storefront window and said, "The cashier tonight must be Sapphire—that means the assistant manager on duty is Ronnie. These people have never seen us before, Gris—how do you want to play it?"

It only took Grissom a moment to decide. "Jim and I'll head straight to the back room—you stay out front and keep an eye on the cashier."

A nod. "You got it."

"Gil," Brass said, his face creased with worry, "I've got to tell you, I think this is the wrong play. There's something going on here that we don't understand, yet. You really think sticking our hand into a blind hole makes sense? We could pull out a bloody stump."

"Hyde has to be somewhere," Grissom said. "He's not at his residence—this is his business. What else do you suggest?"

Without waiting for an answer, Grissom pushed open the glass door and went inside.

"May I help you, sir?" a cheerful voice asked from the cashier's island.

Moving into the brightly illuminated world of shelved videos and movie posters, Grissom said, "Just looking," and kept moving toward the back of the store. He felt Brass behind him, maybe two steps.

Warrick strolled in a few seconds behind them, and walked straight to the cashier.

"Hi," he said in a loud voice. "How are you?"

"Fine."

"Have you got the director's cut of *Manhunter?*"

As Warrick and the cashier chatted, Brass said to Grissom, "You're the evidence guy, for Christ's sake! What can we do here that will hold up in court?"

Still ignoring his colleague, Grissom pushed open the swinging door, despite the PRIVATE sign tacked to it, and almost immediately a figure from inside blocked the way: a kid not any older than the last one they'd met here.

"Hey! Can't you read?"

As the kid pointed to the PRIVATE sign, Grissom took a step back and appraised the youth, who wore a blue polo shirt with A-to-Z stitched over the breast, a pudgy kid with dirt-brown hair and dirt-brown eyes set deep inside a pale face.

"You can't come back here!"

The kid said this loudly—too loudly, as if it were for someone's benefit other than Grissom and Brass.

Grissom leaned in, almost nose to nose with the kid. "We're looking for your boss—Barry Hyde."

"Uh, uh . . ."

From inside the office, a voice called, "I'm Barry Hyde! . . . Let the gentlemen in, Ronnie."

Shaken, Ronnie stepped aside, and Grissom stepped into the small office, Brass following glumly.

Getting up from a desk at the right, where a security monitor revealed four angles of the store (including Warrick and the cashier talking), the man rose to a slim six-foot-one or so. That thin build was deceptively muscular, however. The man—who wore no name tag—was in a black polo shirt and black jeans—wardrobe, Grissom noted, not far removed from his own. He was in his fifties, but youthfully so.

And the man's right hand was wrapped in a large gauze bandage.

"I'm Gil Grissom from—"

"Do you always barge into private places unannounced, Mr. Grissom?" Hyde asked, superficially pleasant, but with an edge.

"From the Las Vegas Criminalistics Bureau," Grissom finished. "This is Captain Brass. We'd like to ask you a few questions."

"We should have knocked," Brass mumbled. "Sorry."

"Apology noted," Hyde said. "And I always like to cooperate with law enforcement, but I'm sure you'll understand if I ask see to your credentials."

"Certainly," Brass said, and they complied with the request.

Hyde studied Brass's badge and Grissom's picture ID a few beats longer than necessary, Grissom thought; a smirk lurked at the corner of Hyde's mouth. This man was not afraid of them, or thrown by their presence: he seemed, if anything, amused!

Handing their credentials back, Hyde gave them a curt nod. "Fine, gentlemen. Now. What may I do for you? And let me assure you that any adult material we rent is clearly within community standards."

Grissom smiled, just a little. "Mr. Hyde, I notice you're wearing a bandage on your right hand—it looks fresh. Would you mind telling us how you injured yourself?"

The mouth smirked, but the forehead tensed. "Is there a . . . context to these questions?"

Brass said, "Could you please just answer."

Hyde's smirk evolved into a smile consisting of small even teeth—something vaguely animal-like about them. He held up the hand in front of him, the bandage like a badge of honor. "Shelving units. Ronnie . . . that's the young man you were intimidating just now . . . Ronnie and I were rearranging some shelves and one of them cut my hand."

"Could I take a look at the injury?"

"Why, are you a doctor?"

"Well, yes . . . in a way."

"I'm going to say no," Hyde said, firm but not unfriendly. "I only just now got the bleeding stopped, and got it properly bandaged. I'm not going to undress the wound so you can look at it, for some unspoken reason. Out of the question, gentlemen."

Grissom fought the irritation rising in him. It must have shown, because Brass jumped in with his own line of questioning. "Mr. Hyde, can you tell us where you were, earlier this evening?"

"I could, but you're going to have to be frank with me, gentlemen, if you want my cooperation."

Grissom laid it out: "This is a murder investigation."

That might have given the average person pause, but Hyde snapped right back: "And that gives you the right to be rude?"

Grissom said nothing.

"Please, Mr. Hyde," Brass said, reasonably, "tell us where you were earlier this evening."

"Any particular time?"

Brass shrugged. "Let's say since five."

"A.M. or P.M.?" Hyde asked, his eyes on Grissom, that tiny half-smirk tugging at his cheek.

"Make it P.M.," Brass said, and took a small notebook from his pocket.

"All right." Now Hyde shrugged. "I've been here at the store."

"Since five?"

"Earlier than that even," said Hyde. "Since around four."

Their earlier visit to A-to-Z had been mid-afternoon; had they just missed their man?

"Witnesses to that effect?" Brass asked casually.

"Ronnie and Sapphire. They both came in at four today."

"Isn't that early?" Grissom asked. "I mean, you open at ten, and go to midnight. I thought the shifts would be divided in half."

A smile split the pockmarked face, a stab at pretended cordiality. "That would make sense, wouldn't it? But today Patrick and Sue had plans—they're something of an item . . . not ideal, a workplace romance, but it happens, and I just hate to be a hard-ass boss."

Pothead Patrick had indeed said good things about their boss; but Grissom didn't mention the other assistant manager—Warrick had negotiated the kid's silence, earlier. Or was there a surveillance tape that Hyde had looked at? Had the killer been reviewing security tapes, too?

Hyde was saying, "The lovebirds left an hour early, and Sapphire and Ronnie came in to cover."

Brass asked, "Did your other two employees see you, today?"

Hyde shook his head. "No, they left right at four, and I wandered in a few minutes after."

"Did you know about their plans?"

"They had permission. Like I said, I try to be a good boss to these kids."

Grissom found himself fascinated by this specimen: if Hyde was the Deuce, Grissom was looking at a classic sociopath. If they could bust this guy, and convict him, he would make a great subject for one of Grissom's lectures.

Brass was asking the guy, "Did you go out to eat or anything? Run errands maybe?"

"No, it's just as I've told you." His tone was patronizing, as if Brass were a child.

Hyde continued: "I was here all evening. Ask my kids, they'll tell you. Oh, Ronnie did go out and get Italian—pizza for them, salad for me. I believe it was about nine o'clock. The three of us ate." An eyebrow arched. "The pizza box, and the little styrofoam salad box, are in the Dumpster out back . . . if you would care for further confirmation."

Grissom had rarely encountered this degree of smugness in a murder suspect before.

Brass asked, "Where did Ronnie go to get this Italian?"

"Godfather's . . . it's a bit of a drive, but that's Ronnie's favorite pizza."

Brass wrote that down, dutifully.

Grissom asked, "You didn't eat any pizza?"

"No. It was sausage and pepperoni—I'm a vegetarian."

"Oh. Health reasons, Mr. Hyde, or moral issues?"

"Both. I try to stay fit . . . and of course I take a stand against wanton slaughter."

Grissom admired Hyde's ability to say that with a straight face. "What's your stand on dairy items?"

"What does that have to do with a murder investigation?"

Grissom shrugged. "I'm just wondering. I have an interest in nutrition. Mind humoring me?"

"Not at all—I'm lactose-intolerant. No cheese on my salad—just good crisp healthy veggies. But I do like some sting in my dressing."

Grissom said, "Thank you."

Brass gave Grissom a sideways you're-as-nuts-as-this-guy-is look, and returned to his questioning. "When was the first time you visited Las Vegas, Mr. Hyde? Prior to moving here, I mean."

Hyde considered that. "Six years ago, I believe—just a month or so before I moved here. I fell in love with the place—was here for a video store owners convention—and moved out here."

"Never before that?"

"Never. I don't have any particular interest in gambling. It was the climate—the beauty of the desert sunsets. That sort of thing."

"All right," Brass said, making a note. "Do you know a woman named Marge Kostichek?"

No hesitation. "No—should I?"

"How about a Philip Dingelmann?"

"No."

"Malachy Fortunato?"

"No . . . and I have to say, I'm growing weary of this game. Who are these people, and why would you think that I'd know them?"

Brass smiled—as enigmatic as a Sphinx. "Why, they're our murder victims, Mr. Hyde."

The smirk lost its sarcasm; the eyes hardened. "And you are suggesting I knew these people?"

Brass said, "We're asking."

Hyde seemed to get irritated, now; but Grissom wondered if it was just another chess move, more cat and mouse.

"You think I've killed these people, don't you? What preposterous, presumptuous . . . this interview is over, gentlemen."

"All right," Brass said.

But Hyde went on: "I've tried to assist you, cooperate with you despite your rudeness, and now you repay my good citizenship by accusing me of murder."

Good citizenship? Grissom thought.

"And within the walls of my own establishment, no less." He went to the door, pushed it open, and waited for them to leave.

Brass began to move, but Grissom gently held him back, by the arm. To Hyde, Grissom said, "Talking here at your . . . establishment . . . might be more comfortable for you."

"Than what? The police station?"

Neither man said a word.

Releasing the door, Hyde returned to his desk, sat, and said, "All right—continue your interview." He gestured to the telephone nearby. "But if you accuse me of murder, if you even imply it, I'll end this interview, phone my attorney, and file charges for harassment."

Grissom noted that the security cam system did not include the office or back room.

"You mentioned gambling, Mr. Hyde," Brass said. "So you don't gamble?"

"I said I had no great interest in it. I live at the doorstep of the gambling capital of the United States, if not the free world. Of course I've tried my luck from time to time."

"Ever at the Beachcomber?"

Grissom could sense the wheels turning behind the controlled if smug facade; but Hyde gave up nothing.

He said, "I've been there. I've been to most of the casinos on and off the Strip, for dining and entertainment, if not always gaming. I've lived here for over five years."

"We'll get to that," Brass said. "You ever use the ATM machine at the Beachcomber?"

Grissom thought he saw Hyde give the slightest flinch. It happened so fast he couldn't be sure. . . .

Hyde said, "I don't believe so."

"But you're not sure?"

"No, uh, yes, I'm sure."

That was the closest to flustered Hyde had been, so far.

Brass said, "There's a security tape that shows you using the ATM machine there almost seven weeks ago."

A disbelieving smile twisted the thin lips. "Shows me? I hardly think so. . . ." This was almost an admission of his avoidance of the casino security cameras, and Hyde quickly amplified: "I've never used my ATM card. . . ."

After his voice trailed off, Hyde seemed lost in thought.

"What?" Grissom asked.

Nodding, Hyde said, "You must have seen the man who stole it."

Brass cocked his head as if his hearing were poor. "How is that?"

"On the tape. The casino security tape—you must have seen the individual who stole my ATM card."

Brass sighed. "You're telling us someone stole your ATM card?"

Hyde nodded. "Yes, around the first of May."

"And when did you report the theft?"

"Just now, I'm afraid," Hyde said, with what seemed an embarrassed shake of his head. "Right after the card was stolen, I got called out of town on business and then I simply forgot about it."

Grissom said, "You forgot your ATM card was stolen?"

Brass didn't wait for a response, asking, "How was it stolen?"

"I don't really know."

Grissom felt the irritation rising again; the man's contempt for them was incredible. "You don't know," he said.

Hyde shrugged. "One day I went to use it . . . in my wallet . . . and it was just gone."

"Then you *lost* it," Brass said, apparently trying not to lose it himself. "Mr. Hyde, that's not the same thing as having it stolen."

Hyde looked at them with undisguised disdain. "I never found it, and the bank never called to say that they had it. So it must have been stolen. . . . I probably left it in a machine when I used it, and someone else simply took it."

Now it was Grissom's turn to feel smug. "How do you suppose this guy got your PIN then?"

Hyde's smile managed to turn even more condescending. "The number was written on the back of the card, at the end of the signature box. I'm afraid I have a terrible memory."

Brass said, "You've been doing pretty well with it tonight."

"Numbers, names, that sort of thing, I'm hopeless. So I just wrote the PIN on the card. You know, to this day, I can't remember my social security number."

Grissom had to wonder if that was because he'd had more than one.

"Then you forgot to report the card's loss," Brass said.

"Yes—precisely. What a fool." Hyde put his hands behind his neck, elbows winged out, as he leaned back, clearly enjoying himself.

Brass flipped a notebook page. "Let's talk about before you moved here, five years ago."

"Let's."

"Where did you live before you moved to Henderson?"

"So many places."

"For instance."

"Coral Gables, Florida . . . Rochester, Minnesota . . . Moscow, Idaho—I even lived in Angola, Indiana, once upon a time."

"Let's talk about Idaho—when did you live there?"

"During college. More years ago than I would like to admit."

Grissom figured there was a lot this guy wouldn't like to admit.

Brass was asking, "So, you went to the University of Idaho?"

Hyde nodded. "Graduated with a degree in English." He removed his hands from behind his head and gestured to the posters. "For all the good it's done me."

"You seem to have done all right for yourself," Brass commented.

"'Education,'" Grissom said, "'is an admirable thing.'"

"'But it is well,'" Hyde said, picking up where the criminalist left off, "'to remember from time to time that nothing that is worth knowing can be taught.'"

"Oscar Wilde," Grissom said, trading a tiny smile with Hyde.

"Speaking of education," Brass said, unimpressed, "can you explain why the University of Idaho has never heard of Barry Hyde?"

He seemed surprised. "No, I can't. I suppose it's possible they've lost my transcript. It has, after all, been quite a few years . . . and a lot of these institutions, when they switched over to computerized systems, well . . . I must have gotten lost in the technological shuffle."

Brass asked, "Is there anyone at the university you knew back then we could talk to now?"

"You must be kidding. My old college chums?"

"Yeah—let's start with 'chums.' "

"I have no idea. I haven't been back since I graduated. You might find this hard to believe, but I was painfully shy and kept to myself."

"And instructors?"

Hyde mulled that over momentarily. "I don't know if they are still there, but Christopher Groves and Allen Bridges in the English department might remember me."

Though not one to make assumptions, Grissom felt sure these were the names of two deceased faculty members.

Brass, jotting the names on his pad, glanced at Grissom. "You got anything else, Gil?"

"Couple questions," he said, lightly. "Were you in the service, Mr. Hyde?"

"The United States Army, Mr. Grissom—why?"

"I was wondering where you were stationed."

Not missing a beat, Hyde said, "I received basic training at Fort Bragg, North Carolina, advanced training in communications at Fort Hood, Texas, and then spent nine months at Ansbach, Germany."

"It's odd," Grissom said, "that your doctor's report says that you've never been overseas."

Hyde's eyes narrowed. "Do you make a habit out of invading the privacy of upstanding citizens, Mr. Grissom?"

"Not upstanding citizens, no."

A sneer replaced the smirk. "Well, in that case, you must have stumbled across the records of a different Barry Hyde." He glanced at his watch—a Rolex—and said, "Now, if you gentlemen will excuse me—while talking with you has been more interesting than I could ever have hoped, it's time to close . . . this conversation, and my store."

He rose, held open the door for them and they went out into the store, where he wordlessly led them to the front door—Warrick was gone, the cashier closing out the register. This door Hyde held open for them, also, nodding, smiling.

Grissom turned to him. "See you soon, Mr. Hyde."

Hyde laughed—once; there was something private about it. "I doubt that very much, Mr. Grissom." He went back inside and locked the door. They watched as he took the cash drawer from Sapphire and retired to the back of the store.

"What did he mean?" Brass asked. "We got a flight risk here?"

"Maybe."

"Cocky son of a bitch."

They found Warrick sitting behind the wheel of the Tahoe. "I got chased out," he said. "Any luck?"

"He was less than forthcoming," Grissom said.

Brass snorted. "That's being generous. What did you learn, Brown?"

"Once you were in back, I showed my ID to Sapphire and Ronnie. They were pretty cooperative—both said Hyde's been here all night, since just after four. Of course when Ronnie went out for pizza, around nine—that left Hyde in the back office, and Sapphire up in the cashier's slot, a post she couldn't leave. They ate carry-out pizza when Ronnie got back, and that's about it."

"Actually," Grissom said, "Hyde ate salad. No cheese, just veggies . . . Which may break this case wide open."

"Huh?" Brass said, blinking.

Getting it, Warrick was grinning. "We'd be shit out of luck, if Hyde was in on that pepperoni pizza."

Brass was lost. "What are you guys *talking* about?"

Warrick cackled and said, "No animal DNA in salad."

"Meet you at the Dumpster," Grissom said to Warrick, and headed to the back of the building.

17

In the layout room, Grissom had arrayed various crime scene photos—of the mummy case, at left, and the Dingelmann shooting, at right—on two large adjacent bulletin boards. He had sent Nick to round everybody up, and Catherine—sipping coffee and eating a vending-machine Danish—was at one of the tables. Nick was already back, sitting next to her, sipping a Diet Coke. Along the periphery, blank computer monitor screens stared at them accusingly—as if it was time to put these cases to bed.

Grissom agreed.

Warrick stumbled in, a coffee in one hand, his other rubbing his face; then the hand dropped away and a tired and puffy set of features revealed themselves, including bloodshot, obviously bleary eyes. "So, boss—what's up?"

Looking equally exhausted, Sara tumbled in on Warrick's heels. She carried a pint of orange juice and half a bagel with cream cheese.

Grissom filled everybody in on anything they might have missed, and Nick had the first question.

Nick said, "Okay, Marge Kostichek hires the Deuce to remove Malachy Fortunato, for reasons that are clear, by now, even to those among us who tend to lag behind. . . ."

"Ease up on yourself, Nick," Sara said.

Nick grinned at her, but the grin was gone by the time he posed the rest of his question to Grissom: "But why kill the lawyer—Dingelmann?"

"Because," Grissom said, "Hyde recognized him."

"Pardon?" Nick said.

"If you study the casino tape, the body language is unmistakable—Dingelmann recognizes the man at the poker machine . . . and the man at the poker machine recognizes him."

"Not a contract hit, you're saying," Catherine said. "Something more spontaneous."

"No, no," Nick said, shaking his head, grinning in disagreement, "silenced automatic, two shots in the back of the head? The Deuce is a hired assassin. . . . He kills for money."

"That's one reason he kills," Grissom said, patient. "But why did he murder Marge Kostichek?"

Sara shrugged. "Every cornered animal protects itself."

"Exactly," Grissom said, pointing a finger at her. "Put the pieces together, boys and girls. We have a hired killer with a very distinct signature."

Nods all around.

Grissom continued: "A signature that hasn't been seen for over five years."

"Not," Warrick said, "since he moved to Henderson."

"So he *is* retired," Sara said.

Nick was shaking his head again. "But what about the traveling?"

"For now, never mind that," Grissom said. "Trips or not, five years ago he came here to make a new life—to live under a new name. The contrived background Warrick and Sara uncovered confirms that."

"And Philip Dingelmann," Catherine said, "was a face out of his old life . . . the mob connections he's turned his back on, for whatever reason."

Grissom smiled. "That's a big 'bingo.' For five years, Hyde's been living quietly in Henderson, running his video store, at an apparent loss, and his only recreation, that we know of anyway, is to come in, twice a week, and gamble a little."

"At the Beachcomber," Warrick said. "At off times. So nobody from his past life might recognize him."

"Right," Grissom said, pleased.

"That's crazy," Nick said, not at all on board. "Even with its family-values facelift, Vegas still has mob roots—plus people from all over the country come here, vacationing. Why would somebody who's tucked himself out of the way, in Henderson, Nevada, come to Sin City twice a week?"

"He can't help himself, man," Warrick said. "He's an adrenaline junkie. All those years doing what he did? Couple days a week, he gets a little taste, gets that buzz that lets him survive in the straight world. Gambling does that for some people."

Grissom said, "It's no accident that more wanted felons are arrested every year at McCarren than at any other airport in the country."

Warrick nodded. "Even in this Disneyland-style Vegas, it's still *the* place where you can find the biggest rush in the shortest amount of time."

"So," Catherine said, almost but not quite buying it, "the mob lawyer just happened to walk into the casino where Hyde was gambling?"

Grissom pointed to a photo of the dead lawyer in the Beachcomber hallway. "Dingelmann was a registered guest at the hotel, yes. Catching some R and R before an upcoming big trial."

"Coincidence?" Sara asked, almost teasingly.

"Circumstance," Grissom said. "There's a difference."

Nick, still the most skeptical of them, said, "And Hyde just happened to have a gun and a silencer with him? Give me a break."

Grissom came over to where Nick and Catherine sat; perched on the edge of the table. "Look at when Hyde gambled. He always picked a time when business was slow. He knew someday, somebody might recognize him . . . and he'd have to be prepared. *That's* why he carried the gun and the noise suppresser."

"Hell," Warrick said. "Maybe that was a part of the buzz."

"Tell us, Grissom," Catherine said. "You can see this, can't you? Make us see it."

And he did.

The .25 automatic, in the holster at the small of his back, brought a feeling of security . . . like that credit card commercial—never leave home without it. On several occasions, he'd almost made it out the front door without snugging the pistol in place, and each time, almost as if the gun called to him, he'd turned around and picked it up.

You just never knew, maybe today would be the day he'd need it. He'd survived this long by being cautious—never scared, just cautious. Dangerous situations required care, planning, consistency. A careful man could survive almost anything.

Over the years, he'd done a number of jobs near Vegas, and he'd always loved the town—Vegas getaways had been something he looked forward to. Now, Vegas getaways from Henderson were twice-a-week oases in a humdrum existence. He derived great pleasure coming to the football field–sized casino at the Beachcomber, but he felt secure: at five-

thirty on a Monday morning, only a couple hundred players would be trying their luck.

In a room this size, this time of day, the gamblers were spread out, making the casino seem nearly deserted. Tourists—the few that ventured this far off the Strip—wouldn't be here at this hour unless they were lost or drunk. These were the hardcores, mostly locals, who never gave him a second glance.

Occasionally, a bell would go off, a machine would ding ding ding, or he might hear a muffled whoop from the half-dozen schmucks gathered around the nearest craps table; but basically, the casino remained as quiet as a losing locker room. He might have preferred a little more action, more glitz, more glamour—but he still had that habit of caution even as he took risks.

He always played at this time of day, fewer people, less noise, hell, even the cocktail waitresses didn't bother him now that they knew him to be a recluse and a shitty tipper. He played on Mondays and Wednesdays, Senior Days at the Beachcomber, when a registered player's points would be multiplied by four.

Though only fifty, his ID claimed he was fifty-six, and the silver hair at his temples made it easier to sell the lie. Right now he had the slot card of a nonexistent registered player plugged into a poker machine closer to the lobby than he would have liked. Normally, he'd play further back in the casino, away from the lobby, but his luck had been bad, and a few months ago, this particular machine had been kind. So, he'd positioned himself here, facing the lobby (his shoulder turned away from the security camera, of course).

He punched the MAX bet button, dropping his running total from twenty-five to twenty. He'd started the session with two hundred quarters when he'd slipped a fifty into the machine only a half-hour earlier. Looking at his hand, he saw a pair of threes, one a diamond, the other a club, plus the six, nine, and jack of diamonds. Sucker bet, he told himself, even as he dropped the three of clubs and tried to fill the flush. He hit the DEAL button and was rewarded with the three of hearts. Naturally.

He cursed under his breath, bet five more quarters, and wondered if his luck could possibly get any worse. Over a month since he won any real money, and he wondered what the hell it would take to turn things around. He looked up to see one of last night's holdouts finally trudging toward the elevators, calling it a night. The guy wore a dark suit, his geometric-patterned tie loose at the neck, puffing like a tan flower from his chest.

The video poker hand came up: two kings, a jack, a queen, a seven. He kept the two kings, dropped the others.

When he saw the man's face, he knew his luck wouldn't be changing today, not for the better anyway. He fought the urge to duck under the machine, but it was too late, the suit looking right at him now, recognizing him—Dingelmann.

The lawyer. His lawyer, in another life. . . .

And right now the ever so cool-in-court counselor's eyes were growing wide in surprise and alarm.

Unconsciously, the player's hand moved toward the back of his slacks, under his lightweight sport coat. He stopped as the lawyer took off at a brisk pace, heading for the bank of elevators to the left and, no doubt, the phone that waited upstairs in his room.

Can't do him here, the player thought, way too fucking public. Be patient, patience is the key. He rose, took a step, the plastic chain attaching him to his player's card reining him in, drawing him back.

He pulled the card, and barely aware of it, looked down as the poker machine started burping out coins. He glanced at his hand, four kings. Damnit. Without another thought, he left the machine and followed Dingelmann. As they neared the elevators, the lawyer's pace quickened and a couple of night owls turned, trying to figure out if the guy was loony or just drunk.

The stalker kept his face blank, though his mind raced, nerve endings jangling, long-lost emotions roiling in his gut. The lawyer, almost running now, got to the elevators, punched the UP button repeatedly and just before the killer could get to him, a car came, Dingelmann entered, and the doors slid shut.

Pounding his fist on the door, he watched as the elevator indicator reported its rise to the second floor; he jabbed the UP button, as the indicator registered the third floor. A car stopped, its door sliding open, but before he stepped on, he looked up at that indicator, which had paused at the fourth floor.

He jumped into the empty car and slapped the four button. By the second floor, beads of sweat were blossoming on his forehead and he was pacing like a caged animal. As the elevator passed the third floor, the pistol seemed to jump into his right hand, his left digging the noise sup-

presser out of the pocket of the linen sport coat. The door dinged at the fourth floor, and he stepped out, screwing the two pieces together.

He listened for a moment. He'd been up into the hotel a couple of times before, with hookers, and he remembered that a steel-encased video camera hung high on the wall at the far end of the hall. The doors for each room were inset into tiny alcoves, making the hall appear deserted; but the Deuce knew better.

Moving quickly, keeping his head down (even though the camera was thirty yards down the hall), he went from door to door. Finally he found Dingelmann, frightened and fumbling with his key card at the door to room 410.

The Deuce pressed the silencer into the back of the lawyer's head and heard the man whimper. A squeeze of the trigger and a round rocketed into Dingelmann's skull, slamming him into the door, and he slumped, slid, to the floor—already dead.

Then, just to make sure, and out of ritual, he fired one more round into the lawyer's head.

A sound behind him—a yelp of surprise—prompted the Deuce to spin, bringing the pistol up as he did, never forgetting the eye of the security camera. Before him, a skinny, dark-haired waiter carrying a tray full of food gasped a second time as he dropped the tray. The metal plate covers and silverware clanged as they hit the floor, spaghetti exploding across the hallway.

Even before the clatter died away, he and the waiter took off running in opposite directions, the waiter toward the elevators, the Deuce directly at the video camera at the far end of the hall. As he took off, his right foot slipped in the lawyer's blood, and his feet nearly went out from under him. Regaining his balance, he flung himself down the hall, the blood smearing off with his first two steps.

As he sprinted he brought his arm up, destroying any chance the camera had of capturing his face on video. He shoved through the fire exit door into the stairwell and tore down the steps two at a time. As he rushed down, his mind worked over the details. Many things yet to be done.

At the first floor exit he stopped. He unscrewed the silencer, slipped it into a pocket. The pistol went into another and he checked himself carefully for splatter. He found a small scarlet blob on the toe of his right running shoe. Using a handkerchief from his pants' pocket, he daubed the spot away, got his breathing under control, stuffed the handkerchief back in his pocket, wiped the sweat from his brow with his left hand, and finally took in a deep breath, then slowly let it out through his mouth. He was ready. He eased the door open and stepped out.

Across the lobby, at the front desk, he saw the waiter screaming at a female desk clerk, and pointing in the general direction of the elevators.

The Deuce, deciding to avoid the lobby as much as possible, turned into the casino, walked past a scruffy-looking blonde girl, probably all of twenty-one, who now occupied his poker machine. The tray was still full of coins from his four kings. Silently cursing, he hoped she pissed it all away.

Avoiding security cameras altogether, often hugging walls, he kept moving, walking not running, not too slow, not too fast, then hustled through the door into the back parking lot, to his car. No rush now—he eased the car out of the parking lot, jogging from Atlantic to Wengert, then finally onto Eastern for the ride home.

The Deuce was free—the lawyer was dead—and Barry Hyde could only wonder whether today had been an example of good luck or bad.

Nick asked, "Then why aren't we busting the guy now?"

"On what evidence?" Grissom asked.

"The videotape," Sara said.

"Can't get a positive ID from that."

Warrick asked, "What about the ATM transaction?"

"Hyde claims his card was stolen. Brass is checking into that now."

"We can match his fingerprints to the shell casings," Catherine offered.

"That's a big one," Grissom said, nodding. "But we have no murder weapon. And nothing that ties Hyde to the murders of Fortunato and Kostichek except the signature."

Greg Sanders leaned in. "Excuse me—oh, Catherine?"

"Yeah?"

"Thought you might like to know—your cigarette butt from Evidence matches the blood you took from the fence."

"All *right!*" she said, jumping to her feet. All around the room, smiles and nods appeared.

Greg wandered on in, eyes dancing, his grin wide even for him. "That 'ASAP' enough for you?"

"Absolutely," she said, sitting back down.

"But like they say at the end of the infomercials," the lab tech teased, holding up a forefinger, ". . . that's not all!"

Everyone looked at him.

Enjoying center stage, Sanders said to Grissom, "Thanks for the take-out salad."

Willing to play along—for a moment—Grissom asked, "You enjoyed it?"

"I think *you* will—the saliva matches the DNA from the blood and the cigarette."

"Salad?" Sara asked.

"From the Dumpster behind A-to-Z Video," Grissom said. "Hyde even invited me to help myself to his garbage."

"Nice guy," Sara said.

Catherine smiled. "What CSI would pass up an all-you-can-eat buffet?"

"Well, I stepped up," Grissom said, "with Warrick's help—and now we have Barry Hyde's DNA at the scene of the Fortunato killing . . . ten years before he claims he ever came to Vegas . . . and we've got that same DNA from the fence he vaulted, behind Marge Kostichek's house."

"What more do we need?" Nick asked.

Grissom said, "Right now, nothing—we've got what we need for the warrant that'll get us even more evidence."

"At his residence," Nick said, finally a believer.

"And the video store," Catherine added.

"I'll call Brass," Grissom said. "With any luck, we'll have a warrant in half an hour . . . Nick, Sara, Warrick—get your equipment together, full search. We're rolling in five minutes."

They all seemed to launch at once. The exhaustion left their faces, and they moved now with enthusiasm and a grim sense of purpose. Grissom watched, a faint smile not softening the hardness of his eyes.

As he was heading out, Warrick turned to Grissom and the two men's eyes locked. "Gris, Barry can run . . ."

"But he can't hide," Grissom said.

18

Maintaining a low profile in this high-rent neighborhood would have been damn-near impossible; so Jim Brass didn't even try. In the early morning sunshine, dew still dappling, the cramped court looked like the Circus Circus parking lot: the two Tahoes and Brass's Taurus were parked in front of the Hyde residence, and two Henderson PD black-and-whites were pulled into the driveway across the street (Brass had not been about to repeat his *faux pas* with the local police, not only alerting them but calling them in).

Neighbors—some in bathrobes, others fully dressed—came out to gawk as the CSI group, led by Grissom and Brass, stepped from their vehicles, a little army removing their sunglasses and snapping on latex gloves. For July, the morning was surprisingly cool, and Warrick and Nick wore dark windbreakers labelled FORENSICS—this was in part psychological, a way to inform the onlookers that this was serious business, and they should keep back and stay away. As the team approached the house, each CSI carried his or her own equipment, each already handed a specific assignment for the scene by Supervisor Grissom.

Warrick would track down the shoes, Nick dust for prints, and Sara handle the camera work. Catherine would join Grissom as the designated explorers, their job to search out the more obscure places, seeking the more elusive clues. Brass—the only one not in latex gloves—would take care of Hyde.

As they marched up the sidewalk to the front door, an aura of anxiety burbled beneath the professionalism.

"Think he might start something?" Nick asked, obviously remembering the close call at the Kostichek house.

At Nick's side, Warrick shook his head, perhaps too casually. "Why should he? Sucker thinks he's Superman. We ain't laid a glove on him yet."

Brass heard this exchange, and basically agreed with Warrick—but just the same, he approached the door cautiously. He held the warrant in his left hand, his jacket open so that he could easily reach the holstered pistol on his hip. Behind him, Grissom motioned his crew— their hands filled with field kits and other equipment, looking like unwanted relatives showing up for a long stay—away from the door, corralling them in front of the two-car garage.

With a glance over his shoulder, Brass ascertained the CSIs were out of the line of fire; then he slowly moved forward. The front door— recessed between the living room on the left and the garage on the right—reminded the detective of the room doors at the Beachcomber, providing a funny little resonance, and a problem: if something went wrong, only Grissom—barely visible, peering around the corner like a curious child—would see what happened.

Nick's words of apprehension playing like a tape loop in his brain—"Think he might try something?"—Brass, within the alcove-like recession, stepped to the right of the door, took a deep breath, let it out . . . and knocked, hard and insistently.

Nothing.

He waited . . .

. . . he pressed the doorbell . . .

. . . and still nothing.

Glancing back at Grissom—who gave him a questioning look— Brass shrugged, turned back, and knocked once more.

Still no response.

Grissom moved carefully forward to join the homicide cop, the rest of the crew trailing behind.

"I don't think our boy's home," Brass said.

Grissom reached out and, with a gentle latex touch, turned the knob.

The door swung slowly open, in creaking invitation, Brass and Grissom both signaling for the group to get out of the potential line of fire.

"Open?" Brass said to Grissom. "He left it open?"

"Cat and mouse," Grissom said. "That's our man's favorite game. . . ."

They listened, Brass straining to hear the slightest sound, the faintest hint of life—Grissom was doing the same.

Long moments later, they traded eyebrow shrugs, signifying neither had heard anything, except the sounds of a suburban home—refrigerator whir, air-conditioning rush, ticking clocks. Drawing his pistol, Brass moved forward into the foyer of the modern, spare, open house—lots of bare wood and stucco plaster and stonework.

Grissom said to Warrick, "Tell those uniformed officers to watch our back. Then join us inside."

"On it," Warrick said, and trotted toward Henderson's finest.

Then Grissom and the other CSIs joined Brass, inside.

A wide staircase to a second-floor landing loomed before them; hallways parallel to the stairway were on its either side, leading to the back of the house—kitchen and family room, maybe. At right was the door to the attached garage, and at left a doorless doorway opened onto the living room.

The loudest thing in the quiet residence was Brass's own slow breathing, and the shoes of the team screaking on the hardwood floor.

In a loud voice—startling a couple of the CSIs—Brass called out, *"Barry Hyde—this is Captain James Brass, Las Vegas PD! We have a search warrant for your home and its contents! . . . Sir, if you are here, please make yourself known to us, now!"*

The words rang a bit, caught by the stairwell, but then . . .

"Simon and Garfunkle," Sara said.

Brass looked at her.

"Sounds of silence," the CSI replied, with a shrug.

Brass eased forward and turned left into the living room, his pistol leveled—a big, open, cold room with a picture window, a central metal fireplace, and spare Southwestern touches, including a Georgia O'Keefe cow-skull print over a rust-color two-seater sofa.

"Clear!" Brass called, when he came back into the foyer, Warrick had already joined Nick, Sara, Catherine and Grissom, who were fanning out—firearms in hand, an unusual procedure for these crime scene investigators, but the precaution was vital.

Opening the door to the attached garage, Nick flipped the light switch and went in, pistol at the ready. After a quick look around, he yelled, "Clear."

They went from room to room on the first floor—Brass, Nick, and

Warrick—checking each one. Grissom and Catherine—weapons in their latexed hands—stood at the bottom of the open stairway, to make sure Hyde didn't surprise them from above.

When Brass, Nick and Warrick returned to the foyer, they all shook their heads—nobody downstairs. Brass then led the way up the stairs, with the same combo of guns and caution, and they inspected the second floor the same way.

"It's all clear," Brass said, returning to the top of the stairs, holstering his handgun. "Barry Hyde has left the building."

"Okay," Grissom said, obviously pleased to be putting the gun away, "let's get to work. You all know what to do."

Sara unpacked her camera, Nick his fingerprint kit and they went to work as a team. Catherine and Warrick disappeared into other parts of the house.

Adrenaline still pumped through Brass as he came down the stairs. "Couldn't the son of a bitch have done us the courtesy of just opening the door and getting indignant about his rights and his goddamn privacy?"

"You're just longing again," Grissom said, "for those days when you could shoot a perp and then say 'freeze.' "

"That approach has its merits."

"So is he not home . . . or is he gone?"

"I said he might be a flight risk."

Grissom nodded, starting up the steps. "I'll check his clothes, his toiletries—see if there are any suitcases in the house."

Brass moved into the living room, where Sara was snapping photos that would comprise a three-hundred-sixty-degree view of the room, working from that central fireplace. As she moved on to another room, Brass poked around. The front wall consisted of one huge mullioned window looking out onto the street, and that lone sapling in the front yard.

A television the size of a compact car filled most of the west wall to Brass's left. A set of shelves next to the TV was filled with stereo equipment, several VCRs, a DVD player, and a couple of electronic components Brass didn't even recognize. On shelves over the television sat a collection of DVD movies, most of which Brass had never heard of. *I have to get out more*, he thought.

Opposite the entertainment center sat a huge green leather couch and a matching recliner squatted along the shorter southern wall. Next to the recliner and at the far end of the couch were oak end tables supporting lighter-green modernistic table lamps with soft white shades. A matching oak coffee table, low-slung in front of the couch, displayed a scattering of magazines with subscription stickers to BARRY HYDE and a few stacks of opened mail and loose papers.

Grissom came in, saying, "No clothes seem to be missing, but it's hard to say. Closet with suitcases seems undisturbed, and all the normal toiletries—toothbrush and paste, aftershave, deodorant—seem to be at home."

"So maybe he's just out for breakfast. Or putting bullets in somebody else's brain."

"You find anything yet?"

Brass pointed at the line of movie cases on top of the television. "I found out I haven't seen a movie since John Wayne died."

Without sarcasm, Grissom asked, "And this is pertinent how?"

The detective shook his head. This was one of the reasons he liked Grissom: the scientist had little use for the outside world, either. His universe consisted of his calling and the people he worked with; beyond that, not much seemed to get Grissom's attention.

"Nothing pertinent about it," Brass said. "Just a social observation."

Kneeling, Grissom started going through the material on the coffee table. Brass plopped down on the couch, watching as the criminalist leafed through Hyde's magazines. Several were vacation guides, one was a *Hustler,* and the last one a copy of *Forbes.*

"Varied reading list," Grissom said.

"Travel, sex, money," Brass said. "American dream."

Loose papers, in with the mail, included various reports from the video store, a folded copy of a recent *Sun,* and an A-to-Z memo pad— an address in black ballpoint scrawled on the top sheet.

Holding up the pad, Grissom asked, "Familiar address?"

"Marge Kostichek?"

"That's right. Why do you think Barry Hyde has Marge Kostichek's address in his home? In the same stack including a newspaper with an account of the discovery of a certain mummified body?"

"I could maybe come up with a reason."

"But if he's expecting us—if he knows he's on the spot—why leave this lying around?"

Brass considered that. "More cat and mouse?"

Grissom's eyes tightened. "Maybe he hasn't been home since we talked to him. Get Sara, would you, Jim? I want a picture of this."

Outside a horn blared, and both men looked through the picture window to see a huge semi-truck, out in the suburban street, apparently somewhat blocked by the two curbed SUVs. The driver of the van blew the horn again, and the Henderson cops—who were parked in the driveway of the home across the street—were approaching.

Sara's voice came from the kitchen. "What's going on out there?"

Brass and Grissom looked at the moving van, then at each other. From Grissom's expression, Brass found it a safe bet that the criminalist had a similar sick sinking feeling in *his* stomach. . . .

"Let's go outside and talk," Brass said, rising from the sofa, his voice lighter than his thoughts.

Grissom got up, too, saying, "You guys keep working."

The CSIs did, but in strained silence; something in Grissom's voice had been troubling. . . .

Following Grissom outside, Brass felt a headache, like a gripping hand, taking hold of him. Every time they got a goddamn break in this case, it evaporated before they could play it out! And he knew, damnit, he just knew, it was happening again. . . .

The coveralled driver—heavyset, about twenty-five, with sweaty dark hair matted to his forehead and a scruffy brown mustache and goatee—had already climbed down out of his cab to talk to the Henderson uniformed men. The latter moved aside as Brass and Grissom came quickly up, meeting the driver in the street, in front of the van. Another guy—a mover—was still seated up in the cab; he had the bored look of the worker at the start of a thankless day.

Brass flashed his badge. "What are you guys doing here?"

Not particularly impressed by the badge, the mover said, "What do you think? We're here to move furniture."

"What furniture?"

He pointed to the Hyde residence. "*That* furniture."

"There must be a mistake," Brass said.

Fishing a sheet of paper from his pocket, the mover said, "Fifty-three Fresh Pond Court."

Brass and Grissom traded a look.

"Show me," Brass said.

Rolling his eyes, the mover handed the sheet of paper over to Brass.

"This seems to be in order," Brass said, reading it, giving Grissom a quick look, then handing the paper back.

Grissom asked, "How were you supposed to get in? Was someone supposed to meet you here?"

The mover shrugged. "Guy on the phone said the police would be here to let us in . . . and here you are."

"When did this work order come through?"

"Just now—I mean, they called the twenty-four-hour hotline. It was a rush job. They paid extra—through the nose, better believe it."

"Son of a bitch," Grissom said, and sprinted toward the nearest Tahoe.

Brass yelled at the mover, "Get that truck out of here—now!"

"But . . ."

"There's a murder investigation going on. You touch that furniture, you're in violation of a warrant."

"Maybe I oughta see—"

"Get the hell out of here!" Brass blurted, and the mover jumped. Brass planted himself and glared at the guy and, finally, the man climbed back into the truck and ground the gears into reverse. As the moving van backed slowly up the court, Grissom was cranking the Tahoe around; then he pulled up next to Brass.

"You coming?" Grissom asked. He seemed calm, but Brass noted a certain uncharacteristic wildness in the CSI's eyes.

Brass jumped into the passenger seat and the SUV flew out of the court, going up on a lawn to get around the semi. As they hurtled down the adjacent Henderson street, Brass—snapping his seatbelt in place—asked, "You want me to drive?"

"No."

"Want me to hit the siren?"

"No."

Accelerating, Grissom jerked the wheel left to miss a Dodge Intrepid. Brass closed his eyes.

As the criminalist ran a red light, Brass flipped on the flashing blue light—still no siren, though. Right now Grissom was jamming on the brakes, to keep from running them into the back end of a bus.

Brass was glad it was such a short hop to A-to-Z Video.

The SUV squealed into the lot and slid to a stop in front of the video store. Grissom was out and running to the door before Brass even got out of his seatbelt. Working to catch up, the detective pulled even just as Grissom pushed through the door and said, "Where's Barry Hyde?"

The cashier said, "Mr. Hyde isn't here right now."

Grissom cut through the store, down the middle aisle, Brass hot on his heels.

Pushing open the back-room door, Grissom demanded, "Where is he?"

Patrick, the hapless assistant manager, merely looked up, eyes wide with fear, and he burned his fingers on his latest joint. With a yelp of pain, the kid jumped out of his chair and backed into a corner.

"Barry Hyde," Grissom said. "Where is he?"

"Not . . . not here. I told you guys before, he won't be back until Monday!"

Grissom pushed through a connecting door into the back room. Brass tagged after. Shelves of videos, stored displays, empty shipping boxes, and extra shelving, but no Barry Hyde. The criminalist and the cop went back through the office, where the assistant manager stood in trembling terror, the scent of weed heavy.

"Sometime soon I'll be back," Brass said, "and if there's any dope on these premises, your ass'll be grass."

Patrick nodded, and Brass went after Grissom, who had already moved out into the store.

As Grissom headed toward the cashier's island, and Brass labored to catch up, a tall blond man in a well-tailored navy blue suit stepped around an endcap, and held out a video box.

The smiling cobra—Culpepper.

"You like Harrison Ford movies, Grissom?" the FBI agent asked casually, his voice pleasant, his smile smug.

"Why am I not surprised to see you here," Grissom said, with contempt.

"This is a modern classic, Gil," Culpepper said. "You really should try it—cheap rental, older title, you know."

And Culpepper held out the video: *Witness.*

Brass frowned, not getting it.

"I haven't seen it," Grissom said. "Is it about a freelance assassin in the Federal Witness Protection Program?"

Oh shit, Brass thought, as it all clicked.

"No," Culpepper said. "But that would make a good movie, too—don't you think?"

Grissom's voice was detached and calm, but the detective noted that the criminalist's hands were balled into fists, the knuckles white. "You weren't looking for your Deuce, Culpepper—you already had him . . . you've had him for almost five years. You were just hanging around criminalistics, to see what we knew, learn what we found, so you could keep one step ahead."

Leaning against the COMEDY shelf, a self-satisfied grin tugging at a corner of his cheek, Culpepper said, "I really can't say anything on this subject. It's sensitive government information. Classified."

"You can't say anything, because then I could have you arrested for obstruction."

Culpepper's smile dissolved. "You're a fine criminalist, Grissom. You and your team have done admirable work here—but it's time to pack up your little silver suitcase and go home. This is over."

Grissom glanced at Brass. "Those short trips Hyde was making, Jim—he wasn't doing hits. The Deuce really was retired—and Barry Hyde was off on short hops, testifying in RICO cases and such. . . . Right, Agent Culpepper?"

"No comment."

"You people made a deal with a mad dog, and now you're protecting him, even though he's murdered two more people."

Now Culpepper turned to Brass. "Maybe you can explain the facts of life to your naive associate here. . . . When cases are mounted against organized crime figures—the kind of people who deal in wholesale death, through drugs and vice of every imaginable stripe—deals with devils have to be made. Grown-ups know that, Grissom—they understand choosing between the lesser of evils."

"Compromise all you want, Culpepper," Grissom said. "Evidence makes no compromises—science has no opinion beyond the truth."

The agent laughed. "You ever consider goin' into the bumper-sticker business, buddy? Maybe you could write fortunes for fortune cookies? You have a certain gift."

"I like the job I'm doing just fine. I'm just getting started on this case. . . ."

"No, Grissom—stick a fork in yourself. You're done."

Grissom's eyes tightened; so did his voice. "When I'm done, Culpepper, you'll know it—you'll be up on charges, and Barry Hyde will be on Death Row."

"Barry Hyde?" Culpepper asked, as if the name meant nothing. "You must be confused—there is no Barry Hyde. Within days the house on Pond Court'll be empty, and in a week, A-to-Z Video will be a vacant storefront."

"Call Hyde whatever you want," Grissom said. "I've got enough evidence to arrest him for the murders of Philip Dingelmann, Malachy Fortunato and Marge Kostichek."

"There's no one *to* arrest. Barry Hyde doesn't exist—it's sad when a man of your capabilities wastes time chasing windmills."

"Barry Hyde's a sociopath, Culpepper," Grissom said. "What's your excuse?"

With a small sneer, Culpepper leaned in close and held Grissom's gaze with his own. "I'm telling you as a brother officer—let it go."

"You're not my brother."

Culpepper shrugged; then he turned and walked quickly out of the store.

Grissom watched the exit expressionlessly, as Brass moved up beside him, saying, "Real charmer, isn't he?"

"Snake charmer."

"Is he right? Are we done, you think?"

"Culpepper doesn't define my job for me—does he define your job for you, Jim?"

"Hell, no!"

"Glad you feel that way. Let's get back to work."

They drove back to the house in silence; both men were examining the situation, from the ends of their respective telescopes. The moving van still sat blocking the court, and Grissom had to park around the corner. As they walked past the truck, Brass was concerned to see no one up in the vehicle. "Where are they?"

Grissom shook his head and headed toward the house. The other Tahoe and Brass's Taurus were still parked out front; the Henderson cops leaned against their squads, sipping something from paper cups. Trotting up the driveway, Grissom led the way through the front door. They found the two movers sitting on the stairs sipping similar cups.

Grissom and Brass nodded to the movers, who nodded back.

"Honey, I'm home!" Grissom announced, voice echoing a bit, in the foyer.

Sara came in from the kitchen, the camera still in her hands. "Where have you been?"

"The neighborhood video store."

Brass said, "Hyde's flown the coop."

Grissom asked her, "Where's everybody?"

With appropriate gestures, she responded. "Nick's printing the bathroom, then he'll be done. Catherine's doing the garage. Warrick found three pairs of running shoes and bagged them. I think he's . . ."

"Right here." Warrick walked down the stairs, stopping just above the two movers. "You guys want some more lemonade?"

They both shook their heads, sliding to one side, so Warrick could come down the stairs between them.

Warrick stood before Grissom and said, "I'm sure one of those pairs of shoes is the right one, Gris. He had three identical pair— really liked 'em."

"Anything else?" Grissom asked.

Nick ambled in from the bathroom. "I've got plenty of prints . . . plus, I found this on the desk in Hyde's office." He held up a plastic evidence bag with a pile of letters inside. "Letters from Petty to Marge Kostichek—which he obviously stole from Kostichek's."

Brass gave Grissom a hard look. "I hope the LAPD catches up with the Petty woman—or that she really knows how to run away and start over. If Hyde has any friends in L.A., we could be looking for another body."

Grissom asked the movers to wait outside, which they did. Then— with the exception of Catherine, who wasn't finished out in the garage—Grissom gathered everyone around him in the foyer and explained the video store encounter with Culpepper.

"Prick," said Warrick.

"You're saying he just made Hyde disappear," Sara said.

"After we talked to Hyde last night," Grissom said, "that was it. Hyde made a call, and they whisked him out of town. He didn't even stop back at home, for fear he'd run into us."

Brass said, "And now they'll start him over, somewhere."

Sara looked dazed. "How can they do that?"

Brass smiled, wearily. "The feds play by their own rules. They don't give two shits about ours."

"So, that's it?" Nick asked, truly pissed. "We bust our butts, and the FBI pulls the rug out from under us? It's just . . . over?"

"I know Gil wants to pursue this," Brass said, "that's my desire, too. But maybe we have to face facts—we've been screwed over by people who were supposed to be our allies. How do we fight Uncle Sam?"

"Let's back up," Grissom said. "Before we march on Washington, let's review what we have, other than a lot of circumstantial evidence. If Barry Hyde walked into this house, we could arrest him—but could we convict him?"

"We could now," Catherine said.

Everyone turned to see her standing in the doorway to the attached garage. An evidence bag dangled from her right hand, inside of which was tucked a 1930's vintage Colt .25 automatic.

Brass felt a smile spreading. "Is that what I think it is?"

"It's not a water pistol. And, if the boss will allow me to make an educated guess, I'm predicting the barrel on this baby will match the bullets we took from Marge Kostichek. And the primer markings on shell casings found at all three murders should tie Mr. Barry Hyde up in one big bloody bow."

Astounded but pleased, Grissom took the bagged weapon, asking her, "Where did you find it?"

"I'll show you."

Catherine led the way into the garage. She stopped in front of a fuse box on the back wall, while the others gathered around her in a semicircle. The gray metal box looked like every other fuse box in the world, with conduit running out the top, disappearing inside the false ceiling of the attic above.

"I noted a fuse box in the basement," she said. "So I wondered why he would have a fuse box in the garage, when there's no heavy duty tools and only two one-hundred-ten outlets."

"Nice catch," Grissom said.

She opened the little gray door, revealing no breakers, no fuses, no anything except the end of the hollow conduit. With her hands in their latex gloves, she removed the gun from the evidence bag to carefully slip it inside the conduit, to demonstrate where she had found it; then just as carefully rebagged the evidence.

Sara, grinning, shaking her head, said, "Almost your classic 'hide it in plain sight.' "

"And the feds lifted him out of this life so fast," Warrick said, "he didn't have to take his favorite toy with him."

"We should look for the black ninja outfit," Sara said. "He obviously made a quick stop here after he killed Marge Kostichek, before going back to the video store."

Everyone was smiling now, proud of Catherine, proud of themselves. That left it to Brass to bring them back to reality.

"Okay," Brass said, "so we have the evidence. But we still don't have Barry Hyde. He's in the FBI's loving arms, helping them bring the really big bad guys down."

"Please," Sara said, making a face. "I may want to eat again, someday."

Grissom did not seem put off by Brass's little speech. "Let's get back to work. Sara's right, let's look for those clothes. . . . We've got a killer to catch."

"But Brass said this was over," Nick said.

"We need to gather our evidence," Grissom said, calmly, "analyze it, prepare it for use in Hyde's eventual prosecution. And, of course, Sara's going to play the major role."

"I am?" she asked, bewildered.

"Don't be modest," Grissom said, with a tiny enigmatic smile. "Let's finish up here, guys—then we'll go back and I'll tell you how we're going to nail Barry's hide to our non-federal wall."

19

Befitting the bitter December weather, the Federal Courthouse in Kansas City might have been fashioned from ice by some geometrically minded sculptor, not an architect working in glass and steel. The interior of the structure, however well-heated, remained similarly cold and sterile. No straight-back wooden chairs for the jury boxes in this building, rather padded swivel chairs and personalized video monitors—though the latter were seldom used, as lawyers so frequently arranged plea bargains before trials began. The justice meted out here seemed to contain no compassion, no humanity, also no punishment in some cases—just judgments as icy as the steel and glass of a structure that seemed a monument to bureaucracy . . . and expediency.

In a courtroom on the second floor, Gil Grissom—in a dark jacket over a gray shirt with black tie, a gray topcoat in his lap—sat in the back row, his eyes on the three-sided frame screen whose white cheesecloth concealed the witness box. Another set of screens blocked any glimpse of the witness's entrance by way of the judge's chambers. Onlookers took up only a third of the gallery.

The twelve jurors—evenly divided between men and women—sat blankly, though the unease of several was obvious; one individual looked as if he'd rather be in a dentist's chair. Behind the bench, the judge was moving his head from left to right, and front to back, apparently trying to work a kink out of his neck.

At the prosecutor's desk a wisp of a woman in a gray power-suit sat next to a bullish federal prosecutor. At the defense table, a nationally known attorney—at least as well-known as the late Philip Dingelmann, whose murder had finally hit CNN, the day the owner of A-to-Z Video disappeared—wore a gray suit worthy of a sales rack at Sears. He had the wild long hair of an ex-hippie, the tangled strands now all gray; he was a character—the kind of lawyer Geraldo loved to book.

Right now he was sucking on a pencil like it was a filterless Pall Mall, speaking in quiet tones to his client. The lawyer had made his bones defending pot farmers and kids charged with felony possession. When the drug of choice shifted to cocaine and the cartels moved in, the attorney had changed—and grown—with the times.

Back here in the cheap seats, Grissom could see only the lawyer's profile, and that of his client, Eric Summers, whose black hair, with its hint of gray, was tied in a short ponytail, his face angular, clean-shaven, with a sharp, prominent chin. Despite his conservative dark suit and tie, this defendant in a major RICO case looked more like a middle-aged rock star, and why not? His forays into the distribution of controlled substances, escort-service prostitution and big-time dot-com scams— the local papers referred to him as "a reputed leader among the so-called new breed of K.C. gangsters"—had allowed him to enjoy a rock-star lifestyle.

Up front, just behind the prosecutor's table, a blond head bobbed up, in conferral with the female prosecutor. Grissom leaned forward, to get a better view—Culpepper, all right.

The witness was escorted in, shadows playing behind the cheese-cloth curtain—probably a federal marshal back there, with him—and then the witness took the chair of honor. The bailiff, on the other side of the screen, swore the witness in, referring to him only as "Mr. X."

Grissom sat forward, not breathing, not blinking, focused solely on the two words that would now be spoken—the words he had shown up to hear, the sound that would make worthwhile his CSI unit finding time for this case, over these last six months, despite whatever demands other crimes might make. It might even justify the overtime Sara Sidle had maxed out on. . . .

And the witness promised to tell the truth, and nothing but, in the traditional fashion: "I do."

Grissom smiled.

The voice was an arrogant voice, self-satisfied . . . the distinctive voice of Barry Hyde.

And Grissom could breathe again. He even blinked a few times. Hours of work, weeks of tracking, months of waiting, had come down to this. Outside were freezing temperatures, an inch and a half of snow, and his colleagues—Warrick Brown, with Sara Sidle, guarding the building's side entrances, Jim Brass covering the back, Nick Stokes standing watch out front.

Grissom and Catherine Willows—in a black silk blouse, black leather pants, a charcoal coat in her lap—sat in the courtroom watching the proceedings, just two interested citizens. Next to Catherine sat Huey Robinson, a Kansas City detective, black and burly, big as a stockyard, barely fitting into his pew. O'Riley knew Robinson—they had been in the army or Marines or something, together—and Brass had recruited the hard-nosed cop, in advance, from the local jurisdiction.

That minor debacle with the Henderson PD had reminded Jim Brass that a little interdepartmental courtesy went a long way; and Grissom had seen from Culpepper's example how a show of contempt for another PD's concerns could rankle.

Sending Grissom, his unit, and Brass to Kansas City for this trial had been expensive; but Sheriff Brian Mobley had been so furious with Culpepper that he'd have spent half a year's budget, if it meant settling scores with the conniving FBI agent.

So with Mobley's help, all the jurisdictional *i*'s had been dotted, and the *t*'s painstakingly crossed. For this exercise to work, everything would have to be by the book.

And right now the object of that exercise was testifying behind a cheesecloth curtain—a vague shadow, but a specific voice.

"It's him," Grissom whispered to Catherine.

Catherine nodded as she looked around the gallery, slow-scanning the faces for possible undercover FBI agents, mixed in with the citizens.

The judge said, "Your witness, Mr. Grant."

Rising slowly, milking the dramatics, the prosecutor said, "Mr. X, you performed a certain task for Mr. Summers, did you not?"

"Yes, sir."

"What was that task?"

"I killed people."

The prosecutor turned to the jury box, letting that sink in; then said, "On more than one occasion?"

"Yes. Three times."

"Did he pay you to assassinate one of his competitors—a Mr. Marcus Larkin?"

"He did."

The prosecutor started to pace in front of the white curtain. "When was this, Mr. X?"

"Just about eight years ago. . . . It'll be eight years, February."

For three and a half hours in the morning, the prosecutor led Barry Hyde through a description of the assassination of Marcus Larkin, a local pimp and drug dealer. When the judge called the lunch break, Grissom and Catherine ducked out of the courtroom, leaving the building, to prevent Culpepper from seeing them. Kansas City cop Robinson—who was unknown to the FBI agent—stayed behind to keep an eye on things.

Catherine suggested grabbing Hyde at the lunch break, but Grissom knew that could put them at odds not just with the FBI, but with a pissed-off federal judge.

"Better we wait," he told her, in the corridor, "till Hyde's testified and the judge doesn't have any further use for him."

So they sat in the rental van, eating sub sandwiches for lunch. The car heater thrummed, throwing out more hot air than the attorneys inside, though never enough to satisfy these desert dwellers, who were literally out of their element in this cold, snowy clime.

"There's Culpepper," Catherine said, pointing to the FBI agent, as he strode up the Federal Courthouse's wide front walk. They watched him disappear into the building.

"That's our cue," Grissom said.

"Yeah. Remember, we got deliveries to make first."

Grissom carried the sandwiches and Catherine the tray of cups of hot coffee—the latter at least a token effort toward thawing the CSIs assigned to standing outside in a wind chill barely above zero.

They came to Sara's station first. In her black parka with the hood pulled up and drawn tight, only her nose seeming to peek out, she looked like a reluctant Eskimo. Hopping from foot to foot, she wore huge black mittens that made her hands look like useless paws.

"Oh, God," she said when they approached. "I thought you'd never get here. I'm freezing. Do people really live in this crap?"

"Stop whining," Grissom said. "How did you survive in Boston?"

"Alcohol—lots and lots of alcohol."

Catherine said, "You'll have to settle for caffeine," and handed Sara a cup of coffee.

"Th–th–thanks."

"Go sit in the van for a while," Grissom said, and he handed her the keys. "This may go all afternoon. The prosecutor took most of the morning, and the defense will take even longer. When you get warmed up, relieve Nick out front."

"I'll never warm up," she groused, accepting the keys and putting them into her pocket.

"This isn't any colder than Harvard yard, is it?"

Sara flipped him off, but the mittens ruined the gesture. He held a sandwich out and she took it and trudged toward the rental vehicle.

"She did a hell of a job on this," Grissom said, watching the young woman trundle off.

"Yes she did," Catherine said.

For these past months, on top of all of her other duties, Sara had kept tab on every mob-related federal trial across the country in an effort to determine when and where Barry Hyde would surface, to testify.

"Somebody better take this post," Catherine said.

"Right."

"Are you staying here or am I?"

"You." He took the tray of coffee cups from her.

"Power corrupts, you know," she said.

"Absolutely," he said.

As he moved off, she called, "Don't be a stranger. Feel free to stop back." She pulled up the hood of her gray coat and jammed her gloved hands into her pockets.

But Grissom was actually on his way to relieve Brass, who in turn took over for Warrick. After an hour, Nick had replaced Catherine, and Warrick had taken over for Grissom, in the back of the courtroom. With a still-shivering Catherine beside him, Grissom finally got back inside the court around three-thirty, easing into their seats beside Detective Robinson.

The defense attorney was attacking Mr. X's credibility. "Mr. X, isn't it true that you would be on Death Row if the government had not intervened and cut a deal with you?"

Behind the curtain, the shadow bounced a little as Hyde chuckled. "No, that's not true. The authorities attempted for years to catch me. Truth is, most federal officers couldn't catch a cold."

This elicited a nervous laugh from the gallery, and a banging of the gavel from the judge—also a warning from His Honor to Mr. X. Frowning, Culpepper turned his head away from the witness stand— almost far enough to spot Grissom. . . .

Catherine glanced at Grissom, who shook his head. *Didn't see us,* he mouthed.

Culpepper was facing front again.

"I turned myself in," Mr. X went on. "I wanted out of that filthy life. You see—I've been born again."

That caused Catherine to smile and shake her head. As for Grissom, despite his antipathy for Hyde, he was enjoying watching the defense attorney search hopelessly for a ladder to help him climb out of the hole he had just dug himself.

Realizing too late his error, the defense attorney finally muttered, "No further questions, Your Honor."

The prosecutor sat back, relaxing just a little.

Grissom rose and moved to the door, Catherine and Detective Robinson falling in behind him.

The judge asked, "Any redirect, Mr. Grant?"

"None, Your Honor."

Pushing the door open, Grissom stepped into the corridor just as Culpepper was getting to his feet. Throwing on his overcoat, Grissom strode quickly down the hall, pulling the walkie-talkie from his pocket. He pushed the TALK button and spoke rapidly. "It's going down now. Everybody inside. Second floor Judge's chambers."

He turned a corner to the right and practically sprinted down the hall so he could be at that door when Hyde came out. Behind him, he heard Catherine and Robinson pounding along step for step.

Opening the door, stepping into the hall, was a marshal, maybe fifty years old with a crewcut on a bowling ball head, and a shabby brown suit jacket a size or two too small. Barry Hyde emerged next, wearing an expensive gray suit and a matching Kevlar vest. Behind Hyde came a second marshal, this one younger, probably in his early thirties, longish brown hair combed straight back, his charcoal suit a better fit than his partner's.

Grissom stepped in front of them, holding up the folded sheets of paper. All three men froze. The older marshal eyeballed Grissom, the younger one reflexively reaching under his jacket.

"Las Vegas Metropolitan Police—I have a warrant."

"Mr. Grissom, isn't it?" Hyde asked, the pock-marked face split-ting into a typically smug smile. "How have you been? Couldn't you find a warmer place for your winter vacation?"

"Sir," the older one said to Grissom, giving Hyde a quick glare to shut up, "I'm afraid you've wandered off your beat. . . ."

"This warrant is legal, Marshal." He held it up for the man to see.

But it was the younger marshal who leaned in for a look.

"Wrong guy," he said. "That's not our witness's name. . . . Now, if you'll excuse us." His hand remained under his coat.

Catherine and Robinson formed a wall behind Grissom.

Then Culpepper's voice came from behind Grissom. "Aw, what the hell is this nonsense?"

But the young marshal was curious, despite himself. "What's the charge?"

"First-degree murder—three counts."

The two marshals exchanged glances, and Hyde's smug grin seemed to be souring.

"You have no legal grounds, Grissom," Culpepper said, moving into the midst of it, anger building to rage. "No jurisdiction . . . This man is a federal witness granted immunity for his crimes."

Warrick, Nick, Sara, and Brass all seemed to appear at once—in their heavy coats, they looked ominous, a small invading army.

Grissom was well-prepared for this assertion from Culpepper; and for all to hear, he said, "This man has no immunity for murders he committed after making his agreement with the government—specif-ically, the murders of Philip Dingelmann and Marge Kostichek."

The marshals exchanged frowning glances, and Hyde's smirk was long gone.

Brass slipped between Culpepper and the rest of the group.

Handing the warrant to the older marshal, Grissom said, "Read it over, Marshal—I think you'll find everything in order."

The older marshal pulled a pair of half-moon reading glasses from his inside suit-coat pocket, and read.

Steaming, Culpepper said to the marshals, "If you two surrender my witness to this asshole, your careers are over."

People down in the main corridor were clustered there now, watch-ing the goings-on in this side hallway.

Robinson, his basso profundo voice resonating throughout the corridor, introduced himself to Culpepper, displaying his badge, and saying, "If you do not surrender this prisoner to these officers, you will be accompanying me, them, and the prisoner to the Locust Street Station."

Brass added, "After which, you can come home with us, to Las Vegas, where you'll be charged with obstruction of justice."

Culpepper's lip curled in a sneer. "Officer Robinson, this is a federal courthouse—and you're in way over your head."

Ignoring this, Robinson moved in beside Grissom, his Kansas City cop's glare firmly in place as he stared at the younger marshal, to whom he also displayed his shield. "And you, sir, would be well served to get that hand out from under your coat."

The younger marshal looked over at his partner who nodded. Slowly, the empty hand came out of the coat and dropped to his side.

"Thank you, sir," Robinson said.

Anger had turned Culpepper's face a purplish crimson; looking past Brass, at the marshals, he said, "We need to get the witness out of here. March him the hell out."

Robinson turned toward him, but Brass was closer, and held up a hand, as if to say, *Please . . . allow me.* Grabbing Culpepper roughly by the arm, Brass said, "You want to be the next FBI agent to go down for obstruction? I got no real problem helping you do that."

Culpepper glared at him, but said nothing, his glibness failing him at last.

The older marshal said to Grissom, "You really think this man," he glanced at Hyde, "killed Philip Dingelmann?"

"It's not an opinion," Grissom said. "I have the evidence to prove it."

"I'll die of old age before you prove it," Hyde said, blustering now, his smugness, his self-confidence a memory. "You haven't got anything!"

"We have something," Brass interjected. "We have the death penalty."

Hyde managed a derisive grin, but the bravado had bled out.

"You're almost right, Barry," Grissom said to the object of the tug of war. "We don't have much. Just you on casino videotape, bullets and shell casings matching your gun, with your fingerprints; then there's your footprints, matching DNA from the Fortunato and Kostichek murder scenes . . ."

Hyde's face drained of color.

". . . but why spoil your attorney's fun? We should leave something for the discovery phase."

"This time you may want to go to a different law firm," Brass advised him, "than Dingelmann's."

Culpepper's hand dropped to his pistol and he said, "This is my witness. This is an illegal attempt to hijack a protected government witness—all of you step aside."

Culpepper didn't see the older marshal draw his weapon, but he certainly felt the cold snout of it in his neck. "Put the gun away, Agent Culpepper—Jesus, didn't you assholes learn anything from Ruby Ridge?"

The FBI agent's face turned white and he was trembling as he moved his hand away. Brass moved toward Culpepper, fist poised to coldcock him; but Grissom stepped between them.

"Calm down, everybody," Grissom said. Then he turned to the devastated FBI man.

The younger marshal holding on to his arm, Hyde said, "You're in charge, Culpepper—remember, you're in charge!"

"Agent Culpepper," Grissom said, "either we're going to walk out of here with Hyde in our custody, or you can go downstairs with us and face the media. How do you think you're going to explain to the American people that you're aiding and abetting a murderer? Obstruction is nothing compared to accessory after the fact."

Culpepper seemed to wilt there in front of them.

Hyde said, "Goddamnit, Culpepper—they're bluffing!"

Time seemed to stop as the two men stared at each other, like gunfighters on a Western street; but Grissom had already won, without using any weapon but his wits.

"Fine," the agent said to Grissom. "Take him."

Hyde, realizing he'd just been sold out, tried to make a break for it, yanking himself free from the younger marshal's grip, running toward the gathering crowd at the end of the hallway. But he didn't get six feet before Warrick and Nick grabbed him on either side. Before he could do more than wrestle around a little, Robinson had his hands cuffed behind him.

"Smart decision, Agent Culpepper," Grissom said. "It's just sad when a man of your capabilities goes tilting at windmills."

"Go to hell, Grissom."

Grissom cocked his head. "Is that any way to talk to a 'brother' officer?"

Culpepper muttered, "Next time," then turned on his heels and headed quickly down the corridor, almost on the run—away from the crowd.

And his witness.

"Culpepper!" Hyde yelled. "What, you're gonna leave me hanging?"

"Actually," Brass said, "it's lethal injection."

"Cul-pepper!" he wailed.

But Culpepper was gone.

Ambling up to Grissom's side, Catherine said, "You know for somebody who smiles as much as he does, Culpepper doesn't seem to have much of a sense of humor."

"He's lucky I didn't cap his ass," Robinson said, "goin' for that gun . . ."

The older marshal extended his hand to Grissom. "Nice piece of work, even if we were on the receiving end of some of it. . . . I'm sorry, what was your name?"

Warrick—who had one of Hyde's arms—said, "Why, that's the Lone Ranger," and Nick—who had Hyde's other arm—grinned big.

Smiling, their boss said to the marshal, "Gil Grissom, Las Vegas Criminalistics Bureau."

As they shook hands, the marshal said, "It's been a pleasure, Mr. Grissom." He nodded toward Hyde, who stood between Warrick and Nick with his head low. "We've been babysitting that stuck-up prick for too long. It'll be good to see him pay for his crimes, for a change."

"See what we can do."

Then the marshal turned to his young partner, saying, "Come on, Ken—we better get goin'. We're gonna be filling out reports on this one for the next hundred years."

Not as enthusiastic as his partner, the younger marshal followed the more experienced man up the hallway with a frown, apparently trying to assess how much damage he had just done to his career.

Brass moved in front of Hyde, gave him a nice wide smile. "You have the right to remain silent . . ."

"Well," Catherine said to Grissom. "You got him—you happy?"

"*We* got him," Grissom corrected. "And, yes, I'm very happy."

"You don't look happy."

"Well, I am."

The killer had been stopped, he was thinking; but what a swath of carnage this sociopath had cut. . . .

As Nick and Warrick led the prisoner toward the elevator—with Robinson accompanying them—Brass, Sara, Catherine, and Grissom all fell in behind.

As they waited for the elevator, Catherine asked Grissom, "So—what do we do now?"

Everyone except Hyde looked Grissom's way.

Bestowing them all a smile, Grissom said, "Let's go back where it's warm."

SIN CITY

For Chris Kaufmann—
the CSI who saw the body

M.A.C. and M.V.C.

*"When two objects come into contact,
there is a material exchange
from each to the other."*

—EDMUND LOCARD, 1910
Father of Forensic Science

Las Vegas—like New York and rust—never sleeps. From dusk till dawn, the sprawl of the city and its glittering neon jewelery enliven the desert landscape, competing with a million stars, all of them so tiny compared to Siegfried and Roy. From the fabled "Strip" of Las Vegas Boulevard to the world's tallest eyesore—the Stratosphere—Vegas throbs to its own 24/7 pulse, hammering into the wee-est of wee hours.

If such modern monuments as the Luxor and Bellagio indicate a certain triumph of man over nature, this shimmer of wholesome sin is nonetheless contained by a desert landscape, including mountains (almost) as green as money, as peaceful as the Strip is not. And a slumbering city—as normal as any urban sprawl, people living, working, loving, dying—exists in the reality of Vegas off the Strip, away from Fremont Street, a world where couples occasionally marry in a real chapel, as opposed to a neon-trimmed storefront where the pastor is Elvis, and "gambling" means getting to work five minutes late, or eating fried food, or cheating on your wife, or maybe trying to get away with murder, figurative or literal.

Nonetheless, as Sinatra said of New York, New York (the town, not the resort), Las Vegas, Nevada, indeed does not sleep. This is a city where, for many a citizen, working nights is the norm, from a pit boss at the Flamingo to a counter clerk at a convenience store, from an exotic dancer in a live nude girls club to a criminalist working the graveyard shift.

1

Millie Blair hated spending nights alone. She had always been anxious, and even being reborn in the blood of Christ hadn't helped. Nor did the nature of her husband Arthur's job, which sometimes meant long evenings waiting for him to get home.

Tonight, Millie couldn't seem to stop wringing her hands. Her collar-length brunette hair, now graying in streaks, framed a pleasant, almost pretty oval face tanned by days of outdoor sports—playing golf or tennis with friends from the church—and she looked young for forty. A petite five-four and still fit, she knew her husband continued to find her attractive, due in part to her rejection of the frumpy attire many of her friends had descended to in middle age. Tonight she wore navy slacks with a white silk blouse and an understated string of pearls.

Millie was glad Arthur still found her desirable—there was no sin in marital sex, after all, and love was a blessed thing between husband and wife—but she was less than pleased with her appearance, noting unmistakable signs of aging in her unforgiving makeup mirror, of late. Frown lines were digging tiny trenches at the corners of her mouth—the anxiety, again—and although she tried to compensate with lipstick, her lips seemed thinner, and her dark blue eyes could take on a glittering, glazed hardness when she was upset . . . like now.

Moving to the window, she nervously pulled back the curtains, peered out into the purple night like a pioneer woman checking for Indians, saw nothing moving, then resumed her pacing. Tonight her anxiety had a rational basis—Millie had heard something terribly disturbing yesterday . . . an audiotape of an argument between a certain married couple.

It was as if some desert creature had curled up in her stomach and died there—or rather refused to die, writhing spasmodically in the pit of her belly. Millie knew something was wrong, dreadfully wrong, with her best friend, Lynn Pierce. A member of Millie's church, Lynn seemed to have fallen off the planet since the two women had spoken, at around four P.M. this afternoon.

"Mil," Lynn had said, something ragged in her voice, "I need to see you . . . I need to see you right away."

"Is it Owen again?" Millie asked, the words tumbling out. "Another argument? Has he threatened you? Has he—"

"I can't talk right now."

Something in Lynn's throat caught—a sob? A gasp? How strange the way fear and sadness could blur.

Millie had clutched the phone as if hauling her drowning friend up out of treacherous waters. "Oh, Lynn, what is it? How can I help?"

"I . . . I'll tell you in person. When I see you."

"Well that's fine, dear. Don't you worry—Art and I are here for you. You just come right over."

"Is Arthur there now?"

"No, I meant . . . moral support. Is it that bad, that Arthur isn't here? Are you . . . frightened? Should I call Art and have him—"

"No! No. It'll be fine. I'll be right over."

"Good. Good girl."

"On my way. Fifteen minutes tops."

Those had been Lynn's last words before the women hung up.

Lynn Pierce—the most reliable, responsible person Millie knew—had not kept her word; she had not come "right over." Fifteen minutes passed, half an hour, an hour, and more.

Millie called the Pierce house and got only the answering machine.

Okay, maybe Millie *was* an anxious, excitable woman; all right, maybe she *did* have a melodramatic streak. Pastor Dan said Millie just had a good heart, that she truly cared about people, that her worry came from a good place.

This worry for Lynn may have come from a good place, but Millie feared Lynn had gone to a very bad place. She had a sick, sick feeling she would never see her best friend again.

As such troubled, troublesome thoughts roiled in her mind like a gathering thunderstorm, Millie paced and fretted and wrung her hands and waited for her husband Arthur to get home. Art would know what to do—he always did. In the meantime, Millie fiddled with her wedding ring, and concocted tragic scenarios in her mind, periodically chiding herself that Lynn had only been missing a few hours, after all.

But that tape.

That terrible tape she and Arthur had heard last night. . . .

Millie perked up momentarily when Gary, their son, came home. Seventeen, a senior, Gary—a slender boy with Arthur's black hair and her oval face—had his own car and more and more now, his own life.

Their son kept to himself and barely spoke to them—though he was not sullen, really. He attended church with them willingly, always ready to raise his hands to the Lord. That told Millie he must still be a good boy.

For a time she and Arthur had been worried about their son, when Gary was dating that wild Karlson girl with her nose rings and pierced tongue and tattooed ankle and cigarettes. Lately he'd started dating Lori—Lynn's daughter, a good girl, active in the church like her mom.

He was shuffling up the stairs—his bedroom was on the second floor— when she paused in her pacing to ask, "And how was school?"

He had his backpack on as he stood there, dutifully, answering with a shrug.

From the bottom of the stairs, she asked, "Didn't you have a test today? Biology, wasn't it?"

Another shrug.

"Did you do well?"

One more shrug.

"Your father's going to be late tonight. You want to wait to eat with us, or . . . ?"

Now he was starting up the stairs again. "I'll nuke something."

"I can make you macaroni, or—"

"Nuke is fine."

"All right."

He flicked a smile at her, before disappearing around the hallway, going toward his bedroom, the door of which was always closed, lately.

Growing up seemed to be hard on Gary, and she wished that she and Arthur could help; but this afternoon's taciturn behavior was all too typical of late. Gary barely seemed to acknowledge them, bestowing occasional cursory words and a multitude of shrugs. Still, his grades remained good, so maybe this was just part of growing up. A child slipping away from his parents into his own life was apparently part of God's plan.

But the problem of coping with Gary, Millie realized, was something to be worried about after this mess with Lynn got cleared up. The woman let out a long breath of relief as she peeked through the drapes and watched Arthur's Lexus ease into the driveway.

Finally.

A moment later she heard the bang of the car door, the hum of the garage door opener, and—at last!—Arthur stepped into the kitchen.

Stocky, only a couple of inches taller than his wife, a black-haired fire hydrant of a man, Arthur Blair—like Millie—had retained a youthful demeanor. Even though he was older than his wife (forty-four), his hair stayed free of gray; God had blessed him with good genes and without his wife's anxious streak. Black-framed Coke-bottle glasses turned his brown eyes buggy, but Millie's husband remained a handsome man.

Arthur had first met coed Millie ("Never call me Mildred!") Evans at a frat party back in their undergraduate days. A sorority sister and a little wild, she had dressed like, and looked like, that sexy slender Pat Benatar, all curly black hair and spandex, and she took his breath away. Immediately recognizing that she was out of his league, the bookish Arthur wouldn't have said a word to her if she hadn't struck up a conversation at the keg. Throughout the course of the evening they'd exchanged glances, but no further words. He could tell she was disappointed in him, but he'd been just too shy to do anything about it, at first; and then, pretty soon, he'd been too drunk. . . .

The next semester they'd had an Econ class together and she had recognized a familiar face and sat down next to him. Now, twenty years later, she still hadn't left his side.

Walking through the kitchen, Arthur moved into the dining room, set his briefcase on the table, tossed his suit jacket onto a chair and passed straight into the living room to find Millie standing in the middle of the room, holding herself as if she were freezing. Her face seemed drained of color, her eyes filigreed red. She'd clearly been crying. . . .

"Baby, what's wrong?" he asked, moving to her, taking her into his arms.

Arthur knew his anxious wife might have been upset about anything or nothing; but he always took her distress seriously. He loved her.

"It . . . it's Lynn," she said, sobs breaking loose as he hugged and patted her.

It was as if his arms had broken some sort of dam and she cried uncontrollably for a very long time before she finally reined in her emotions enough to speak coherently.

Arthur held her at arm's length. "What's wrong, baby? *What* about Lynn? Has that tape got you going . . . ?"

"Not the tape . . . I mean, *yes* the tape, but no . . ." Gulping back a last sob, Millie said, "She phoned this afternoon, about four—real upset. Said she had to see me, talk to me. Said she was on her way over."

"Well, what did she have to say, once she got here?"

"Arthur, that's just it—she never showed up!"

She told him about trying to call, getting the machine, and how she just *knew* Lynn had "disappeared."

Her husband shook his head, dismissive of the problem but not of her. "Honey, it could be anything. There's no point in getting all worked up . . . at least, not until we know what happened."

She stepped out of his embrace. Her eyes moved to the drawer handle of the end table across the room. His gaze followed hers—they both knew what lay in that shallow drawer: the tape. That awful audiotape that they had played last night. . . .

"Just because . . ." He stopped. ". . . this doesn't mean . . . necessarily . . ."

She drew in a deep breath, calming herself, or trying to. "I know, I know . . . It's just that . . . well, you know if she'd been delayed, she would have called, Arthur. Certainly by now she would have called."

He knew she was right. After a sigh and a nod, he asked, "Is Gary home?"

She nodded back. "In his room, of course. Behind the closed door."

"It's normal."

"He . . . sort of gave me the silent treatment again."

"Really?"

"Well. No. He was polite . . . I guess."

Arthur walked to the foot of the stairs and called up. "Gary!"

Silence.

A curtness came into Arthur's voice, now: "Gary!"

The clean-cut young man peeked around the hallway corner, as if he'd been hiding there all the while. "Yes, sir?"

"Your mother and I are going out. You okay with getting your own dinner?"

"Yes, sir. Already told mom I would microwave something. Anyway, I have to go into work for a couple of hours. Maybe I'll just grab something on the way."

"Well, that'll be fine, son. . . . We'll see you later."

"Yes, sir."

The boy disappeared again.

Millie, shaking her head, said, "All I get are shrugs. I can't believe how he opens up to you. He really respects you, Art."

Arthur said nothing, still staring up the stairs at where his boy had been. He wondered if his son's respect was real or just for show—assuming the kid even knew the difference. Arthur had had the same kind of relationship with his own father, always "yes sirring" and "no sirring," thinking he was doing it just to stay on the old man's good side, then eventually finding out that he really did respect his father. He hoped Gary would some day feel that way about him . . . even if the boy didn't do so now.

He turned to his wife. "Come on, sweetie," he said. "And get your coat. Some bite in the air, tonight."

"Where are we going?" she asked, even as she followed his directions, pulling a light jacket from the front closet. Also navy blue, the jacket didn't quite match her slacks and she hoped at night no one would notice.

"I think we'll drop by at our good friends, the Pierce's."

She didn't argue. For a woman with an anxious streak, Millie could be strong, even fearless, particularly when the two of them were together. Arthur realized going over to the Pierces was the course of action she'd wanted all along, she just hadn't wanted to be the one to suggest it.

Her respect for him was real, Arthur knew. Anyway, their church taught a strict, biblical adherence to the husband's role as the head of the household.

They moved to the door, but—at the last second—Millie hurried back to the living room, grabbed the small package out of the end table and tucked the audiotape into her purse.

The drive to the Pierce home took only about twelve minutes. Traffic had thinned out and the cooler autumn temperatures had settled in, apparently convincing many a Las Vegan to stay inside for the evening. Millie wondered aloud if they should listen to the tape again, in the car's cassette player, as they drove over.

"No thanks," Arthur said, distastefully. "I remember it all too well." Then he shook his head and added, "I don't think I'll ever forget the . . . thing," almost swearing.

Though Owen and Lynn Pierce were supposed to be their best friends, Arthur and Millie Blair both loved her, and barely tolerated him. Arthur found Pierce to be a vulgar, cruel, Godless man, an opinion with which Millie agreed wholeheartedly. Arthur also believed that Owen dabbled in drugs, or so the rumors said; but he had no proof and kept that thought to himself. He feared that Millie wouldn't allow Gary to continue dating Lori Pierce if she thought there were drugs anywhere near the Pierce home—even if Lynn *was* her best friend.

The Pierce house looked like a tan-brick fortress, a turret dominating the left side of a two-story structure that presided over a sloping, well-landscaped lawn, sans moat however. Inside the turret, a spiral staircase led to the second floor (the Blairs had been guests at the Pierces' home many times). The front door sat in the center of this mini-Camelot with a three-car garage on the right end. With just the one turret, the house seemed to lean slightly in that direction, giving the place an off-kilter feel.

When the Lexus pulled into the castle's driveway, Arthur said, "Now let me handle this."

Again, no argument from Millie on that score. She just nodded, then—almost hiding behind him—she followed her husband up the curving walk to the front door.

Arthur rang the bell and they waited. After thirty seconds or so, he rang it again, three times in rapid insistent succession. Again they waited almost a half a minute, an endless span to spend standing on a front porch; but this time as Arthur reached for the button, the door jerked open and they found themselves face-to-face with Lynn's husband—Owen Pierce himself.

Muscular in his gray Nike sweats, with silver glints in his dark hair, Pierce had striking blue eyes, and a ready, winning smile that displayed many white, straight teeth. Pierce's face seemed to explode in delight. "Well, Art! Millie! What a nice surprise—what are you doing here? I mean . . ." He chuckled, apparently embarrassed that that might have sound ungracious. "How are you? We didn't have plans for dinner or something tonight, did we? Lynn didn't say anything . . ."

The therapist's grin seemed forced, and his words came too fast and were delivered too loudly. Arthur again considered those drug rumors. "No, no plans tonight, Owen. We were hoping to speak to Lynn."

"Lynn?" Pierce frowned in confusion, as if this were a name he'd never heard before.

"Yes," Arthur said. "Lynn. You remember, Owen—your wife?"

An uncomfortable silence followed, as Pierce apparently tried to read Arthur's words and tone.

Finally, Millie stepped forward. "Owen, Lynn called me earlier, and said she was coming to see me . . . then she never showed up."

"Oh!" He smiled again, less dazzlingly. "Is *that* what this is about. . . ."

Millie said, "It's just not *like* her, Owen. She would have called me, if she had a change in plans."

Pierce's smile finally faded and his eyes tightened. "Her brother called. She barely took time to tell me! Something about an illness, and how they needed her there. You know how she jumps to, when her family's involved. Anyway, she packed a few things and left, lickety split."

What a load of bull, Arthur thought. He knew Lynn Pierce wouldn't leave the city without telling Millie where she was headed, and how long she'd be gone—particularly when Lynn had told Millie she was coming "right over"! Something was definitely not right here.

Arthur considered the tape in Millie's purse. Should he confront Pierce about it?

As Arthur was mulling this, his wife took a step nearer to Pierce, saying, "I'm sorry, but I don't believe you, Owen. Lynn would never . . ."

A frown crossed Pierce's face and Millie fell silent. The expression replacing the phony smile was all too sincere: as if a rock had been lifted and the real Owen had been glimpsed wriggling there in the dirt.

Over the years, the Blairs had both seen Pierce lose his temper, and it was never a pleasant sight—like a boiler exploding. Arthur took Millie gently if firmly by the arm and turned her toward the car. "Excuse us, Owen. Millie's just concerned about Lynn, you know how women are."

Pierce twitched a sort of grin.

As the couple moved away, Arthur said, "Hope Lynn has a good trip, Owen. Have her give us a call when she gets back, would you? . . . Thanks."

And all the time he spoke, Arthur steered Millie toward the car at the curb. She did not protest—she knew her place—but when he finally got her in the car, backed out of the driveway, and drove away from Owen Pierce and the castle house, she demanded an explanation.

"Don't you worry, darling," Arthur said. "We'll do something about that evil bastard."

Sometimes, when a swear word slipped out of him, she would scold him. He almost looked forward to the familiarity of it.

But tonight, she said only, "Good. Good. Good."

And she sat beside him in the vehicle, with her fists clenched, the purse in her lap . . . and that tape, that terrible tape, in the purse.

2

Captain Jim Brass ambled down the hall toward the washed-out aqua warren of offices that served as headquarters for the Las Vegas Criminalistics Bureau, a coldly modern institutional setting for the number-two crime lab in the country. The sad-eyed detective was sharply attired—gray sports coat over a blue shirt, darker blue tie with gray diagonal stripes, and navy slacks—and his low-key demeanor masked a dogged professionalism.

A cellophane bag dangled from the detective's right hand, an audiotape within. Slowing to peer through various half-windowed walls, Brass passed several rooms before he found the CSI grave-yard-shift supervisor, Gil Grissom, in the break room at a small table, hunkered over a cup of coffee and a pile of papers. Dressed in black and wearing his wire-framed reading glasses, the CSI chief looked like a cross between a gunfighter and a science geek, Brass thought, then realized that that was a pretty accurate mix.

Grissom—one of the top forensic entomologists in the country, among other things—was in his mid-forties, with his boyishly handsome features seemingly set in a state of perpetual preoccupation. Brass liked Gil, and felt that what some considered coldness in the man was really a self-imposed coolness, a detachment designed to keep the CSI chief's eye on facts and his emotions in check.

Brass pulled up a chair. "Latest issue of *Cockroach Racing Monthly*?"

Grissom shook his head, and responded as if the detective's question had been serious. "Staffing reports. Scuttlebutt is the County Board wants to cut the budget for next year."

"I heard that, too." Brass sighed. "Doesn't election time just bring out the best in people?"

Grissom gave him a pursed-lipped look that had nothing to do with blowing a kiss.

"Maybe you need something to put you in a better mood, Gil— like threats of dismemberment."

Grissom offered Brass another look, this one piqued with interest.

Brass held up the plastic baggie and waved it like a hypnotist's watch, Grissom's eyes following accordingly. "Among your state-of-the-art, cutting-edge equipment . . . you got a cassette player?"

Nodding, rising, removing his glasses, Grissom said, "In my office. What have you got?" He gathered up the pile of papers, the cup of coffee, and led Brass out into the hall.

The detective fell in alongside Grissom as they moved down the corridor. "Interesting turn of events, just now, out at the front desk."

"Really?"

They moved into Grissom's office.

"Really."

Brass had only lately ceased to be creeped out by Grissom's inner sanctum, with its shelves of such jarred oddities as a pickled piglet and various embalmed animal and human organs, and assorted living, crawling creatures—a tarantula, a two-headed scorpion—in glassed-in homes. At least the batteries had finally worn down on the Big Mouth Billy Bass just above Grissom's office door.

A desk sat in the middle of the methodically cluttered office, canted at a forty-five-degree angle, two vinyl-covered metal frame chairs in front of it. Brass handed the bag over to Grissom, then plopped into a chair. Behind his desk, Grissom sat and placed the bag on his blotter like a jeweler mounting a stone. From the top righthand drawer, he withdrew a pair of latex gloves and placed them next to the bag.

"Is this all tease," Grissom said, hands folded, "or do you plan to put out?"

Brass sat back, crossed his legs, twitched a non-smile. "This couple comes in tonight, to the front desk. Nice people, late thirties, early forties—straight as they come. He's in the finance department at UNLV."

Grissom nodded.

"Arthur and Millie Blair. They say their friend, woman named

Lynn Pierce, has disappeared . . . and they think something 'bad' has happened to her."

Grissom's eyes tightened, just a little. "How long has Lynn Pierce been missing?"

Checking his watch, Brass said, "About seven hours."

Grissom's eyes relaxed. "That's not twenty-four. She may be gone, but she's not 'missing,' yet."

Brass shrugged. "Officer at the desk told 'em the same thing. That's when they pulled out this tape."

Grissom glanced at the bag. "Which is a tape of what?"

Brass had to smile—Grissom was like a kid waiting to tear into a Christmas present. "Supposedly an argument between Lynn Pierce and her husband."

"Husband?"

Brass pulled a notebook from his jacket pocket and flipped it open, filling Grissom in on the particulars—Owen Pierce, successful physical therapist, married eighteen years to the missing woman.

"Clinic—'Therapeutic Body Works'—in a strip mall out on Hidden Well Road. East of the Callaway Golf Center."

One of Grissom's eyebrows arched in skeptical curiosity. "And the Blairs are in possession of this tape because . . . ?"

"This is where it gets good," Brass said, shifting in the chair. "The Blairs say Mrs. Pierce showed up on their doorstep last night—with this tape in her hot little hand. Mrs. Pierce told her friends the Blairs that she'd hidden a voice-activated tape player in the kitchen. Wanted to prove what kind of verbal abuse she'd been suffering, of late."

"I like a victim who provides evidence for us," Grissom said.

"Well, then you'll love Lynn Pierce. Her hidden microphone caught a doozy of an argument, it seems. Anyway, the Blairs said that Mrs. Pierce gave them the tape for safe keeping, then she sat with them and talked and talked about her marital problems, and trouble with their daughter, Lori . . ."

"Lori is whose daughter?"

"The Pierces. But most of all, Lynn was tired of the constant threats of violence her husband had been making."

"Let's hear the tape."

Brass held up a palm. "You still haven't heard the best part."

The detective told Grissom about the Blairs going to the Pierce home, where Owen Pierce claimed his wife had gone to visit a sick brother.

"Is that the best part?" Grissom asked, unimpressed.

"No—the best part is, while the Blairs are talking to one officer at the front desk, the other officer is taking a phone call from guess who."

"Owen Pierce."

"Owen Pierce. Calling to report his wife missing. He now claims that she got pissed off after a 'misunderstanding,' and he figures she left him, and he doesn't know where the hell she went."

Grissom was sitting forward now. "Did the wife take anything with her?"

"A couple of uniforms went to the house," Brass said. "Pierce told them he didn't see her go. But she took her own car—a '95 Avalon—also a suitcase, some clothes."

"Let's listen to the tape."

Brass raised both eyebrows. "Why don't we?"

Slipping on the latex gloves, Grissom removed the tape from the bag. He rose, moved to a small boombox behind the desk, and slid the tape into the holder. After closing the door, he pushed PLAY with a latexed fingertip—Brass noted that Grissom brought the same anal-retentive precision to the simple procedure of playing an audiotape cassette as he would to one of his bizarre experiments involving blood-spatter spray patterns or insect eating patterns.

The sound was somewhat muffled; apparently the couple had been standing across the room from the secreted tape recorder. But the words soon became clear enough, as the Pierces raised their voices in anger.

"If you don't stop it, just stop it, I swear I'll do it! I'll divorce you!"

That had been the woman's voice.

Now the man's: *"Stop it? Stop what? What the fuck are you talking about?"*

"I'm talking about the cocaine, Owen—and your slutty women! I've already talked to a lawyer—"

"You bitch—lousy rotten bitch . . . go ahead, go ahead and file for divorce. I'll make sure you don't get a goddamned thing—including Lori!"

Brass glanced at Grissom, but the criminalist's face was blank, his focus complete.

"*Owen . . .*" The woman's voice had turned pleading. "*I just want us to be a . . . family, again. Do you think what I really want is a divorce?*"

The man's reply was mostly inaudible, but they heard three words clearly: "*. . . give a fuck.*"

The woman spoke again, and she too was inaudible, but then her voice rose, not in anger, but as a conclusion to a speech: "*I just want you and Lori to find the peace that I've found serving our Lord!*"

"*Oh, Christ! Not that Jesus crap again. I've told you a thousand fucking times, Lynn—I believe what I believe.*"

"*You don't believe in* anything."

"*That's my choice. That's America. That's what your forefathers died for, you dumb . . .*"

At the next word, Grissom shot a look at Brass.

The man was saying, "*You need to give Lori the same space, too, Lynn. She's a young adult. She deserves a little respect.*"

"*She's a child.*"

"*She's sixteen! Hell, in half the world she'd be married already! Old enough to bleed, old enough to breed!*"

"*Owen!*"

"*I'm just telling you what I do, what our grown* daughter *does, is none of your goddamned Bible-beating business.*"

"*Maybe . . . maybe I should get a divorce then.*"

"*Knock yourself out. . . . But remember, you don't get one dime, not one fucking thing.*"

"*Is that right? I hired the best divorce lawyer in town, Owen— and when I get around to telling him about the drugs and the women and you screwing the IRS by skimming off the top of the 'Body Works'? Well, then we'll just see who gets custody of Lori!*"

The woman sounded triumphant, Brass thought, and for a moment the husband had no response. The woman's time on top of the argument didn't last long.

"*You do,*" Pierce said, "*and I'll kill your holier-than-thou ass . . .*"

"*Owen! No! Don't say—*"

"*And then I'll cut you up in little pieces, my darling bride. I will scatter your parts to the four winds, and they will* never *put Humpty Dumpty back together!*"

The argument lasted only a couple of more minutes, none of it coherently audible—the couple had apparently moved farther away from the hidden machine—before the detective and the criminalist heard the sound of a door slam and then the tape clicked off.

"What do you think?" Brass asked. "We got enough to go out there? Or is that just the road company of *Who's Afraid of Virginia Woolf*?"

Grissom stood. "I think we need to go out there. Everybody's in-house, at the moment—let's take the whole crew."

Brass winced. "Don't you think we should try for a warrant, first?"

Grissom gave Brass that familiar mock-innocent smile. "Why? Mr. Pierce called the police. He's concerned about his missing wife. We should help the poor guy, don't you think?"

"Yeah, who needs a warrant to do that?" Brass said, grinning, climbing out of the chair. "What about the tape?"

"What tape?"

"Yeah," Brass said, eyes narrowing. "Obviously Pierce doesn't know it exists. No need to tell him that we do."

"I don't know what you're talking about," Grissom said. "Let's go see what there is to see."

Ten minutes later, six colleagues—all but Brass in dark FORENSICS windbreakers—met in the underlit parking lot.

Lanky, loose-limbed, African-American Warrick Brown stood a few inches taller than the athletically brawny Nick Stokes; both men were in their very early thirties.

Off to one side were the two women on the team, Grissom's second-in-command, Catherine Willows, and the relatively recent addition, Sara Sidle.

The Willows woman had a checkered past, Brass knew, but her experience had made her a valuable counterbalance to the overly cool Grissom. Brass had less confidence in Sara Sidle, despite her status as a former Grissom pupil handpicked by Gil for the job. Sidle seemed to be a Grissom-in-the-making, similarly obsessed with work—and with people skills rivaling those of her tactless mentor.

Grissom filled his people in, quickly, on the contents of the tape and the potentially missing woman.

"So we have a verbally abusive husband," Grissom said, tone as tight as his eyes, "who threatened his wife with dismemberment."

"But we're pretending to help him out," Warrick said.

"I didn't hear that," Grissom said, sweetly.

Warrick, Nick, Catherine, and Sara rode in the Tahoe, Grissom rode with Brass in the detective's Taurus. Just before midnight, they arrived at the castle-like house on the impressive sloping lawn, lights shining out downstairs windows, sending sword-like shafts of light into the dark.

Brass and Grissom led the way to the front door. The detective rang the bell and had to wait only a moment before the door opened to reveal a muscular man in dark slacks, black T-shirt, and black loafers, dark hair peppered with gray. The man stood before Grissom like a mirror reflection—only, Brass thought, this was Gil Grissom on steroids.

Brass smiled, mildly. "Mr. Pierce?"

The man nodded. He seemed anxious. "You're the police?"

Touching the badge on his breast pocket, Brass affirmed, "We're the police—sorry it took us so long to respond to your call. . . . We had to round our people up."

Grissom flicked Pierce an insincere smile. "We're a full-service operation, Mr. . . . Pierce, I assume?"

Still not inviting them in, Pierce nodded.

Grissom lifted the necklace I.D. "Gil Grissom, Las Vegas Criminalistics. This is Captain Jim Brass, and this is our Criminalistics crew."

Pierce regarded the considerable assembly overflowing his front stoop. "Then . . . you haven't found my wife?"

"No, sir," Grissom said, "I'm sorry, as yet we haven't."

Pierce shook his head. "I don't understand what you're doing here. I gave all the information to the officer, on the phone. Shouldn't you be out looking for Lynn, Detective . . . Griswald, is it?"

"It's Grissom, Mr. Pierce, only I'm not a detective. I'm a supervisor of Criminalistics." He flashed another empty smile. "And we *are* out looking for your wife. That's why we're here. You see, we handle crime scene investigation."

A puzzled look tightened Pierce's face. "Crime scene? I don't understand. This isn't a crime scene—my wife walked out on me."

"Sir, my understanding is, you don't know that for sure. She might well have been abducted."

"Well . . . that's possible. Maybe I hadn't wanted to . . . admit that to myself."

Grissom nodded in supposed sympathy. "Also, there's the matter of the Blairs."

"The Blairs."

"Yes. Your wife called them in the afternoon . . . said she would come by, never materialized. They said they spoke to you."

Pierce sucked in air, his expression turning sheepish. "Oh. I see . . . look, when they came by, I was embarrassed. I told them that Lynn went to visit her brother to, you know, get rid of them."

Frowning, Brass asked, "You wanted to get rid of them?"

"They mean well, Detective . . . Brass?"

"Yes. Brass."

"They're kind of busybodies, Detective Brass. Judgmental types—Bible beaters? And the wound was fresh, Det . . . uh . . . Mr. Grissom. I needed to be alone while I sorted some things out."

Grissom shrugged one shoulder. "Then why did you telephone the police?"

He shrugged both his. "I wanted someone to help me find her. I thought maybe Lynn and I could find a way to work out our problems."

"So, then, you really don't know where she is?"

Pierce shook his head. "Nope, no idea."

"And you weren't here when she left?"

"No. I was at my office . . . my clinic."

"That makes abduction a real possibility, Mr. Pierce. And that's why we're here."

He frowned. "Just because I have no idea where Lynn is? And because she made a phone call?"

"Yes, sir." Grissom's expression turned almost angelic. "We want to help you. Maybe we can find a clue as to what happened to your wife."

"But," Brass said, with half a smile, "we can't help you out here on the stoop."

Pierce sighed again, shrugged with his eyebrows this time. "Well—if it'll help find Lynn . . . of course, come in."

The response surprised Brass a little, and he exchanged glances with Grissom, who the detective figured had also been expecting objections from Pierce, not cooperation—particularly if a crime had gone down within these castle walls, earlier today.

Pierce stepped back inside and held the door as the group trooped in, moving through a small entryway into a larger anteroom of a home whose walls were cream-color stucco with dark woodwork. A winding staircase disappeared up a landing at left, and a hallway was at left also, with the dining room visible through one arched doorless doorway, in the facing wall, and, to the right, a living room yawned through another archway. The furnishings were colonial, tasteful enough, but a bit at odds with the castle-like architecture.

Brass asked, "Is there anyone else in the house, sir?"

"Just my daughter."

Grissom asked, "Was she here when your wife left?"

"No. I'm afraid not."

A teenage girl stepped down the winding stairs into view. She wore Nikes, nice new jeans, a big white sweatshirt, with her long blonde hair pulled back and held in place with a blue scrunchy. Her pretty face—she resembled her father, though the eyes were wider set—was well scrubbed and her bright blue eyes were rimmed red. She glanced down at the contingency in the anteroom, and froze on the landing.

"This is my daughter," Pierce said, "Lori."

The girl gave a barely perceptible nod, then turned and disappeared back upstairs.

Pierce sighed again and said, "You'll have to forgive her, please. This has been hard for both of us, but especially for Lori. She's taken it pretty hard, the idea of her mother . . . abandoning us."

Brass nodded. Grissom was looking around, taking in the framed wildlife artwork.

"Will you have to . . ." Pierce looked for the words. ". . . disturb Lori, when you make your search?"

Brass glanced at Grissom, who gave a little shrug.

"I don't think so, sir," the detective said. "We'll leave her alone for now . . . though it's possible we might have some questions later."

"I understand."

Grissom approached Pierce, standing a little too close, as if having a better look at an insect specimen, and said, "Mr. Pierce, if you and Captain Brass will wait in the living room, we'll get to work. Then we'll talk to you when we're finished."

"All right."

For the next two hours, the CSI crew—in latex gloves but wielding little else of their elaborate equipment—crawled over every inch of the house, examining everything from the basement to the garage, speaking to the teenage girl only to ask her to step out of her bedroom for a few minutes. When they had finished, they conferred in the kitchen, careful to keep their voices down as they discussed what they'd found, and hadn't found.

An eyebrow arched, Catherine said to Grissom, "There are gaps in the closet. Some clothes and shoes gone, apparently."

"Consistent with Lynn Pierce packing up and leaving," Grissom said.

Catherine smiled humorlessly, nodded.

Sara was nodding, too. "Yeah, and there's a row of suitcases in the basement, with a space in it—so maybe one of them is gone. Space on the shelf above, where a train case could've been."

Warrick piped in: "Only one toothbrush in the master bathroom. Some empty spaces on her makeup table, like she took perfume, makeup, stuff like that."

"No sign of her purse," Nick said. "And there was no blood in the drains, no knives missing that I could tell, no sign anyone did . . . what he said he would . . . on the tape."

"I'd sure like to bring a RUVIS in here," Catherine said, referring to the ultraviolet device that would show up blood stains.

"I don't think we can justify that," Grissom said. "If there *is* a crime here, we don't want to do anything that would be thrown out of court. . . . So what does this house tell us?"

"She may have gone," Catherine said.

Sara's eyebrows were up. "Or somebody may have made it look like she left."

"Gris," Warrick said, "I did find one thing that could be significant." He showed them a clear evidence bag with a hairbrush in the bottom.

Grissom took the bag, held it up and looked at it as if it held the secrets of the universe; several blonde hairs dangled from the brush. He asked, "Does a woman pack up and go, and leave her hairbrush behind?"

"Maybe Sara," Nick said with a grin, and Sara grinned back and elbowed him, a little.

Grissom focused on the hairbrush in the bag. "Why don't we ask Mr. Pierce about this?"

They followed their supervisor into the living room where Pierce and Brass (his notepad out) sat on a couch in front of a thirty-six-inch Toshiba in an early-American entertainment hutch (just like George and Martha Washington used to have); CNN was going, with the mute on.

"Anything you'd like to share?" Brass asked Grissom.

"You'll be relieved to know," Grissom said, "that there are no signs of a struggle anywhere in the house."

"I could have told you that," Pierce said.

Catherine said, "We don't see any overt indications of abduction."

"That's a relief, anyway," Pierce said, letting out a big sigh—too big, maybe.

Grissom offered up his patented smile. "What can you tell me about this, Mr. Pierce?"

And he held up the bag with the brush.

"Well . . . that's Lynn's," Pierce said.

Catherine asked, "Would you say your wife is well-groomed, Mr. Pierce? Takes pride in her appearance?"

Pierce bristled. "She's a beautiful woman. Of course she's . . . well-groomed."

Catherine's smile was utterly charming, her words casually heartless. "Does she usually go off without her hairbrush?"

"Maybe she has more than one." Pierce held his hands out, palms open. "How should I know? . . . Anyway, she only uses a brush when her hair is long. Lynn had her hair cut recently—it's barely over her ears. I've seen her combing it, but not brushing."

Sara said, "I noticed three computers in the house, Mr. Pierce."

He nodded. "Yes. Lori's is in her bedroom, mine is in the basement—I have my business programs on that—and in the spare bedroom, Lynn has her own for e-mailing her friends and, I don't know, whatever else she does."

Grissom said, "We'd like to take Lynn's computer with us, if you don't mind."

Pierce winced at that one. "You want her *computer?*"

With a brief nod, Grissom said, "May help us track her movements. See if your wife e-mailed someone to notify them that she'd be coming for a visit. Can you access her account?"

"Afraid I can't. She has her own password. . . . Even the closest couples have privacy issues—who doesn't want to have a few secrets?"

Grissom said, "Secrets don't stay secret long, in my world, Mr. Pierce."

Catherine asked, "How about a cell phone? Does Mrs. Pierce have one?"

"Why, yes—she carries it in her purse, all the time."

"Have you tried to call her since she turned up missing?"

"Of course!"

"And?"

A shrug. "And it comes back 'out of service.' "

Catherine thought about that, then asked, "May we see last month's bill?"

Starting to look mildly put-out, Pierce said, "Well . . . all right."

"And her credit cards and bank statements?"

Pierce gave Grissom a sharp look, as if to say, *Can't you keep this underling in check?*

Grissom turned on the angelic smile again. "It's an old, old theory, Mr. Pierce—follow the money. Wherever Mrs. Pierce is, she's spending money, somehow or other . . . and unless she left carrying a massive amount of cash, there should be a credit-card trail to follow."

The color had drained from Pierce's face. "Well . . . Now, she could have taken cash with her, quite a bit of it. But I wouldn't know."

"You had separate accounts?"

"Yes."

Catherine said, "Privacy issues?"

Pierce ignored that, looking instead at the CSI chief. "Lynn's from a wealthy family, Mr. Grissom. She has a considerable amount of money beyond what I earn. . . . There's her money, my money, and our money—lots of couples are that way." With yet another sigh, he rose. "I understand you're just trying to help. . . . I'll get you the papers you need."

Brass, still seated, asked, "Do you have a recent photo of your wife we could take?"

"Yes. Of course. I'll get one for you." Pierce left the room, and they could see him going up the stairs; in a few minutes he was back, handing Brass a five-by-seven snapshot. "This was taken at her birthday party, just two months ago."

Grissom took the photo away from Brass and looked at the casual image of a haggard, haunted-eyed blonde standing rather somberly next to several laughing female friends, a HAPPY BIRTHDAY banner in the background. In her late thirties, early forties, with short hair that flirted with the collar of a blue silk blouse, Lynn Pierce had blue eyes that matched her daughter's, high cheekbones with a touch too much blush, a long but graceful nose, nicely full lips, and a stubby flat chin. She was neither beautiful nor unattractive—a "handsome" woman, as they used to say. As she stared up at him with clear, piercing eyes, Grissom got the impression that she was a no-nonsense, down-to-earth person.

The somberness of her expression, however, seemed almost to speak to him, as though there were something she needed to say.

Fifteen minutes later, after forced-friendly handshakes and good-byes with their host, the group trooped back out of the Pierce home, Catherine's arms piled with papers, Nick lugging Mrs. Pierce's computer.

As the rest of the CSI team loaded what they'd taken into the Tahoe, Catherine, with arms folded like a Sioux chief, faced Grissom. "Your tape not withstanding . . . the evidence shows no signs that any crime has been committed on those premises."

Nearby Brass was rocking on his heels. To no one in particular, he said, "You really think Owen Pierce is the distressed husband he claims to be?"

"You looking for an opinion?" Grissom asked. "I don't do opinions."

Catherine was smiling, though, regarding her boss with cat's eyes. "You don't fool me."

Grissom's brows rose. "I don't?"

"Something's wrong in that house, and you know it."

Grissom frowned at her. "I *don't* know it," he said.

And he stalked back toward the Taurus, Brass following him, throwing a shrug back at the quietly amused Catherine.

"Retaining water," Catherine said to Sara.

"And me fresh out of Midol," Sara said.

Grissom got in on the rider's side and sat and brooded. He *didn't* know that something was wrong in that house—but he *felt* it.

And he hated when that happened.

For now, he had nothing to go on. Nothing to do but return to HQ and wait for a real crime to come in.

And hope it wasn't a murder, and the victim: Lynn Pierce.

3

A day later, and Lynn Pierce remained among the missing—the only change in status was that she was now officially listed as such.

Grissom was seated at his desk in his office, dealing with paperwork. The CSI supervisor would not have admitted it under torture, but the face of the sad-eyed blonde in that snapshot haunted him.

Still, at this stage, little remained appropriate for his CSI team's attention: no sign of foul play had been found. There was only the husband's threat to kill his wife to go on . . . and how many husbands and wives, in the heat and hyperbole of an argument, had threatened as much?

He had assigned Sara to the case, and she had drawn upon her considerable computer expertise to track the woman's credit cards; but none of the cards had been used since Lynn Pierce's disappearance, and the woman hadn't been to an ATM or used a phone card either. E-mails from friends were piling up unanswered and none of her recent cyber-correspondence mentioned a trip or hinted that she might be preparing to run away.

If she was alive, she would leave a trail—this Grissom knew to a certainty; the absence of such, so far, only substantiated his conviction that she had been killed. This was not a hunch, rather a belief built on the circumstantial evidence thus far.

Sara, sitting at her computer, had looked up at him with eyebrows high, and said, "She could be paying her way with cash—she does have money of her own."

"Check for withdrawals, then."

"Maybe she kept a stash of cash, somewhere."

"What, under a mattress? No, if that's the case, it'll be in a safety deposit box—check with her bank on that, as well."

Sara smirked at him. "But that's the point of safety deposit boxes—nobody knows what goes in and out, banks included."

Grissom lifted a finger. "Ah, but the banks record *who* goes in and out, to have a look at their safety deposit boxes. . . . See if Lynn Pierce has done that, lately."

Sara, nodding, went back to work.

Even as he sent Sara scurrying to check, Grissom didn't hold much stock in the notion that Lynn Pierce was funding her disappearance, paying as she went. From what he had gathered thus far, this was a woman of faith and family who spent little money on herself.

The phone rang. Grissom, who hated having his thoughts interrupted, looked at it like the object had just flipped him off. It rang a second time, and finally, he reached for the receiver.

He identified himself, listened for several moments, writing down the information, and then told Jim Brass, "I'll have a team there in under fifteen minutes, and see you in five."

Grissom glanced at his own notes.

A dead woman—not Lynn Pierce—needed their attention.

Catherine Willows—typically stylish in a formfitting green V-neck ribbed sweater, tailored black slacks and ankle-high black leather boots—was peeling an orange when Grissom walked into the break room and handed her his notes.

"Dream Dolls?" she asked, peering over the edge of the note at Grissom. Her expression split the difference between a smile and a frown. "You're kidding, right?"

Grissom risked just the hint of a smile. "You know the place better than anybody else on staff."

"What's that, another excerpt from *The Wit and Wisdom of Gil Grissom?*" She tossed the scrap of paper on the table next to the orange peels. "A very slender volume, I might add."

He took a seat beside her. "You *can* handle this? It's not a problem, is it? Is this . . . a sensitive issue with you?"

Her eyes were wide and unblinking as she said, "You'd know this, why? Sensitivity being your long suit and all." She sighed, nibbled an orange slice. "A dead stripper, and you immediately think of me— should I be complimented?"

Grissom thought about that for a moment. "You may have my job one day, you know."

"It's been offered to me before," she reminded him, adding wryly, "Sometimes I wonder why I didn't take it."

"Me too," Grissom admitted. "If you were supervisor, and one of your CSIs was a former stock-car racer, and you had a case turn up at a speedway . . . who would you send?"

She sighed. "Point well taken." She glanced at the notes again. "How did the woman die?"

"That's what the coroner will tell us . . . Looks like strangulation."

"All right," she said. "You're not coming?"

He shook his head. "I'm meeting Brass in five minutes. He's invited me along—interviewing the Blairs, the friends who reported the Lynn Pierce disappearance . . . now that it's official."

Catherine was cleaning up her trash, depositing the peels and her Evian bottle in a bin, when he told her, "I said a CSI team'd be right out."

She bestowed him her most beautiful sarcastic smile. "I'll shake a tailfeather."

On her way out of the break room, he called, "And take Sara!"

Catherine nodded, threw him a wave over her shoulder, and strode down the hall.

Catherine found Sara Sidle huddled over her computer monitor, her mouse racing around the pad as she studied something on the Internet. Wearing dark bell-bottom jeans and a dark blue scoop-neck top under her baby-blue lab coat, she looked more like a clerk at Tower Records than a dedicated scientist. Her dark curly hair bounced as she bobbed in time to some internal rhythm.

"Sorry to interrupt," Catherine said, "but we've got a call."

Sara barely glanced at her. "Uh, Grissom assigned me to this Pierce disappearance."

"Well, he wants you to accompany me on this one. We've got a live one."

"You mean a dead one."

Catherine shrugged.

"Just give me another minute," Sara said, her gaze glued to the monitor.

Catherine leaned in for a look.

"I've been checking hotel reservations and check-ins for the last two days," Sara said, "and nothing."

"We'll find her," Catherine said, "or she'll turn up on her own. Nobody disappears 'without a trace,' no matter what you hear."

They gathered their equipment, jumped in one of the department's black Tahoes—Catherine tossing the keys to Sara—and strapped themselves in for the short drive to Dream Dolls.

"So," Sara said, with a sideways glance, "this is one of the older, uh, clubs in town, isn't it?"

"That's right. And yes, Dream Dolls *is* one of the clubs I worked at."

"Oh. Really. Interesting."

"Is it?" Catherine turned and folded her arms and faced the windshield. "Grissom assigned me to this, he says, because I worked there, and have an advance knowledge of the place."

"Makes sense. But . . . why'd he send me?"

"Probably because he figured it would be less awkward for me than taking Nicky or Warrick . . . assuming Grissom could be that sensitive."

Sara mulled that a moment or two. "Maybe he figures, since we'll have to deal with a lot of women, you know, at the club . . . sending two women kinda makes sense."

"Maybe."

The club sat in the older part of downtown, blocks away from the renovation of Fremont Street. Though it wasn't that far from headquarters, and she had passed the place numerous times, Dream Dolls—and that life—seemed to Catherine worlds away from where she was now. She wondered if Ty Kapelos still ran the show there. He'd always seemed just one brick short of a pimp; but he had, at least, always been fair.

"Even *your* looks won't last forever," he'd told her. "Start saving. Think up a future for yourself."

In a way, that had been an important point on the winding road to the straight life she now lived.

Sara pulled the SUV into a parking space beside two squad cars, whose rollers painted the night alternately blue and red. The two women climbed out of the Tahoe, gathered their equipment, and turned toward the club, a one-story faded bunker of a redbrick building.

Catherine looked up at the garish glowing neon sign on a pole looming over the sidewalk, featuring a red outline that suggested an overly endowed woman, sliding down a blue neon firepole; when the neon stripper reached the bottom, giant green letters . . . one at a time . . . spelled out DREAM DOLLS, then held and pulsed . . . before the sequence started again.

Smirking, shaking her head, Catherine figured Ty must have finally decided to spend a few bucks on the business. Hearing footsteps on the cement, she looked toward a young male uniformed officer coming their way from where he'd been positioned at the front door.

"CSI?" the officer asked.

She read his nameplate: JOHNSTON. A newbie, right out of the academy she'd bet, all wavy blond hair and blue-eyed, vacant stare— was this his first crime scene?

"Catherine Willows and Sara Sidle," she said with a nod toward her partner. "Pardon the expression, but it's kinda dead out here."

His voice was a breathy tenor. "I was told not to let anyone in or out, 'cept you guys and the detectives."

She nodded and strode past him.

"Real mess," he said, hollowly.

Spinning to face him, Catherine demanded, "You were in there?" All she needed was for some rookie to contaminate her evidence. "You saw the scene?"

Eyes bright and glistening, he nodded. "Just for a second—from out in the hall." He swallowed. "Never seen anything like that."

"But you didn't go near the body?"

"No."

She studied his face for a second, then—satisfied he'd been frank with her—said, "Good," turned back to the club and pulled open the front door. Behind her, Sara tossed a hip to hold the door open. They entered a small alcove with still another door between them and the bar; already the smoky, spilled-beer-stench atmosphere assailed them. To their right, behind a small table, sat a good-looking if steroidally burly doorman in a white shirt, red bow tie, and black jeans.

"You ladies . . ." He seemed to have been about to say one thing, in his pleasant baritone, then—perhaps noting Sara's silver flight-case field kit—finished by saying something else. ". . . are with the cops?"

Catherine said, "Crime scene investigators."

He nodded, gesturing toward the club, as if there were anywhere else to go.

Catherine opened the inner door and the blare of amplified rock almost knocked her back into the entryway. The music hadn't been this loud back in her day—or at least she didn't remember it that way. Stepping inside, the two women let the door swing shut behind them.

The stage was where it had always been, still about the size of Wayne Newton's yacht, filling the center of the room, a brass pole anchoring either end. No dancers were on stage at the moment, though the lights continued to blink to the beat of the music. A few customers dotted the chairs near the stage and most of the girls huddled in a faraway corner with two uniformed officers. In the corner to the left an elevated DJ booth oversaw the room like a prison tower, the sentry a scrawny guy in headphones, a scruffy beard, short blond hair and a fluorescent DREAM DOLLS T-shirt. His head moved to the music like a head-bobbing toy. He seemed oblivious to the fact that another employee was dead and the stage was empty.

Detective Erin Conroy stood at the long bar at the right, a notepad in hand, talking to someone Catherine couldn't see.

Still moving slowly, Catherine and Sara made their way to the bar and Conroy looked up, her green eyes tight, whether from the situation or the smoke, who could say? On the other side of the bar stood a short, bald, fat man, the sleeves of his white shirt rolled up, the top three buttons left open to reveal the sort of gold chains it takes hours to win at a carnival.

Catherine had to yell to be heard. "Hey, Ty!" She jerked a thumb toward the DJ, then slashed her throat with a finger.

His mouth dropped open, as he recognized her, but he obeyed. Tyler Kapelos looked over at the DJ's corner and yelled. *"Worm!"*

The DJ glanced up—the club owner, too, dragged a finger across his throat, the DJ nodded and the sound system went quiet, though Catherine figured she'd be hearing the echo for hours. Minus the blare of music, the club's essential seediness seemed to assert itself.

"Cath," Kapelos said, a smile spreading like a rash over his ample face. "Jeez, it's good to see you. What's it been . . . ten, fifteen years? I was starting to think you didn't love me no more. I heard you were with the cops, but still . . . never expected to see you in my place. You know me, I run a clean shop—no drugs, no hooking."

"I'm not a cop, Ty—I'm a scientist."

His dark eyes danced; he was in a good mood, considering. "You *did* make good!"

Sara—apparently feeling left out—said, "Crime scene investigators—my name is Sidle."

Kapelos acknowledged Sara with a nod, then turned his sweaty grinning countenance back on Catherine. "I just knew you'd make something of yourself." He gestured with a wag of his head to the squalid world around them. "You were always too good for this place."

"Okay," Catherine said, all business, "we're officially all caught up—now, what happened here?"

Kapelos began to speak, but Detective Conroy stepped in, glancing occasionally at her notepad. "We have a dead dancer in the back, in one of the private rooms. Goes by 'Jenna Patrick'—don't know if that's her real name or not. Late twenties, strangled—apparently by a john."

"Excuse me," Kapelos said, mildly indignant, "but they're not 'johns.' This is not the Mustang Ranch, y'know. They're customers. Patrons."

"Speaking of which," Catherine said to Conroy, "if you don't mind a suggestion—we could use a couple more detectives to question those customers. We can't release them without preliminary statements, at least."

But Conroy was ahead of her. "I have a call in. O'Riley and Vega are on the way. . . . Crime scene?"

The detective led the way, Catherine and Sara falling in line behind her as they moved to the back. With the music off and the echo subsiding, the customers and dancers corralled out there were talking too loud, yelling to be heard over music that had gone away.

As the trio of female investigators edged into the cramped hallway in back, Catherine noticed a small video camera overhead. She paused and pointed it out to Sara, who had seen it, too.

"We'll get the tapes before we go," Sara said.

The hallway contained six doors, three on each side, all standing open; this area was not part of the building's original design, and had not been here during Catherine's tenure—strictly contrived out of sheetrock, cheap trim and black paint, to accomplish a specific purpose.

Looking through the first door on the left, Catherine saw a room the size of a good-sized closet with a metal frame chair facing the door. The walls back here were black, too, and the carpeting looked like some cheap junk maybe picked up at a yard sale. Each cubicle had a mounted speaker to feed in the DJ's tunes.

"Private dance rooms," Conroy said. "Lap dances, they call 'em."

Table dances—where a dancer, between sets, would work the room, squeezing dollars out of patrons for up-close-and-slightly-more-personal glimpses at a girl—were as far as things had ever gone, in Catherine's day. Nothing to compare with the likes of "lap" dances and the stuff that went on in these private rooms, on the current scene.

"There are doors on the rooms," Conroy pointed out, "but no locks."

"If a customer gets out of line," Sara said, thinking it through aloud, "a bouncer can respond to a shout or a scream, and put a stop to it."

"In theory," Catherine said. "But that doesn't seem to have helped, here. . . ."

Peeking over Sara's shoulder, Catherine got her first look at the body. Nude except for a lavender thong, Jenna Patrick lay in a fetal position, her long blonde hair splayed away from her face and bare back, something thin and black tight around her throat. Her head faced left, one sightless brown orb staring at the place where the wall and floor met. Full dark lips were frozen in a parody of a kiss and a tiny mole punctuated the corner of her mouth. She had full, heavy breasts and the strong, muscular legs of a dancer. She wore black patent-leather spike heels that would have been a bitch to walk, let alone dance, in.

"That looks like an electrical tie," Catherine said.

"Looks like it," Conroy said.

The women remained in the hallway, huddled around the doorway, maneuvering around each other for a better view.

Sara said, "Cut off the carotids—she was out in seconds . . . and dead in under a minute."

Catherine said to Conroy, "How many men was she in here with tonight?"

The detective shook her head, ponytail swinging. "Kapelos said they never settled up till the end of the night—he and the dancers split the take, back here . . . twenty-five dollars a dance."

"Plus tips," Catherine said, "which the girls wouldn't share, even if they were supposed to."

Conroy went on: "Jenna came in at five and was scheduled until twelve—only a couple of bathroom, cigarette breaks. No lunch break."

Catherine nodded; she knew the drill.

"That normal?" Sara asked, wincing.

"Yeah," Catherine said. "Most of the girls don't eat much anyway, gotta stay in shape. If they want a meal, they brown-bag it in the dressing room. . . . Jenna here would've worked straight through till midnight, getting out before the crowd got too out of hand. . . . Those last hours of the night are the worst."

Sara was doing a lousy job of hiding how fascinated she was, hearing Catherine's inside scoop on the skin business.

"Or," Catherine went on, "if there were some high-rollers and she thought she could make some real bucks, maybe she'd stick around another hour or so. That's pretty typical."

Sara asked, "When did you quit doing this . . . yesterday?"

Conroy piped in: "Am I catching the drift of this, correctly? You used to dance for Kapelos? *Here?*"

"About a hundred years ago, I did. Got my degree, and got out—any other questions?"

"No," Conroy said. "None. Glad to have your, uh, insights."

The two CSIs unpacked their tools in the tiny hallway and went to work. First, Catherine used an electrostatic print lifter to get footprints off the floor of the room, and then the hallway. She'd have to take shoe prints from the cops, Sara and herself, to eliminate them, but she still had hope of getting something. They photographed everything, dusted the chair and the door knobs for prints; then Catherine bent close to the victim's neck for a better look at the weapon that had taken Jenna Patrick's life.

"About three-eighths of an inch in diameter," Catherine reported. "Standard black electrical tie, available in every hardware store in the free world."

Picking a spot that looked clean, she used a small pair of wire cutters to snip the tie, which she then bagged. It wasn't very wide, but even if they snagged a partial print, that'd be useful.

Over the course of the next two hours, they lifted hairs, samples of stains, fibers, dirt, anything that might help them identify who had killed Jenna Patrick in that room. Using the RUVIS—a sort of pistol-gripped telephoto lens—they turned up occasional white splotches on the carpet, indicating probable semen spills from happy customers.

"Greg's going to love us," Sara said sarcastically, referring to their resident lab rat, Greg Sanders, whose job it would be to wade nose deep in the DNA cesspool they uncovered tonight.

"This cubicle could be a career for him," Catherine said with a smile. "But oddly . . . there's not as much as I thought there would be. Place like this should be wall-to-wall DNA."

Sara nodded, shrugged. "Yeah. What's up, y'suppose?"

Catherine thought Sara's question over for a few seconds, then said, "I'll be back."

Walking across the club—the lights on now, exposing Dream Dolls as the dingy nightmare it was—she saw that the place had emptied out except for cops and employees. She nodded to Detectives O'Riley and Vega, who were interviewing a waitress and the red-bow-tied bouncer. The dancers were in the dressing room in back where Conroy would be questioning them; the DJ in his corner was covering his equipment under tarps. Catherine moved to the bar, behind which Tyler Kapelos moped with a cup of coffee.

"How long am I gonna be closed down, Cath?" he asked as he poured her a cup, too.

"You can probably reopen tomorrow if you want. We'll be done soon."

"That's a relief, anyway." He nodded and sipped from his cup. "Pretty ugly in there."

"Shame. She was a nice kid."

Catherine knew that whichever one of his dancers had died, Kapelos would likely have said the same thing.

"But, y'know, funny thing," she said casually, "it's not as bad as it could have been." She sipped her coffee, hot, bitter, but better than the break room swill. "You got a cleaning woman coming in daily or something?"

He smiled a little, shrugged. "Spent some money, fixed stuff up, some. How d'you like the new sign?"

"Class," she said, only half-sarcastic. "What did you do in the back? And when?"

"Fresh paint, new carpet." He rubbed a palm over his forehead, then back over his balding scalp, distributing the sweat. "Maybe a month ago, two, no more'n that."

"I should thank you. You're making our job a little easier."

"Yeah? How so?"

Now she shrugged. "Normally, a place like this—we'd be sifting through DNA until we all retired."

A defensive frown formed on his Greek Lou Grant face. "I told ya, Cath, this is no hooker haven. With these lap dances, guy makes a mess, it's in his pants."

"Even so—there'd be some of that on the floor, and hairs and sweat and . . . well, the general residue that follows a good time being had by all."

"That wicked sense of humor." His smile was feeble but sincere. "Almost wish you was still here, kid."

"That makes one of us, Ty."

"Seriously. You still got the looks, and Lord knows you got style."

Interrogation was Conroy's job, but the detective was busy, and Catherine knew her familiarity with Kapelos might make him more open with her. "Any idea who would do this to her, Ty?"

He sucked in a breath. "Probably that son of a bitch Ray Lipton. . . . I guess I shoulda thought to tell that female detective about that prick. Nice looking woman, that detective." He glanced back toward the hallway. "And you know that kid you come in with, what's her name? Siddon?"

"Sidle."

"She could make a few bucks here, too. What's the PD policy on a little innocent moonlighting?"

Catherine ignored that. "Who is this Ray Lipton?"

"Jenna's boyfriend. He hated her workin' here." He shrugged. "Old story."

Very old story, Catherine knew. Half the guys dating dancers hated what their women did for a living; the other half only dated the women *because* they danced. Sometimes the first group had started out in the second. "Ray and Jenna, they fight?"

Kapelos snorted a laugh. "Cats and dogs. It got so bad I had to get a damn restraining order against the guy."

Catherine frowned. "Did he hit her?"

"Well . . . not exactly—he would kinda manhandle her, sometimes. Anyway, he kept coming in here, making scenes, causin' trouble. Hell, Lipton practically choked one of my regulars here, once."

The image of the strangled woman leapt into Catherine's mind. "You call the police on him?"

"Naw. You remember how it is, Cath—like I said, the guy Lipton got into it with, he was a regular. Didn't want no trouble, either. After that, I got the restraining order to keep Lipton out."

"Could we talk to this regular?"

Kapelos found a glass to dry with a dirty towel and considered that. "You ain't gonna make no trouble for him, Cath, right? I mean, he's a right guy."

In other words, married.

"No trouble, Ty," Catherine said. "The detectives'll just want to ask a couple questions."

Kapelos shrugged again and said, "Guy's name is Marty Fleming."

"Know where we can find him?"

The bar owner thought about that and dried two more glasses. "He ain't been in for a while. Last I heard, he was dealing over at Circus Circus."

"When did this run-in with Jenna's boyfriend happen?"

"Oh, three . . . maybe four months ago."

She patted the man's hand, where it rested on the counter. "Thanks, Ty. By the way, restraining order or not—you didn't happen to see Lipton in here tonight?"

Kapelos shook his head. "Nope; but I was in the back, in the office, most of the time. Ask the girls, or maybe Worm."

"The DJ?"

"Yeah. He knows Lipton. Anyway, I've seen 'em sit and chew the fat, before."

"Thanks for the coffee," Catherine said, and had a final sip.

The CSI was starting away when Kapelos said, "She was a nice girl, Cath—like you. Mighta got outa the business one day. . . . Do me a favor?"

"Try to."

"Catch the son of a bitch?"

She grinned at him. "That's why they pay me the medium-sized bucks."

Catherine crossed the room to the opposite corner where the DJ was just pulling on his jacket. "You speak to a detective yet?"

He shook his head. Worm was maybe twenty-five, his black satin jacket bearing a Gibson guitar logo on the left breast. He wore black jeans, Reeboks, and a black T-shirt with a MUSIC GO ROUND logo stenciled across the front. "That lady cop, she told me to wait around for her."

Catherine nodded. "Detective Conroy. Shouldn't be long. As soon as she's done in the dressing room, she'll be out here."

"It's all right," he said, with a good-natured shrug. "I've got nothin' better to do anyway. Still on the clock."

"So they call you Worm?"

He flashed an easy smile. "Name's Chris Ermey. Why they call me Worm's a long story—let's just say it involves a tequila bottle."

"I'll take your word for it," Catherine said, with a little smile. "Ty mentioned you know a guy named Ray Lipton."

"Yeah, sure, I know Ray."

"See him in here tonight?"

Worm thought about that for a long moment. "I might have."

Catherine cocked an eyebrow. "*Might* have?"

"Gets pretty smoky in here, but I thought I saw him, across the room—see, Ray usually wears that one jacket of his."

She nodded, letting him tell it in his own way, his own time.

"It's kinda like a letter jacket, 'cept it's denim with, like, tan cotton sleeves. Has the name of his company—Lipton Construction? On the back."

"And you saw him tonight."

"I saw a jacket like that, across the bar tonight—near the private dancer rooms? Guy had a cap on and dark glasses, coulda been Ray— only I think he had a beard."

"Does Ray have a beard?"

"When I first met him he did. Then he didn't. And I haven't seen him for a while, so he coulda grown it back. Hell, come to think of it, it probably *was* Ray. He hated Jenna working here, y'know."

"Thanks, Mr. Ermey," Catherine said.

"Am I done now?"

"No—I was just getting a little background. The detective will be with you soon, and go over all of this again."

The DJ nodded, said, "Fine with me, still on the clock," plopped on a chair, fished a pack of cigarettes out of somewhere and lit up.

Catherine went back down the hall, where she found Sara packing up the last of their gear. Conroy, moving briskly, came down the hall from the dressing room end.

"Get anything?" Catherine asked.

"Her boyfriend seems prime." She glanced at her notepad. "One Ray Lipton—lot of the girls mentioned him. Said he had an attitude about Jenna dancing here."

"Yeah, I heard that story too," Catherine said, and quickly filled the detective in on what Ty had told her.

"Doin' my job again, Catherine?" Conroy asked, kidding.

"I figured Ty might open up to me," Catherine said, lifting her shoulders and putting them down again. "For old time's sake."

"Well, evidently the Patrick woman lived with another dancer, a . . ." Conroy checked her notes. ". . . Tera Jameson. They say Jameson used to work here, too, but took a job at another club, Showgirl World, about three months ago."

"Movin' on up," Catherine said.

"I'm going to talk to the DJ," Conroy said, "then follow up with Kapelos—half an hour, I'll be done here."

"We're wrapping up now," Sara said.

"If I can find Ray Lipton tonight," Conroy said, moving off, "I'll be bringing him in for questioning—you two want a piece?"

Sara and Catherine traded looks, then both gave Conroy nods.

Catherine said, "Let us know when you get back to HQ. In the meantime, we'll run our findings over to the lab and get the DNA tests started."

The two CSIs had the SUV loaded up when Sara remembered the videotapes; Catherine went back inside to talk to Ty Kapelos one last time.

"Ty," Catherine said, "we're going to need tonight's security tapes."

Kapelos was seated on a bar stool now, on the customer side of the counter; he was smoking the stubby remains of a foul cigar. "No problem, Cath. Got 'em in back."

Five minutes later he handed her a grocery bag brimming with videotapes.

Her eyebrows rose. "These are all from *tonight*?"

"Yeah, sure," Ty said, as he swept his hand around the bar, a king gesturing to his kingdom. "Eight cameras—can't be too careful, in this business. One over the door, one on each corner of the stage, two behind the bar, and that one at the end of the hallway. Seems like every other asshole who walks in the place is lookin' to sue me over some goddamn thing or another. Tapes don't lie."

"Thanks, Ty," Catherine said, arms filled with the bag, the heft of it reassuring. "We'll get these back to you."

"Keep 'em till ten years from Christmas," he said, "if it'll help get that son of a bitch."

Catherine glanced around, to make sure no one was looking, and gave the bar owner a kiss on the stubbly cheek.

Then—once again—she was out of there.

4

Arthur and Millie Blair lived in an anonymous, cookie-cutter white-frame two-story with a well-tended barely sloping lawn on a quiet street in a fairly well-to-do neighborhood not far from the UNLV campus, where Mr. Blair worked. The effect of the Lynn Pierce disappearance on the Blairs was at once apparent, when Brass and Grissom rolled up in the unmarked car: every light in the house was on, lighting the grounds like a prison yard.

To Brass, the Blairs seemed like nice people, salt-of-the-earth church-goers who kept to themselves mostly, worked hard, saved money, raised their only son the best way they knew how. Then, one day, their lives had changed forever—just because of who they were acquainted with.

Happened every day. Somebody had to live next door to JonBenet and her parents; someone had to take the apartment next to Jeffrey Dahmer; John Wayne Gacy had nextdoor neighbors on his quiet street; O.J.'s wife Nicole had girl friends close to her.

Lynn Pierce was Millie's friend, Arthur's too, and had trusted them with the tape that might now be the only link to what Brass still hoped was just a missing persons case, and not a murder. Even though the disappearance was in no way the fault of this nice couple, Brass could see the guilt there on their faces.

He could tell they felt they should *know* where she'd gone, even though they couldn't possibly have that information. Like most people caught up in a tragedy, the Blairs battled the feeling that somehow, some way, they should have done something, anything, to prevent this terrible situation . . . and they hadn't.

Yes, they could have come to the authorities with the tape right after Lynn brought it to them; but the Pierce woman had asked them to hold onto it for her. They couldn't have realized she might have anticipated her own murder, and was leaving a smoking gun behind, to identify her killer.

Only right now Brass did not have a murder—just a missing person. Nonetheless, he had brought Gil Grissom along, since at present the criminalist and his people were the only ones really, truly looking for Lynn Pierce.

The couple sat on their tasteful beige couch across from Brass and Grissom. Mr. Blair was in the white shirt, striped tie, and gray slacks he'd probably worn to work that day. Nervously, the man pushed his dark-rimmed glasses back up his nose, so thick-lensed they exaggerated his eyes—to comic effect in other circumstances. Next to him, his wife Millie had on black slacks and a black-and-white striped silk blouse—dignified attire, vaguely suggesting mourning. She kept her arms crossed in front of her, clutched to herself, as if they could somehow keep out the problems that now faced them.

Grissom, like a priest in black but without the collar, perched on the edge of a tan La-Z-Boy, as if afraid to sit lest the thing might swallow him whole. Grissom, it seemed to Brass, seemed uncomfortable with comfort. On the other hand, Grissom surely knew as well as Brass that this was not going to be a pleasant interview.

After clearing his throat, Brass asked, "So, Mrs. Blair, you don't believe that Mrs. Pierce would abandon her husband and daughter?"

"No, I don't." She looked at him curiously. "Do you?"

Brass smiled meaninglessly. "It's not important what I believe, ma'am. What's important is that we find Mrs. Pierce."

Mrs. Blair unfolded herself a little, revealed the tissue in her right hand, and dabbed at her eyes. "Lynn would never run off like that, and not tell anyone where she's going. That's just not her. Not at all."

"Help me get to know her, then."

"She's . . ." Mrs. Blair searched for the word. ". . . sounds corny but . . . she's sweet." The woman glanced toward her husband, who took her hand in his. "We met a year or so ago, when she joined our church . . . then our women's Bible study group."

"You didn't know the Pierces before that?"

"No." She smiled—it was half melancholy, half nervous. "I think Lynn had a change of heart, a change of . . . spirit . . . direction."

"I see," Brass said, not seeing at all. Grissom was looking at the woman as if she were something on a lab slide.

"Before she met the Lord, Lynn had a different set of values, a different social circle . . . but since she joined our group, she and I became good friends—best friends."

"Would you say Lynn is reliable? Could she ever be . . . flighty?"

Mrs. Blair smiled at the absurdity of the thought. "Oh, Detective Brass, you can always count on Lynn. If she says she's going to do something, she does it."

"I see."

"That's why I was so surprised last night when she phoned to tell me she was on her way over—*right* over—and then never showed up."

"Tell us about that phone call," Brass said. "How did she sound?"

She glanced at her husband; they were holding hands like sweethearts. "I feel so bad about that . . ."

"Darling," Mr. Blair said, "it's all right."

His wife went on: "I've thought and thought about it since last night. I knew at the time she was upset, but I should have heard it then—she sounded distraught. Even terrified, but trying to . . . you know . . . hide it a little."

"You're sure about this?" Brass asked.

She shook her head, sighed. "I'm not sure about anything, anymore. I've replayed it so many times in my mind, I don't know if she *really* sounded distraught or if I'm putting my own feelings into it. . . . I won't lie to you, Detective Brass, I have . . . nervous problems. Sometimes I take medication."

Brass glanced at Grissom, but the criminalist's eyes were fixed upon the woman. The detective said, "Is that right?"

"Yes—Prozac."

Her husband added, "A small dosage."

"Well," she said. "Prozac or no Prozac . . . I think Lynn was distraught. Really and truly."

"Any idea what was troubling her?"

With a tiny edge of impatience, Arthur Blair said, "Maybe it was her husband threatening to cut her up in little pieces."

Brass nodded. "I don't mean to downplay the tape. But remember, some husbands and wives make those kind of idle threats all the time—"

"We don't," Mr. Blair said.

Brass continued: "And, at any rate, that was an argument from the day before. Did you get a sense of what *specifically* was troubling her the afternoon she called?"

Glumly, Mrs. Blair shook her head. "No. She didn't tell me what it was, exactly . . . and I'd have no way of guessing."

"Was she upset with her husband? I mean, this is a woman who went to the trouble of capturing her husband's verbal abuse on tape, after all."

"That was my assumption, but when I asked her, directly, if it was another argument with Owen, she kind of . . . dodged the issue."

Mr. Blair sat forward. "It must have been about Owen. Lynn calls Millie all the time when Owen becomes . . . uh . . . overbearing."

"That's happened a lot?"

"I don't know if it's fair to say 'a lot,' " Mrs. Blair said, thoughtfully. "She does call other times, though."

"Has she ever called upset about something other than her husband's abusive behavior?"

"Lori," Mr. Blair blurted, before his wife could answer. "Their daughter—she aggravates Lynn almost as much as Owen."

"That's true," Mrs. Blair admitted, shrugging one shoulder, raising one eyebrow. "Lori gave Lynn fits . . . although—and I don't like to brag—they seem to've had a lot less trouble with her, since Lori started dating our Gary."

Brass smiled. "Then Gary's a positive influence on the Pierce girl?"

Mr. Blair smiled and nodded. "He's a good boy—follows the Lord's teachings and studies hard in school."

Brass wondered what planet this was, but said, "That's great. You're very lucky."

"No question," Mr. Blair said. "Gary's helped settle Lori down. She was a little . . . wild, before."

"Wild?" asked Brass. "How so?"

Mr. Blair was searching for the words, so Mrs. Blair answered for him: "Impetuous, I would say. She made some mistakes with boys . . . drugs. It's an evil world out there, Detective Brass."

"I've noticed."

Mrs. Blair went on, in a pleased rush: "But between Gary's good influence, and Lynn's good parenting, they got her straightened out."

"Despite her father," Mr. Blair grumbled.

"Anyway," Mrs. Blair said, "I would say the girl's doing fine now. Better grades, active in church, doesn't try to dress like those . . . slatternly singers that are so popular now—like Lori *used* to."

"Even so," Brass said, "it would seem Lynn's had more than her share of stress in her life—would you agree?"

The Blairs exchanged searching looks.

Then, at the same time, Mr. Blair said, "Yes," as Mrs. Blair said, "No."

The two laughed in awkward embarrassment, and Brass waited for them to sort it out themselves, each saying, "You first," and "No, you." Finally, Mrs. Blair said, "Lynn has stress, but I'm not sure it's any more than anyone else, you know, in these troubled times."

Brass sat forward. "You mean to say, you don't consider her problems with her daughter, and her abusive husband, exceptional?"

Mrs. Blair shrugged with her eyebrows. "Well, I think the trouble with Lori, at least, is behind them."

"But what about with Owen?"

Mrs. Blair turned to her husband. Arthur Blair's lips peeled back and his eyes narrowed. The calm Christian removed his mask to reveal an angry human beneath. "Owen Pierce is a worthless, Godless son of a . . ." Blair's voice trailed off and his knuckles turned white on the arm of the sofa as he struggled to control his emotions. His wife slipped her arm around his shoulder, comfortingly.

Captain Jim Brass had spent enough time with the Blairs, and people like them, to know that for Arthur Blair to come as close as he had to calling that son of a bitch Pierce a son of a bitch indicated an unfathomable depth of anger toward Owen Pierce.

"I take it you listened to the tape?" Blair asked, his voice still edged with an unChristian viciousness.

"Yes, sir." Brass nodded toward Grissom. "We did."

Blair sighed heavily. "Then you know what that monster must be capable of, to threaten his wife with that." He shifted on the couch, sitting forward. "Understand something, Detective—I wouldn't have allowed Gary to get involved with Lori if I didn't think that Lynn was going to . . . divest herself of Owen, and soon."

Millie Blair patted her husband's arm in an effort to calm him.

"Normally," Mrs. Blair said, "our faith discourages divorce. But

Pastor Dan says, when a spouse has fallen into satanic ways, a person must protect one's self, and children."

Brass winced. "You don't mean . . . literally . . . that Owen Pierce practiced satanism?"

"Of course not," Mr. Blair said, sitting back, calmer. "But he's a . . . devil . . . a demon himself. Capable of the worst atrocities. . . ."

For the first time, Grissom spoke. "So, then, Mr. Blair—I take it you think Owen Pierce has made good on his threat to cut her into 'little pieces'?"

Arthur Blair's eyes became huge behind the lenses and his wife's curled-fingered hand went to her mouth, where she bit a knuckle. Grissom might have slapped them, the way his words registered.

"That is what you think, isn't it?" he pressed. "Isn't that why you brought the tape to us?"

Mrs. Blair stared at her lap and covered her face with one hand and began to cry, quietly. Mr. Blair, slipping an arm around his wife's shoulders, gave a tired nod.

Yes, Brass thought, *Gil really has a way with people.*

Grissom pressed on. "Do you think there are any circumstances at all under which Lynn might have just . . . left?"

Trembling with tears, Mrs. Blair shook her head.

Calmly, Grissom said, "Mr. Pierce said his wife had a significant amount of money in her own name and could have used it to disappear."

"She had money," Mrs. Blair conceded, the tears subsiding, "but it was all tied up in investments . . . stocks, bonds, CDs."

Mr. Blair concurred: "None of it was liquid enough for her to get to easily."

Nodding, Mrs. Blair went on. "She complained about that. It was something Owen talked her into. Even though she had her own money, she had little cash. I don't think I ever saw her with more than, say, fifty dollars in her purse. Even though the money was hers, Owen seemed to keep her on a tight leash."

The interview continued for a few minutes, but neither Brass nor Grissom found any new ground to cover. The Blairs had been unfailingly cooperative, but they were weary, and the detective and the criminalist knew nothing more was to be learned here, at least not right now.

On the way back, Grissom rode up front with Brass.

"Do *you* think Owen Pierce is the devil?" Brass said to the CSI, half-kidding.

"No," Grissom said, seeming distant even for him. "But he's a hell of a suspect."

At headquarters, back from the strip club, Catherine sat down in the layout room, with a notepad and pen, the Dream Doll tapes, and a VCR. Meanwhile, Sara took their findings to Greg Sanders so he could begin testing.

The tapes weren't labeled, so each one was a new adventure. The first one had been from the back right corner of the stage, the camera farthest from the door, the bar, and far to the left of the hallway. Only the chairs around the stage on the backside were visible from this angle.

No one fitting the description of Ray Lipton came into view. Catherine flew through the tape on fast forward, knowing she would view the tape more carefully later. For now, she just wanted to see what Worm, the cheerful DJ, had seen. Ejecting that tape, she moved on to the next one. This camera hung behind the left side of the bar, nearer the front door.

Halfway through the tape, Catherine was about to give up and move on, when she glimpsed, on the fuzzy black-and-white picture, a two-tone jacket. Stopping, she rewound the tape until the jacket came into view, and went in reverse, then pushed PLAY.

The guy came into view wearing the denim and tan jacket, a ball cap pulled low, dark glasses, and jeans. He walked through the shot and out the other side. She rewound it, ran it again. Something on the guy's face . . . a beard? Worm had said Lipton might have grown his beard back; hard to tell with this tape. Popping the cassette out, Catherine went to the next, then the next—one after another, until she finally got through them all.

This Lipton guy, it seemed, had gone out of his way to avoid the camera. He hadn't walked over to the bar, for a drink; and the camera above the door had gotten barely a glimpse of him . . . none of the stage cameras caught more than a snatch of him. Of course, Catherine told herself, with that restraining order, Lipton wasn't supposed to be in there anyway, so maybe he was just being careful.

Only the camera at the head of the hallway got a decent shot of him, and that was of his back as he led busty, leggy Jenna through the door. Even with the poor quality of the tape, Catherine was able to make out the words Lipton Construction on the back of the jacket, as the couple disappeared out of frame.

Catherine sped the tape forward, until the figure in the jacket . . . bearded, all right . . . returned for a quick exit—alone.

"Conroy's back."

Catherine spun to see Sara standing in the doorway.

Sara ambled over to the monitor. "Anything good on?"

Catherine nodded. "Looks like Lipton was there, all right—got a good shot of his jacket going down the hallway with Jenna Patrick."

"Time on those tapes?"

"Yeah . . ." Catherine pointed to her notes. "Time jibes. And Lipton, or anyway a guy in a Lipton Construction jacket, comes back out of the lap-dance cubicle . . . alone."

"Interesting," Sara said. "But why watch TV, when a live performance is available? . . . Come on. Conroy's got the star of your show in interrogation."

They walked quickly down several connecting hallways and ducked into the observation room next to interrogation. Through the two-way mirror, they could see Ray Lipton, directly across from them—sitting alone, eyes cast down, the streaks of tears drying on his cheeks.

"He must've loved her," Sara said. "Crying for her."

"Love's the motive of choice," Catherine said, "of many a murderer."

Lipton's hands were balled into fists and lay on the table like objects, forgotten ones at that. The denim jacket with the tan sleeves hung over the back of the chair. He was thinner and shorter than Catherine would have expected from someone in construction, with hazel eyes, a long, narrow nose and, to her surprise, no beard.

Could she have been mistaken about what she'd seen on the video? He might have shaved, but . . . no, his cheeks were shadowed blue with stubble, indicating Lipton hadn't shaved for many hours.

A moment later, Detective Erin Conroy entered the interrogation room, a Styrofoam cup of water in one hand, notepad in the other. She placed the cup in front of Lipton, said, "There you go," and sat at the end of the table, giving her observers a view of both of them. Lipton picked up the cup, sipped from it, returned it to the table, then leaned his elbows on the wood, running his hands through his longish brown hair.

"I can't *believe* she's dead," he said, his voice quiet and raspy, a rusty tool long out of use.

Catherine looked at Sara as if to say, "What's he trying to pull?"

Lipton looked across at Conroy, his expression pitiful. "We were going to be married, you know."

"Again, Mr. Lipton, I'm sorry for your loss," Conroy said. "But there are some things we need to talk about."

Lipton looked down, shaking his head, tears again trailing slowly down his cheeks. "Can't it . . . can't it *wait?*"

"No. The first hours of a murder investigation are vital. I'm sure you understand that."

"Murder . . . a gentle soul like Jenna . . . murdered. . . ."

"For Jenna being a 'gentle soul,' Mr. Lipton," Conroy said, no inflection in her voice, "you two seemed to fight a great deal . . . especially for a couple about to be married."

"But . . . we didn't fight," he sputtered. Then his eyes moved in thought. "Well . . . no more than anybody else. *All* couples fight."

Conroy shook her head. "All couples don't include a partner with a restraining order on them . . . like the one the court issued on you, to keep you away from where Jenna worked—right?"

"Oh Christ," Lipton said, all the air rushing out of him. Catherine and Sara watched as, before their eyes, sorrow turned to despair. "You . . . you think *I* killed her!"

"I didn't say that, Mr. Lipton."

"Do I . . . need a lawyer?"

Conroy ducked that. "No accusations have been made. I simply asked if there isn't an in-force restraining order against you."

"You must know there is," he said, sullenly. Now his voice grew agitated: "I loved Jenna, but I *hated* her job—everybody knew that. But that doesn't mean I killed her. Jesus, she was going to quit! We were going to be married."

"Where did you meet Jenna?"

"At . . . Dream Dolls."

"You were a customer."

"At first, but. . . ." His look was more pleading than angry now.

"How do you explain being in Dream Dolls tonight?" Conroy asked. "Considering the restraining order."

Now he sat up, alert suddenly. "Dream Dolls? I wasn't in Dream Dolls! You think I want to go to jail?"

Conroy didn't answer that.

"Lady, I was home all night."

"That's not what everyone at the club says."

"What do you mean by 'everyone'? Who *says* I was there?"

"Just the owner, the girls, and the DJ."

"What the hell . . ." Lipton's voice was incredulous; he shook his head, desperately. "Well, they're mistaken. They're wrong! Or maybe lying!"

"All of them? Wrong? Or lying?"

"That fucking Kapelos, he hates me. He's the one took out the restraining order! He'd say *anything*. Where was he when Jenna was . . . was . . ."

He couldn't seem to say it.

Conroy said, "And the rest of them? Lying? Wrong?"

He sighed, shrugged. "I don't know what else to say—I was home all night. Honest to God. I swear."

"Anybody to verify that?"

"I live alone, except . . . when Jenna stays over."

And he began to cry. To sob, burying his face in his hands.

Catherine left the observation room, circled to the other door, and strode in. Lipton jumped in his seat, looking up, though Conroy didn't even turn.

"Who . . . who are you?" Lipton asked, face a wet smear, eyelashes pearled.

"Crime scene investigator, Mr. Lipton. Catherine Willows." She came around and sat opposite him. "Would you like to know how I've been spending the night?"

He swallowed thickly, shrugging as if nothing could rock him now—he'd been through it all. But he hadn't.

Catherine said, "I've been watching videotape of you at Dream Dolls—videotape captured on security cameras . . . tonight."

His eyes widened, lashes glistening. "What? But that's . . . that's just not possible." His voice had a tremor, as if he was about to break down, utterly.

Still Catherine pressed, gesturing to his jacket. "I saw Jenna going into one of the back rooms, with a man about your size, wearing your jacket."

"My jacket?"

"The jacket had your Lipton Construction logo on the back. Denim with tan sleeves—just like that one."

Something close to relief softened his face. "Oh, well shit. I had those made up for all my guys, and even a few of our better customers."

Conroy, poised to write in her notepad, asked, "How many jackets like this exist?"

Another shrug. "Twenty-five . . . maybe thirty."

"Could you be more exact?"

"Not off the top of my head. Probably my secretary could. At work."

A bad feeling in the pit of her stomach started to talk to Catherine, and she wished those security cams had caught a better face shot of the person wearing the jacket in the bar. *Was it Lipton or not?*

Catherine asked, "Have you ever worn a beard, Mr. Lipton?"

"What? Yeah . . . yes."

"Recently?"

"No. That was last year."

"You didn't shave off your beard, this evening."

"No! Hell no."

Catherine studied the man. Then she said, "I'll need your jacket, Mr. Lipton."

"Sure. But I'm tellin' you—I wasn't there."

"Jenna was strangled with an electrical tie."

Lipton flinched, then shook his head. He could obviously see where this was going.

She said, "And when I search your truck, I'm going to find electrical ties in the back, aren't I?"

"You . . . you could search a lot of trucks and find that."

Catherine could tell Conroy was starting to have her doubts about the suspect, too, particularly when the detective tried another tack.

"While you were home alone tonight, Mr. Lipton, did you call anybody?" Conroy asked. "Anybody call you?"

He thought for a moment, then shook his head.

"D'you order pizza or something?"

This required no thought: "No."

"What *did* you do this evening?"

Lipton lifted his hands, palms up, and shrugged. "I watched TV— that's it."

"What did you watch?"

"Was it . . . a football game?"

Conroy leaned forward now. "What, you're asking me?"

"No, no, I know! Yeah, I watched a football game."

"What game, what network, what time?"

He collected his thoughts. "I didn't see the whole thing—I came in during the third quarter. Indianapolis Colts against the Kansas City Chiefs."

Conroy was writing that down.

Lipton went on: "Just as I sat down, Peterson kicks a field goal for the Chiefs . . . then on the kickoff, some guy I never heard of ran it back for a touchdown."

"That was the very first thing you saw?" Conroy asked.

"Yeah. Very first. Field goal. Peterson."

"We'll check that out, Mr. Lipton," Catherine said. "If you're innocent, we'll prove it. But if you're guilty . . ."

His eyes met hers.

". . . we'll prove that too."

"I'm not worried," he said.

But he sure as hell looked it.

5

Amid pine trees in a deceptively peaceful setting, a low-slung non-descript modern building played host to a maze of hallways connecting the conference rooms, labs, offices, locker room, and lounge of the Las Vegas Police Department's criminalistics division. A sterile, institutional ambience was to be expected, but the blue-tinged fluorescent lighting and preponderance of mostly glass walls gave CSI HQ an aquarium-like feel that Nick Stokes, at times, felt he was swimming through.

In one of these hallways, Nick rounded a corner and all but bumped into Grissom, who had just returned from the interview with the Blairs.

Grissom paused, as if it took him a moment to register and recognize his colleague, who had also paused, flashing his ready smile.

The CSI supervisor did not smile, nor did he bother with a hello. "Nick, Sara's teamed with Catherine on the stripper case—I need you to take over the search of the Pierce records."

Nick shrugged. "No problem."

"It's all in Sara's office—work there . . . she won't mind. Look at the Pierce woman's computer, her bank accounts, ATM, calling card, the works. Find us something."

"How far has Sara gotten?"

"Start over. Fresh eye."

"Okay." Nick risked half a smirk. "I don't suppose you considered assigning me to that exotic dancer case."

Grissom's bland baby-faced countenance remained expressionless. "No. Not for a second. Warrick, either. He's on the Pierce case, too."

"You gotta admit, this doesn't sound like as much fun as interviewing nude girls."

Now, finally, Grissom smiled a little. "But you're like me, Nick— only interested in truth and justice, right?"

Then Grissom was gone, leaving Nick to wonder if that had been sarcasm. . . . Sometimes it was damn tough to tell, with that guy.

Nick set himself up in Sara's office—she was out in the field with Catherine, but Grissom was probably right, she wouldn't mind. Sara was that rare individualist who relished being a team player. Though his specialty was hair and fiber analysis, Nick—like all the CSIs Grissom had assembled—was versatile enough to step in and take over any other criminalist's job. And a video-game buff like Nick was hardly a stranger to computers.

With a sigh and a mental farewell to his bevy of beautiful dancers, Nick Stokes buried himself in the computer records of Lynn Pierce. E-mails were still coming in, mostly junk, but one from her brother indicated she hadn't gone to visit him . . . unless something really clever was going on—a possibility that, however far-fetched, had to be considered.

Another e-mail, from a Sally G., whose handle was AvonLady, was even less promising. Several mass e-mailings from Lynn Pierce's church indicated a limited and specific social circle. But Nick kept digging and had been at it about an hour when Grissom stuck his head in Sara's office and announced their first real chunk of evidence.

"You coming with?" Nick asked.

"No. Take Warrick."

Less than two minutes later, Nick strode into the locker room, where Warrick sat on the bench in front of his locker, his head hanging down, a jock who just lost the big game.

"Who cleaned your clock?" Nick asked.

Warrick gave him a slow exhausted burn. "Me, myself, and all that overtime."

"Well, guess what—we just bought some more."

Looking up, alert suddenly, Warrick asked, "What gives?"

"Grissom got a call from Brass—Lynn Pierce's Toyota's turned up in long-term parking at McCarran."

Warrick was on his feet. "Yeah, I was hoping to put in a few more hours—let's go before I change my mind."

McCarran International Airport was one of the five busiest airports in the nation, and one of the most efficient. In the wee hours, dawn not yet a threat, airliners still screamed hello and good-bye, and cars made their way in and out of the parking lot.

Twenty-five minutes after leaving HQ—five minutes of which had been taken up dealing with security at the parking-lot entrance—Nick and Warrick's black Tahoe pulled to a halt behind a squad car that blocked in a white 1995 Toyota Avalon. As they climbed down from the Tahoe a uniformed officer got out of his squad and came back to meet them.

"Anybody been near here?" Warrick asked.

The uniformed man, a fair-haired, weathered pro in his forties, shook his head; his nameplate read JENKINS. "Airport security, making the rounds, recognized the car from our wants list and matched the plate, then gave us a call."

"Good catch," Warrick said.

Officer Jenkins nodded. "They've been making more frequent visits out here ever since September eleventh. Security guy stayed by the car until I got here, but he never got out of his Jeep."

"Good," Warrick said.

"You take a look?" Nick asked.

"Yeah," Jenkins said. "Walked around it once, cut it a wide swath, though—looks locked. Didn't touch shit. Didn't smell anything foul comin' from the trunk area, so I just got back in the squad and waited for you."

"Not your first time at the rodeo," Warrick said. "Thanks."

Jenkins liked that. "You fellas need me to stick around?"

"Naw," Warrick said.

Nick asked, "You call for a tow truck?"

Jenkins shook his head. "Should I have?"

"Naw, that's cool," Warrick said. "We'll get it."

"All right then," Jenkins said, and let out some air. "I'm gone."

"Thanks again," Nick called after him.

The officer waved but never turned back. He climbed into the cruiser, fired it up, and rolled away—Nick's guess was the officer's shift was also long since over and the guy had likely logged more than his own share of overtime.

Warrick used his cell phone to call for a truck. The parking lot was well lighted and, at first, they didn't need their Maglites for their work, which they began by photographing the car from every angle. Then they dusted the handles, the hood, and the trunk for prints.

"Wipe marks on the handles," Nick said.

Warrick smirked humorlessly. "Trunk too."

"Kinda makes you think maybe it wasn't Mrs. Pierce who parked it here."

"Don't let Grissom catch you at that."

Nick frowned. "At what?"

"Thinking."

Nick grinned, and Warrick motioned for them to go back to the Tahoe, and wait, which they did.

"You know, if you're in the trunk of a car," Nick said, "you're doing one of two things."

"Yeah? What's that?"

"You're a corpse waiting to get dumped, or you're sneakin' into a drive-in movie."

Warrick smiled a little. "They still got drive-in movies in Texas?"

"Last time I was home, they did."

It took forty-five minutes for the flatbed truck to arrive and another three or four for Warrick to stop Nick from bitching out the driver for taking so long. In under ten minutes, the driver—a civil servant in coveralls impervious to Nick's complaints—had hooked up the car and dragged it onto the bed.

"Well, that *was* quick," Nick admitted to the guy.

"You made my night," the driver said with no sincerity whatsoever, and disappeared into it.

Once they had the car out of the way, the pair of CSIs got out their flashlights and searched the parking space carefully, even getting down on their hands and knees—but found nothing. Satisfied they hadn't overlooked anything, they drove back to the CSI garage to take a more careful look at the car.

After putting on coveralls, they entered the bay where the Avalon sat like a museum exhibit. Fluorescent lights gave the car a bleached, almost ghostly cast. Warrick used a slim-jim to undo the lock.

"Twelve seconds," Nick said with a chuckle. "Man, you're slippin'."

"Want me to lock it back up, and give you a shot?"

Waving his hands in surrender, Nick said, "No, no, that's okay—if I showed you up, you'd lose the will to live."

"Yeah, well I'm just hangin' on as it is," Warrick harumphed, and opened the door. He dusted the driver's door handle, the armrest, the steering wheel and the gear shift. Nick did the passenger side handle, armrest, and the glove compartment. Again, they noticed that the car had been wiped.

"Somebody's hiding something," Warrick said.

"Usually are," Nick nodded, "or we wouldn't be involved—we're just going to have to look harder."

"Yeah, well I better start looking with my eyes open, then," Warrick said. He stared down at the armrest of the open driver's door. "You see that funky power-window button?"

Nick glanced down at the passenger arm rest. "Yeah, it's got that weird . . . lip, in the front."

"So . . . how do you suppose one would go about raising the window?"

Nick frowned—was this a trick question? "Well, 'one' would put his finger under the lip . . . and pull up."

"Which should leave the clever team of criminalists with . . . what?"

Nick smiled, wide. "A fingerprint on the underside . . ."

"Very good, class."

So Warrick printed the underside of the power-window button . . . and got a partial. He got another partial off the back of the gear shift lever, and Nick lifted a pretty good print off the passenger-side window button. The prints would go into the computer as soon as they finished with the rest of the vehicle. They would also need to take Owen Pierce's prints, of course, and daughter Lori's.

"You got a preference over the trunk," Nick asked, "or the interior?"

Warrick shrugged. "Whichever."

"I'll take the trunk."

"Go for it, drive-in boy," Warrick said dryly, and opened the passenger-side door. Sinking to his knees, next to the car, he shone his Maglite on the floor and started going over the carpeting, inch by inch. After his inspection he would vacuum the floor as well; but for now, he just wanted to see the car, up close and personal.

The two CSIs worked in church-like silence, each focused on his particular task. Nothing on the passenger-side floor, nothing in the glove compartment, nothing wedged into the seat. Warrick looked in the cup holders, in the console storage area, even ejected the plastic sleeve of the CD player and found nothing.

Moving around to the rear of the vehicle, Warrick stopped for a moment. "Anything?"

Nick was bent over the trunk, his face buried under the spare tire. "Nothing—you?"

"Zip squared. Somebody's cleaned this car within an inch of its life. It's like it just came off the showroom floor. It's got everything but the new car smell."

Nick beamed at him, mockingly. "I know where you can get a little spray can that'll provide that, if you want."

"I'll pass."

"So we keep lookin'?"

"Keep looking," world-weary Warrick said, and moved to the driver's side of the car.

As he went to lean in, the beam of his flashlight swept over the headrest and . . . *something glinted.*

It was there, then it was gone—like the car had winked. Warrick frowned. The Avalon had tan cloth seats . . . what could've glinted?

He swept the flashlight over the headrest a couple of times, but nothing showed up. The car did not wink at him. He leaned in, inspected the headrest, saw nothing. He raised the Maglite so that the beam shone straight down. Leaning in closer, he looked at the seam that ran across the top of the headrest. Then he saw it . . .

. . . gleaming up at him: *a tiny piece of glass.*

After photographing the mini-shard at rest, Warrick tweezered the fragment free. He carefully studied it for a moment, but its miniscule size kept its origin a secret.

After bagging his prize, Warrick went back to the seam. Moving slowly, a stitch at a time, he found first one blonde hair, then another. Both hairs, like those on the brush already in evidence, could easily belong to Lynn Pierce. Then he found another hair—shorter, darker.

Bingo, he thought.

He stored all three hairs in separate baggies and went back inside the Avalon for one last look at that helpful headrest—first the side on the right, then the top, and finally down the left side, nearest the door. He shone the light at the underside of the headrest and picked up on a tiny spot on one of the stitches, about the size of a period. His experience told him the answer to a question he didn't bother to ask.

"Found it!" he yelled, but his voice remained cool.

"All right," Nick said, coming around from the back. "Found what?"

"Blood."

Nick leaned in. "Where?"

Warrick showed him.

"I think we have a crime scene," Nick said.

Warrick said, "I think we have a crime scene."

They got a photo of the blood speck, after which Warrick carefully scraped the tiny dot into an evidence bag.

Grissom strolled in and looked through the open driver's door. "Clean car."

"Too clean," Nick said.

"And yet not clean enough," Warrick said.

"Give," Grissom said.

They explained what they had found so far.

"What's next?"

"Luminol," Warrick answered, shrugging as if to say, *What else?*

"If there's one spot of blood in that car," Grissom said, nodding, "there's probably more."

When they sprayed the luminol on, any other blood would fluoresce. No matter how carefully the car had been cleaned, blood would glow blue-green at even one part per million.

"Before you hit that interior with luminol," Grissom said, "are you otherwise through in there? Anything else you found? Noticed?"

Nick could sense they were being sucker-punched, but nonetheless he shrugged and said, "No, that's it."

Warrick, though, said, "Why, Gris? You got something?"

Grissom leaned inside the car for a look of his own; his eyes were everywhere. "How tall was Lynn Pierce?"

Nick thought that over. "Five-four?"

"That's right," Grissom said, withdrawing himself from the vehicle. "And if she was five-four and drove her car to the airport and left it parked there . . . why is the driver's seat all the way back?"

Nick and Warrick traded *how-the-hell-does-he-do-it* looks.

Grissom asked, "Or did you move the seat, Warrick? Going over the interior?"

Warrick shook his head.

Grissom turned to Nick, asking pleasantly, "You?"

Another head shake.

Grissom looked at Warrick. "Thoughts?"

Warrick sighed to his toes, holding up his hands in admission of frailty. "I'll fingerprint the power-seat button . . . *then* we hit the interior with luminol."

"Smart thinking," Grissom said, then he turned and left.

"I hate him," Nick said, admiringly.

"Yeah," Warrick said. "He's good."

The power-seat button stuck out from the side of the seat like a tiny shiny peanut. Warrick dusted it . . . and found out it too had been wiped.

"This is starting to piss me off," Warrick said as he reached for the luminol. "Every time we get hold of something, it grins and gets away."

Warrick started at the floor and worked his way up, spraying the luminol on the driver's-side floor mat, the seat, and then the headrest. Instantly, the surfaces became dotted with bluish green pinpoints.

"Nick," Warrick said, "you gotta see this."

Nick peered in from the passenger side. "Uh oh . . . I don't think Lynn Pierce caught her flight."

Gravely, Warrick shook his head. "Flew apart, maybe. . . ." He sprayed luminol over the backseat and the passenger side, but all the blood seemed to be concentrated in the driver's seat. "Let's get the seat covers off, and see what's underneath."

The two used utility knives and, whenever possible, followed seams, to cause as little damage as possible, preserving the seat covers. Nick climbed in the back and attacked the driver's seat from the passenger side, while Warrick knelt on the floor next to the car and started cutting the edges on his side. In short order they had the covers off the seat, the back and the headrest.

Then they were staring in disbelief at the foam rubber cushions. Dark stains spread ominously from the headrest down the back to a low spot on the back edge of the seat.

Finally Nick said, "Somebody got shot in the head . . . would be my guess."

"Educated guess," Warrick said, eyebrows lifted. "Damn. . . . Let's find out if it was Lynn Pierce."

"We got hairbrush hairs," Nick said. "But DNA testing is going to take a while."

"Then the sooner we get the ball rolling with Greg, the better. . . . After that, let's talk to Gris—but I think I already know what he's going to say."

Warrick shot Polaroid photos of the interior while Nick took a small scraping from the seat to use in a DNA test. After stopping by Greg Sanders in his lab, they called on Grissom, who was buried in paperwork in his office.

They explained their findings and showed him the photos of the blood-spattered seat. Grissom stared at the photos long enough to make Nick uneasy.

Finally Grissom said, "All right . . . first thing, line up one of the dayshift interns to start calling the glass companies in town."

Warrick nodded. "To see if anybody's replaced the driver's side window of a white '95 Avalon in the last few days."

Nick, nodding, too, said, "On it."

Grissom studied one of the photos again. "It's probable that fragment of glass you found came out of the original window."

"Yeah, that's our take on it," Warrick said.

"But we need to know, don't we?" Grissom tossed the grisly photo on his desk and his grin was a horrible thing. "And now we get a search warrant and go over the Pierce house again. Only this time . . . we do it right."

Nick tilted his head. "But we don't have enough to arrest Pierce—do we?"

The CSI supervisor considered that for a long moment. Then, he rattled off his mental findings, clinically: "There's the tape where he threatened to cut up his wife and there's blood in the car, but there's no body, no weapon, no DNA match for a while—I don't think we can even speculate on a motive, yet."

"In a bad marriage," Warrick said, "you won't have to look very hard."

"But we haven't looked yet," Grissom reminded them. "And the DA isn't going to want to even *talk* to us, if we don't find something better than what we have now."

"That's a crime scene," Nick said, frustrated. "Broken glass, blood spatter . . ."

Warrick was nodding, punctuating his colleague's points. "Nick's right, Gris."

Grissom said, "I'll go along with you on that, Nick—that's a crime scene . . . but what's the crime? Who's the victim? Isn't it also possible that the short dark hair and the fingerprints belong to a victim who isn't Lynn Pierce?"

Warrick rolled his eyes and asked, "Who else *could* it be?"

"Or maybe it's not a victim at all. Maybe it's the daughter—maybe she or her mom had a nosebleed."

"Ah, man," Nick groused, "you don't believe that!"

"I don't believe anything yet, Nick. The evidence will show us the way—we just need more of it."

Warrick leaned a hand on the desk. "Odds are the blood is Mrs. Pierce's, Gris. I mean, we can't find her, she doesn't seem to be using any of her credit cards or her phone card—the blood's in *her* car . . ."

"The odds say it's her," Grissom agreed. "But we don't play the odds. We put all our money on science. . . . Now, we start with the Pierce house again and find out the truth. You two go on out there. I'll call Brass and meet you there—we don't have enough for an arrest . . . yet . . . but I know just the judge to give us a search warrant."

An hour later, as dawn was breaking, Captain Jim Brass parked his Taurus behind the black Tahoe in the Pierces' driveway. "I don't see your people," Brass said.

"Maybe they're already inside," Grissom said.

"Without a warrant."

Grissom gestured with open palms. "Maybe—Pierce has cooperated so far."

"I don't like him—he's an arrogant prick."

"You have some evidence, Jim, that led you to that conclusion?"

The detective gave the criminalist a tired smile and pointed to his own gut. "Yeah, this—it's my prick detector."

Grissom's smile was skeptical. "A judge and jury may want more."

Brass summoned half a smirk. "That's what's wrong with our judicial system."

The two men climbed out of the car and walked up the sidewalk to the front door. Grissom was about to ring the bell when Warrick pulled the door open.

"He let us in," Warrick whispered, stepping out onto the stoop. "He didn't even bitch about getting woken up."

Grissom asked, also sotto voce, "What have you told him?"

"Nada," Warrick said, doing the umpire "you're out" gesture. "Not even that we found the car. Just that his wife was officially missing now, and we needed to step up the investigation . . . apologized for the early hour."

Brass was impressed. "Nice work, Brown."

Warrick ignored the compliment, saying to Grissom, "You can give him the warrant, though—he's in the living room."

His voice still low, Grissom asked, "Find anything?"

"No. . . . Either this guy is really good, or there's nothing to find."

"Stick with it."

Warrick headed in and disappeared down the hall to the left, as Grissom and Brass walked into the living room where Owen Pierce stood in fresh blue jeans and tasseled loafers, a blue Polo shirt open at the neck; he was unshaven, and sipping a cup of coffee.

"Morning," Pierce said. "Can I get you guys some coffee?"

"No thanks," Brass said, though the smell of it was tempting. He handed Pierce the warrant, who accepted it without looking at it.

"May I ask why you believe you need a search warrant?" He seemed more hurt than indignant. "Haven't I made my home available to you, in every way?"

Brass gave Grissom a look and the CSI supervisor stepped forward. "We've located your wife's car, Mr. Pierce."

"You . . . the Avalon, you mean?" He sounded genuinely surprised, his expression hopeful.

"Yes, sir," Brass said. "A few hours ago at McCarran."

Pierce tried out a smile, looking from the detective to the criminalist. "Well, that's a break for our side, isn't it?"

Brass wasn't sure who exactly was on "our side," as Pierce defined it. "It's a break in the case, Mr. Pierce. But I'm afraid the situation has taken a serious turn."

Grissom, flatly, declared, "We found blood on the driver's seat of your wife's car."

"The driver's seat was . . . there was blood?" His hopeful expression vanished, but nothing replaced it—an alert sort of blankness remained. He set his cup down on a nearby coffee table.

"Actually, the car was clean, sir." Grissom shrugged. "Well, except for a drop of blood on the headrest."

Pierce's face remained impassive as he stared Grissom down. "One drop?"

"One drop—but that was to enough to indicate we should look . . . closer."

Curiosity filled the void of his expression. "And how did you do that?"

"We peeled off the seat covers. Those can be cleaned, but underneath? Practically impossible. And we discovered a large quantity of blood on the seat's cushions."

Now confusion colored Pierce's face. "Under the seat covers? What the hell does that mean?"

"The amount of blood indicates the probability of something violent happening in the car. . . . The absence of blood on the seat covers indicates someone covering up that violence."

Shaking his head, seemingly feeling helpless, Pierce said, "I don't know what to say, Mr. Grissom . . . Detective Brass. Other than, I hope to God Lynn's all right."

God again, Brass thought. *He's all over this goddamned case.*

Grissom was asking, "Have you had an automobile accident, in the Avalon? Was it necessary to repair the driver's-side window of your wife's car recently?"

"No—why?"

"We also found glass in the car . . . and we believe it came from the driver's-side window."

Pierce began to pace a small area. "I don't know how that could be possible . . ." His eyes were wide, a frown screwing up his face. "That window's never been broken."

Grissom changed direction. "Do you own a gun?"

"What? No. Of course not."

"Never? With all these outdoorsman prints, ducks and geese and deer, I thought maybe you were a hunter."

"No. Not since I was a kid, with my dad. . . . I just like looking at a landscape that isn't desert, once in a while. Where are you going with this, Mr. Grissom?" Then a mental light bulb seemed to go on for Pierce, his eyes flaring. "You're here looking for a gun. . . . You think I killed my wife!"

Brass stepped forward. "We're not making any accusations, Mr. Pierce."

Pierce was shaking his head, his eyes wild now. "There's blood on the seat of my wife's car . . . so that means I *killed* her? This is absurd—you should be out looking for her! She's alive, I'm sure! You don't have any evidence."

Grissom said, pleasantly, "That's why we brought the search warrant, Mr. Pierce."

Warrick stepped into the living room and said, "Gris? A word?"

Grissom turned to Pierce. "May we use your kitchen, to confer?"

"Oh," Pierce said with a sarcastic wave, "be my guest! By all means!"

Other than not bothering the sleeping Lori Pierce, Nick and Warrick had searched the house from top to bottom, giving the home a much more thorough going over than the first time.

"No gun," Nick told Grissom and Brass, leaning against the kitchen counter. "No bullets, either—nothing to indicate that there's ever been a gun in the house."

"No significant new evidence?" Grissom asked glumly.

"Not of murder," Warrick said, and gave them a cat-that-ate-the-canary grin.

Grissom and Brass just looked at him.

Warrick milked it for a few seconds, then he spilled: "I found this little darling in a vent in the basement . . ."

And he held out a clear plastic bag containing a small amount of white powder. The baggie had a small red triangle stamped in one corner, a dealer's mark.

"Coke?" Grissom asked. "Pierce has cocaine in the house?"

"That's right," Warrick said, pleased to be the man of the hour.

"Not very much, though," Grissom said.

"Misdemeanor," Brass said.

"But enough to book his ass," Warrick pointed out. He held up the baggie. "You recognize this?" He showed Grissom the triangle, Brass too.

"Never seen that mark before," Grissom said.

Neither had Brass.

Grissom asked, "And there's nothing else pertaining to Mrs. Pierce?"

Nick shrugged. "Sorry, Gris. No gun, no bullets, no blood, no nothin'. We went through everything, even the drains . . . zippo."

They followed Brass and Grissom into the living room, the detective heading for Pierce, who was seated on the sofa, sipping his no doubt cold-by-now coffee.

"Mr. Pierce," Brass said, "I'm placing you under arrest."

The therapist's eyes widened, but the hand holding the coffee cup remained steady. "For . . . murder?"

Brass shook his head. "Possession of cocaine."

Grissom held up the evidence bag for Pierce to see.

Pierce made a face, tried to wave this off. "Oh, Jesus, that's *years* old! I forgot it was even in the house."

Brass put on his patented grin. "I know this'll be hard for you to believe, Mr. Pierce, but that's not the first time I've heard that."

"Hey, I used to snort some, but I haven't used since, hell . . . forever. It's an innocent mistake. When I got off it, that's one little stash I missed, when I threw out the rest."

"Interesting defense," Brass said.

Pierce let out a weight-of-the-world sigh. "Fine, fine. . . . Will I need my lawyer?"

"This small amount is just a misdemeanor, Mr. Pierce," Brass said. "Probably not, but of course it is your right to seek counsel."

"No, to hell with it," Pierce said, standing. "Let's just get this over with, so you can get back to the business of finding my wife. . . . Are you going to slap on the cuffs?"

Brass beamed at him. "Not unless you're going to make a break for it."

"I'll try to restrain myself," Pierce said. "My daughter's still in bed . . . I need to leave her a note."

"Go ahead."

"Very generous of you."

Soon the five of them were marching through the front door of the Pierce castle into the sunshine. Brass guided the suspect into the backseat while he and Grissom climbed in front. Nick and Warrick took the Tahoe.

Traffic was already heavy. They were almost halfway back before either of them said a word.

Finally, Nick asked, "There is a crime here, right? Besides misdemeanor controlled-substance possession?"

"What we have here," Warrick said, "is a crime scene . . . in search of a crime."

6

Something about Ray Lipton—his grieving manner, more than his words—made Catherine Willows want to believe his story. Of course, Catherine had also believed her ex-husband, Eddie, and she knew how well *that* had turned out.

However much her heart wanted Lipton not to have done it, the evidence told another story: the videotape (beard or no beard), the history of fighting, the weapon . . . everything pointed toward Ray. Odds were, he'd done the murder—and these were a hell of a lot better odds than you could get at any casino in town.

Greg Sanders poked his spiky-haired head into her office. "No prints on that electrical tie."

Catherine looked up from the pile of papers on her desk with a frustrated frown. "Not even a partial?"

"Of the killer, I mean." Sanders stepped inside the office, hands on hips. "Couple of smudges and a couple on the sides—all the vic's." He shook his head. "Poor baby only had a few seconds before the strap would've cut off the blood flow to her brain, y'know."

Catherine nodded gravely.

The often jokey Sanders was dead serious. "She gave it her best— tried to get a hold of it and failed. So she was an exotic dancer, huh?"

"That's right."

"Yeah, okay . . . well, I'll just get back to it, then."

Sitting back and closing her eyes and sighing, Catherine let her weight rock the chair. She sat there for a long moment, just thinking, processing the new information, sorting out her emotional reactions and putting them in one mental pile (marked "Catherine"), placing the facts in another (marked "Grissom").

Something tiny gnawed at the back of her brain . . . small but tenacious.

"Hey."

With a start, Catherine sat forward to see Sara standing in front of her.

"Hey," Catherine said.

"You ready to go?"

". . . Sure."

Sara frowned as she studied Catherine. "Sorry, I didn't mean to startle you . . . I just thought we'd go check out Lipton's truck."

Catherine rubbed her eyes. "Good idea. I could stand getting out of here."

Sara gestured toward the PD wing. "Conroy has to book Lipton, and then she wants to meet us at Jenna's apartment, to search it? And to tell her roommate the bad news." A little what-the-hell shrug—"I thought we could do Lipton's truck on the way. We probably oughta log the overtime while the case is still fresh."

Catherine nodded and rose. "Okay."

Lipton Construction had a corner building in an industrial park east of the airport. A one-story stucco affair with smoked-glass windows, dating back decades—ancient history in this town—it crouched like an ungainly beast near the entrance to the park, far away from the heavier industry. A couple of pick-ups and a Honda Accord sat in the otherwise empty parking lot out front. To the left, behind a gate and an eight-foot cyclone fence, lurked a few heavy-construction machines. Down the side of the building, two garage doors opened onto the fenced-in lot.

Sara pulled the Tahoe into the parking lot and eased into the spot next to the green Accord. Catherine wondered if any of these people knew what had happened to their boss—and their boss's fiancée—last night. They parked and climbed out of the SUV, Sara lugging a field kit.

Sara, as if reading Catherine's mind, asked, "You think they know?"

"Probably not."

"Just the same, walking in there, cold. . . . Any ideas?"

Holding up a finger in a "wait" manner, Catherine said, "Just one." She plucked her cell phone from her purse, punched in a number, pushed SEND, and waited.

Finally, a voice on the other end picked up. "Conroy."

"Willows. Lipton still being cooperative?"

"Yeah. Still claims he was home alone, too."

"Innocent people don't always have alibis, you know."

"Is that what you think he is?" the detective asked. "Innocent?"

"I think he's a suspect. And if he still wants to impress us with his cooperative attitude, why don't you have him call his construction company and pave the way for us?"

"You really think that's necessary?"

"Detective Conroy, if Lipton makes the call, his people just might be more anxious to help than if we just barge in and tell them that we've arrested their boss on suspicion of murder."

"Good point. Where are you?"

"At Lipton Construction—in the parking lot."

"Sit tight," Conroy said. "I'll call you back in five minutes."

Conroy more than kept her promise, Catherine's cell ringing in just under five.

"Lipton made the call for us," Conroy said. "He told them to play ball. They're expecting you."

"Good. Thanks."

"Catherine, I'll be questioning Lipton's people later today; but if you hear anything interesting, during the course of your evidentiary search, write it down, and let me know when we meet up at Jenna's apartment—so I have the info, going in."

"I hear you," Catherine said with a smile, and clicked off.

"We got the go-ahead?" Sara asked.

"Yeah. Lipton's staff is waiting for us . . . and Conroy gave us her roundabout blessing for a little off-the-cuff interrogation."

They walked into a roomy, undistinguished office with cream-colored walls, a handful of desks and a few file cabinets. Just inside the door they were addressed by a young woman sitting behind a metal desk, immediately to their left.

"You the cops, already?" she asked, her voice cold.

"LV Metro PD," Catherine said, displaying her I.D. "Crime scene investigators."

At a cluttered desk farther to the left, behind the woman's tidier one, sat a heavy-set thirty-something guy in an open flannel shirt and a Bulls T-shirt, eyeing the two female callers suspiciously over a mountain of papers. To his left, in the back corner, was a closed door; nearer them in the back, off to the right, a third desk sat empty.

"Ray said you were coming," the ash blonde said sullenly. "What, were you out in the parking lot all the time?"

Sara stepped forward, to the edge of the woman's desk. "Do you have a problem?"

Catherine quickly moved beside Sara, touching her arm, and said to the woman, pleasantly, "Who runs the office, please?"

"Mr. Lipton does." The ash blonde's voice was trembling and it seemed like she might cry. "And he's innocent. Ray Lipton has his faults, but he's not a killer."

"We don't decide that," Catherine said, rather disingenuously. "We just gather evidence."

The heavy-set man used the desk to help him rise. "Crime scene investigators, huh?" He had a deep, boomy voice that rattled up out of his chest like he was speaking from inside a trash can.

Catherine moved away from the secretary/receptionist's desk, to make eye contact with the hulking figure. "That's right. We'd like to see Mr. Lipton's office and his company truck."

Stepping out from behind the desk, which looked like a a playhouse toy next to him, the mountainous man lumbered forward, talking as he went: "Was that girl killed here or something? You saying this is a crime scene? Are you kiddin'?"

Sara, who did not suffer fools gladly, looked about to burst, and Catherine could just see the citizen's complaint forms come flying into the office, after the Sidle social skills went into full force.

Holding Sara back gently, Catherine said, "We need to investigate all aspects, all avenues, of a crime . . . not just the scene of the crime itself."

The big man deposited himself before them. "Ray's a stand-up guy," he said, his eyes burning into Catherine's. "He's not the killer type."

Chin up, Sara asked mock-innocently, "Is he the restraining-order type?"

The big man turned his gaze on the younger woman, sucking in air—the buttons on his flannel shirt threatening to pop and reveal the Bulls T-shirt in toto. Then the air rushed out: "That was *bull*shit. He never did *nothin'* like that!"

"Like what?" Sara pressed.

Catherine stepped between them. "Sir, we're not going to debate the issue. This is police business. As I said, we're only here to have a look at Mr. Lipton's office and truck."

Still staring at Sara, the big man seemed to buckle a bit; then he said, "Well, all right—but we're only cooperatin' 'cause Ray told us to."

"So that's what this is," Sara said. "Cooperation."

Wincing, Catherine raised a hand. "Thank you, sir. We understand. And you should understand that we are here as much to look for evidence to exonerate Mr. Lipton as anything else."

He considered that, doubtfully, then said, "This way, ladies."

Catherine fell in alongside him, and Sara brought up the rear.

"I'm Catherine Willows, and this is Sara Sidle. And you are?"

"Mike. Howtlen."

He opened the door at the rear of the office, leading them into a corridor with another door on the left and one at the far end. "Ray's office is here." He gestured toward the closest of the doors. "And the truck, it's in the bay, in back."

The big man opened the office door and they all stepped inside. This was a colorless oversized cubicle with a messy desk, two filing cabinets, a couch against one wall, and—for the man who thought it unacceptable for his girl friend to be a stripper—a Hooters calendar.

"What's your job here, Mr. Howtlen?" Catherine asked.

"One of the job foremen."

"I see. And how long have you worked for Mr. Lipton?"

"Ever since Ray went into business for himself. . . . Six years."

"Do you have a Lipton Construction jacket?"

He looked at her funny. "Why do you ask that?"

"I'd appreciate it if you'd just answer, sir."

He shrugged, nodded. "Yeah, sure. I got a jacket. We all do."

"Define 'all.' "

Another shrug. "Twenty employees, here at Lipton Construction. We all got one. Ray's generous, and we're cheap advertising."

Well, Catherine thought, Howtlen would make a hell of a billboard, at that.

Sara had slipped on latex gloves and now moved around to the rear of the desk. She opened the top righthand drawer and fingered Scotch tape, a ruler, pencils, rubber bands. Slowly, she worked her way toward the back.

Howtlen's eyes were riveted on Sara—whether in suspicion or interest or just because Sara Sidle was cute, Catherine couldn't say.

What she could say, to Howtlen, was, "Can you put together a list for us, of everyone who has one of those Lipton Construction jackets?"

The foreman said nothing as he watched Sara shut the top drawer and move down to the next one. His face turned pink and he seemed to be gritting his teeth. So it wasn't Sara's good looks that had his attention: Howtlen was bridling at the indignity of their CSI invasion of Lipton territory.

Catherine took a step and gently laid a hand on his arm. "Mr. Howtlen?"

He shook his head and looked down at Catherine. "I'm sorry, what?"

"Sir, remember—what we find may clear Mr. Lipton."

"Should I believe you?"

"Off the record, sir—I have a hunch Mr. Lipton's innocent myself."

Sara flinched, but pretended not to hear it.

Howtlen said, "You're not just sayin' that."

"No. But it's my job to find out, either way—if Ray did kill his girlfriend, you wouldn't want him to have a pass, would you?"

"I . . . no. Of course not."

"Good. Now about that list, Mr. Howtlen? Of jackets?"

"Yeah, sure—puttin' that together shouldn't be a problem."

"Mr. Lipton told us he gave them to preferred customers, too."

"Oh, shit, come to think of it, yeah . . . but I have no idea who that'd be. But Jodi, that's the gal out front, she'd probably know. . . . Yeah, no problem. We'll get you that list."

The now truly cooperative Howtlen left then to fill Catherine's request, and the CSIs got down to work. Ninety minutes later they had pretty much dissected everything in the office and found nothing of value. The business records in the file cabinet, Catherine decided, could be left behind, for now; and there was no computer in here.

Gathering up their gear, they moved down the hallway into the bay.

Two roll-up garage doors dominated the left wall of the high-ceilinged concrete chamber. Men's and women's bathrooms took up the rest of the side they'd entered through. A workbench ate up a large chunk of the righthand wall; some green metal garden furniture and, at the rear of the room, a couple of wood-and-metal picnic tables comprised the break area. The center of the room held two blue pick-ups with Lipton Construction stenciled in white-outlined red on their sides. The one parked nearest to them had "Ray" in white script letters over the driver's side door. The back of the pickup was filled with tools and various piles of gear, as well as a steel toolbox mounted on the front end of the bed.

"I'll take the box," Sara volunteered, "if you want the cab."

Catherine shrugged her okay. "Dealer's choice."

They took photos of the truck from every angle, fingerprinted the doors and tailgate, and then each went to investigate their own part of the truck. In the cab, Catherine found very little beyond an empty soda cup and a McDonald's sack with a Big Mac wrapper and an empty french fry container.

"Got it," Sara said from the back.

Catherine came out of the cab. "Got what?" She moved down the driver's side of the truck to find Sara pointing the camera at something in the bottom of the truck bed. Following the line of the lens, Catherine saw what "it" was: a nest of black man-made snakes in a plastic bag. . . .

Black electrical ties identical to the one that had squeezed the life from lovely Jenna Patrick.

The floor shook as Howtlen strode in, a piece of paper dangling from his massive paw. "Got your list, for ya!"

But Catherine was on to other things. "Mr. Howtlen, do you recognize this?" She pointed toward the bag.

Joining her alongside the truck, Howtlen looked down into the box, shrugged. "Sure—'lectrical ties. We use 'em all the time. I got a bag of them in back of my truck, too." He gestured at the other pickup. "Why? Is that important?"

"An electrical tie like these," Sara said, studying the man, "was the murder weapon."

"No shit! Really?"

Catherine gave him a hard look. "Really—tied around Miss Patrick's neck."

"Hell of a way to go." He was cringing at the thought, the tiny features almost disappearing into his fleshy face. "Don't ever think, just 'cause she was a stripper, Jenna wasn't a sweet kid . . . 'cause she was."

"Ray is said to have a temper," Sara said. "And yet you don't think he was capable of that? In the heat of anger?"

Howtlen shook his head quickly. "I've worked for Ray for six years—known him a hell of a lot longer than that . . . and, yeah, he can lose his top. But this is a sweet guy . . . and no killer."

Everybody was "sweet" to Howtlen, it seemed.

Sara didn't let up: "You do know the Dream Dolls club's manager was able to get a restraining order against him?"

The big head wagged, side to side, sorrowfully. "Yeah, yeah, I know . . . Ray caused scenes in there more than once. Sometimes when a guy dates a stripper, at first it's really great, and then it makes 'em crazy, other guys lookin' at their lady, naked."

"How crazy?" Catherine asked.

"Not *that* crazy, not Ray! He never hurt nobody in his life. Even that time when one of the bouncers hit him . . . with those brass knuckles? Ray yells, but he's not violent. Not really."

"Well if you're right," Catherine said, "our work will help clear him."

Howtlen held up the paper to Catherine. "Then take that list you said you wanted. I never had no idea just how many jackets Ray passed out . . . I admit I'm a little surprised, 'cause they're pretty expensive. But, anyway, Jodi found the receipts. Thirty-five."

Catherine accepted the list. "And how many of the jackets are accounted for on this list?"

"Twenty-seven we're sure of, who he gave 'em to, and a few maybes. The others . . . who knows? Maybe Ray can help. He'll probably remember."

"May we have copies of the receipts too?"

Howtlen nodded. "I'll get Jodi to do that for you right away."

"Thank you. And we'll need to take the ties from your truck too. Just to be sure."

"All right." He turned and lumbered to the door, then stopped and turned, sheepish—the big man was a big kid. "Hey, uh . . . sorry about before. You girls seem nice. You gotta understand—Ray's my friend, and he's a good guy."

"It's all right, Mr. Howtlen," Catherine said. "And we do understand—one of our coworkers was accused of murder, last year."

"How did that come out?"

Sara said, "He was innocent."

Catherine gave Howtlen a genuinely friendly smile. "Happy endings are still possible, you know."

"Yeah," Howtlen said, shaking his pumpkin head, "but not for that sweet kid, Jenna."

Ten minutes later they left Lipton Construction with the list, the photocopies of receipts, and two bags of electrical ties from both trucks. Catherine phoned Conroy again and the detective said she was on her way to Jenna Patrick's apartment. Did they still want to meet her there?

Catherine said yes, then clicked off, and said to Sara, "You don't mind? You are up for that?"

"We put in this much overtime," Sara said, at the wheel, with half a smirk, "why not?"

Catherine laughed silently. "Would you rather do your job than sleep?"

"Sure. So would you, Catherine."

Catherine said nothing; it was true. She loved her job, she loved solving puzzles. She just feared that she might become Grissom or, for that matter, Sara.

Jenna Patrick's apartment was off Escondido near the UNLV campus. Conroy's Taurus already sat in front of the building when Sara pulled up and parked across the street. From the outside, the three-story building looked like an early sixties motel, all rust-color brick and crank-open windows. Concrete stairs ran up the right side of the building, and there seemed to be a small parking lot out back.

The three women—one detective and two criminalists—met up at the curb, where Catherine and Sara filled Conroy in on what they'd learned at Lipton Construction. Then the trio paraded single-file up the stairs (Conroy, then Catherine, then Sara) to the third floor, around the back and up the far side of the building to 312. A picture window faced them, curtains drawn over it keeping out any sunlight that might try to sneak through.

Strippers worked the night shift, too.

Conroy knocked on the white wooden door. Nothing. They waited, then Conroy knocked again and said, loudly, firmly, *"Police."*

Slowly, the door cracked open, chain latch still in place, and a tired woman peered out. "What? . . . Awful early . . ."

Conroy flashed her badge. "Are you Tera Jameson?"

The one visible eye widened enough to take in the badge. "That's me."

"Ms. Jameson, could you open the door, please?"

"Yeah. Sure." A sigh, and the door closed; they heard the chain scratch across the latch, then the door opened again. The voice of their hostess was more alert, now: "What's this all about?"

The three stepped in, Tera Jameson closing the door behind them. She was a buxom woman, her curly brunette hair flowing down her back but also framing her heart-shaped face. Tallish, maybe five nine, she wore only a 49ers football jersey about five sizes too large for her and a pair of baggy gray cotton shorts.

The living room was tidy if crammed with rent-to-own-type furniture. A low-slung dark coffee table with a glass top and piles of magazines crouched in front of a couch, and an overstuffed brown chair sat against the right wall with a hassock in front of it. In the opposite corner a twenty-five-inch color TV occupied a maple wall unit with a stereo, VCR, DVD, and the attendant software.

"Thank you, Ms. Jameson," Conroy said, and she gestured to the couch, adding, "Maybe you should sit down. I'm afraid I have some bad news."

"What kind of bad news?" The woman's dark eyes flared, but she took Conroy's advice, sliding over to the couch and taking a seat. Sara sat down on her far side, not crowding the woman, and Catherine took the overstuffed chair, while Conroy got down on her haunches in front of Tera Jameson, parent to child.

"It's about your roommate," Conroy said. "I know you were friends."

"Best friends," Tera said. Then the eyes widened again, and she said, ". . . *were?*"

Conroy sighed and nodded. "I'm sorry to report that Jenna Patrick died last night."

Tera's hand shot to her mouth, her teeth closing on a knuckle as tears took the path over her high cheekbones down her face. "Oh, my God. But . . . she was in perfect health!"

"I'm afraid she was killed, at work, last night."

"What do you mean, 'killed'? An accident of some—"

"Murdered."

Tera covered her face with her fingers and began to sob.

Conroy eased forward, a hand rising to settle soothingly on the dancer's shoulder. "Ms. Jameson, I'm very sorry."

Now a certain anger seemed stirred into the sorrow. "What . . . what in hell *happened* to her?"

"Jenna was in one of the private rooms . . . and she was strangled."

"I *told* Ty those lap-dance rooms were dangerous. Goddamnit! I wouldn't work them . . . I refused. Goddamnit."

Catherine asked, "You did work at Dream Dolls, at one time, Ms. Jameson?"

"Yes . . . I've been at Showgirl World for, I don't know . . . three months?" Tera pulled a tissue out of a box on the coffee table and dabbed at her eyes. "Did you get him?"

Conroy, still on her haunches, blinked. "Excuse me?"

"That asshole Ray Lipton. It was him, wasn't it? It must have been."

Sitting forward, Catherine asked, "Why would you think that? He was her fiancé; he loved her."

She sneered, her lip damp with tears. "He's a fucking nutcase. He *hated* that she danced . . . *and* he hated that she lived with me, another dancer . . . I was a 'bad influence'! He fucking *met* her at the club! Jesus."

Catherine tilted her head. "Mr. Lipton said they were going to be married, soon. Was he lying?"

"Yes. No . . . I mean, yeah, that was the plan—they were getting married. Jenna was barely even my roommate anymore. To keep Ray happy, she moved out of here about a month ago."

Sara asked, "Was she quitting dancing for him?"

"Eventually, she planned to. I mean, most of us plan to get out, sooner or later. I have a nursing degree, you know. But she wanted to keep dancing for a couple of years, *after* they got married, to help build a nest egg. I mean, do you have any idea what those tits of hers cost?"

"Around ten thousand," Catherine said.

Conroy asked, "Well, was she living here, or not?"

"Her name's still on the lease, but she'd pretty much moved in with Ray. She still had a few things here, but it was mostly just stuff she hadn't picked up yet."

Conroy—squatting must have been getting to her—moved to sit down on the other side of Tera. She asked, "And why do you think Ray would kill her?"

"Probably over the dancing. That she hadn't quit, that she wanted to keep going with it. . . . He hated that she danced even more than he hated her living with me. I mean, she liked it here—our hours were similar, it was close to work—but she moved in with him, to . . . what's the word? Placate the prick."

Conroy asked, "You think Ray hates you?"

Tera looked uncomfortable. "I *know* he does. You know about the restraining order Ty had against him, and what caused it?"

"We know that he tried to choke a customer," Catherine said.

"Well, that was just one particularly juicy time. It was me pulled his ass off that poor nerdy guy he jumped. More than once, when I was still at the club, he started trouble over our friendship, Jenna and me. He'd see us sitting together, or standing at the bar, laughing, and get all paranoid we were laughing at him. He'd start screaming at me. He probably yelled at me as much as he did Jenna."

"Why was that?" Conroy asked.

"You know how guys can be—jealous over their girlfriend's best friend. It's stupid, such a guy thing. He thought I had some . . . I don't know, kinda power over her. That I was this wicked witch trying to keep them apart."

"Why would he think that?"

Tera pulled her knees up under her, sat that way. Her chin was up. "Because I told her not to take any crap off him. If they were gonna be married, she still had to be her own person, and stand up for her rights, like dancing if she wanted to. I just generally encouraged her to do what she wanted to do."

"And Ray didn't like that."

"Oh, hell no. Ray's a typical control freak. He thought getting her away from me would make her fall in line with his plans. Get her to live with him, stop dancing, do whatever he said."

"Ray ever try to get physical with you?"

"No." She sat up straighter. "He's a coward, too—he knows I trained in tae kwan do. He figured, lay a hand on me and I'da sent his balls up to live in his throat . . . and he figured right."

"Okay," Conroy said, an uncomfortable tone creeping into her voice. "You mind if we look around?"

"Not at all. Anything that'll help." Tera shook her head, the dark locks shimmering. "Her bedroom's the one on the left, opposite the bathroom. Or it used to be."

Suddenly Tera's tough talk dissolved into another round of tears, and that quickly built into racking sobs.

Conroy stayed and held the dancer, tried to comfort her as Catherine and Sara moved to the bedroom. They slipped on latex gloves and entered.

Tera hadn't been kidding—Jenna had moved out, all right: no bed, no dresser, no furniture of any kind, just a few stray clothes hanging in the closet and a small pile of CDs sitting inside the door, the final artifacts remaining of Jenna Patrick's life in this tiny apartment.

The two criminalists went back to the living room where Conroy still sat on the couch next to Tera Jameson, holding the woman's hand—something she doubted Jim Brass would have done, and which would have mystified Grissom. Catherine caught Conroy's gaze and shook her head—they hadn't found anything.

Conroy rose, looking down at the young woman with a somber smile. "Ms. Jameson, we're sorry for your loss."

Tera, who was drying her eyes with a handkerchief, nodded bravely.

Conroy joined the CSIs at the door. "If we have more questions," she said to Tera, "we'll get back to you. . . . You have my card, if you think of something you consider important."

"I do, yes—I will . . . and thank you."

"Have you ever been back to Dream Dolls," Catherine asked suddenly, "since you quit?"

Tera shook her head, her long dark hair swinging. "No way. Good riddance to that hellhole."

Catherine knew the feeling.

"Thanks," Catherine said, and exchanged polite smiles with the woman.

Soon the trio from LVMPD were standing next to Conroy's car. Catherine asked, "You didn't search Lipton's place yet?"

"No," Conroy said, "just picked him up and brought him in. We should get to that."

"Since he's in custody," Sara said, "maybe it could wait till tonight—we're way past the end of shift, and I'd hate to get the dayshift's sticky fingers in this."

Conroy said, "That should work out fine. Meantime, I'll ask Lipton if he'll give us the go-ahead, and see if we have to get a search warrant or not."

"You think he'll stop cooperating?" Catherine asked.

Conroy arched an eyebrow. "Wouldn't you, if you were about to go down for murder?"

"Yeah, I suppose I would . . . unless I was innocent."

"Which you think he is?"

"Well, he's cooperated with us so far—hasn't hidden a thing."

Sara asked, "Tera didn't paint a very pretty picture of him."

"She also didn't paint that violent a picture of him," Catherine pointed out. "Lipton and Tera hated each other, but it never went past shouting matches, didn't come to blows."

The three traded expressions that were made up of equal parts exhaustion and perplexity.

Catherine gave Conroy a wave, and she and Sara headed back to the Tahoe. They had plenty of work to do, though some of it could wait till tonight and, she hoped, the evidence would provide the right answers.

Concentrate on what cannot lie, Grissom liked to say: *the evidence.*

Hearing footsteps, Catherine turned to find Conroy right behind her. "I'm thinking of stopping at Circus Circus on the way back . . . you girls interested in some more overtime?"

Catherine looked toward Sara, and they both sighed and shrugged—at this point, what was the difference?

Twenty minutes later they pulled into the parking garage next to Circus Circus; then they were walking through the maze of halls to the second-floor casino where the familiar casino sounds—spinning slots, dealers calling out cards, rolling roulette balls—belied the breakfast hour. This large area was filled with slots, about half of which were in action; the cashier's cage stood immediately to the right, an Hispanic security guard making small talk with a cute redhead on the other side of the bars.

Conroy approached him and displayed her I.D. and a professional smile. "Who could I talk to about one of your employees?"

The stocky, wispily mustached guard had a radio mike clipped to the epaulet of his left shoulder. He used the mike to check with a Mr. Waller, who would receive the Las Vegas Metropolitan Police contingent in his office, which proved to be on the first floor, past the front desk, and down a deserted corridor behind a door labelled SECURITY.

A tall, thin man in a well-tailored gray suit and black and gray tie extended his hand to Conroy even as the guard showed them in. With a smile just a little too wide and teeth just a little too white, the casino man introduced himself as Jim Waller, and I.D.'s were proffered, hands were shaken, Catherine finding the man's grip limp and his palm slightly moist.

Waller moved behind the desk and sat in a massive maroon leather chair, a computer whirring behind him, the screensaver showing fish swimming around. He motioned toward the three leather-covered chairs in front of his large darkwood desk.

Waller was a typical casino security man: unfailingly polite and helpful to the police, but wary as hell. "What can I do to help you, officers? Something about an employee, I understand? Is it a criminal matter?"

"Yes, Mr. Waller, it's criminal," Conroy said, and the security man's smile vanished, all those big shiny teeth tucked away in his face. "But the crime doesn't involve your employee."

Conroy explained the situation and soon Waller was using a walkie-talkie to summon Marty Fleming.

"Should only be three or four minutes," Waller said.

It was five, a security guard showing up, escorting a slump-shouldered, medium-sized man in his late forties with sandy hair, a bad complexion and gold-rimmed bifocals. A walking cast peeked out from the man's left pant leg; Catherine found him a rather pitiful-looking character. Waller rose, came around the desk and approached the man.

"Marty," he said, speaking to the dealer (though in a facility this size, the odds were scant Waller actually knew the employee), "these police officers need to talk to you."

The dealer's face turned anxiously inquisitive as his attention turned from Waller to the women.

"Detective Conroy," Waller continued, "I'll be at the front desk, when you've finished using my office."

"Very kind of you," Conroy said.

Then the security guard and Waller and the latter's shit-eating grin left them alone.

"Wh-what is this about?" Fleming asked.

Sara got up and vacated the chair next to Conroy, gesturing to Fleming to take it, saying, "Why don't you have a seat, Mr. Fleming, that cast doesn't look very comfortable."

He sat down, Conroy made the introductions, and explained the purpose of their visit, including the tragic death of Jenna Patrick.

"Damn it, anyway," Fleming said, shaking his head. He had a perpetual "why me?" demeanor. "I told Ty it was no big deal. Now he goes around telling the police."

Catherine said, "Mr. Fleming, it is a big thing—Mr. Kapelos did the right thing informing us. If Ray Lipton did attempt to strangle you, it might represent a pattern—a pattern of violence that culminated with him killing that young woman."

Fleming shook his head. "That's so sad . . . she was just the nicest girl. So beautiful. Nice and beautiful."

Catherine pressed: "Is Ty Kapelos telling us the truth? Did Ray Lipton choke you at Dream Dolls three months ago?"

Slowly, Fleming nodded; he seemed embarrassed. "About that— maybe a little longer ago. He saw me coming out of one of the backrooms with his girlfriend—I had, uh . . . you know, a private dance with her. Listen, you're not gonna talk to my wife, are you?"

Conroy said, "No, Mr. Fleming."

"I mean, she'll kill me, and then you'll be investigating *that.*"

"Tell us about that night, Mr. Fleming—the night Ray Lipton attacked you."

He sighed, thought back, pushing his glasses up on his nose— they didn't stay there long. "Jenna, she gave me a hug, you know, as we were comin' out of the booth—that's not something they usually do, I mean, when the dance is over, it's over. But she was a nice girl, and I used to have a dance from her, I don't know, a couple times a week."

Catherine nodded just to keep him going.

"Anyway, she hugged me and I gave her a peck on the cheek and the next thing I know, this guy is all over me, like ugly on a bulldog. Knocks me down, pins me to the floor in that, you know, that narrow hallway? On the floor there, digging his fingers into my throat. His face was all red . . . mine probably was, too. The girl was screaming and all, and I started to black out. I tell you, I thought I was dead."

Conroy asked, "Then what?"

He swallowed, pushed his glasses up again. "This brunette, another of the dancers, grabbed him by the hair and pulled him off. Saved me, sort of. She wasn't a very nice person . . . kinda cold, the other one, dark-haired. I had a private dance from her, once, too . . . brrrrr! But she did save me, I guess, from that Lipton guy. Anyway, she doesn't work there anymore."

"Tera Jameson, you mean?" Sara asked.

Fleming shrugged. "I didn't pay any attention to her name—I didn't like her. Anyway, the girls danced under different names, different nights. . . . So, then he and her started screaming at each other. He looked like he wanted to punch her, but he kept his distance. I just got up and a couple of the girls helped me back into the dressing room . . . only time I was ever back there."

He stopped and smiled as he thought back to that experience.

Conroy prompted him: "Mr. Fleming?"

"Yeah, anyway—I stayed back with the dancers, in their dressing room, till Ty and that Worm DJ guy hustled this Ray out of the club."

"Did you get the cast from that attack?"

Looking a little sheepish, Fleming said, "No. Got that about a month ago—accident at home. You know. Most accidents happen there."

Maybe his wife *would* kill him, Catherine thought.

Conroy asked, "That night at the club, that the last time you had contact with Ray Lipton?"

"Yeah."

"You're sure?"

"I'd remember."

"Guess you would." Conroy gave him a smile. "Thank you, Mr. Fleming."

He sighed, nodded. "You won't talk to my wife?"

"We won't talk to your wife."

Fleming rose and went out, and the trio lingered in Waller's office briefly, then did the same.

They stopped at the front desk and Conroy thanked Waller, and they made their way out of the gaudy casino, that pioneer in making Sin City family friendly.

Then they drove back to HQ, where they finally ended the night that had long since turned to day.

7

Lake Mead was born of Hoover Dam stemming the Colorado River's flow; downstream Davis Dam had given birth to Lake Mohave, and together the pair of man-made bodies of water—and the surrounding desert—comprised Lake Mead National Recreation Area, a million and a half acres set aside in '64 by the federal government for the enjoyment of the American tourist. Lake Mead's cool waters were ideal for swimming, boating, skiing, and fishing.

But some people had a peculiar idea of fun, which meant the CSIs were no strangers to the recreation area. They were at the end of another long shift, the day after the Toyota Avalon had been found at McCarran, when a phone call had come in, just as Nick Stokes and Warrick Brown were about to head home. Grissom had headed them off, announcing another discovery, this time a grisly one.

And now, once again, three nightshift CSIs, including their supervisor, were dragging their weary bones into the sunshine. Or at least Warrick and Nick were weary: Grissom never seemed tired, exactly, nor for that matter did he ever seem particularly energetic—except when evidence was stirring his adrenaline flow.

Soon Warrick was steering one of the team's black Tahoes out Lake Mead Boulevard, Route 147, past Frenchman's Mountain and on toward the recreation area as he followed the twisty road west of Gypsum Wash and then down the Lake Shore Scenic Drive. The landscape was as untamed and restless as the Old West itself, rugged, chaotic, God working as an abstract artist, sculpting rocks in countless shapes in a raw rainbow of colors—snowy whites, cloudy grays, gentle mauves, and fiery reds.

When Warrick swung into the parking lot for Lake Mead Tours, Brass's Taurus pulled up and parked next to them.

The autumn morning was cool enough for their windbreakers. None of them bothered with field kits yet—they would get the lay of the land, first—or maybe the lake, the endless expanse of which glistened nearby. Grissom and Nick climbed down and followed Warrick a few steps to where a man in a tan uniform stood next to a U.S. Fish and Wildlife pickup. Brass caught up quickly.

"Warrick Brown," the criminalist said, pointing to his necklace I.D. "Las Vegas CSI."

"Jim Tilson, U.S. Fish and Wildlife."

The two exchanged polite smiles and handshakes—the latex gloves weren't on, yet.

"This is Nick Stokes, CSI," Warrick went on as the rest of the group caught up with him, "and our supervisor, Gil Grissom, and Captain Jim Brass from Homicide."

Tilson nodded to them—more polite smiles, more handshakes.

Warrick was studying the guy, brow knitted. "I feel like I know you, Mr. Tilson."

A real smile creased Tilson's face now, revealing a row of uneven but very white teeth. "I played a little ball—Nevada Reno, then the CBA, couple years . . . till I blew my ankle out."

Snapping his fingers, Warrick said, "Yeah, yeah, I remember you! Jumpin' Jimmy Tilson. You spent some time with the Nuggets, too."

Tilson nodded. "That was a while ago."

"Mr. Tilson," Grissom said, "why did you call us?"

Tilson led them around his truck. "Over here . . . Not pretty."

Grissom smiled thinly. "They so seldom are."

They walked across the parking lot and down to the edge of the lake, where the water lapped at the sloping cement, and Tilson's USFW flat bottom boat was tied to the cruise boat's dock. If they looked hard, they could see the tour boat down at the far end of the basin; but that wasn't what they'd come to see. Warrick gazed into the flat bottom's bottom, where a canvas tarp covered something in the middle of the boat.

"I was on the lake this morning taking samples," Tilson said, a grimness in his tone.

"Samples?" asked Brass.

Tilson shrugged. "Testing chemical pollution in the lake, at various depths. It's an ongoing USFW concern. Anyway, I bring up my container, then start hauling up the anchor to move to another spot. Well, the damn anchor snags on something." Another shrug. "Happens once in a while. Lotta shit's ended up in this lake over the years."

"I can imagine," Brass said, just moving it along.

"So," the wildlife man said, "I start pullin' the anchor chain back in, and damn, it's heavy as hell." Tilson moved close to the boat, then glanced up toward the parking lot—to make sure they were undisturbed—and pulled back the tarp. "And this is what I found."

Even Grissom winced.

"That's one nasty catch of the day," Nick said, softly.

The lake had bleached the slab of flesh the gray-white of old newspaper. Someone had severed the body just above the navel and near the top of the femurs, leaving only the buttocks and vagina and the tops of the thighs. The unctuous odor of rot floated up and Warrick forced himself to breathe through his mouth.

"This is all you found?" Nick asked, frowning down at the thing.

"That's it."

Grissom was gazing out at the lake now. "Mr. Tilson, can you tell us where exactly you found this body?"

Now Tilson looked out across the water, gesturing. "Straight out—half a mile or more."

"You have GPS?"

Global positioning system.

Nodding, Tilson said, "I took a reading, but the damned thing flamed out on me. Bad batteries, I guess."

"We can send divers down," Nick suggested.

Grissom and Tilson both shook their heads at the same time, but it was Brass who said, "Too deep."

"Nearly six hundred feet in places," Tilson added.

"Besides which," Grissom said, "there's no telling how many different places parts were dumped into the lake."

"Whatever happened to dragging the lake?" Nick asked.

Tilson said, "You don't drag a lake that covers two hundred forty-seven square miles . . . and, man, that's just the water, never mind the seven-hundred miles of shoreline. And you take in the whole area, you've got twice the size of Rhode Island to deal with."

"And you have over ten million visitors a year, right, Mr. Tilson?" Grissom asked.

"That's right, sir."

"Lotta suspects," Warrick said.

And yet all of them knew, if this torso belonged to a certain missing woman, that one particular suspect would head their list. Warrick also knew that Grissom—whose mind had to be buzzing with the possibility of this being what was left of Lynn Pierce—would never countenance such a leap.

"I get the picture," Nick was saying. "So . . . what can we do?"

Warrick twitched half a humorless smirk, and said, "We can do a DNA test on what we have, and hopefully identify the body."

Again, neither the criminalists nor the police detective said what they all were thinking.

"Mr. Tilson," Brass said, a mini-tape recorder at the ready, "can you tell us exactly what happened this morning? In detail?"

Though this version of the tale took longer, it added very little to the original, more succinct story Tilson had told earlier.

"Did you see anything unusual on the lake this morning?" Brass asked.

Tilson looked at Brass with wide eyes, and gestured down into the boat.

"Besides that," the detective said quickly. "Other boats, suspicious activity, anything at all noteworthy?"

The USFW man considered that carefully. Finally he said, "There were some boats . . . but, I mean, there's always boats. Didn't see anything odd, not like somebody dumpin' stuff into the water or anything. And we keep an eye out for that kinda thing."

For several minutes, Brass continued to question Tilson, without learning anything new. Tilson requested permission to confer with some of the recreation area personnel, who were nervously hovering at the periphery. Brass—after glancing at Grissom, for a nod—okayed that.

Finally, Brass said to Grissom, "We can't exactly go door to door with a picture of this, and ask if anybody recognizes her."

They were near the flat-bottom boat. Grissom was staring at the torso, as if waiting for it to speak up. Then he said to Brass, "There's a body of evidence, here."

"Are you kidding?"

Grissom tore himself away from staring down at the torso to give

Brass a withering look. Then he returned his eyes to the evidence and said, "Look at the edges."

The criminalist pointed first to the waistline, then the jagged cuts to the thighs. Warrick and Nick were looking on with interest.

Grissom was saying, "We'll figure out what made the cuts—that will help. She'll talk to us. . . . She already is."

Nick took pictures while Warrick carefully searched the boat for any other trace evidence. Once he had photos of the torso, where it lay in the boat, the two CSIs removed it from the snarled anchor chain and gently turned the body over.

Nick winced. "That left a mark . . ."

"Gris!" Warrick called. "You're gonna wanna see this!"

Striding over from where he'd been conferring with Brass, Grissom called, "What?"

Warrick raised an eyebrow and gestured in *ta-dah* fashion at the torso.

Glancing down, Grissom saw intestinal tissue sticking out of a slice in the back, like Kleenex popping out of a box.

Brass joined the group. "Something?"

"Whoever cut her up made a mistake," Grissom said. "He tried to cut through the pelvic bone. Whatever he used got jammed up, and when he pulled it out, the blade snagged on the intestines."

Warrick didn't know which was grislier: the torso, or the glee with which Grissom had reported the butcher's "mistake." But Warrick also noted Grissom reflexively referred to the unknown killer as "he."

In the hour it took the CSI team to finish, the paramedics showed up, as did news vans from the four network affiliates. Uniformed officers held the reporters and cameramen at a distance, but there was no way Brass would get out of here without talking to them.

Gil Grissom did not envy Brass this part of his job. The CSI supervisor watched as the detective moved over to the gaggle of reporters. It was a calculated move on Brass's part: if the cameras were focused on him, they'd be unable to shoot the body being loaded into an ambulance.

Grissom watched as the four reporters and their cameramen vied for position, each sticking his or her microphones out toward Brass's unopened mouth. Grissom recognized Jill Ganine. She had interviewed him more than once, and he liked her well enough, for media.

Next to her, Stan Cooper tried to look like he wasn't shoving Ganine out of the way. Kathleen Treiner bounced back and forth around the other two like a yappy terrier until her brutish cameraman managed to elbow in next to Cooper and give her some space.

Ganine got out the first question. "Captain Brass, is that the body of Lynn Pierce, the missing Vegas socialite?"

Leave it to the press to ask the question none of them had spoken. And just when had Born-Again suburban mom Lynn Pierce become a "socialite," anyway?

Grissom wished the TV jackals hadn't jumped so quickly to the conclusion that it was Lynn Pierce; more than that, he wished he could keep himself from making that jump. The torso could, after all, be any of hundreds of missing women. *Evidence*, he told himself, *just wait for the evidence and all will come clear.*

"We have no new information on Lynn Pierce," Brass said.

Cooper jumped in. "But you did find a body?"

Brass seemed unsure how to answer that. "Not entirely true," he finally said.

That was a nice evasion, Grissom thought; but as he listened to the reporters and the detective play twenty questions, Grissom kept his eyes on Ned Petty. Working carefully, the innocent-looking reporter was nearly around the tape line set up by the uniformed officers, as he and his cameraman moved toward the ambulance. The reporter was to Grissom's right, and slouching as he moved, no one—other than Grissom—seeming to notice Petty closing in.

Slipping behind the ambulance, to block the media's view of him, Grissom moved around until he was hidden by the ambulance's open back door, waiting.

With the body bag riding atop it—the rather odd shape of its contents plainly visible through the black plastic—the gurney was rolled by the EMS guys to the back door of the ambulance. Petty stepped forward, his microphone held up as he said, "Clark County paramedics load the body . . ."

"May I help you?" Grissom interrupted pleasantly, stepping out from behind the door and directly into the path of the cameraman's lens.

Petty didn't miss a beat.

The reporter swiveled, said, "On the scene is one of Las Vegas's top crime scene investigators, sometimes the subject of controversy himself—Gil Grissom. Mr. Grissom, what can you tell us about the victim?"

And Petty thrust the microphone toward Grissom, like a weapon.

Maintaining his cool, Grissom gave the camera as little as possible—a blank face, and a few words: "At this point, nothing."

Petty fed himself the mike, saying melodramatically, "That didn't *look* like a human body on that stretcher."

The mike swung back toward him, but Grissom said only, "That isn't a question."

"Do *you* believe you've found Lynn Pierce?"

Another shrug, this one punctuated by a terse, "No comment."

Finally the ambulance doors closed behind him, the paramedics all loaded up now, and the ambulance left—no siren; what was the rush? But the newspaper contingent made a race out of it anyway, peeling from the lot in pursuit of the emergency vehicle.

Having the scene to themselves again, Nick, Warrick, and Grissom gathered their gear, and left, finally letting Lake Mead start the process of getting back to normal—tourists would soon enjoy the sunshine shimmering off the lake, unaware of the gruesome events of the morning.

That night, a few hours before the official start of his shift, Grissom—blue scrubs over his street clothes—slipped into the morgue where Dr. David Robbins still had the torso laid out on a table.

A whole body, a female body, Lynn Pierce's body. She is already dead. In a sparse bathroom, the body sprawls in a tub, unfeminine, undignified. A chainsaw coughs and sputters and spits to life, then growls like a rabid beast.

First it gnaws through the arms at the shoulders, then the legs below the hip sockets. The gnawing blade eats through the neck, severing spinal cord, nerves, and muscle. The body is limbless, headless.

The animal feeds on, but its keeper aims too low and the saw grinds to a halt in the middle of the pelvic bone and that blade is pulled out savagely, bringing with it a rope of intestine. With a snarl the blade shivers back to life, and this time the keeper aims higher, severing the body, just above the navel.

Pieces are packed into garbage bags with something to weigh them down, and hefted into the trunk of a car, driven to Lake Mead,

loaded onto a boat beneath cover of night, dumped into the dark wa-
ters, here, there, scattered to the sandy bottom to never be found—
save for one piece somehow freed, escaping the depths, floating,
armless, legless, finding its way into the boat of the Fish and Wildlife
man.

As Grissom approached, Robbins looked up. The pathologist had
been at Grissom's side for so many autopsies they had both long ago
lost count. Robbins, too, wore a blue smock.

"You know," the coroner said, gently presenting the obvious, "the
DNA test is going to take time . . . no getting around that."

Grissom shrugged. "I came to find out what you know *now.*"

Using his single metal crutch, Robbins navigated around the table.
"I could share my preliminary findings."

Just the hint of a smile appeared at the corner of Grissom's mouth.
"Why don't you?"

"There's this." Robbins pointed toward the victim's episiotomy
scar. "She's had at least one child."

Grissom nodded curtly, and moved on: "Dismembered before or
after her death?"

"After death." Robbins gestured. "No bruising around where the
cuts were made. If she'd been alive . . ."

"There'd be bruises at the edges of the cuts. If the dismemberment didn't kill her, what did?"

Robbins shook his head, lifted his eyebrows. "No other wounds.
Tox screen won't be back for a couple of days, at least. . . . Truthfully,
Gil, I haven't got the slightest idea how she died."

"She is dead."

"Yes. We agree on that. But if the tox screen doesn't reveal something—and I doubt if it will—we may never know cause of death."

"Any other good news?"

"One very good finding—birthmark on her left hip." Pulling the
light down closer to the torso, Robbins highlighted the spot, which
Grissom himself had glimpsed, earlier, at the lake.

Grissom rubbed his forehead. "Be nice to have a little more."

"Well, really we're just getting started," Robbins said, touching the
corner of the table as if that might connect him to the victim in front
of him.

"What's next?"

"We'll deflesh the torso."

"Good. Maybe the bones will talk to us."

"Yes. Let's hope they have something interesting to say."

"They often do," Grissom said. "Thanks, Doc. I'll be back."

"I'm sure you will."

Grissom made his way back to the break room where Warrick and Nick each sat with a cup of coffee cradled in hand. The coffee smelled scorched and the refrigerator in the corner had picked up a nasty hum. Although he liked working graveyard—because it helped him avoid dealing with much of the political nonsense, and obtrusive building maintenance, which happened nine to five, as well—Gil Grissom wondered why his dayshift counterpart, Conrad Ecklie, never seemed to get around to getting that fridge fixed . . . much less teach his people not to leave the coffee in the pot so long that it became home to new life-forms. That was one scientific experiment Grissom was against.

Filling Nick and Warrick in on what Robbins had told him, Grissom concluded, "I want to know who she is."

Warrick shook his head. "Well, that could take a while."

Grissom's voice turned chill. "I want to know now. Not in a month or even a week, when the DNA results roll in—*now*. Find a way, guys," Grissom said, heading for the door, "find a way."

Still shaking his head, Warrick called out, "Gris! Two hundred people a month disappear in this town, you know that . . . a lot of them women. How are we going to track down one of them without DNA?"

From the doorway, Grissom said, "Eliminate the missing women who haven't had children."

Warrick, thinking it through, said, "And any that aren't white."

Nick was nodding. "And then we'll track one down who had a birthmark like that on her left hip."

"See," Grissom said, with that angelic smile that drove his people crazy. "We have a lot."

Moments later, Grissom was back in his office, seated behind his desk, jarred specimens staring accusingly at him from their shelves. A voice analysis report of the audiotape provided by the Blairs was waiting on his desk, and he read it eagerly.

He never would have admitted it to the reporters, and certainly not to his team, but Grissom was battling a small yet insistent voice in

the back of his mind that kept telling him that they had just found
Lynn Pierce.

And since one of his chief tenets was that the evidence didn't
come to you, you went to it, Grissom picked up the phone and got
Brass on the line.

"Jim, did you get a detailed description of Lynn Pierce beyond the
photo her husband gave us?"

"I didn't, but the officer that spoke to Owen Pierce on the
phone . . . he did. Why, what do you want to know?"

"Distinguishing marks?"

He could hear Brass riffling through some papers.

"A small scar on her left hand," Brass read, "an episiotomy scar, a
bluish birthmark on her right shoulder . . ."

The torso didn't have a left hand or a right shoulder.

". . . and another birthmark, uh, on her left hip."

Grissom let out a long, slow breath.

"Jim, that was her in Lake Mead."

"Damn," Brass said, the disappointment evident in his tone. "I was
hoping . . ."

"Me too."

"But if she's been killed, at least we have something to go on. We
need to get over to Pierce's before the media . . ." The phone line
went silent.

"Jim, what is it?"

"I just turned on a TV, to check . . . we're too late. It's already on
channel eight."

"I'll call you right back." Grissom hung up and strode briskly toward the break room, pulling his cell phone and jabbing in Brass's
number, on the move. In the break room (Warrick and Nick long
gone), he turned on the portable television on the counter and
punched channel eight. He heard the phone chirp once, and Brass answered.

"I've got it on," Grissom said.

They watched as Jill Ganine stood next to Owen Pierce, the physical therapist, in dark sweats, towering over the petite reporter, on the
front stoop of his home.

"Mr. Pierce," Ganine said, her voice professional, her smile
spotwelded in place, "as you know, the severed remains of a woman

were pulled from Lake Mead this morning. Do you believe this to be your wife?"

Pierce shook his head. "As I've told the police, Lynn left us . . . both my daughter and myself. Lynn and I'd had some problems, and she wanted time by herself. . . . We *will* hear from her."

"But, Mr. Pierce—"

"I *have* to believe that the poor woman found today is someone else . . ." He touched his eyes, drying tears—or pretending to. "I don't wish anyone a tragedy, but . . . I . . . I'm sorry. Could I . . . say something to my wife?"

The camera zoomed past a painfully earnest Ganine in on Pierce. The big man steadied himself, rubbed a hand over his face, then looked into the lens.

"I'd just like to say to Lynn, if you're listening or watching—please, just call home, call Lori . . . that's the important thing. We so need to hear your voice."

Giving a little nod of understanding, Ganine turned to the camera, as Pierce disappeared behind his front door. "That's the story from the Pierce house, where the little family still holds out hope that Mrs. Pierce is alive and well . . . and will soon get in touch with them. . . . Jill Ganine for KLAS News."

Grissom clicked off the television.

"You believe that shit?" Brass asked in Grissom's ear.

"What I believe doesn't matter. Melodramatic TV news is irrelevant. What matters is the evidence."

"Like the birthmark?"

Grissom said, "And the audiotape."

"Shit! Damn near forgot about that tape."

Grissom said, "I just got the voice analysis back—and it's definitely Pierce talking. He threatens to cut his wife up in little pieces and now we have a piece of a woman . . ."

"Not a 'little' piece, though."

"No . . . but one with a birthmark identical to a marking his wife's known to have. Can I assume, Captain Brass, you'll be on your way to call on Owen Pierce, soon?"

"Meet me at my car."

8

At the same time Gil Grissom was meeting up with Jim Brass in the parking lot, Catherine Willows sat before a monitor at a work station in her office. The TV remote in hand seemed grafted there, as grainy images slipped by on the screen, rewinding, then playing again, rewinding. . . .

Despite her glazed expression—Catherine had been at this three hours—she was alert, and the unmistakable aroma of popcorn penetrated Catherine's concentration. Keenly tuned investigator that she was, she turned toward the doorway. There stood Sara Sidle, typically casual in jeans, blue vest, and cotton blouse, holding out an open bag of break-room microwave popcorn like an offering to a cranky god.

"If that smelled any better," Catherine said to her colleague, "I'd fall to the floor, and die happy."

Sara placed the steaming bag on the counter, away from the stack of tapes they'd been plowing through, and wheeled her own chair up beside Catherine's. "Careful—don't get burned."

"In this job? When *don't* you get burned . . . ?" Taking a few kernels, Catherine blew on them, then popped the popcorn into her mouth. "You know, normally I have a rule against eating while I work—I don't have your youthful metabolism."

"Yeah, right. . . . Anyway, when was the last time you had a meal? Christmas?"

"Well . . . maybe New Year's. . . ."

Sara smirked triumphantly. "My point exactly. We've got to eat something sometime, don't we?"

"We'll *take* a break when we *come* to a break. . . . I just feel . . . I don't know, guilty somehow, taking off before anything's been accomplished."

"Feeling guilty is one thing," Sara said, shoving the bag at her again. "Feeling faint is another."

Catherine glanced at Sara—when an obsessively dedicated coworker tells you to slow down, maybe you ought to listen. And yet Catherine kept at it, the grainy video images crawling across the screen. Right now she was viewing the angle behind the bar. In the frame, the guy in the hat, dark glasses, and Lipton Construction jacket, strolled through then disappeared. Rewind. Again.

"That might be Lipton," Sara said, leaning in, eyes narrowed. "Then again, with this picture, it might be Siegfried or Roy."

"Or their damn tiger." Catherine sighed, shook her head. "We've *got* to get a better look. Where's Warrick, anyway?"

Audio-visual analysis was Warrick Brown's forensic specialty.

Sara shrugged. "Off with Grissom and Nick. They're neck-deep in the Pierce woman's murder."

Catherine looked sharply at Sara. "That torso's been identified positively?"

"Close enough for Grissom to call it science and not a hunch. And I think our likelihood of borrowing Warrick for this, in the foreseeable future, is—"

"Hey! You remember that one guy?"

Sara's eyebrows went up. "I'm good, but I need a little more than that to go on."

Then Catherine traded the remote for her cell phone and punched in Grissom's number.

"Grissom," the supervisor's voice said, above the muted rumbling of motor engine and traffic sounds that told her he was on the road; he was, in fact, on his way with Brass to Owen Pierce's residence.

"Gil, I've got a problem."

"Jenna Patrick?"

"Yeah," Catherine said. "The videotapes are so grainy, not even Lipton's mother could ID our suspect. I'm assuming you can't spare Warrick—"

"Normally when you assume you make an ass of u and me. This is one of the rare other occasions."

Catherine rolled her eyes at Sara; a simple "That's right" would have been sufficient. Into the phone, she asked, "Gil, who *was* that guy?"

Again Sara raised her eyebrows. Grissom, however, had no problem deciphering who Catherine meant, answering without hesitation: "Daniel Helpingstine."

"Helpingstine," Catherine echoed, nodding. "That's right, that's right."

"Anything else?"

"Can I borrow Warrick?"

"No."

"Then I have to spend a little money."

"That's what we have—a little money. But do it."

At that, they both clicked off, no good-byes necessary. She rose and moved behind her desk. Sitting down, she quickly found the leather business-card folder in a drawer and riffled the plastic pages.

"Helpingstine?" Sara asked, still perplexed; she hated not knowing what was up.

"Yes." Catherine was flipping pages. "I guess you must've been out in the field, when he stopped by—manufacturer's rep from LA, who was here, oh . . . maybe six months ago. . . . Here you are! . . . He was pushing this new video enhancement device called Tektive—not computer software, a stand-alone unit."

"What's it do?"

Catherine started punching buttons on the cell phone again. "Just about everything short of showing the killer on the Zapruder film, if Helpingstine's to be believed. He might be able to out-do even Warrick, where this security tape's concerned."

On the other end of the line, the phone rang once, twice, three times, then a recorded message in Helpingstine's reedy tenor came on, identifying the West Coast office of Tektive Interactive.

Catherine waited for the tone, and said, "I don't know if you'll remember me, Mr. Helpingstine, this is Catherine Willows, Las Vegas Criminalistics. If you could call me, ASAP, at—"

She heard the phone pick up, and the same reedy tenor, in person, said, "Ms. Willows! Of course I remember you, pleasure to hear from you."

"Well, you're really burning the midnight oils, Mr. Helpingstine."

"My office is in my home, Ms. Willows, and I just happened to hear your message coming in—you're nightshift, if I recall."

This guy was good. But she could practically hear him salivate at the prospect of a sale.

"That's right," Catherine said, "nightshift. Never dreamed I'd get a hold of you tonight—"

"It's been what, Ms. Willows—six months? How may I help you? Are those budget concerns behind you, I hope?"

Maybe she could pull this off without spending even "a little money." "Mr. Helpingstine, are you still willing to give us an on-the-job demonstration of the Tektive?"

He was breathing hard, now. "Happy to! As I told you when we met, as good as our prepared demonstration is, it's far better for us to help *you* with something, and, uh . . ." She could hear pages turning quickly. ". . . how is Thursday?"

"I know it's terribly short notice, but . . . could you possibly fly in here tomorrow?"

Silence indicated he was considering that. "This isn't just . . . *any* demo, is it?"

"No," Catherine confessed. "It's a murder."

"Let me check on flights and I'll get back to you."

"You have my number?"

"Oh yes. In my little book."

She could almost hear his smile.

Catherine hung up, and with a wry smirk said to Sara, "He thinks he's got my number."

"That's only fair, isn't it?" Sara batted her eyes. "I mean, you've got his."

They returned to the tapes and the popcorn, and less than a half hour later the desk phone rang.

She answered, and Helpingstine asked, "Can you have someone pick me up at McCarran?"

Catherine smiled; now this was service. "Tell me what gate and what time, Mr. Helpingstine. Someone will be there, possibly my associate Sara Sidle or myself."

She could hear his pen scribbling Sara's name, then he gave the information, finishing with, "And would you please call me Dan?"

"Happy to, Dan. And it's Catherine. See you soon."

Catherine hung up and Sara asked, "How soon?"

"Six-thirty."

"Tomorrow evening?"

Catherine grinned. "No—this morning."

Sara grinned, too. "He have a thing for you, or what?"

"I think he has a thing for money—this little item sells in mid five figures." She sighed. "That means we can stop looking at these grainy videotapes until he gets here and concentrate on other things."

"For instance?"

"We could grab some food, if you like."

Sara half-smirked, lifted a shoulder. "Actually, I'm kinda stuffed."

"Demon popcorn. There's always searching Lipton's house."

Sara's eyes brightened. "About time!"

Reaching for her desk phone, Catherine said, "I'll call Conroy."

An hour later they met Detective Erin Conroy—crisply professional in a gray pants suit—in the driveway of Ray Lipton's house on Tinsley Court, not far off Hills Center Drive. A baby-blue split level built in the 'eighties, the house perched on a sloping lawn, looking well-taken care of in a neighborhood of other well-maintained homes, always a quiet area, particularly so at this hour of the night. The driveway ran alongside the house, a two-car garage around back.

The detective stood next to her Taurus, warrant in her hand, at her side, almost casually. "I've got it—let's go in."

"How are we getting inside?" Sara asked.

"Look what our buddy Ray gave me . . ." Conroy flashed a key. "The warrant's just to dot the i's. Lipton's still cooperative—insists he's innocent."

Innocent men always do, Catherine thought; *but then so do most guilty ones. . . .*

The three of them pulled on latex gloves, then the detective unlocked the door and they stepped inside.

"You want upstairs or downstairs?" Catherine asked her coworker.

"Cool stuff's always in the basement," Sara said, with a smile of gleeful anticipation. "I'll take that."

"Let's clear it first," Conroy said.

So the three of them walked through the basement, then Conroy and Catherine went up.

Stairs from the entryway opened onto the living room. Catherine noted the good-quality brown-and-tan carpet, and heavy brown brocade drapes hanging from ornamental rods, shut tight, the sunlight managing only a hairline or two of surreptitious entry. With everything shrouded in darkness like this, the house gave the impression it'd been closed up much longer than twenty-four hours. Only yesterday's *Las Vegas Sun*, on the coffee table and open to the crossword puzzle, indicated ongoing life. Beyond the coffee table, the cream-color plaster wall was occupied by an oversized brown couch accented by a couple of tan throw pillows; a starving-artist's-sale desert landscape hung straight above the couch. However neat the living room might be, one aspect seemed to indicate a male presence: the room had been turned into a formidable home entertainment center.

A thirty-six-inch Toshiba color TV ruled the room from a wheeled stand in a corner of the room, while a tan highback armchair sat to Catherine's left, where she stood at the top of the entry stairs, the chair's twin across the room next to the sofa. Both were placed at angles to the couch so they faced the TV. Speakers were mounted to the walls around the room and she noticed a black sub-woofer on the floor next to the TV stand. A DVD player and VCR were stacked on the lower shelf of the stand and through a smoked-glass door below that, she could make out a row of DVDs.

"Why go out to the movies?" Conroy asked.

"It does beg the issue," Catherine said.

"So maybe he *was* home watching football."

"We'll see. . . ."

Using her Maglite, Catherine took a quick look at the DVDs, then at the other shelves of the TV stand, one of which had a few prerecorded tapes and a lot of T-120 cassettes, some with notations: "Friends season closer"; "Sat Nite Live w/ John Goodman"; and so on.

She checked the VCR: no tape. Question was, had Lipton recorded the Colts/Chiefs game, watched it after committing Jenna's murder, then hidden (or thrown away) the incriminating tape, just so he could have his TV ball game alibi?

Stranger things had happened, of course, but Catherine had a hard time buying that Lipton had strangled his girlfriend, come home, maybe had a beer while he watched the taped game, while at the same time getting his story ready for when the police came around. That seemed a reach to her.

Nonetheless, she gathered all the videotapes, including the prere-
cords, stacking them in front of the TV; she told Conroy to collect any
video cassettes she might run across, and called the same instructions
down to Sara. They would box them all up as evidence.

Catherine and Conroy checked the cushions of the furniture and
behind the framed landscape over the sofa, finding nothing, not even
loose change. They moved through the dining room, Conroy pausing
briefly to riffle through the pile of mail on the table. She found nothing worth bagging.

The kitchen, a small galley-type affair, had a U-shaped counter at
the far end, home to a double-basin sink with a couple of dirty plates
and a glass in one side. The stove and refrigerator were a matching
off-white, and Catherine found healthier food in the fridge than she
would expect from a single guy. In the freezer and cupboards, she
found nothing noteworthy.

The refrigerator had a piece of note paper held to the door by a
Wallace and Gromit magnet: a list of names and phone numbers.
Conroy put the list into an evidence bag and replaced the magnet on
the refrigerator.

"Not much so far," the detective said.

"Well, we know Jenna was living here," Catherine said. "Or do you
know a man who could keep a house this tidy?"

"Not many," Conroy admitted.

They moved down the hallway to where two doors stood opposite
each other. The one to the right was a spare bedroom, the one to the
left the bathroom. Conroy took the bathroom, Catherine the bedroom. Sparsely furnished with only a tiny dark dresser and a single
bed covered with a tan quilt, the room with its bare cream-color plaster walls looked like a nun's cell.

A closet hid behind wooden, sliding double doors. Catherine
opened one side and saw shoe- and other boxes stacked from the floor
to the shelf, with more boxes occupying that space.

She heard Conroy pad in from the bathroom.

"Nothing in there," the detective said. "I'm going to check out the
master bedroom."

"All right. I'll be going through these boxes."

The fourth box down in the back row, a flowered Mootsie's Toot-
sies shoebox, presented Catherine with the prize. Opening the box—

the only woman's shoebox in the stack—she found a false beard, mustache, and a small brown bottle of spirit gum.

She felt her hopes that Lipton might be telling the truth start to fade, as this discovery seemed to confirm what she'd seen in the videotape . . . that he had, indeed, worn a fake beard and mustache to throw people off the track, and yet still had the bad sense to wear a coat with his company's name on the back.

Lipton didn't seem that thick, but plenty of other criminals had done dumber things in the commission of their crimes. She recalled one Don Dawson, who had worked at Castaways Bowling Center. Dawson had been smart enough to know the boss had a camera in the office, so when he'd gone in to crack the safe he'd worn a mask-style stocking cap. The cap had gone nicely with the satin jacket with Castaways Bowling Center embroidered on the back, and his name, "Don," on the breast. Dawson had lasted through almost thirty seconds of interrogation before he'd copped to the robbery.

Such stories abounded in national CSI circles. Like the two star athletes who robbed a local Burger King where their pictures hung in honor on the wall; or the numerous bank robbers around the country who would write their robbery notes on their own deposit slips.

Over the years, Catherine had seen enough reasonably bright criminals do enough dim things to know that anything was possible. She carefully dropped the beard and mustache into an evidence bag, the spirit gum into another, and the shoebox itself into a third.

Sara appeared in the doorway. "Any luck?"

Holding up the bag with the fake beard, Catherine said, "Jackpot."

Sara came over with "wow" in her eyes and had a look at the treasures Catherine had dug up.

Catherine asked, "How about you?"

"Well, I found a box in the basement with two Lipton Construction jackets in it. They look new, or anyway they've never been worn."

"Anything else?"

Sara shrugged, a little frustrated. "There's some stuff down there that doesn't fit Ray. Most of it looks like Jenna's—diet books, *Men Are From Mars, Cosmo*'s, and some other fashion magazines, buncha *Vogue*'s."

Conroy came back in from the master bedroom. "Nothing in

there. Clothes from both of them. Obviously, Jenna was living here. You want to take a quick look around?"

This was addressed to Catherine, but Sara said, "I'll go, while you finish in here, 'kay?"

Catherine nodded. " 'kay."

She spent another hour going through boxes, but found nothing. When Sara and Conroy came back from the bedroom with a bag containing Ray Lipton's work boots, Catherine looked at the evidence curiously.

Sara said, "You lifted boot prints, didn't you, from the lap dance room?"

"Right," Catherine said, smiling, "and Lipton was wearing *tennies* when Conroy hauled him in . . . Good catch, Sara!"

"Thanks."

"That the only pair of boots in the house?"

"Didn't see any others."

"Well, Warrick says it always comes down to shoe prints . . . we'll see."

Back at HQ, the two CSIs and the detective logged in evidence for several hours. Catherine instructed Sara to line up some interns to go over the box of video cassettes, to check for a tape of that Colts game.

Shift was almost over, and the sun freshly up, by the time Catherine was back in one of the Tahoes, taking the 515 to 15 South, so she could get to the airport without having to fight morning traffic on the Strip.

Helpingstine was coming in on Southwest 826, which meant Gate C of Terminal One. A long hike, but after a cooped-up night of sitting in front of a monitor, then crouching in a closet at Lipton's, and finally logging evidence at CSI, the walk would seem like an invigorating relief.

As she made her way through the concourse, Catherine struggled to put a face with the name of the man she was picking up. They had met only once, briefly, about six months ago. Her memory was finally jogged, when the tall, fortyish man—glasses riding a pug nose, straight dark hair parted on the left, graying at the temples, his light gray suit looking suitably slept in—recognized her instantly, and strode up to her with a wide smile and a hand outstretched.

"Ms. Willows," he said, in a nasal but not unpleasant twang that indicated Chicago somewhere in his background, "good to see you again."

"Mr. Helpingstine," she said, smiling and allowing him to pump her hand, "you're very kind to come at such short notice, and so quickly."

He raised a gently scolding finger. "It's Dan, remember?"

"And Catherine," she said, falling in alongside him as he walked.

"Afraid we'll have to go to baggage claim to pick up the Tektive. They're understandably fussy about carry-ons."

Helpingstine's luggage consisted of a nylon gear bag with a Lakers insignia on it, and a square silver flight case on wheels that Catherine assumed contained the Tektive.

She led the way back to the Tahoe, with the salesman's small talk running to how well the Tektive was going over with various major metro police departments. But when Catherine tried to turn the conversation to the Jenna Patrick case, the manufacturer's rep waved a meaty hand. "Let's wait till I've had a chance to look at the tape."

"Fair enough, Dan. We'll follow your lead."

"I do have one other request."

"Name it."

"They didn't feed us anything on the flight. Can we go through a drive-thru or something?"

Suddenly she remembered her popcorn snack with Sara, a hundred years ago; her stomach growled its opinion. "I think I can manage that request."

They got McDonald's breakfasts, went back to headquarters and ate in the break room.

Sara ducked her head in. "I smell something very nearly like real food . . . What'd you bring me?"

Catherine handed her a breakfast burrito—vegetarian, of course—and Sara pulled up a chair and soon was digging in like she hadn't seen food since the Reagan administration.

"Dan, the dainty flower to your left is Sara Sidle."

Sara nodded and kept chewing.

"Dan Helpingstine," he said. "Tektive Interactive."

"Heard all about you, Dan—can't wait for you to work your magic." Between burrito bites, Sara said to Catherine, "Lots of footprints in the lap-dance room, and in the hall."

"Yeah, dozens," Catherine said between bites of a bagel sandwich. "Lots and lots of high heels. I remember."

"But just the one pair of work boots."

"I remember that, too."

Sara shook her head, shrugged, started a second burrito. "I haven't compared them up close yet, nothing Grissom-scientific yet . . . but the eyeball test says the boots we brought in tonight, from Lipton's, are larger than the prints we lifted at the strip club."

Catherine said, "We'll check that out more thoroughly, as soon as we're finished with the video."

Setting up in Catherine's office, they got Helpingstine settled at a work station and lined up with the Dream Doll security tapes.

"First we'll digitize them," he said, working in his shirtsleeves, "then we shall see what we shall see."

"How long's the digitizing take?" Catherine asked.

"How long are the tapes?"

Catherine explained what they had, what they wanted, and why, for now, they were going to concentrate on just small segments representing two cameras: the one from behind the bar and the one from the end of the hallway.

Leaving the Tektive rep to his work, they went back to the footprints. Working in the layout room, they took prints from Lipton's boots and compared them to the one they got from the strip club.

"This print," Sara said, meaning what they'd just created, "is definitely shorter than the lap-dance boot."

"Are we *sure* Lipton had the boots on that night?" Catherine asked. "Is it possible that it's somebody else's boot, and we missed Lipton's print? Maybe he's one of the running shoes we found."

Sara shook her head. "The tennie he was arrested in's been ruled out . . . and the boot print was the oddest we got at the strip club, as well as the freshest, I mean it was on top . . . so we assumed it had to be the killer's."

Catherine wasn't sure whether to feel good or bad about this indication of Lipton's innocence; Grissom would advise her not to "feel" anything.

So she calmly said, "We'll check the videotape first, then if we get nothing, we head back to Lipton's to bring in all his shoes."

"It's a plan."

They returned to Catherine's office to find Helpingstine hunkered over his black box with its keyboard and built-in monitor screen.

"You ready for us?" Catherine asked.

The tech nodded. "These tapes are for shit, of course. Not exactly broadcast quality."

Catherine leaned in and patted his shoulder. "Which is why you're here, Dan, right?"

He gave the two women a little sideways half-smile. "You came to the right man. . . . I've cleaned up the images some, already, and I can isolate your guy in a couple of them."

"Any shots of his shoes?"

He returned his attention to his machine. "Let's see."

Catherine and Sara sat down on either side of him, facing the Tektive monitor, Helpingstine stationed at the keyboard. He punched some keys and the screen came to life, the angle on the tape playing from high behind the bar.

"That looks just the same to me," Sara said. "No offense."

"None taken," Helpingstine said. "Just wait." He tapped some more keys and the picture improved, sharpening, the video garbage clearing somewhat.

But it was still disappointing, and Catherine groaned, "Dan, I was hoping for better . . ."

"Hey hey hey," the tech said, sounding mildly offended. "A mini-miracle I can do on the spot. You want an act of God, it's gonna take some time."

"Okay, show us a mini-miracle."

With a few keystrokes, Helpingstine outlined Lipton in the frame. Then the screen went blackly blank, except for the figure of the killer center screen.

"Now that is interesting," Sara said.

The murderer had no legs below the level of where the bar would have been, but was intact from the waist up except for a spot on his shoulder where a customer's head had been between him and the lens. They could barely make out the Las Vegas Stars logo on the ball cap, and the large dark glasses gave him the appearance of an oversized insect.

"Can you give us better detail on his face?" Catherine asked.

More work on the keys and the picture became slightly less blurry. "Quick fix," Helpingstine said, "that's what you get."

Catherine leaned forward in her chair. "That *is* a fake beard, isn't it?"

"Yeah," Sara said. She jabbed at the monitor screen. "And a mustache too. . . . Could be what you found at Lipton's."

Catherine asked the rep, "Any other quick tricks for us?"

Using a mouse, Helpingstine moved the killer's image into a corner. Then, fingers flying over the keys, he brought up another still, this one showing the killer from behind as he towed Jenna Patrick down the hallway, toward the private dance room where she was killed. A few more clacks from the keyboard and everything in the bar disappeared except for Lipton and Jenna.

A few keystrokes later, the grainy image sharpened further, the Lipton Construction lettering on the back of the jacket springing into sharp relief. From this angle, just barely able to see one side of the killer's partially turned head, they could clearly discern the fake beard.

"Is that a shoe?" Catherine asked, pointing at a dark spot at the end of the killer's leg.

Helpingstine said, "It would appear to be the toe of some kind of boot."

Catherine and Sara traded looks.

The killer stood practically upright, bent only slightly as he extended his hands back to Jenna's. She seemed taller than he was, but then she was wearing those incredible spike heels.

"Did you monkey with the aspect ratio on this?" Sara asked. "Is the picture squeezed or stretched in any way?"

"Not at all," the rep said. "That's reality, as seen by a cheap VHS security camera."

"And cleaned up by an expensive electronic broom," Catherine pointed out.

Sara pressed: "What's wrong with this picture?"

They all studied the frozen image for a long time.

Finally, Helpingstine said, "His head seems too big. Is that what you mean?"

The question was posed to Sara, but it was Catherine who said, "That could be part of it . . . but there's something else."

"What?" Sara asked. "It's driving me crazy . . . it just looks . . . *wrong* to me."

Catherine pointed. "Look at the shoulders—doesn't Ray Lipton have broader shoulders than that?"

"You're saying that's not Ray Lipton," Sara said.

"Call it a hunch," Catherine said.

Sara gave her a wide-eyed look. "You know what Grissom would say. Leave the hunches to the detectives—we follow the evidence."

"Let's follow it, then," Catherine said. To Helpingstine, she said, "Can you stay at this a while?"

"Absolutely," he said.

"Sometime today, call a cab, check yourself in to a hotel . . . there are a few in town . . . and save your receipts."

"Hey, Catherine, I'm here to help—no charge."

"You're here to make a pitch for your product; but we're not going to take advantage. You may have to stay over a night. We'll cover it."

He shrugged. "Fine."

She explained that their shift started at eleven P.M., but gave him her phone and pager numbers, should he come up with something sooner.

"Are you clocking out now?" Helpingstine asked.

"No, Dan. I have a little more work to do, before I call it a night."

"Or day," Sara said, hands on hips. "What do you have in mind?"

"I'm going to check Ray Lipton's alibi."

Her eyes getting wider, Sara said, "But he doesn't *have* one."

Catherine shrugged, smiled. "Let's follow the evidence, and see if you're right."

9

Not as many lights were on in the Pierce castle, tonight—a few in the downstairs, one upstairs. Distant traffic sounds were louder than those of this quietly slumbering neighborhood, the only voices the muffled ones of Jay Leno and David Letterman.

Out on bond on his possession charge, Owen Pierce opened the door on Brass's first knock—as if he'd been expecting them—the physical therapist's handsome features darkly clouded, the blue eyes trading their sparkle for a dull vacancy. He slouched there in a black Polo sweatshirt, gray sweat pants, and Reeboks, like a runner too tired even to pant. His eyes travelled past the Homicide captain to Grissom.

"What you found . . ." Pierce began. "Is it . . . Lynn?"

But it was Brass who answered: "Could we come in, Mr. Pierce? Sit and talk?"

He nodded, numbly, gestured them in, and soon Brass and their host sat on the couch with its rifles-and-flags upholstery, while Grissom took the liberty of pulling a maple Colonial arm chair around, so that he and Brass could casually double-team the suspect.

"It's Lynn, isn't it?" Pierce said, slumped, arms draped against his thighs, interlaced fingers dangling.

"We think so, Mr. Pierce," Grissom said. "We won't have the DNA results for a while, but the evidence strongly suggests that what we found was . . . part of your wife's body."

Pierce stared at the carpet, shaking his head, slowly. *Was he trying not to cry?* Grissom wondered. *Or trying to cry . . .*

Grissom had a Polaroid in his hand; he held it out and up, for Pierce to see—a shot close enough to the torso to crop out everything but flesh. "Your wife had a birthmark on her left hip—is this it?"

Swallowing, he looked at the photo, then dropped his head, his nod barely discernible but there. "Is it . . . true?"

Brass asked, "Is what true, Mr. Pierce?"

He looked up, eyes red. "What . . . what they're saying on television . . ." Pierce's voice caught, and he gave a little hiccup of a sob; a tear sat on the rim of his left eye and threatened to fall. ". . . that Lynn was . . . cut up?"

Brass sat, angled toward the suspect. "Yes, it's true. . . . I'd like you to listen to something, Mr. Pierce." Pulling a small cassette player from his suitcoat pocket, already cued up, Brass pushed PLAY.

Pierce's angry voice came out of the tiny speaker: *"You do and I'll kill your holier-than-thou ass . . ."*

Another voice, Lynn Pierce's terrified voice, said, *"Owen! No! Don't say—"*

"And then I'll cut you up in little pieces."

Brass twitched half a humorless smile. "Gets a little ugly after that. . . . Wouldn't want to disturb you in your time of sorrow."

Pierce had a poleaxed expression. "Where did you get that?"

Brass ignored the question. "Maybe now would be a good time to advise you of your rights, Mr. Pierce."

The therapist's dull eyes suddenly flared bright, as he rose to loom over the detective and the criminalist, and the sorrow—possibly fabricated—turned to unmistakably real rage. "You're *arresting* me? What for? Having an argument with my wife?"

"You threatened to cut her into pieces," Brass said, "and shortly thereafter . . . she was in pieces. We don't view that as a coincidence."

"That tape probably isn't even admissible. Who gave it to you? What, the Blairs? Those religious fanatics? Probably doctored that tape . . . edited it. . . ."

"We've had the tape closely examined," Grissom said. "It's your voice, and the tape is undoctored."

A half-sigh, half-grunt emanated from the therapist's chest, and he sat back down, hard, shaking the couch, jostling Brass a little.

Pierce fixed his red-rimmed blue eyes onto Grissom. "Are you a married man?"

"No."

Then Pierce turned to Brass. "How about you, detective? Married?"

Brass said, "My marital status isn't—"

"Ha!" Pierce pointed at the Homicide captain. "Divorced! . . . And I suppose you never threatened your wife? You never said, I could just *kill* you for that? One of these days, Alice, pow!, zoom!, straight to the moon?"

"Ralph Kramden," Grissom pointed out, "never threatened to dismember his wife."

Brass glanced at the criminalist, surprised by the cultural reference.

Backing down now, Pierce ran a hand over his forehead, removing sweat that wasn't there. "I see your point, guys, I really do . . . I have a nasty temper, but it's strictly . . . verbal. I'm telling you, those words were just me losing it."

"Your temper," Brass said.

"Yes. No question."

"Lost your temper, killed your wife, dismembered her. You're a physical therapist—you have some knowledge about anatomy."

"I *didn't* kill her. It was just an argument—we had them all the time, since her . . . conversion, that Born-Again crapola. But do you honestly think I would kill my wife over *religious* differences?"

Brass was about to respond when the front door opened and a teenage girl stepped into the foyer.

Grissom didn't recognize the girl—she had short, lank black hair, a pierced eyebrow, enough black mascara to offend Elvira, black form-fitting jeans, and a black Slipknot T-shirt. He wondered if this was a friend of Pierce's daughter, Lori, come to visit.

"Daddy, what is it?" the girl asked in a mousy voice that didn't go with her punky Goth look.

Pierce's eyes went from Brass to Grissom to the girl. "Lori," he said slowly. "These officers have some information about Mom."

Grissom looked harder—this was indeed Lori, formerly blonde and rather wholesome-looking, perhaps getting an early start on Halloween.

The girl froze, her eyes wide, the whites of them making a stark contrast with the heavy black mascara. "Is she . . . al . . . all . . . right? What they found . . . on TV . . . was it . . .?"

Pierce was on his feet, nodding gravely, motioning to her. "Come here, baby . . . come 'ere."

A short, sharp breath escaped her, then Lori ran to her father's arms and he held her tight, saying, "She's gone, honey . . . Mom's gone." They stayed that way for a long time. Finally, Pierce held his daughter at arm's length.

"What *happened?*" Lori asked, her pseudo-adult makeup at odds with eyes filled with a child's pain.

Pierce shook his head. "No, honey. It's not the time for that. . . . I have to deal with these . . . the authorities."

"Dad . . ."

"Lori, we'll talk about this later."

She pulled away from his grasp. "I want to know, *now.*"

Grissom had a shiver of recognition: he'd said almost exactly the same thing about Lynn Pierce to Warrick and Nick.

Brass was on his feet. He moved near the father, and said, almost whispering, "Why don't you let me talk to her, Mr. Pierce. I have a daughter, not much older than her. . . ."

Turning to face him, Pierce said, rather bitterly, "Your compassion is noted, detective. But I don't think that's such a good idea."

"I do need to ask your daughter some questions," Brass said. "I'm sure you want to cooperate . . . both of you?"

The girl's eyes were tight, her expression paralyzed, as if she couldn't decide whether to scream, cry, or run.

"Lori's had a great shock," Pierce said, reasonably. "Can't this wait until later?"

"Frankly, Mr. Pierce . . . no. This is a murder investigation. Delays are costly."

Exasperated, Pierce turned to Grissom. "Can't you stop this? You seem like a decent man."

With a tiny enigmatic smile, Grissom rose and said, "You seem like a decent man, too, sir. . . . Maybe you and I should leave Lori and Captain Brass alone, so they can talk . . . and you can show me the garage."

Pierce was looking at Grissom as if the criminalist were wearing clown shoes. "What?"

"Your garage," Grissom said, pleasantly, pointing. "It's this way, isn't it?" He started toward the kitchen.

Reluctantly, with a world-weary sigh and one last glance at his daughter, Pierce followed the CSI.

"Sit down, Lori, please," Brass said, gesturing toward the sofa. "You don't mind if I call you Lori?"

"Do what you want," Lori sniffled. Tears were trailing down her face, mascara painting black abstract patterns on her cheeks. She looked at him skeptically, then demanded, "Are you going to tell me what happened to my mother?"

"Lori . . . please. Sit."

She sat.

So did he.

"I'm Detective Brass. You can call me Jim, if you like."

Her response was tough, undermined by a teary warble in her Sniffles the Mouse voice: "I feel so close to you . . . *Jim.*"

Brass took in a deep breath, let it out slowly through his mouth. No sugarcoating this; the girl had seen the television news, after all. He said, "Your mother was murdered."

He watched her as she took that in. Her face auditioned various emotions, one at a time, but fleeting—surprise, fear, anger— as she struggled to process and accept what he'd just told her. Her internal struggle, barely letting any emotion out beyond the unstoppable tears, reminded Brass a great deal of his own daughter. He wondered if Ellie had cried when his wife told her that he had left them; he wondered where Ellie was now, and if she still hated him.

"Are you all right?" he asked the girl.

"No, I'm not all right! . . . Yeah, right, I'm fine, I'm cool! You got a *touch,* don't ya?"

Brass felt a fool—just as his own daughter had so often made him feel. Of course Lori wasn't "all right," and for that matter, probably never would be. Mothers were not supposed to get murdered.

Then the girl's toughness dropped away. "I . . . I can't believe it," she finally managed.

"It's hard to lose family," he said. "Especially a parent. Even if you had trouble with them. Sometimes that only makes it harder."

The streaky face looked at him differently now. "You . . . ?"

He glanced around, making sure they were alone. "Yeah, both of mine are gone. Not as rough as you, Lori."

"No?"

"Natural causes, and I was an adult."

"But . . . it was still hard?"

"It's always hard. Lori, I don't like this, but we all owe it to your mother to find out what happened to her, and clear this up as much as possible."

"What, like that'll bring her back?"

"Of course it won't bring her back. But it could mean . . . closure, for you. And your dad."

"Closure, huh? Everybody talks about closure. You know what I think, Detective? Closure's way fucking overrated."

". . . You may have a point, Lori. . . . Now, I've got to ask you some questions—you up to it?"

She took a deep breath and nodded, what the hell.

Brass hated this part of the job, and wondered where he should start. If he hit a raw nerve, the girl—who had warmed to him some—might come unglued; and then he'd have a hell of time getting her to answer any questions. If she truly broke down, he'd have to call in the Social Services people, to provide the girl counseling . . . and his investigation would take a backseat.

Best to tread carefully, he thought. "Did you get along with your mother?"

Shrug.

"You're what, Lori? Sixteen?"

Nod.

"So, how did you get along with your mother?"

"You already asked me that."

He'd gotten *some* words out of her, anyway. "Yes, Lori, but you didn't really answer me."

Another shrug. "Not good, really. She didn't want me to do, you know, anything."

"What do you mean . . . 'anything'?"

"You know—go out with guys, go to concerts, get a job. She wanted me to be the girl in the plastic bubble. She barely tolerated my boyfriend, Gary."

"Tell me about your boyfriend."

This time the nod carried some enthusiasm. "Gary Blair. He's cool."

"Cool? Aren't the Blairs a pretty straight-laced family?"

A tiny smile appeared. "Basically. I don't know about lace, but he's pretty straight. His parents are in a church group with Mom . . . otherwise, I don't think she'd even let me go out with him."

"How strict was your mom?"

She snorted. "She's way past strict into . . ." Her expression turned inward. ". . . I mean, she *was* way past strict. . . ."

Brass could have kicked himself for the past-tense slip. She'd just been opening up, when he made the faux pas, and now he had to find a way to save the interview, before the kid caved.

"What do you and Gary like to do together?" Brass asked. "Movies? Dancing?"

Lori, lost in thought, didn't seem to hear him. She was still on his previous question, mumbling, "Yeah, Mom made the 700 Club look like, you know, un-psycho."

"You and Gary?"

She seemed to kind of shake herself out of it. "We, uh . . . you know, go to the movies, we hang out at the mall. Sometimes we just stay here."

"Ever go to the Blairs?"

"Not much. His mom is really weird, kinda . . . you know, wired? Like a chihuahua on speed?"

Brass smiled at that, though the drug reference was disturbing. "So when you and Gary hang out here, what do you do?"

Yet another shrug. "Listen to CDs in my room, watch DVDs, stuff like that. Sometimes surf the 'net. Go in chat rooms and pretend to be people, you know, like pretend I'm a nympho or a dyke or somethin'—typical shit."

Brass was starting to wonder if the shrugging was a nervous tic, or simply generational—his sullen daughter had shrugged at him a lot the last time he'd seen her. Somewhere along the line, shrugging had become a substitute for speech. "Gary ever around, when your parents argued?"

She gave him an odd, sideways look. Her response turned one syllable into at least three: "No."

"But you did? See them argue?"

"I . . . I don't know if I should be talking about stuff like that. . . . That's personal. Family shit."

"It's all right, Lori. I'm a . . . public servant. I'm just trying to help you . . . help your family get through this."

She drew back. *"That's* bullshit."

He froze, then laughed. "Yeah . . . I guess it is, sort of. Lori, this is a crime. I have to find out what happened to your mom. If you don't talk to me, you'll have to talk to somebody, sometime. Why not get it out of the way?"

Lori considered that for a moment before answering. "Yeah, well. They fought sometimes. All parents do. All married people do, right?"

"Right."

"I don't think they fought any more than anybody else. I mean, I never saw Gary's parents fight, but they're such . . . pod people. My other friends' parents fight, at least the ones that are still together do."

Out in the large, tidy garage, Pierce stood on the periphery, arms folded, while a latex-gloved Grissom poked around.

One of the two parking places stood empty, the therapist's blue Lincoln Navigator occupying the other. A workbench made out of two-by-fours and plywood ran most of the length of the far wall, tools arrayed on the pegboard above it, larger power tools stored on the shelf below. Three bikes and two sets of golf clubs in expensive bags lined the nearest wall. A plywood ceiling held a pull-down door with stairs that gave access to the crawlspace up there.

"Do you own a chain saw?" Grissom asked affably.

"A chain saw!" Pierce's eyes and nostrils flared. "I resent this harassment! I'm trying to—"

Holding up a traffic-cop palm, Grissom interrupted. "I'm not harassing you, Mr. Pierce."

"That's how it looks to me."

"I'm sorry you see it that way. I'm doing my job, which is to find and eliminate suspects based upon the evidence."

"I'm automatically a suspect, I suppose, because I'm the husband."

"Based on that tape you heard Captain Brass play, it's fair to say you had argued with your wife, threatening her with violence . . . and when she turns up dead in just the manner you described, you tell me? Are you a reasonable candidate for the crime?"

The therapist looked dumbfounded. "Well . . ."

"Your cooperation helps me eliminate you as a suspect. Remember that."

Pierce turned conciliatory, sighing as he walked over to the criminalist. "I'm sorry, Mr. Grissom. I guess I lost my head, because I do know how it looks."

The question, the CSI thought, *is how did your* wife *lose her head?* But Grissom had enough sense and tact not to blurt as much.

Instead, Grissom said only, "Understandable, sir. Understandable."

"Lynn and I had some really good times, before she was . . . *born* again. I'm telling you, it's like she joined a cult. Do you know that she told me, once, that she felt it was so sad that good people like Gandhi and Mother Teresa had to go to hell, 'cause they hadn't been saved, like she had? I can't lie to you, Mr. Grissom—we were definitely in the divorce express lane."

"The chain saw?"

Pierce sighed, pointed. "Under the workbench. . . . Want me to . . . ?"

Grissom nodded, followed him over and watched as Pierce pulled out two chain saws and hauled them, one at a time, up on the bench. One, a brand new STIHL, was still in the box.

"This box is sealed," Grissom said, giving it a close, thorough look.

"Yeah, just bought it yesterday. Got the receipt."

The other, an old Poulan, was so rusty that Grissom could tell just by looking that the saw wouldn't even start, let alone cut through a human body.

"What do you generally use a chain saw for, Mr. Pierce?"

"Cutting firewood, mostly. Pile out back."

Grissom nodded at the door leading outside. "May I?"

"Be my guest."

Behind the house, in the moonlight, Pierce showed Grissom to the woodpile. Using a pocket flash, the CSI knelt and inspected several of the cords.

"These are freshly cut, Mr. Pierce." He stood. "You've got one saw that's inoperable, and another still in the box. How is it you have fresh cut firewood?"

Pierce didn't miss a beat. "Nextdoor neighbor. Mel Charles, he loaned me his chain saw."

"When?"

"Couple of days ago. I like to watch a fireplace fire . . . helps me think, relax. So, I cut some wood. That's relaxing, too—use some muscles I don't, in my work."

Grissom nodded; he'd have Brass check with the neighbor.

They went back into the garage, Pierce saying, "Is that all, Mr. Grissom?"

"Crawlspace?"

Pierce pulled the steps down, and Grissom and his Maglite went up for a look—nothing. He would send Warrick and Nick in for the fine-tooth comb tour, later.

The physical therapist ushered Grissom back into the house, where Brass and Lori were just wrapping up their interview. Brass glanced up as they came in, but continued the interview.

"Lori, you've gone through some pretty big changes," Brass said. "The dyed hair, the pierced eyebrow, weren't you worried about what your mom would say when she came home?"

Lori's eyes shot to her father's, but she said nothing.

Pierce, sitting next to his daughter, putting a hand on her shoulder, said, "Lori was so upset when we thought Lynn had abandoned us, well . . . I thought a few changes wouldn't hurt anything, and would help Lori's state of mind."

"But wouldn't her mother have been furious?" Brass asked.

Pierce waved that off. "Lori had every right to be angry. At least, she thought so at the time."

Brass's eyes moved to Grissom. The CSI supervisor shook his head: nothing in the garage. Rising, Brass said, "Thank you, Lori—I really appreciate your cooperation."

The girl shrugged—but a tiny one-sided smile indicated the slight but significant rapport Brass had established.

To Pierce, Brass said, "I'm sure we'll have more questions for Lori, as the investigation continues. But I promise you we'll keep her best interests in mind."

"I'm sure," Pierce said dryly.

"We'll also have more questions for you."

"Then you're not arresting me?"

"No," Brass said, a "not at this time" lilt in his voice, "but you may wish to consult with your attorney."

Pierce's reply was quietly sardonic: "Because you have my best interests in mind."

The investigators moved to the door and Pierce shut it wordlessly behind them.

Out in the yard, Grissom gestured to the sprawling stucco ranch-style house next door. "We need to stop by the neighbor's house."

"Kinda late."

Grissom explained what Pierce had told him about the chain saw. "I want that chain saw, now."

"Are you saying Owen Pierce borrowed his neighbor's chain saw to cut up his wife?"

"He could have. Any way you look at it, I want that chain saw."

They crossed the well-manicured yard, a dwarf fruit tree perched in the middle of a brick circle surrounded by a moat of mulch. Brass rang the bell.

"They're gonna love us," Brass said.

But it was only a moment before an auburn-haired woman of about thirty answered the door. She wore jeans, tennis shoes, and a T-shirt with the "Race for the Cure" logo splashed across the front. Green-eyed with milky skin, she had a small rabbit-twitch nose and an inquisitive expression—but she didn't look annoyed.

The muffled sound of Conan O'Brien came from the living room. *Good,* Brass thought. *We didn't wake anyone.*

"I don't normally open the door at this time of night," she said, and her voice, though quiet, carried a backbone of authority. "But I've seen you before, stopping next door, and on TV, too—you're the police officers on the Lynn Pierce case, aren't you?

Brass already had his I.D. out to show her. "That's right, ma'am. I'm Captain Jim Brass and this is crime-scene investigator, Gil Grissom. Is Mel Charles here?"

"Mel is my husband—I'm Kristy Charles." Her smile disappeared. "The house is kind of a mess—you mind if I bring Mel to you?"

"Not at all," Brass said. "This shouldn't take long."

"Any help we can give, we're glad to—Lynn's a great gal, but her husband . . . well, I'll get Mel for you."

Soon Mel Charles filled the doorway, his wife staying just behind him, taking it all in. She seemed to have a satisfied expression, as though relishing this call by the police.

"Mr. Charles," Grissom said, "did you loan a chain saw to your nextdoor neighbor, Mr. Pierce?"

"Couple days ago," Charles said.

"Have you loaned him the saw on other occasions?"

Charles considered that for a moment, then shook his head. "Never needed it before. He had his own. He's always out there cutting wood."

"Why'd he need yours?"

"Said his had rusted up on him, and he hadn't had a chance to get a new one."

"Are you and Owen Pierce close, Mr. Charles? Hang out, shoot the breeze, loan each other garden tools and so on, pretty casually?"

"No. We just nod at each other. . . . Kristy and Lynn are friendly, share a cup of coffee now and then . . . I wouldn't say 'close.' "

"Obviously, you've seen the news about the disappearance of Mrs. Pierce, and what was found out at Lake Mead, today . . ."

Mrs. Charles's face was etched with dread. "You don't mean . . . he used *our* chainsaw to . . . oh my God. . . . Excuse me."

And she was gone.

Brass said, "Your wife liked Mrs. Pierce."

Eyebrows rose above the Buddy Holly rims. "You make it sound like Lynn's dead, Captain Brass."

"The evidence leans that way, yes."

Charles shook his head, mouth tight. "Well, that's a damn shame, God, a pity. She was real nice—kind of straight-laced? But nice."

"Straight-laced?" Brass echoed, remembering using the term himself when questioning Lori.

"You know—Born-Again Christian, conservative as hell."

"How about Mr. Pierce?"

With a shrug, Charles said, "We don't know them that well, really. But I get the idea he wasn't the church-going type, himself."

"What makes you say that?"

Charles was clearly trying to decide how much it was fair to say. ". . . I've seen rough characters stop by the house."

"Any you might be able to identify?"

"There was this one guy . . . I don't want to sound prejudiced."

"Black? Hispanic? Asian?"

"Black guy—dreadlocks, jewelry, baseball cap backwards."

"Often?"

"No. Few times, when Pierce's wife was away. He had different women in the house, too, when Lynn was visiting relatives or even just off doing some church thing."

Brass frowned. "Different women? Not one woman?"

"Hookers, is my guess. Right in his own house."

"What about his daughter? Would she have witnessed it?"

"She wasn't home that much, especially when the mom wasn't around."

Mrs. Charles's voice chimed back in; she'd returned, drying her eyes with a tissue—maybe she'd been off throwing up. "That daughter's got a smart mouth . . . but I suppose people think the same thing about our kids."

Brass was not surprised the Charleses and the Pierces weren't close—typical for neighbors in a city growing as fast as Vegas. It was one of the things Brass hated about living in the fastest-growing city in the United States. In the last ten years, the population had expanded by the size of Minneapolis, and every single day the equivalent of Salt Lake City came to visit. He lived in a city of strangers, some good, some bad, and one of them had killed and dismembered Lynn Pierce.

Mel Charles did not object when Grissom collected the chain saw into evidence.

As they drove back, Brass turned to Grissom. "What do you think?"

"If Pierce used this chain saw, all the cleaning in the world didn't get the blood off. The luminol will tell."

But an hour later Grissom was in his office, on the phone to Brass. "This chain saw hasn't cut anything but cord wood."

"Jesus," Brass said into the phone. "This guy Pierce has an answer for everything."

"Too many answers, Jim—and too pat. Don't despair—this tells us a lot."

"What does it tell us? A chain saw with no blood on it? That doesn't tell us a damn thing!"

Patiently Grissom said, "It tells us there's a missing chain saw—probably at the bottom of Lake Mead."

"Where we'll never find it—but how do you figure . . . ?"

"I should have known," Grissom said, disgusted, "when Pierce all but walked me over to that nextdoor neighbor. He was sending us on a wild goose chase, Jim, while trying to build a sort of alibi. Doesn't wash, though."

"Because there's a third chain saw?" The skepticism in Brass's voice was thick.

"No, there are *four* chainsaws. Think it through, Jim—Pierce has an ancient, rusted-out chain saw. That thing hasn't been used for some time. Yet the neighbor has seen him, fairly recently, cutting cord wood."

"There's also a brand-new, in-the-box chain saw."

"Yes—to replace the chain saw used to dismember Lynn. The one now, presumably, at the bottom of the lake."

Brass was getting it. "And after he tossed that chain saw in the lake, he borrowed his neighbor's . . . to cut some firewood, and to throw us off the trail."

"Exactly. To make it appear that there had never been a chain saw in the Pierce household between the old rusted one and the new-in-the-box."

Brass grunted a humorless laugh. "Well, Gil—I'll let *you* walk your new proof over to the D.A. That's about the most circumstantial circumstantial evidence I ever heard."

"I didn't say it would hold up in court. But it's a piece of the puzzle, and we need all the pieces we can get our hands on."

"Particularly since we only have one piece of Lynn Pierce. Can you make the picture out yet, Gil, of this puzzle you're working?"

"I can tell you Owen Pierce cut up his wife with the missing chain saw."

"After he murdered her?"

"That," Grissom said, "I can't say."

"Great. If we can prove he cut his wife up, but not that he murdered her first, we can book him on his other crime."

"What other crime?" Grissom asked.

"Littering."

And the phone clicked in Grissom's ear.

10

Well past the end of her shift, the long hours suddenly catching up to her, Catherine Willows sat at her desk, on the phone, talking to a lawyer—and the hell of it was, it had been her own idea.

She was speaking to Jennifer Woods, in "legal" at ESPN, and had introduced herself. The woman—whose voice was alto range, self-confident, professional—did not seem at all surprised, or for that matter impressed, to be hearing from a Las Vegas PD criminalist.

"How may I help you, Ms. Willows?"

"Ms. Woods, we have a suspect in a murder case who claims he was watching television at the time of the murder."

"Our network, I take it."

"That's right."

"What day, what time?"

Catherine read from her notes: "Thursday, October twenty-five, from five thirty Pacific time until, let's say midnight."

"And what are you after, Ms. Willows?"

"First, your program listing. Second, a VHS dub of your file tape, assuming you keep such a thing. As I said, we're checking a murder suspect's alibi."

A pause—ducks were being gathered into a row. "All right, Ms. Willows, here's how it works. We need a letter of request sent to us. If it's not in writing, it doesn't exist."

"May I fax it?"

The lawyer's silence indicated consideration. "You may fax it to get the process started, but I can't really divulge any information or share any videotape until we have the letter mailed to us."

"This is a murder investigation."

"Exactly, Ms. Willows. And we're the legal department of a major company."

"I would appreciate any help you can provide," Catherine said, holding her temper in check. As much as she wanted them to rush, the truth was she did understand their hesitancy—right now, Catherine Willows was just a voice on the phone. "I'll fax you a copy in ten minutes and overnight the letter. What's the fax number and the address?"

Woods told her, then added, "I'll begin looking into this now; I'll call you when I have something."

Catherine recited all her phone numbers and said, "Thanks—you getting started on this really means a lot."

"No promises."

And the lawyer hung up.

Five minutes later, Sara strolled in, less than bright-eyed after another endless shift. "Find out anything?"

Shaking her head, Catherine said, "Only that even when a lawyer does me a favor, I don't like 'em much."

"Is the network going to help?"

"After their lawyers assure them that there's no way anybody can ever sue them for doing their civic duty, I think so."

"What do we do in the meantime?"

"Here's a thought—why don't we go home?"

Sara's eyebrows lifted and she nodded. "It's an idea."

"You up for coming in a hour or two early? Maybe by then the elves will have polished all our boots for us." Catherine was reaching for her purse.

"Elves like Greg Sanders," Sara said, as they walked down the hall toward the locker room, "and Dan Helpingstine?"

"Great big elves like that, yeah."

And the women went home, like Vegas headliners, to sleep away the day.

The city wore the blue patina of dusk, the sky streaked a faded orange along a horizon made irregular by the lumpy spine of the slumbering beast of the dark blue mountain range; dark gray clouds, like factory smoke, encouraged the night.

In her stylish black leather jacket, a turquoise top, and new black jeans and black pointed-toe boots, Catherine Willows walked briskly across the parking lot, feeling fresh, well-rested, and ready to get back to solving Jenna Patrick's murder. She had not yet admitted to herself that this case was special, that her emotions had been touched by the thought of a young woman, about to leave that life, having hers ended prematurely.

She collected Sara in the break room, where the brunette criminalist was giving the dayshift's coffee a down-the-drain mercy killing.

"Hey," Sara said.

"Hey," Catherine said. "Let's see what the elves have come up with."

"Greg first?"

Catherine nodded. "Greg first."

Greg Sanders was hovering over one of his state-of-the-art machines. God, he was young, Catherine thought; with his spiky hair and mischievous smile, he looked more like a kid than a gifted scientist— still, there was no doubting his ability.

Catherine stood across from the slender blue-smocked figure, Sara leaning on the counter, not yet awake. This was morning to them, after all.

"What do you have for us?" Catherine asked.

Sanders shuffled some papers, and smiled—a smile that might mean disaster or triumph, one never knew. "Last things first, I guess. The fake beard and mustache you found in Lipton's house? Human hair."

"Human scalp hair," Catherine said.

Sara was frowning, not quite following.

Sanders picked up on Catherine's thought. "Human scalp hair's what they use to make really high-quality wigs." He brought out two plastic bags with the beard in one and the mustache in the other.

"Okay," Catherine said, with Sanders and yet not with him. "So what does that tell us?"

He turned his palms up. "Well, the hair in the beard and mustache, that you took from Lipton's closet, doesn't match any hairs you collected in Dream Dolls."

"No?"

He held up a tiny bag with a single straight brown hair in it. "No— for example, this is from the club, and I identified it as wig hair, but the cheap variety . . . *not* human hair: rayon."

"Okay," Sara said, not ready to process this information just yet, "what else?"

Sanders showed them two more evidence bags. "The spirit gum bottle, and the shoebox you got all this stuff from? The only fingerprints belong to the victim, Jenna Patrick."

Sara shrugged. "So Ray Lipton wore gloves, or wiped off the bottle and box."

Sanders was already shaking his head. "Not likely."

"Why?" Catherine asked.

"No wipe marks, but plenty of clear prints—the Patrick woman's prints would've been smeared, if the box'd been wiped. Near as I can tell, only Jenna Patrick ever touched this stuff."

"Okay," Catherine said, "so Ray Lipton didn't touch any of it. Maybe this is some other fake mustache and beard, hard as that might be to buy. . . . What about the back room at the strip club?"

"Yeah," Sara said, eager, "any sign of our man back there?"

Sanders sighed, took a swig of coffee, shook his head. "You brought in a ton of stuff; I'll still be going through this evidence when I reach retirement. Y'know, I never knew female pubic hair could be such a bore."

Sara made a face. "Thanks for sharing, Greg."

"Anyway, none of the fingerprints belong to Ray Lipton. His hair wasn't back there, either."

Sara suddenly seemed animated—finally awake. "Wait, Greg— what are you telling us . . . Lipton didn't do it?"

"I'm not saying that. Anyway, you've still got the videotape, don't you?"

Catherine said, "That's starting to look a little iffy, its own self."

After another sip of coffee, Sanders raised his eyebrows, shrugged and said, "It's not that Lipton *couldn't* have done the deed—it's just that there's no real evidence from the strip club that he did, other than the security videotape. And if you think that's not him on the video . . . well . . . where does that leave you?"

Sara turned to Catherine. "Where does that leave us?"

"Where else?" Catherine said. "Back to square one: find evidence that Lipton did it . . . or evidence that exonerates him."

"And, hopefully, points to someone else," Sara said. "Greg, you got anything else for us?"

"Fingerprints, lots of them. Hair, fibers, and DNA. We just don't know who they go with. I need samples from the dancers and the customers."

Catherine shook her head. "We've got the customers who were there when the murder was discovered—O'Riley and Vega have been interviewing them, collecting fingerprints; maybe dayshift can help us out and gather those samples for you."

"That'll help," Sanders said.

"As for customers who might've been there earlier that day or night," she went on, "or more crucially, any who slipped out before Jenna's body was found . . . there's no way to track them down."

"Unless they were regulars," Sara said, "and that Kapa-what's-it guy'll give us their names."

"Kapelos," Catherine said. "He might help." She used her cell phone and caught Detective Erin Conroy, telling her, "We need another visit to Dream Dolls."

"Got a lead?"

"We may have, after you've done some questioning. . . . Meet Sara and me there, and I'll fill you in when I see you."

Fifteen minutes later, they met the detective in the mostly empty parking lot of the strip club, the fancy DREAM DOLLS sign doing its neon dance for no one in particular.

"Why so dead?" Sara wondered aloud.

Catherine surveyed the vacant spaces. "Early evening . . . weeknight."

Still, strip clubs in Vegas rarely had empty parking lots, no matter what hour it was.

"You mind telling me," Conroy said, her mouth a tight line, "why we've returned to this delightful scene of the crime?"

"Ray Lipton," Catherine said quietly, "may not be our guy."

A convertible Mustang rolled by, a male passenger catcalling at the three women standing in the parking lot, possibly mistaking them for strippers on their way into the club. A low-rider BMW drove by, its bass speaker rattling windows in the surrounding older buildings.

"Lipton not our man?" Conroy asked, numbly.

Catherine shook her head.

Conroy was frowning. "What the hell? We have him cold, on videotape."

"That might not be him," Sara admitted. "If it was, he somehow managed not to leave any prints."

"You CSIs ever hear about gloves?" Conroy asked.

"It's not that easy," Catherine said.

She filled Conroy in on Greg's reading of the evidence, and Helpingstine's preliminary enhancement of the video, which seemed to bring out a figure that didn't entirely resemble Lipton's build.

Rather glumly, Conroy asked, "Suggestions?"

Catherine said, "Sara and I'll get hair and blood from the dancers, and I thought you might want to re-interview."

"Yeah," Conroy said, "probably a good idea. But maybe you should chat with the owner some more."

The two CSIs gathered their equipment from the Tahoe, Conroy giving them a hand, and headed into the club. While Sara and Conroy kept a respectful distance, Catherine approached Ty Kapelos, who ruled the roost from behind the bar, wearing what appeared to be the same white long-sleeved shirt as the other evening.

"Hey, Ty," she said.

"Hey, Cath . . . knew you couldn't stay away—missed me, didn't ya?"

"That's it, Ty," Catherine said. "You're irresistible."

The club was quiet, only a handful of college-age guys, hanging out near the stage, and a few white-collar types at tables, whether conventioneers or local businessman "working late," Catherine couldn't hazard a guess. The music was thankfully silent—Worm in his booth, going through CDs looking for tunes, reminding her of Greg Sanders examining clues—and no women were currently on the stage.

"Jeez, Ty," Catherine said. "I'd like to have the tumbleweed concession in this place, about now."

Kapelos shrugged. "Changeover time, Cath. You know how that is. Girls are in the back."

"That the *whole* story, Ty?"

His good humor evaporated, and he answered her, but in a hushed tone. "Nothing like a murdered dancer to chase business away."

"Sure—your patrons like things discreet. Murder happens, you never know when the cops are going to show back up."

"You said it, Cath, I didn't—at least, the sheriff had the decency to send around pretty cops."

"You're still a charmer, Ty," she said, and explained what they needed.

"Sure, go ahead," Kapelos said.

Catherine turned to Conroy, who gave her a look. The CSI nodded just a little, getting it, and said, "You two go ahead. . . . I'll catch up."

Conroy smiled a little as she and Sara moved toward the hallway in back.

Returning her attention to Kapelos, Catherine asked, "Which of your dancers makes the most money?"

He shrugged as he polished a glass.

"Come on, Ty—I'm not the IRS. I don't want to bust anybody's chops, particularly not yours—I just want to know if Jenna was the object of jealousy."

Another, more cooperative shrug. "Yeah, some—she was really cute, y'know, had this girl-next-door kinda thing goin'. She did pretty well even before her boob job, which came out great, and made her even more popular. . . . Some of the girls didn't like that. You know how it goes."

Catherine was aware that Jenna's life at Dream Dolls wouldn't have been easy. Under the added pressure of her jealous boyfriend, Jenna couldn't have been very happy; no wonder she'd wanted out. "Had Jenna ever talked about quitting?"

Kapelos waved off the question. "Yeah, sure. They all do."

"So, you didn't take her talk of quitting seriously?"

"Question is, did *she* take it serious. I mean, hell, I knew this boyfriend, Lipton, wanted her to quit . . . even though he *met* her here . . . and she usually talked about it, right after they argued. 'Maybe Ray's right, maybe I am prostituting myself.' I learned a long time ago not to put too much stock in that kind of talk. These are messed-up kids—you know, Cath . . . low self-esteem, high drug abuse, and more incest victims than a week of Springer."

"Was Jenna a drug user?"

"I don't know about her private life. I don't have to tell you, I don't allow none of that shit in here, not in my business . . . but what they do on their own time, how they spend all this money they make, that's *their* business."

"Jenna ever mention anything about her and Lipton getting married?"

"Yeah, but I figured she was just talkin' about that to keep Lipton on the hook. Sure he's a hot-headed prick, but he's also a good-looking fella with a successful small business."

"So you figure she did want to marry him?"

"I think so, but my take is, she wanted to work a few years, and put a little money away, of her own, before she walked away from show biz to be a baby-making machine."

"Did she say that? Indicated Lipton wanted a big family?"

"Yeah. She'd be a normal housewife, those were the words she used. Look, I don't have to tell you Dream Dolls and even the glitzier clubs, like Showgirl World and Olympic Gardens, ain't exactly Broadway or Hollywood . . . but it's still show business, and Jenna was a star, in her little universe . . . and it's hard to walk away from that kind of attention."

"But Jenna did want to marry Ray," Catherine said, pressing Ty, "if not now, eventually?"

Kapelos turned up his palms. "Who can say? You ever know anybody talkin' about marriage didn't have their head up their ass?"

Suddenly her ex-husband Eddie's face popped up in her memory, like a jack-in-the-box, and she shook her head to dismiss the image.

"Damn straight," Kapelos said, misreading that as a gesture of agreement with him.

Catherine didn't bother to correct him. "Which of these dancers would you say disliked Jenna the most?"

Kapelos harumphed. "Hell, take your pick. It ain't like the old days when you girls watched out for each other. These days, these girls just as soon spit at each other as say hello. This is a more lucrative business than when you left, Cath. Some of these girls are makin' a good six figures."

Catherine squinted—had she heard right? "You serious?"

"As a heart attack . . . and Jenna was one of those girls. She did the circuit, made some serious green, but this was home for her. . . . Y'know, when she did L.A., she had the porn producers hounding her, all the time."

"She interested?"

A groove of thought settled between his thick eyebrows. "Frankly, I think she mighta been considering it. She told me that some of the top girls in the adult industry work a few years, and retire millionaires."

"Did Lipton know she was considering a porn career?"

"If he did, well . . ."

"Well what, Ty?"

"I was gonna say . . . he'd kill her."

Their gazes held for several long seconds, then Catherine twitched a smile and said, "Thanks, Ty. I'm going to the back, to help out. I know Detective Conroy's going to have some more questions, possibly about regulars. I'd appreciate if you'd be as open with her as you have been with me."

Kapelos grinned. "Not a chance, Cath . . . not a chance."

She chuckled, as Kapelos turned his attention to one of college kids, who'd ambled up to the bar.

Pushing through the curtains at the corridor's end, Catherine entered a different facet of the world of Dream Dolls.

The dressing room was much brighter than the dark bar and it took a moment for her eyes to adjust. Once the tiny stars dissipated, she found herself in a room deeper than she remembered, going back a good thirty feet and leaving space for nine tiny dressing tables along each side wall. Globe lights on four ceiling fans ran down the center of the ceiling. At least, Catherine thought, Ty had finally got rid of those fluorescents that painted the dancers a ghostly white. Walls a pastel green, the room felt soft and inviting compared to the overbearing blackness beyond the heavy curtains.

Conroy was in the far left-hand corner interviewing a lithe, chocolate-skinned dancer wearing a red sequined g-string and nothing else. About halfway back on the right side, Sara was taking a blood sample from a blonde woman in red bikini lingerie, a voluptuous girl of maybe twenty.

Seven or eight other women stood around in various stages of undress, none of them the least bit modest or seemingly even aware of the three fully clothed women in their midst. The unforgiving illumination revealed cellulite, stretch marks, scars and other imperfections that the low, blue-tinged lighting out front would conceal; a couple of them wore a shiny patina of perspiration that told Catherine they had been dancing recently.

A redhead with breasts as fraudulent as her hair color strode forward on spike heels that lifted her to a height of six feet. Probably pushing thirty or even thirty-five . . . ancient in this trade, Catherine knew . . . the busty dancer had the cold eyes of a veteran and a narrow severe face framing a small round mouth that looked perpetually angry. She used a large white beach towel to dry herself as she walked over, saying, "You with them?" The woman tilted her head toward the back of the room.

Nodding, Catherine introduced herself, adding, "Crime scene investigator—and you are?"

"Pissed off . . . Thanks for askin'." She saronged the towel around herself, plucked a package of cigarettes from the nearby dressing table and lit herself up. She blew smoke and said, "I was just wonderin' when you people are gonna be done with this place so we can go back to makin' money."

Ignoring the stripper's belligerent attitude, Catherine asked, "You have *my* name—yours is . . . ?"

Chin high, proud of herself, the dancer said, "Belinda Bountiful."

Catherine laughed out loud. "That wouldn't be a stage name, by any chance?"

The redhead glanced around, making sure no one was listening, and whispered, "Pat Hensley."

"Don't the other girls know your real name?"

"We're not that close. I like to keep my private life private, that's all. . . . I got a husband and two kids to feed."

Catherine sat on the edge of a dressing table. "So, the money's dried up around here?"

With a shake of her ersatz-auburn mane, the dancer said, "It was hard enough to make money here when Jenna was alive—this ain't exactly the Flamingo, you know. But now . . ."

"What about now?"

"Whose fantasy is it, to go into the club where there's been a murder, anyway? Jeffrey Dahmer's maybe? Ted Bundy's? And those two ain't been hittin' the club scene much, lately. Plus which, we've had cops in and out of here, almost nonstop since Jenna bought it."

That was touching. "You have a few customers out there. It's early, yet."

"Probably as big a crowd as we'll see all night."

Trying to catch the dancer with her guard down, Catherine asked, "Bother you at all, how much money Jenna was pulling down?"

The Hensley woman scoffed at that. "Hell, no. You're kidding, right?"

"You were making your fair share then?"

Moving a well-manicured hand to her cleavage, the dancer asked, "You know anything about this life, then you know that as long as I have these, I'm going to make my fair share."

"You happen to know if Jenna Patrick was using her real name?"

The belligerence was gone, now. "That was her real name—had the right sound, y'know? Lots of 'Jennas' around the strip circuit, right now. Hot porn star name."

"You knew that was Jenna's real name, but she didn't know yours?"

"Hey, just 'cause I'm belly-achin' about business, don't think I'm glad Jenna's gone. Truth is, we were friends. I get along with her roommate, too."

"Tera Jameson, you mean?"

"That's right—ever see that one dance? Now she is class; she was born with a great rack, and she studied ballet and shit. Yeah, before Tera left for Showgirl World, the three of us was pretty close."

Catherine cast an eye toward Conroy who was still talking to the African-American dancer. "Has Detective Conroy talked to you yet?"

The dancer shrugged. "Last time you guys was here."

"Not this time around?"

"No, why?"

"I had the impression," the CSI said, "that the girls around here weren't all that tight."

Pat nodded. "That's true enough, but I'm kinda the . . . den mother, I guess. And the three of us, Tera and Jenna and me, we hung out together quite a bit. Shopping, the occasional breakfast after we got off, stuff like that."

"How well do you know her boyfriend?"

"Hothead Ray? Not all that well." Pat smirked sourly. "I was a little surprised when Jenna hooked up with *his* ass."

"Surprised, why?"

Again the dancer looked around to make sure they weren't being overheard. "I never knew what was goin' on with Jenna and Tera, not exactly, not really . . ."

Catherine nodded, even though she didn't know what she was agreeing with.

". . . but I just assumed . . . well . . . you know."

The CSI's antennae were tingling as she said, "No—I don't know."

"Knowing that Tera was a lez, I just assumed that Jenna was too. Anyway, that's why I was so surprised when Jenna hooked up with Lipton. I mean, I didn't know Jenna was bi—but what the hell? Whatever gets you through the night . . . or workin' *these* hours, the day!"

Catherine's eyes bored into those of the dancer.

"Ooooh shit," Pat said, eyes as big as her bosoms. "You didn't know Tera leaned that way, did you?"

"Never came up before. All we knew was, she and Jenna lived together; but nobody mentioned a relationship between the two, other than that they were roommates."

"Didn't you talk to Tera yet?"

"Yes. She didn't say a word about it."

The dancer shrugged. "Well, even these days, people don't always advertise it."

However you figured it, Catherine knew, this little sexual tidbit would call for another trip to Tera Jameson's apartment.

The criminalist decided to push on; she had in Pat a close friend of the deceased, after all. "Any idea who would be jealous of Jenna, either here in the club, or, I don't know . . . maybe somebody out of Lipton's life? Coworker at the construction company, maybe?"

Pat looked slowly around the room. "Here at Dream Dolls? Any of these girls who haven't saved up for new ones were jealous of her. And she had really nice work done . . . I'm saving up to get mine overhauled."

Catherine's eyes travelled around the dressing room and she realized Pat's words might apply to all of these other dancers. That meant if Lipton really was innocent, they would have no shortage of suspects.

Sara strolled up and looked at Pat. "You ready to give at the office?"

Before Catherine's eyes, Pat Hensley disappeared and in her place stood Belinda Bountiful, returning in all her bitchy glory. "Is this trip really necessary? Ain't it enough you're keeping us from makin' a livin'?"

Sara shrugged with her mouth. "You can either do it voluntarily, or we can get a court order. Do it now and we're out of your hair—your choice."

Making a real production out of it, star stripper Belinda Bountiful finally agreed to follow Sara back and have the blood drawn. Turning privately to Catherine, Pat peeked out from behind the Belinda mask to whisper, "Can't ever let 'em forget who the real diva is around this hellhole."

While Conroy and Sara finished up, Catherine moved back to the tiny room where a murder had occurred. Using her Swiss Army knife, the CSI sliced through the yellow-and-black crime-scene tape and eased the door open. Having been closed up for this long a time, the cubicle hit Catherine in the face with a hot, fetid aroma, as if not an atom of air conditioning had penetrated the police seal.

Pulling on latex gloves, she stepped in. They were missing some-thing—something *important*, she thought; and maybe they had missed it in here. . . .

Standing there at the threshold of the murder, Catherine saw it happen.

Lipton—in a fake beard and mustache, dark glasses on, cap pulled down tight, the LIPTON CONSTRUCTION lettering on his jacket standing out in bold red letters against the denim background—walks down the hall, leading Jenna Patrick down the familiar path to the lap-dance cu-bicles. Naked except for the flimsy lavender thong, Jenna trails behind a few steps, an apprehensive smile on her pretty face as she wonders why her boyfriend is tempting fate by coming in here. Still, it excites Jenna, knowing that he would disguise himself so they could be to-gether here, at the forbidden place that Dream Dolls has become. . . .

They enter the little room, he sits on the chair and Jenna closes the door. She goes to him; perhaps they even kiss. He is, after all, no ordi-nary customer. Jenna spins around, sits on his lap and begins to gyrate to the music filtered in through the speakers, even as behind her back, he pulls on gloves, takes the electrical tie out of his pocket, and at the critical moment, slips it down over her head, and around her slender throat.

He yanks it tight. Within seconds it cuts off the blood in her carotid arteries. She struggles to get a grip, her eyes wide with fear and pain and betrayal and sorrow; but it's too late. . . . Essentially un-conscious, brain death only a few short minutes away, she stops fight-ing as the electrical tie does its terrible work. All Lipton has to do is sit quietly and watch her die.

When she is dead, dropped to the floor, he need only rise, and make his way through the bar, out the door, and into the cool night, where a new life awaits, where he will find some new woman who will not betray him with this sorry, sordid lifestyle.

"You all right?" Conroy asked.

Catherine shook herself to awareness. She hadn't even heard the detective come up behind her. "Yeah—fine. I was just thinking it through."

Sara strolled up in the hallway. "Four of the girls aren't here, but they're scheduled to work tomorrow. We can go to their apartments, or stop back, then."

"Tomorrow'll do fine," Conroy said, as the three women confabbed in the corridor. "We got plenty to work on."

"You get anything interesting?" Catherine asked them.

Conroy shrugged. "Hard to say. The dancer that spoke to you . . ." She checked her notes. ". . . Belinda Bountiful, aka Pat Hensley?"

"Yeah?"

"She brought out some things that might be worth looking into. Especially if you're still unsure about Lipton."

"Namely that Tera Jameson is gay," Catherine said, "and Jenna bisexual."

"Well," Sara said, taking this new information in stride. "I think we need to drop around at the roommate's again."

"Yeah," Conroy said. "That's a swell idea." The detective let loose a long sigh. "So—should we kick Lipton, you think? Are you sure he's not the guy?"

"Not sure at all," Catherine said. "We've got Jenna potentially in a love relationship with her roommate, but Ty tells me Jenna was being courted by Los Angeles pornographers, offering the world to her on a blue movie platter. Other than his half-assed alibi and the security videotape, it's all pretty shaky where Lipton's concerned . . . and if this tech we've got working on the tape says that's *not* Lipton . . . well . . ."

"That doesn't really answer my question," Conroy said. "Do we kick him loose, or don't we?"

Catherine thought about it. Then she asked, "How long can you hold him?"

"Without pressing charges?" Now Conroy thought about it. "We may be pushing it already. He'd be on the streets by now, if he'd asked for a lawyer."

Sara asked, "Can't you hold him as a material witness?"

Conroy turned up her palms. "How? If Ray boy wasn't here, then he can't be a witness . . . and if he *was* here, that makes him our number-one suspect. Ladies, you better talk to your videotape expert, and find out where we really stand."

A little over half an hour later, with Detective Conroy's blessing, Catherine was back in an interview room with Ray Lipton. A lidded medium-sized evidence box was on the table before her.

The construction mini-magnate looked like hell. The last forty-eight hours had seemed to chew him up pretty bad, his eyes red and puffy and locked into a vacant, not-quite-there holding pattern. He hadn't shaved or bathed and he carried the heavy, sour scent of sweat that came from living in the same clothes in the same small cell for way too long. He sat alone at the table, his head hanging. Though physically much smaller, the CSI towered over him.

His voice was low, strained, as if he hadn't taken a drink of water since the last time they had seen him. "I need a lawyer, don't I?"

"If you want one, you have every right to make that phone call." In her one hand, Catherine held a fax from Jennifer Woods of the ESPN legal department. Along with a stern reminder to make sure the letter was in the mail, Woods had sent a log of all programming from noon until midnight, October 25, 2001; a videotape had been Fedexed.

"But before you make that call," Catherine said, "I'd appreciate it if we could talk, just a little more, about your alibi."

"I don't have a damn alibi." He shook his head. "I told you, Ms. Willows—I was home alone, watching a football game."

"That's my point, Mr. Lipton. The football game can help give you an alibi."

He looked up. "You're shitting me, right?"

"No—not one iota, Mr. Lipton. It won't clear you, but it would be a good start. Now . . . what time did you say you started watching the game?"

Lipton shrugged. "Game started at five-thirty. Got home about seven, took a shower, nuked some dinner, probably sat down just about seven-thirty. Second half had started. Like I told you before, Peterson kicked a field goal; then this guy I never heard of ran the kickoff back for a touchdown."

Catherine checked the sheet in her hand. According to the ESPN log, Dominic Rhodes ran back a kickoff for a touchdown with 4:50 left in the third quarter. The action occurred at 7:34 P.M. Pacific Time. "Dominic Rhodes ring a bell?"

Lipton brightened. "Yeah! That's the guy."

"Then what?"

"Couple of minutes later, the Chiefs scored a touchdown. It was a hell of a half—I think there were four touchdowns in the fourth quarter alone."

"Do you recall how many were made by each team?"

"Two," he said, with confidence. But then his expression dimmed a bit. "Now . . . can you tell me something?"

"I'll try."

"How does this help me?"

"The game was broadcast live, right?"

"Yeah. Of course. I don't care about that tape-delay shit."

"Did *you* tape it?"

This had apparently not occurred to him. Lipton shook his head.

"I'm pretty sure of that myself," Catherine told him. "There was no tape in your machine, and we've checked every videotape in your residence, and the game hadn't been recorded on any of them. You would have had to tape it, watch it, and dispose of the tape before the police arrived. More importantly, you'd have had to anticipate we would ask you specifics about the game, and you'd have to be ready for our questions. Not impossible, but in real life, in the time frame we're talking about, highly unlikely."

His eyes had come alive. "Does that mean I'm finally free?"

Catherine gave him a "sorry" smile, and shook her head. "Not just yet. We're still working on the security videotape."

The contractor retained his hopeful expression, nonetheless. "I'm not worried—that's not me on the tape, 'cause I wasn't there. . . . And you don't think it's me on the tape yourself, do you, Ms. Willows?"

With a quick glance at the two-way mirror where she knew Conroy and Sara were watching, she said, "This isn't about my opinion, Mr. Lipton."

"Sure it is. You can't tell me you people don't look at this evidence from some kind of point of view. Everybody knows that instincts are just as important as facts."

Gil Grissom would disagree, Catherine knew; but she said, "Let's just say I'm not entirely convinced one way or the other."

That took some of the air out of him.

"Also, I need you to explain these." She took the lid off the box that contained the evidence bags from the house: the beard, mustache, spirit gum, and shoebox.

Lipton looked in at them without touching anything. He shrugged. "That's Jenna's stuff."

"A beard and a mustache?"

"Yeah—it's from her act."

"Her act?"

Lipton nodded matter of factly. "She had this routine where she'd put this stuff on, dance around the bar dressed as an old man. She didn't make a stage entrance, you know? And another girl would still be dancing. Jenna'd just sort of show up out in the club, kinda sneak out there." He grinned, shaking his head, remembering. "She'd have 'em all fooled."

"Did she?"

"Oh, yeah, she was really good. She'd rub against these guys as she moved through the bar, drove 'em batty—they thought she was an old gay guy tryin' to get lucky or somethin'! Eventually, she'd work her way to the stage and got up there with the girl that was dancing at the time, and rub all over her."

"Uh huh."

"It's just about the only bit I ever liked about her dancing. See, the other dancer would pretend to be grossed out by the old man and'd leave the stage . . . then this 'old man' would start stripping. When the stiffs finally figured out they had pushed *her* away, they went ballistic. She had them all in the palm of her hand."

"That must have got under your skin," Catherine said.

"Naw," Lipton said, shaking his head. "Just the opposite. That act wasn't about cheap sex, her act was . . . social commentary. Jenna liked making that point; she was smart, you know, and sensitive. Don't turn someone away until you get to know 'em. It was subtle, but it was about a hell of a lot more than just Jenna taking off her clothes. Like I said, it was the only bit of hers I liked."

"Why hasn't anyone mentioned this act before?"

"Well, she hadn't done in quite a while. After she, you know . . . had her augmentation surgery, it wasn't so easy for her to pretend to be a man. . . . Does this clear me?"

"No."

His face fell.

She continued: "I need to confirm that this act really existed."

"That Kapelos character'll tell you."

"I'll call him right now and find out," she said. "You see, it's like I told you when this started, Mr. Lipton."

The suspect's eyes were poised between hope and despair, now.

"If you are innocent," she said, "we'll find that out, and we *will* catch the killer."

"Not for my sake," he said.

She wasn't following him; her expression said, *What?*

"For Jenna's," he said.

11

At the same time Greg Sanders was giving Catherine Willows and Sara Sidle the skinny on wig hair, Gil Grissom—in a loose long-sleeve dark gray shirt and black slacks—was striding down the hall, a file folder in one hand, his heels clicking softly on the tile floor. Finally arriving at his destination, he knocked on a door with raised white letters spelling: CAPTAIN JAMES BRASS.

"It's open," came the muffled voice from the other side.

Grissom walked in and granted Brass a boyish grin; the detective was sitting in a large gray chair behind a government-issue gray metal desk.

The office was a glorified cubicle, the wall to the left filled with file cabinets, a chalkboard all but obscuring the wall at right, with a table covered with stacks of papers camped beneath it. Brass's desk, however, was tidy, bearing only the open file before him, a telephone, and a photo of his daughter, Ellie.

"Chic," Grissom said.

"You came by for a reason, or just to brighten my evening?"

Standing opposite Brass, ignoring a waiting chair, Grissom deposited his own file on top of the one Brass had been perusing. "Results of the tox screen on our torso—no drugs, no alcohol."

"Sounds like a good Christian corpse," Brass said, cocking an eyebrow over the file. "But is it Lynn Pierce?"

"Still waiting on DNA confirmation. Replicating the DNA, heating it and cooling it, over and over, takes time."

Brass nodded, put down the file, locked eyes with the CSI. "Tell me we've got something to hold us over till then."

"Doc Robbins defleshed the torso, and used the bones to run

some numbers, which reveals significant information, through wear."

Though Brass had once supervised CSI himself, he still considered much of Grissom's information to sound like gibberish. "Which in English means what?"

Nick Stokes—in a long-sleeve tan T-shirt and dark tan chinos—appeared in the open door, but didn't interrupt. Brass waved him in, and Nick moved to the side and leaned against the corner file cabinet.

"It means," Grissom said, "that the torso belonged to a white woman between the ages of thirty-five and forty-five, weight approximately one-ten, height about five-four . . . and she was definitely dismembered with a chain saw."

With an amazed shake of his head, Brass asked, "Robbins got all that from the pelvic bones?"

"Yeah, that and that she was in a heavy exercise program . . . did a lot of sit-ups."

"You can tell me all this, including her dismemberment by Black and Decker . . ."

"We don't know the brand name. Yet."

"But you can't confirm who she is or how she died."

"That's true to a point. But we have the husband's identification of the birthmark, and now, a lot more."

"Such as?"

"Female between thirty-five and forty-five, weighing one-ten and standing five-four . . . who does that remind you of?"

Brass shrugged one shoulder. "Sure, those figures fit Lynn Pierce . . . but how many other missing women?"

Slowly, Grissom said, "Factoring in the birthmark, and the episiotomy scar? . . . Not another in Nevada."

Silence stretched in the little office.

"Well . . ." Brass sighed. "We already knew it was Lynn Pierce, didn't we? . . . And yet we still don't have a thing to hang on that bastard husband of hers."

Grissom held Brass's eyes, and then slowly moved both of their gazes over to Nick, standing on the sidelines, leaning against that file cabinet.

Wearing a tiny enigmatic smile, Nick straightened. "We may have him. . . . You tell me."

"I will," Brass said. "Go on."

"I've been working on the Lynn Pierce computer and credit-card records."

"Any movement since her disappearance?" Brass asked.

"Nothing on the e-mail front. She's still getting them, a few friends, church announcements, spam; but she hasn't answered any of 'em, since the day before she went missing. And nothing new on the credit cards or ATM."

"What woman does not use her charge card?" Grissom asked.

"A dead one," Brass admitted.

Nick said, "Hey, I got more—something really interesting. Going through the old credit card receipts, I found this." He stepped forward holding out a slip of paper.

Brass took the slip and studied it. "A receipt for a box of forty-four-caliber shells . . ." His head went sideways. "Didn't Pierce say . . ."

". . . that he never owned a gun?" Grissom finished. "Yes he did. . . . Gentlemen?"

Somehow, Brass managed to arrive in front of the Pierce home in less than ten minutes. The sun had long since dipped below the horizon, leaving the sky the purplish hue of a huge bruise. The evening was cool and only a few lights were on in the castle-like house. Grissom and Nick hurried to keep up with Brass, who moved onto the porch, skipped the bell, and pounded on the front door with his fist.

Pierce, in an open-neck navy Polo shirt and dark blue jeans, opened the door displaying the same hangdog expression they'd seen on their last visit. He had not shaved; perhaps, Grissom speculated, the physical therapist had stayed home from work again today.

Brass held out the photocopy of the receipt like a bill collector demanding a payment way overdue. He didn't even wait for their reluctant host to speak. "You lied, Pierce! You told us you never owned a gun—so how do you explain a receipt for bullets you bought?"

The detective kept walking as he spoke, backing Pierce inside the house with the force of his words and forward motion. Grissom and Nick followed them in, the former even shutting the door behind him, as the group gathered in the foyer by the winding stairway.

"And don't bother feeding us some bull about buying them for a friend," Brass ranted. "This time, I want the truth." Finally, when the detective stopped to take a breath, Pierce got a word in.

"All right!" the therapist said. "All right, I admit it. . . . I . . . I had a gun in the house . . . for a while."

Brass seemed ready to blow again, but that statement brought him up short. He looked hard at Pierce. "*Had* a gun?"

"*Had* a gun," Pierce repeated.

Brass's open hand shot to his right temple, as if he were either fighting off a vicious migraine or a sudden stroke. Neither option struck Grissom as positive.

The therapist held up his hands in a fashion that was equal parts surrender and calming gesture; then he led them into the living room, gesturing to the rifles-and-flags sofa. "Please, please . . . sit down. Let me explain."

In a stage whisper in Grissom's direction, Brass said, "This should be prime."

But Brass took a seat on the couch, while Grissom again sat at the edge of the maple chair opposite; Nick hovered in the background, while Pierce settled in chummily beside the skeptical detective.

"I know what you're thinking," Pierce said, reasonably, with a tone usually reserved for children. "Cocaine in the house, gun in the house, Born-Again wife . . . he had to have killed her."

"Now that you mention it," Brass said.

Running a hand over his unshaven face, the therapist sighed in resignation. "Okay. I had a gun. A .44 Magnum I bought from . . . an acquaintance."

"And of course it wasn't registered."

"Your negative attitude, Captain, doesn't keep that from being any less true."

"The name of the acquaintance?"

Pierce hesitated.

The sarcasm in Brass's tone had been replaced with matter-of-fact, almost cheerful professionalism. "One of you is going to jail this afternoon, Mr. Pierce—either you or the person who sold you an illegal weapon. You make the call."

"I can't tell you, Captain."

"Can't? *Won't*, you mean."

"I bought it from the man I was buying cocaine from. He doesn't even know my wife—he's no suspect in this."

Brass frowned in shock. "And you're *protecting* him?"

"I'm protecting myself and my daughter. Do I have to tell you that these kind of people are dangerous?"

Grissom said, "You were friendly enough with this person to purchase a weapon from him . . . what, to protect your family from the likes of the man you *bought* it from?"

"You might say . . . Guys, fellas . . . this is hard to admit."

Brass smiled an unfriendly smile. "Try."

Pierce sighed. "For a while, I was . . . when Lynn got involved with her church, gone all the time . . . well. She used to be . . . God!"

Grissom said, "Mr. Pierce, if you are innocent, you need to be frank us, so we don't waste our time going down your road. Do you understand?"

Pierce swallowed thickly, nodded. "My wife used to be a wild-cat . . . in the bedroom? Do I really have to say more? . . . Anyway, when she . . . got religion, certain things suddenly seemed . . . perverted to her. We hardly . . . had relations at all, anymore. . . . I need something to drink. Just water."

"Nick," Grissom said, and gestured toward the kitchen.

Nick nodded and went away.

"I'm not proud of it," Pierce said, "but . . . I started seeing prostitutes. They're not exactly tough to hook up with in this town. Sometimes I brought them to my office, sometimes to a motel, and sometimes . . . I brought them here."

The son of a bitch was confirming the nextdoor neighbor's story!

Nick delivered the glass of water, Pierce took it, saying, "Thanks . . . You know how some of these girls, these women can be. How they sometimes bring their pimps or whoever around . . . and my . . . my coke connection said I should be careful. Said I needed protection in the house. . . . So I bought the Magnum."

Brass said nothing; then glanced at Grissom, who shrugged. It was a good story.

"Okay, Mr. Pierce," Brass said softly, "then where's the gun now?"

Pierce looked at the floor, then at Brass, and back at the floor. "I had second thoughts about having it around the house, and, anyway, I stopped seeing those kind of girls."

"You haven't answered my question."

"I threw it away."

Grissom, wincing, said, "You threw the gun away?"

"Yes."

"Where?"

"Lake Mead."

Grissom felt as though he'd been slapped; he glanced at Brass, whose expression said he felt the same.

Brass asked, "You own a boat?"

"No. I went out on one of those excursions. Just tossed the thing overboard when nobody was looking."

Grissom said, "Don't suppose you kept the receipt for that ride?"

"No. Why should I? Wasn't deductible."

Brass rose, reaching for his cuffs. Grissom, still seated on the edge of the chair, touched the detective's elbow, then—with his head—signaled for Brass to come with him.

Rising, Grissom said, "We'll be right back, Mr. Pierce. If you don't mind, we're going to borrow your kitchen for a moment."

Pierce sipped his water. "Be my guest."

The three of them adjourned to the kitchen.

"Lake Mead?" Brass said, eyes wide with fury, though he kept his voice low. "He's rubbing our goddamn faces in it!"

"No, that's good," Grissom said, with a hand gesture and a little smile. "He's cute. He thinks he's smarter than us."

"Maybe he *is* smarter," Brass said.

"Than some of us . . . maybe." And Grissom grinned sweetly, while Brass shook his head in utter irritation—only some of it at Pierce.

"You *are* going to arrest him for the pistol?" Nick asked Brass, also keeping his voice low.

"Damn right," Brass said. "That much we *do* have on the son of a bitch."

Now it was Grissom shaking his head. "It'll never hold up, Jim—you know that. There's no gun. All we really have is a receipt for bullets dated six months ago."

"He confessed to having a gun!"

"Remind me—which one of us read him his rights?"

Brass's face was red; he was breathing hard. "I can't believe this! It's crazy. Insane . . . That evil bastard killed his wife, cut her up, and dumped the pieces of her in the lake. There's gotta be something here! Where's the justice?"

"No justice yet," Grissom said, gently, touching the detective's sleeve. "But there will be. Now, let's get out of here before we screw something up."

They took their leave quietly, and let Pierce have the last word.

At the doorway, he said, "I hope I've been of some small help."

Nick Stokes parted company with Grissom and Brass at HQ, and headed into the lab where Warrick had been working. He found Warrick practically spotwelded to the monitor of a computer.

"What's up?" Nick asked.

"I'm trying to track down that red triangle we found on the bag of dope at Pierce's."

"Timely," Nick said. "Pierce just copped to getting not just coke from a dealer, but a gun as well."

Nick filled Warrick in on the latest visit to the king of the Pierce castle, including the therapist's refusal to I.D. his connection.

Nick asked Warrick, "Getting anywhere?"

"Not yet . . . but I just know I've seen that signature somewhere, it's ringin' a bell . . . a distant one, anyway. I'm gonna keep diggin'."

"All right." Nick yawned. "I'm fried—Grissom had me in early today, to keep at those computer records . . . I gotta go home and catch some z's."

"It's a plan. . . . Later."

"You may want to try getting some sleep one of these days yourself," Nick said, at the doorway. "Latest thing—they say it's really catching on."

Warrick expended half a smirk. "Not around here."

Warrick Brown stayed with it, going through file after file looking at drug dealers the LVMPD had busted in the last few years. An hour later, he was still rolling through files looking for the odd little red triangle.

A knock at the doorframe took him away from his work, and he turned to see one of the interns, a young, dark-curly-haired guy named Jeremy Smith, slight of build, in a black UNLV sweatshirt and blue jeans. A criminal justice major at the university, Smith had been working part-time for the last few months, sometimes days, occasionally nights.

"Hey, Jeremy," Warrick said, mildly annoyed to be interrupted. "What's up?"

Smith stepped gingerly into the lab, as if not sure he had permission. "I talked to every glass company in the metro area—remember, to see if they replaced the driver's side window of a '95 Avalon?"

"Right. And?"

The young man shook his head. "Zip zally zero."

Warrick muttered a "damn," but the kid was stepping forward, more sure of himself now.

"Then I thought I better check the car dealerships too."

"That was good initiative, Jeremy—any luck?"

"Not really."

"Yeah. Well. Good thought, though. Thanks."

"All right, then . . . Warrick?"

Warrick sighed to himself, suddenly sorry he'd told the kid to call him by his first name.

Smith was beside the computer, now, bright-eyed as a chipmunk. "Anything else I can do for?"

Why not tap into all this energy? Warrick considered the offer for a long moment, then said, "Junkyards, Jeremy—try the junkyards."

Smith nodded, grinned. "I'm on it."

The kid was halfway out the door when Warrick called out, "One more thing, Jeremy! You ever see this before?"

The intern came back over and Warrick passed him the evidence bag with the baggie of coke inside.

Turning it over and over, Smith studied it, then handed it back. "Yeah, I've seen this mark."

Warrick knew the intern had been working a lot of days, and gave him the benefit of the doubt. "Bust you were in on?"

The intern shook his head, saying, "No, this is something I've seen on campus. . . . Small-time dealer, sells mostly grass. I don't know if he's been in the system or not."

"He wouldn't have a name, would he?"

"Well, I don't know his real name—his street name is Lil Moe. Supposed to be once you've tried his stuff, you always want . . . a little mo'."

Warrick just looked at Smith.

Jeremy gave him a quick nervous smile and patted the air with his hands, like an untalented mime. "Hey, that's just what I heard."

"Uh huh."

"Honest, Warrick!"

Smith used some of his nervous energy to haul his ass out of there, and Warrick immediately tried "Lil Moe" in the database, coming up blank. He checked pending files and struck out again. Finally, he went in search of Jeremy the intern and found him in the break room with a phone book in one hand and a phone in the other, a notepad and pencil before him.

The kid looked up, saw Warrick, and said, "Starting on the junk-yards. Some of 'em work at night, y'know. Anybody I can't talk to, at least I can have a list of numbers ready for tomorrow."

"Table that. Would you know Lil Moe if you saw him?"

"Sure."

"Help *me* know him."

"Five-nine, -ten maybe, a hundred twenty-five or thirty. Real skinny. He's got dreadlocks to his shoulders and always wears this big Dodgers stocking cap."

"Stocking cap in Vegas?"

Smith shrugged. "Makes him easy to find."

"Find where?"

"He kind of bounces around the edges of the campus . . . but he'll probably be somewhere around the Thomas & Mack Center."

Easy for students to find him, Warrick thought, and nodded. "Thanks."

"What now?"

"Junkyards."

"Junkyards," Jeremy said, and got back to it.

Warrick found Brass in his office and shared his new information. "Lil Moe, huh?" Brass said.

"A little is better than nothing at all." Warrick stood with his hands on his hips, his eyebrows high. "You wanna go for a ride, and see if we can score?"

Brass was already on his feet. "Let's do that—even a drug dealer'll feel like a step up from Owen Pierce."

The home of the Runnin' Rebels basketball teams squatted on the far southwest corner of the UNLV campus, but the Taurus came at the Thomas & Mack Center from the campus side. The detective made the trip just below the speed limit, but not too slow. The Tau-rus stuck out enough without them crawling along in an obvious search. It wasn't midnight yet, and the campus hadn't quite yet gone to sleep.

People (kids mostly) dotted the sidewalks here and there, quiet students heading to their dorms, louder ones off to the next kegger, the occasional professor walking with briefcase and sometimes a young teaching aide, a few joggers working off the stress of the day in the cool of the night . . .

. . . and another strata more in the shadows, harder to see, unpredictable, even dangerous, some searching for drugs, and—more important to Brass and Warrick—some selling. On their first lap, as their eyes probed the shadows and recesses of doorways, they didn't see anyone fitting Lil Moe's description . . . and not on the second lap, either, or even the third.

By lap four, midnight had come and gone, the sidewalks had thinned, and they hadn't gotten even a whiff of Lil Moe.

"Maybe he's not out tonight," Brass offered.

"Or maybe he's making the car. Just 'cause it's unmarked, that doesn't mean Moe doesn't know a police car when he eyeballs it."

"We could disguise ourselves," Brass commented dryly from the wheel, "as cheerleaders."

"I got a better idea. . . . Let me out."

Brass just looked at him. "You have your weapon, Brown?"

"No—I don't wear it around the lab."

"We're not in the lab. You're asking to do some kind of half-assed, impromptu undercover dance, and that's not—"

"C'mon, Brass! I'm not saying leave me alone. Just back me up from a distance. Let me see if I can smoke this guy out."

"You're a criminalist, Brown—not a cop."

"And you're a middle-aged white guy. Which of us stands to score easier?"

Brass considered that. "Well, it's plain this plan isn't working."

"All right then—Plan B."

Hopping out at the corner of Harmon and Tarkanian Way, Warrick ambled down the street named after the legendary UNLV basketball coach. Taking his time, not wanting to appear anxious or in a hurry, Warrick strolled toward the arena, enjoying the cool evening. In the dusky light he could barely make out the sign for the Facilities Management Administration Building (whatever that was) across the street. Passing the single-story building, he continued inexorably toward the Thomas & Mack Center.

Warrick turned left, keeping the basketball arena on his right as he circled the building. The streetlights spaced their pools of light about every ten yards, giving a sense of security to a gaggle of passing coeds, but only made Warrick feel more like a moving target. The shadows deepened and became fathomless in contrast to the spheres of white.

He glanced up to see Brass's Taurus turning off Gym Road into the Thomas & Mack parking lot near Tropicana Avenue. Then he shifted his gaze around, as if aimlessly looking at this and that, so that anyone watching him wouldn't realize he'd been keeping tabs on the unmarked car.

The CSI had almost made it to the Jean Nidetch Women's Center when a male voice called out to him from the shadows. "Bro!"

Warrick swiveled that way but stayed on the sidewalk. He said nothing.

The voice from the darkness said, "You lookin' for somethin'? Or you jus' lost?"

"That depends. What kinda map you sellin'?"

A figure took a step closer, remaining in the shadows, but now visible as a slight, sketchy presence. "Roadmap to bliss, bro—happiness highway."

Warrick settled into place on the sidewalk. "Who couldn't use a little happiness?"

The guy took another step toward the light. Warrick got a better look at him now: a tall, gangly man in a silk running suit, a Dodgers stocking cap perched atop a tangle of dreadlocks. Just a kid, Warrick thought, maybe twenty-one tops.

"You lookin' for happiness, I got it. Just not out there, man—light hurts my eyes. Ease on down the road."

After a glance around, Warrick stepped out of the pale circle of streetlamp light, and into the shadows in front of the guy . . .

. . . who fit the intern's description of Lil Moe like a latex glove. *Long time since I hit a jackpot in this town,* Warrick thought.

The dealer was saying, "What kind of happiness you in the market for?"

"You might be surprised what makes me happy."

"Hey, bro—I'm strictly pharmaceutical . . . strange sex stuff, try the yellow pages."

"Not sex, Moe . . ."

Eyes and nostrils flared. "How you know my name? I never done bidness with you."

"Information, Moe—that's all I want."

"You want infor*mation* from me? Do I look like a fuckin' search engine? What am I, some Yahoo Google shit?"

Lil Moe snapped his fingers, and before Warrick could move, a third party grabbed his left arm, wrenched it behind him, and pain streaked up his arm, spiking in his shoulder. He heard a sharp metallic *snick*, and suddenly felt the point of a blade dimple his throat, next to his Adam's apple. He froze—and hoped to hell that somewhere Brass was watching this, somewhere *close*, calling in some backup.

"I'm gonna ask you again, homey," Lil Moe said, moving in on Warrick, the dealer's face contorted, waving his hand like a pissed-off rapper. "Why you want information from *me*?"

The knife pressed deeper, and Warrick felt the sting before something warm began trickling down his neck. Behind him, whoever held his arm was strong, and kept Warrick's hand high between his shoulder blades, the muscles stretching and ready to explode, if the assailant snapped the bone.

In front of Warrick, the young man in the Dodger stocking cap hopped from foot to foot, as if the sidewalk were a bed of coals under his expensive sneakers. "Who *sent* you, man? What's this about?"

Forcing himself to slow his breathing and to remain calm despite the situation, Warrick's mind raced over possible outcomes—most of them grim.

"I'll pay for what I want," Warrick managed.

"Oh, you gonna pay, all right! Who you workin' for? You with Danny G?"

His unseen assailant's breathing came in sharp, rapid gulps, breath hot on Warrick's neck and reeking of liquor and garlic. The assailant sucked his teeth as if trying to control his salivating over the urge to plunge the blade into Warrick's throat.

And the dealer was singsonging, "You better fuckin' talk, boy, while you got your vocal cords."

Rasping, his voice little more than a hoarse whisper, Warrick asked, "You don't wanna cut me."

Looking older suddenly, Lil Moe eyeballed the CSI, the anger shining through even in the darkness. "Aw fuck this, Tony—fuckin' *cut* him, man!"

Even as Warrick tensed for the cold invasion of steel, he felt the pressure go slack on his arm and the blade drew away from his neck. Then he heard steel clatter to sidewalk, followed by Brass's quiet voice saying, "Smart move—and I didn't even have to tell you to drop it."

Lil Moe's eyes went wild, his mouth dropped open; no words exited, but he did: spinning on his heel, he ran like a starting gun had sounded. Turning, Warrick saw his assailant, a wiry black kid, this one in baggy UNLV jersey and baggier jeans and no more than sixteen, the nose of Brass's automatic kissing the boy's right temple.

"You just gonna stand there bleeding?" Brass asked Warrick. "Or are you gonna go catch him?"

Warrick took this gentle hint, and spun and sprinted after the drug dealer.

Moe had a good twenty-yard head start. But he was also stoned and pumping his arms wildly, his knees pistoning up and down, his stride lengths varying as the drugs kept him from running smoothly. And instead of heading toward the mass of buildings to the east, where he would have had options for escape and possibly obstacles to benefit his youth, he had taken off across the vast expanse of the parking lot.

Before he'd got halfway to Tropicana Avenue, Moe started to slow, and—by the far side of the lot—Warrick caught up and grabbed his jacket, slowing him as they both ran. "Stop! . . . It's over!"

Lil Moe fought frantically with the zipper, trying to escape the jacket and still keep running at the same time. The drugs prevented him from doing either very effectively. Suddenly lurching to the right, Moe snatched the jacket from Warrick's grasp, but tumbled, elbows and feet flying at odd angles, and he whumped onto the cement and rolled and came to a skidding stop at the parking-lot curb, in a fetal position, one hand going to his face, the other arm wrapping around ribs that were at least cracked if not broken.

Barely breathing hard, Warrick bent down over him. "That's it—there ain't no Moe."

Sweat beading on his face and looking like he couldn't decide whether to bawl or vomit, the young man stared up, all the fight gone from his face. "Okay, man, okay—so I'm Lil Moe. You five-oh?"

Warrick grinned. "Criminalist."

"What-the-fuck 'ist'?"

"Don't sweat the details—you're still in a world of trouble."

Brass strolled up, towing the other one by his elbow, the kid's hands cuffed behind him. "Brown—you caught him," the detective said, looking very pleased. "Nice job."

Touching the small wound on his neck, Warrick returned his attention to Lil Moe. "You got a customer named Owen Pierce?"

The young man was shaking his head before Warrick finished the question. "Never heard of the dude and I ain't sayin' shit till I see my lawyer."

Looking down at the dealer, Brass asked, "You got a name?"

"Told you! Talk to my lawyer."

"He admits he's Lil Moe," Warrick said.

"What's your real name?" Brass asked.

"Lawyer me up, or kick me, Barney Fife!"

Brass sighed. "Who's your lawyer?"

Lil Moe shrugged. "P.D. my ass."

Brass rolled his eyes and Warrick felt himself growing very weary. Public defender—this was going to be a long night.

"I got Band-Aids in the glove compartment," Brass said.

Warrick said, "I've been cut worse shaving."

"Probably." Brass managed one of his rumpled smiles. "But that you can't brag about."

And they hauled the drug dealer and his scrawny "muscle" back to the Taurus.

12

At just before two a.m., waiting in the parking lot for Catherine Willows and Sara Sidle, Detective Erin Conroy for the umpteenth time questioned the wisdom of her decision to apply for a police position in Las Vegas. How glamorous it had sounded, how inviting the travel books had made the desert mecca seem, how foolishly she had booked Rat Pack-era images into the theater of her mind.

Only recently had Erin admitted to herself that she missed her family—her folks, her sister and husband; and almost immediately she'd longed for the changing of the seasons. There were no beautiful autumn colors in Nevada, no leaves putting on their last mighty show before exiting to make way for the white blanket of winter—no sledding, no sleigh rides . . . and you could get hot chocolate, sure, but what was the point?

In the desert, they had . . . the sun. Winter sun, spring sun, summer sun (with the bonus of unbearable heat), and now, in the fall, just for a change of pace, more sun . . . with these cool desert nights the only respite.

Erin Conroy fought to shake off her melancholy and tried to dismiss the thought of another Christmas with no snow, no family, and not even the prospect of a New Year's Eve date.

"You all right?" Willows asked.

The homicide detective hadn't even seen Willows and Sidle exit CSI. "Uh, yes, sure, fine."

"We signed out a Tahoe—we'll follow you over."

The trio planned to call on the late Jenna Patrick's roommate, Tera Jameson.

"Oh?" Erin said.

"Yeah," Willows said, "we have to meet our video wizard, Helpingstine, back here at four A.M."

"Has an early flight out," Sidle said.

"Does he have anything good for you?" Erin asked.

"Guess we'll see."

The CSIs in their Tahoe followed Detective Erin Conroy in her Taurus through typically bustling Vegas wee-hours traffic to the three-story motel-like apartment house where Tera Jameson (and Jenna Patrick had once) lived.

Again Erin led the way up the stairs to the third floor and around the building, stopping in front of Tera Jameson's door; no light filtered through the window curtains. The detective knocked and got no answer, knocked twice more and again got no response. The three of them looked at each other for a long moment.

"She does work nights," Sidle said.

Willows raised her eyebrows. "Should we try Showgirl World, you think?"

"She isn't scheduled there tonight," Erin said. "I already checked."

"Maybe she's asleep," Sidle offered.

Erin used her cell phone, dialed the police department switchboard and got Jameson's number. She dialed again and they could hear the phone ringing, inside. Finally, the machine picked up: "It's Tera. You know the drill: no message, no call back . . . 'bye."

"We could use a warrant about now," Sidle said.

Erin left a message for Tera to contact her, then punched END and turned to start the long walk back around the building and down the stairs. "You two go on back and keep your date with that video techie."

"Gonna stake the place out?" Sidle asked.

"Maybe . . . but first, I'll think I will drop around Showgirl World and see if maybe I can't get a line on her, there. Maybe she traded shifts with somebody, last minute."

"Call us if you need us," Willows said, in step with the detective. "And sooner is better than later—Mobley's on our case about all the overtime."

Erin nodded and kept walking. She'd gotten the same memo;

problem was, some nightshift work simply had to be done during the day, and there was a rivalry between them and dayshifts that discouraged helping each other out.

Soon the Tahoe was peeling off in one direction, and the Taurus in the other, as Erin Conroy drove across town, to Showgirl World . . .

. . . which was everything Dream Dolls and so many other strip clubs in the greater Vegas area wanted to be when they grew up. The exterior was black glass and blue steel, the sign a green-and-blue rotating neon globe with SHOWGIRL WORLD emblazoned across it in red neon letters that chased each other to a finish. Erin parked in the massive lot, which was almost full—though it was approaching three in the morning, that was prime time in Party Town.

She opened the door, took a step inside a foyer whose gray-carpeted walls were arrayed with framed black-and-white photos of the featured dancers and had to pause until her eyes adjusted from the brighter parking lot. With the spots before her eyes dissipating to a hard white glow, Conroy approached the doorman—a big, bald, olive-skinned, Tony Orlando-mustached ex-linebacker in a white shirt, black bow tie, and tuxedo pants.

"Fifteen bucks," he said, voice naturally gruff but tone noncommittal, his eyes on hers nonjudgmentally. Erin plucked her I.D. wallet from her purse and showed the doorman her badge and a smile.

"Or not," he said, and—completely unimpressed—waved her on through.

Stepping through the inside door, Erin had to again stop and allow her vision to adjust, as the club itself was much darker than the foyer. The ventilation was better in here than Dream Dolls, but a mingled bouquet of tobacco, beer, and perfume nonetheless permeated. Techno throbbed through the sound system at a decibel level just a notch below ear bleed, and Erin could feel the beat pounding in her chest, like a competing heartbeat.

Where Dream Dolls had cheap industrial-strength furniture, Showgirl World had heavy black lacquered wooden tables surrounded by low-slung black faux-leather chairs. Each table accommodated five chairs and those along the mirrored walls squatted within partitioned-off nooks that largely screened patrons from view while allowing a full view of the stage. Even the chairs lining the stage were comfortable swivel affairs, albeit bolted to the floor.

Right now, the main, kidney-shaped stage—around and over which red and blue lights flickered in sequence—held two statuesque if bored-looking women, gyrating more or less in time to the music, occasionally draping themselves on one of two brass poles to swing their forms around, sometimes upside down. To the left, a bar extended toward the back, behind which a four-foot-high mirror ran its length. Three bartenders in tuxedo shirts and black ties worked briskly, mixing drinks and raking in money as fast as possible.

Erin approached the nearest one, a guy older than she would have expected to find working in a place like this; he was in his mid-fifties, easy, with short, neatly trimmed gunmetal-gray hair, darker-gray-rimmed glasses and the burly bearing of a cop or, anyway, security man.

Pulling out the badge-in-wallet again, Conroy asked, "The boss around?"

"We're clean, detective," the bartender said, reflexively defensive. "Everything here's aboveboard."

"That's a good answer—I just don't remember asking a question that goes with it."

He made a face. "All right, all right, don't get your panties in a bunch—I'll get him." The burly, bespectacled bartender moved to a phone on the back counter, punched a button, spoke a few words, listened a second, then hung up. He returned with his expression softened, seeming even a little embarrassed. "Boss'll be right out. . . . Look, detective, I didn't mean to give you attitude."

"I'll live."

"No, really. It's just that I used to be on the job, myself, and I know these guys run a clean joint. I just don't like to see 'em hassled."

"No problem. Vegas PD?"

The guy shook his head. "Little town in Ohio. Moved out here when I retired. Looking to get away from the midwest winters."

Conroy nodded, smiled. "Only now, you miss them. How long were you on the job?"

"Twenty-eight years."

Erin frowned, curiously. "Why didn't you stay for a full thirty?"

"They put me behind a desk and I couldn't take it. . . . *Now* look what I'm behind."

She chuckled, and a door she hadn't realized was even there, down at the far end of the bar, opened like an oven to blast a wide shaft of light into the darkness of the club, only to be sucked away as the door swung shut. A brown-haired, thirtyish, stocky man in a dark business suit approached her warily. He glanced at the bartender, who nodded her way, then seemed to get very busy farther down the bar.

The new arrival stuck out a hand. "Rich McGraw," he said, his voice deep.

She introduced herself, practically shouting to be heard over the blare of music. She showed McGraw her I.D wallet, but the fine print was lost in this pitiful light, though the glint of her badge made its point.

"What can I do for you, Detective Conrad?"

"Conroy," she said, almost yelling, and explained the situation. A new song came on but the intensity of the volume had lowered just enough to make conversation possible, if not easy. Now and then she had to repeat herself.

"She's not here," McGraw said.

"I know—I called earlier. I don't think it was you I talked to, Mr. McGraw."

"Must not've been."

"I'm hoping to get in touch with her tonight, or tomorrow at the latest. When does she work next?"

"You tried her place? You got that address?"

"Yes, sir." Then she repeated: "When does Tera work next?"

But he shook his head. "She won't be back till day after tomorrow, earliest. Said she wanted a few days off."

A sinking feeling dropped into the detective's gut. *Where the hell was Tera Jameson? And why had she picked now to disappear?* "Say where she was going?"

Again, McGraw shook his head.

Erin wondered how he managed that so well without the benefit of a neck. "And you don't know when she'll be back?"

"Nope. Maybe day after tomorrow." Shrug. "She's gonna call in."

In the mirror, Erin noticed that the two girls dancing to Samantha Fox were not the ones who'd been on when she arrived—a bosomy brunette and a leggy black girl were reigning over their male court.

"You seem to give Tera a lot of leeway, Mr. McGraw."

"She's popular. Exotic. She was in *Penthouse*, you know."

"No, I didn't. Could I see her dressing room?"

"She's okay, no prima donna, like some of them. So I give her leeway, yeah."

"Her dressing room?"

The oddly handsome features beamed at her. "You got a warrant?"

Erin shook her head.

He half-smiled, his expression almost regretful. "I don't mean to be a prick about it, lady, but I do have to protect the privacy of my employees—and we are talkin' about one of my star dancers, here."

"You know I'll just be back, once I've got a warrant."

He nodded. "And at that time I will personally escort you to her dressing room."

Detective Erin Conroy left the club wondering if the management had just covered for Tera; maybe the dancer was even camped out there, in a back room or dressing area. One thing the detective knew: she needed search warrants for both Jameson's apartment and dressing room and she needed them now.

She would check with Captain Brass for his advice on which judge to wake up.

Catherine Willows was at a table having coffee in the break room, killing a few minutes while Helpingstine—who had arrived after checking out of his hotel to make a presentation of his evidence to them—got his fifty-thousand-dollar toy up and running again.

Sara ambled in, with the latest from Greg Sanders. Getting herself an apple juice from a fridge that thankfully held no Grissom experiments at the moment, Sara said, "None of the shoes from Ray Lipton's house match the prints from Dream Dolls."

Catherine couldn't find it in her to be surprised. "Did our boy Ray ditch them, y'suppose?"

Sara shrugged, sat, sipped. "Don't know . . . but what I do know is, the top print is the killer's, and Ray Lipton's shoe size is *way* bigger than the print. I'm starting to agree with you."

"About what?"

"That he's innocent."

"I didn't say he was. We don't have any evidence that proves he *didn't* do it either."

"Jeez, Cath—do you want him to be guilty, or innocent?"

"Yes," she said.

On that note, they finished their drinks and made their way down the hallway until they reached Catherine's office, where the door was open, Dan Helpingstine pushing his glasses up on his nose and waving for them to join him.

The tall, pug-nosed manufacturer's rep had his Tektive video machine all fired up, and he motioned for them to sit on either side of him. Catherine eased down on Helpingstine's left, Sara to his right, while on the monitor screen they could see the security tape from the front door at Dream Dolls.

"I spent a very long day getting to know these tapes," he said.

"Find anything?" Sara asked.

"I think so—you'll have to be the judge."

Catherine felt a spark of hope.

"This," Helpingstine said, "is your killer coming in."

They watched as their suspect moved through the door, face turned away from the camera, trying to slide through the frame quickly. The tech did his thing with the keyboard and the picture cleared somewhat. Again he separated their suspect from the surroundings and improved the picture even more.

"Freeze that for a moment," Catherine said.

Helpingstine obeyed.

"Look at the shoulders," she said. "Remember we said they didn't look broad enough to be Lipton's?"

"Yeah," Sara said slowly.

"Now look at the hips."

Helpingstine was smiling. "I was hoping you'd notice that. Men's shoulders are wider than their hips—women are the opposite."

Catherine and Sara traded significant looks, while Helpingstine unfroze the image and allowed it to move in slow motion, even as he worked on it some more.

From this high angle, they now were looking down on the figure from the side. All they could see of the head was the ball cap, an ear, the glasses, the beard, and the corded muscles of the neck.

"Freeze that again!" Catherine said.

Helpingstine did.

"Can you zoom in?" Sara asked.

Catherine and Sara again traded glances—they were on the same page.

Helpingstine zoomed in on the head. Though they got significantly closer, the resolution grew worse accordingly, and it wasn't a big help.

Sara pressed closer, her nose practically against the screen, pointing. "What's that dark spot on the ear?"

The others leaned in closer too.

"I can't make anything out except a discoloration," Catherine said.

Helpingstine punched the keyboard and the ear blossomed to fill most of the screen.

"Is that just . . . pixelation?" Sara asked.

"No way," the tech said. "It's *something*—I just can't squeeze out enough res to tell *what*. Earring, maybe. Probably, in fact."

Eyebrow raised, Sara said, "Lipton doesn't have a pierced ear, does he?"

"No," Catherine said.

They sat back and looked at each other.

"Ray Lipton *is* innocent," Sara said.

Catherine nodded. "And Tera Jameson hated him."

"Well," Helpingstine said, "based upon unequivocal standards of anatomy, your killer is a female—in fake facial hair."

Catherine stood, pacing; Sara stood also, but planted herself. The wheels were turning now, for both of them.

"One of the strippers at Dream Dolls," Sara said, "told you Tera was a lesbian, and indicated Jenna was bisexual, right?"

"Right," Catherine said. "She also suggested that maybe Jenna Patrick and Tera Jameson weren't just roommates."

"But we don't have any evidence that they were having an affair," Sara said.

"Yet," Catherine said.

Sara rose. "Better call Conroy."

Catherine already had her phone out and was punching in numbers. By the time Catherine and Conroy had compared information, they came to the mutual conclusion that they needed to meet back at Tera Jameson's apartment.

"Let's roll," Catherine said to Sara.

"Conroy meeting us there?"

"Oh, yeah—with a warrant and the landlord."

But before they exited the office, Catherine went to thank Helpingstine. "Your next trip to Vegas," she said, "will be entirely on us—we may need you to testify."

"My pleasure," Helpingstine said, grinning. "Anything to get the word out about my baby. . . . Will you recommend to your superiors that they buy a Tektive?"

"Dan," Catherine said, pausing halfway out the door, "I'll recommend we invest in the company."

In the hallway, coming around a corner, Catherine and Sara almost collided with the burly, crew-cut Sergeant O'Riley.

"Just the lady I was lookin' to see," O'Riley said to Catherine, pleasantly. "Those jackets you had me tracking down—the Lipton Construction jackets?"

"Yes?"

He dug a notepad out of his breast shirt pocket, referred to a page as he said, "Twenty-six positive I.D.'s out of the twenty-seven . . . and all three that the Lipton Construction office girl had marked 'maybe' were correct. No idea about the other five . . . or the one we're short, outa the positive list."

"Nice work, Sergeant. Thanks."

He gave Catherine a little grin. "Getting along out there all right, without me?"

Catherine smiled at the big man. "Yeah—but don't think you're not missed."

"Holler if you need me," he said, and headed back toward the PD wing.

Thirteen minutes later, Catherine and Sara pulled up in their Tahoe to find Conroy standing on the sidewalk out in front of the brick apartment house, speaking with a silver-haired senior citizen in a gray sweater, white slacks, black socks and sandals.

"This is the landlord, Bill Palmer," Conroy said. "I've already apologized for bothering him, this time of night."

"Morning," the older man corrected, trembling slightly as he shook their hands. He had wireframe trifocals, and one gigantic overgrown white eyebrow that looked like a caterpillar had died on his forehead.

"I've served Mr. Palmer with the warrant," Conroy said, "and he's about to let us in."

"Let's get on with it," Palmer said.

The three women followed him up the stairs and around behind the building. They'd made this trip enough that Catherine was considering adding it to her normal exercise routine. Palmer worked his way through half a dozen different keys—apparently there was no single master—before he finally managed to unlock the door of the apartment. Once they were inside, Conroy escorted the landlord back outside, to clear the scene, while Catherine and Sara snugged on their latex gloves and went to work.

As was so often the case in their job, they didn't know what they were looking for, exactly; so they started right there in the living room. Moving slowly, the two CSIs went over the single-armed couch, the chair, the hassock, and the rest of the living room, finding nothing of any apparent significance.

"If you take the bathroom," Sara said, "I'll take the kitchen."

"What a deal."

"I'll buy breakfast later, if you do."

"That is a deal."

In the bathroom, a gold-metal basket sat empty on the back of the toilet lid and Catherine knew at once that Tera Jameson had taken all of her cosmetics and such with her. Nonetheless, Catherine opened the medicine cabinet, but found nothing of use in there.

Whether the killer was Lipton or Tera or someone else, they would need DNA evidence on each of their suspects. Using a forceps like a spoon, Catherine dug around in the sink drain and came up with a wad of hair. Actually, she noticed two different colors of hair—Tera's and Jenna's, most likely. She stuffed it all into an evidence bags and slid over and did the same thing with the tub drain.

Sara came in from the kitchen and stuck her head in the door. "Nothing."

"Not much here either. Hair for DNA samples."

"Care for a double-team in the bedroom?"

"Sounds like more fun than it will be."

A king-sized bed with an ornate bookshelf headboard dominated the far wall of Tera's bedroom. A good-sized matching dresser stood against the left wall, a small television perched on top of it. The right

wall was all closets and the wall with the door was home to a small dressing table, with a framed *Penthouse* magazine cover on the wall nearby . . . and Tera—wearing a golden chainmail outfit that most of her flesh showed through—was the cover girl.

Sara went directly to the dressing table, while Catherine started with the headboard. Dark oak and sturdy, the headboard contained two shelves and a drawer on either side. The top shelf was lined with paperbacks, mostly Grisham, King, Koontz, and various other thrillers. The bottom shelf held magazines and a small electric alarm clock radio. Opening the nearest drawer, Catherine looked inside and found a tie-on seven-inch sex toy.

"Well hello, big fella," Catherine said.

"What?" Sara said.

"Have a look at this."

Sara came over and peered into the drawer. "DNA on a stick!"

Catherine snapped several photos of the device then she carefully slipped it into an evidence bag. "I'll let *you* drop this one off with Greg," she said.

Sara gave her a "gee thanks" expression, then said, "Found a couple of wigs, but nothing like the short-hair one in the security video. And no mustache, beard, or spirit gum."

"Let's keep looking. There's a surprise in every drawer. . . ."

"Be nice to find a Lipton Construction jacket."

Sara went from the dressing table to the closet. The second drawer of the headboard was empty and Catherine moved to the bed. The RUVIS showed a few spots of bodily fluids on the spread and Catherine bagged the spread, too. Recently washed, the sheets were clean under the ultraviolet. Stripping off the sheets, Catherine immediately saw small dark stains in numerous places on the mattress.

Sara was pulling several pairs of jeans from the closet; these and a couple of baseball caps, she bagged, saying, "No boots."

"None?"

"Cowboy or otherwise—nothing."

After taking pictures, Catherine took scrapings from the dark spots on the mattress. It appeared to be menstrual blood, but she bagged each scraping separately.

They spent hours combing the apartment, but never found any

boots or Lipton Construction jackets or any other evidence that seemed to point toward Tera Jameson's guilt.

Finally finished, they packed up their silver field kits and met Conroy and the landlord outside.

"Anything?" the detective asked.

Catherine shrugged. "Some material to send through the lab . . . then maybe we'll know more."

Conroy frowned. "No jacket? No beard?"

"No jacket. No beard."

The elderly landlord was looking at them like they were speaking in Sanskrit.

At the bottom of the stairs, a sporty black Toyota eased by them, and Catherine recognized the woman behind the wheel: Tera Jameson.

The car parked, the engine shut off, and the woman unfolded herself out of the car and started in on a brisk walk. Carrying a purse on a shoulder strap, she wore tight denim shorts, a black cropped T-shirt exposing her pierced navel, and high-heeled sandals. Her bushy brown hair was tied back in a severe ponytail.

Then she saw the little group at the bottom of the stairs and froze in mid-stride.

"Is that my stuff?" she asked, her voice shrill, angry. "What the hell are you doing with my stuff?"

Conroy stepped forward and held out the folded paper. "Tera Jameson, we're serving you with a search warrant."

The exotic eyes were wide, nostrils of the pretty face flared like a rearing horse; she did not accept the warrant. "What the hell *is* this? I got rights like anybody else, you know!"

Conroy's voice was coldly professional. "Ms. Jameson, this warrant allows us to search your residence for evidence, which we have done in your absence."

"Evidence of fucking what?"

Catherine stepped forward and said, "Ms. Jameson, we're gathering evidence in the case of Jenna Patrick's homicide."

Tera shook her head angrily, the ponytail swinging. "You've *got* that abusive son of a bitch in custody, don't you? Why aren't you searching *Lipton's* house?"

"We have," Catherine said, calmly.

"Well . . . isn't *he* the *killer?*"

With a noncommittal shrug, Conroy said, "We have several suspects."

"Oh, and I'm one of them now? I was *working* the night Jenna was killed. Jesus! He's a crazy jealous asshole! He did it, you *know* he did it."

"Well we do know one thing for sure," Conroy said. "Lipton never lied to us."

"Right!" she laughed, bitterly. "Lie is all Ray Lipton does." Then she stopped as she realized what Conroy meant. "Wait . . . you think *I* lied to *you?*"

"I don't remember you telling us you were a lesbian."

Tera Jameson backed up a step, horrified and offended. Words flew out of her: "Why the hell does that matter? What business is it of yours? What could it possibly have to do with Jenna's death?"

Catherine asked, coolly, "Ms. Jameson—were you and Jenna involved?"

"No! We were just friends."

"We've been told Jenna was bisexual."

"Who by? That cow Belinda? That's crazy! That's nonsense! Jenna was straight—you think gays don't have straight friends? Odds are one of *you* three is a lesbian!"

"Jenna was straight?" Conroy repeated, arching an eyebrow.

"Yes, she was straight! So why should I have mentioned my sexual preference? It has nothing to do with this."

Sara asked, "So you two just lived together?"

"I told you—Jenna wasn't like that. What, you think we were a couple of teenage girls playing doctor? Get real."

"Well," Catherine said, edging past the dancer, the bagged bedspread piled under one arm, "we'll know soon enough."

"Is that my bedspread? Are you taking my bedspread?"

Catherine said nothing.

Now Tera was following them as they headed for the Tahoe. "What *else* of mine are you taking?"

"Some jeans," Sara said, casually, "some other stuff."

"Shit! You lousy bitches!"

Conroy swung around and faced the dancer. "Maybe we should take you in, too."

Tera's face screwed up in rage. "For what?"

Catherine knew Conroy wanted to say murder . . . but right now? They had no proof.

So the CSI stepped forward and said, in a friendly manner, "Ms. Jameson—you liked Jenna. She was your friend. Let us do our job. We're just trying to eliminate you as suspect . . . that's all."

Tera thought about that, and said, "Yeah, right," not seeming to believe Catherine, but not as worked up, either.

Then the dancer was heading quickly up the stairs, ponytail bouncing.

When Tera was out of sight, Catherine said, "Greg had better come through for us, or we might find ourselves on the crappy end of the lawsuit stick."

Conroy sighed. "Thanks for playing diplomat, Catherine—I was kind of stepping over the line, there. And with the mood Mobley's been in lately, I don't want any part of pissing off the sheriff."

"I hear that," Sara said.

But Catherine knew it was worse than just department politics. Detective Erin Conroy had taken in one bum suspect, and doing that a second time could make the case practically impossible to prosecute . . . if they ever got that far. Any decent defense attorney would make mincemeat of them for arresting two wrong suspects—talk about reasonable doubt—and Jenna Patrick's killer, whoever he or she might be, would walk smiling into the sunset.

"Well, if I can't come up with something solid," Conroy said to the CSIs as she helped them load up the SUV, "you ladies better find it for me, somewhere in all this evidence we've been gathering . . . and soon."

Then the detective went to her Taurus, and Catherine and Sara to their Tahoe, to head back. The sun was coming up, and another shift was over.

13

The next night's shift had barely begun when Warrick Brown stuck his head into Grissom's office, waving a file folder. "Lil Moe's real name is Kevin Sadler."

Grissom looked up from files of his own. "The pusher you busted? What was that about? Bring me up to speed."

Warrick remained in the doorway. "Sadler's a two-bit dealer, done some county time, never handled enough weight to go the distance."

"And this has to do with our case how?"

Warrick offered up a sly smile. "Sadler stamps his bags with a little red triangle."

"Like the bag of coke we found at Pierce's?"

"Exactly like."

Grissom rocked back. "So—does this mean we have a new suspect?"

Warrick leaned against the jamb. "You mean, did Owen Pierce hire this scumbag to off his wife? Or maybe did Owen and his connection have a falling out, and Lynn Pierce caught the bad end of it?"

Impatiently, Grissom said, "Yes."

"No," Warrick said. "Sadler was in lockup for three months—grass bust. Just got out."

"Just?"

"Two days after Lynn Pierce went missing."

Grissom made a disgusted face. "Didn't take him long to jump back into business. Well, at least you got him off the street. . . . What's next?"

"Gris, Little Moe's *not* a dead-end."

"There's mo'?"

Warrick actually laughed. "That wasn't bad, Gris. Anyway, just two short years ago, Sadler was a baseball player at UNLV. Guess who his physical therapist was?"

Grissom's eyes glittered. "Does he live in a castle?"

"How's this for a scenario? Kevin Sadler, aka Lil Moe, enters his new, lucrative line of chemical sales. And maybe his physical therapist is not just a member of the Hair Club for men . . ."

Grissom frowned thoughtfully. "He's the president?"

Warrick shrugged a shoulder. "People who come to massage therapy are hurting—and massage isn't cheap. Pierce pulls down seventy-five an hour for a session . . . so he's obviously attracting a clientele who could afford recreational drugs to help ease their pain."

Still frowning, Grissom—already on his feet—asked, "You run this by Brass?"

"Oh yeah—more important, he's about to run it past our friend Kevin . . . which is to say Moe." Warrick checked his watch. "They should be heading into the interrogation room about . . . now."

Through the two-way glass they could see the slender, dread-locked Sadler, in one of the county's orange jumpsuits, sitting sullenly at the table, a bandage on his forehead. Seated beside him was Jerry Shannon, the kind of attorney who was glad for whatever scraps the Public Defender's office could toss his way. Short and malnourished-looking, the attorney looked superficially spiffy in a brown sportcoat, green tie and yellow shirt, which on closer inspection indicated his tailor shop of choice might be Goodwill.

Brass was on his feet, kind of drifting between Sadler and his attorney, whose arms were folded as he monotoned, "My client has nothing to say."

Warrick and Grissom exchanged glances: they'd encountered Shannon before; low-rent, yes, thread-bare, sure . . . but no fool.

Brass directed his gaze at Sadler, and with no sympathy, asked, "How's the ribs?"

"They hurt like a motherfucker!" Sadler said, and grimaced, his discomfort apparently no pose. "I'm gonna sue your damn asses, police brutality shit. . . ."

The skinny attorney leaned toward his client and touched an orange sleeve. "You don't have to answer any of the captain's questions, Kevin—including the supposedly 'friendly' ones."

"You prefer Kevin, then?" Brass asked. "Not Moe?"

The dealer looked toward his lawyer, then back at Brass, blankly. Shannon leaned back in his chair, folded his arms again, smiled to himself.

Brass was saying, "Found a lot of grass on you last night, Kevin—not to mention the coke and the meth, and the pills. County just won't cover it. This time you're gonna get a little mo' yourself . . . in Carson City."

Trading glances with his attorney, Sadler tried to look defiant and unconcerned; but the fear in his eyes was evident.

"You positive you don't want to answer a few questions for us? Help us out?"

"Hell no! You—"

But Sadler's attorney had leaned forward and touched that orange sleeve again, silencing his client.

Pleasantly, Shannon inquired, "And what would be in it for my client? If he 'helped you out.' "

"That would depend on the answers he gives," Brass said.

Shannon shook his head. "You want Kevin to answer your questions, and *then* you'll offer us a deal? That's a little backwards, Captain Brass, isn't it?"

Brass shrugged. "Fine—we can let the judge sort it out. What do you think, Kevin? You're young enough to do ten years standing on your head—you won't even be all that old when you get out."

"Captain Brass," Shannon began.

But Sadler shook the attorney's hand off his sleeve and said, surly, "Ask your damn questions."

Brass took the seat next to Sadler. He even smiled a little as he asked, "Kevin—last night you told us you didn't know Owen Pierce . . . was that true?"

Sadler's forehead tightened in thought.

"I guess ten years isn't such a long time," Brass said, reflectively. "You might even be out in five. They even have a baseball team at Carson City—how is the knee, anyway?"

Sadler got the message, and shook his head, disgustedly. "I only know him *that* way . . . Pierce worked on my knee, some. That's it. End of story."

Brass rose, and looked toward the two-way window.

"That's my cue," Warrick said to Grissom.

Moments later Warrick entered the interrogation room waving a clear evidence bag; carrying it over to Sadler, Warrick let him see the bag within the bag, the red triangle winking at him. "How did this end up in Owen Pierce's house, if he was just your physical therapist?"

The attorney said, "Pierce could've got that from anybody. There are countless sources in this town."

Warrick showed the bag to the attorney, now. "But those sources don't use this particular signature. . . ." And now the CSI turned toward the dealer. "Do they, Kevin?"

Sadler turned away from Warrick's gaze.

"Were you paying Pierce in coke, Kevin?" Warrick pressed. "Is that how it worked? Him tradin' you physical therapy for his chemical recreation?"

The dealer settled deeper into sullen silence.

"The hell with this!" Brass said, roaring in off the sidelines. "Kevin can rot in jail for the next decade or so—that's a given." The detective leaned in and grinned terribly at the sulky face. "But I will promise you this, Mr. Sadler—when we put Pierce away for murder, I'll find a way to latch onto you as an accessory."

Brass motioned with his head to Warrick and they headed toward the door.

"Accessory?" Sadler blurted, his eyes wide, batting away his lawyer's hand. "Hey, man I ain't accessory to shit!"

Brass stopped, his hand on the knob. "Did you know Lynn Pierce?"

"I never even met the wife. I was never over there when she around—mostly we did business at his office."

Brass strolled back over. "What kind of business, Kevin?"

Sadler looked at his attorney a beat too long. They had him.

"I seen the papers and TV," Sadler said, tentatively. "Is she . . . missing or, she dead?"

"Mrs. Pierce?" Brass said, conversationally. "Dead. Cut up with a chain saw."

That stopped Sadler, who blew out some air. "Man, that is cold. . . . I had nothing to do with that. You sound sure he did it . . ."

Warrick said, "If he didn't, we want to prove that, too."

Sadler snorted a laugh. "Yeah, right—I forgot all about where the police was into justice and shit."

Tersely, the attorney said, "Kevin, if you *must* speak . . . think first. And check with me if you have doubts about—"

"I'm on top of this," Sadler said sharply to Shannon. Looking from Brass to Warrick and back, he said, "That stuff last night . . . the blade and all—that was goin' no place. You dig? That's just, you know—theater."

Warrick, who still had a small Band-Aid on his neck, said, "Theater."

"Yeah—people got to take this shit serious."

"Dealing, you mean."

Sadler shrugged. "Anyway, I never killed nobody. I scare people if I have to—to buy me, you understand, *street* cred."

Brass said, "Kevin—when your knee went south, and you dropped out of school, and entered your new line of work . . . did Owen Pierce help you line up clients by introducing you to certain of his patients?"

". . . If I answer that, it'll help clear up this murder? Won't be used to nail my sorry ass to the wall?"

Brass said, "All we want is Lynn Pierce's killer. I'm a Homicide captain—I don't do drugs."

"That's a good policy," Sadler admitted. Then, smiling broadly, the dealer said, "It is a sweet deal—his clients, my clients, got a lot in common, y'know: money and pain."

"Are you and Pierce still in business together?"

"Oh yeah, we tight—ain't shit could come between us. I even let him borrow my boat."

Brass's eyes widened. *"You've* got a boat?"

"Yeah," Sadler said, misreading the detective's reaction. "What, a brother can't own a boat?"

Warrick asked, "What kind of boat is it?"

"Three hundred eighty Supersport. That is one fast motherfucker, man."

Brass again: "And you let Pierce borrow it?"

"Sure . . . We might come from different places, but, hey—we understand each other, 's all 'bout the benjamins, baby. Hell, he even kept an eye on my crib while I was in the lockup—brought my mail in, let the housekeeper in and shit."

"This was during your recent vacation with the county?"

"Yeah—I only jus' got out. Don't you got that in your computer?"

Leaning in alongside the dealer, Brass said, "Kevin, you seem to have heard about Lynn Pierce's disappearance."

"Yeah. I don't live in a fuckin' cave."

Warrick, seeing where Brass was going, dropped in at the young man's other shoulder. "Then you heard about the body part that was found at Lake Mead?"

"Yeah, sure, I . . ." Once more, Sadler looked from Warrick to Brass and back again, this time with huge eyes. "Oh, shit . . . are you sayin' he used *my* boat to . . ."

The attorney said, "Kevin, be quiet."

"Your good friend Owen Pierce," Warrick said, "made an accessory-after-the-fact out of you."

"But I was in jail!"

"An accessory doesn't have to be present, just help out—lend a boat, for example."

The attorney said, "Gentlemen, I think my client should confer with me before this goes anywhere else."

But Brass said, "How would you like a pass on the drugs?"

Sadler said, "Hell, yes!"

And his attorney settled back in his chair, silently withdrawing his demand.

"Then," Brass continued, "give us the address and key to your house, and the location of your boat."

Sadler frowned. "Just let you go through all of my shit?"

"That's right—and we don't need a search warrant, do we? After all, you're going to be a witness for the prosecution."

Shannon was way ahead of his client, leaning forward to say to Brass, "And anything you might find, beyond the purview of your murder investigation, goes unseen?"

Brass thought about that, then glanced at the two-way glass.

Moments later, Grissom entered the interrogation room, conferred briefly with Brass, who then said, "We can live with that."

Sadler looked at his attorney, who was smiling. Shannon said, "So can we, gentleman," with a smugness not at all commensurate with how little the lawyer had had to do with the deal.

Gil Grissom, Jim Brass, Nick Stokes, and Warrick Brown—the latter behind the wheel—rode together in one of the black SUV's, their first stop the Quonset hut–style storage building where Sadler kept his speedboat. One of half a dozen adjacent cubicles, the oversized shed was at the far end of a U-Rent-It complex not far from where Sadler lived.

Warrick dusted the metal door handle for prints, but the CSI found nothing; no surprise, as the desert air caused fingerprints to disappear sooner than in more humid climes.

With that pointless task completed, they swung the overhead door up and moved inside to have a look at the drug dealer's very expensive boat. With no electricity in the garage, they compensated with flashlights. Forty feet long, the sleek white craft was crammed into the shabby space with barely enough room to shut the door, a beautiful woman in a burlap sack. Triple 250-horsepower Mercury motors lined the tail and, as Brass played his beam of light over the engines, he let out a long low appreciative whistle.

"Fast boat," he said.

"If you say so," Grissom said, eyes on the hunt for something pertinent.

Nick and Warrick climbed up into the craft while Brass and Grissom remained on the cement floor. Warrick started at the stern, Nick in the bow, and they worked toward the center. To the naked eye, the boat appeared pristine, and the lingering scent of solvent and ammonia suggested a fresh cleaning.

"When was the last time Sadler had the boat out?" Nick called down.

Shining his flashlight on his notebook, Brass said, "If our charming cooperative witness can be trusted, right after the Fourth of July. He was in lockup most of the time after that."

Nick glanced back at Warrick. "Then where's the dust?"

"Boat's way too clean," Warrick said, shaking his head. "Ask me, somebody used it, and cleaned it."

From below, Grissom said, "Don't ask yourself—ask the evidence."

Nick and Warrick dusted the controls and the wheel for prints. Everything had been wiped. Opening the fish box, Nick shone his beam inside and saw that it too had been hosed clean.

"There's nothing here," Warrick said finally. "There'd be more dust and dirt if it had come straight off the showroom floor."

"Keep at it," Grissom said, working the cubicle itself.

Up in the boat, the indoor/outdoor carpet covering the cockpit floor was a mix of navy, light blue, and white swirls. Even on his hands and knees, with the beam of his light barely six inches off the deck, Warrick doubted he would see anything even if it was there. Fifteen minutes of crawling around later, he had proved himself correct.

Nick jumped down onto the cement, nimble for the big guy he was. "I don't know what to say, Grissom."

Grissom's smile was barely there. "Remember the old movies when the Indians were out there, about to attack? 'It's quiet . . .' "

" 'Too quiet,' " Nick finished, with a nod. "And this is too clean, way too clean for sitting as long as it's supposed to . . . but we can't find anything."

Grissom's head tilted and an eyebrow hiked. "If a dismembered body was disposed of from the deck of that boat, Nick—what should we expect to find?"

Nick smiled, nodded, went to Warrick's field kit, picked out a bottle and tossed it up to him.

"Luminol, Gris?" Warrick called down. "You don't really think he cut her up on the boat, do you?"

"I don't know," the supervisor said. "I wasn't here when it happened . . . see if anything's *still* here that can tell us."

Nick walked forward to where Brass stood with his arms crossed.

"I thought we had the bastard," said the detective.

Shrugging, Nick said, "Grissom's right—the cuter they think they are, the smarter they think they are, the surer a bet that they slipped somewhere." He looked down, his gaze falling on the end of the trailer. "Anybody dust the hitch?"

Brass looked at him, a tiny smile beginning at the corners of his mouth. "Not yet."

With the luminol sprayed over the cockpit, Warrick turned on the UV light source. He moved from bow to stern on the port side: nothing; going the opposite way on the starboard side, Warrick made it as far as the console before he saw the first glow . . .

. . . a fluorescent dot.

His breath caught and he froze, willing the tiny green spot to not be a figment of his imagination. Two more drops to the side, one more on the gunnel, and Warrick knew he was seeing the real thing. Retracing his steps to the center of the boat, he opened the fishbox. Though it had appeared clean at first glance, it now had a tiny fluorescent stripe on the bottom, against the back wall. One bag of body parts had leaked, he thought.

"Got blood," he called down, coolly. "Not much, but it'll give us DNA."

Grissom smiled at Brass. "If Lynn Pierce's dismembered body took a trip on that boat, we're going to know."

Removing the tape from the trailer hitch, Nick shone his light on the tape to reveal a nice clean thumb print. "Got a print off the trailer hitch!" he called.

The quartet locked up the garage feeling pretty good about themselves—they knew to a man that they were finally making progress in this frustrating case.

"Next stop," Grissom said, "the home of Kevin Sadler."

"And more puzzle pieces?" Nick asked.

"Maybe," Grissom admitted. And then he went further: "Maybe enough pieces to tell us what picture we're putting together."

The house, a rambling ranch in need of repair and paint, squatted on one of those side streets that never made it into the "Visit Vegas!" videos, much less the travel brochures.

Brass unlocked the door and the CSIs moved in, carrying their silver field kits in latex-gloved hands, their jobs already assigned by their supervisor, the detective ready and willing to pitch in on the search. Nick took the kitchen, Grissom the bedroom and bathroom, Brass the living room, and Warrick the basement.

Arrayed with contemporary, apartment-style furnishings, many of them black and white (the walls were pale plaster), the place was tidy, perhaps—like the boat—too tidy. On the other hand, Sadler had been away for some months, and only recently returned; so it was not surprising that the place had been cleaned while he was away (while watching the place, Pierce had let the housekeeper in, the dealer had said), nor was it startling that Sadler hadn't had time yet to get it very dirty, since.

The television in the living room was smaller than a Yugo—barely; next to it, stacks of electronic equipment thumbed their noses at Brass, who knew what little of it was. A large comfy-looking white leather couch dominated the center of the room with chairs set at angles facing the television on either side. Thick white pile carpeting squished beneath the detective's feet, the type that particles of evidence could hide themselves away in; still, Brass knew there was little hope of finding any evidence in here, which (he also knew) was why he'd drawn this room in the first place.

In the bedroom, on the nightstand, Grissom found an ashtray full of smoked joints and, in a drawer of the nightstand, a large resealable plastic bag full of grass. As he went through the closet, Grissom began to realize he wasn't going to find anything to help him in here. He had hopes for the bathroom, but found nothing there, either. To his surprise, luminol showed no blood in the tub . . . or the sink. . . .

In the kitchen, Nick found some blood in the drain, as if someone had washed it off their hands. And luminol showed a few spots of blood in the sink. He took samples of all of it, but found nothing else.

"You're gonna wanna see this!" Warrick called from the basement.

They trooped downstairs, an eager Grissom in the lead. The windowless room was illuminated by a single bulb dangling from the ceiling, *Psycho*-style. In the far corner, a shower head was attached to the wall, feeding a drain in the floor a few feet away. Though a curtain rod made a square enclosure, the shower curtain was long gone, bits of it still entangled in the metal rings of the rod.

The latter detail struck Grissom as possibly significant.

Next to the shower, a large sink was mounted on the wall, with a toilet along the same wall beyond that, no walls around any of the fixtures.

With the others looking on, a calm but focused Warrick said, "I sprayed the shower, the floor, the sink and the toilet with luminol."

No one said anything as the lanky CSI turned on the UV light. Nor did they speak when the entire room seemed to supernaturally fluoresce before them, freezing even these seasoned investigators into shock.

Shaking his head, Brass finally said, "Oh, my God . . ."

His expression grim, Grissom hung his head, the vision of it playing before his closed eyes.

Pierce has a key to the house. He comes down here, into this cement dungeon, with the body of his wife. He places her in the shower like the lump of flesh she's become, and goes back upstairs for his chain saw. Soon, he returns, and fires it up. . . .

Trying to keep the mess to a minimum, he begins a one-man assembly line, cutting off a piece of his dead wife, then cutting off part of the shower curtain—with scissors?—and wraps it up like a piece of meat from the grocery store. Then he puts the pieces in garbage bags, taking care to weight down each bag—rocks? sink weights?—before he ties it off.

All the time he's doing this, Pierce has no emotional response to the fact that he's chopping up his wife. It's a job—nothing more. He has had so many bodies stretched out before him on his massage tables that the human body has no surprises for him—bones, muscles, fat, his fingers know them all so well.

If anything, he takes a grim satisfaction that he's obliterating Lynn's identity, this new identity, this born-again prude who replaced the woman he married. It somehow isn't enough to just kill her—she had been so concerned with spiritual matters, so obsessed with the heavenly world beyond this one, well, he would just relieve her of that cumbersome suit of flesh, removing it from existence: no body, no Lynn.

He also relishes outsmarting the police. If they somehow do come after him, and he is cornered, he will blame that squalid little dope dealer.

"Sadler did it," he will say. "Drug deal went bad for him, and he was desperate for cash—and I owed him money, and couldn't pay up."

But Sadler was in jail, when your wife disappeared, *the cops would say.*

"That's what Sadler thought you would think," he says. "The perfect alibi—but he had one of his 'homeys' do it for him."

And of course the police will believe him—in Pierce's mind, who wouldn't take the word of an upstanding white citizen over that of some black drug dealer?

But even dead, Lynn proves to be a pain in the ass—she pisses him off one last time, when he tries to slice through the pelvis, and the saw jams up in the bone, dragging the intestines out as he pulls the saw free. He feels foolish, for a moment, supposed expert at anatomy that he is.

But the moment passes, and before very long, he's finally finished down here. He cleans up the blood, making a thorough job of it, con-

vinced he's left no traces for investigators to find. He loads up his SUV with his chain saw and his bags of "meat," hauls the saw and the bags over to Sadler's boat in the nearby storage shed, takes the boat out under the cover of darkness, onto Lake Mead, and rides around the rest of the night, dropping bags—and a chain saw, and maybe a gun—over the side.

The only thing Pierce misses is that one of the bags has a pinhole leak, dripping blood in the fishbox, on the deck, and on the gunnel before he finally gets it over the side. His subsequent thorough cleaning of the boat cannot remove these blood trails; but he does not know that.

Nor does the anatomy "expert" foresee the pelvic piece, still filled with gas, breaking free from its weighted bag, starting for the surface only to be caught up in the anchor chain of the Fish and Wildlife worker, Jim Tilson.

All Owen Pierce knows is that he has one last thing to do: he must turn himself into a distraught husband unable to find his runaway wife.

Grissom wondered where the body had been when they were in the house that first night. Had Pierce already brought his wife's remains here? And where had Lynn's car been during all of this?

He asked Warrick, "You got pictures and scrapings?"

"Doing it now," Warrick said.

"Nick," Grissom said, "you help him in here. Also, check upstairs for scissors Pierce might have cut the curtain with. Take a sample of what's left of those curtains, too."

"On it," Nick said.

"Jim," Grissom said, "you want to come with me?"

"Where to?" Brass asked.

"Outside—one more thing I want to check."

Around behind the house, invisible from the street, sat a small clapboard shed of a garage, barely big enough for a car and a few tools. It had two old swing-out wooden doors held together with a chain and padlock.

"You have the key for this?" Grissom asked.

Using the key ring Sadler had provided, Brass tried one key after another until, on the fifth attempt, the lock gave. Each of them grabbed a door and tugged. Slowly, rusty hinges protesting, the doors swung open.

No car occupied the dirt floor and only a few tools hung on the wall around the place; seemed Sadler wasn't much of a handyman. In the far corner sat a rusted garbage can. Striding over to the dented receptacle, Grissom poured flashlight light down into it. Shiny glints winked back at him. "I think I just found the driver's-side window of Lynn Pierce's car."

"Anything else?" Brass asked as he joined Grissom at the trash can.

Bending over, Grissom withdrew a wadded-up piece of paper, which he carefully smoothed out in a latexed palm. "Receipt for a replacement window for a 'ninety-five Avalon." Grissom flashed a smile at the detective. "Paid cash at a U-Pull-a-Part junkyard."

Brass wasn't smiling, though, when he said, "You think he'll have cute answers for all of this?"

"Why don't we call on him, and see?"

14

At the start of shift, Sara Sidle felt she had drawn the short straw—Catherine was on her way to Showgirl World to serve the warrant on the dressing room, while Detective Conroy was heading back to Dream Dolls to reinterview Belinda Bountiful and the other strippers—again. That left Sara to supervise the lab work at HQ, in particular following up on anything Greg Sanders might have come up with. With Grissom, Warrick, and Nick all tied up with the Lynn Pierce case, she felt like a ghost haunting the blue-tinged halls of CSI.

In particular, she hoped to take care of one frustrating detail. They had been trying to track down the Dream Dolls private-dance cubicle carpeting ever since Jenna Patrick's body had been found. Ty Kapelos provided Sergeant O'Riley with the name of the cut-rate retailer who sold it to him. O'Riley'd been having difficulty getting in touch with the retailer, a guy named Monty Wayne, who ran a small discount business in the older part of downtown.

"Guy's been on vacation," O'Riley told Sara yesterday, "and his only other employee is this secretary whose English ain't so hot."

But this evening, upon getting to work, Sara found, on her computer monitor screen, a Post-it from O'Riley saying Wayne was back from his vacation. Even better, the retailer had provided his home number, saying it was okay to call up till midnight.

Sitting behind her desk and punching in the numbers, Sara tried to fight the feeling that she was spinning her wheels while everyone else on the CSI team was doing something really productive, not to mention more interesting. The phone rang twice before it was picked up.

"Wayne residence," a rough-edged male voice intoned.

"Mr. Wayne?"

"Yes."

"This is Sara Sidle, Las Vegas P.D. criminalistics. You spoke to Sergeant O'Riley, earlier?"

The voice brightened. "Ms. Sidle, yes . . . been expecting your call. How can I be of help to the police?"

"Sergeant O'Riley spoke to you about this carpeting in the back of Dream Dolls—"

But Wayne was all over that, wall to wall: "Oh yeah, I remember that shit. And it *was* shit—that Kapelos character got it cheap because I could barely give the stuff away."

"Why is that?"

"Came from this manufacturer in South Carolina—Denton, South Carolina. I used to buy a lot of stuff from them, but they been slipping. I took these two rolls as a sample."

"Would you know if anybody else locally carries it?"

"Hell, I doubt it. I happen to know I was their only Vegas client, even in their heyday. And now, hardly anybody buys from Denton anymore . . . might say they're hanging on by a thread."

He seemed to be waiting for her to laugh; so Sara forced a chuckle, and said, "Please go on, Mr. Wayne."

"I doubt if there's any more of that cut-rate crap in the state, let alone the city."

"Thanks, Mr. Wayne. Would you have the Denton manufacturer's number?"

"I already gave it to that Sgt. O'Riley, and I don't have it at home. Why don't you check with him? He and I went over pretty much the same ground."

Probably including the "hanging by a thread" gag, she thought; but she said, "Well, thank you, Mr. Wayne, you've been very cooperative," which was true.

He said it was his pleasure and they said good-bye and Sara hung up, quickly dialing O'Riley's desk; she got the message machine so she tried his cell, catching him in his car on his way to the aftermath of a convenience store robbery.

"Yeah, I talked to Goldenweave in Denton," O'Riley said. "They didn't sell that carpet to anybody else in Vegas, or even in the southwest. Is that helpful?"

"Could be," she said, thinking about it, the carpet suddenly seeming to Sara like the fabric version of DNA.

Finally feeling a little spring in her step, she bounced over to Greg Sanders in his lab, but found him sitting in a chair by a countertop, not working on anything, not even goofing off with a soft drink or video game or anything . . . just sort of sitting morosely.

"I was kind of hoping you might have something for me," Sara said from the doorway.

But the spiky-haired lab rat just sat there, as if he hadn't heard her.

She waited for a moment, then said, "Greg? Hello?"

He didn't move.

Finally, she went to him, placing a hand on a shoulder of his blue smock. "Greg, what is it?"

Shaking his head, he looked at her. "This stripper case of yours . . . I hate it."

"You hate it."

"Can you believe that? A case involving exotic dancers, and I'm longing for a decomposing corpse or maybe another skinned gorilla."

Sara pulled up a chair and sat beside him. "Be specific."

His sigh lifted his whole body and set it down hard. "Okay—you bring me enough raw evidence to fill a warehouse, and yet I get nothing from the prime suspect, but a ton of stuff from all the coworkers. I mean, they've all been in that room . . . but Lipton? Never. And there's enough DNA in that cubicle to start an entirely new species, only none of it belongs to him."

"What about the roommate?"

Greg turned to look at her, eyes narrowing. "Yeah, I was gonna ask about her."

"Why's that?"

"Well, first understand that there's carpet fibers on the clothes of all those Dream Dolls dancers—any of them, all of them could've been in that private dance cubicle at any time."

"We knew that. What's that got to do with the roommate? Tera Jameson?"

Greg offered her a palm, to accompany the only halfway interesting information he had: "She's got the carpet fibers on her stuff too."

"Hmmm. She's our other good suspect."

Greg brightened. "She is?"

"Yes . . . but she used to work at Dream Dolls, herself."

"Oh. Her DNA's in the mix, too, by the way."

"Could be the same reason. You get anything from the mattress or the sex toy?"

Another sigh. "Doing that next. I believe this is the first time you've brought me a vibrator."

She smiled a little but, heading for the door, said only, "Don't go there, Greg."

Sanders managed his own little smile, before his expression turned serious as he returned to his work.

Sara, on her way to the office, had the nagging feeling she'd missed something, that the puzzle pieces were all before her now, and she wasn't quite putting them together.

Detective Erin Conroy and Pat Hensley sat on metal folding chairs in the dressing room at Dream Dolls, a few of the dancers in various stages of undress milling about, applying expensive makeup and cheap perfume. Pat's alter ego, Belinda Bountiful, didn't go on for another half hour, and she was relaxing, enjoying a cup of coffee; so was Conroy, keeping it casual, not even taking notes.

Her back to the dressing table, almost plain without makeup, the garishly redheaded Hensley wore a low-cut lime top that shared much of her ample cleavage with the world; her jeans were funkily frayed and form-fitting, and she was barefoot, her toenails bloodred. But it was the Dolly Partonesque cleavage that kept attracting Conroy's attention.

Catching this, Belinda said good-naturedly, "If you got it, honey, flaunt it. I paid good money for these and I intend to get a whole lotta mileage out of 'em."

The refreshing bluntness of that made Conroy laugh. Then she said, "We were talking about Tera Jameson."

"Right. What else can I tell you?"

"Is Tera's sexual preference widely known in your circles?"

Hensley shrugged. "She don't advertise it, but she doesn't hide it, neither."

"What about Jenna?"

Hensley sipped her coffee. "She *didn't* advertise it."

"That she was a lesbian?"

"No. Anyway, like I told that other female dick, the other day—Jenna liked both flavors."

"She was bisexual, you mean."

"Yeah, I said that before. What are you getting at?"

Conroy chose her words carefully. "Another friend of hers claims Jenna was strictly straight."

Hensley smirked. "Couldn't have been somebody who knew Jenna very well."

Conroy sat forward conspiratorially. "What if I told you it was Tera Jameson herself who made that claim?"

"I don't care if Oprah told you: it's a crock. Tera's lying. Why, I have no idea."

"*Were* Tera and Jenna having an affair?"

"Well, they *did* have one . . ."

"Right up to the time of Jenna's murder?"

"No—it was over months ago. They still roomed together, but Jenna told me, in no uncertain terms, that she and Tera were history. Still friends! But history."

"Because of Ray Lipton."

Hensley nodded. "Jenna fell hard for the guy. . . . You mind if I start putting on my makeup?"

"Not at all."

Hensley turned her back to the detective, began applying her makeup, and talking to Conroy in the mirror. "I can see why Tera didn't like Ray, though."

"Because he stole Jenna away?"

"Well, yeah, I guess, but . . ."

"Because he was a hothead?"

"That, too—though Lipton was mostly talk. I saw him do stuff like grab Jenna, by the wrists, y'know? But never hit her or anything."

Conroy kept trying. "What else didn't Tera like about Ray Lipton?"

"He looked down on Tera . . . he was very, what's the word? Provincial in his thinking. To him, it was perversion, girls with girls."

In the dressing room mirror, Pat Hensley was turning into the garishly attractive Belinda Bountiful. Conroy asked, "Pat . . . Belinda—this is important. Are you sure Jenna and Tera were involved, romantically? Sexually?"

A laugh bubbled out of the stripper. "Oh, yeah—I know for a fact!"

"Are you saying . . ."

Now the stripper turned and looked at the detective dead on. "Don't spread this around, okay? I got a husband, and two kids. But I work in a kinda bizarre line of business, you might have noticed, and I don't always see things, or do things that . . . conventional society would put their stamp of approval on."

Knowing the answer, Conroy asked, "How do you know Tera and Jenna were involved, Belinda?"

And Pat *was* Belinda now, when she said, "'Cause one horny drunken afternoon, girlfriend, I let the two of 'em make a Belinda Bountiful sandwich . . . that's *how* I know."

Taking a long swig from her coffee, Detective Erin Conroy smiled. "You like our Dream Dolls coffee, huh? It's not bad, for a dive."

"Not bad at all," Conroy said, rising, placing the empty coffee cup on the dressing table. "Delicious, in fact."

Almost as good, Conroy thought, *as catching Tera Jameson in another lie.*

In the dimly lighted, smoke-swirling cathedral of skin that was Showgirl World, Catherine Willows—in a black leather coat, canary silk blouse, and black leather pants—stood at the mirrored bar and waited, her silver field kit on the floor next to her.

The music pounded and a blonde pigtailed dancer in a schoolgirl micro-mini-skirt outfit was up on stage, toward the start of her set, and a few other girls in lingerie were meandering through the audience, even though the place was barely a quarter full, an early evening lull.

The bartender, a fiftyish guy in gray-rimmed glasses, came back from the telephone. "Mr. McGraw will be right out."

"Thanks."

A blade of light sliced into the darkness from the left, bouncing like a laser off the mirrors, and then as quickly disappeared. Stocky Rick McGraw—in a dark blue suit and lighter blue shirt without a tie—emerged from his office." "What can I do for you, Detective?"

"Crime scene investigator," she said, handing him the search warrant. "I'm here to search the dressing room."

The stocky club manager slipped the folded paper into the inside pocket of his suit without a glance. "Sure."

Catherine lifted one eyebrow and showed him half a smile. "You told Detective Conroy you wouldn't let her search the place without a warrant."

A small shrug. "And you brought one."

"Tera Jameson been in today?"

"Here now, but doesn't go on for a while. Wasn't scheduled—filling in for a sick girl." He gestured. "She's working private dances. You need her?"

"No. The night Jenna Patrick died, over at Dream Dolls—Tera worked that night, right?"

"Yeah. I told the cops all about it."

"Tell me again."

"Well, she was here, all right. We were kind of shorthanded, and she wound up doing sets at the top of every hour, for a while there."

"Do you have any kind of record of that? Is there a sheet that logs which dancers went on and came off when . . . that sort of thing?"

"What do you think? They sign in, they sign out; that's the extent of it."

"But you would testify she was here all night?"

McGraw nodded. "Six P.M. to three A.M."

Shaking her head, Catherine sighed and asked, "Dressing room in the back?"

"Yeah." He gestured toward the back with his head. "Don't you want me to round up Tera for you?"

Glancing this way and that, not seeing the Jameson woman anywhere, she shook her head. "Just the opposite. I wasn't planning on her being here. . . . Keep her out, while I'm in there, if you can."

"See what I can do. . . . No promises."

Only two dancers occupied the dressing room when Catherine—lugging the silver field kit—entered. Back here, the accommodations weren't much better than those of Dream Dolls. It didn't matter how nice a club was, the dressing rooms were all the same.

The nearest dancer was touching up her makeup. She gave Catherine a noncommittal nod in the mirror, her wide brown eyes sizing up the competition.

Catherine asked, "Tera Jameson's table?"

The dancer nodded toward the back. "She has the whole rear stall—she's a *star*, y'know." Turning from the mirror to look Catherine up and down, rather clinically, she added, "I didn't know she had a new squeeze."

Catherine said, "I'm with the police," and flashed the CSI I.D.

"And that makes you straight?"

Catherine arched an eyebrow. "The Jenna Patrick homicide?"

Now the woman got it, but she didn't seem to much care. "I didn't know her," she said, turning to herself in the mirror.

The other dancer had flopped onto one of the sofas, on her back, and was smoking a cigarette; she looked bored beyond belief.

At the far end, Tera had given herself some privacy by moving in a small clothes rack of her own, which she'd positioned as a wall between her and the next station. A window onto the rear parking lot was next to her table and obscured from view of the rest of the dressing room by that same clothing rack. Her makeup table and mirror was at right, while across the way—where there had once been another makeup station—another small rack of clothes was hanging with shoes below.

Tera's station itself was neatly organized. The chair was pushed in under the table, makeup case closed and sitting on the left side of the table, a box of tissues on the right corner nearest the mirror, a towel folded in quarters in front of it, another draped neatly over the back of the chair. The routine was readily apparent to someone who had once been in the life. Catherine eased into the latex gloves and went to work.

The makeup kit looked more like a jewelry box with a lid that flipped up and three drawers down the front. The top opened to reveal some small jars and brushes, and lipsticks laid in a neat row in a padded section on the right side.

But among the jars of nail polish and makeup, Catherine found a bottle of spirit gum.

Pleased, she bagged that and moved to the top drawer, where she found more lipsticks, rouges, bases, and powders. The second drawer contained much the same thing and Catherine wondered how much makeup one dancer needed. In the bottom drawer, she saw a stack of fashion magazines; she almost shut it again, then stopped and removed the magazines, and—crammed down under them—found a fake mustache and beard.

The beard/mustache combo looked as though it could match the rayon fibers they had found at Dream Dolls. With a satisfied sigh, Catherine bagged this major find and set it on the makeup table.

Catherine casually flipped through the garments on the rack nearest the station. She knew how it improbable it was that the Lipton Construction jacket would be hiding out here in plain sight, but she had to look. The circumstantial evidence was mounting, but she could already hear some lawyer saying Tera had decided to imitate her friend Jenna's old man act, and that's why she had spirit gum and blah blah blah.

But if that jacket turned up here, that would really sell a jury. . . .

She tried the other clothes rack and found nothing but stripper attire; however, when she checked down below, looking through the shoes, hoping to find a pair of man's boots, she noted a small suitcase and a matching train case. Pulling them out from where they'd been tucked away, Catherine snapped the suitcase open and found various street clothes; the train case held, among other things, the cosmetics that had been missing from Tera's bathroom this morning.

Suddenly Catherine knew this was Tera's final night at Showgirl World. The woman would gather her last night's wages—and this week's check, due tonight—and book it out the window to the parking lot.

Catherine punched Sara's number into her cell phone.

"Sara Sidle."

"It's me. I found spirit gum and the fake facial hair. There's even a damn window right by Tera's dressing table, for her to slip out of."

"Wow! Why did she keep that stuff around? Why didn't she dump it?"

"She's here now," Catherine said. "Maybe I'll ask her. You touch base with Conroy lately?"

"Yeah, I'm in the car with her now, heading your way. Conroy wants to question Jameson."

"What do *you* have that's new?"

"Greg's done with the tests on the evidence from the woman's apartment," Sara said. "Seems the sex toy has Jenna's DNA on it, and the menstrual blood stains from the mattress? They're from *both* women—Tera and Jenna, sharing a bed."

"So Tera's lover dumped her for a guy," Catherine said. "Ray Lipton, a homophobic hypocritical hothead. Tera decides to get even and kill her unfaithful lover, then frame the interloping boyfriend."

"She could have it all," Sara said.

"It's a motive," Catherine said, "but we still need something to tie her directly to the killing—beard isn't going to be enough."

"Look," Sara said, "keep Tera there till we get there."

"I had better," Catherine said. "She's a definite flight risk. Bags are packed here at the club . . . next to that window."

"Give us ten minutes. Oh yeah, one more thing Greg found—rug fibers from the lap-dance room at Dream Dolls turned up on jeans we took from Tera's apartment."

"Okay. I'll see you . . ." Catherine's voice trailed off. Then she said: "We've *got* her. She *did* it."

"Huh? How so?"

Catherine smiled into the cell phone. "If there were fibers from the private dance room at Dream Dolls, on Tera's clothes? She's guilty."

"But Tera worked there, too!"

"Yeah, she worked there *before* that carpeting was laid. Tera left Dream Dolls three months ago, and hadn't set foot in the place, since—or so she said."

"And the carpeting went in *two* months ago!"

"That's right. We've got her."

Sara spoke to Conroy, bringing her up to speed.

Suddenly Conroy was on the phone. "Keep Tera busy, if you can. Don't play cop: I'll make the arrest."

Cell phone back in her purse, Catherine returned to the makeup station to gather her things, but the plastic bag with the beard had slipped to the floor.

When Catherine bent to retrieve it, she looked under the table and saw a vent in the wall near the floor. Pulling out her Mini Maglite, she shone the beam at the screws and saw that the paint on them had been freshly chipped. From her field kit she got a small screwdriver, and crawled under the table to unscrew the four screws; then she pulled off the grate.

Inside the vent lay a dark garbage bag. She pulled it out and allowed herself a little smile as she opened it. In the bottom of the bag were the Lipton Construction jacket and the men's boots Tera had worn that night.

And now Catherine could see it happening, in her mind's eye . . .

. . . back in her quiet corner of the dressing room, Tera tapes down her breasts and dresses in clothes similar to Lipton's. She shoves her hair up under a ball cap, glues on the fake beard and mustache, and dons the dark glasses and the Lipton Construction jacket that she'd obtained from either one of his workers or a customer. She opens the window, watches for a quiet moment, drops into the parking lot where her car waits. Then, in drag, she drives to Dream Dolls, and somehow coaxes Jenna into the back room—either the disguise fooling the dancer in the dim lighting, or Jenna titillated by her former lover's masquerade.

Once in the lap-dance cubicle, Tera slips the electrical tie around Jenna's neck and yanks it tight. She watches the woman who betrayed her squirm in pain, then die.

Leaving the club, Tera returns—still in drag—and parks in the Showgirl World rear lot, waiting for the right moment to slip back through the window into the club, where she removes the disguise and hides the beard under some Vogue's and the jacket and boots in the vent. Soon she is to be back on stage, entertaining the masses, never having left the club.

When the police come to her apartment, she puts on the act of the grieving former roommate, certain that the plot will work and Ray Lipton will spend the rest of his life in prison.

In building her alibi, Tera had run so tight a timetable that the damning evidence—the fake facial hair, the jacket, the boots—had been stowed away at Showgirls, for future disposal. But with cops coming in and out of the club, and all these eyes on her, Tera hadn't yet dared sneak them out.

Catherine bagged the jacket and the boots, and then she closed up her field kit and gathered everything—it was quite a haul—and set them on the floor next to Tera's station. Toward the front of the dressing room, the black dancer was about to go out in a silvery nightgown over silver bra and thong.

"Are you on next?" Catherine asked her.

"In about half an hour. I'm gonna go out and stir up some business, first."

Catherine showed her a five-dollar bill. "A favor?"

The dancer snatched the fivespot out of Catherine's fingers, then asked, "What?"

"Just go out there and see if Tera's occupied."

The dancer shrugged, went out, came back in less than a minute.

"She's giving a private dance. Way down on the end—it's a separate room, but no door. Slip out past the bar during a song, and she probably won't see you. Between songs, she might."

"Thanks."

Catherine lugged the evidence outside and locked it in the Tahoe. As long as Tera hadn't seen her, Catherine wasn't worried about the woman splitting—she was giving a private dance, and still had no idea that Catherine was even on the premises, let alone what evidence the CSI had found.

With the Tahoe locked, Catherine checked the magazine on her pistol and reholstered it. Maybe she wouldn't be making the arrest herself, but Catherine knew she was dealing with a killer. She glanced up the street, saw no sign of Conroy and Sara, and decided she better get back inside.

Inside again, she stopped at the bar where that fiftyish bartender was using a damp cloth on the countertop. She said to him, "Detective Conroy tells me you're an ex-cop."

The guy nodded.

"You know who I am?" she asked him.

"CSI."

"That's right. If there's trouble, what are you going to do?"

He eyeballed her for a long moment. "Call 911."

"Right answer."

He absently wiped his cloth over the bar. "Is there gonna be trouble?"

Shrugging elaborately, Catherine said, "Anything's possible."

"I've heard that theory."

Catherine instinctively liked this guy—not too excitable, no nonsense, just the sort of mentality needed in a place like this. "Detective Conroy and another CSI are on their way here now."

The bartender waited for the rest.

"When they arrive, tell them I'm in the private room." She pointed at the doorless doorway down on at the far end.

"No problem . . . Tera's in there now, y'know, with a couple patrons of the arts."

"Yeah."

"She in trouble?"

"Oh yeah."

Again he wiped the towel over the bar. "Wish I was surprised."

"But you aren't? Everybody else seems to like her."

He shook his head. "They're not paying attention. She's a wrong chick, and I'm not talkin' about her sexual inclination. It's just . . . her train don't run all the way to the station."

Catherine smiled. Cops never stopped being cops, retired or not. "Can you make something happen?"

"Try me."

"I don't want any other dancers and customers going in that room. Not till I come back out, or Detective Conroy goes in."

"I can do that."

Several moments later, Catherine slipped inside the private-dance room, which was much bigger than the closet at Dream Dolls. It was actually more semi-private, able to accommodate two "private" dances at a time; the music in here was strictly from the outer club, leaching in through the doorless doorway—"I'm Not That Innocent," Britney Spears. Two black faux-leather booths without tables were in there, so a dancer could essentially enter the booth and entertain; mirrors covered the walls, and right now no one occupied the table nearest Catherine.

In a red jeweled g-string and nothing else, Tera danced in front of the other booth, though her image danced on all of the mirrored walls. Catherine stepped forward so that the two guys sitting at the table could see her. They were burly guys wearing cheap suits, blue-collar bozos at a bachelor party maybe, one with a buzz cut, the other with longish dark hair. Tera turned her backside to her audience, looked at Catherine, nothing registering on the exotic features, and kept dancing.

"You want to join in, honey?" the longhaired guy asked when he spotted Catherine.

"You're a little overdressed, ain't ya?" the buzz cut wondered, and laughed drunkenly.

The criminalist said nothing, just leaned against a mirrored wall and waited; Conroy would be here soon, and if Tera wanted to dance the time away, that was fine with her.

But Britney Spears had run out of protestations about her inno-

"Yes. Fibers on your jeans prove you were at Dream Dolls that night. It's over, Tera."

On cue, Debbie Harry stopped singing, while Conroy stepped into the mirrored room, reaching behind her to pull out her cuffs; Sara Sidle entered and stepped up alongside the detective. Catherine saw Tera's eyes narrow, sensed the woman was about to act, and reached out . . .

. . . but the stripper was too fast for Catherine, and whirled to grab Sara by the wrist, and—showing surprising strength—flung Sara into Conroy, knocking the two women into the wall behind them, smashing into one of the mirror panels, shattering the glass.

In the outer club, the bartender was rounding up patrons and herding them out into the parking lot.

Just as the mirror broke, Sara's head careened off the wall; then she fell forward to the floor in a semiconscious heap, the deadly glass falling behind her like sheets of barely melting ice. Conroy stayed on her feet somehow, and was trying to pull her pistol. Neither woman seemed to have been cut, some part of Catherine's brain noted, even as she got to her feet and whipped the pistol off her hip, filling her hand, pointing it at Tera, who swiftly, nimbly snatched up a long shard of glass.

As Conroy turned to face her, the stripper—clutching the shard like a knife, unafraid of cutting her own hand—jammed the jagged glass into the detective's shoulder, and reflexively Conroy dropped her gun. Pain etched itself on Conroy's face, as she slumped to the floor, clutching her bleeding shoulder.

Sara Sidle pushed herself up to her hands and knees, fragments of glass sliding off her back, and looked up to see Tera grabbing Conroy's pistol off the floor. Still battling the pain reverberating in her skull, Sara reached for the pistol on her belt. Just as her fingers touched it, she felt something cold and metallic against her temple.

"Freeze."

Her back to the open doorway, Tera clamped onto a handful of Sara's hair and pulled the CSI to her feet. Sara opened her eyes to see Catherine standing directly before them, her pistol drawn and aimed at a spot just past Sara's head. *They had solved a murder,* Sara told herself; *they'd been so close to success and in just a few seconds, it had all gone so wrong. . . .*

cence, and as soon as the song finished, Tera stopped dancing, and smiled coolly at the guys. "More?" she asked them; she had numerous bills stuffed in the side of her g-string.

"What about your friend?" the buzz cut asked, nodding toward Catherine. "Get her to join in!"

That was enough: flashing her ID, Catherine walked over and said, "You two have had enough fun."

The two burly guys exchanged looks and decided she was right, and split, leaving Catherine and Tera alone, just as a new song came on.

"I'm working," Tera said, and flipped the greenbacks at the side of her g-string with a red-nailed finger.

"Not at the moment, you aren't."

Tera put her weight on one leg and smirked humorlessly at Catherine. "I have to get ready to go on. . . . I promised a guy . . ."

"How much is a table dance?"

"Twenty-five."

Catherine took a twenty and a five from her purse and held them out.

Tera's full lips pursed in a smile. "I *said* one of you three cops would be gay . . . didn't think it was you, though. . . . What's your name again?"

"Catherine."

Swaying seductively to the music, Tera asked, "Are you on duty, Catherine?"

"No," Catherine lied. "I just . . . had to see you again."

Still undulating, keeping time with her body, Tera smiled, and danced closer and closer to Catherine. Speculative. Unaware, and drawing closer, Tera leaned in, her lips almost close enough to Catherine to kiss her. Through the doorless doorway, Catherine could see the ex-cop bartender pointing the way, and Conroy (Sara just behind her) barreling through the club, a hand going to the pistol on her hip.

Just before their lips seemed about to touch, Catherine said, over the din of the throbbing music, "I know you did it."

Tera's eyes popped open, and she froze.

"I found the jacket in the vent, the beard under the *Vogues*."

The stripper took two quick steps back, like she'd been punched. "No . . ."

That was when it dawned on Sara that these might be her last few seconds on Earth.

Catherine Willows pointed her automatic at the fierce-eyed woman holding Sara hostage. With Conroy in the way before, Catherine hadn't been able to drop the hammer on the dancer. And now . . . now . . .

"Easy or hard, Tera," Catherine said, as matter of factly as possible. "Your choice."

The stripper held Sara in front of her, only a sliver of her face showing from behind Sara's skull. For all the confidence she was projecting, Catherine knew she didn't have a prayer to make this shot.

"Drop the gun, Catherine," Tera said, "and let me walk out of here . . . or this skinny bitch dies."

"I can't do that." Catherine glanced at Conroy who was on her knees to Tera's left. The injured detective slumped slightly forward, her good hand digging under her coat.

Tera pressed the gun harder into Sara's temple. "They say the second time is easier than the first . . . and the first time? Wasn't hard at all."

Slowly Catherine shook her head. "You know we can't just let you walk out of here."

"Sure you can, Catherine." Those exotic eyes were unblinking, and very, very cold. "Drop the gun—now."

Catherine swallowed thickly, sighed, and said, "All right, all right . . . you win."

"I thought I might."

Bending at the knees, Catherine held the gun slack in her hand, leaning toward the floor, about to put the weapon down. That was when Conroy's hand came out of her coat and she shouted, *"Tera!"*

The stripper spun, roughly dragging Sara with her. When Tera saw something metallic in Conroy's hand, she fired—not at Sara, but at Conroy, the bullet striking the detective in the chest, sending her sprawling backward, her hideaway spare pistol tumbling from her hand.

At the same instant, Sara had ducked to her left, the pistol explosion deafening her, the muzzle flash practically blinding her. But as she went down, she managed to jam her elbow into Tera's ribs, breaking the stripper's grip on her, creating a slice of daylight between them.

Catherine's pistol spoke.

Tera made a brief, strange cry as the bullet entered her chest, mist erupting from her torso, the shot straightening her, momentarily, before collapse came. The murderer of Jenna Patrick was dead before she hit the floor, leaving Catherine Willows—with a gun in hand—to look at her own dazed reflection in the wall of mirrors opposite.

After kicking the pistol away from Tera, Sara reached down and sought a pulse, but found nothing. She turned to see Catherine bending over Conroy, and moved to join them.

The detective opened her eyes, closed them, opened them again. "Well, *that* hurt!"

Nodding, Catherine said, "You gave me a scare . . . didn't know you were wearing your vest."

Wincing in pain, Conroy's good hand went to her chest. "The suspect?"

"Dead."

"Good." Conroy, helped to her feet by Catherine, added, "Politically incorrect as it may be . . . I say she deserves what she got . . . Sara, you okay?"

Sara, helping Catherine guide Conroy to a chair, said, "Fine—thanks to you two. How's your shoulder?"

"Not so good," Conroy said, the cloth around the wound blood-soaked. "Fingers are numb. You wanna call an ambulance?"

"Why don't I do that," Sara said and disappeared.

Catherine brushed a strand of hair out of Conroy's face. "Just sit there—stay quiet. Ambulance will be here soon."

"You know, I've been thinking about quitting . . . going back home to be closer to my folks?"

"You think now's a good time to be talking about this?"

Conroy shrugged with her one good shoulder. "I think maybe I'll visit my folks, and then come back to work a while. Before I decide."

"Good plan," Catherine said, humoring the woman, who was clearly already in shock.

Sara returned. "Bartender called nine-one-one when he heard the first shot. Ambulance and backup should be here any second."

Catherine rose and went over and knelt beside the sprawled-on-her-back lifeless body of the dancer.

Catherine Willows had rarely bothered wondering what her life would be like today, if she hadn't gotten out of these damn clubs and into college and CSI. But now, looking at Tera Jameson looking back at her with dark dead eyes, Catherine couldn't help but see herself there, on the floor, a lovely woman turned by a bullet into a piece of meat.

Or did places like Showgirl World and Dream Dolls turn women into pieces of meat, even without bullets?

She rose.

Sara asked, "You okay?"

"You know me—never doubt, never look back."

Nonetheless, inside of her, Catherine Willows wondered if she had just killed a part of herself.

15

The moon had turned the evening an ivory-tinged shade of blue; a few lights were on in the Pierce stronghold, both upstairs and down, the curtained windows emanating a yellowish glow.

Warrick Brown and Nick Stokes, in the Tahoe, drew up at the curb just as Jim Brass and Gil Grissom were getting out of the Taurus. Catching up with the detective and their supervisor, Nick carried his field kit, but Warrick—like Grissom—brought nothing but himself, as Brass led the way up the walk that curved across the gently sloping, perfect lawn. The detective rang the bell, the rest of them gathered on the front stoop like trick-or-treaters who'd arrived a bit early for Halloween.

The door opened on the first ring, as if they'd been anticipated; and Grissom—at Brass's side—found himself face-to-face with a young man he did not recognize. None of them did, in fact.

Brass tapped the badge on his suitcoat breastpocket, saying to the kid, "Would you tell Mr. Pierce he has company?"

"I'm sorry, sir, but he's not here right now." He was a clean-cut, slender, tallish black-haired boy of sixteen or seventeen, in a green Weezer T-shirt, Levi's, and black-and-white Reeboks. "Mr. Pierce has gone to pick up some carry-out."

"I see."

"But he should be back in a few minutes. . . . I don't know if I should let you in . . . but you could wait out front. . . ."

Grissom asked, "Who are you, son?"

An easygoing smile crossed the young man's pleasant face; the kid seemed familiar to Grissom, though he remained certain he'd never seen him before. The boy's response explained that: "Why, I'm Gary Blair."

Brass said, for the benefit of Nick and Warrick, "Your folks reported Mrs. Pierce's disappearance."

Gary nodded.

"And you've been dating Lori?"

"Yes." The kid looked from face to face of the crowded little group on the doorstep. "I guess it would be okay if you wanted to come in. . . . Like I said, Mr. Pierce'll be back in just a few minutes."

They flowed into the foyer, all of them standing around uneasily.

"Is Lori home?" Brass asked.

"She's upstairs changing her clothes. We're going out after dinner. She should be right down . . . why?"

Grissom could sense Brass's uneasiness. On the way over, the detective had mentioned that he didn't like the idea of arresting Pierce in front of his daughter, but saw no way around it.

With this in mind, Grissom suggested, "Maybe we can catch Mr. Pierce at the restaurant."

Picking up on that, Brass asked the boy, "Where did Mr. Pierce go to pick up the carry-out?"

Gary shrugged, shook his head. "All I know is, he's going for Chinese."

The muffled sound of the garage door opening ended this exchange, and Grissom and Brass traded glances—they knew the arrest would have to go down in front of the kids.

Her hair now a garish orange, as if her head was on fire, Lori came trotting down the circular stairs in gray sweat pants and a Fishbone T-shirt of which the bottom six inches had been cut haphazardly off to reveal her pierced navel and flat stomach. Though she looked less Goth, her blue eyes were again held prisoner within black chambers of mascara.

To Jim Brass it seemed that every time they visited this house, the daughter had taken another step away from the conservative religious beliefs of her late mother. He hoped she could find some sane middle ground, once they got her into foster care.

Lori and her boyfriend trailed after, as Brass led the CSI team into the kitchen, to meet Pierce as he came in from the garage, his arms laden with paper bags, his back to them as he shut the door, the unmistakable aroma of Chinese food accompanying him.

When he turned, the therapist's dismayed expression told them their presence in his kitchen was no surprise: he had seen the SUV and the unmarked car parked in front of his house . . . again.

Pierce, in a blue sweatshirt and black sweatpants, set the brown bags on the kitchen counter, and waited for what he knew would be coming.

And it came: "Owen Pierce," Captain Jim Brass said. "I'm placing you under arrest for the murder of Lynn Pierce."

"You're making a mistake," he said. "You're needlessly ruining lives, when you have nothing to go on but supposition."

Grissom said, "We've just been over at Kevin Sadler's house."

Pierce went ghostly, ghastly pale, and he leaned against the counter, as if to keep from collapsing.

Grissom continued: "The basement, the broken glass in the garage, the receipt, we have it all."

Lori ran to her father, and there was no accusation, just pained confusion in her voice, as she said, "Dad! What's he *talking* about?"

Pierce opened his arms and she filled them; he patted his daughter's head as she wrapped her arms around him, his eyes going to Brass, then Grissom. He seemed about to say something comforting to the child, but what came out was: "They're arresting me for killing your mother."

Gary Blair swallowed, and staggered over to a chair and sat at the kitchen table, slumping, leaning his elbows on the table and catching his face in his palms; his eyes were wide and hollow.

"It's not true," Lori said.

Slowly he shook his head. "It *is* true. . . . I hated her, Lori. I'm sorry."

His daughter drew away and stared at him, eyes huge within their black mascara casings, shaking her head. "You can't be serious. . . ."

"She kept pushing and pushing. Do I have to tell *you* how she was? Jesus this, Jesus that—I finally had enough of her. We loved her once, Lori, both of us . . . but you know as well as I that she was a different woman. . . . I shot her."

The girl drew away from her father's arms, and somehow her eyes grew even larger. "What?"

He reached out and took her by the arms and pulled her back to him, so he could look in her face. "You have to understand, Lori—*I shot her.* You have to accept that."

Brass, who had never before heard a more bizarre confession, looked sharply at Grissom, who seemed lost in thought.

Lori Pierce was shaking her head; across the room, at the kitchen table, her boyfriend was covering his face with one hand, as she said, "No, Daddy, no."

"Yes!" Pierce said. "You have to accept it. I shot her and—to protect myself—I did a terrible thing. I got rid of her body. . . . - Don't make me say how."

Tears began to stream down the girl's cheeks, making a mess of her mascara; she was trembling as Pierce pulled her to him again, holding her, soothing her.

Brass got on his cell phone and called Social Services. Soon he clicked off, muttering, "Damnit," and turned to Grissom. "There's no field agent available now."

Grissom winced. "That means juvenile hall."

His daughter still weeping against his chest, Pierce—his eyes flaring—snapped, "I won't have you putting her in jail!"

"It's not jail," Brass began.

"Yes it is," Pierce said, biting off the words.

Brass did not argue; the father was right.

Gary spoke up. "She can stay at our house, in the guest room."

Brass thought about that, said, "What's your number, son?"

The boy gave it to him, Brass punched the numbers in, and soon had Mrs. Blair on the line.

"A social worker will be around in the morning," he told her, "first thing."

"We'll be glad to look after Lori till then," Mrs. Blair said.

With that settled, Nick accompanied the girl upstairs for her to pack an overnight bag.

With his daughter gone, Pierce—seeming strangely calm now, to Grissom . . . shock?—turned a penetrating gaze on the seated Gary Blair. "I need you to watch out for my daughter, Gary."

Gary said, "Yes, sir."

Grissom noted that the boy did not seem to have lost any respect for Pierce, upon learning the man had shot his wife and butchered her body for disposal.

Pierce was saying, "I know it's a lot to ask."

Gary rose, and when he spoke, his voice had surprising authority. "Don't worry, Mr. Pierce—I'll take care of her."

They all stood around awkwardly until Lori and Nick returned, Lori carrying a backpack and a small suitcase. Dropping the bags, the girl again ran to her father, throwing her arms around him, desperately. The pair hugged tightly, Pierce again telling his daughter that he loved her.

"It's going to be all right, Lori," he said. "I have to pay for my crime."

Nick accompanied Gary and Lori to the door, and Brass kept tabs through a window as the clean-cut boy and the Goth-punk girl walked hand-in-hand down the sidewalk, then crossed the street to a blue Honda Civic parked there, which soon pulled away.

Brass turned and faced Owen Pierce and gave him his rights. The therapist held out his hands, presenting his wrists.

"I'm supposed to cuff your hands behind your back," Brass said. "But if you're going to be cooperative . . ."

"When have I not been?" Pierce asked.

The guy had a point. Brass allowed Pierce to keep his hands in front of him for the cuffs, then led him out to the Taurus and put him in the backseat. Grissom climbed in front with Brass while Nick and Warrick got back into the Tahoe.

As they followed the Taurus back to CSI Division, a troubled Nick asked, "What the hell was that about?"

The normally unflappable Warrick, whose own expression was dumbfounded, shook his head. "Weirdest confession I ever heard."

"In front of his damn *daughter!* Why would he do that?"

"I don't know," Warrick admitted. "Just being honest . . . better to hear it from him than somebody else. I guess."

"It's sick."

With a shrug, Warrick dismissed the subject. "Hey, can't ever tell what they're going to do or say, when they finally get busted."

Grissom joined Warrick and Nick behind the two-way mirror to watch as Brass led a low-key Pierce into the interrogation room. Brass turned on the tape recorder; a uniformed officer was in the corner manning the digital video camera.

Brass asked, "Your name is Owen Matthew Pierce?"

"Yes."

"And you've been advised of, and understand, your rights?"

"Yes."

"And do you wish to make a statement?"

"Yes." There was a long silence before Pierce spoke again. "My wife Lynn and I had an argument."

"Go on," Brass said.

"We'd been arguing a lot lately."

"I see."

"Her religion, it drove us apart. She almost died, or thought she almost died, anyway, and made some sort of . . . deal with God or Jesus." He shook his head, numbly. "When we were younger, she was great. Beautiful. Used to say she'd try anything once. The sex was unbelievably hot. . . . She'd do anything."

Nick and Warrick, behind the glass, exchanged glances; Pierce discussing his wife in these terms, during the confession of her murder, was both inappropriate and weird. Grissom, on the other hand, showed no reaction—a hand on his chin, he was studying Pierce like a bug.

"I mean *anything*," Pierce was saying, and he was smiling now, reminiscing, "with *anybody.* We got into some wild shit over the years, and we both liked it."

"Is that where the drugs came in?"

Pierce pressed his hands flat on the table, sighed, the smile fading. "Yeah . . . back when we were swinging, we used to get high, grass, pills, but the most extreme thing we did was coke. In fact, it was the drugs that made Lynn get religion."

"You said before she got religion when she almost died."

"That was the drugs. She O.D.'d on some coke, had a seizure, I took her to the emergency room . . . it came out fine, but she freaked anyway. Next thing I know, she's going to church every twenty minutes and yammering about my almighty soul."

"Describe what happened on the day of your wife's death."

"We argued."

"Tell it in detail."

Another sigh. "Well . . . we argued. Lynn wanted to send Lori to some private school, some religious institution, in Indiana. Lori didn't want to go, and I was against it, too. Lori could never stand up to her mother, so I was the one who took her on. Anyway . . . the argument escalated."

"Why did Mrs. Pierce want to send Lori away?"

Pierce shifted in his seat. "Before Gary Blair came along, Lori was pretty wild—Lynn found grass in her room, once, and she was dating some rough boys. That's when the talk started, about this Jesus school."

"This has been an issue for a while?"

"Yes. Maybe six months. Lori started going to church, dating Gary, to please her mother. But it wasn't enough: Lynn still wanted to ship her off to holy-roller class, to get her 'closer to God.' Lynn wanted to turn Lori into a goddamn clone of herself!"

"And you didn't buy that."

"Well, of course I didn't want my daughter to become the same uptight, judgmental asshole my wife had turned into."

"So—the argument escalated. Go on."

"We were yelling at each other, and Lynn went out to the garage, kind of . . . saying she didn't want to talk about it anymore. She'd made her mind up and that was that, and if I tried to stop Lynn, she'd . . . turn me in for my own drug use."

"Were you still using?"

He nodded.

"Please state that, Mr. Pierce."

"I was still using drugs."

"The argument moved into the garage?"

"Yes . . . yes. Lynn said she wanted to go for a drive to get away from me, but I wanted to settle the issue." Pierce closed his eyes, his head sagged forward. "I had a gun hidden in the garage . . . I felt I needed protection."

"Who from?"

"Kevin Sadler. Lil Moe, they call him. My connection, my dealer. I owed him money. That's why I had a gun."

"All right. Go on."

Pierce shrugged. "I went and got it from my toolbench, where I kept it. I pointed it at her, just to scare her, really. Told her not to leave or . . . She said I was a sinner and would go to hell. That's when I shot her."

"Where was Lynn, Mr. Pierce? Standing there in the garage, when you shot her?"

He shook his head. "No. Lynn had already gotten into the car and started it. I shot her through the driver's side window."

"Then what?"

Shrugging, Pierce said, "Well, hell—I panicked. I knew I had to get rid of the body. In my job, I know a little about anatomy; I'm not squeamish about anything to do with the human body. With Lil Moe in jail, I figured I could use his house, without anyone finding out."

"When did you do this?"

"That same night, late. As soon as I shot her, I put Lynn's body in the trunk, wrapped in an old tarp in the garage, and cleaned up the car, and drove it over to Lil Moe's. Put it in the garage, there. Then I walked to a commercial area and caught a cab and came back home, just before the Blairs showed up, pounding on my door, looking for Lynn. . . . See, I didn't want Lori to know what I'd done, obviously . . . and I'm always home for dinner. So I came home, and went back to Lil Moe's well after dark. I drove my SUV on that trip."

"Then what?"

"I carried Lynn inside the house, down into the basement and . . . cut her up with my chain saw." Finally Pierce's cool mask began to crack; tears started rolling down his face, though he didn't seem to notice. "I wrapped her up in the shower curtain, or anyway pieces of it, then put the . . . packages in garbage bags, along with the chain saw. I folded the bloody tarp up and put it in another bag. I used rocks from a garden nextdoor to Lil Moe's to weight them down. After that I spread more garbage bags on the floor of the SUV and put her in there. I picked up Lil Moe's boat . . . there's a trailer hitch on my SUV . . . and went to Lake Mead. I just rode around dropping bags into the lake until they were all gone. It was . . . peaceful. A beautiful night."

"Is that all?"

Pierce sagged. "Isn't that enough?"

Soon a uniformed officer came in to escort Pierce away, while Brass joined the CSIs in the adjacent observation room.

"How's that for chapter and verse?" Brass asked, pleased with himself.

Grissom said nothing, his face blank but for a tightness around his eyes.

"What's the matter, Gil?" Brass asked, a bit exasperated. "He copped to it! Life is good. We got the bad guy. Which is the point of the exercise, right?"

Grissom twitched something that was almost a smile. "We got *a* bad guy . . . but we don't have Lynn Pierce's murderer."

"What? Gimme a break! The son of a bitch confessed."

"The 'son of a bitch' lied," Grissom said.

Warrick stepped up. "That was one elaborate lie, then, Gris. . . ."

"Like all effective fiction, it had elements of truth. . . . For example, he cut up the body all right, that part of the confession was true. He just didn't kill his wife."

Nick's eyes were tight and he was smiling as he said, "You notice he didn't start crying, till he talked about cutting her up? Killing her, he was cool as a cuke."

Brass looked like somebody had poured water on him; of course, he looked like that much of the time. Still, his aggravation was obvious as he said to Grissom, "Do you have any idea how much I hate it when you do this to me?"

Grissom smiled his awful angelic smile. "I hate to be the bearer of bad news, Jim . . . but the evidence doesn't lie."

"People do," Nick said.

"Pierce does," Warrick said.

Brass held up palms of surrender. "Okay—tell me why."

Grissom's expression turned somber. "Pierce said he stood outside the car and shot his wife through the car window, correct?"

"Yeah."

"We know from our tests that there was hardly any glass *inside* the car, and the blood was confined to the driver's seat. If Lynn Pierce had been shot from the outside, the glass would have blown in and her blood would have been splashed and spattered all over the passenger side of the car. And he said it happened in the garage. That garage was clean."

Brass's face managed to fall further. "So we still have a killer out there?"

"Yes," Grissom said with a nod. "But we know who it is."

"We do?" Brass asked.

Warrick's expression, and Nick's, asked the same question.

Grissom raised a lecturing forefinger. "You recall when we arrested Pierce, he made that drawn-out, unnatural confession to his daughter?"

"I'll say we recall," Warrick said. "Nick and I both thought that was way beyond weird."

Grissom asked, "And why would a father confess to murdering mommy, in front of darling daughter, unless . . . ?"

Nick's eyes popped and his head went back, as he got it. "Unless they were getting their *stories* straight!

"Damn," Warrick said. "And right under our nose."

"We need to go back to the castle, one last time," Grissom said. "The queen is dead, and the king is covering up for the princess."

16

By this time, Catherine and Sara were back. Grissom took the two into his office, where they filled him in on the wrap-up of their own case. Both of them looked a little shell-shocked, and Grissom told them to take the rest of the night off.

"You'll talk to the psychologist tomorrow," he told Catherine.

"Great," she said with a humorless smirk.

"And then the shooting board."

"It was righteous," Sara said, shaking her head.

"I'm sure. Go home, you two, and get some rest."

Catherine was studying Grissom. "Well, what are you so excited about?"

"Me? Excited? I don't get excited."

"Sure you do . . . finding bugs at crime scenes, for example . . . or when you're coming down the home stretch of an investigation."

He owned that he, Brass, Warrick, and Nick were about to search the Pierce homestead one last time.

"We're coming along," Catherine said.

"Absolutely, we're coming," Sara said.

"No. Go home, I said."

"Shift isn't over," Sara said.

"It's a big house," Catherine said. "Four more hands to find evidence. . . ."

Less than half an hour later, Brass and the nightshift CSIs again stood in the foyer of the Pierce home—all of them: Nick, Warrick, and Grissom . . . Sara and Catherine, too.

Grissom was looking hard at Catherine, who stood there with field kit in hand. "Are you sure you're up to this?"

"No," Catherine said, "I'd rather sit at home thinking about what I'm going to say to the department shrink tomorrow."

"I'm going to take that as sarcasm," Grissom said.

"Why don't you," Catherine said. "Can we get started?"

Grissom led them into the living room, where everyone snapped on latex gloves, including Brass; all five CSIs had their field kits. With the family gone, the house was deathly quiet, almost tomblike. Despite the high that accompanied what Catherine had described as "the home stretch," Grissom felt remorse slithering through his belly, regretting not only what had happened to Lynn Pierce, but for what would happen in the coming hours. . . .

Nick asked, "Do we think that .44 was the murder weapon?"

"A strong possibility," Grissom said.

"I'll tell you what's a strong possibility," Warrick said. "Strong possibility that gun's in a garbage bag at the bottom of Lake Mead."

"Not if this family's concerns about Kevin Sadler were real," Grissom said.

"Which means it may still be here," Warrick said.

"Where?" Nick asked.

"Yeah," Sara said, mildly mocking, "just ask Grissom—he'll know."

But Grissom's expression had turned cagey. "Where is the one place in this house we haven't looked?"

"You kiddin', Gris?" Warrick asked. "We've turned this place upside down, like twelve times."

"Gil," Brass said, "I'm here more than I'm home."

"Remember that first night?" Grissom asked. "What was the one thing Pierce requested we do?"

"Not disturb his daughter," Nick said, not missing a beat. "She was too traumatized."

"That's right," Grissom said. "And which of us has searched Lori Pierce's room since then?"

Their looks traveled from one face to the next, none of them able to come up with an affirmative answer. The group followed Grissom quickly up the winding stairway, and soon they were crowded into the hallway, outside the daughter's room.

Plush pink carpeting covered the floor and a pink canopied bed dominated the left side of the room, half a dozen stuffed animals making the pink-and-red spread their jungle. Directly across from the door, a white student desk contained a monitor, keyboard, and mouse, with a single drawer in the center. The computer tower sat on the floor to the left of the desk. On the right side stood a four-drawer white chest, more stuffed animals herded on top. Along the right wall, a television and stereo perched on a small white entertainment stand with the closet door beyond that.

The Goth girl was still living in the little girl's room she'd grown up in.

After unloading their tools in the hall, they split up, doing their best not to trip over each other—it was actually a goodsized bedroom, but with six of them working there, the space seemed impossibly cramped. Catherine took the desk and dresser, Grissom the bed, Warrick the closet, Nick and Sara worked the components of the entertainment center. Using the RUVIS on the bed, Grissom was the first to sing out.

"Someone's been having sex on this bed," he said, like a bear finding signs of Goldilocks.

Everyone looked over at the multiple blossoms of white showing up under the ultraviolet.

"Lots of sex," Catherine said, raising an eyebrow.

Sara and Nick dismantled the television and stereo, finding nothing, reporting as much to Grissom.

Catherine pored over the dresser, found nothing on top or behind it, then went through the drawers one at a time. Except for a stash of condoms in the third drawer, she found nothing other than the girl's clothes. However . . .

"Traces of white powder on the desk," she said.

"Cocaine?" Brass asked.

"Greg will have to confirm, but take my word for it . . . that's coke."

No one argued with her. Their grave expressions indicated a mutual understanding that, despite the little-girl surroundings, Lori Pierce had grown up, and not in a good way.

The tower, monitor, and keyboard yielded nothing, but Catherine discovered a tiny bag inside of the mouse, the source of the white powder. Smaller than the bag they found in the vent in the basement, this one too carried the little red triangle that was Lil Moe's logo.

Catherine shared her discovery, then asked, "You suppose Pierce knows his daughter's buying drugs from his partner?"

"Remind me to ask Daddy," Brass said, "right after I present him with his Father of the Year award."

The top shelf of the closet contained boxes, books, and even more stuffed animals. Warrick leafed through the hanging clothes in the closet, a peculiar mix of the Goth girl and the preppier Lori; but again found nothing.

Not surprisingly, the closet floor was cluttered with shoeboxes; propped against the wall, behind the hanging clothes, leaned a tennis racket and softball bat, a glove nearby, and a pile of magazines—*Sassy, Spin, Sixteen.* After moving all this stuff out, Warrick went over the flooring, his flashlight beam illuminating his way.

In the corner, he found a tiny pile of dust. Loose floorboard, he thought, and pried at the board with a screwdriver. Slowly, one end came free and he eased the board free, then the one next to it, then one more. Craning his neck over the hole and shining his light down inside, he made a wonderful, terrible discovery.

Warrick felt a nausea burning a hole in his stomach as he realized what this meant. "*Got it*—I've got the gun."

Everyone traded looks of mixed emotion—no one had wanted this to come down this way.

Warrick bagged the .44, then went back into the hole, found the box of bullets, and two more bags of coke. "This just keeps getting better," he said glumly.

"Next stop the Blairs?" Grissom asked Brass.

Brass used Lori's phone book to get the number and punched it into his cell. ". . . Mrs. Blair, this is Captain Brass—would you check on your son, and Lori?"

"I don't understand. They're both in bed, asleep, Captain . . . Gary in his room, Lori in the guest—"

"Wake them, get them dressed, and . . . just sit with them, till we get there. Involve your husband, would you?"

"Captain Brass, I still don't understand."

Not wanting to alarm the woman, Brass said, "We just have some new questions that have come up, and it really can't wait."

". . . All right, then. Please hold."

Brass waited, everyone's eyes on him. Several endless minutes went by, when the woman's voice jumped into the detective's ear. "They're both gone! I can't find them anywhere in the house!"

"Calm down, Mrs. Blair. We'll handle it."

"But . . ."

"You and your husband just stay put. Someone will be around. We'll find your son and his girlfriend."

"Like you found Lynn? . . . I'm sorry. That was uncalled for, I . . ."

"Please, Mrs. Blair. You and your husband, stay put."

Brass pushed END and said to Grissom, "They're not there. Lori's gone missing—Gary, too."

"Where are they off to?" Sara asked.

"Are they on the run?" Nick asked.

"I don't think so," Grissom said. "I think they're coming here."

"Here?" Sara asked.

"Homeward bound," Brass said, nodding his agreement with Grissom's unstated thinking; he gestured to Warrick's findings. "Far as Lori knows, we're long gone, and Daddy's in lockup. But we might be back during the course of our investigation, and she's got drugs and the gun here."

"She'll want to ditch the gun," Warrick said.

"And use the drugs," Catherine said.

The detective pressed quickly on, urgency coloring his tone: "Let's pull the vehicles around the corner. If Lori is coming, let's not tip her off that we're here."

Warrick, Nick, and Sara moved the cars; Grissom, Catherine, and Brass put the room back together, but did not replace the evidence in its hiding places. When the car-parking trio returned, all six of them spread out through the house. Warrick and Nick took the basement, Grissom and Sara the first-floor rec room, and Brass and Catherine went upstairs to the master bedroom.

A few minutes later, the garage door whirred up, then down, and Grissom heard voices coming in through the kitchen.

A muffled voice, recognizable as Gary Blair's, said, "I'll wait here. . . . Hurry up."

And Lori Pierce's voice said: "You don't wanna go upstairs? Party a little?"

"No! I wanna get back before my parents miss us. Don't fool around, Lori!"

"I thought you liked to fool around . . ."

"Just get that stuff, and let's go!"

From their rec room post, Grissom and Sara heard her feet padding up the winding stairs.

Within seconds, Lori's reaction at realizing her stash had been discovered echoed through the house: *"Shit! Shit shit shit!"*

The girl came flying down the stairs, wild-eyed, just as Grissom and Sara came around to meet her. She froze on the stairs, a few steps from the bottom, then glanced over her shoulder—Catherine and Brass were just above and behind her. Warrick and Nick entered the foyer, the latter hauling a bewildered-looking Gary Blair by the arm.

"Lori Pierce," Brass said, in a neutral tone that was nonetheless chilling in the teenagers' ears, "you're under arrest for the murder of your mother, Lynn Pierce."

"What?" Gary Blair blurted. He shook himself free from Nick's grasp, but didn't go anywhere; his expression was that of a kid who'd just heard the truth about Santa Claus. "Her *father* did it—he confessed!" Gary looked around at the adults clustered in the foyer. "You heard him, you *all* heard him! *I* heard him."

Grissom's eyes weren't on Gary, but on Lori, as he said, "Mr. Pierce lied, son. . . . He lied to protect his daughter."

"My *father* killed my mother," Lori insisted, desperation edging her voice, her face, her gestures, animated. "Gary and me, we *heard* him confess—just like you did!"

Grissom walked up several stairs to face Lori, where she was caught between the two groups of grown-ups. "We heard him confess," Grissom acknowledged, "but we also heard him lie."

Lori's voice was filled with typically teenaged contempt. "How do *you* know?"

"We know because the evidence is at odds with what your father 'confessed'—your mother's murder couldn't have happened the way he said, Lori. And the fingerprints on the gun and the box of bullets are going to be ID'ed as yours."

"I didn't kill Mom," Lori said. "I loved her! *Daddy* hated her—that's why he killed her!"

Brass came down and took her gently by the arm and Grissom got out of the way, as the girl was read her rights and handcuffed.

The detective was about to escort the girl from the castle when Gary Blair said, to no one in particular, "I . . . I need to go home."

Lori swung her face toward the boy and gave him a withering look. "You suck," she said.

Brass walked the girl out, and Grissom answered the boy's question: "You're coming with us, Gary. You're a material witness."

Back at HQ, Brass chose to interview Gary Blair first. Grissom was in the interrogation room with them, the rest of the team watching through the two-way glass. The boy's parents had been called, and were on their way.

Brass and the Blair kid sat on opposite sides of the table. Tears rolled down the young man's cheeks and he was trembling.

"Do you want to wait till your parents get here, Gary, before we talk?"

"No . . . I'd . . . I'd rather talk without them here."

"Well, they're coming."

"You better ask your questions, then, 'cause once they're here, I'm zipping it."

"Okay, Gary. What happened that day?"

"Wh . . . what day?"

"What day do you think?"

The kid swallowed snot and tears, and tried to get his crying under control before answering. Finally, staring at the table, he said in a small, very young voice, "Her mom, Mrs. Pierce . . . her mom caught us in bed together, in Lori's room. She wasn't even supposed to come home until hours later, 'cause she had church . . . but her meeting was cancelled and she came home early and she caught us . . . doing it." He shuddered at the thought. "We'd been doin' some, you know, lines, too, and Mrs. Pierce, she found the coke on the desk. Boy, did *she* come unglued! I just shut up and tried to stay out of it, but they had this huge screaming match, Mrs. Pierce threatening to go to my mom and see that Lori and me were split up. Mrs. Pierce told Lori she was sending her to a special school, somewhere out of state, to repent and get tight with Jesus. Crazy stuff like that—but mostly, Mrs. Pierce was saying over and over that Lori and me could never see each other again."

Grissom asked, "Where was the gun, Gary? Somewhere in the garage?"

"No—in Lori's backpack."

Brass frowned. "Why there?"

He shrugged. "She'd started buying coke from this guy who was her father's connection, too."

"Did Mr. Pierce know about this?"

"No! Hell, no! But Lori met this guy at the house a couple times, when he came to do business with Mr. Pierce."

"The gun, Gary."

"I'm getting to that. Lori was afraid of this guy."

Frowning, Grissom said, "Lil Moe?"

"Yeah—Lori said he was hitting on her and she didn't want him to. She said that the next time he, you know, sexually harassed her, she was going to put a stop to it, and threaten him with the gun."

Frowning in thought, Grissom asked, "Where did this gun come from?"

Brass picked up on that. "Was it her father's gun, Gary?"

"Yes . . . she got it out of a drawer somewhere, and her dad didn't even miss it."

Brass took a deep breath, let it out, and said, "So, Gary—what happened after Mrs. Pierce went ballistic?"

"Mrs. Pierce said she was going to drive straight over to my parents' house, and tell 'em what was going on."

"Your parents have no idea that you're sexually active? That you've used drugs?"

He shook his head.

Brass said, "Mrs. Pierce threatened to go your parents. What then?"

"Lori followed her to the garage, arguing all the way, but more . . . trying to reason with her now, and begging her and stuff. She got in the car with her mom, to try and talk her out of it. And they drove off, still yelling at each other."

"Did you know Lori had taken the gun with her?"

"No. It was in the kitchen, on the counter—the backpack?"

"What did you do then, Gary?"

He shrugged. "I just got my stuff and went home, praying that Mrs. Pierce didn't show up to blow my world apart. And then when Lori and her mom didn't show up, I figured Lori and her mom had worked it out—that she talked her mom out of telling my folks. Later that night, Lori called to say her mom had taken off somewhere. You know, needed time to think and stuff, after the shock of what she found out about Lori and me."

"You didn't know Mrs. Pierce was dead?"

"Oh, no. Lori told me that you people thought her mom was dead, but I didn't really know till I heard her father confess. I thought he was telling the truth. . . . Are you sure he wasn't?"

The interview continued a while, but nothing new was revealed; and then the Blairs were there, and Brass and Grissom left them alone with their son, after telling the young man to be frank with his folks.

"You tell them, Gary," Brass said, "or I will."

The interrogation with Lori Pierce did not go well, at first. Again Grissom accompanied Brass, while the rest of the CSIs looked on through two-way glass. The girl refused to budge off her father's story.

Watching the interrogation, Catherine said to Sara, "She's a smart kid. Knows if she keeps her mouth shut, her old man will take the rap."

"That's cold," Nick said.

Sara said, "So is killing your mother."

Grissom hadn't asked any questions yet; protocol gave that honor to Brass, but the detective was not getting anywhere, and was clearly frustrated, giving Grissom a wide-eyed look that granted the CSI supervisor permission to take a shot.

"Lori," Grissom said, "I'm a criminalist."

Lori Pierce looked up, her face haggard, years added to her features with each passing hour. She summoned some contempt for the adult: "And I care why?"

"Do you know what a criminalist is? What he does?"

The girl stared straight ahead, avoiding Grissom's casual but penetrating gaze.

"I work with evidence," he said. "Like finding your fingerprints on that gun."

Lori didn't seem to be paying any attention to this.

"Do you know what the evidence in this case is telling me?"

The girl gave him a patronizing look. "Don't talk to me like I'm twelve."

"The evidence tells me both you and your father are lying."

Within their mascara caverns, Lori's eyes seemed suddenly nervous.

With a smile that seemed friendly enough, Grissom said, "You're not going to tell me what really happened, are you, Lori?"

The girl showed him a middle finger and said, "Sit and spin."

"How about I tell *you* what happened."

"Who told you, genius?"

"The evidence. The evidence says you argued with your mother over her catching you and Gary in bed and finding drugs."

She sneered at him. "You mean, Gary told you that. He is so ball-less."

Grissom continued: "Your mother was going to the Blairs to force Gary's parents into making Gary break up with you; then your mother was going to send you to private school."

"Gary. Again, Gary. *He's* not evidence. He's just a little weasel, and a *big* disappointment."

"You're right, Lori— that much Gary did give us. But after that, the evidence takes over the tale. You rode in the car with your mom. You were trying to calm her down, but she was in the grasp of religious fervor and there was no reasoning with her."

The first chink in her tough teenage armor appeared as a tear rolled down Lori's cheek, trailing mascara. "She didn't understand that I loved Gary . . . or thought I did."

"Your mother's religious beliefs were . . . unforgiving."

"Mom, she was like a Nazi, with all this religious junk. She was like Jim Jonesing my ass!"

"You tried to talk to her but she wouldn't listen. But there's something the evidence hasn't told us yet. . . . It will. But it hasn't yet. Where did you go, Lori? You never made it to the Blairs. Where *did* you go?"

She swallowed. Her lips were trembling, her eyes spilling tears. "The church."

Brass leaned forward. "The church?"

The girl nodded. "It's out past the Strip, on the outskirts of town . . . almost in the desert. It's got this big parking lot. I asked Mom if we could go there and . . . pray together."

Grissom said, "No one was around?"

"No other cars in the lot. Later that evening, there would be church stuff goin' on, but sorta over the supper hour . . . no. It was pretty deserted. But Mom had her own key; she was one of the church leaders, you know—we coulda gone in and prayed together."

"But you didn't go in and pray," Brass asked, "did you?"

"No. We sat in the car and I tried to talk to her, I really tried. Only she was so wrapped up in 'God's will' and how we're all sinners and need to be punished that . . . She was mental, she really was."

Grissom asked, "You grabbed the gun from your backpack on the kitchen counter, Lori, and took it with you, when you jumped in the car with your mother."

She nodded numbly. "Mom didn't see the gun. I had it wrapped in my jacket."

Brass looked like his head was about to explode. "You manipulated your mother into going to that church parking lot . . . so you could shoot her?"

"No! No . . ." Tears erupted full force now, long violent, racking sobs.

Catherine Willows, watching through the glass, could not bear any more of this; however hardboiled a CSI she might be, Catherine was also a mother. She exited the observation booth and entered the interrogation room, glaring at the two men as she sat beside the girl, and comforted her.

After a while, Lori—Catherine holding her hand—said to them, "I didn't mean to shoot her, it was an accident. . . . I just couldn't bear to have Gary taken away. He was the only good thing in my life. He was all I had."

"Why did you have the gun with you?" Catherine asked.

"So I could threaten to kill myself. And that's exactly what I did: I told her I would kill myself right there, in front of her, if she didn't promise to let me finish high school here, and keep seeing Gary, and not tell his parents. I meant it, too! I even said I'd stop the drugs and Gary and I wouldn't have relations, anymore. Didn't do any good."

"How did your mother die, Lori?" Catherine asked, gently.

"It was an accident! She grabbed for the gun . . . I think she thought I was going to use it on myself, and . . . it just went off. The window blew out, and . . . it was awful. It was an awful nightmare!"

Grissom asked, "How did you get home?"

"I spread my jacket on the floor, on the rider's side? And I put mom down on the floor there, on the jacket, y'know? And I drove home. I don't know how. I wasn't crying or afraid or anything. It was like I was outside myself, watching."

"And then?" Grissom asked.

"Then I drove the car into the garage and got Daddy. Told him what happened, and . . . he took care of it. I know he went out to the church parking lot and kind of . . . cleaned up out there. Otherwise . . . he didn't tell me how or anything; all I knew was the car . . . and mom . . . were gone."

"Your father understood about the drugs, and you and Gary?"

"Actually, I . . . I never told Daddy about the coke. Just about the sex. . . . He said that was my business and Mom should have left me alone. He was great, really—perfect father, the best—never cared what I did."

"And with your mother gone," Grissom said, "the rules around the house loosened."

Brass asked, "How long had you been doing coke before your mom caught you?"

She shrugged. "A few months. Gary and I, we just fooled around with it, a little. But after Mom died, every time I went to sleep, I saw her face, her . . . bloody face. The coke made that easier to deal with. I could stay up for a long long time, then I'd pass out. And the good part was, I didn't have dreams."

Catherine sat with her arm around the girl, who again began to cry. Brass gestured to Grissom to step out into the hall.

Brass asked, "Is she telling the truth?"

"Her story and the evidence are compatible."

"I didn't ask you that, Gil."

"I can only tell you what the evidence tells me."

Brass was shaking his head. "That girl was ready to let her father take the fall for her. . . . She may have cold-bloodedly killed her mother, lured her to that church parking lot, and . . . Jesus!"

"We'll go out to that church and see what we can find," Grissom said. "We should find glass, and blood . . . but without the rest of Lynn Pierce's remains . . ." He shrugged.

Brass said, "I guess she's going to Juvenile Hall, after all."

Warrick, Nick and Sara exited the observation booth, joining Brass and Grissom.

"So Pierce walks?" Warrick asked, fire in his eyes. "He cuts up his wife with a chain saw, and *walks?*"

Brass shook his head. "Not hardly—accessory after the fact and possession. Don't forget his business arrangement with Kevin Sadler;

Sadler will testify against his former silent partner. Pierce'll be gone a good long while."

"What about Lori?" Sara asked.

Brass said, "If they try her as an adult, she could get life."

Nick said, "I believe her story."

"So will a jury," Warrick opined.

"So she gets away with it?" Sara asked, vaguely disgusted.

"Lori Pierce has given herself a life sentence," Grissom said. "A life sentence of knowing she killed her own mother."

"All the coke in the world won't make that go away," Warrick said.

No one disagreed.

17

At the end of shift, Gil Grissom invited Catherine Willows to his town house, offering to fix her some breakfast. She accepted.

Sitting with her legs tucked under her on the small brown leather couch by a window whose closed blinds were keeping out the early morning sun, Catherine watched Grissom scramble eggs, standing in his sandaled feet on the hardwood floor in the open kitchen with its stainless-steel refrigerator and counterspace that spilled into the living room of the spacious, functional condo. Where they weren't lined with bookcases or stacked electronics, the white walls were home to framed displays of butterflies—beautiful dead things that Grissom could appreciate.

Catherine was sipping orange juice; actually, a screwdriver, the juice laced with vodka at her request.

"Like a bagel with this?" he asked, poised over the eggs with the same quiet intensity he brought to any of his experiments.

"That'd be fine—no butter, though."

He shuddered at that thought, but continued with his work.

"You know, I took this job because I like puzzles," she said.

"Me too."

"And I like the idea of finding out who is responsible for the senseless violence that seems to be all around us, chipping away at what we laughingly call civilization."

She was a little drunk.

Grissom said, "Again, we're on the same page." He, however, was not drunk; only orange juice in his glass.

"I never expected," she said, "in a job where I only carry a gun 'cause it's part of the job description . . . where I'm investigating the *aftermath* of crimes, not out on the streets like so many cops are . . . I never . . . never . . . never mind."

He lifted his head from the eggs and looked over at her. "You saved Sara's life . . . and Conroy's. You should feel good about yourself."

"Would you feel good about killing someone?"

". . . No." He used a spatula to fill a plate with eggs. Half a bagel—unbuttered, lightly toasted—was already deposited there.

Sighing, she pulled her legs out from under her and sat up on the couch. "You didn't do me any favor, you know, sending me back into that world."

Grissom walked over, her plate in one hand, utensils and napkin for her, in the other. "You mean, those strip clubs?"

"Those strip clubs. That young woman I shot . . ." And the tears came, and Catherine covered her face with a hand.

Grissom, stunned, sat down next to her, but gave her plenty of space, her plate of eggs in one of his hands. He waited patiently for her crying to cease, then when she looked at him, handed the plate toward her.

She took it, but he left his hand there for a long moment, and for that moment they held the plate, together; their eyes met and finally they both smiled a little . . . friends.

Soon he'd gone to fetch his own plate of eggs, and his own bagel—buttered, untoasted—and sat next to her on the couch, where they ate in silence, other than an occasional compliment from Catherine on his cooking, which he did not acknowledge.

"This guy Pierce," she said, and sipped her drink.

"What about him?"

"I don't know, I just can't wrap my mind around the guy. . . . He's not a monster. I mean, he must love his daughter—he tried to take the blame for her. But he also coldbloodedly cut up his wife with a chain saw."

"*We* look at dead people dispassionately," Grissom said. "Bodies become evidence, to us. Some would consider us coldblooded."

"Maybe. But that man loved that woman once . . . Lynn Pierce used to be a vibrant, happy woman who Owen Pierce loved. How could even a coldblooded bastard like him learn to live with what he's done? And that his daughter murdered her own mother? His wife, a woman he must have once adored? How can he handle it? How can he *deal* with it?"

"Oh I don't know," Grissom said, and took a bite of bagel. He chewed, swallowed, and—conferring Catherine his angelic smile— added, "Maybe in prison, he'll get religion."

COLD BURN

For Anthony E. Zuiker—
without whom . . .

M.A.C. and M.V.C.

"With method and logic
one can accomplish anything."

—HERCULE POIROT

"Data! Data! Data!
I can't make bricks without clay."

—SHERLOCK HOLMES

1

Like the beacon over Bethlehem, the fallen but bright star called
Las Vegas had long ago guided wise guys from the east to this un-
holy city where Christmas of a sort was celebrated year-round. Ever
since Ben "Bugsy" Siegel had died for the sins of tourists everywhere,
men had journeyed across the desert, lured by the glowing neon temples called FLAMINGO and SANDS and CAESAR'S, summoned by
celestial bodies with names like Liberace and Sinatra and Darin, to
worship at the altar of the elusive fast buck.

Right now, with Christmas less than a month away, gamblers were
high-rolling into town like a horde of last-minute shoppers, bucking
the odds and dreaming of a green Christmas.

Driving through the Lake Mead National Recreation Area in the
predawn darkness, Ranger Ally Scott—like most residents of Las
Vegas—was contemplating the upcoming holiday in terms that had
nothing to do with gambling. That is, except for the gamble she
would take buying anything for her perennially hard-to-shop-for father. Then there was her sister Elisa . . . a gift certificate, that would
just be cold.

Which was exactly what Ally was at the moment. She didn't have
the Park Service Bronco's heater on and the vehicle's interior wasn't
any warmer than the night she plowed through, the temperature
hovering around a crisp forty. Ally had bundled herself up in her
heavy jacket and Thinsulate gloves, but like so much of the Las
Vegas population she had grown up somewhere else. Iowa in her
case—so she damn well knew the difference between *real* winter
and what Las Vegans only *thought* was winter.

Thin, practically scrawny, and barely over the mandatory Ranger height minimum, Ally enjoyed the relative chill of the December Vegas night as she tooled along the two-lane blacktop that snaked its way through the entire twenty-mile length of the Lake Mead facility.

The flat-brimmed campaign hat covered most of Ally's blonde hair, the rest ponytailed back and tucked inside the collar of her jacket.

Ally had joined the Park Service right out of college and had spent the six years since then working her way up the ladder. Barely a year ago, after bouncing from station to station in the Southwest, she'd landed this plum assignment, here at Lake Mead. Now and then, she drew the night shift like this, but she didn't mind. She was comfortable in her own company.

Headlights slashing the darkness, the Bronco rounded a curve, and the ranger felt (more than actually saw) a blur of motion to her left. Slamming on the brakes, she jolted the vehicle to a stop just as a creature tore across the road in front of her and disappeared into the blackness to her right.

Coyote.

Out here, the lights of the city were a glow on the horizon; otherwise, under a moonless desert sky scattered with half-hearted stars, the landscape remained a mystery. Still, Ally felt something—off to the passenger side of the Bronco.

With the windows rolled up, she could hear nothing, yet her well-trained senses were tingling. *Was* that . . . something? Some muffled sound, out there in the night . . . ?

She shoved the gearshift into park, let out a deep breath, and pretended the goosebumps on her arms were from the cold. Opening the driver-side door, she dropped onto the blacktop and stilled as she listened, intently. At first, only the wind whipping through the foothills, like the ghost of a mule train driver thrashing his team, broke the silence. Then, between lashes of wind, Ally heard something else. . . .

Something animal.

The ranger unsnapped her holster and rested her hand on the butt of her Smith and Wesson model 10, like a western gunfighter ready for the worst. Though most cops these days carried automatics, Glocks, Brownings, the Park Service still issued their rangers traditional, standard Smith and Wesson six-shooters with four-inch barrels. Ally wished she had something with a little more stopping power and, considering her prowess with the weapon, several more rounds at her disposal.

Stepping cautiously, quietly around the open door and walking to the front of the Bronco, Ally could see nothing, although her ears picked up something, something that might have been a far-off conversation. No words could be made out, but the ranger thought she heard voices. . . .

Then, in one chilling moment, she understood what the "talk" was. The coyote that'd crossed her Bronco's path was over there, and the creature wasn't alone—a minor critter convention was under way. Ally didn't bother pretending that the shiver up her spine was caused by the wintry wind.

Ally clambered back into the Bronco and slipped the gearshift into reverse, backing the vehicle, blocking the road, and cranking the wheel so the front beams threw their small but insistent spotlights up onto the desert hillside.

Six . . . no, seven coyotes huddled around and hunkered over a large white lump on the ground. For just a moment, the shape was abstract in the harsh headlights. Then Ally knew. As acid rose in her stomach, Ally Scott recognized the lump as human flesh—the nude body of a woman, sprawled on her side.

The body wasn't moving.

Even with the presence of the coyotes, Ally held out hope that the woman might still be alive, that this was an unconscious body and not a dead one, despite the scavengers. She again hopped down from the Bronco, pulling her pistol to fire a round into the night sky.

The shot splitting the night and then echoing across the desert did get the attention of the animals, the coyotes' heads popping up, turning in her direction . . . but it didn't spook or disperse them.

Ally lowered the pistol and fired off another round, only a foot or so over the heads of the coyotes this time. The critters jumped and moved away, a few feet, claws scratching the desert floor, but most still lingered near the prone nude form.

And that pissed Ally off.

She charged right at them, screaming and firing off several more shots, and the animals finally took the hint, relinquishing their prize and scampering like evil puppies into the night.

Making more noise than necessary, to help make sure the scavengers didn't return, Ally pulled off a glove and knelt next to the body.

The woman—a brunette—appeared to be dead, after all. She lay on her side, as though she were sleeping . . . but she wasn't. Reaching down, Ally touched the woman's neck and, trained cop though she was, drew back her hand quickly as if she'd touched a hot stove.

What she had sensed was quite the opposite—the flesh felt more like cold rubber than anything warm and human. The woman's lank hair felt damp—had the woman crawled up here from the lake? Was this some skinny-dipping party gone awry?

Ally's stomach flipped and the ranger knew that her supper was about to make a return trip. She started panting on purpose, like a dog, just like her orthodontist had taught her back when she was a teenager getting braces. While Dr. McPike had taken that mold of her mouth, he'd instructed her that panting would help her overcome her gag reflex.

You just never know, she thought, *when these little life lessons are going to come in handy.*

Ally searched for a pulse—finding nothing stirring under the cold, clammy flesh. This was a dead body, clearly . . . and that put Ally right smack in the middle of what she knew damn well was a crime scene. The urge to drag the body back to the Bronco was nearly overwhelming, but Ally knew not to disturb the scene any more than she already had, rushing in to chase off the coyotes.

Pistol still in her hand, Ally backed carefully to the vehicle, her eyes sweeping the dark beyond the body and the Bronco beams, just waiting for the first coyote to creep back into the wash of the car's headlights, for her to pick off. She knew, too, that if this was a murder, the perpetrator could possibly still be in the area . . . though she doubted that. The coyotes wouldn't have made their move until they were alone with the corpse.

Her eyes still searching the hill, Ally reached inside, plucked the mike from its dashboard perch, pulled the long cord out so she'd have an unobstructed view of the body and pushed the talk button.

"Dispatch," she said, "this is mobile two."

No response from the base.

"Dispatch, this is mobile two. Aaron, it's your wake-up call! Get off your ass—I found a dead body."

The low-pitched male voice sounded groggy, which was hardly a surprise. "Ally? What the hell did you say?"

"Call the city cops, Aaron—we got a d.b."

A summer intern brought back on temporarily to help out during the holiday vacations, Aaron Davis had little experience beyond handing out maps to tourists and flirting with teenage girls come to swim in the lake.

"Aren't we supposed to notify the FBI, Ally?"

The mild irritation Ally felt was a relief compared to the creepiness that had come over her, touching that cold corpse.

"We will, Aaron," she said with feigned patience, "but the Fibbies won't make it for days." She sighed. "The Vegas P.D. will be here within the hour. Call 911."

"But we're the cops, aren't we, Ally?"

"Well . . . I am."

"You mean, cops can call 911, too?"

"Aaron . . . just make the call. Then you can go back to sleep."

"You don't have to be mean," Aaron said.

She clicked off then and the ridiculousness of the conversation made her laugh. She laughed and laughed, tears rolling down her cheeks, and then she thought to herself, *Laughin' like a damn hyena,* and that made her think of the coyotes.

And then she didn't laugh any more.

She just watched the still white lump of flesh, guarding it from scavengers. Ally Scott could protect the dead woman from the coyotes, no problem; but if the woman was a murder victim, it would take a different breed of cop to find the animal who had done this.

2

Standing at the edge of the blacktop, Catherine Willows—Las Vegas Metro P.D. crime scene investigator—let the headlights of the Park Services Bronco, blocking the road, give her her first view of the body.

The dead naked woman lay on her left side, arms folded chastely across her bosom, legs pulled up in a tight, fetal ball. At this distance, no signs of violence were apparent and Catherine wondered if this death could somehow be natural. According to the ranger, the woman's hair was damp and, even from here, Catherine could make out the dampness of the ground beneath the corpse. Maybe the woman had been swimming in the lake; perhaps this was a romantic tryst that had got out of . . .

Catherine stopped herself. Unlike her boss and colleague Gil Grissom, she almost always allowed herself to play with theories before all the facts were in. But she knew the practice could be dangerous if left unchecked, particularly this early on.

On their first case together, Grissom had said, "It's a capital mistake to theorize before one has data. Insensibly one begins to twist facts to suit theories, instead of theories to suit facts."

"That sounds like a quote," she'd said.

"It is," Grissom had said, with no attribution, just glancing at her with that little half-smile and smug twinkle of the eye she now knew so well.

Even so, the tryst notion was one of the few logical explanations that came readily to mind to answer the musical question, what was a nude woman doing wandering around the Lake Mead National Recreation Area in the middle of the night . . . ?

Two squad cars, their rollers smudging the night with alternate smears of red and blue, blocked the road a hundred yards on either side of the scene. Detective Jim Brass's unmarked Taurus sat on the shoulder of the road near where Catherine and her partner tonight, Warrick Brown, had left their Tahoe.

Ever the gentleman, Warrick was pulling their flightcase-like field kits out of the back of the SUV while Catherine had stepped to the edge of the road for an overview of the crime scene. Her hair whispered at her ears, thanks to the gentle desert wind—which had a bite to it, as the sting at her cheeks attested.

Captain Brass ambled up next to her. Despite the temperature, Brass wore no topcoat, just a plaid sportcoat over a gold shirt with a blue-and-gold striped tie. When she had first known the detective, Brass had been a rumpled sort, with the unkempt aura of the recently divorced; but time passed and the detective had long since spiffed up.

A small cloud huffed out as he spoke. "Dead nude woman."

As if that were the beginning and the end of it.

Catherine asked, "No ID?"

"Nude, Catherine," he said, dryly. "She wasn't strolling around buck naked with her purse."

"I don't go anywhere without mine."

"Nonetheless . . . we got nothing here."

"Not yet." Catherine smiled at him, teasing just a little. "Warrick and I'll have a look, if you don't mind."

"Knock yourself out."

Following her flashlight's beam, she slowly walked over the sandy ground, careful not to disturb any potential evidence as she approached the corpse.

Brass remained on the edge of the road.

She heard Warrick behind her, field kits clanking. Then he was beside her, asking, "How's it read?"

Tall, with a shaggy, modestly dreadlocked haircut, Warrick Brown had skin the color of coffee with just a hint of cream stirred in. He was a man with a ready smile, though Catherine knew him to be serious and even inclined to melancholy.

He watched as Catherine played the flashlight along the woman's back, as if painting an abstract picture. Then she crouched and shone the beam on the woman's disturbingly peaceful face: the eyes closed, a puggish nose above full colorless lips . . . but no sign of violence, no immediate cause of death visible.

"She doesn't have much to say yet," Catherine said. "Fortunately, the coyotes were just getting started when that ranger interrupted 'em—this could be a lot worse."

"Maybe not from Miss Nude Vegas's point of view," Warrick said, in his deadpan way. "Dumped, y'think?"

Catherine nodded. "Probably dropped here, yes—other than paw-and-claw prints, no signs of a struggle on the ground. But, damn . . . who is she?" Then to the corpse, "Who are you?"

"She went out of this life," Warrick said softly, "same way she came in—naked."

Catherine frowned. "Maybe not . . . I think I saw some sort of impression, maybe from underwear. Still, it's not a lot to go on."

"Well, you know what Gris would say."

She nodded. " 'Just work the evidence.' "

"That's it."

"Well, even if that's what 'Gris' might say, allow me to point out that while we're 'working' the evidence, our fearless leader and his trusty aide will soon be sucking up room service in a first-class hotel."

Graveyard shift supervisor Grissom and another CSI, Sara Sidle, would be leaving early this morning for a forensics conference at a mountain lodge in upstate New York, where they would be teaching. Though forty degrees might be cold in Vegas, Catherine knew that where Grissom and Sara were headed, a minus sign would likely be in front of the temperature before the weekend was over. She really didn't envy the pair a bit.

Warrick made a clicking sound in his cheek and said, "Explain to me again why we're not there?"

"I didn't go because I declined the opportunity."

"You declined? A paid vacation?"

"Yes. Unlike some people, I have a life, and I didn't want to leave my daughter with a babysitter for that long."

"I have a life."

"Let's say you do. Even so, you hate the cold."

Warrick sighed. "Yeah, well. That cushy hotel, it's got heat, doesn't it?"

Catherine allowed that it probably did.

"And the classes are indoors, right?"

"Grissom's will be," she admitted. "There may be some outdoor crime scene stuff, but you don't bring people in from Vegas to teach criminalistics in the snow."

"Thank you. You make my point—I'm tellin' you, Cath . . . that could've been us on that trip."

She nodded. "If I hadn't declined . . . and you weren't such a baby."

"Hey—that's cold."

"See? Bellyachin' about the weather already."

Finished with her examination of the corpse, Catherine rose and faced her partner. "Time to go to work, before I start thinking you don't love your job."

He shook his head. "You can love your job, and still need a little R&R."

"Well," she said, as they headed back to the Tahoe, "how about, for fun, you find us a usable tire track on the shoulder of the road, before all these people tromping around turn Lake Mead into a dust bowl."

Catherine snapped off photos as fast as the flash would recharge, little pops of daylight in the night, two photos of each angle, for safety, covering the body five ways: from the right; the left; top of the head down; bottom of the feet up; and overhead.

Warrick poked around the side of the road, occasionally bending, now and then taking his own photos. Finally, satisfied he'd found all the pertinent, usable tire tracks, he spritzed them with hair spray to hold them together, then got his field kit and mixed up some goo—casting powder and dental stone—so he could cast some of the different tracks he'd marked.

Catherine didn't think about it, but nobody spoke to them while they processed the scene—and this was not unusual. Crime scene investigators, working their scientific wonders, created in those around them a quiet reverence, as if all the kneeling she and Warrick were doing was praying, not detecting.

Or maybe it was the dead woman, in the midst of the CSI rituals, who inspired the silence.

Over on the blacktop, Brass interviewed the ranger who'd found the body, while the uniformed men stood around and did their best to look official. Truth was, once the CSIs had shown up, a uniformed cop at a crime scene usually had just about the most boring job in the law enforcement book.

Under the bright light of some portable halogens, Catherine went over the corpse as carefully as she could—nothing seemed wrong, other than a few nibble marks on the arms and legs where the coyotes had begun. No signs of struggle, no skin under her fingernails, no black eyes or bruises—nothing to say this woman wasn't just sleeping, except for the absence of breath.

An indentation showed the curve of the victim's panty line, but Catherine could find not so much as a thread for evidence. It was as if the sky had given birth to Jane Doe and let her fall gently to the sandy ground—stillborn. Finally, as night surrendered the desert back to the sun, Brass approached with cups of coffee for the two criminalists.

"Life's blood," Catherine said as Brass handed her the steaming Styrofoam cup.

Warrick saluted with his and took a sip. "Here's to crime—without it, where would we be?"

Brass raised both eyebrows and suggested, "In bed, asleep?"

They watched as the ranger climbed into her Bronco—she paused to nod at them, professionally, and they returned the gesture—and then she slowly pulled away.

Using her coffee cup to indicate the departing vehicle, Catherine asked, "She seemed competent."

"Yeah," Brass said with a nod. "We got lucky, having her find our girl."

"She see anything?"

"Nearly hit a coyote with her Bronco." Brass shrugged one noncommittal shoulder. "About all she saw was coyotes, gathered around the corpse."

"Singing Kum-bayah," Warrick said dryly.

"Did those little doggies mess up your crime scene much?"

Catherine shook her head. "Hardly any marks on the body."

Eyes tightening, Brass asked, "What's that tell us?"

"Our vic probably did not just wander out here and die," Warrick said.

Brass looked at him.

"She's barefoot," Warrick continued, "and there's no bare footprints anywhere. You don't have to be an Eagle Scout to figure, if she was wandering dazed and nude, coyotes woulda got to her before she made it this far into the middle of the park. Somebody dropped her off."

Brass returned his gaze to Catherine. "That how you see it?"

"Makes sense to me," she said. "Lady Godiva's probably a dump, all right . . . but if the coyotes were around her and the ranger scared them off, she couldn't have been on the ground for very long, or else there wouldn't have been much left after the coyotes chowed down."

Frowning, Warrick asked the detective, "Ranger didn't see or hear a car?"

"Nope," Brass said. "She did mention that five bucks buys a car a five-day pass to the Lake Mead recreation area. Tourists can come and go as they please, whenever they please."

Warrick said, "Ever wonder what it's like to do this job in a town not crawling with tourists?"

"Oh but that would be too easy," Brass said. His sigh started in his belly and dragon-breathed out his nose. "Could be any car and it could be anywhere by now. You said there were no bare footprints—how 'bout shoeprints?"

"No," Catherine said, "whoever brought her in must've blotted them out, when they were leaving."

Almost to himself, Warrick said, "Ten million tourists a year visit this place."

"Yeah," Brass said grumpily. "Fish and Wildlife guy told us so, last time we had a dead naked woman out here."

Last autumn a woman's torso had been dredged from Lake Mead.

"We caught that guy," Warrick reminded Brass.

"How about cars?" Catherine asked. "How many in the park now?"

Brass offered up a two-shouldered shrug. "No records. It's a vacation spot—casual. Your guess is as good as mine."

Catherine frowned. "So they never know who's in the park?"

"Just happy campers—happy *anonymous* campers."

"So," Warrick said. "We have a dead naked woman . . . no ID, nothing around the body, and the only evidence we have is a track off a tire that could belong to just about any vehicle."

A grin put another crease in the rumpled detective's face. "And that's why you guys make the medium-sized bucks."

They exchanged tired smiles, which faded quickly as the trio watched two EMTs struggling to maneuver the gurney bearing the black-bagged body down to the road. The EMTs loaded the black bag—the woman finally clothed, in a way—into the back of the ambulance, closed the doors with two slams that made Catherine start a bit, then climbed in around front. The flashing lights had been on when the vehicle barreled in, and now came on again, automatically; but the driver shut them off, and the vehicle rolled away.

No hurry, not now.

"What's next?" Warrick asked.

Glancing at her watch, Catherine said, "We call it a night."

"We haven't even identified her yet," Warrick said to Catherine, but his eyes cut to Brass. "First twenty-four hours—"

"We don't even know," Brass interrupted, "if we have a homicide. . . . And if we did, can you point at any evidence that's time-sensitive here?"

Catherine shook her head.

After a moment, so did Warrick.

The detective held up his hands in front of him, palms out, his way of saying this was neither his fault nor his problem. They all knew that Sheriff Brian Mobley had put the kibosh on overtime except homicides, and even then on a case-by-case basis. Mobley was eyeing the mayor's seat in the next election and wanted to be seen as fiscally responsible, and that meant cutting most OT.

Catherine said to Warrick, "If it was up to me, we'd work this straight through—since homicide seems a possibility."

Brass, who'd had his own share of battles with the sheriff over the years, said, "We're all slaves to policy. You're on call, as usual—something pressing comes up, your beeper will let you know."

"I think our vic deserves better," Warrick said.

"Is she a vic? Do we even know that, yet? . . . Get some rest, come in tonight and look at this again, with a fresh eye."

In the rider's seat of the Tahoe, Catherine sat quietly, letting Warrick brood, and drive.

Truth be told, for Catherine the moratorium on overtime was sometimes a blessing of sorts. Sure, she wanted to find this woman's killer . . . if the woman had been killed . . . as much as Warrick or God or anybody; and she knew damn well the longer they waited, the colder the trail.

On the other hand, Mobley's penny-pinching gave her the chance to spend a little more time with daughter Lindsey after school. As much as she loved her job, Catherine loved her daughter more, and

Lindsey was at that stage where the girl seemed to have grown an inch every time Catherine saw her.

But this was a homicide. She wouldn't say it out loud just yet, but she knew in every well-trained fiber of her being that some sicko had left that woman out here as meal for the coyotes.

And that just wouldn't do.

When she came in that night, right after ten, Catherine Willows was already dragging. She'd slept through the morning, catching a good four hours, but did housework and bills in the afternoon, then spent the evening helping Lindsey with her homework. The latter, anyway, was worth losing a little sleep over.

Until Sheriff Mobley's recent fiscal responsibility manifesto, the CSIs had worked whatever overtime was necessary to crack the case they happened to be on. Catching a case on the night shift meant that certain tasks just couldn't be accomplished during their regular shift. And the level of cooperation with the day shift was less than stellar— Conrad Ecklie, the supervisor on days, considered Grissom a rival, and Grissom considered Ecklie a jerk. This did not encourage team playing between graveyard and days.

Now, with OT curtailed, the CSIs just had to try to cram more work into a normal shift. Although the new policy might pave the way for Mobley's advancement, Catherine knew that rushing to cover so much ground in such a short time could lead to sloppiness, which was the bane of any CSI's existence.

Her heels clicked like castanets on the tile floor as she strode down the hall toward the morgue. When she arrived, she found what she had hoped to find—Dr. Robbins, hard at work on her case. His metal crutch stashed in the corner, the coroner—in blue scrubs, a pair of which Catherine would put on over her own street clothes—hovered over the slab bearing their Jane Doe, a measuring tape in his hands, sweat beaded on his brow.

The balding, chubby-cheeked coroner, his salt-and-pepper beard mostly salt by now, was the night shift's secret weapon. His sharp dark eyes missed nothing and, despite having to use the metal crutch after a car crash some years ago, he moved around the morgue with a nimbleness that ex-dancer Catherine could only envy.

"Getting anywhere?" she asked lightly.

He shrugged without looking up. "Catherine," he said by way of acknowledgment, then answered her question with: "Early yet."

For all the time she'd spent studying the dead woman under her flashlight beam, Catherine moved in eagerly for a good look under better conditions. Crime scene protocol had meant Catherine had left the woman in her fetal position; now the nude female was on her back on a silver slab.

Her flesh ashen gray, Jane Doe had a pageboy haircut, wide-set closed eyes, and full lips that had a ghastly bleached look. A nice figure, for a corpse.

"Funny," Catherine said.

"What is?"

"She kinda looks like Batgirl."

Robbins glanced up, then returned to his work.

"From the old TV show," Catherine explained. "Not that you'd—"

"Yvonne Craig." Robbins flicked her a look. "You don't want to play Trivial Pursuit with me, Catherine."

"I'll keep that in mind. Sex crime?"

"No evidence of it. When she died, she hadn't had intercourse in a while."

Catherine gestured to the woman's waist. "What about the visible panty line?"

"She died clothed—marks from a bra too."

"Cause of death?"

"Asphyxia, I would venture." He thumbed open one of Jane Doe's eyelids and revealed red filigree in what should have been the white of an eye. "She has petechial hemorrhaging in the conjunctivae."

Catherine leaned in for a closer look. "That's asphyxia's calling card, all right. Strangulation?"

"Strangely, doesn't appear that way—no ligature marks, no bruising."

Catherine pondered that a moment. "So . . . you've ruled out what, so far? Suicide?"

He smiled. "Unless you know a way she might have killed herself, then stripped off her clothes."

"Where are we, then?"

He shrugged. "As I said . . . early. Printed her and gave them to Nick to run through AFIS."

Nick Stokes was another of the graveyard shift CSIs. He'd been working his own case last night, so he hadn't joined them on the trip out to Lake Mead.

"Nick's in already?" she asked.

"Few minutes before you. Closed his case before he went home last night and was looking for something to do."

"We all feel a little lost without Grissom around," she said, attempting to be sarcastic and yet not completely kidding.

"Couple of odd things that will, I think, interest you," he said. "Have a look. No charge. . . ." He pointed to the victim's right arm.

Catherine moved around where she could get a better view. The victim had an indentation in her left arm above the point of the elbow—a faint stripe, resembling a hash mark.

"And here," Robbins said, pointing to the victim's left cheek, which had been out of sight at the crime scene.

"Any ideas?" asked Catherine as she looked at a small, round indentation that appeared as if the tip of a lipstick tube . . . or a bullet, maybe . . . had been pressed into the woman's cheek.

Again Robbins shook his head. "I was hoping you might have one. . . . Found postmortem lividity in the buttocks, lower legs, and feet, as well as the left cheek. I checked your photos and they show her lying on her left side."

Catherine shrugged. "That's the way we found her."

"Well, it almost looks like she was in a sitting position, after she died." Robbins then abruptly changed the subject. "Tell me—how cold did it get last night, anyway? What did the temp get down to?"

Thrown by this seemingly out-of-left-field question, Catherine shrugged again, more elaborately this time. "Chilly but no big deal. Forty, maybe."

Robbins shook his head again, but this time it was more an act of bemusement than disagreement. "Body's pretty cold—colder than I would have expected."

"She was cold to the touch last night, too."

"And the hair was wet, you said?"

"Yeah—damp."

"Does it seem reasonable to you that someone might have been swimming in the lake on a night that cold?"

"No . . . but we run into people doing a lot of things that don't seem reasonable, Doc."

"That's true. That much is true. No pile of clothing found?"

"Not a scrap."

"Interesting."

And with this, he fired up the bone saw and got ready to start the more in-depth procedures.

Frustrated, Catherine wandered off to find Nick. She checked the AFIS computer room—no sign of him. Wandering the aquamarine halls of the facility, a glass-and-wood world of soothing institutional sterility, she passed a couple of labs and Grissom's office before she finally tracked Nick down in the break room. He sipped his coffee and took a bite of doughnut as Catherine walked in.

"Hey, Nick," she said, trying to sound more nonchalant than she felt. Solving Jane Doe's murder would be a lot easier if they could ID her quickly.

Using the Styrofoam cup, Nick gave her a little salute as he finished chewing his doughnut.

Catherine dropped into a chair across the table from him and waited, knowing the doughnut just might be Nick's dinner. The break room always seemed to be undergoing some sort of massive cleanup, but no matter what either they themselves or the janitorial staff attempted, the room still smelled like one of Grissom's experiments gone awry. The refrigerator against the far wall held items that looked more like mutant life-forms than food, and the coffeepot was home to a sludgy mass that reminded Catherine too much of things she'd seen on the job.

She asked, "Any luck with AFIS?"

"Nope," he said, then took another bite of doughnut.

"So we don't know any more about her now than we did this morning?"

He shook his head. "I put her into the Missing Persons database, but . . ." He made a sound that was half snort, half laugh. ". . . you know how long that can take."

Catherine nodded glumly.

Warrick came in, wearing a brown turtleneck, brown jeans, and his usual sneakers. "Hey," he said.

"Hey," said Catherine.

Nick nodded and finished chewing the last of his doughnut. "I'm on the Jane Doe with you guys, now."

"More the merrier," Warrick said. "Anything new?"

Catherine said, "Robbins thinks asphyxia—but not strangulation, and not a sex crime. How about you?"

"Nothing on the tire mark so far, but the computer's still working."

A familiar voice squawked on the intercom. "Catherine, you in there?"

She spoke up. "Yes, Doc—with Nick and Warrick."

"Well," the voice said, "I have something to show you."

They exchanged looks, already getting to their feet, Catherine calling, "We're on our way!"

Nick slugged down the last of his coffee and the three of them moved silently but quickly to the morgue. When they walked in, in scrubs, they found Robbins bent not over the corpse—opened like a grotesque flower on the slab nearby—but a microscope. Immune from Sheriff Mobley's overtime edict, the doc regularly put in punishing hours, a habit that was helpful to the CSIs in this current Scrooge-like climate.

"Notice anything odd about this body?" he asked, directing the question to Catherine, senior member of the group.

"Nothing we haven't talked about already," she said, with a glance over at the autopsy-in-progress. "For some reason her hair was wet, and she was cold, but why not? It was chilly out last night."

Robbins nodded and gestured with an open palm for her to take his place at the microscope. "Yes, but was it this cold?"

Sitting down, Catherine gave Robbins a look, then pressed her eye to the eyepiece of the microscope. On the slide he'd prepared, she saw what appeared to be a flesh sample with several notable oddities—specifically, distortions in the nuclei of some cells, vacuoles, and spaces around the nuclei of others.

Catherine looked up at Robbins. "Is this what I think it is?"

He nodded. "Your Jane Doe was a corpse-sickle."

Warrick and Nick exchanged glances.

"Say again?" Warrick prompted.

"A frozen treat," Robbins said again, in his flat, low-key way. "What Catherine is looking at under the microscope is a tissue sample from Jane Doe's heart."

"She *froze* to death?" Warrick asked, his usually unflappable demeanor seeming sorely tested.

Robbins shrugged one shoulder. "Still working that one out. Suffocation is cause of death, but I don't know the circumstances for sure."

First Nick, then Warrick took turns gazing into the microscope. Robbins said, "Notice those discolorations, vacuoles, and spaces?"

Warrick nodded, eyes glued to the slide.

The doctor continued: "Ice crystal artifacts."

"So she was frozen," Nick said, trying to process this information. "But maybe after she was dead."

"Frozen God knows when . . . and rather carefully frozen, at that."

Warrick's eyes were wide and his upper lip curled. "And then what?"

"And then," Robbins said, "thawed . . . which is why her hair was damp. Catherine, the ground beneath the body was damp, I believe?"

She nodded. "Wet underneath and in a small area downhill from where she lay."

"Suffocated," Warrick said. "Then frozen."

Robbins did not answer immediately. But, finally, he said, "Yes."

Catherine's mind was racing. She expressed some of her thoughts: "And because Jane Doe was frozen, we can't pinpoint when she died."

Robbins grunted a small laugh. "Pinpoint isn't an issue. It could've been a week ago, it could've been six months, or even longer, for that matter."

Nick was shaking his head. "Well, hell—how did we not notice she'd been frozen?"

The doctor raised a finger. "As I said . . . she was 'carefully frozen.' Someone took precautions to avoid freezer burn. Wetted her down— a spray bottle would be enough. Kept wetting her down, all over, as the freezing process continued. And that is what kept her from getting freezer burn."

"So," Catherine said. "Our killer knew what he was doing."

"Or she," Nick put in.

Robbins sighed, nodded and then explained his theory.

Jane Doe has probably been either sedated or restrained or both. She's still clothed at this point, then something clean cuts off her breathing, plastic over her nose and mouth maybe, and she's out within five minutes. . . . Dead in not much more than that.

The killer strips her, then seats her inside a chest-style freezer. Could be an upright, but a chest freezer would be easier; then he . . . or she . . . cranks the freezer up to its highest setting . . . but is careful to use a pitcher or a squirt bottle, maybe even a hose, to wet down the corpse. The killer checks on her at least once a day, and wets the body every time he checks the progress of the freezing. After some unspecified time, the killer pulls her out and allows her to defrost naturally . . . then dumps her body in the Lake Mead National Recreation Area.

Warrick's eyes were tight with thought. "If he . . . or she . . . thought we'd be fooled into thinking we had a fresh body, then—"

"Then on that effort, our killer failed," Catherine said. "But even so, we've still had the time of death stolen from us, here."

"Exactly," Robbins said.

"So . . ." Catherine lifted her eyebrows, smiled at her colleagues. ". . . if we can't determine when she died, let's start with who she was."

"Which'll lead," Nick said, arching an eyebrow, "to finding out who wanted her dead."

"Which'll lead," Warrick said, with finality, "to putting the bastard on ice."

3

Initially, the idea of a getaway weekend with her boss had appealed to Sara Sidle, for all kinds of reasons. But somehow in the thirteen hours between when she'd left her apartment and fallen gratefully onto this cloud of a bed in a posh hotel, she had gotten lost in some newly discovered circle of Hell.

Grissom had picked her up just after 10 P.M., the time they normally would have been heading into the lab. Instead, they drove to long-term parking at McCarran and schlepped into the airport with their carry-ons as well as two suitcases of equipment for their presentation; the attendees would mostly be East Coast CSIs with the instructors flown in from around the country. Typically, the boyishly handsome, forty-something Grissom wore black slacks, a black three-button shirt, and a CSI windbreaker.

"That's the coat you're taking?" she had asked. Sara had a Gortex-lined parka on over her blue jeans and a plain dark T-shirt.

He looked at her as though a lamp had talked. "I've got a heavier one in my bag."

She glanced at his two canvas duffels, both barely larger than gym bags, and wondered how he got a heavy coat into either of them. Deciding not to think about it, she got into the check-in line right behind her boss. Both were using their carry-ons for clothing, and checking their suitcases of equipment on through. No need to freak out the security staff, who would not be prepared for X-ray views of the sort of tools, instruments, chemistry sets, and other dubious implements that the CSIs were traveling with.

Sara spent the flight from McCarran to O'Hare squashed in the middle seat in coach—Grissom took the window seat, not because he was rude, she knew, but because it was his assigned seat, and Grissom never argued with numbers.

Sara dug into an Agatha Christie mystery—the CSI could only read cozy mysteries, anything "realistic" just distracted and annoyed her with constant inaccuracies—and Grissom was engrossed in an entomology text like a teenager reading the new Stephen King.

The whole trip went like that—the two of them reading their respective books (Sara actually went through two) with little conversation, including an O'Hare breakfast that killed some of their four-hour layover in Chicago. Then it was two hours to Dulles in D.C., another forty-five minutes on the ground, and a ninety-minute flight to Gordon International, in Newburgh, New York. Grissom was better company on the trip than a potted plant—barely.

They were met by a landscape covered with four or five inches of snow that, judging by its grayish tint, appeared to have fallen at least a week ago. The cold air felt like the inside of a freezer compared to what they'd left behind in Vegas, and as the pair stood outside the airport waiting for the bus that would haul them and their gear the twenty miles from Newburgh to New Paltz, Grissom glanced around curiously, as though winter in upstate New York was one big crime scene he'd stumbled onto.

Sara, on the other hand, felt at home—spiritually at home, anyway. The temperature here, just above thirty, took Sara back to her days at Harvard; the frigid air of winter in the east had a different scent than the desert cold of Vegas.

At the curb in front of the New Paltz bus station, an old man in a flap-ear cap, chocolate-colored Mackinaw, jeans, and dark work boots, waited next to a purring woody-style station wagon, the side door of which was stenciled: MUMFORD MOUNTAIN HOTEL.

Carry-ons draped over them like military gear, Grissom and Sara made their cumbersome way toward their down-home chauffeur. As soon as the codger figured out they were headed his way, he rushed over and pried one of the suitcases from Sara's hand.

"Help you with that, Miss?"

But he'd already taken it.

"Thanks," she said, breath pluming.

The Mumford man was tall, reedy, with wispy gray hair; his hook nose had an "S" curve in the middle where it had been broken more than once.

After slinging Sara's bag in the back, he turned and took one from Grissom and tossed it in. The man's smile was wide and came fast, revealing two rows of small, even teeth.

"Herm Cormier," he said, shaking first Grissom's hand, then Sara's. "I've managed the hotel since Jesus was a baby."

"Gil Grissom. Honor to be picked up by the top man himself."

"Sara Sidle. We're here for the forensics conference . . . ?"

"Course you are. You're the folks from Vegas."

Grissom smiled. "Is it that easy to spot us?"

Cormier nodded. "Your coat's not heavy enough," he said, with a glance toward Grissom's CSI windbreaker. "And you both got a healthy tan. We got nobody comin' in from Florida or California for this thing, and I knew two of you were coming from Vegas. . . . Plus which, all but a handful of you folks won't be in till tomorrow."

Grissom nodded.

"You, though, Miss," Cormier said, turning his attention to Sara, "you've been around this part of the country before."

Though anxious to get into that warm station wagon, Sara couldn't resist asking: "And how did you reach that conclusion?"

The old man looked her up and down, but there was nothing improper about it. "Good coat, good boots, heavy gloves—where you from, before you lit in Vegas?"

"San Francisco."

"No, that ain't it." His eyes narrowed. "Where'd you go to college?"

She grinned. "Boston."

Cormier returned the grin. "Thought so. Knew you had to've spent some time in this part of the country."

The driver opened the rear door of the wagon and they were about to climb in, when another man sauntered up. A husky blonde six-footer in his late thirties, the new arrival had dark little eyes in a pale, bland fleshy face, like raisins punched into cookie dough. He wore a red-and-black plaid coat that looked warm, aided and abetted by a black woolen muffler. In one black gloved hand was a silver flight case—this was another CSI, Sara thought, and that was his field kit—and in the other a green plaid bag that jarred against the competing plaid coat.

"Gordon Maher," he said to all of them.

Cormier stepped forward, shook the man's hand and made the introductions, then said to the new arrival, "You must be the forensics fella from Saskatchewan."

They piled into the station wagon, Grissom and Maher in the back, Sara and Cormier in the front. Despite the snow blanketing the area, the roads were clean. As the station wagon wended its way through the countryside toward Lake Mumford, Sara allowed herself to enjoy the ride, relishing the wave of nostalgia she felt, watching the snow-touched skeletal trees they glided past.

Harvard had been where Sara first took wing, first got out from the shadow of her parents. She sought out kindred spirits, overachievers like herself, and soon she was no longer seen as too smart, too driven, too tense.

The very air in this part of the country smelled different to her now—like freedom, and success. She didn't know when she fell asleep, exactly, but suddenly Cormier was nudging her gently. The car was parked on the shoulder and, when she looked around, Sara realized that Grissom and Maher had gotten out.

"Thought you might like to catch the hotel and lake," Cormier said, "from their best side."

Slowly, Sara got out of the car, the chill air helping her wake up; she stretched. Grissom and Maher stood in front of the car, staring at something off to the right. Going to join them, she looked in that direction as well, shading her brow with her hand as she gazed down the hill through the leafless branches at an ice-covered lake surrounded mostly by woods.

In preparing for this trip, Sara had understandably assumed Mumford Mountain Hotel would perch atop a mountain. Instead, the lodge hunkered in a valley between two mountains, overlooking the lake—and from this distance, situated as it was on the far side of the frozen expanse, the sprawling structure brought nothing so much to mind as a gigantic ice castle from the fairy tales her mother had read to her as a child.

It wasn't beautiful, really, more like bizarre—and mind-numbingly large, which was especially startling out here in the middle of nowhere. A hodgepodge of five interconnected structures, Mumford Mountain Hotel might have been a junkyard for old buildings: in front, near the lake, sat a squat dark-wood ski chalet; to the right and behind the chalet, a huge gray castle complete with turrets and chimneys rose seven stories. That gothic monstrosity was flanked by two functional-looking green four-story buildings that might have been the boys' and girls' dormitories at an old private school.

The one on the right had a deeply sloped, gabled roof, while its fraternal twin at the other end had a flatter roof with a single sharp point rising like the conical hat of a Brothers Grimm princess. If those buildings didn't supply enough rooms for Mumford's guests, a last building—what looked like a two-story gingerbread house—had been cobbled together on the far right end. The whole unlikely assembly seemed to shimmer under a heavy ice-crystal-flung dusting of snow.

"The Mumford Mountain Hotel," Cormier said, pride obvious in his voice.

"Can't say I've seen its like before," Maher admitted, arms folded against himself. "What's the story on the various building styles?"

"Well, that castle part came first—then wings were added, to suit whoever was running the place at the time. The hotel just sort of grew over the years. It's hard for people to get an idea of how big she is, when they're up close. I like to give folks the chance to see it from a distance, get a little perspective."

Sara said, "You could get lost in that place."

Cormier nodded, breath smoking. "Over two hundred fifty guest rooms, grand ballroom, complete gym, meeting rooms, tennis courts, golf course."

"The lake get any action in the winter?" Maher asked.

Again Cormier nodded. "They'll clear the snow off and play hockey on it when the weather gets a mite colder."

Soon they were back in the car and following the narrow road that wound down the mountain and ended at the check-in entrance of the hotel, which was alongside the building—otherwise the guests would have had to maneuver the flight of stairs to the actual main entrance and the vast covered porch where countless rocking chairs sat unattended. A light snow began to fall as Cormier directed several bell-boys to unload the station wagon, piling the guest luggage onto carts, a process Grissom watched with suspicion—his precious tools and toys were in those bags.

They checked in, having just missed lunch, but Grissom shared with her a fruit basket the conference chairman had sent, and Sara left him at his room, where he was eating a pear as he unpacked. She headed down the wide, carpeted hall for her own accommodations, eating an apple along the way. She felt like Alice gone through the mirror into a Victorian wonderland—dark, polished woodwork; soft-focus, yellow-tinted lighting; plush antique furniture; wide wooden stairways; and little sitting areas with fresh-cut flowers and frondy plants and their own fireplaces.

Now, midafternoon, having gotten the nap she so desperately needed (sleeping in the car had actually made her feel worse), Sara felt an irresistible urge to go exploring—there were only a few hours left before sundown. She wondered if Grissom would feel the same.

Of course he wouldn't.

He was probably curled up with that damned bug book again. Not that she didn't understand his almost hermit-like behavior—she was a loner herself. But ever since the Marks case, Sara had tried to force herself out into the world more, to have a life beyond the crime lab, after noting the work-is-everything, stay-at-home, shop-out-of-catalogues existence that had contributed to the death of a woman way too much like herself.

She had come to Mumford with a plan to embroil Grissom in an outing and Sara Sidle was nothing if not thorough. Quickly she changed from her traveling clothes into black jeans, a heavier thermal undershirt and a dark flannel blouse. She slipped into her parka, snatched up her camera, briefly considered taking along her collapsed portable tripod, then decided not to be encumbered. Maybe later. She locked the door behind her and went to Grissom's room.

Her first knock inspired no answer, and she tried again. Still nothing. On the third, more insistent knock, the door opened to reveal Grissom, entomology text held in his hand like a priest with a Bible—it was as if she'd interrupted an exorcism.

"Hey," she said, chipper.

"Hey," he said, opening the door wide. "You look rested."

Wow—that was one of the nicest things he'd ever said to her.

Encouraged, she tried, "You wanna go for a walk?"

He glanced toward the window on the far side of the room, then turned back to her. "Sara—it's snowing."

She nodded. "And?"

He considered that for a while.

"I don't do snow," he said. He was still in the black slacks and black three-button shirt. Gesturing with the bug book, he said, "It's cozy, reading by the fire. You should try it."

That almost sounded romantic. . . .

He frowned at her and added: "Don't you have a fireplace in your room?"

". . . I finished my books already."

"The first thing the pioneers did was build shelter and go inside. Out of respect to them, I—"

"Did you know there are 274 winter insects in eastern New York state alone?"

He stilled, but clearly sensed a trap. "You made that up."

Grinning, she handed him the printout. "Snow-born Boreus, Mid-winter Boreus, Large and Small Snowflies, and the Snow-born Midge . . . just to name a few."

After a quick scan of the page, he said, "If you've got your heart set on it, I guess I'll get my coat."

To Grissom's credit, the coat he withdrew like a rabbit out of a hat from his canvas carry-on—a black, leather-sleeved varsity-type jacket, sans letter or any other embellishment—was heavier than the windbreaker, though still not really sufficient for this weather. He slipped some specimen bottles into the pockets, zipped up the coat, yanked on black fur-lined leather gloves, and they were off.

The first hour or so they spent hiking through the snow-covered woods, Grissom stopping every now and then to look for insects on the ground and on trees. Sara—who found Grissom's behavior endearingly Boy Scout-ish—snapped off about a dozen nature shots, barely putting a dent in her Toshiba's 64-mb memory card; but after a while the snowfall made that impossible. It was getting heavier, and Sara knew they should head back.

But she was having too good a time. The wintry woods were delightful, idyllic. A charmingly gleeful Grissom actually found several specimens that he had carefully bottled for transport back to the hotel. He was close to her, their cold-steam breath mingling, showing her one of his prizes, when they heard it.

A pop!

They swung as one toward the forest.

Frowning, Sara asked, "Hunters?"

Grissom shook his head, but before he could speak, four more pops interrupted.

Shots—no doubt now in her mind, and clearly none in Grissom's, either.

Even though the shots were in the distance, they both found trees to duck behind.

"If it's hunters," he said, looking over at her, "they're using hand-guns."

"Where?"

"Can't tell. . . . Over there, maybe," he said, pointing to their left. Without another word, he took off walking in that direction, and Sara fell in behind him.

"Should we really be moving toward the gunfire?" she asked.

He threw her a sharp sideways glance. "It's our job, Sara."

"I know that, but we're not in our jurisdiction and we're not armed. What are you going to do if we meet the shooter?"

They were moving through the trees, twigs and leaves snapping underfoot; and the snow was coming down now, really coming down.

"What if it's a hunter?" she asked. "We aren't in bright clothing—Grissom! Stop and think."

He stopped. He thought.

Then he made a little shrugging motion with his eyebrows. "Maybe we ought to turn around," Grissom admitted. "Could be someone just doing a little target practice."

"Good. Yes. Let's do that."

But he made no move to go back. Snow now covered their boot tops and threatened their knees. They were deep in the woods, deep in snow, somewhere on the slope behind the hotel—they could still make out its towers through the skeletal branches and haze of snow. Soon it would be dark, and they'd have to navigate by the lights of the hotel.

Looking at Grissom, Sara realized that his varsity jacket wasn't doing him much more good than his windbreaker would have. The CSI supervisor was working to hide it, but he obviously was shivering. His cheeks were rosy, the snow in his hair making it appear more white than gray.

Still, she knew him well enough to know the cold wasn't what was on his mind.

Just ahead, a round wooden pole peeked above the drifting snow, bearing two signs: one, pointing left, read Partridgeberry Trail to Lakeshore Path (whatever that was); the other, pointing to the right, said Forest Drive.

"Either of these paths get us back faster?" Grissom asked.

Sara shrugged. "As long as we can see the hotel, we're okay."

"But we can go back the way we came, right? You do know the way."

She twitched a sheepish smile. "Well, to be honest . . . when we were looking for those snowflies, and we cut through the woods . . ."

"Sara, if we're lost, say we're lost."

"We're not lost," Sara insisted. "If you look through there, you can see the hotel."

He turned to look at the path they'd carved coming up the trail. Already the snow filled in their tracks and, if they tried retracing their steps, the guesswork would soon begin. . . .

"Look, I've got my cell phone," she said. "Why don't we just call the hotel and tell them where we are?"

Without answering, Grissom looked down where the Partridge-berry Trail ought to be, then back in the direction they'd been going, then sharply back toward the Partridgeberry Trail, his nose in the air, sniffing the wind.

"Grissom," Sara said. "This is no time to be a guy. Asking for directions is nothing to be ashamed of."

He kept sniffing.

She continued: "Let's just phone the hotel and tell them we're . . ." Something about the look on his face stopped her. "What?"

His nose still high, the snow turning his eyebrows white, he asked, "You smell that?"

Now Sara sniffed the air. "Grilling, maybe?"

"In this weather? No . . . I recognize that smell!"

And Grissom took off running, kicking up snow as he struggled to sprint through the deepening white stuff. Without thinking, Sara plunged after him; it was like trudging through sand.

"Grissom! Wait up!"

But he did not slow for her.

She didn't know why they were running, where they were going or what had set Grissom off; but she suspected what it was and knew she wasn't going to like it.

Grissom just kept running, his head swiveling, and when he finally stopped it was so sudden she almost barreled into him.

She let out a squeak, and lurched to the right to avoid colliding with Grissom, who turned and sprinted left into the woods.

Sara slipped, gathered herself, then tore off after him again. "Grissom!"

He fell to his knees, maybe ten yards in front of her, as if seized by the urge to pray. When she caught up and bent to help him, she realized he was scooping up handfuls of snow, and throwing them at a burning human body.

The snow hissed and steamed when it struck the flames. Swallowing quickly to avoid being sick, Sara dropped to her knees and joined him in flinging handfuls of snow at the burning body.

Finally, after what seemed like hours, but was probably only a couple of minutes, of heaping snow on the body, the fire was extinguished. For the most part, the flames seemed to have been centered on the chest and face of a male who lay on his back, his arms at his sides, his legs slightly splayed.

Reaching carefully, avoiding the still steaming torso, Grissom felt the man's wrist for a pulse.

"Damnit," Grissom said bitterly, as if this were his fault. "Dead."

"What happened here? Not spontaneous combustion, certainly."

Grissom took a quick look around. "No. There are other sets of tracks here." He pointed further down the hill toward the hotel. "Give me your cell phone; I'll call 911. You start taking pictures of everything—fast. The way this snow's coming down, this crime scene will be history in fifteen minutes."

"It's a digital camera. . . ."

They both knew that in some states, photographs taken on a digital camera were inadmissible in court—digital doctoring was simply too easy.

"It's what we have," Grissom said. "We can both testify to that. Get started."

A comforting sense of detachment settling down on her, Sara tossed Grissom the phone and got to work.

She'd start with the body, then work her way outward from there. She logged the facts in her head as she took her photos. He was a white man between nineteen and twenty-five, judging from his young-looking hands—tall, maybe six feet, six feet one, 175 to 185, dark hair, most of it burned off, wearing a navy blue parka, mostly melted now, over a T-shirt (black possibly, but that might have been the charring), jeans, boots and, surprisingly, no gloves.

Sara devoted a couple dozen shots to the body—already planning to erase the nature photos, if need be—and was careful to capture as much detail as she could. Then she moved to the tracks in the snow. They were already filling in; she took close-ups and distance shots, wishing she had the tripod after all, using one of her gloves to show scale.

Five sets of tracks: three sets coming from the hotel, two sets going back. With the way the snow was coming down, Sara couldn't even tell if the other sets were the same approximate size, let alone whether they had been made by one set of boots or two. And her hand was freezing.

Grissom walked up to her. "How's it going?"

"Lost cause," she said, glumly. "Boot holes are filling up—no way to get a decent picture."

"That's the least of our problems," Grissom said. His voice was tight; he was either irritated or frustrated—maybe both. "I just got off the phone with the Ulster County Sheriff's Office."

"On their way?"

"Not exactly. Deputy says they might have a car out here . . . tomorrow."

She brushed snow off her face. "That's not funny."

"Am I laughing? It's snowing so hard they've closed the roads."

"Well . . . I guess that's no surprise."

"Add to that, they've had a major chain reaction accident up on Interstate 87. . . . All the available deputies and state troopers are working that scene."

"Shit." She was hopping now, trying to stay warm.

"So we're on our own."

"On our own. . . ."

Grissom gestured toward the smoldering human chunk of firewood. "Our victim was already dead when the fire started, or he would have been face down."

"I'm too cold to think that one through. Help me."

"Sara, nobody alive stays on his back in the snow with his face on fire."

"I see your point."

Grissom headed back to the corpse. "We need to try to determine cause of death."

She fell in with him, slipping her camera in her parka pocket. "Okay. But with this snow coming down, we can't treat the body with the respect it deserves."

"That's a given."

They bent down over him, one on either side, and began carefully wiping away the snow, which already threatened to bury him.

"No visible wounds other than the burns," Sara said. "Were you thinking those gunshots we heard—"

"I'm not thinking anything yet. Just observing." Slowly, Grissom rolled the body onto its right side. He pointed to a spot in the middle of the victim's back. "Entrance wound."

"Looks like a .38."

"Or a little smaller."

Sara, teeth chattering, let out a nervous laugh and Grissom looked up sharply at her.

"Sorry," she said, and held up her gloved hands in surrender. "My bad . . . I was just thinking of something you taught me when I first joined CSI."

"What?"

She sighed a little cloud and said, "First on the scene, first suspect. . . . And this time it's us."

He reacted with an eyebrow shrug. "Other prime suspects include people the victim knew, relatives, friends . . . and we're strangers."

"Lots of people are killed by strangers."

He nodded, looking toward the tracks in the snow. "How do you see this?"

Sara squinted, thinking it quickly through. "Well. . . . He's being followed by two people . . . with a gun, or guns. They've brought him out here to kill him."

"Then why all the shots? I only find one wound."

"All right," Sara said, processing that. "Two people chasing him, missing him, finally one of them got him, then they set him on fire."

A branch cracked behind them and Sara reflexively reached for the pistol that wasn't on her hip as she spun toward the sound.

"Whoa, Nellie!" Herm Cormier said, holding up his hands in front of him. "It's just me and Constable Maher."

Sara noted that Cormier had a .30-06 Remington rifle slung over a shoulder, the barrel pointed down. He'd traded in the Mackinaw for a heavy fur-lined coat; a stocking cap came down over his ears, and he wore leather gloves.

Maher was encased in a parka and wore a backpack. He too wore gloves and a stocking cap. "What the hell happened here?" he asked.

"Gunshot wound to the back," Grissom said. "At some point the victim was set on fire . . ."

"Jesus H. Christ," Cormier said, his voice hollow. He had stepped around them, and now stood looking down at the charred body in the snow.

Sara asked, "You know him, Mr. Cormier?"

Shaking his head and turning away, an ashen Cormier said, "Hell's bells, he's burned so damn bad, I . . ."

"But do you know him?" Sara pressed.

Cormier choked like he might heave, then swallowed and said, "I can't rightly tell."

"How about the clothes?" Grissom asked.

Glancing at the body, then turning away again, Cormier said, "That don't help. . . . We better call the sheriff."

Grissom filled them in on that score.

"Did you check for a wallet?" Maher asked.

"Just getting ready to," Sara said. "You want to give me a hand?"

Maher propped the body on its side while Sara patted the pockets; nothing.

Looking from one man to the other, Grissom asked, "What are you two doing out here?"

Swiveling toward Grissom, Cormier said, "Jenny—that's the little gal at the desk Ms. Sidle spoke to about the weather—she told me you two were out walking . . . and that she'd told Ms. Sidle the snow wouldn't be too bad. Turns out this could be one of them hundred-year storms."

"Really," Grissom said.

Cormier nodded. "Weather Bureau's predicting as much as twenty-four inches in the next twenty-four hours."

Maher piped in, "Mr. Cormier decided he better come find you two. I overheard his conversation with the desk clerk and, since I track in the snow for a living, I offered to come along."

"We better start gettin' back," Cormier said.

Sara dusted snow off herself. "How are we going to get this body back to the hotel?"

Cormier said, "For now, we got to leave it here."

"We can't do that," Sara said. "That body is evidence, and this crime scene is disappearing as we speak."

Cormier shrugged. "Ms. Sidle, we try to carry him with us, he could end up being the death of us all. These storms get worse 'fore they get better."

"But . . ."

"This is a murder," Grissom said, gesturing about them. "What about the evidence?"

Maher stepped forward now. "Dr. Grissom, excuse me, but I've been working winter crime scenes my whole career. The evidence is going to be fine."

"In a blizzard."

Maher nodded, once. "The snow will help preserve it, not destroy it. But you and Ms. Sidle are right—we can't just leave the scene unguarded. For one thing, predators could come along and make a meal of our victim."

Sara asked, "What do you suggest?"

"I suggest," Maher said, "we take turns guarding the scene—the three of us. I can help you work the crime scene after the storm breaks."

Sara had no better idea, and when she looked Grissom's way, she could almost see the wheels turning in the man's head. The only two people she figured for sure weren't suspects were Grissom and herself.

Everybody else was a candidate.

But her gut said to trust Maher. He'd come to the conference alone and, like them, didn't seem to know anyone here.

"Any other options?" Grissom asked.

Maher shook his head. "We stay out here now and Mr. Cormier's right. There'll be five deaths to investigate."

Grissom said, "All right—how do we get back?"

Sara said, "Grissom . . . are you sure about—"

"Constable Maher is the expert here, not us. We'll have to take his word for it."

Maher turned to the hotel manager. "Mr. Cormier, I'm going to need your rifle."

"Why?"

"So I can take the first shift."

"I'm not as keen on this idea," Cormier said, "as you and Mr. Grissom."

Maher pointed toward the hotel. "In two hours, I want you to lead one of these two back up here to relieve me. You can find this spot, in the dark, right?"

"Course I can, no problem . . . but that ain't the issue. This weather, it's beautiful from a distance . . . up close, it can get god-damned ugly."

"Can't leave the crime scene unsecured," Maher insisted.

Grissom said, "Mr. Cormier, please."

Reluctantly, Cormier held out the rifle.

Maher said, "Hold that just another minute, eh?"

The Canadian withdrew something shiny from his backpack. He unfolded what looked to be a large silver tablecloth.

"Space blanket," he explained with a smile. "Good for holding in the heat. Thought one of you might need it. Dr. Grissom, if you could give me a hand. . . ."

Grissom took one side, Maher the other, and the pair covered the corpse.

"This will help preserve the site," Maher said. "Once the snow stops we can investigate the scene."

"But it'll be under two feet of snow by then," Sara pointed out.

Maher gave her a lopsided grin. "And that's a bad thing?"

"Of course!"

His smile straightened out and widened. "Ms. Sidle, I know a few tricks—if we were in the desert, wouldn't you?" Then a gust of snowy wind blew through, and seemed to carry off Maher's smile. "I don't want this man's killer to get away any more than you do."

Grissom surprised her by putting a hand on her shoulder. Sara stared at the fingertips touching her coat. She tried to analyze her feelings, but suddenly felt paralyzed. Then, with the wind picking up to a near howl, she heard Grissom's voice from what sounded like far away. "Whoever did this won't get away from us."

"Now," Maher said, "I need you to take the long way out of here—back the way you two must have come, judging from the tracks."

Finally, Cormier handed over the rifle to the constable. "Sure I can't talk you out of this lunacy?"

"Positive. Just remember, I need you to bring one of them back here to relieve me."

Nodding, Cormier said, "All right, but it's crazy."

Maher turned to Grissom. "I know you two don't have much experience with winter, but we're going to have to guard this scene until the snow stops."

Sara stepped up. "All night?"

"However long it takes."

Grissom said, "Makes sense. Two-hour shifts sounds good. I'll come up next, then Sara."

Maher nodded.

Cormier said, "We better get going—be dark soon, and we don't want to spend those two hours getting down to the hotel."

Maher took a small black box out of his coat pocket. "GPS," he said.

Sara knew that it would be easier for them to find this spot again with the use of Maher's global positioning unit.

"That's a small one," she said, admiringly.

"Yeah, brand new, eh? Just breakin' it in." He punched a few buttons and handed the gizmo to Grissom. "Use this to find your way back," the Canadian advised.

"Anything else?" asked Grissom.

"Yeah, bring coffee on the return trip—for me and you."

Sara asked the Canadian, "Any suggestions for when we get back to the hotel?"

"Check around the buildings for footprints. If the killer or killers went all the way down this slope, they had to come out somewhere. If they went straight down, the tracks'll probably start around the back of the building."

"All right," Grissom said.

Cormier seemed to be working hard to keep his back to the corpse, even though the space blanket and the beginnings of a layer of snow already covered it. And when Maher gave him the high sign to start back up the trail, Cormier was obviously eager to go. Sara and Grissom dropped in behind him.

"How do we know," Sara asked Grissom quietly, making sure

Cormier, whom they'd lagged behind somewhat, couldn't hear, "that we can trust Maher?"

"We don't."

"Then why . . . ?"

"If we accept him at face value," Grissom said, "he's a real boon to us—an expert on winter crime scenes, which we're not."

"Granted. But, not counting us, he and Mr. Cormier were the first on the scene . . . making them suspects."

"Well," Grissom said, "if we've left the murderer behind with the body of his victim, he will try to cover his tracks . . . and not just with snow."

"You mean . . . he'll give himself away."

"Yes. We didn't mention that you'd taken extensive photos of the victim and the crime scene, before he and Mr. Cormier got there."

Sara smiled slyly at her boss. "And we won't mention it, will we?"

Grissom answered with a smile and a shake of the head, and as they trudged after Cormier, toward the towers of the hotel, their cozy, shared conspiracy almost made her feel warm.

Almost.

4

Seated on a stool in a musical equipment shop on Tropicana Avenue, Warrick Brown strummed the C.F. Martin DSR guitar, forming a mellow C major 7 chord.

"Sweet," Warrick said. "How much you say, again?"

Sitting on a Peavey amplifier nearby in a MUSIC GO ROUND T-shirt, Mark Ruebling stroked his chin thoughtfully. "They're going for $2,499 new . . . I can let you have that beauty for $1,400."

The shop had opened a little over four months ago, and Warrick had been one of the first customers through the door. Always on the lookout for good musical gear, he'd liked how Ruebling, the owner, gave him fair value for trade-ins and didn't try to gouge on new items.

Like the DSR Sugar Ray, for example, a solid-body mahogany; Warrick knew—having been to the Martin company's website—that the store owner spoke the truth about the retail price. Still, nobody sold anything full retail these days, and fourteen hundred was a lot of green.

Warrick had been getting heavier and heavier into his music, partly because what had been the other great passion of his life—gambling— he now knew was a sickness. He already had an acoustic guitar, a decent, funky old Gibson he'd picked up in a pawnshop; but not one anywhere near as fine as this Martin.

"That's a tempting offer, Mark."

The store owner nodded, his chin still in his hand.

"But," Warrick said, "you know I been trying to deal with my temptations."

Ruebling smiled slyly. "Not all temptations lead to sin, my friend."

"True. But even at that price, it's a sinful lot of money for a public servant . . . How about I think on it, get back to you?"

"No problem. I'll hold it for you, few days. Just let me know what you want to do."

Now it was Warrick's turn to nod, playing it coy and low-key, when both of them knew damn well he'd end up taking the guitar. But maybe Mark would carve off another C note or so. . . .

And in the meantime Warrick could work on convincing himself that spending that much money wouldn't break him. Funny thing was, Warrick had never worried about having enough money back when he gambled. Like all degenerate gamblers, he always figured he'd win and then there would be plenty to spread around.

Reading his customer's mind, Ruebling said, "Seems to me, Warrick, cleaning up and livin' the straight life has turned you kinda conservative."

"Gotta be, with you so liberal with my money."

The two men exchanged smiles, as Warrick handed the guitar back to Ruebling, then checked his watch—time to head in.

Warrick liked how late the stores stayed open in this town—even a graveyard shift zombie like him could do a little shopping on the way to work. Growing up in Vegas made him prejudiced, Warrick knew, but there was nowhere else in the world he would rather live . . . even though with his gambling jones, no other place could be worse for him.

Generally Warrick showed up at CSI a half-hour early, with Nick maybe five or six minutes behind him. He went straight to the break room, poured himself a cup of coffee and strode to the locker room to change. The leather jacket he wore into work would never see a crime scene. He changed pullover sweaters as well, trading this month's tan one for last year's gray one.

Locker closed, he plopped onto the bench, sipped from his coffee and imagined himself in his living room playing that Martin acoustic. The thought gave him a warm feeling—like hitting twenty-one at blackjack. He closed his eyes and leaned back, his head resting against the cool metal of his locker.

"Asleep on the job already?" Nick's voice.

Keeping his eyes closed, Warrick said, "Let a man daydream."

"Is that possible on night shift? . . . What's she look like?"

"You must know, I'm playing my new guitar I haven't bought yet."

"Oh boy—the Lenny Kravitz fantasy again?"

Warrick opened one eye and looked up at Nick, who stood over him with a smile on half of his face. "Now, Nick, don't be dissin' Lenny."

"I wasn't dissin' Lenny. I would never diss Lenny. . . . You, maybe. But not Lenny."

Warrick opened the other eye and couldn't stop from smiling. "You're gettin' an early start. . . . Seen Catherine yet?"

Nick shook his head, going to his own locker. "I came straight in here." He quickly changed shirts, then the two of them went off in search of Catherine Willows, currently their acting boss.

They spotted her moving briskly down the corridor just outside the layout room. Warrick took one look at her and thought, *If she can afford that wardrobe, I can swing that Martin.* Today—tonight—fashionplate Catherine wore an oxblood leather jacket with a silk scarf of white, gold and maroon flowers. Nick fell in on one side of her, Warrick the other.

"Where we headed?" Warrick asked.

"Where is it always lively around here?" Catherine asked rhetorically.

"The morgue," Nick said.

"Right you are, Nick," Catherine said. "Our vic is still the only body of evidence we have . . . though that's about to change."

"I like change," Warrick said. "I'm in favor of change."

She brandished a file thicker than a Russian novel. "We've ID'ed our vic," she said, flashing a triumphant smile. "And you're never going to guess who she is."

"Gris doesn't let me guess," Nick said.

Warrick said, "Amelia Earhart?"

"Not that big a media star," Catherine admitted, as they walked along. "Does the name Missy Sherman ring any bells?"

"One or two," Nick said. "Missing housewife, right?"

"Had her fifteen minutes of infamy, a year or so ago," Warrick added. "She our ice queen?"

"She is indeed," Catherine said. "Missing Persons database coughed up her prints, this afternoon."

They stopped and she showed them a photo of the Sherman woman—it was their frozen victim, all right, and she was warmly beautiful, dark bright eyes flashing, pert-nosed, with a vivacious smile. Warrick had the sick feeling he often had, toward the start of a murder investigation, as he registered the reality of the human life, lost.

"So, then, day shift told the husband?" Nick asked.

"No," Catherine said, and put the picture away. She started walking again and Warrick and Nick fell in like nerds in a high school hallway tagging after the prom queen. "They're under the same OT restrictions we are—if it's night shift's case, it can wait till night shift."

"Jesus," Warrick breathed. "Guy's sitting at home, his wife's dead and nobody tells him 'cause of budget cuts?"

"We have to specifically request day shift help—in triplicate," Catherine said, with a humorless smile.

"I don't want to tell the husband," Nick said. "It's not CSIs' job to tell the husband."

Catherine nodded and her reddish-blonde hair shimmered. "I have a call in to Brass—we want to be there for that, though. Anyway, I want to go through the file one more time, before we have a look at Mr. Sherman."

They stepped into the anteroom of the morgue, the area where the CSIs would wash up and get into their scrubs, if an autopsy were going on. Warrick said, "You know the case, Cath? All I remember is, housewife evaporates, details at eleven."

"You're fuzzy on it," Catherine said, " 'cause Ecklie's people worked that one—Melissa 'Missy' Sherman, married, white female, thirty-three, no children. She and her husband, Alex, lived in one of those new housing developments south of the airport."

"Which one?" Nick asked.

"Silverado Development." She thumbed quickly to a page in the file. "Nine six one three Sky Hollow Drive."

"I lived in Vegas all my life," Warrick said, "and I have no idea where that is."

"Across from Charles Silvestri Junior High," Catherine said.

"Home of the Sharks," Nick put in.

Warrick and Catherine just looked at him.

"Football," Nick said, as if that explained it all.

"That's twisted, man," Warrick said, then asked Catherine, "was hubby ever a serious suspect in her disappearance?"

"Well, you know he was a suspect," Catherine said.

The spouse always was.

"But," she continued, "serious? Let's just say Ecklie and the day shift detectives didn't find anything."

Warrick smirked humorlessly. "Ecklie couldn't find the hole in the doughnut he's eating."

"No argument," Catherine said, "but apparently this was a fairly mysterious missing persons case. That was part of why the media was attracted to the story—June Cleaver vanishes."

Warrick frowned. "And nothing at all on Ward?"

"They were college sweethearts at Michigan State, got married and moved out here when Alex Sherman graduated from college. Missy finished her finance degree at UNLV."

"Maybe they're not Ward and June," Nick said. "Maybe they're Barbie and Ken."

Catherine shrugged. "Looks like a perfect life, till the day she and her girlfriend went out shopping and for lunch, after which Missy was expected to drive straight home."

"Instead, she drove into the Bermuda Triangle," Warrick said.

Nick asked, "Wasn't the car found?"

Catherine nodded. "In the parking lot at Mandalay Bay, a 2000 Lexus RX300. That's an SUV. She and her friend ate at the China Grill . . . then poof."

Nick's eyes narrowed. "You mean, she never even made it to the car?"

"Oh she got that far. Ecklie's people found a doggy bag in the Lexus. But after that . . ." Catherine held her hands up in a who-knows gesture.

The trio found Dr. Robbins behind his desk, where he was jotting some notes; he looked up as they neared.

"Hey Doc," Catherine said. "Got ya an ID on Jane Doe."

Robbins gave her a satisfied smile. "Melissa Sherman. We've met."

Catherine frowned. "Did somebody call you with the missing persons info?"

The coroner's smile expanded. "No. Some of us are just good detectives."

"You figured out this was Missy Sherman?" Warrick asked. "Where do you keep the Ouija board?"

"In her stomach," Robbins said. "That is, the clue was in her stomach. And what's interesting is, it gives us a more reasonable window for time of death. Freezing or no freezing."

Catherine was nodding, half-smiling, as she said, "Let me guess—Chinese food."

Robbins tapped the tip of his nose with his index finger. "Undigested beef and rice in her stomach. When she was killed, the body stopped working and the freezing kept the contents from decomposing."

"And the Chinese food led you to Missy Sherman how?" asked Warrick, not sure whether he was annoyed or impressed.

"It reminded me of the doggy bag they found in her car when the Sherman woman went missing. I checked the original evidence report and it stated Missy Sherman's doggy bag contained Mongolian beef and rice. That, in turn, prompted me to recall we'd gotten a copy of her dental records when she first disappeared . . . just in case, you know, a body turned up, as it too often does in these cases . . . and I just finished matching those dental records to the body you brought in yesterday."

"Wow," Nick said. "Good catch, Doc."

"You are the man," Warrick admitted. "And now nobody can say we don't have a homicide."

Catherine already had her cell phone in her hand. She punched the speed dial and waited. After a few seconds, she said, "Jim, it's Catherine. We've ID'ed the body from Lake Mead: Missy Sherman—that missing persons case from—"

She waited while Brass spoke, then looked at her watch, and said, "You want to go at this hour?"

Brass said something else, then Catherine said, "All right—we'll meet you there."

Punching the END button on her phone, she turned to Warrick and Nick. "Brass was out on a call. He'll meet us at the Sherman place."

Before long, they were turning right off Maryland Parkway onto Silverado Ranch Boulevard; then the Tahoe swung into the Silverado Development and followed a maze of smaller streets back to Sky Hollow Drive, a neighborhood peaceful under a starry sky with a sliver of moon, asleep but for a few windows flickering with TV watching, and Warrick could've sworn he could hear the muffled laughter from the Conan O'Brien show audience.

A handsome mission-style stucco, 9613 was a tall, wide two story with a tile roof that seemed more pink than orange under the mercury-vapor streetlights. Large inset windows were at either end of the second floor with a smaller window, a bathroom maybe, in the center. A two-car garage was at left, flush with the double archways of a porch at right, leaving the dark-green front door in shadows.

For so nice a home, the lawn was modest—true of all the houses in the development—and had turned brown for the season, though evergreens along the porch provided splashes of green while blocking the view of the front-room picture window, whose drapes were shut, though light edged through. An upper-floor window, with closed curtains, also glowed.

The temperature again hovered around the forty-degree mark, just crisp enough to justify Warrick and Nick putting on CSI jackets. Brass, in his sportscoat, didn't seem to notice the chill; this was typical of the detective, Warrick knew, as the man had spent a large chunk of his life in New Jersey, where a winter like this would rate as tropical.

They did not go up to the front door immediately. Instead, the detective and the three CSIs stood in the street next to the black Tahoe parked behind Brass's Taurus, and got their act together.

"What do we know about this guy?" Nick asked.

"I remember this case," Brass said. "I wasn't on it, but I sat and talked to the guys working it, often enough."

"What did they say about Sherman?" Warrick asked.

Brass shrugged. "Guy did all the right things—full cooperation, went on TV, begged for his wife to contact him or, if she was kidnapped, for the kidnappers to send a ransom demand. You probably saw some of that."

Nick was nodding.

With a shake of the head, Brass said, "They say Sherman seemed genuinely broken up."

"What does your gut say?" Warrick asked the detective.

"Just wasn't close enough to it to have a gut reaction. But in the car, on the way out here, I called Sam Vega—he caught the case, was lead investigator."

They had all worked with Detective Sam Vega when he did graveyard rotation. He was a smart, honest cop.

Catherine asked, "What did Sam have to say?"

"Well," Brass said, "at first, as convincing as Sherman seemed, Sam figured this was a kidnapping . . . but then when no ransom demand came in, he started looking at the husband again."

"Was Mrs. Sherman unhappy in her marriage?" Nick asked. "Could she have just run off, to start over someplace?"

Brass shook his head. "By all accounts she was a happy woman with a happy life, and if she was going to run off, why leave a doggy bag in the car?"

"People rarely carry leftovers into their new life," Catherine said.

Brass went on: "If she did run off, consider this: Missy Sherman took no money, no clothes, never called anyone from her cell phone, never e-mailed anybody—this woman just flat out disappeared, and didn't even bother with the puff of smoke."

"So she didn't run off," Warrick said.

"Anyway," Brass went on, "the longer this case dragged on, the harder Vega looked at the husband. This guy came up so clean, water beaded off him."

Catherine asked, "What was Sam Vega's bottom line on the husband?"

"Sam says Sherman seems like a right guy, who hasn't done anything weird or different or outa line, since Scotty beamed the poor bastard's wife to nowhere. No new girlfriend, no attempt to collect on the wife's life insurance policy, which wasn't that substantial, anyway—nothing."

"How'd he pay for that hacienda?" Warrick asked, with a nod toward the formidable stucco house.

"Very successful computer consultant," the detective said. "He's got some real estate too."

Nick asked, "What kinda real estate?"

"Apartments. Sherman makes good money. Pretty much pool the four of our salaries, and you got his annual income."

They stood there, contemplating that.

Then Catherine said, "Maybe we better stop loitering in the street before somebody in this nice quiet neighborhood calls the cops about the riffraff."

They followed Brass to the dark-green front door of the Sherman home; the four of them barely fit on the shallow porch. From the living room, they could hear voices—loud, animated.

"Movie," Nick said.

"Sounds like *Bad Boys*," Warrick said.

"Bad what?" asked Brass, wincing.

"*Bad Boys*," Nick said. "You know, Will Smith, Martin Lawrence—they're cops . . ."

"If they're cops," Brass said, "I'm a police dog."

Warrick and Nick exchanged he-said-it-not-us glances.

Smirking sourly, Brass turned back to the door.

Warrick was listening to the sounds from within. "That's a high-end sound system. He's watching a DVD."

"I'll be sure to put that in my report," Brass said, and rang the doorbell.

They waited. The loud movie voices ceased, then a few seconds later the door cracked open; one brown eye behind one wire-framed lens peeked cautiously out. "Yes?"

Brass held up his badge on its necklace. "Mr. Alex Sherman?"

The eye narrowed, examining the badge; then the door swung open wide, revealing another eye and the rest of his wire-framed glasses, and the rest of him.

Alex Sherman—six-two, easily, and in his midthirties—wore his black hair short, razor cut, and with his high cheekbones, dark brown eyes and straight nose he had a vaguely Indian look, though he was only moderately tanned. In his stocking feet, he wore gray sweatpants and a green tee shirt with a white Michigan State logo; his build said he worked out.

"What can I do for you, Detective?"

"May we come in?"

Sherman motioned for them to enter, eagerly, saying, "It's about Missy, isn't it? Is it about Missy?"

They stepped into a foyer with a small, round table next to the door and a framed black-and-white photo of Missy Sherman on top of it.

"Is there somewhere we can sit down, Mr. Sherman?" Brass asked evasively.

Anxious, Sherman led them to the right into a living room smaller than the Bellagio casino, though Warrick would've needed a tape measure to be sure. A massive wide-screen plasma TV monitor hung on the far wall; beneath it a small cabinet held stereo and video components with speakers scattered strategically around the room. A tan leather sofa ran under the picture window, its matching chair and hassock angled toward the television; to the right of the sofa was an easy chair in rough fabric with a faux Navajo design.

Sherman sat on the sofa, Brass next to him, while the others fanned out in front of them. Brass quickly identified himself and the CSIs by name.

"This is about Missy," Sherman said, "isn't it?"

"I'm afraid so," Brass said. "We saw a light on upstairs—is someone here with you?"

"No—I turn that light on so I don't have to walk up to the bedroom in the dark. Now, what news do you have about my wife?"

Brass paused; he swallowed. "I'm sorry, sir. Your wife was found—"

"You've found her?" Sherman said, jumping in, dark eyes wide.

"Her body was found, Mr. Sherman. Early this morning by a park ranger at Lake Mead."

"She's dead," he said incredulously, clearly not wanting to believe it.

"She's dead, yes."

Sherman covered his mouth with a hand, and then the tears began. And then he flung his glasses to the end table beside him, hunkered over and began to sob.

Warrick looked at the floor.

Catherine handed the man a small packet of tissues. Warrick could only admire her—she was always prepared, wasn't she?

After perhaps thirty seconds, Sherman said, "Missy can't be . . . why, after all this time . . . ? I thought . . . I hoped . . . you hear about amnesia, and . . ."

More comments, only semicoherent, tumbled from him, but within another thirty seconds, the sobbing had ceased, and he seemed to have hold of himself.

Brass asked gently, "Is there someone you'd like us to call for you? You probably shouldn't be alone now."

Sherman's reply had building anger in it. "I shouldn't be *alone* now? I shouldn't have had to be *alone* for all these months, but I was! Why didn't you find her last year? Maybe she'd be alive! She would be here, with me. . . . Missy's everything to me. You people, you *people* . . . !"

Catherine stepped forward, hands raised before her. "Mr. Sherman—we're very sorry for your loss. It's not good for someone who's had a blow like this to be alone."

Sherman appeared startled that someone had interrupted his tirade, and in such a compassionate manner; and that brought him back.

In a low, trembling voice, he said, "I'm sorry . . . I'm really sorry. I shouldn't be angry with you. I'm sure you did everything you could. . . . Where's Detective Vega?"

"We're with the night shift," Warrick said. "Detective Vega works days, right now. He'll be informed, and I know he'll be concerned. I'm sure he'll talk to you."

Nodding, lip trembling, Sherman said, "He . . . He tried . . . tried very hard."

Then Sherman just sat there, collapsed in on himself, like a child trying not to cry.

How Warrick hated this part of the job. But he knew that Gris would only remind him that the CSIs worked not just for the victims, but for their loved ones. Warrick and his associates couldn't make the pain of losing a wife or a sister or a friend go away; but at least they could try to provide some answers and—when the system worked the way it was supposed to—a modicum of justice.

Nick appeared from somewhere with a glass of water and handed it to Sherman, who took a short sip, then a longer drink. Hand shaking, he set the glass on the end table. "Thank you, Officer."

Nick just nodded.

"I love my wife very much," Sherman finally said. His voice had a quaver, but he had regained some composure. "And for a whole year I've had only questions with no answers. I just wanted Missy back alive. I should have known that after this long . . . Ever see that movie, with John Cleese?"

Brass frowned at the seeming non sequitur. "Sir?"

"He's trying to get somewhere and can't make it on time, just one damn thing after another . . ."

"Clockwise," Catherine said.

"Is that what it's called? Well, in that movie, John Cleese, he says, 'It's not the despair . . . I can handle the despair. It's the hope!' "

And Sherman began to laugh, only the laughter turned to tears again. But briefly, this time. "Like the big dope I am, I just kept hoping."

"In your position, we all would, Mr. Sherman," Catherine said. "We all would."

"And sir?" Warrick said. "You'll have plenty of time now, to come to grips with this. Don't beat yourself up."

Catherine glanced at Warrick, a bit of surprise in her expression, then said to Sherman, "You will make it through this. And, for what it's worth, we will be working very hard to find out who did this."

Sherman looked up at her, his forehead tightening. "You make it sound . . . She was killed?"

Brass said, "Yes, sir."

"Oh my God . . . oh my God . . ."

They let him cry. Warrick watched Catherine and Brass exchanging a series of looks that were a silent conversation about whether they should press on with any questioning, or if Sherman's grief made that impossible.

Brass seemed to want to stay at it. To give the man a chance to get himself together.

The tears slowed, then stopped. Sherman dried his face with some of Catherine's tissues. "There was a time when I . . . I can't believe I'm admitting this, but there was a time I actually wanted her to be dead."

Catherine said, "Mr. Sherman, you should—"

"If her body was found, that at least would mean the end of wondering. I sit here, sometimes all night, watching mindless movies, trying not to think where she might be. The later it was at night, the more horrible the possibilities. Now . . . now, that it's finally happened, I have a thousand questions, a million questions. Who would do this to Missy? *Why?*"

"This investigation is just starting," Brass said.

"It's not—You don't consider it just an old case that . . ."

"No. It's very much on the front burner. We hope to be able to answer some of your questions soon."

Swallowing hard, turning sideways toward the homicide cop, Sherman asked, "Was she . . . ? Did someone . . . ? Was . . . ?"

Brass didn't seem sure what Sherman meant, but Catherine said, "She was not sexually assaulted, Mr. Sherman. She died of suffocation."

"Suffocation . . . Missy?" Leaning forward and grasping Brass's hands, startling the detective, Sherman implored, "Jesus Christ man, what can you tell me? Where has she been for the last year? Who had her?"

"She wasn't strangled, sir," Catherine said. "We're not sure of the circumstances, where her suffocation is concerned. But she was not strangled."

"And we can't tell you where she's been all this time," the detective said. "But she appears to have been killed shortly after she disappeared."

"You said . . . Lake Mead. A ranger found her?"

Brass nodded.

"But that's . . . such a public place!" Sherman was growing outraged again. "How could she not be found, in over a year?"

Catherine stepped forward, crouched in front of the man and touched one of his hands, as if he were a small child she were comforting. "We understand how difficult this is for you, Mr. Sherman. But even though your wife was killed over a year ago, the person who committed that crime—or some associate of the murderer—only this morning placed her body in the park. That makes this a very new, active case . . . and we need to get right to work."

Sherman swallowed, nodded. "Anything you need. Anything."

"Well . . . to begin with, we must ask you to go over this one more time. It's been a long time since anyone looked at your wife's case with fresh eyes. And since we didn't work the case before, maybe we can find something that got overlooked the first time."

Gazing at her, his eyes still damp, Sherman nodded that he understood. "Where do we start?"

Catherine rose and backed up a little, giving Brass some room as the detective took over again. "From the beginning," he said. He withdrew the small tape recorder from his sportscoat pocket, adding, "And with your permission, we'll record this interview."

Turning sideways again, to look right at the detective, Sherman said, "No problem, Detective uh—what was your name, sir?"

"Brass."

Sherman took several deep breaths; he had another long drink of water. Then he said, "Whatever you need. Ask whatever you need to."

"All right. You last saw your wife when?"

"Thursday, December 6, 2001. That morning, before I went to work."

"Was everything all right that morning?"

Shrugging as he said it, Sherman said, "Fine. Great. We were a happy couple, Detective Brass."

"Tell us about that morning."

"Well . . . Missy was going shopping with her friend Regan

Mortenson; then they were supposed to finalize plans for the four of us to have dinner and a movie Saturday night."

"The four of you?"

"Missy and me . . . Regan and her husband, Brian."

"You two couples socialized frequently?"

Sherman nodded. "They've been our best friends for, oh . . . years. I don't think I would have made it through the last year without them. Regan's always stopping by to check on me, Brian and I have lunch, oh, twice a week, anyway."

"How and when did you meet them?"

"Missy and Regan went way back. Hell, they were sorority sisters at Michigan State—Tri Delts."

Warrick repressed a smile, reflexively remembering the old joke from his days at UNLV. Don't have a date? Tri Delt.

"After we moved out here," Sherman was saying, "Regan came out a year later. They weren't just sorority sisters, Missy and Regan, they really were like sister sisters. Anyway, Regan met Brian out here, and they got married."

"Brian Mortenson," Brass said, more for his own benefit than Sherman's.

"Yes. Great guy. Wonderful guy."

"And what does he do?"

"He's Events Coordinator for the Las Vegas Convention Center, sets up their programs and conventions . . ."

Heavy-duty job, Warrick thought.

Brass nodded. "And his wife?"

"Regan? She solicits funding for Las Vegas Arts."

"Is that a job, or volunteer work?"

"Volunteer."

"How long have you known Mr. Mortenson?"

"Oh, ten years, easily. . . . We met not long after Missy and I moved to Vegas. In fact, we introduced them, Regan and Brian. He and I were playing basketball at the health club we both belonged to; still do. He was sixth man at Bradley, Brian was."

Brass shifted on the couch. "Back to the day in question. You say Missy was here when you left for work."

"That's right."

"Presumably, then she went shopping with Regan."

"No presumably about it. Ask Regan—they went shopping, and had lunch together."

"And when did you first suspect something was wrong?"

"Almost immediately. From when I got home from work, I mean. If Missy wasn't planning to have supper, she'd have said something. And if there'd been a change of plan, she'd have called on the cell, or at least left me a note."

"So you were concerned."

"Well . . . not overly. Didn't get too worried at first. Her car wasn't here, I figured she ran up to Albertson's for something."

That was a local grocery chain.

"Or maybe ran out to get some carry-out," Sherman was saying. "If she got too busy to fix supper, she'd sometimes stop for Chinese or Italian."

Brass nodded. "How long before you started to worry?"

Sherman considered that. "I waited . . . maybe an hour. Then I called Regan. She said she hadn't seen Missy since lunch. I couldn't think of where she might be."

"Then what?"

"I called our usual take-out places—they hadn't seen her. I started in on all of her friends that I could think of, and none of them had seen her, either."

"Is that when you called the police?"

"No. I called Regan again, to see what kind of mood Missy'd been in. Regan said normal, fine, real good spirits. And then the paranoia set in . . . I mean, we were happy, but we had our arguments."

"Such as?"

"Well, I'd been on her about credit cards; she was buying a lot of clothes. I handle the finances, and she was kind of, you know, irresponsible at times. I told all this to Detective Vega."

"You'd had words about it recently?"

"Not . . . words. We bickered about it, not the night before she disappeared, but the night before that. Still, that was enough to get me stewing. I even went upstairs to see if her clothes were still in the closet. You know, thinking maybe she'd left me or something—not for real, just ran to her mom's or one of her sister's in a huff maybe. But everything was there."

"Did you call her family? Her mother, her sisters?"

He nodded glumly. "None of them had heard from her."

"So, Mr. Sherman—when did you call the police?"

Looking a little uncomfortable, Sherman said, "I heard that you can't file a missing persons report until someone has been gone twenty-four hours."

Brass shook his head. "Not always the case."

Sherman shrugged. "Well, that's what I believed. . . . So I waited all that night and didn't call 911 until the next morning."

Her voice low, Catherine said to Warrick, "That's why day shift got it instead of us."

Brass was asking, "What did you do that night, while you waited?"

Sherman sat slumping, his hands loosely clasped. "I . . . tried to think of where she might go and went driving around looking for her car. First, the grocery store, Albertson's, the one over here on Maryland Parkway." He pointed vaguely off to his right. "If she was mad at me, maybe she was driving around the city, pouting. . . . She could pout, at times. So I just started driving around, all over the place. The Strip. I started with Mandalay Bay where she'd last been seen."

"That's where officers found her car," Nick put in, "the next day, right?"

Sherman nodded vigorously. "Yes . . . but I didn't see it there. Somehow I missed it."

Warrick noted this: the first real inconsistency, the only striking anomaly in the husband's story, so far.

"2000 Lexus," Brass said. "Nice car."

"You wouldn't think I could've missed it, but I did. In my defense, I was pretty worked up at this point . . . frantic. And it is a huge parking lot."

Brass nodded. "So, you just drove around all night?"

"Not all night. Only till about ten . . . and then I came home. I suppose I hoped that she'd've come home while I was out . . . but, of course, she hadn't."

"So what did you do then?"

"What I always do when I want to get my mind off my troubles—put in a movie." He sat up and a faint near-smile crossed his lips. "Missy and me, we're kind of movie buffs. . . . You can see the home theater here, pretty elaborate. We watched a lot of movies."

"So," Warrick said, "you just popped a DVD in and waited."

"Yes," Sherman said, looking up at Warrick. "I didn't want to worry—I didn't want to be ridiculous. But I kept looking out the front window every five minutes to see if she was pulling up. At some point, I finally just dropped off to sleep. When I woke up and found she still wasn't home, I called 911 right away."

"Then the police took over," Brass said.

"Yes."

Brass said, "Thank you, Mr. Sherman," and clicked off the recorder.

"Is . . . is that it? Is that all?"

"Actually, Mr. Sherman," Brass said, "we would like to take you up on your offer to help."

"Certainly. . . . Anything at all."

"Good. Because I'd like to have our crime scene investigators take a look around."

Warrick winced—that was a poor choice of words, considering . . .

Sherman flushed. "Crime scene . . . ? Are you saying that after all I've been through, I'm a suspect, now? In my wife's murder?"

Brass began, "Mr. Sherman, please . . ."

His spine straight, his eyes wild, Sherman almost shouted: "You come to tell me she's dead after a year of me praying for a fucking miracle that she might be alive and I open up my heart to you and you have the goddamn audacity to accuse me?"

"Mr. Sherman, no one's accusing you of anything—" Warrick protested.

"It sure as hell sounds like it! Crime scene my ass!"

"Sir," Nick said, "we know it's been a year, and that things have changed, but we have to look."

"I don't have to let you," he said, almost petulantly. "You need a search warrant, don't you?"

"You don't have to let us," Brass acknowledged. "But I was taking you at your word, when you said you wanted to help."

For several long seconds, Sherman just sat there, his hands balling into fists that bounced on his knees; he was clearly struggling to decide what to do.

Catherine crouched in front of him again. "You loved your wife—we can all see that. But if there's so much as a shred of evidence in this house that might lead us to her killer, wouldn't you want us to find it?"

Slowly, the fists unballed. "Of . . . of course."

She kept her voice low, soothing. "Then let us do our job. We want to catch your wife's murderer as much as you want us to. But to do that, we need to examine everything pertinent to the case . . . and that includes this house. Unless you've gotten rid of her things, Missy's home will have a lot to tell us about her."

Sherman swallowed and sighed . . . and nodded. "I understand. I'm sorry I lost my temper. It's just . . ."

Catherine touched his hand. "No problem."

"And I haven't gotten rid of her things, I could never do that. Everything's exactly the way it was the day she left. I haven't moved so much as her toothbrush. I always hoped the door would open and she'd walk in and we'd just pick up from where we left off. . . ."

He began to cry again.

Several awkward moments crawled past, as the CSIs looked at each other, wondering if they should get started or not.

Then Sherman said, "If . . . if it will help, take all the . . . all the time you need. You won't be keeping me up. It's not like I'll be sleeping tonight."

Diving right in, Warrick asked, "I have to ask this, sir. Do you own a freezer?"

"Not a stand-alone freezer. Just the little one in the top of the refrigerator."

"Not a chest-style freezer, either?"

The man shook his head.

"Ever had one?"

"No." He looked curious about their questions, but pale, and Catherine could almost see him deciding he didn't want to know why they were asking.

They went out to the Tahoe and got their equipment; inside the house, they split up. Catherine took the bathroom and the master suite; they didn't want Sherman getting upset about one of the men pawing through Mrs. Sherman's things, so Catherine volunteered for that duty. While Brass talked informally with Sherman in the living room, Nick and Warrick divided up the rest of the house. Nick started in the kitchen, Warrick in the garage. As with most houses in Vegas, there was no basement.

Warrick didn't expect to find anything in the garage, really, at least not as far as the freezer was concerned. Even if Sherman had at one time had a freezer, and used it to freeze his wife, it would be long gone by now. But the criminalist did check the floor for telltale marks of a freezer or any other appliance having been dragged across; nothing. A small workbench with a toolbox atop it hugged the near wall. Warrick looked it over and checked the toolbox but again came up empty.

Missy's Lexus, returned by Ecklie's people months ago, sat on the far side, Sherman's Jaguar parked beside it. The garage had sheet-rock walls, a large plastic trash can and a smaller recycling receptacle in the corner nearest the double overhead door. One of those pull-down stair-cases led to a storage space above the false ceiling. Walking around the cars, Warrick saw some gardening tools and a lawn mower against the far wall.

The place seemed only slightly less sterile than a hospital. Shaking his head at the cleanliness, Warrick tried the door of the Lexus and found it unlocked. Even though the Chinese food had sat in the car for some time, the smell was gone. In fact, Warrick noticed, the car smelled new. Too new—it had been professionally cleaned. Looking down at the carpeting, then studying the seats closely, confirmed his diagnosis: the SUV was cleaner than the day it had left the showroom.

After closing the door, he walked around between the cars and pulled the rope for the pull-down stairs. He climbed the flimsy ladder, pulled out his mini-Mag and light-sabered it around the darkened storage space. A few cardboard boxes dotted the area, mostly close to the opening, and when Warrick touched them, they seemed empty.

Moving the beam from right to left, he paused occasionally, looked at something a little closer, then slid the light further along. Nothing seemed out of the ordinary. Putting the butt of the mini-Mag into his mouth, he leaned over and undid the folded flaps of the nearest card-board box. Inside he saw the Styrofoam packing that came on either end of the DVD player he'd seen inside. The next box had held the re-ceiver for the home theater system. It too contained only original pack-ing. Warrick finished quickly and rejoined the others back inside.

The search had taken nearly two hours and they had nothing to show for it. As they packed up and prepared to leave, Warrick wan-dered into the living room where Brass and Sherman still sat. "Mr. Sherman, I take it you had your wife's car washed?"

Sherman started. "Why, yes . . . yes I did. At one of those places where they really give it the works. Did I do something wrong? The other officers told me I could, they said they were finished with the Lexus and it was covered with what they said was fingerprint powder. I mean, the car was really filthy."

Warrick nodded. "You didn't do anything wrong, sir."

"You guys about ready?" Brass asked.

"Catherine's done and Nick's just putting the drain back together in the kitchen. We're done."

Brass rose and shook Sherman's hand. "I'm sorry for the intrusion, but I'm sure you understand. And we are very grateful for your cooperation."

"Whatever you need. Whenever you need it."

Catherine trooped in, looking beat.

Sherman sat up. "Any luck?"

Dredging up a smile, Catherine said, "Too soon to tell. Thank you again, sir."

All of them thanked their host and paid their sympathies, then followed Brass outside onto the sidewalk. The houses around them were dark now, and silent.

"Anything?" Nick asked Catherine, his voice a strained whisper.

She shook her head and, with her eyes, posed the same question of Warrick.

"Nothing," he whispered. "Can't blame him for wanting to wash the fingerprint crap and luminol outa his vehicle."

Nick was shaking his head, his expression discouraged. "A year's a long time," Nick said.

Brass heaved a sigh, then said, "I'll talk to the Mortensons tomorrow—maybe they can tell us something."

"It's no wonder we found ice inside Missy," Warrick said, "with a case gone this cold."

And they got in their vehicles and drove back to HQ.

5

Walking single file through the snow, Herm Cormier remained in the lead, followed by Sara, with Grissom bringing up the rear. They had trudged through a winter landscape tinted blue by twilight, though by the time they could see the hotel again, night had swallowed dusk, and the lights of the wonderfully ungainly conglomerate of buildings glittered in the darkness as if the lodge were a colossal jewel box.

By the time they reached the back parking lot, Sara's breath was coming in short, raspy gulps. Despite the cold, she was perspiring, her hair lank and wet against her cheeks, forehead, and nape of her neck, and inside her coat she could feel a trickle of moisture down her back. Mostly it was from the exercise of the forced march down the mountain; but some of it was excitement, nerves.

Less than a dozen cars were scattered about the mostly deserted lot, all of them covered by various depths of powder, ice particles sparkling back the reflected lights of the hotel. The snow showed no sign of letting up—if anything, it seemed to be coming down harder now, as if God couldn't wait to sweep their evidence under a gigantic white rug.

"Is Maher going to be all right out there?" Sara asked, as they stopped in the lot, convening in a little huddle. "Storm's getting worse. . . ."

"The constable knows what he's doing," Grissom said. "He's better suited to thrive under these conditions than we are."

With a chuckle, Cormier said, "Constable Maher lives in weather like this, Ms. Sidle. . . . He'll be fine. We just don't want to leave him up there alone for too long a spell."

A spell? she thought. This guy was a fugitive from a Pepperidge Farm commercial.

Sara, who was usually game for anything in an investigation, was not looking forward to her own shift at the snowy crime scene. And she found it difficult to accept that the cold and snow would preserve the crime scene; she was glad to have those photos to fall back on, digital or not.

"Any idea how long this'll keep up, Mr. Cormier?" Grissom asked, looking up into the falling snow, white shimmering along his eyelashes.

Squinting up into the snow himself, the hotel man said, "Storm like this'll usually blow itself out, oh, in a day or so . . . no more'n two."

"What happens to the conference?" Sara asked.

Shaking his head, flinging snow, Cormier said, "It may be just you two and Constable Maher. Not many were coming in early . . . instructors like you folks mostly . . . and those that come in today on later flights, well they sure as H aren't gonna join us. Only a few other guests got here before the downfall commenced . . . but when we get inside, I'll check the register, just the same."

"You don't expect anyone to trail in tomorrow," Grissom said.

As if the storm had its own answer for Grissom, a howl blew through the parking lot, stirring up a new storm of snow.

"We won't see anyone else make it in for at least twenty-four hours . . . unless it's by sled or sleigh."

Grissom wiped moisture from his face and asked: "Did anyone leave, after the storm started?"

Cormier shook his head again. "Can't rightly say—guests usually check out no later'n one or one-thirty, but somebody mighta had somewhere to go tonight, in town maybe, and when the snow started, tried to beat the storm to where they were goin'."

"You can check, though."

"I'd have to—I don't know who come and went, while we were in the woods."

"The victim could've been a guest."

"That's a fact."

Sara said, "And the killer or killers may well still be in the hotel."

Cormier said, "Seems reasonable, too. Don't cherish the thought, but I can't rightly argue with it."

"You have neighbors?" Grissom asked. "Anyone live in a cabin nearby, for example? Is there a private home tucked away up here?"

"No. The hotel owns all this land—everything your eye can see, Mr. Grissom."

Glancing around at the billowing storm, Grissom said, "My 'eye' can't see much right now, Mr. Cormier."

"Well, if the sun was shining, and I made that statement, it'd still be no exaggeration."

"Any of the staff live on the premises?"

"Only my wife and me—rest're in New Paltz, and drive up here to work. Just before we went lookin' for you two, I let the bellboys and the housekeeping staff go on home . . . and I'm pretty sure none of the night shift even tried to make it in."

Grissom glanced at Sara, then said to the hotel manager, "Who does that leave, Mr. Cormier?"

"Well, let's see. . . . Me and the Missus, Jenny, the desk clerk, Mrs. Duncan, the head cook, and maybe two or three more of the kitchen staff, maybe a dozen or so other guests, and the three of you."

The wind wailed.

"We have to consider them all suspects," Sara said.

"It's not as many as I thought we might be dealing with," Grissom admitted. His gloved hands were in the pockets of the black varsity jacket. "But questioning them indiscriminately won't get us anywhere."

Sara nodded, sighing, "We could use Brass about now, couldn't we?"

Cormier, not understanding, said, "Oh I wouldn't say that, Ms. Sidle—I got the utmost confidence in you folks . . . and the constable, of course."

Grissom smiled a little and said, "Thank you, Mr. Cormier. But what Sara means is, interrogation isn't our strong suit. We follow the evidence."

"Although if it leads us to a suspect," Sara said, "we will interrogate that person, to the best of our abilities. It's just not our specialty." Then she turned to Grissom and said, "Trouble is, the evidence is two miles that way . . ." She pointed up the mountainside. ". . . under a foot of snow."

Grissom twitched a smile. "Some of it is. But that's not the only evidence. . . . The killer got to that body the same way we did—he walked."

"Or killers," Sara reminded him. "We saw two sets of tracks coming and going before they got buried, too. That is, two sets besides the victim's."

Grissom nodded. "And from what direction were the tracks coming?"

"Well, right down here." Sara thought back, imagined the footprints she'd photographed. She could have checked on her digital Toshiba, but she did not want to reveal to Cormier that she had the camera with her. "There were three sets, the victim and the other two."

"Go on," Grissom said.

"Probably pretty close to the route we took to get back. As if they came straight up from this rear entrance."

"So what should we be doing now?" Grissom asked.

"Looking for boot or shoe prints."

Moving carefully, Grissom and Sara started toward the edge of the lot that bordered the incline. Sara had gone barely ten feet across the lot when Grissom said, "Whoa, Sara . . . don't step down."

She froze (not hard in this weather), with her foot hovering just above the snow.

"There's an indentation just under your boot," Grissom said, making his way toward her, watching his own steps carefully. "These prints have almost filled in—hard to spot."

"I'm gonna lose my balance here!"

"Just put your foot down to the left—a good six or seven inches, please."

Sara did so. Grissom, at her side now, pointed to a series of the indentations—they were so nearly filled in, she had missed them; the snow coming down—and the accumulation the occasional wind gust was blowing around—had been no help, either.

Sara nodded that she saw the prints, then said, "We need to mark these!"

"And fast," Grissom said.

"What can we use?"

Cormier said, "I'll be right back! You two wait here."

When Cormier had disappeared inside the hotel, Grissom said, "Quick—snap photos."

Sara understood immediately—Gil wanted the photos but didn't want the hotel manager, who was still a suspect, to know that she had a camera. She was having trouble seeing the indentations but Grissom would guide her; and once he had, she'd see the print immediately. Her flash did well by her and, despite the darkness and snowfall, she got decent shots. Idly she wondered if digital photos were admissible as evidence in New York State.

For a guy in a coat too light for the heavy weather, Grissom hardly seemed to be feeling the effects of the cold. To Sara, the man seemed like he always did when he was working—content.

Finally, Grissom said softly, furtively, "Put it away."

Cormier—who'd been gone less than five minutes—stood at the edge of the parking lot, brandishing a handful of metal rods.

"My tomato stakes!" the old boy called, clearly proud of himself. "Got them from the toolshed!"

Grissom directed Cormier on a route to join them without disturbing the footprints. He handed over the tomato stakes and helped them plant one near each footprint, though the tracks were barely visible now.

When that task was complete, Grissom pointed to a blue Pontiac Grand Prix, perhaps a decade old, in the far corner of the lot. "That vehicle's got less snow on top, and more snow underneath, than the others."

"Nice catch," Sara said.

"That's our last arrival. You know who owns that car, Mr. Cormier?"

"Amy Barlow's ride—she's a waitress, here." He checked his watch. "She came in a little early—probably wanted to beat the weather. She's never missed a day. Hard worker."

Grissom led the way over to the car. The vehicles on either side were top-heavy with snow; the Grand Prix wore only a shallow hat of snow. A path of divots led from the driver's door to . . . nowhere, really. Grissom couldn't find any tracks—they'd all filled in.

"Maybe she's the last to arrive," Sara said, finding a few indentations near the rear entrance. "But she's been here long enough for her footprints to fill almost completely in."

"Could have seen something interesting," Grissom said.

Sara tilted her head. "Like somebody leaving in a car, maybe?"

"Or a person or persons, trudging up that slope, perhaps."

Picking up the thread, Sara said, "Or down it."

Grissom beamed at Cormier. "Name was Amy Barlow, was it? Now Amy is someone we do need to talk to."

"Not a problem," the hotel manager said. "But, uh . . . we're not going to just barge in and announce there's been a murder, are we?"

Grissom and Sara exchanged glances—admissions on both their parts that neither had considered this, as yet. Again, that was Jim Brass's bailiwick.

Grissom seemed gridlocked; Sara decided to carry the ball.

She said, "If we don't inform the guests and staff, and someone else dies, aren't we at least partially responsible?"

"Legally, you mean," the hotel manager said, keenly interested, "or morally?"

Suddenly the old man didn't sound like Pa Kettle; she was starting to think his cornpone patter was strictly color for the rubes.

"Possibly both," Sara said.

Grissom was nodding. "On the other hand, the killer or killers don't know that we know a murder's been committed . . . and we might be able to do a little investigating on the QT without tipping our hand."

"You mean, if the perps aren't aware that someone's investigating them, that puts the guests and staff in less jeopardy."

"And us in a better position to uncover evidence. The only exception would be if we're talking about a murderer poised to strike again . . . a serial killer or a multiple murderer with an agenda. Revenge murders against jury members, for instance."

Grissom was sounding like he was the one who'd been reading Agatha Christie.

"That strikes me as statistically unlikely," Sara said.

"I'd have to agree, Sara."

"Excuse me," the hotel manager said, "but don't I get a vote?" They both looked at him.

"I don't think any good comes from scaring the bejesus out of the people in there." He yanked a thumb toward the looming hotel. "I mean, they're stuck here, no matter what. And we don't even know for sure that the killer's in there. Or killers."

"Good point," Grissom said.

"And as for any litigation that might arise," Cormier said, a city savvy showing through the country-speak again, "I'd have more exposure if I panicked these folks, and if they went running off in the storm . . ."

Grissom flicked half a smirk. "A different kind of exposure would become an issue."

"What are we going to do?" asked Sara.

Glancing down at his watch, Grissom said, "It's almost dinnertime. Let's go inside and get warmed up."

"And we say nothing about the murder," Sara said.

"Not just yet." He turned to the hotel man. "Mr. Cormier, can you make sure that Amy Barlow is our waitress tonight?"

Cormier, whose relief at Grissom's decision was obvious, said, "That shouldn't be hard. None of the other waitresses probably made it in."

Grissom shot hard looks at both Sara and the hotel owner. "Right now, we need to just keep our wits about us . . . and process the evidence as soon as we can."

"That evidence is all ruined," Sara said glumly. "That crime scene's a joke . . . an unfunny one."

Grissom bestowed her a quiet smile. "Don't be so sure, Sara. Constable Maher's been working winter crime scenes a long time. There's tricks to this weather . . . just like we work our own magic in the desert."

Working a desert crime scene was, after all, one of the topics they would have been discussing at the conference. So Grissom made a valid point—as usual. For the first time since they'd stumbled onto that murder scene, Sara felt hopeful.

"Now," Grissom said, turning his attention to the hotel man, "what can we do about getting the authorities here?"

Cormier shook his head. "Lived here all my life, and this is all too familiar. . . . By now the roads are closed, phones are probably dead, and we'll be lucky if our power lasts through the night."

Sara got out her cell phone. "What's the state police number?"

Cormier told her, and she punched it in.

All she got was a robotic voice informing her that her call could not be completed; she reported as much to Grissom.

"When God decides to give technology the night off," Cormier said, "ain't a thing a man can do about it."

Grissom frowned, curiously. "Who said that?"

"Well, hell, man," Cormier said. "I did! Just now."

Sara said, "I'll keep trying."

Grissom said, "Good—in the meantime, we're agreed on how to proceed?"

Sara and Cormier both nodded. Sara didn't like the hotel owner knowing what they were up to; he was, after all, still a suspect. But she felt sure Grissom was keeping that in mind, lulling the man into a false sense of security.

Sara said to Grissom, "Let's get you inside, already. You look like the frostbite poster boy."

Snow clung to his hair, his eyebrows, and both his cheeks and ears were tinged red. "All right," he said, obviously oblivious to how he felt, much less looked.

Twenty-five minutes later, Sara—having treated herself to a quick hot shower and a mug of hot chocolate, courtesy of the coffee machine in her room—felt like a new woman (or anyway, a thawed one) and ready to begin their investigation anew. She pulled on a brown long-sleeved crewneck T-shirt and tugged on tan chinos. Over the tee, she climbed into a tan-and-brown wool sweater. Then she bopped down to Grissom's room and knocked on the door.

Again she waited, but nothing happened. She knocked harder, and this time Grissom opened the door and stepped into the hall, his gloves in one hand and a stocking cap in the other.

"Cormier donated this to me," he said, by way of greeting, holding up the cap.

"You'll need it," she said. "You smell good—what cologne is that?"

His eyes tightened as he processed the question. Then he said, "Thanks . . . it's aftershave," and pulled the door shut.

In the elevator, Grissom said, "Cormier seems fine, but be discreet around him."

"Sure. If the victim turns out to be local, that makes him a prime suspect."

"Constable Maher's on the suspect list, too."

Sara studied Grissom's profile, but nothing was to be learned there. She said, "But what motive would a CSI from Canada have to kill somebody in upper New York State?"

He turned and gave her that maddening smile. "We discover two sets of tracks, Sara, moving away from the murder victim . . . and we hear shots. Soon after, we find a burned body with a fatal bullet wound . . . and shortly after that, two men walk out of the woods . . . one with a firearm."

"I still don't see what possible motive a Canadian constable would—"

"Everything we know about Maher, either Cormier or Maher himself told us. That his name is Maher, that he's a constable, that he's from Canada and so on. They could be in this together."

For a moment, it was as if Grissom had punched her in the stomach. Then she managed, "Where does that leave us?"

His smile turned angelic. "Well, for one thing, we're left with photos of the crime scene that neither suspect knows about."

A high-ceilinged chamber of dark carved wood in the Victorian manner, the lobby had an elegant old world feeling with the expected lodge ambience. The far wall was mostly a picture window that looked out at the snow falling on the frozen lake, beyond which rose rocky ledges and towering evergreens, surreally semivisible in the blend of blizzard and night; it was partly blocked by a tall, narrow, well-trimmed Christmas tree. Five people—Herb Cormier and four individuals Sara assumed to be among the guests—stood before the picture-postcard-like vista, watching the lovely, terrible storm.

To Sara's left stretched the front desk, attended by Jenny, the busty, redheaded female clerk who'd assured her the snow would let up soon. The desk clerk smiled and waved. Clearly perplexed by this gesture, Grissom raised a hand waist-high in response, much the way a Roman emperor might reluctantly acknowledge a subject; Sara, who would like to have throttled the woman, forced a smile.

The wall at right was dominated by a massive wood-and-brick roaring fireplace; above a mantel decorated with pine tree boughs hung a large framed oil painting of Mumford Mountain House in the summer season. Spread out before the fire on an oriental carpet were various velvet-covered settees, overstuffed couches and leather chairs, crouching between tables covered with well-thumbed magazines and vintage books. Three more guests sat reading by the soft yellowish light of tabletop lamps.

Herm Cormier—in a rust-colored corduroy jacket over a buttoned-to-the-neck white shirt, blue jeans and boots—caught their reflection in the picture window, turned and came quickly over to them, meeting them at the edge of the chairs and sofas.

In a voice barely above a whisper, he said, "Lookin' out that window, the world's so peaceful, so pretty—can't hardly believe what happened."

Not interested in such ruminations, Grissom asked, "Who else is here from the forensics conference?"

"Just you two and the constable. . . . Everybody else couldn't get into the airport in Newburgh, and of course some folks weren't comin' in till tomorrow, anyway. The phones've been out for a good hour, now, so we're not sure exactly what's what, in a lot of cases."

"Have you arranged for that waitress, Amy Barlow, to wait on us?"

"I've told my wife Pearl, she's the hostess. Amy's the only waitress made it in, though we do have a waiter workin'." Cormier looked Grissom over. "You're dressed warmer, I see—you look like you can survive a few hours out there. . . . I'll get my things and meet you in five or ten minutes. Here in the lobby?"

"No," Grissom said. "I'll be with Sara in the dining room."

"Fine with me," Cormier said, and took off toward the check-in counter, disappearing behind it, through a door marked HOTEL MANAGER—PRIVATE.

Sara and Grissom followed the arrowed DINING ROOM signs past the lobby down a hallway lined with framed photos of Mumford Mountain Hotel staff and management dating to roughly the beginning of time. At the end of the hall, to the left, was a wide stairway to the dining room.

The Victorian theme continued in the expansive restaurant, with its open-beamed two-story ceiling and scores of tables with white linen cloths and hardwood chairs, the quiet elegance of a bygone era reflected in the "M"-engraved sterling flatware and green monogrammed china. With only a handful of diners, the hall seemed absurdly large, the chandeliers bathing the all-but-empty chamber in soft yellow light, as if Sara and Grissom had wandered into an abandoned movie set on some vast soundstage.

They waited as the hostess showed another couple to a table. Heavyset, in her early sixties, her gray hair in a short shag, the hostess wore a midcalf gray knit dress dressed up by a white-and-red corsage, and sensible black shoes.

She trundled their way, greeting them with a big, wide smile, bifocals on a cord draped around her neck. "Good evening, folks," she said, hands folded before her; she looked like a fifth-grade schoolteacher scrutinizing her new pupils.

Grissom just stood there, as if the woman had been speaking esperanto.

"I think you should have a reservation for us," Sara said. "Either under Grissom or Sidle."

The woman's only jewelry, Sara noted, was a watch and a wedding ring with a good-size diamond.

"You must be the folks Herm told me about," she said, extending her hand. "I'm Pearl Cormier—Herm's wife."

Grissom shook the woman's hand and said, "I won't be dining with you this evening, but I will have a cup of coffee with Ms. Sidle."

"Right this way," she said. She steered them to a table not too close to the other couple (the only other diners at the moment), and they sat down.

"We serve family-style," Pearl told Sara. "Your choice of meats tonight is fried chicken or medium-rare roast beef." With a knowing nod and a wink, she added, "Amy will be right with you."

They had expected Mrs. Cormier to know they wanted to talk to Amy; nonetheless, Sara glanced at Grissom, who also seemed to be wondering what else Herm had told the missus.

Sara sat with her back to the kitchen, Grissom on her right, the varsity jacket slung over his chair, the CSI windbreaker exposed. Sara had barely gotten her menu open before a cheerful voice chimed, "Hi, I'm Amy. I'll be your server tonight."

They smiled up at her.

Amy smiled back and said, "Frankly, I'm just about everybody's server tonight."

Sara laughed politely and, after a beat, so did Grissom.

Their prospective witness was tall and thin, in her late twenties, her dark hair tied into a loose ponytail that ran halfway down her back. Amy Barlow's smile revealed wide teeth stained yellow, probably by cigarettes. She wore black slacks and a black bow tie over a white blouse whose buttons were tested by an ample bosom. A gauze bandage encircled her left hand.

"Start you folks off with a drink?" she asked.

Pleasantly, Grissom asked, "What happened to your hand, Amy?"

She shook the hand like it still hurt. "Cut myself cutting up an onion—they're short in the kitchen tonight."

"You all right?"

She nodded. "It don't need stitches—but boy, it . . . Listen, you're sweet to ask, only there are better subjects to whet your appetites. Take your drink orders?"

"Coffee, black," Grissom said.

"Hot chocolate," Sara said.

When Amy returned with their beverages, Grissom said, "I heard you were one of the last to get here tonight, before the storm closed the roads. Or was it still afternoon?"

As she gave Sara the steaming mug, Amy said, "Afternoon. Two-thirty or three, I guess. But it was getting pretty slick out even then."

"Lucky you made it in at all," Sara said, over the rim of her mug.

"Yeah, I wanted to beat the storm in; don't like missin' a night's work . . . I can use the money."

"I hear that," Sara said. "You were lucky nobody hit you, rushing home, when you were coming in."

"I did see a couple cars, and it made me nervous—didn't want any slidin' into me, that's for sure. Some of these guests, with rental cars, if they're from some part of the country where it doesn't snow, well!"

"We're from Vegas," Grissom said.

"You're dangerous, then!" the waitress said, with a good-natured chuckle. "You people who aren't used to winter driving, you're lethal weapons on wheels."

"Sounds like you almost got hit," Sara said.

"Not really. It wasn't on the mountain drive, anyway, it was down on the road between here and New Paltz. Anyway, you decided on choice of meat?"

Grissom explained he was only having the coffee, and Sara asked for just the vegetable dishes.

And off Amy went.

"We need to talk to Amy in depth," Grissom said. "One of those cars may have been driven by the killer."

"If so, then our perp is off the premises, and even if that waitress has a photographic memory and gives us a license plate number, what are we going to do about it? With the phone lines down and cells dead and . . ."

Grissom shrugged. "How did detectives solve cases before all the technology came along?"

Sara paused. "By observing. By asking questions."

"That's what we need to be doing."

"That and guarding our snowbound crime scene, you mean."

"My turn now," Grissom said. "Yours will come soon enough. . . . Remember, Sara, Sherlock Holmes was a scientist too."

"Grissom—Sherlock Holmes was a fictional character."

"Based on Joseph Bell—a scientist."

Amy brought a basket of rolls and breads and butter, and Herm Cormier seemed to materialize next to them, an apparition in a heavy parka, bearing two thermoses of coffee.

With a thin smile, the hotel manager asked, "Ready to rough it, Dr. Grissom?"

Grissom nodded, got up, slipped on his varsity jacket.

A few other guests had found their way into the dining room and Cormier kept his voice low, trying not to alarm the customers starting to fill the restaurant. "I'm on record that this all-night vigil with the . . . the thing . . . is a bad idea."

"Duly noted," Grissom said. Then to Sara, he said, "See you in two hours. In the lobby."

"If I'm not there," she said, "call my room—case I fall asleep."

Grissom nodded and the two men headed for the door, Cormier's voice far too loud as he said, "And if there's anything else we can do to make your stay more comfortable, you just let us know!"

Sara finished her veggie dinner—mixed vegetables and parsley potatoes (she figured she'd ingested a stick and a half of butter)—and chatted some more with Amy, but got no real information out of the waitress. Pushing any harder would've been too obvious—she and Grissom would eventually have to interrogate the woman, Sara knew.

As she indulged in a sliver of pecan pie, Sara watched Amy and a tall, thin waiter handle what little there was of a dinner rush. Amy worked the cluster of tables around where Sara was seated, and the thin, dark-haired waiter worked some tables toward the entrance. He too wore a white shirt, black bow tie, and black slacks, and seemed to possess the same energy to please that inhabited Amy Barlow.

Back in her room, seeking a little privacy and maybe even some rest, Sara pulled out her cell phone—it paid to keep trying. She flipped through the local White Pages, and tried the county sheriff, the New Paltz P.D., the state patrol, and even the phone company, all with the same lack of success.

On a whim, she punched in Catherine's cell phone number. Surprisingly, the phone rang! . . . and Sara felt a little jolt shoot through her.

"Catherine Willows," the familiar voice said, a nice clear, strong signal.

"Catherine! It's Sara."

"Well, hi, stranger. I see on the Weather Channel you're getting some snow."

"Are we. And you're not going to believe what happened, here . . ."

"Yeah, well you're not going to believe the case you missed out on. You may be the one hip deep in snow, but we've got the frozen—"

And the line went dead.

Sara quickly hit redial and another familiar voice—the robotic one—returned with the news that her call could not be completed and to please try again later.

Though Grissom and Constable Maher were, technically at least, nearby . . . just up that slope . . . Sara suddenly felt very alone.

Usually a person who didn't mind a little seclusion, Sara Sidle found herself wishing she could speak to just one person beyond the world of Mumford Mountain Hotel. But, for now at least, that appeared impossible.

Heaving a sigh, Sara returned the phone to her purse, placed it on the nightstand and took a nap with the light on. In part this was because she didn't want to fall too deeply asleep, with the two-hour stint of crime-scene duty ahead of her. But it was also because, for some inexpressible reason, she didn't feel like being in the dark, right now.

Before they'd left the hotel, Cormier loaned Grissom a muffler, but as the two men trudged up the rocky slope through the snow—the hotel man again leading the way—the CSI kept the woolen scarf off his face. Cold or no cold, he had questions to ask.

Grissom had to work his voice up over the wind. "Mr. Cormier . . ."

"Call me Herm!"

"Herm, now that you've had some time—any idea who the victim was?"

"Be a long time," Cormier said, " 'fore I forget that sight."

They were taking the same circuitous route up the slope as they'd used getting down. Trodding behind the man, in the howling storm, Grissom had to strain to hear; but even without Mother Nature's wintry distractions, he'd have had trouble catching the man's words.

"The truth is," Cormier went on, "that poor bastard's body was just too badly burned for me to recognize! If that was my own brother, I don't know that I could tell you."

"I understand!" said Grissom, practically yelling to be heard over the wind. He picked up his pace and fell in alongside Cormier, but the old man was far more at ease with the weather and terrain, and Grissom really had to work to keep up. "How many of the staff are actually here?"

"Those I already told you about—Amy, Mrs. Duncan, the head cook, Jenny at the desk, Pearl, and me."

"Didn't I see a waiter in the dining room?"

"Oh, Tony! Tony Dominguez. He's one of our best workers, even if he is a little . . ." He bent his wrist.

"Gay?"

The hotel manager smirked humorlessly. "Let's just say Tony ain't the macho-est guy around. But he does a helluva good job for us."

"Any other staffer you might've overlooked?"

They plodded along and the wind picked up in intensity for about a minute and a half. Just when Grissom was wondering if Cormier had either forgotten or ignored the question, the hotel man said, "Bobby! Bobby Chester made it in. . . . Lunchtime fry cook! He's also Mrs. Duncan's dinner-hour helper."

Grissom did the tally: Cormier, his wife, Pearl, and five others. Seven.

The wind kicked back in and shrieked at them until Grissom was forced to cover his face and fall back behind Cormier and let any other questions wait. And he had plenty more, but the pitch of the path had turned more steeply upward and every lungful of air now came with some effort. For now, Grissom would concentrate on just getting up the hill again and reaching that snow-blanketed crime scene.

Finally, Cormier said, "This is it," though Grissom would never have known it. Between the drifted snow and the darkness, they might well have been on the moon. Nor could the CSI see the constable, anywhere. . . .

Cormier called out to the man, who yelled back: "Over here!"

They followed the Canadian's voice and soon saw what he'd been up to while they'd been gone. Maher had carved himself a nook out of the snow at the base of a tree and hunkered down for the wait. The constable had apparently anticipated that even with Cormier guiding Grissom, it would take the Vegas CSI longer than two hours to get back up here; in fact, they were pushing three.

Not that that seemed to have bothered the Canadian. He had the bearing of a man who enjoyed the solitude of the woods and winter, and, of course, he'd had Cormier's .30-06 if anything had tried to disturb his serenity.

"You kept busy!" Cormier said.

"Got to work just after you left," the Canadian said. "Thought I better, eh, before the light faded too much!"

Cormier poured Maher a cup of steaming coffee from one of the thermoses while Grissom played a flashlight over the area. He immediately noticed changes that Maher had made at the crime scene. The tips of four sticks poked up out of the whiteness, indicating that impromptu stakes had been driven into the snow, forming a ten-by-twenty-foot square.

"You want to explain the sticks?" Grissom asked.

Maher grinned as he sipped the coffee. "Happy to! Thanks for the coffee, Mr. Cormier—I was starting to think you fellas forgot about me!"

"Sorry we took so long," Grissom said, almost hollering over the wind. "The sticks?"

As Grissom pointed his flashlight at one of the stakes, now nearly buried in the snow, Maher explained, "I found two tiny tracks in the snow on either side of the body. Did you two see them?"

Grissom nodded. "Sara and I saw them, but I have no idea what they were." He did not mention that Sara had taken photographs. "Misses, maybe."

"That's exactly what they were," Maher said. "Missed shots."

"And now they're buried under all this snow."

Maher smiled. "You pick things up fast, Dr. Grissom."

Pursing his lips, Grissom said, "And somehow you're going to use these sticks to find those bullets?"

The constable nodded. "Yes, sir. Soon as the snow stops."

"How?"

"I'll explain it when I do it. I was going to give a demonstration on that very thing this weekend . . . but I guess you and Ms. Sidle will be the only ones to see it."

Grissom filled him in on the parking lot shoeprints.

"I'll take a look at 'em after I get warm," Maher said. "Ms. Sidle going to be all right, pulling her shift, or should I come up early to relieve her?"

"Don't come up here a minute early," Grissom said, "or you'll just be insulting her."

"She's a good man?"

"As tough and smart as any CSI anywhere. You try to baby her, she'll only resent it."

"Take your word for it."

"She'll probably deal with the cold better than me."

Maher nodded. "I'll relieve her after her full shift. In the meantime, here's the rifle." Maher handed the .30-06 over to Grissom.

"Any advice?"

"Yeah," Maher said. "Don't move around much. The more you move around, the more chance you'll disturb evidence. I don't mean to be insulting, Dr. Grissom, but snow is fragile. Right now, it's our friend."

"Preserving our evidence," Grissom said.

"Exactly. But it won't take much to turn it into a liability."

Cormier handed Grissom the second thermos of coffee. "You'll probably be wanting this."

Grissom nodded his thanks.

"Be my guest," Maher said and pointed. Grissom's flash followed, swinging around, and found the dugout next to the tree. "That'll keep you out of the wind. Keep your face covered."

"Got it."

Cormier said, "I'll be back in a couple of hours with Ms. Sidle. I'll give you plenty of warning, now . . . so don't you go pluggin' us!"

"Just yell good and loud," Grissom said. "Get your voice up over this wind!"

"No problem. But don't you be trigger-happy."

"Don't worry, Mr. Cormier, if I can't see it, I won't shoot at it." He gave them a rueful smile that they probably couldn't make out in the pitch darkness of the woods.

Several minutes later, Grissom was straining to see the departing pair; but they'd already disappeared into the snow. Depositing himself in Maher's hideaway against the tree, Grissom eased down, his back against the bark, and did his best to relax.

Two hours wasn't such a long span, a mere 120 minutes; still, Grissom knew that out here—where darkness meant black, and the neon-bright night of Vegas was almost a continent away—two hours could be a relative eternity. As snow continued to fall, Grissom, clutching both the rifle and the thermos of coffee, settled in.

If the snow would just stop around daybreak, they could get to work at this crime scene, and let Constable Maher demonstrate his bag of tricks. Grissom was always willing to learn something.

On the other hand, if Maher was a fraud, a killer in disguise, Grissom was more than willing to teach a lesson himself.

6

The one thing Las Vegas didn't need was more flashing lights. This town trying to dress itself up for Christmas, in the opinion of Captain Jim Brass, was an exercise in overkill. How did you decorate a city already adorned with millions of lightbulbs, a desert oasis that glowed like a three-billion ka-gigawatt Christmas tree all year round?

And yet they still tried. As he rolled by the Romanov Hotel and Casino in his police department Taurus, an elaborate flashing display spelled out Merry Christmas and Happy Hanukkah over flickering Nutcracker Suite images; and Santas and elves and reindeer, it seemed, danced Rockette-style on every casino's electric marquee. Brass shuddered to think what Glitter Gulch would be like—neon Santa hats on the towering cowboy and cowgirl? The nightly overhead laser display with Sinatra singing "Luck Be a Lady" shifted to "Jingle Bells," rolling dice traded in for mistletoe and holly?

The Taurus cut confidently through heavy evening traffic, Brass weaving in and out between rental cars with the gawking tourists and various vehicles bearing blasé locals headed to dinner or a movie, or homeward bound. Darkness had settled over Las Vegas, with the temperature once again falling precipitously toward the freezing mark. The cars with their headlights only added to the light show.

In the passenger seat, Nick Stokes lounged in his dark-brown sport shirt and lighter-brown chinos, looking dreamily out at the Strip. "Don't you just love Christmastime in Vegas?"

"Yeah," Brass said, "it's nice to have the place livened up a little. You clock in early? If so, end of shift, you better clock out the same way—Mobley hasn't approved this case for OT."

"I know that. I didn't clock in yet." Nick beamed at Brass. "I'm your 'Ride Along' buddy."

"You're my *what*?"

A tiny smile traced the CSI's square-jawed countenance. "You know how the sheriff has been encouraging citizens and police to have better interaction— through the Ride Along program?"

"Oh, please."

"Now, Captain Brass—like any other interested citizen, I'm entitled to a police 'Ride Along,' long as I meet the criteria and sign the waiver."

Brass just stared at his passenger, who finally pointed toward the windshield and said, "Jim—the road?"

The detective returned his attention to his driving and barely avoided clipping a minivan.

"And as a citizen," Nick added, "I must say I expected the police to observe better highway safety procedures."

"You're pushing your luck," Brass said, meaning with Sheriff Mobley.

"I've signed my waiver," Nick said, plucking a folded-up piece of paper from the breast pocket of his sport shirt. "And I've met the criteria by being duly interviewed by a member of the LVMPD."

"What member was that—Warrick Brown?"

"Your detective instincts never fail to impress, Captain. Yeah, Warrick interviewed me for the Ride Along program, and signed off. And I duly interviewed and approved him, too."

The detective shook his head again, and couldn't keep the smile from forming. "You guys are pushing it, I tell you."

"Like you wouldn't try this, if you had a case that needed the extra hours."

Brass grinned over at Nick. "Maybe I'm disappointed I didn't think of this scam first. But my guess is, before long, Mobley'll clear the Missy Sherman case for overtime."

Nick nodded. "Media attention."

Brass nodded back. The missing housewife finally turning up had won Missy Sherman another fifteen minutes of headlines and TV news. That the body had been frozen, Brass and company had thus far managed to withhold—once that got out, the tabloid sensibilities of the media would really swing into high gear.

The detective got off Interstate 215 at Eastern Avenue and drove south to Hardin. After taking a left, Brass drove until he could turn back north on Goldhill Road. The house he eased to the curb in front of was a near mirror image of the Sherman place—similar stucco two-story mission-style but with the two-car garage on the right, and the roof tile more a dark brown. A black Lincoln Navigator and a pewter Toyota Camry sat in the driveway.

As they got out and Brass strolled around the Taurus, Nick asked, "You ever run into the likes of this before? Ice-cold trail, no evidence . . ."

At Nick's side now, Brass said, "In the days before all the high-tech stuff kicked in, yeah. You'd catch a case that you just knew you'd never crack, 'cause there was jack squat to go on."

"But you'd hang in there, right?"

"Right. Months devoted to dead ends, and the end result—another folder for the cold case file. You guys and your toys . . . you find a hair on a gnat's ass and match it to a pimple on a perp in Southeast Bumfuck, Idaho."

Nick chuckled and admitted, "Sometimes it's that easy. Only, this one doesn't feel that way. I'm afraid I've got that nagging feeling that we'll never crack this thing."

They were at the porch, now.

Brass shook his head, placed a hand on the young CSI's shoulder. "You'll crack this one, Nick. It's just . . . they can't all be easy."

Nick nodded, and smiled. "But it would be nice. . . ."

The front door resembled the Shermans' too, except not hunter green, rather a rich, dark brown. Brass used the horseshoe-shaped knocker, waited, and then waited some more. The detective glanced at Nick, who glanced back and shrugged. Brass rang the bell, waited a few seconds and rang it again.

The door opened and the doorway filled with a large man, like a frame that could barely encompass a picture. Six-five easy, Brass thought, the guy was a muscular two-fifty; his head, just a little small for the massive build, like his growth had gone as far as it could when it got past his bull neck. His eyes were dark brown, his hair a close-cropped light brown with matching close-trimmed goatee. He wore black running shorts and an expensive black-and-white pullover sweater with the sleeves pushed halfway up his formidable forearms. His sandals cost more than Brass's house payment.

Brass tapped the star-shaped badge on his breast sport-coat pocket and said, "Captain Brass, Las Vegas police. Mr. Mortenson? Brian Mortenson?"

The big man nodded, his expression somber. "This must be about Missy." He shook his head. "How can I help?"

"We'd like to talk to you and your wife. Is she here?"

"Well, she's here, but this has got her very upset. Could we do this another time?"

"If you do want to help, sir, now is better. With you both home. . . ."

"Do I need an attorney?" he asked.

Brass shrugged. "Do you?"

The big man in the doorway thought that over. Then he said, "You know, Regan and I already told that Detective Varga everything we know. It's all on the record."

Brass's tone grew more businesslike. "It's Detective Vega, and you were questioned in the context of a missing person case. This is a murder."

He sighed heavily. "Don't misunderstand, I want to help. We want to help. It's just, I don't want Regan any more upset than she already is."

"I do understand that, Mr. Mortenson. May we come in?"

Mortenson stepped out of the way and let them into the foyer. "I talked to Alex today. . . . He's shattered by this. It's terrible. Awful."

Like the Shermans' foyer, this one had a Mexican tile floor, albeit in a lighter shade. A cherry table next to the stairway to the second floor was home to a large glass vase filled with fresh-cut yellow roses, the pale yellow plaster walls contrasting with the brightness of the flowers. An open archway led into a cozy living room decorated with a floral sofa and overstuffed chairs and two maple end tables. In front of the sofa sat a matching coffee table littered with several remotes and a few fashion, sports, and fitness magazines.

"Make yourself comfortable," Mortenson said, nodding toward the living room, his tone much less defensive now, "and I'll fetch Regan. She's upstairs in her office."

Mortenson went up the stairs two at a time; he had the easy grace of a natural athlete, which not all brutes possessed. Brass led Nick through the archway into the living room, where they claimed the two chairs that framed the sofa, leaving it open for the Mortensons.

After only a minute or so, the couple entered the living room, the small woman leaning against her husband, one of his big arms around her. Regan Mortenson seemed frail beside her husband, her mane of long blonde hair hanging loose, partly obscuring her heart-shaped face. Tanned and fit, with long legs, Regan no doubt played a lot of tennis or golf. She wore denim shorts and a white tee shirt bearing a transfer that looked familiar to Brass (Nick recognized it as Picasso's lithograph of Don Quixote), the words "Las Vegas Arts" in loose script below the transfer. Though she was in her mid-thirties, Regan had a college coed, California-girl air.

Brass and Nick rose as the couple walked to the sofa, the husband saying, "Dear, these are the police officers who want to talk to us."

Brass made the introductions, then said, "We know you and Mrs. Sherman were very close, ma'am, and we're sorry for your loss. We will try to make this as brief and painless as possible."

"You're very kind," she said with a nod, brushing the blonde hair out of her face.

The couple sat, Mortenson making the couch whimper in protest; in contrast, Regan perched on the edge, poised to fly at the slightest provocation.

"What is there I can tell you?" she said, her voice tiny. Both Brass and Nick had to strain to hear. "Last year, we told that nice Hispanic detective everything we could remember."

"As you already know," Brass said, his tone official yet solicitous, "Missy Sherman's body has been found."

Brian said, "It was all over the news."

"And Alex called us, too," Regan said.

"The coverage was vague," the husband said, "about where she was found. Something about Lake Mead."

"Yes," Brass said. "Off the road that runs through the park."

"How terrible," Regan said, shuddering. "She did love that area. We used to swim there, sometimes, Missy and I—sometimes we took midnight swims."

"Is that right?"

"Under the stars. We'd even been known to, uh . . . this is embarrassing."

"Go on."

"We used to swim on impulse. Which means, you know . . . skinny-dipping?"

Brian gave her a look. "Really?"

She nodded, even mustered a little smile. "We didn't invite you guys along for that."

Brian's expression was distant; probably, Brass was thinking, the husband was contemplating missed opportunities.

Now Regan appeared thoughtful. "Only . . . this seems like a little late in the year for that. You know . . . too cold?"

"Yes it is," Brass said. "I do need to go over some old ground."

"Please."

He took out his minicassette recorder. "And it's best I record it."

"No problem."

"But you will need to speak up a little." He clicked it on and asked, "How long have you known Missy?"

She sighed, shook her head, the blonde hair shimmering; she was a lovely woman—ex-jock Brian appeared to be a lucky man.

"Since Michigan State," Regan said. "We were both Tri Delts. Then, it turned out that our hometowns weren't that far apart—she grew up in Kalamazoo and I was from Battle Creek. We'd both been cheerleaders in high school and our towns played each other and . . . well, we were kindred spirits. So, anyway, we started riding home together for holidays and stuff. She was a year older than me, and helped me adjust to college and sorority life. We became best friends and . . . and have been ever since."

Her lower lip was trembling, her eyes moist. Nick handed her a small packet of tissues and she thanked him; but she remained composed.

Brass asked, "You moved out here because of Missy?"

"In part. I was looking for a new start, and Missy and Alex made it sound like such a great place to live. She'd keep talking about fun and sun, and me stuck in Michigan—anything to get the hell out of there!"

"Not much for winter?" Nick put in, with a friendly little smile.

She shook her head. "I just hate winter, I despise snow. Plus, I was having sinus headaches and my doctor recommended I go somewhere warm, with a more steady climate. And my best friend and her husband were here."

She was speaking louder now, more animated.

Brass asked, "What can you tell us about the last time you saw her?"

The upbeat attitude faded, her eyes clouding over. After a while she said, "It was such a typical day for us girls. Nothing special about it, but if you had to pick a representative day for what our friendship was all about, and what we did together, that day would've served just fine. Shopping, lunch, then . . ."

Her voice broke.

Brass paused in his questioning while Brian Mortenson put a comforting hand on his wife's shoulder. Regan choked back a sob, digging into the tissues. She dabbed at her eyes. Her makeup did not run, however—studying her, Brass realized Regan's eyeliner was tattooed on.

"I . . . I'm . . . I'm sorry," she finally managed.

They gave her a long moment to compose herself, then Brass went at it again. "I do need more detail, Mrs. Mortenson," he said. "Let's start with what time you and Missy got together that day."

Regan thought back. "We were in separate cars. We usually didn't pick each other up or anything, we'd meet someplace. That morning . . . We met at Barnes and Noble, the one out on Maryland Parkway . . . by the Boulevard Mall?"

Brass and Nick both nodded.

"Anyway," she went on, "that was around ten. We had coffee and a scone, then browsed for a while. Alex had a birthday coming and he's such a movie freak that Missy wanted to get him this special movie book."

"And did she?" Brass asked.

Nick remembered that although the Chinese food had been found in Missy's Lexus, no other packages remained.

"She did," Regan said. "Missy found just the right book for Alex— this biography of Red Skeleton."

Nick smiled a little; but neither he nor Brass corrected her: Skelton.

She was saying, "Alex is into the old movie stars—but, actually . . . I wound up giving it to him."

"You gave it to him," Brass repeated, not following.

Twisting the tissue in her hands, she said, "We were planning to have Alex's birthday at our house—we've done that before."

Brian nodded.

She went on: "The store wrapped it for her and she just gave it to me to keep, till the party." Regan's voice shrank even more. "Of course, we never had that party, not after Missy disappeared."

"And you gave him the book."

She nodded.

"When?"

For a second she seemed to not understand the question, then said, "On his birthday," as if that should have been obvious. "I stopped over and gave him the package, and told Alex it was from her."

"This was a month after she disappeared."

Another nod. "I thought he'd appreciate that. That it would seem . . . special."

"And how did he react?"

She smirked sourly. "I guess it wasn't the smartest thing I ever did— he really broke up. He cried and cried."

And then she began to cry too, muttering, "Stupid . . . stupid . . . stupid . . ."

Mortenson rubbed his wife's neck. "Don't beat yourself up, baby. You were just trying to be nice."

Picking the momentum back up, Brass asked, "Okay, where to after the bookstore?"

"Caesar's—the Forum shops for a couple hours. It's expensive but there's lots of fun stuff to see."

"So you were just window shopping?"

"Mostly, but Missy did buy a nice sweater at . . . I don't remember which store, for sure. It was a year ago. . . ."

"Think, for a moment."

". . . Saks, maybe? Only, we pretty much made the rounds that day and hit almost every store. She could have bought that anywhere. And maybe something else . . . But anyway, I'm positive she was carrying some bags when we went back to our cars."

"Okay. You get through shopping at Caesar's. Then what?"

"Lunch. It was after one by then and we decided to go to the China Grill at Mandalay Bay."

Nick, in his friendly way, asked, "That's kind of a tourist trap, isn't it?"

"Yeah, sort of, but the food is really good. And Missy and me, we're people watchers. We both get a kick out of watching the tourists and guessing who they are and where they're from. It's better than the zoo."

"Do you remember what you had for lunch?"

"Grilled mahimahi. That's what I always have there. It's great." Her grief over Missy appeared momentarily displaced by her enthusiasm for her lunch. "They grill it with pea pods, yellow squash, carrots, leeks, and shitaki mushrooms."

"What about Missy? Wouldn't happen to remember what she ordered?"

"She had a fave, too—Mongolian beef. Without fail, that's what she'd order. Great girl, but no sense of adventure when it came to food."

"What did you two talk about over lunch?"

Regan shrugged, her mood upbeat again. "Missy and I decided to get the boys to take us to see the Harry Potter movie."

Brian Mortenson rolled his eyes just outside his wife's line of vision.

"You girls talk about anything else?" Brass asked. "Was Missy having trouble at home?"

Regan shook her head. "Not really—she thought the world of Alex, and he's been crazy about her since college."

"When you say, 'not really,' that implies . . ."

"Well . . . she was a little miffed about him getting on her, for spending too much on clothes. She said sometimes Alex treated her like he was the breadwinner and she was the little woman."

"Missy didn't work outside of the home?"

"No, but she managed their apartments. She had a finance degree, y'know. So I think she resented, just a little, being treated like a stay-at-home housewife. But I don't want to give you the wrong impression. Missy wasn't bent out of shape or anything. Every marriage has its little bumps. . . . Right, dear?"

Brian nodded.

Brass asked, "How long did lunch last?"

"An hour, maybe two."

"And all the two of you talked about was going to see a movie? And that Alex had been on her lately about her shopping?"

Shrugging, Regan said, "The rest was the same stuff we always talked about—just girl talk."

"Girl talk."

"What we're reading, who's getting divorced, who's fooling around on who—the usual gossip."

"What was she reading?"

"Nick Hornby."

"Any of the divorce or 'fooling around' talk have to do with Missy herself?"

Regan's face hardened. "Now, I'm willing to help you, but Missy wasn't like that. She loved her husband and he loved her—a storybook marriage, the kind most people can only dream about."

Brian Mortenson sat forward now. "These are our friends you're talking about, Detective. Like Regan says, we'll help, but have a little common decency, would you?"

"Sir, you don't have to like the questions I ask," Brass said. "I don't even like them . . . but these are the things that have to be asked in every homicide case."

Fuming but saying nothing, Mortenson sat back.

His wife put a hand on his leg just above the knee. "It's all right, Brian."

Nick said, "You're mourning the loss of a friend. But Missy didn't just pass away—she was murdered. We don't have the luxury of common decency, in the face of indecency like this. . . . Not if we want to do right by Missy."

Brian was still scowling, but his wife looked up at him sweetly and said, "They're right, honey. We have to help. We have to do whatever it takes to find out who took Missy away from us."

Mortenson sighed heavily, then nodded. "I don't know, baby. This is getting a little . . . weird."

Nick rose and, seemingly embarrassed, said, "My timing is lousy, I know . . . but I wonder if I could use your bathroom?"

"Sure," Regan said.

"Down the hall, off the kitchen," Brian said, with a dismissive gesture.

Nick offered a chagrined smile, and said, "I'm afraid department policy requires I be accompanied by the homeowner. You know how it is—things turn up missing, lawsuits. . . . Could you show me there, Mr. Mortenson?"

"Oh for Christ's sake," Mortenson said. "What next?"

But he got up, reluctantly, and escorted Nick out of the room.

Suddenly Brass felt very glad he'd allowed Nick Stokes to be his "Ride Along"—there was no such department policy as the one Nick referred to. Nick had clearly sensed Brass's desire to speak to the wife without the husband around, and had made it happen.

"When you were shopping, Mrs. Mortenson, did you see anyone suspicious, maybe someone following you?"

"No! No one."

"What about at the restaurant?"

"Of course not."

"Please think back, Mrs. Mortenson. If someone was stalking Missy, you might have noticed."

She chewed her lip in thought, big ice-blue eyes wide, gently filigreed with red.

Brass tried again. "Nobody talked to you or hit on you? A couple of attractive women out shopping, could be a guy might take a run at one or both of you."

She smiled, almost blushing. "Well, in a town full of showgirls, a woman my age can only thank you for a compliment like that . . . but no. No one talked to us, other than the workers in the stores and our waiter at lunch."

"Did any of the clerks get overly friendly? How about the waiter? More interested in you two than usual?"

"If so, Detective, it flew over my head. You think a stalker was watching us?"

This was getting nowhere. "Did you actually see Missy get into her car? In the restaurant parking lot?"

"Well, I walked Missy to her Lexus, then went on to my own car. It was parked farther out."

"Then you did see her get into the SUV?"

Regan nodded, and a pearl-like tear rolled down her tanned cheek, glistening like a jewel. "She already had the door open. She set her doggy bag inside, then ducked back out and . . . we hugged. How was I to know we were saying good-bye, forever?"

"You couldn't have known."

Regan swallowed. "I said we'd see her and Alex on Saturday, then she got in, and I walked away."

"That was the last thing you saw? You didn't see her drive out?"

"No."

"Did she start the engine?"

"I don't . . . don't remember."

"Could there have been someone hiding in the car? In the back, maybe?"

"She put the doggy bag in front, side and rear windows are tinted. . . . Maybe. But I really don't think so."

"Where did you go from the restaurant?"

"I had another appointment."

"With whom?"

The onslaught of questions was clearly getting to her. "Really, Detective, is that important?"

Brass shrugged. "Probably not. But I have to check everything."

Nodding, Regan said, "I serve as a fund raiser for Las Vegas Arts."

Alex Sherman had mentioned that.

"Sometimes," she was saying, "I meet with artists. I met with one that day."

"Which artist? What's his name?"

"Her name," she corrected. "Don't be sexist, Detective."

"Sorry."

"Sharon Pope."

"Where can I contact her?"

"She's in the book."

Brass was reflecting, trying to think if he had any other questions for the woman, when he heard Brian Mortenson yelling from the back of the house.

The detective and the blonde exchanged looks, then got up and quickly followed the sound of the voice down the hall, the hostess leading the way.

Even if it wasn't really department policy.

Five minutes before, when Nick had requested a guide to the bathroom, Mortenson had led the CSI past a formal dining room dominated by a huge oak table and through a hall-of-mirrors kitchen with its stainless-steel appliances. Off the kitchen to the left, Mortenson pointed toward the bathroom.

"Knock yourself out," the man said sourly.

Nick had used the bathroom and took his time washing up. Joining his host in the hallway again, Nick pointed past Mortenson toward an open door that led into the empty garage.

"You might want to shut that," Nick said. "Letting in the cold."

"Hell," Mortenson said, looking around. "Thanks . . . I was getting ready to put the cars into the garage when you and your partner knocked out front."

Mortenson moved toward the door, but before he could close it, Nick—at the man's side—was pointing into the garage at a white appliance against the back wall. "That a chest freezer?"

"Yeah."

Boldly, Nick stepped through the door out into the garage. Voice pinging off cement, he said, "I've been thinking about getting one. . . . This baby expensive?"

Mortenson followed the CSI. "Not that much—less than $500."

Nick whistled. "Hey, that's not bad at all." He gave Mortenson the look you give a used-car dealer. "Has it been good to you?"

Mortenson nodded, shrugged, then glanced back in the direction of the living room, mildly imposed upon, but not knowing what to do about it. "Had it three years," he said. "Not a lick of trouble."

Nick stood studying the freezer, admiringly. "Doesn't hurt it any, to be out in the garage?"

"Naw," Mortenson said, getting sucked into the seemingly mindless conversation. "Runs a little more, but there's nowhere in the house for it. This works fine." He opened the lid so Nick could peer inside.

While proud homeowner Mortenson droned on, Nick checked out the freezer, though not for the reason the other man likely thought. Three-quarters filled with white-butcher-paper-wrapped packages with very clear dates printed in Magic Marker, the Mortensons' freezer was better organized than Nick's office. Beef on one side, chicken and fish to the back, pork to the right and vegetables in the front. Though only about eight or nine cubic feet—and stacked with enough food to keep a homeless shelter going for weeks—the freezer did appear big enough to hold Missy Sherman's body. A small layer of frost coated the walls, but Nick could still see every seam and the smoothness of the surface along the back.

What he did not see was something that could have made the round mark on Missy Sherman's cheek.

Nick asked, "How often do you have to defrost one of these?"

Mortenson shrugged. "Once a year, maybe. Not so bad—there's a drain plug in the bottom. Some of the more expensive ones coming out now are frost-free."

"Sounds good. Looks like you defrosted yours, recently?"

"Yeah—maybe three weeks ago."

Nick looked from the bottom of the freezer to a floor drain in the center of the garage floor. Pulling a plastic bag from his pocket, he asked, "Would you mind if I lifted a sample from your drain?"

Mortenson looked at him like he was crazy, then slowly, the man's eyes narrowed. "Why?"

The best Nick could come up with was, "It might be helpful. You said you wanted to help."

"In Missy's murder investigation."

"Right."

"In my garage."

"Uh . . . yeah."

"Which, means . . . what?" The eyes on the little face over the big body tightened; the goatee was like dirt smudged on his chin. "You suspect me of Missy's murder?"

Shaking his head, Nick said, "I don't suspect anybody yet. . . . I'm just doing my job."

"And here I thought you were just this nice guy interested in buying a freezer."

Risking Brass's ire, Nick revealed: "Missy Sherman was frozen."

Mortenson frowned. Trying to make sense of it, he said, "She was frozen to death? In Las Vegas? How the fuck cold was Lake Mead that—"

"No. Frozen. As in a freezer."

"What, now you suspect us? Are you high?"

"No. I'm just a crime lab investigator who needs to check that freezer." And Nick pointed to the appliance.

His voice rising and bouncing off the enclosed space, Mortenson yelled, "Alex told me you took his place apart, too! You really don't have any goddamn decency, do you?"

Nick glanced toward the house, afraid that the man's voice would carry and bring out the wife and Brass.

"Sir," Nick said tightly, one ex-jock getting into the face of another. "You said you wanted to help. I need to have a look at that freezer."

Looking down at Nick, noses almost touching, Mortenson blared, "There's some murdering lunatic out there, and you people come around and bother us! The people who knew and loved Missy! Isn't it enough that we lost our friend, that Alex lost his wife?"

Regan and Brass appeared in the doorway off the kitchen.

"Brian, what's wrong?" Regan asked, her voice rising, ringing off the cement, making her sound a little like Minnie Mouse in an old movie house. She rushed to her husband's side.

Brass trailed after, shooting a look at Nick, who could only shrug and nod toward the freezer.

The detective got the significance at once, and turned to Mortenson, who seemed just ready to launch into the next wave of his tirade.

Cutting him off, Brass said, "You're right, Mr. Mortenson, there is a lunatic out there, a murderer, and we don't have any idea who it is . . . so we have to suspect everyone, if only to start ruling people out."

Trembling, the big man said, "You have no right, no right at all . . ."

"We can do this now," Brass said, "and you can cooperate . . . or we can get a warrant and do it later. Either way, whatever evidence my criminalist wants, he's going to get. The question is, do you want to slow us down, or not? You choose."

Mortenson seemed to shrink a little, from King Kong to the son of Kong, his wife slipping an arm around his waist.

She said, "Just let them do what they want to do, Brian, and get them out of our house."

He gave her a sick look. "This guy says Missy was frozen, that somebody stuffed her in a damn freezer or something. They think . . ." And he looked toward the appliance.

Regan paled, horror-struck, but nonetheless said, "Don't make them come back here—I don't ever want to see these terrible people again. Please, Brian, I'm begging you—just let them do what they want, take what they want, and leave us alone."

"All right, baby," he said with a sigh. Then he looked from Nick to Brass. "Do what you have to . . . then get the hell out of my house."

Brass stood in the garage with the Mortensons, trying to make peace with them, while Nick went to the car, got his camera and his silver toolkit. When he returned, the husband and wife stood watch accusingly, near the door to the kitchen. Brass had parked himself close by, but no further words were exchanged with the couple.

Nick snapped off several shots of the freezer from both a distance and up close, concentrating particularly on the seams and side surfaces on the inside. When he was done, Nick set the camera aside, pulled on latex gloves, bent down to the floor drain, removed the cover and fished out whatever he could from the shallow trap; then he placed his findings in the bag. The tense silence in the room and the eyes of the Mortensons boring into his back as he worked weighed on him and he wished Brass would say something to break the hush, but the detective seemed content to stand by without comment.

Nick sealed the bag, replaced the cover on the drain, rose and nodded to Brass. He ended by taking another half-dozen photos, this time of the drain. Without a word, Mortenson pushed the button on the wall that activated the garage door opener. As the double door whirred upward, the detective and CSI took the hint and walked out into the evening and down the driveway to the Taurus at the curb.

Nick glanced back and saw Regan Mortenson silhouetted in the corner of the doorway, while Brian walked out of the garage onto the driveway, stopping next to his wife's Camry. Mortenson stared at them until the car pulled away.

"That went well," Nick said.

Brass said, "You know, outside of Grissom and Ecklie, I don't know anyone who pisses people off like you do. At least they have an excuse, they're supervisors, they're supposed to piss people off. But you . . ."

"Some people like me," Nick said, mildly amused by this rant. "Some people love me."

"Probably not the Mortensons."

Nick hefted the bag of slime and grinned. "But I did win their door prize."

Nodding toward the bag, Brass asked, "And if that turns out to be nothing?"

Nick shrugged. "Ruling out innocent people is just as important as finding guilty ones, right?"

"I guess," Brass said, obviously not convinced.

Back in the lab, Nick went to work processing the goop from the Mortensons' drain. The glass-walled DNA lab was one of the most elaborate in the CSI facility. Closed off by two sets of double glass doors, one on the north and another on the west, the room comprised five workstations, not counting the microwave oven. One station was

for the thermocycler, one for each of the two polarized light microscopes, another for the gas chromatograph and mass spectrometer, plus the one where Nick was hard at work.

He was almost finished when Catherine came in and dropped onto the chair at the station immediately behind and to the left of him at the stereo microscope. Hunching over the tool, he used reflected light to study in three dimensions the grime from the drain.

"Hey," she said.

Looking up, he said, "Hey." Tonight, she wore brown slacks, a burnt-orange turtleneck sweater, and a look of either exhaustion or frustration, Nick couldn't tell which.

"Where've you been?" he asked.

"Best Buy."

He grinned. "Consumer heaven." He looked at his watch. "They're not open this late."

She tapped her ID. "I had a special get-in-after-hours card."

"Looking for the perfect DVD player, huh?"

Catherine closed her eyes and rubbed her forehead. "Is that all men think about?"

"No," Nick said, carefully considering the question. "There's sex and sports, too. Then comes toys like DVD players."

She finally gave in and grinned.

"What were you up to, after closing at Best Buy?"

Sighing, stretching, she said, "I was going over every freezer in the place, trying to find one that matched the mark on Missy Sherman's face."

"Any luck?"

She shook her head. "I'll try another store tomorrow." Frowning, she asked, "Where's Warrick, anyway?"

"Still working the tires, I think. Haven't seen him for a while."

"What are you up to?"

"Went with Brass to interview the Mortensons—the Shermans' best friends?"

She nodded, interested.

He filled her in, building to the chest-freezer punch line and the slime he was currently processing.

Catherine perked up. "What did you get?"

"Just what you did."

"Shit."

Nick grunted a laugh. "I don't know where Missy Sherman's been for the last year, but it sure wasn't in that freezer."

A throat cleared, and they turned to see Warrick draped in the doorway. "FBI computer is taking its own sweet time with that tire mark."

Nick said, "With no more of a casting than you got, it's not going to help us much, anyway. We find a car to match it to, groovy . . . but for now . . ."

"I know," Warrick said. "Coldest case ever . . . You guys catch any luck?"

"Same kind as you," Catherine said.

Nick leaned on the counter and turned to Catherine. "What have we got so far, besides no overtime?"

Catherine flinched a little nonsmile. "A dead woman who has been frozen for the last year."

"A few tire tracks," Warrick added. "An indentation in the victim's cheek. Another longer, narrower indentation on her arm. Some Chinese food in her stomach . . ."

"And no fortune cookie," Nick said. "But I have ruled out one of the many chest freezers in Las Vegas. How many more d'you suppose there are to check?"

Warrick just looked at Nick, while Catherine sat there, apparently wondering whether to laugh or cry.

7

Sara Sidle's nostalgia for the bracing weather of her Harvard days had long since blown away with one of the many gusts of winter wind. Ensconced in the shelter Constable Maher had made in the snow, huddled against a tree, rifle gripped in fingers going numb despite Thinsulate gloves, Sara now clearly recalled why she'd gone west after graduation.

Guarding a snow-covered crime scene in the midst of a blizzard was a duty that neither training nor experience had prepared her for. Thank God the two hours were almost up. She wondered if, on her return, she should round up Amy Barlow—not that the woman would likely go anywhere, in the middle of this snowbound night. But the waitress remained the closest thing to a witness they had.

Prior to taking her first crime-scene shift, Sara had returned to the dining room, where she spoke briefly to Pearl Cormier. The half-hearted dinner rush was already over, and Amy was nowhere in sight.

Pearl, holding down the hostess station, explained: "Amy's helping in the kitchen—short-handed back there. Short-handed everywhere in the hotel."

"You'll provide her with a room tonight?"

"Can't hardly make Amy sleep in her car, honey."

"Could you let me know the room number?"

And Sara had gone up to catch a little sleep, which the phone interrupted in what seemed like a few seconds, with Pearl informing the CSI that Amy Barlow had room 307; but right now the waitress was still working, helping waiter Tony Dominguez set the massive dining room for breakfast—a big task for two people.

Which meant that before Sara could follow up with the waitress, she had her outdoor duty to do. And so she'd followed Herm Cormier over the hill and through the woods to babysit a snowbound corpse who had not been content just to be shot, he had to be half-burned to a crisp, too.

When she'd thought about this duty, she had, frankly, pictured a winter wonderland, despite the dead body—sparkling crystal on white rolling drifts, reflecting the moon and stars. The reality? Clouds covered the stars and what little moon there was, and she was miles away from the nearest streetlight, and even the hotel wasn't in view. This was a darkness like she'd never known, an all-encompassing inside-of-a-closed-fist nothingness that embraced her in its frigid fingers—and also disconcerted the hell out of her, despite her hardheaded, scientific bent.

She had her flashlight, but was loath to turn it on for fear of taxing the batteries, which would really put her in hot water . . . well, cold water, anyway. Nestled there in her pocket, the flashlight provided a small reassurance, a promise of light more important to her, at the moment, than the light itself.

Pushing the button on her watch, illuminating the dial, Sara noted that another fifteen minutes remained before Maher was due to relieve her. Leaning the rifle against her shoulder, she pulled off one glove, reached carefully into her pocket and withdrew her flash.

Going left to right, she made her arc of the crime scene with the beam. The sticks that Maher had planted in the snow were all but buried. Grissom had told her that several inches had been exposed, when he'd noticed them. Now, the stakes would soon be memories under the white blanket. She continued the arc past where the body should be, the other set of sticks and on around to her right.

She saw nothing—no animal, no person. That was comforting. Also creepy.

Switching off the light and tucking it away again, a sudden sense of loneliness descended on Sara, heavier even than the falling snow. It was as if extinguishing the light had somehow shut off the lights on the entire world and every soul in it, and Sara—who normally didn't mind a little quiet time to herself—felt like the only person left. That was when she heard something crunch in the snow.

She held her breath and strained to hear over the wind as her fingers clawed for the flashlight in her pocket; what she heard, first, was her own heart pounding.

Then, another crunch—this one to her right.

She fumbled with the Maglite, then the beam came to life and she thrust it out like a sword toward the sound.

She saw nothing.

Then, panning left, the light caught a flash of . . . fur!

Whatever-it-was had outrun her beam, and she whipped the shaft of light in pursuit, catching a glimpse of a furry form, going past it, then coming back to settle on the cold brown beautiful eyes of a big cat.

Not a house cat: a bobcat or a lynx.

Poised to leap, the beast bared its teeth and snarled—the sound was brittle in the night, yet it echoed. With each fang as long as one of Sara's fingers, the cat seemed torn between its desire to get at the corpse and being almost as afraid of Sara as she was of it.

Trying to raise the rifle with one hand, in a steady motion—not wanting to make a swift move that might inspire an attack—and yet keeping the beam on the growling animal, Sara knew that the cat could cover the ground between them in mere seconds. Carefully she traded hands, shifting the flashlight to her left, the rifle to her right, propping the rifle against her shoulder—all with no sudden moves. Once she had the rifle more or less in place, her right index finger settled on the trigger. . . .

Sighting down the barrel as she'd been taught, she kept the light trained on the growling cat, muscles rippling under its fur, and exerted pressure on the trigger. Don't jerk it, she thought, just squeeze . . . nice and easy. . . . When the trigger was about halfway down, she heard a loud pop!

But she had not fired.

A bullet thwacked into a tree behind the cat, and the animal jumped to one side—beautiful, graceful—and sprinted off, a brownish blur dissolving into the night.

Sara swiveled toward where the shot had originated—just behind her, and to her left, her ears still ringing from the rifle report—and captured Maher and Cormier in the Maglite's beam.

The Canadian handed a rifle over to the hotel owner. Both men looked like Eskimos, wrapped up in those parkas, hoods up, only the centers of their faces truly visible in the beam of the flashlight, perhaps ten yards from her.

"You scared the shit out of me!" Sara screamed, the adrenaline of the moment somehow combining to ratchet the volume of her voice in these woods, where the only other sound was the dying echo of Maher's gunshot.

Maher looked stunned for a moment, then smiled and said, "You're welcome."

"I mean . . . thank you. . . . But I did have the situation in hand."

"I know you had that cat in your sights, and I know I missed. I wasn't trying to save you."

"What?"

"I was saving the cat."

". . . The cat?"

Walking toward her, Cormier at his side, Maher said, "The cat's a North American lynx. Endangered species."

"Lynx?"

"*Lynx canadenis* to be precise," Maher explained, a few yards away now. "You seldom see them this far south. . . ."

Cormier butted in. "Not unheard of either. Seen my share of 'em in my day. You can get in trouble shootin' 'em, Ms. Sidle."

Sara swung the Maglite to Cormier and said, "Maybe I should've let him chow down on our corpse—or offer him one of my legs to chew on."

"I just wanted to scare it off before anything happened," Maher said, squinting at the light.

Finally realizing she was blinding the men, she pointed the flash at a more downward angle. "Sorry, guys . . . didn't mean to lose it."

"No problem, eh?" Maher said.

"If I'd been any more scared," she admitted, "I don't mind telling you, I'da wet myself."

"Wouldn't worry none," Cormier said. "It woulda froze up right quick."

Sara arched a half-frozen eyebrow at the hotel manager. "You know, if you get any folksier, the next time I aim, it might not be at a lynx."

Cormier grinned, and so did Maher. "Let's get you back down to the hotel, little lady."

She looked at Maher. "Did he just call me 'little lady'?"

"I believe he did," an amused Maher said.

"Herm," she said to the hotel man, "I'm taller than you are, okay?"

"You are at that . . . but you don't mind if I lead the way?"

Every bone in her body felt leaden and every muscle ached, even burned, and now that the adrenaline rush had subsided, she thought her legs might betray her. Taking a deep breath, she moved around a little, hoping to encourage some blood flow to her extremities.

"Ready?" Cormier asked.

"Ready," she said. Then turning to Maher, she asked, "Anything I can do down at the hotel? It's only what . . . ten-thirty?"

Maher shook his head. "Just get some rest, 'cause we'll be keeping up the rotation. Snow seems to be letting up, some. Maybe by first light we'll finally be able to go to work."

Sara exhaled breath that hung there like a small cloud. "I am ready to do more than sit."

"Just sit and scare off bobcats, you mean?"

Sara grinned. "Constable, that was a lynx. I thought you knew your stuff out here, in the woods."

With tight smiles and nods, they bid their goodbyes. Maher returned to the cubbyhole he'd dug, thermos of coffee and Remington rifle both handy, while Sara took off after Cormier. The movement, rather than wake her up, only made clear to Sara just how exhausted she was, and any thought of interviewing Amy Barlow, or anyone else for that matter, evaporated from her mind. Making their way slowly down the rocky slope in the darkness, aided by flashlight beams, they trudged down toward civilization.

Which right now Sara Sidle defined as a warm bed.

The rest of the night passed uneventfully.

On that cloud of a bed, Sara fell deeply asleep, and when the wake-up call came, she arose groggy, really dragging; she had slept in her clothes and bundled into her coat, stocking cap, muffler and all, she sleepwalked down to the lobby and fell in with Herm Cormier.

Once outside, the cold air snapped her back to bitter reality. And at the crime scene, she never once drifted off to sleep—it was if anything colder than before, though the snow was half-hearted and, by the end of her watch, all but stopped.

She returned to the hotel for three hours of deep, blissful sleep; this time she beat her wake-up call. She felt refreshed, and—after a shower—invigorated, ready to make her way up that mountain and relieve Grissom.

Just after seven-thirty, she stepped off the elevator into a lobby deserted but for Mrs. Cormier behind the front desk. The older woman gave her a wave and Sara waved back, and was about to ask where Pearl's husband was when Herm Cormier materialized at her side.

"Rarin' to get at it?" he asked.

"Actually, yes. Last night was so odd, it's almost like looking back on a dream, or maybe a nightmare."

Cormier pointed a mildly scolding finger. "I wish you folks woulda let me take a turn or two out there."

She shook her head. "Really needed to be one of us, at all times. That'll be much better when this case eventually gets to court."

He grunted a laugh. "No bad guy yet, and already you're thinking about court?"

She nodded, grinned. "That's really where all of the work we do ends up. Where is everybody?"

"Things usually are a little livelier around here," he said, glancing around. "We're a big haunted house this weekend—they say Stephen King wrote that book about this place."

"The Shining?"

"I guess," he said, with a shrug. "What guests we have are probably takin' breakfast. Amy, Tony, Mrs. Duncan, and Bobby Chester are working the kitchen, naturally."

"Where's Constable Maher?"

"He's in the dining room, too. That's why I was out here, on the lookout for you. Mr. Maher asked, when you come down, I request you join him. And me, too. He says we all need to eat—it's going to be a long day."

"Sounds like a plan."

Soon they were entering the vast dining room where ten people, mostly couples, were seated centrally, having breakfast. Stares and whispers followed Sara.

"I guess word's out," she said, as Cormier led her past gawking guests toward a table where Maher waited.

"Well, you know how it is—in an environment this small, news travels fast. Especially with the four of us running in and out every couple of hours."

She nodded. "In other words, you told your wife."

He nodded. "Told my wife."

Maher stood as Sara approached and they exchanged good mornings. He'd been smoking a cigarette—this was the smoking section—but he stabbed it out as Sara neared. His eyes were as red-rimmed as hers, but he too seemed energized.

"I think you're going to enjoy today much more than yesterday, Ms. Sidle."

"Call me Sara, please," she said, sitting.

"All right," Maher said, taking his seat, Cormier doing the same, "if you'll call me Gordon . . . or even Gordy."

"Gordon, if you can make that crime scene shake off the snow and talk to us, I'll call you a genius."

The other diners were slowly returning to their food, if occasionally glancing over at the detectives in their midst.

The menu was a small single page, with only a handful of items—basically, a choice of ham, bacon, or sausage and various combinations of eggs and cakes—and she was still studying it, as if looking for hidden meaning, when a loud crash made her—and everyone else in the dining room—jump half out of their chairs. She whirled to see the waiter, Tony Dominguez, kneeling over a tray on the floor, half a dozen plates upended, food scattered.

"First time that ballet dancer ever got clumsy," Cormier muttered, and hustled over to help the waiter clean up the mess.

The pair worked fast, starting with carefully piling the broken pieces of dishes and glasses onto the serving tray. Sara caught sight of a pink stain on the left arm of the waiter's white shirt—from juice maybe; the stain looked dry, so it hadn't come from nicking himself due to this spill. Cormier went off to the kitchen for more cleaning utensils.

Turning back to her table, Sara leaned forward resting an elbow, touching a hand to her face. So much for waking up refreshed—the crash and clatter of china and silverware had almost made her leap out of her skin, and she realized how frazzled she still felt. So much for a peaceful getaway with Gil Grissom. . . .

"Brace up, eh?" Maher said. "We'll be getting to work before you know it—and I have a hunch you're the kind who's never happier than at a crime scene."

He seemed to be describing Grissom more than her, but Sara nonetheless brightened at the prospect. "I guess you planned on having more than just two students."

"With 'students' like you and Dr. Grissom, it's a master's thesis class. Limited enrollment."

A haggard Amy Barlow trod up to their table, little of yesterday's spring in her step. Her hair, though tied back in a loose ponytail, looked haphazardly combed, dozens of stray strands seeking escape; and she wore no makeup. She had on the same black slacks and white shirt but no bow tie, the crisp pressed look of last night's uniform absent. The only thing she seemed to have changed was the bandage on her left hand.

"You're one of those crime lab people, aren't you?" Amy asked Sara. "In for the conference that got canceled."

"That's right," Sara said, rather startled by the question.

"Then maybe you'll know—I asked Herm but he just said stay about your business."

"Know what, Amy?"

"Is it true?" She glanced in the direction of the mountainside. "That there's a body out there somewhere?"

Sara glanced at Maher, who nodded.

"I'm afraid so," Sara said. "The police can't make it up here in the snow, so we're doing what we can."

"What can you do?" Amy frowned curiously. "What happened?"

"A man was killed," Sara said.

" 'Nother skiing accident? Exposure . . . ?"

"No. It was intentional. Homicide."

Amy frowned. ". . . Murder?"

"Yes."

Somehow Sara had wound up on the wrong end of the Amy Barlow interrogation. Taking back the initiative, the CSI asked, "Can you tell us anything about the cars you saw on the road yesterday?"

Amy frowned again, in thought this time. "Would that have something to do with this?"

"Might. What did you see? What do you remember seeing, on your way in to work?"

The waitress shook her head, as if her response would be negative, then said, "One was an SUV, that much I can tell you . . . a Bronco, or Blazer? They all kinda look alike to me."

"That's a good start, Amy," Maher said. "What about color?"

Amy's eyes tightened as she searched her memory. "Dark red, like a maroon?"

That had been more a question than an answer, but it was something, anyway. "You're doing fine," Sara said. "What about a license plate? If not the number, were they New York State plates? Out of state . . . ?"

Amy drew in a breath, exhaled through her nose, shook her head, ponytail flouncing. "Didn't notice."

"And there was another car?" Maher pressed.

That had been the waitress's implication.

"Yes," she said. Then, proud of herself, she gave the following detailed description: "Something big and black."

Sara hid her frustration, while Maher kept at it, asking, "New or old?"

"On the newer side," Amy said. "Like a Toyota or a Honda—I don't know cars very well. That's Jimmy's thing."

"Jimmy?"

"My guy," she said, with a shrug. "Can I give you a piece of advice, hon?"

"Sure," Sara said.

"Never date a guy younger than you. Young boyfriend, they'll drive you crazy. You feel like you're raisin' a kid, sometimes."

Sara had been in that position once or twice, and smiled in recognition.

Back from mopping the floor, Cormier was sitting down with them again, and had caught the tail end of that. "James Moss," he said, filling in information. "Jimmy. He's a waiter here too." He looked up at Amy. "Wasn't Jimmy supposed to work yesterday too?"

She nodded. "Didn't make it in, in time. With the phones down, I ain't even talked to him."

"You two usually ride in together," Cormier said.

Another nod. "Not yesterday—Jimmy said he had some errands to run. Somebody he had to see, he said."

"That new restaurant in New Paltz is hiring," Cormier said. "Kid asked for a raise last week and I turned him down."

Maher kept his attention on the hotel man. "Did Jimmy call in?"

"I'd have to ask Pearl, but I don't believe so. But lots of the help didn't call in, and of course it wasn't long before the phones were down. Listen, in this part of the world, with this kind of weather, we're used to the help not calling when they can't make it in."

Amy smirked. "Probably holed up playing with his damned Game Cube, praying for snow all weekend. . . . Folks ready to order?"

They did, and Amy went away.

"Well, the snow has stopped," Maher said. "Any word from the outside?"

"Phones're still down," said Cormier. "I do have a ham radio, though."

"And?"

"Guy I talked to in Mexico hears we had a hell of a storm."

Sara laughed; so, after a moment, did Maher.

Cormier was continuing, "The county guys were probably up all night, with that damned chain reaction accident out on the interstate. If they get out here today at all, it probably won't be till afternoon."

Maher turned to Sara. "Cell phone?"

"Oh, I haven't tried it yet this morning." She took it from her purse, punched in Catherine's work number—it was what, 3:30 A.M. back there? She got nothing, not even the robotic voice.

Sara shook her head glumly, returned the cell to her purse.

"Snow might have screwed up the tower," Cormier said, with a twitch of a humorless half-smile. "Happened before."

The waitress returned with coffee for the men and tea for Sara. "Breakfast'll be up in a few shakes," she said.

"So," Maher said, sighing, "we're still on our own."

"Looks that way," said Cormier.

"If I'm not out of line," Sara said to the constable, "you don't seem horribly disappointed."

A smile flickered on the Canadian's lips. "I like a challenge."

"Me, too. So we're getting to work?"

Maher nodded curtly. "Mr. Cormier's going to help us gather some gear, and I've got some things in my room I brought for lecture purposes. Breakfast first."

Sara sipped her tea. "You're the boss. . . . Just don't tell Grissom I said that."

He chuckled. "We've got a lot to haul—any problem with that?"

She grinned. "The bellboys went home, so I'm ready. Bring it on."

He nodded to her. "That's what I like to hear."

Amy brought their food and, as they ate, Maher outlined the morning's plan, then turned to Cormier. "I'm going to need a medium-speed snow dispersal device."

Scratching his chin, Cormier gave the Canadian a cockeyed look. "I don't believe I've got one of those, much less heard of one, before."

"Are you sure, Herm?" Maher grinned. "Aka, a leaf blower?"

"Well, hell! Sure, I got a beauty—gas-powered too. Which is a good thing, 'cause I'm not sure there's enough extension cords in the whole hotel to reach up the side of that mountain."

After breakfast, they went off respectively for their outdoor apparel, collecting their various equipment, and reconvened outside the rear entrance, for one last check. Sara had both her case of equipment and Grissom's (Pearl at the desk had loaned her Gil's spare room key), her camera and tripod. Maher also had two cases, one of which held his metal detector. Cormier looked as though he'd cleaned out the toolshed—scattered around the edge of the parking lot were a leaf blower, two shovels, a push broom, a kitchen broom, a whisk broom, a roll of garbage bags, and a toboggan.

"That's your wish list," the hotel manager said to Maher.

"Good job, Herm," Maher said. "Leaf blower gassed up?"

Cormier said, "You could disperse snow from here to New Paltz with that sucker."

"And the toboggan's a fine idea."

"Thanks."

Sara asked, "Too steep for snowmobiles?"

"Yeah, too steep and too many trees up there, too easy to wind up twisted around one of 'em. Rocky, too. Toboggan's safer."

They loaded their equipment aboard the sled, then Cormier and Maher lashed everything down. Though clouds still covered the sun, daylight filtered through, and the reflective shimmer of ice crystals on the snow was breathtaking. That the snow had stopped was a blessing. A good foot of white had fallen since Sara and Grissom had come upon the burning corpse, and despite the Canadian constable's confidence, she wondered if there would truly be any evidence left to collect.

"At least it was a wet snow," Maher said.

He and Cormier still looked like Eskimos to her, in their parkas. "Is that good?" she asked.

"Real good, for us—limited drifting."

"Won't that make snow dispersal harder?"

"It'll be harder to blow; but as long as it doesn't go slushy on us, it'll hold together better, and give us good detail." Nodding to himself, he added, "If there's such a thing as an ideal winter crime scene, this should come close."

Then they marched up the hill, Maher and Cormier taking turns leading the way, and pulling the sled; Sara offered to take her turn dragging the heavy toboggan, but somehow it never happened. Instead, she wound up bringing up the rear, to one side of the thing, making sure nothing tumbled off, due to hitting a rocky patch.

The walk to the crime scene—which before had taken just short of half an hour, in the deep snow—took nearly an hour as the load constantly shifted, causing them to stop again and again, and check it and reset everything.

After the fourth time this happened, Sara said, "I thought this was the twenty-first century."

"Back at the lodge it is, just barely," Cormier said. "Out here, time isn't just relative, it's pret' near nonexistent."

They were already late and Sara started to worry that maybe they'd get up there and find Grissom frozen to that tree. Or maybe that lynx would be standing there studying Grissom, with Grissom more than likely studying it back.

When they arrived at the site, however, Grissom was already pawing in the snow near the body, like a kid on Christmas morning who hadn't waited for his folks to get up before getting at his presents.

"Dr. Grissom!" Maher called.

The CSI supervisor continued on as if he hadn't heard. Leaving the toboggan with Cormier, Maher strode on ahead and called Grissom's name again. This time Grissom, looking comical in the stocking cap and muffler, turned.

"Plenty of time to do the body later," Maher said.

"All right," Grissom said, stepping away. "What's first?"

Maher was at Grissom's side now. "If this was a crime scene back in Vegas, what would you do first?"

"Take photos of everything—I presume Sara brought her camera today." Grissom was nicely ambiguous about that, Sara noted.

Maher was nodding, saying, "What else?"

"Look for footprints."

"Then let's do that." Maher gestured to the white landscape. "We don't want to risk trampling the killer's footprints, so let's find them."

Sara had joined them, by now, and asked, "How, exactly?"

Maher extended a hand, like a hypnotist before a subject. "Grid it out in your mind—like you would any other scene. Ignore the snow."

She stared at him, eyebrows arched. "Ignore the snow?"

Maher gave her a gentle smile. "Just for now."

She looked all around the buried crime scene. "All right, Gordy . . . I've got it."

Grissom said, "Gordy?"

Maher said, "That's my name. Feel free to use it, too, Dr. Grissom."

Grissom said nothing, just glanced at Sara, who shrugged.

"Mr. Cormier," Maher said.

"Yes, sir?"

"Would you unpack the leaf blower, please?"

"You got it."

Soon the hotel owner was bending over the toboggan, untying ropes.

"Now, Dr. Grissom," Maher said, "and Sara—you two remember about where the footprints were, correct?"

"Well," Sara said, pointing, "the victim ran a fairly straight line. So . . . from the body down the hill."

Grissom said, "The other four sets—the two up and the two back—were scattered sort of on either side of the victim's."

Maher nodded, breath pluming. "We're going to have to work these from the outside in. Where would you say the tracks were the furthest out?"

Pointing to a tree slightly downhill from their position, perhaps ten feet to their left, Grissom said, "Just this side of that tree."

"All right." Maher turned toward the old boy at the toboggan. "How you doing there, Mr. Cormier?"

"Comin' along!"

Maher turned back to the Vegas CSIs and said, "Okay, for a few minutes I'll be doing all the work . . . but it won't be long and there'll be plenty for everybody, eh?"

They nodded.

"For now, Sara, you better start finding a way to warm your camera."

"It's digital."

"Yes, and you won't want the lens fogged, and the batteries don't like the cold, either."

"How about inside my coat, Gordy?"

"That may be a little too warm, but it's better than any idea I've got."

Sara went back to the sled, carefully unpacked her camera and slipped half-out of the coat—God, it was bitter!—and withdrew an arm from one sleeve, slung the strap over her shoulder and put the camera against her side. Then she tugged the coat back on and zipped up. Maher's concern wasn't misplaced—the camera already felt cold, even though it had made the journey up here in its leather case. She hugged it close and hoped it would warm up quickly.

Grissom followed Maher as the constable circled down to the point the CSI had indicated, and they stood just on the wrong side of the tree from where the footprints had been before being buried under all that snow.

"This is the tree?"

"Yes," Grissom said, pointing toward the area on the other side. "The prints were right over there."

With a Cheshire cat grin, Maher asked, "Do you get a kick out of experiments?"

Grissom said simply, "Yes," which was the understatement of the new century.

"This isn't exactly an experiment, Doctor, but I think you're going to like it."

Before very long, Maher fired up the leaf blower, yanking the cord, and aimed it at the new-fallen snow. Wet though it was, the white powder still flew in every direction as the leaf blower eased over it. Despite the use of forced air, the Canadian worked carefully.

Moving down to join them, careful to take the same path they had taken, Sara and Cormier came down to watch the show. The camera felt warm against her now and Sara decided to snap off a couple of preliminary shots, getting photos of Maher at work. She looked over at Grissom, who studied Maher in rapt fascination and even admiration.

Quiet and still, Grissom seemed mesmerized as the leaf blower cleared layer after layer. Within a few minutes Maher shut down the leaf blower and signaled them to join him. He had blown open a circle about fifteen by fifteen inches and—in the bottom, dug into the five inches of snow already packed there when they'd arrived yesterday—Sara saw a pristine boot impression.

She turned to Grissom. "No way."

Shaking his head, Grissom said, "I just saw him do it."

They had a little sunshine now, but Maher's smile was brighter. "Medium-velocity snow dispersal device. Pretty cool, eh?"

"Pretty cool, indeed," Grissom said. "I trust the term is designed to sound impressive in court?"

"That, and 'leaf blower' just has no charm."

Looking like an overgrown demented kid in that stocking cap, eyes gleaming, Grissom asked, "May I?"

"Sure," Maher said. "You saw how I did it—just be careful and don't hit the area too directly."

"I'm all over it."

"Just be all over it—carefully." The Canadian refired the leaf blower and handed the business end to Grissom. "Take her for a spin."

Grissom moved just under a yard downhill and a little to the left. The impression Maher had unearthed—or more accurately, un-snowed—was of a right footprint. That meant the next one should be a left, which was the reason for Grissom moving just a few inches off line.

While Grissom worked with the blower, Sara put a ruled scale next to the footprint and snapped a couple of photos.

"Wait," Maher said. "You need the scale, you're exactly right . . . but for it to be accurate in a photo, it should be at the same depth as the impression." He dug out beneath the scale and set it down. Sara took two more photos, then slipped the camera back inside her coat to keep it warmed up.

"You'll see the difference once you get those up on a computer screen," Maher continued. "Use your tripod too—that and some oblique lighting should raise the detail."

"Thanks. I will."

Maher moved to where Grissom was blowing away more snow. With a small amount of guidance from the Canadian, Grissom eventually uncovered another footprint.

"Got a left foot," Grissom said, his smile almost feral.

"You comfortable doing this?" Maher asked.

"I'm always at my most comfortable," Grissom said, "at a crime scene."

Maher said, "All right, then—you keep moving. Do one more set from this row, then try to find the other three and we'll do two molds each from each row."

"Sounds good."

"And while you're doing that, Sara's going to take more pictures, while I'm melting the sulfur."

Grissom just nodded and went back to work.

"Sulfur?" Sara asked.

"Never made sulfur casts?" Maher asked her, as he led her back up the hill.

"Can't say I have."

"Just dental stone, huh?"

"That's what works best in our climate."

Opening one of his cases on the toboggan, Maher withdrew a Sterno burner and handed it to Sara.

"Take this," he said, then pulled out a small saucepan and handed it to her. "And this."

Finally, he brought out a yellow block slightly smaller than a brick and a cooling rack with extended legs.

"Come on, Sara," Maher said, "and I'll show you how this alchemy works."

Clearing a spot in the snow, he lit the Sterno burner and—while it got going—he dumped the yellow brick into the saucepan. As Sara watched, Maher put the saucepan on top of the cooling rack he'd opened up and set over the flame.

"Okay, Sara—this is going to start stinking to high heaven before long, so why don't you set your tripod up, and take your pictures, before I pour the sulfur in. We're only going to have a small window before our sulfur smells real ugly."

"Anything you say, Merlin," she said, and grabbed her tripod off the toboggan.

"And while you're there," Maher said, half-turning, "could you bring me that can of gray primer?"

She looked in the nearest bag and found the paint. "Got it."

As she set up the tripod, so that the camera would be directly over the footprint, Maher shook the paint, then sprayed a light layer of primer over the print.

Alarmed, Sara said, "Hey—you're disturbing evidence!"

He shook his head. "I'm enhancing the visibility. And besides, you already have pictures of it, au naturel."

Grissom turned off the leaf blower and, watching where he was going, walked over to them.

"Look what the Mountie did," she said, pointing at the print.

Maher was taking out his own mini-Maglite; he set it in the hole he'd cleared, so that it shone at an oblique angle across the impression.

"The visibility is a lot better," Grissom said. "I've read about this a couple of places."

"You have?" Sara asked.

"Kauffman's guide to winter crime scenes is pretty much definitive; and there's a good paper, done by two Alaska CSIs, Hammer and Wolfe. Still, reading about it's one thing—working it out in the field . . . that's the ticket."

"But paint?" she said.

Her supervisor shrugged. "No different than us using hair spray on tire tracks."

Sara thought about that.

"That's a good one," Maher said, giving them a thumbs-up. "I love my Aqua Net."

With a quick nod, Grissom turned and moved back to the leaf blower.

Looking through the viewfinder, Sara had to admit, the prints seemed better-defined. She snapped off several shots from various heights. The rotten-egg smell of the sulfur floated down to her and she fought the urge to gag. It wasn't her way to give in, and she prided herself on her strong stomach, so she decided to risk her breakfast and get a closer look. Edging up, she saw Maher stirring the sulfur as it melted into a translucent amber liquid.

"You were right," she said. "That impression looks great, Gordy. Sorry I snapped at you . . ."

"It may smell like Daffy Duck's backside," he said, "but, damn—it works, eh?"

"You prefer it to dental stone?"

"Detail with sulfur is even higher. Cures faster too. The downside is, it's a lot more expensive, and a pain in the ass to work with, sometimes. You let it get too hot, it'll either ignite or get flaky. . . . Then you have to cool it down and start from jump."

Sara wondered if any of this would ever come in handy at home. Chances were, probably not; still, it never hurt to learn new techniques.

"The optimum temperature is about 119 degrees. But you've got to be careful because the flashpoint is 207 degrees and the self-ignition point is only 232. Once it's at the right temp, though, all we have to do is pour it in and wait. . . . You ready?"

She nodded.

Maher took the pot off the flame and carried the brew toward the print. Eyes wide, he said, "And, oh yeah—never use this stuff indoors!"

Grinning a little, she said, "Kinda guessed that. Noxious fumes aren't my favorite." She watched as he carefully filled the impression with the liquid sulfur. "That won't melt the impression?"

He shook his head. "Not enough to matter. The detail'll still be better than dental stone, and we don't have to take a week off, waiting for it to cure. Besides, if you use dental stone, you'll mix it with potassium sulfate and that reaction creates enough heat that if you don't put it in the snow while it mixes, it'll completely melt your impression."

A short while later, Grissom came over to them again. "I've uncovered two sets in each row."

"Good job," Maher said.

"Just looking with the naked eye," said Grissom, "I'd say all four sets were made by the same person."

"No kidding? Not two killers, then?"

"Looks like one. Smaller person, too—men's size eight or nine, woman's nine or ten."

"So—what happened?"

Grissom explained what he knew so far.

The killer chases the victim away from the hotel. The victim sprints up the slope and the killer is shooting at him, at least three shots fired.

So the killer fires and misses, fires and misses, then connects, putting one in the victim's back, the victim pitching forward. Then the killer rolls him over and sets the victim on fire. To disguise the body, perhaps, or even . . . to punish the corpse, disfigure it vengefully.

"But what about the other tracks?" Sara asked.

"That doesn't make sense," Grissom admitted, eyes tightening with thought, "unless . . ."

Still kneeling over the impression, Maher asked, "Unless what?"

"Unless the killer didn't have the gasoline along, and had to go back for it."

"Or," Maher offered, "the killer may have had the gas along, but left something behind here at the scene—in the heat of the moment, eh?—and had to come back for it."

"Possible," Grissom granted.

Pulling the first cast up, Maher said, "One other thing."

"Yeah?"

He held the casting of the impression where they both could see it. "Our killer has new boots. I couldn't get a better casting in the parking lot of a shoe store with boots right out of the box."

"So," Grissom said, "we've finally got some real evidence."

Rising, Maher said, "Sara, take your photos of the rest while I bring Grissom up to speed, with the sulfur process."

Pulling her camera out again, Sara asked Maher, "And what are you going to be doing?"

"Well, we've got the killer's feet. Be nice to know his weapon too, eh?"

She just looked at him.

"When I've got both of you working the footprints, I'll go to find our missing bullets."

The sun was hiding and the air was growing colder. Was it going to start snowing again? No wonder Maher was trying to work fast.

Cormier, who'd been a spectator on the sideline for some while, came up to them then. "You folks gonna be much longer?"

"Some time, yes," Grissom said.

"Then I'm goin' back down to the hotel and see if anybody's tryin' to dig us out or anything . . . and find out if the phones are workin' yet. Be back in an hour, okay?"

"Should be fine," Maher said. "And bring up some more coffee, eh?"

Sara whispered to Grissom, "Good day, eh?"

But the reference was lost on him.

Cormier waved and started down the trail.

"Smallish feet for a man," Sara pointed out as the hotel manager disappeared in the trees.

"He doesn't have new boots, though," Grissom said.

"At least, not that he's wearing."

"Then," Grissom said, "we can't eliminate him—or anybody else—as a suspect, yet. So let's get back to work and dig up some more evidence."

Grissom rejoined Maher over by the Sterno burner. Sara went back to work taking pictures, using the tripod and digging down with the scale. She even sprayed the gray primer in a couple of the prints. Sneaking a look at Grissom, she noticed that again he seemed utterly content in his work. Sara wondered idly if she looked that happy as she was spray-painting snow.

Somehow, she doubted it.

8

Catherine Willows could think of only one place to go, on a case this cold: back to the beginning. Under her direction, the CSIs watched old security videotapes from Mandalay Bay, the Chinese restaurant; they read original reports of the detectives and the day-shift crime lab, combing them for any lead that might have been missed thus far. Nothing promising had yet emerged.

Catherine refused to be intimidated by the year they had lost. Nor would she accept the option that they'd run into a killer smart enough to get away with murder. Some murderers did go unapprehended, of course—rare ones who really did outsmart the police; and others who were lucky enough to draw second-rate detectives and third-rate crime labs. Most killers—even the smart ones—made at least one mistake, often many more than one, in the commission of their homicides.

Tonight, Catherine was playing Grissom's role, checking in with her people, cheering them on, exchanging ideas, priming pumps. Walking down the hall through the warren of labs under the cool aqua-tinged lighting, she ran into Greg Sanders, the young, spiky-haired lab rat who looked more like an outlaw skateboarder than the bright young scientist he was. Under his white lab coat, Sanders wore a black T-shirt with a Weezer logo.

"Tell me you found something," she said.

"I have checked every result from the day-shift lab reports."

"Tell me," she repeated, "you found something."

"I have personally examined every bit of evidence collected by Ecklie's people: random hairs, fibers, even the Chinese food container from the Lexus."

"Tell me. You found something?"

He pursed his lips as he thought, carefully; then, abruptly, he said, "No."

She placed a hand on the young man's shoulder. "Tell me when you find something."

Catherine moved on.

She found Warrick Brown—still working on the tire marks—at a computer terminal, fingers flying on the keyboard. His manner was cool, deceptively low-key. Catherine considered Warrick an intense, even driven investigator—the sharp, alert eyes in the melancholy face were the tell.

"Anything?" she asked.

He looked up at her glumly. "The tire mark closest to where Missy got dumped is a General. It's an aftermarket tire that fits a lot of SUVs."

"Which tells us an SUV stopped along the stretch of road where Missy Sherman was found."

"Yes—an SUV that may or may not have been driven by the killer who dumped the body there. With a tire distinctive enough to say it belongs to an SUV, but not narrowing it down much."

"So," Catherine said, "nothing."

"Not nothing," he said. "It's a start."

"Some people say the glass is half-full."

"Grissom says, dust the glass for prints and see who drank the water."

Catherine chuckled softly. "What about the other marks you casted?"

"Two motorcycles."

"Probably not significant."

"Probably not," he agreed. "One tire from an ATV, which is a possibility, but a stretch; the others still unknown."

Catherine nodded. "Keep working it."

"You know I will."

As she moved down the hall, Catherine savored the sweet thought of solving a case day shift had dropped the ball on. That was hardly the top priority, of course—finding the truth and making it possible for justice to be meted out remained much higher on her list; but she'd be lying to herself if she didn't admit the appeal of outshining Sheriff Mobley's lapdog, Conrad Ecklie.

First-shift supervisor Ecklie, after all, gloated over each perceived victory, and had a ready excuse for every loss. He'd made his bones badgering the other two shifts at any opportunity. It would be nice, Catherine thought, if they could find a way to shut him up, if only for a little while.

In the morgue, Dr. Robbins was doing only marginally better than the others.

"Definitely, suffocation," he said. "And it was a plastic bag."

"We know this because . . . ?"

The bearded coroner showed her a sheet of paper. "Read for yourself—tox screen came back, heightened CO_2 level."

"All right," she said, "at least that's something."

"Yeah, but that's all I can tell you on the subject. If you're waiting for me to identify the type and brand of the plastic bag, you'll be disappointed."

Catherine shook her head, patted his shoulder. "You're never a disappointment to me, Doc. . . . Just keep looking."

That left Nick and the videotapes. She found him in the break room with an open bag of microwave popcorn, a Diet Coke, and the remote. His three-button gray shirt had flecks of popcorn salt on the front, his black jeans, too.

Draped in the doorway, she said, "Midnight movies, huh? What's playing—*Rocky Horror*?"

"Well, it's the time warp, all right," he said, and his grin had a little pride in it, which encouraged Catherine.

"Meaning?" she said, at his side now.

"These year-old tapes gave up something. I think. You tell me. . . ."

She pulled up a chair and said, "Pass the popcorn."

He did, and she nibbled, while he went on: "First, you have to understand that there are no cameras on any of the exits at the Mandalay Bay . . . so we have nothing of cars leaving the premises."

"Well, we wouldn't want it to be too easy, right?"

"That's a sentiment I've never quite grasped." He backed up the tape a ways and hit PLAY. "This is at just about 1:35 P.M."

The tape rolled and Catherine, munching the popcorn but glued to the screen, watched the grainy black-and-white image of cars turning into the Mandalay Bay parking lot from the Strip. The camera looked down at the cars and made it impossible to see inside the vehicles.

Three or four cars rolled by before she saw what Nick wanted her to see, a Lexus RX300, pulling into the lot.

"That's Missy?" Catherine asked.

"Yeah. Their Lexus had a Michigan State sticker in the rear window, and it's tough to see at this angle, but, if you know it's there . . ."

He showed her what he meant, and Catherine was able to catch the sticker with its helmeted Spartan head, despite the high angle, or enough of it anyway to sell her on this being Missy's Lexus.

"Now the next car . . ." Nick backed the tape up again, and let the tape play again until the Lexus pulled through the camera shot once more, and was replaced by a dark, boxy car. ". . . is Regan Mortenson's gray Camry."

"All right. Both women were at the Chinese restaurant. Any security tapes available from inside the place?"

He nodded. "The two of them walking through to the restaurant and again when they're leaving. One on one camera, other on another."

"They arrived together," Catherine said, no big deal, "they left together."

"The tape doesn't lie. It's just like Regan told Brass and me, only . . . look at this."

Nick fast-forwarded the tape, the clock in the corner rolling over in high speed. Just after 11:45 P.M., he slowed the tape and brought it to normal speed.

As the grainy images flickered across the monitor screen, Nick said, "I was going through the rest of the tape at high speed . . . probably the same way Ecklie's guys did it . . . but my soda took a tumble and as I reached out to catch it, I stopped the machine right about here."

Cued up properly, the tape revealed several cars rolling past the entrance without pulling in. A few made the turn into the lot, then at 11:49—according to the timer in the corner—an SUV slowed as it approached the entrance, rolled by, then sped up and disappeared.

Catherine froze, a half-handful of popcorn paused in midair. "Holy . . . That looks like . . ."

"It sure does," Nick said, and he backed the tape up until the SUV was once again in front of the entrance, then still-framed the image and—using a nearby computer keyboard—punched keys, zooming in on the side of the vehicle, a Lexus RX300, same color as the Shermans'. It wasn't terribly clear, but in the rear window was the white-and-green Michigan State sticker, Spartan head and all.

Catherine returned the handful of popcorn to the bag. Quietly, as if in church, she said, "And Ecklie's people never noticed this?"

"Apparently not—no record of it." Nick shrugged. "I might've missed it, too, if I hadn't almost knocked over my Coke. We were all looking for cars coming in the entrance, not passing it by. . . . Let me tweak this a little. . . ."

He zoomed in even closer and tried to clear the picture. It remained a little pixilated, but the sticker was unmistakably the Michigan State sticker on the passenger rear window of a Lexus RX300.

"What," Nick asked, "are the odds that this is someone else's Lexus with exactly the same Spartan sticker, in the same position on the same window?"

"Grissom would give you a figure," Catherine said. "I'll just say, slim and none. But, Nick—that car was found in the parking lot!"

He nodded. "That's a fact." Gesturing at the still frame again, he added, "Another fact: this is the main entrance. There are other ways into that lot, and not all are covered by security cams."

Catherine, amazed, said, "Can we ever see the driver?"

"I don't think so. We'll try some image enhancement, but with the angle, and reflections . . . Probably not gonna be lucky on that one."

"Nick, what about talking to the people inside the hotel, when the SUV drove by?"

"Even assuming the driver came inside at some point, there'd be thousands of people in that casino alone. And that was over a year ago. How are we going to track them down?"

"You're right," she admitted. "If this crime had gone down yesterday, we'd be facing tough odds—a year later. . . . So Missy was abducted in her own car, and driven off, and after her murder, the Lexus was returned to the lot?"

"Looking that way."

She thought for a moment. "If the Chinese food in Missy's stomach is undigested, then by the time her car comes back to the hotel . . ."

"She's dead," Nick said.

Perplexed, Catherine pointed at the screen. "Then who the hell is driving that Lexus?"

"Maybe somebody who owns a chest freezer."

"May," Catherine said, "be." She pushed a button on the intercom. "Warrick?"

His voice crackled back over the line. "Cath?"

"Head over to the video lab, would you?"

Soon they were showing Warrick the tape; then they shared with him what they'd surmised.

"If you're thinkin' I need to put my proctology tool up that Lexus," Warrick said, shaking his head, "I gotta tell ya—that baby wasn't that spotless at the dealership. Anything I find could've been easily displaced when Sherman had the interior professionally cleaned."

Catherine asked innocently, "You ID those other tires yet?"

Warrick twitched half a smirk. "That's a work-in-progress."

"Which is the better lead?"

"The Lexus."

"Well, then," she said. "Round up a detective and head back to the Sherman place."

Warrick stood and gave her a grumpy look. "You know, if Gris was here—"

"He'd send your ass out to the Shermans to pick up that Lexus."

Warrick considered that for a second. "Yeah, he would," he admitted, and was gone.

Jim Brass drove Warrick back to the quiet upper-middle-class housing development; calling on people so late at night—it was approaching midnight—was something Warrick could never get used to, rolling into slumbering neighborhoods, delivering nightmares.

Again, one light was on upstairs, and another in the living room of the mission-style house on Sky Hollow Drive. No loud TV emanated, however, and Alex Sherman answered on the first knock. For a change, they were expected: Brass had called ahead, though the detective had given the man no details.

His white sweatshirt (with green Michigan State logo) and green sweatpants rumpled, Sherman greeted them with the hollow look of a man who was either sleeping way too much or hardly at all.

"Do you know something?" he asked, his tone at once urgent and resigned. He had lost his wife and even the best news could not bring her back.

"We do have a lead," Brass said. "You remember Warrick Brown, from the crime lab?"

"Of course."

Warrick picked up the ball. "Could we step inside? We need to talk again."

"Sure . . . come on in. I made coffee."

They did not refuse the offer. This time it was Warrick who sat beside Sherman on the couch, while Brass perched on the edge of a nearby chair. Sherman's dark razor-cut hair stuck out here and there at odd angles, and the man's glasses rode low on his nose. He hadn't shaved in a while.

"I'm a little out of it," he admitted. "I'm getting calls from Missy's relatives, and . . . I haven't even made the funeral arrangements yet."

Brass said, "It's hard getting used to the idea of your wife being gone."

Sherman looked sharply at the detective. "I was used to her being gone. What I'm not used to is her being back . . . and murdered . . . and . . ."

Warrick thought the man might weep, but it was clear he was way beyond that. Nothing to do but get into it. . . .

"Mr. Sherman," Warrick said, "did you ever wonder why it was that you couldn't find your wife's SUV that night?"

Sherman shrugged—not just his shoulders, his whole body seemed to capitulate. "I assumed I was just . . . too screwed up. Too worried and anxious to tell my ass from a hole in the ground."

"It never occurred to you that the car actually may not have been there."

Frowning, Sherman said, "What are you talking about? It was found right there in the lot."

Warrick nodded. "What did you say at the time, when you were questioned?"

"I said, I know my own car, and it wasn't there or I would have seen it."

"You were right."

Sherman didn't grasp Warrick's meaning yet. "But like I said, I've come to realize I must've been so out of it . . . ." Sherman's features had a hard, almost sinister look as he turned a burning gaze on the CSI. "Or . . . are you saying something else?"

"I'm saying something else, sir. Tonight, we finally figured out why you didn't see the Lexus."

"My God," Sherman said, jumping ahead a step, sitting up; it was almost as if he'd been woken with a splash of water. "You mean it really wasn't there?" Sherman finished for him, his eyes widening a little behind his glasses.

Warrick nodded slowly.

"Well, where the hell was it, when I was looking for it?"

"That's just it—we don't know."

"Then how do you know it wasn't there?"

Warrick explained, in some detail, what had been discovered by Nick, going over the surveillance videos.

Sherman's voice rose, and possessed a tremble that might have been sorrow or anger or perhaps both, as he said, "Why, after more than a goddamn year, are you people just now figuring that out?"

Warrick searched for words. Should he tell the grieving husband that the reason was because Nick spilled a pop can? Or maybe share with him the superiority of Grissom's graveyard crew over Ecklie's day shift?

Brass, who'd been quietly sitting drinking the coffee, now sat forward and bailed Warrick out. "A year ago," he said, "a whole different set of investigators, assigned to a missing person case, were looking for cars coming into the hotel. Now, one of our crime lab investigators, new to the case . . . the murder case, Mr. Sherman . . . caught a glimpse of what looked like your car driving past the entrance."

This seemed to placate Sherman, who said, "Well, you told me fresh eyes would be a good thing for the investigation. And I appreciate the validation of my original statement . . . but what good does it do?"

"Plenty," Warrick said. "We think Missy was abducted in her own car, driven away and the car brought back to the Mandalay Bay and parked again."

"To confuse the issue," Brass said.

"All right." Sherman seemed more alert now. "What can I do to help?"

Warrick said, "Allow us to take your van into custody and search for evidence again."

This seemed to disappoint him. "The police didn't find anything a year ago. And the van has been cleaned since then. Stem to stern."

"We know. But with this new information, we need to take another look. We hope you won't ask us to go to the trouble of a warrant, because that will slow us down."

Sherman said, "Whatever it takes. It means a lot to me that you people are doing something."

As Brass went back to the Taurus to call for a tow truck, Warrick said, "We appreciate this, sir. And we'll stay at it until we find whoever did this."

Sherman's expression seemed doubtful. "No offense, but you hear a lot about unsolved cases, and even about people who get caught and then walk . . ."

"We have high arrest and conviction rates, Mr. Sherman. We're ranked the number two crime lab in the country."

Sherman found a smile somewhere. "Well, I guess I know what that means."

"Sir?"

"You try harder."

Warrick returned the man's smile.

"I'll get you the keys," he said, and went off.

The tow truck showed up quickly and, within an hour, Warrick had the SUV in the CSI garage, ready to do his own search of Missy Sherman's Lexus.

The exterior was clean and he checked for prints, but came up with only a few, probably mostly Sherman's, and maybe those of employees at the car wash. Warrick had already asked Brass to contact Premium Car Wash and take employees' prints. Any employees who'd quit in the meantime would have to be tracked down; once again, Warrick was glad not to have Brass's job.

He compared the prints from the Lexus with Sherman's prints on file; one of two sets of prints on the driver's door and the hood belonged to Sherman. The other set belonged to some John Doe— a car wash employee, maybe . . . but almost certainly not Missy's killer.

Being essentially a liquid, fingerprints on the exterior of the vehicle would have long since evaporated in the dry Vegas heat. A fingerprint found in, say, Florida, where the humidity was much higher, would evaporate more slowly. The only way that fingerprint belonged to the killer was if the killer had touched the van a hell of a lot more recently than when murdering Missy.

Warrick also got prints, some full, some only partials, from the other door handles on the vehicle and also from the hood; but all proved to be Sherman's. Getting trace from the tires—to see where the vehicle had been during its missing time—would be useless after the car wash, and Ecklie's people had neglected to do it at the time of discovery because they'd assumed they knew where the SUV had been the whole time.

And when we assume, as Grissom was wont to say, *we make an ass of you and me.*

Warrick opened the rear hatch and combed the carpeting for clues. As he expected, Alex Sherman's cleaning up after Ecklie's people had left little evidence behind: a scuff mark here, a stray hair there.

The scuff mark on the plastic seemed to have come from something black and rubber, but probably not from Missy Sherman's shoe. Chances were that if she had been thrown back there and scuffed the plastic with the heel of her shoe, more than one such mark would've been left.

As for the hair, it was black and short, more likely from Alex Sherman than from his wife or her killer.

Still, Warrick took a scraping from the scuff mark and bagged the hair. He just didn't expect them to pan out.

More of the same awaited him in the backseat, where he bagged a fiber or two and another hair, the latter looking like it was indeed from Missy—black, but much longer than a stray from Alex's razor-cut, where it might have fallen from the driver's seat. He drew a blank on the front passenger seat, then finally made his way to the driver's side.

Using his mini-Maglite, Warrick went over every square inch of the seat and the back. He was about to give up when he glimpsed something pressed between the headrest and the top of the seat. He moved in closer: a blonde hair. Missy's hair was black; also, this hair was longer than Missy's hairstyle would have given up. He plucked it carefully with his tweezers, then bagged it.

As Warrick closed the last door, Brass strolled in, looking bored; but then the detective always appeared bored, even at his most interested. "Anything?"

"Few hairs and a couple of fibers, but this wagon's been cleaned so thoroughly, I was lucky to find 'em."

Warrick stood looking at the SUV for a long moment, as if this were a showroom and he was seriously considering buying. What had he missed? His gut . . . which he listened to religiously, despite Grissom's warnings . . . told him there must be something.

But if there was, why hadn't Ecklie's people found it?

Then he said to Brass, "Is Ecklie a dick?"

"Does a bear shit in the woods?"

"Is graveyard crime lab better than day shift?"

"You're better than just about any CSI shift in the country."

Warrick, surprised by this admission from Brass, said, "Yeah, I know. Thanks. I don't think I'm done here. . . ."

The criminalist went to the driver's side door, bending, looking hard . . . the top ridge, the window, the handle, the . . .

Hoooold it, he thought.

The handle.

Just like the guys on Ecklie's crew, he'd dusted the outside, but what about the underside? Getting out his mini-Maglite, he knelt next to the door and shone the beam up at the underside of the door handle.

"Something?" asked Brass.

"Another brilliant idea . . . nets another nothing."

Warrick stood, stepped back, surveyed the vehicle again. Then he opened the door, glanced around the interior. Looked at the steering wheel, the dash, the windshield and, finally, looked up at . . .

. . . the visor.

"Jim, get me a forceps out of my bag, would ya?"

Brass withdrew the instrument from the silver case and brought it to Warrick. "Got something?"

"Don't know yet."

Using the forceps, Warrick slowly pulled down the visor. Next to the airbag warning label lay a small plastic lid. He used the forceps to raise the plastic and a tiny light came on next to a business-card-sized mirror. Warrick looked at himself in the mirror, and also at a small bit of fingerprint on the corner of the glass.

"There you are," he said, as if to his own image.

Brass was alongside the vehicle now. "Like what you see?"

"It's more than just my handsome face—it's a fingerprint that Eck-lie's people missed."

"How'd they manage that?"

"Didn't pull down the visor. And I bet once I dust the plastic lid, we may have more."

"I thought you didn't bet anymore," Brass said.

"Not often," he said, climbing out of the car to go after his finger-print kit. "And I couldn't tell you what the odds are, here . . . other than that they've just improved."

A white plastic Sears bag in hand, Catherine Willows walked briskly down the corridor, like a shopper at a mall heading for a really great sale.

Catherine, however, had already made her purchases. After mak-ing the rounds of just about every appliance store in Clark County, Catherine had finally ended up "where America shops," to quote a slo-gan from bygone years. The Sears bag held—potentially—two of the most elusive answers in the Missy Sherman inquiry.

She barged right in, startling Dr. Robbins, who was at his desk tak-ing care of paperwork.

"Need a look at one of your customers, Doc," she said, striding over to the vault where Missy Sherman still resided.

"Catherine—what are you doing?"

Setting her bag on a nearby worktable, Catherine opened the vault, slid out the tray bearing Missy's body, then turned and grabbed some-thing from the shopping bag. As she did, Robbins came hustling over, barely letting his metal crutch touch the floor.

"You're pulling a Grissom, aren't you?" Robbins asked.

"I prefer to think of it as a Willows." She held up a small blue piece of rubber that looked a little like a pudgy bullet, rounded at one end, flat on the other end, barely an inch long.

"What do you have there, Catherine?"

Carefully brushing the hair away from the face of the victim, Catherine placed the rounded tip of the rubber nipple against the dead woman's cheek.

The indentation matched perfectly.

Smiling triumphantly and holding up the blue rubber object be-tween thumb and forefinger, Catherine said, "Doctor, you are looking at a frost warning device found in Kenmore chest freezers sold at Sears."

"So," Robbins said, "she was kept in a Kenmore freezer."

"That's the theory. Give us girls a hand, would you?"

"My pleasure."

Grunting, Catherine said, "Here—let's sit her up . . ."

"Okay . . ."

They lifted Missy's corpse so that she . . . it . . . was now sitting on the slab, leaning a little left toward Robbins, almost as if Missy were trying to lay her head on Robbins' shoulder, restfully.

Then, while Robbins held Missy more or less upright, Catherine removed the other item from the bag, a metal rack covered with white plastic, designed to sit across the opening of the freezer and hold smaller items.

Catherine held the tray to the hash mark on the back of Missy's arm.

"Shit," Catherine said.

It didn't match.

Perplexed, she stepped back. "Why didn't that work?" she said.

Robbins looked at the corpse's arm, then at the rack and finally back at the arm. "Flip the rack," he suggested.

She did, then placed it against Missy's arm—perfect!

"That's more like it," she said with some satisfaction. "Now we know what kind of freezer we're looking for."

She helped Doc Robbins lower Missy back down. As the coroner covered his charge carefully, and eased the slab back inside the vault, he asked, "How are you going to track down the specific unit?"

She shrugged. "Frankly, Doc, I have no idea. I'm just happy to put a couple of the pieces together, and start making out a picture. What do you think? Should I go door to door?"

He closed the vault, consigning Missy Sherman's remains to cold storage—again. "How many Kenmore chest freezers with racks and little blue plugs are there in Vegas?"

"Haven't the foggiest. No database I know of would be any help at all."

"What about sales records?"

"Possibly," she said, "but if we go back to when Kenmore started using the blue plug and the rack, that might be a year ago or it could be twenty. Haven't checked, yet."

"If it's twenty," Robbins said, "I would imagine Sears has sold its share here in Vegas."

"And who's to say the freezer was sold in Vegas? Hundreds of people move here every month, bringing their freezers and other things along in the back of their covered wagons."

Robbins nodded. "No offense, Catherine, but I'm glad I don't have your job."

Catherine glanced toward the vault where Missy resided. "You may find this hard to believe, Doc, but I don't spend much time envying you, either."

He smiled at her. "Nice work, Catherine."

"Thanks. Later, Doc."

For almost five minutes, Catherine raced around CSI HQ looking for Warrick and Nick, going room to room with no luck. Finally she found Warrick in the fingerprint lab.

"You wouldn't be in here," she said hopefully, "if you hadn't found something in that Lexus."

Warrick reported his findings, concluding, "The hair and fibers are at Trace, and I'm doing the print off the mirror."

"And?"

"And it doesn't belong to either Alex or Missy Sherman."

"Dare I hope . . . ? But it could be someone from the car wash."

"Could be," Warrick admitted. "And we won't be able to print and eliminate any of them until the car wash opens in the morning."

"You don't have to wait till morning to run it through AFIS, though."

"That's my next step. . . . You've got that look, Catherine."

"What look?"

"Cat? Canary? What have you come up with?"

She told him what she'd learned about the freezer.

"Sweet," Warrick said. "Forward movement. Gotta love it."

Nodding, she said, "Stay on those prints."

"Try and stop me."

She was barely out the fingerprint lab door when her cell phone chirped; she answered it.

"It's Nick." In the background, she could hear the familiar howl of the Tahoe's siren.

Talking and walking, she said, "Where are you rolling to?"

"Murder scene! I think you need to be in on this."

"We're focused on the Sherman woman. You've gone solo before, Nick—what's the problem?"

Nick worked his voice up over the siren: "Radio chatter I been listening to, street cops think it's a strangulation. But no ligature marks!"

Like Missy Sherman.

"Who's the vic?"

"As-yet-unidentified woman about Missy Sherman's age. If she's a thawed-out corpse-sickle, too, we could have a whole 'nother deal, here."

Just what they needed: another serial killer.

"Where's the crime scene?" Catherine said, almost yelling into the phone, which leached siren noise.

Nick was almost yelling, too. "Charleston Boulevard—all the way out at the east end."

"Nick—there's nothing out there."

"Just our crime scene . . . and some houses, up the hill."

"I'll grab Warrick and we'll meet you there." She clicked off without waiting for his response.

In the Tahoe's front passenger seat, Warrick said, "This damn case didn't make any sense when it was just a missing person turned murder. Now you're telling me it might be a double homicide?"

Deciding not to get him stirred up with her serial-killer notion, Catherine—behind the wheel—shook her head. "We don't know the murders are connected."

"Then why are we heading out to the crime scene?"

She shrugged. "Back Nick up."

After that, the pair drove mostly in silence, Warrick unsuccessfully fiddling with the radio trying to scrounge up the same kind of chatter Nick had overheard. They surely would have arrived at the scene a minute or two sooner if Warrick had been driving, but his race-car tendencies made Catherine nervous, so she'd slid behind the wheel. She had enough stress right now.

Soon, she was easing to a stop near Nick's Tahoe. They exited their Tahoe into the chilly night with field kits in latex-gloved hands, their breath visible. Streetlights didn't reach this far past the end of the paved road and halogen work lamps had been set up near the body.

Charleston Boulevard dead-ended at the foot of a mountain, near where several half-million-dollar homes nestled on a ridge, modern near-mansions with a view on rocky, scrubby desolation. Little more than a hundred yards to the south from the houses, near the entrance to a construction road that led off around the mountain, a ditch on the very edge of the desert had become a dumping ground for trash—bulky waste items like carpeting and old sinks, and—tonight—the nude body of a slender white woman around thirty years old.

Just off the side of the construction road, on her back, arms splayed, legs together, the corpse rested amid the garbage, alabaster skin glowing under the brightness of the halogen beams. The glow intensified every time the strobe on Nick's camera went off.

Catherine and Warrick came closer. The uniformed officers were divided into three pairs, their cars blocking the eastbound lane of Charleston Boulevard and a gravel area to the left of the CSI Tahoes. The first pair of officers stood guard near the body, the second pair were assigned to keep any cars coming up Charleston from stopping and gawking, and the last pair stood between the dead woman and a handful of concerned, confused residents who'd wandered down from the expensive homes in the mountain's shadow.

"She frozen?" Warrick asked.

Nick snapped off two more quick pictures. "You'd have to ask Doc Robbins, but I'd say no—none of that moisture under the body found at the Lake Mead scene."

"Strangled, you think," Catherine said.

"Suffocation, anyway," Nick said.

The woman's eyes were open, staring skyward at nothing—with the distinctive petechial hemorrhaging of asphyxia.

"Want me to check for tire marks?" Warrick asked.

"Please," Catherine said.

Moments later, Catherine glanced over to see Warrick slowly looking over the gravel area at the end of the road, in search of tire tracks from the vehicle that had dumped the body. Catherine walked up to the detective who'd caught this case, Lieutenant Lockwood, a tall, athletically built African-American. He gave her a grim smile as she approached.

"Lieutenant," she said.

"Catherine," he said.

"Any witnesses?"

"None we know of."

"Who called it in?"

He nodded toward one of the squad cars, where an Hispanic woman sat quietly in the back, a tissue to her face. Catherine watched until the lady dropped the tissue and Catherine could get a better look at the woman's profile. About all Catherine could tell from here was that the woman's black hair was tied back in a bun. "Who is she?"

"Lupita Castillo," Lockwood said. "Domestic." He turned and pointed toward a rambling two-story stucco.

"Who lives there?"

Tilting his notebook toward the halogen work lights, Lockwood checked. "Jim and Catherine Dietz. He's a honcho with the Democratic party, she's a high-powered attorney. Ms. Castillo, off work, was making her way to the bus stop, couple blocks from here. Stumbles on our dead naked woman."

Looking at the rocky ground, Catherine said, "And Mr. Democrat and Mrs. Mouthpiece can't drive their maid home, or at least to the bus stop?"

"I had the same thought," Lockwood said. "Ms. Castillo says her employers usually drive her to and from work, but they're out of town. Comes by the house every other day just to make sure everything's okay."

"The Dietzes are where?"

"Disney World with their six-year-old daughter."

"Where'd Ms. Castillo call from?"

"She went back up to the Dietz house."

"What was she doing there so late on a Saturday night?"

Lockwood chuckled. "Jeez, Catherine, we think alike."

"Great minds."

"I asked her and she said that she came over after Mass, made herself dinner and watched a cable movie. She said the family lets her do that, when they're away—makes it look like someone's home."

"Sounds credible," she said. She gave Lockwood a tight, businesslike smile. "Time to go to work."

With Nick taking photos, Catherine was free to do a detailed study of the body.

The woman's blonde hair spiked a little on the top and, on the back and sides, was no longer than Nick's. Tiny, junkie-thin, with nearly translucent skin, the woman reminded Catherine of the dancers she used to work with who were locked in clubs all night and their apartments all day. They never saw the sun and their skin took on a ghostly pallor. This woman shared that unhealthy skin tone, but for the crimson slashes of lipstick.

With her eyes open, the dead woman seemed to float above the garbage pile; she might have been on her back in a swimming pool, looking up at the piece of moon and the scattering of stars.

Catherine sensed someone at her side.

Nick.

"Just threw her away," he said, his expression grave. "Like another piece of trash." He shook his head.

"Oh yeah," Catherine said. "We have to nail this monster, Nick . . ." She gave him her loveliest smile. ". . . for leaving us a garbage dump to process as a crime scene, if nothing else."

He nodded, eyebrows high, a smile beginning to dig a dimple in one cheek, and said, "You got that right."

And they went to work.

9

The crime scene was still and lovely, sunlight dancing off the white expanse, with almost no wind. Sara was taking photos when the hotel manager trudged back up into the crime-scene area, a thermos under either arm. His expression was grave, but he sounded cheerful enough as he called, "Hot coffee!"

Grissom and Maher immediately slogged over to where Cormier had set up shop at the tree that served as their watch post. Maher in his parka might have been reuniting with his Eskimo brother, when he approached the similarly attired Cormier. The hotel manager poured the brew into Styrofoam cups he'd withdrawn from a coat pocket. Sara finished her latest series of photos, then joined the group. Cormier handed her a steaming cup, which she blew on before taking a hesitant sip.

"I was just telling your partners here," Cormier said, "the sky's plannin' to dump more snow on us."

She looked from Grissom to Maher, their faces as grim as Cormier's. "More snow," she said.

Cormier nodded. "Weather report is not encouraging. Could be as many as ten more inches."

"So much for the forensics conference," Grissom said.

"Officially canceled," Cormier said. "Got an e-mail from two of the state board members who set it up."

Maher sighed over his cup, and the cold steam of his breath mingled with the hot steam of the coffee. "Is anybody getting in?"

With a quick head shake, Cormier said, "No one gettin' out, either. I don't look for the State Police to even try, till later."

"Define 'later,'" Grissom said.

"Not right now," Cormier said, ambiguously.

Sara sighed a cloud, and in exasperation said, "What next?"

Grissom turned to her and spoke over the ridge of his muffler. "Finish our coffee and go back to working the crime scene. Just because it snows doesn't change the job, Sara."

Yes, out here in the beautiful snowy woods, Sara was experiencing a true Grissom moment. Only her boss would provide a literal answer to what a billy goat would have easily perceived as a rhetorical question.

Grissom was asking the Canadian, "What's the story with the sticks over there?"

Sara had been wondering that herself.

"It's a technique developed by two Saskatchewan game wardens," Maher said. "Buddies of mine—Les Oystryk and D. J. McGill. Come on, I'll show you."

Maher led the CSIs to the stick he'd planted at the downhill end of his line. "It's a pretty simple theory, really," he said, gesturing with a gloved hand, as if passing a benediction. "I placed a stake where the bullet entered the snow."

Eyes tight, Grissom asked, "Denoted by the beginning of the streak you saw yesterday?"

"Exactly. Normally, we'd run a string or flagging tape twenty feet to a second stake, aligning it with the streak in the snow that showed the bullet's path. But with snow this deep, I simply ran the second stake as straight as I could, and planted it without the string."

Sara asked, "And the bullet never deviates from the path in the snow?"

" 'Never' isn't in my lexicon," Maher said. "If the slug hit a rock or something, deviation is possible, even probable—but with snow like this to slow the bullet, the path won't be altered much."

Grissom gestured back toward the toboggan. "Which is where your metal detector comes in."

"Yes," the constable said. "Lucky I brought it along for my presentation, eh? . . . I think we'll find the bullet within three feet of that line, on either side."

"This technique," Grissom said. "How often is it successful?"

"Most of the time . . . 'Always' isn't in my lexicon, either." He turned toward the hotel manager, who was still under the tree, and called, "Mr. Cormier!"

"Yes, sir?"

"Need a favor!"

Cormier came over. "What can I do you for, Mr. Maher?"

Pointing just beyond and to the left of the body, Maher said, "Take the shovel and clear me a space in the snow, oh, three by three feet."

Nodding, Cormier asked, "How deep?"

"Down to the dirt, please. We're creating a control area."

"Shovel's just about my level of high tech," Cormier said, and marched off to the toboggan, where he fetched the shovel and went over to start digging.

While Grissom worked on casting footprints, Sara helped Maher get his metal detector assembled and running. Giving him room, she accompanied the Canadian as he and it traveled back and forth over the track the bullet had taken. Every time he pointed at a spot, she placed a smaller stick.

She'd marked only two spots when he stopped, stared at the ground in confusion, and said, "Well, that's weird, eh?"

"What is?"

"Gettin' a beep here, on something a whole lot bigger than a bullet."

"Any idea what?"

Maher shook his head. She inserted a stick at the spot and he kept moving. When he finished, four different places had been marked by Sara in that fashion.

Sara asked, "Now what?"

"We run the metal detector over our control area," Maher said.

She watched as he ran the detector over the bare spot Cormier had created.

"All right," Maher said. "It's clear—no metal in the dirt. Sara, get a garbage bag from the sled, would you?"

Sara trotted over, grabbed one of the black bags, came back and handed it to Maher.

As he ripped out the seams, Maher said, "Now we'll cover the bare spot Mr. Cormier made for us."

"Oh," Sara said, understanding. "We're going to put the snow we marked onto the plastic, and sift through it."

Maher nodded. "But first we dig. You take those two," he said, pointing at the two marked spots nearest the downhill end of the line.

Then he went over and knelt in the snow, next to two spots further up the line. "And I'll take these two."

Sara had hardly begun to dig down when she saw something pink, and froze. "Constable! Grissom! . . . I think you both better see this."

They came over.

Grissom crouched over her find. "Blood . . ."

Maher, hovering, asked, "What the hell's that doing here?"

Reflexively, they all glanced back toward the snowy hump of the body almost ten yards uphill; but the victim wasn't talking.

Maher looked from Grissom to Sara. "Didn't you say the only blood was near the body?"

"That's right," Sara said. "We didn't see any this far down."

Grissom asked, "Could this patch of blood have already been covered by snow?"

"I don't think so," Sara said. "Not in the time between our hearing those shots and coming onto this crime scene."

Maher's expression, in the fuzzy cameo created by the parka, was thoughtful. "Could be someone covered it on purpose, hastily kicked snow over it. . . . Besides those footprints, you see any other disturbed snow?"

Grissom said, "No," and Sara shook her head.

Then she asked her boss, "Do you have one of those bug specimen bottles on you?"

A small bottle materialized in Grissom's gloved palm; he handed the container over to her.

Using the cap, she shooed the pink snow into the bottle, then closed it. She handed the little bottle to Grissom and went back to her digging, only now she was more careful, much slower, searching every inch to make sure she didn't miss any evidence. Maher went to work on his spots, and Grissom returned to footprint duty.

Stripping off her gloves, she started digging with her fingers, not trusting the shovel or even her gloves to keep her from contaminating any more evidence. The cold and wet of the snow was kind of refreshing at first, but it only took a couple of minutes before her fingers turned red and the tips started to numb up.

She was just starting to think taking off the gloves was a really dumb idea when she touched something hard.

Her hand jumped out of the hole as if she'd been bitten by a snake.

"Are you all right?" Grissom asked, running over to her. He sounded genuinely concerned.

"Something metallic," she said. "Not small . . ."

They both looked toward Maher, working at his own spot; but his eyes were on them, as well. The constable came over and drew a forceps from a pocket. "Can you get it with this?"

"Should be able to." She accepted the tool, inserted her bare hand and the forceps down into the hole. Maneuvering carefully, she worked the ridged jaws around the object. Squeezing, she dragged the object out of the snow, like pulling a tooth. It felt heavy and came out slowly. When the object finally appeared from the snow, they all froze, as if the cold had finally caught up with them.

Only it was not cold, rather shock.

"A knife?" Maher asked, as if he wanted confirmation of what his eyes had shown him. "You said our vic was shot."

"He was," Grissom said.

Sara held up the knife in the jaws of the forceps, squinting at it. The thing wasn't that big—blade no more than four inches long.

"Our victim was shot, all right," she said. "And so . . . how do we explain this?"

"More blood," Grissom said, almost admiringly.

A pink sheen covered much of the blade.

They all traded looks.

"There's no knife wounds in the body, right?" asked Maher.

"None plainly visible," Grissom said. "Does this mean our killer took defensive wounds away from this scene?"

All three looked up the hill to where the body lay, almost thirty feet away. *Still not talking . . .*

"Blood," Maher said. "How is that possible?"

"There's not much blood here," Sara said, meaning both the knife blade and the snowy stuff she'd gathered.

"Which means?"

It doesn't start out as a chase. The victim-to-be and a companion come partway up the hill together. They're talking, arguing even, and a verbal confrontation turns ugly and physical . . . and the vic-to-be stabs the companion, who pulls a gun in self-defense . . .

. . . and now it's a chase, beginning somewhere down the slope. The companion is running and shooting, and by the time the two reach this

point, the killer's missed twice, two wide shots. The vic drops the knife, in the process of trying to escape, running for his life; but he only makes it another ten yards, before he catches a bullet in the back and goes down. Then the companion goes to the fallen victim, dead now, and decides to disfigure or disguise the body. The killer goes back to the hotel, collects the gas can, and returns for the impromptu funeral pyre.

"It plays out similarly with three participants," Sara said with a shrug.

Grissom and Maher were both nodding.

"It's a scenario that suits the evidence we have," Grissom said. "Let's keep working and get some more data, and see what we can build from that. . . . Sara, put your gloves back on. We don't want to have to amputate your fingers."

Ruefully, Maher said, "Looks like our vic was one of those poor bastards who brought a knife to a gunfight."

"Not much of a knife, at that," Sara said.

"Still," Grissom said. "Pretty big for a pocket knife."

"But not big enough," Maher said, "to go up against bullets."

Moving in from the sidelines, Cormier asked, "Is . . . is that blood the killer's?"

Maher said, "Good chance of it."

"Don't mean to tell you experts how to do your job," the hotel man said. "But can't you just get the killer's blood type from that, and identify him?"

"In a lab we could," Grissom said. "Not out here." He spread his gloved hands, indicating the forest. "Anyway, the blood on that blade froze overnight, and the red cells will all have ruptured. If we had the lab, we could type it through the plasma, but not under these conditions."

Going back to work, they carefully emptied the snow from the other holes one shovelful at a time. When they had emptied twelve-inch circles around each of the markers and placed the snow on the spread-out garbage bag, Maher went over the smaller pile again with the metal detector as Sara and Cormier watched.

When Maher got a hit, Sara dropped to her knees, and slowly sifted through the area. After a moment, she found it. Holding it up, she stared at the tiny ice ball with the dark, lead center. "What happened?"

With a little grin, Maher said, "Snow happened. The hot bullet melted it, then the condensation froze around the cartridge as it slowed the bullet down."

They repeated the process with all the snow from the places they'd marked, but they found only one more bullet and a coin, a quarter.

"Here ya go, Gordy," she said, flipping the quarter to the Canadian.

"Not that much less than I usually get," Maher said, catching it.

"Yeah," Sara said, with a grin, "but that's American."

"Good point, eh?"

Moving over to Grissom, Sara said, "Two bullets. When I get the ice off 'em, we'll have a better idea what we've got."

"Good work," he said. Then, rising from the print he was working on, he picked two different left-foot castings from the line he'd done. "What do you think of this?"

She studied the castings. "They're the same boot."

He nodded. "Two different sets of tracks made by the same boots. One killer, two trips out and back."

"That confirms my reconstruction."

"Far as it goes . . . We need more evidence."

Maher joined them. "How are the castings coming, Dr. Grissom?"

"Finished. Just getting ready to pack up."

"All right. I've got the bullets. Don't think there's anything else we can do here."

Sara asked, "What about the body?"

Maher gave Grissom a hard look. "What do you think, Dr. Grissom? Are we done with the scene?"

Grissom glanced around, eyes tight with thought; then, slowly, he nodded.

"I agree," Maher said. "I suggest we take the body with us . . . which is part of why we brought the toboggan."

"Hold on!" Cormier called from the sidelines, where he'd been listening. "How come you can take the body now, when you couldn't before?"

"Before," said Grissom, "it was part of an active crime scene. Now that we've worked the scene, we can remove the body."

Shaking his hooded head, the old man walked away.

Maher glanced toward the sky, saying, "If we can pack up quick enough . . ."

"We have a shot at the parking lot," Grissom finished.

"Let's go sledding, then," Sara said.

Grissom and Maher carefully dug out the body, wrapping it tightly in the space blanket and binding it to the toboggan. As they worked with the remains, Sara gathered up the tools and added them to the load. Within fifteen minutes, they were starting back down the slope.

Again, Cormier was in the lead, Maher dragging the toboggan, Grissom and Sara bringing up the rear, making sure their package stayed wrapped up. As they trudged along, they discussed what to do with the body.

When they reached the edge of the parking lot, its scattering of vehicles so topheavy with snow they resembled big white mushrooms, the CSIs were still hashing over the subject.

Maher said, "Maybe we should just bury it in the snow again."

Sara made a face. "We just dug it out!"

The Canadian nodded, saying, "Yes, but the killer set it on fire for a reason . . ."

Grissom said, "And you're worried that by bringing it into the hotel, we're giving the killer a chance to finish the job."

The constable shrugged. "It is a consideration."

"If we bury it outside again, we'll have to set up another rotating shift," Maher said, "to guard it from predators."

"Please God," Sara said, the hotel and its promised warmth so nearby, "let there be another way."

They had reached the shoveled area near the rear door of the hotel, parking the toboggan alongside.

Grissom looked toward the manager. "Mr. Cormier, do you have a walk-in cooler?"

Cormier snorted a laugh. "Can't run a hotel this big without one. . . . You're not . . . ?"

Cormier's eyes followed Grissom's to the blanketed body strapped to the toboggan.

Grissom asked, "Does the cooler have a lock?"

"Well, padlock, yeah, but—"

"Who has keys?"

"Me, the Missus, and Mrs. Duncan, she's the head cook. But you can't seriously—"

"What about the fry cook?" Maher asked. "What's his name?"

Cormier said, "Bobby Chester. He doesn't have a key. Usually, he only works during the day, and the Missus or me is always around. But gentlemen, you can't honestly be considering . . ."

Grissom and Maher were trading looks.

Then Maher said, "Mr. Cormier, we're going to have to ask you to collect the keys and give them to us."

The hotel man was shaking his head. "You can't really be suggesting we stow that . . . corpse, in the walk-in cooler?"

Grissom and Maher just looked at him. Sara, astounded herself, was enjoying watching this play out.

"There are sanitary issues," Cormier was saying, "there are laws we'd be breaking . . ."

"Not more serious than murder," Grissom said. "We have to insist. We're commandeering your cooler."

"Tell me this is some sick joke," the hotel manager said. "What would I tell the health inspector?"

Maher said, "Mr. Cormier, it's really the only option that makes sense."

"But the guests, what will they say?"

"You're not to tell them," Grissom said. "The fewer people that know what we're doing, the better."

"Well, now," Cormier said, "finally we agree on somethin'!"

Maher smiled pleasantly, but in an entirely businesslike way. "Would you get us that padlock key, please?" He turned to Grissom. "We really should start to hurry on the parking lot."

The hotel man sighed and it hung in the air. "Be back in a few minutes."

Cormier started away, and Sara called out: "Sir!"

He turned. "Yes, Ms. Sidle?"

"You might not want to mention this to Pearl."

The hotel man's eyebrows rose, then he nodded, saying, "Good thought, Ms. Sidle. Good thought."

They watched as the dejected-looking Cormier went inside.

Maher asked Sara, "What's this about Mrs. Cormier? We got another suspect?"

"If our host really wants to keep the news about a stiff in the cooler from the guests," Sara said, "he'll be wise to keep it from his wife. . . . She's one of the few communications systems around here not affected by the storm."

"Ah," Maher said.

"Now about the blood on that knife blade," Sara said.

Maher and Grissom faced her.

"What about it?" her boss asked.

"That waitress, Amy Barlow? She's got a bandage—cut on her hand."

Grissom nodded, remembering. "She said she got it slicing onions in the kitchen. Do we believe her?"

Sara shrugged. "She's the only person I've seen with a cut."

"There's the waiter," Maher said.

Sara frowned. "The one who dropped the tray?"

"Spot on his sleeve, eh?"

Sara smiled. "Oh, you noticed that. . . . I couldn't tell what it was. He's working with food and liquids, so that stain—"

"Might have been blood," Maher said. "Could explain why he dropped that tray. Weak arm, sore arm."

"Have we narrowed the list of suspects," Grissom asked, "or increased it?"

Maher shook his head. "We still don't really have any significant evidence pointing toward anyone."

Sara asked, "Is there any way to cross-match the blood on the knife?"

Grissom shook his head as well. "Doubtful the hotel has the tools for that."

Cormier emerged and trailing him—surprisingly enough—was Tony Dominguez, the tall, slender Hispanic waiter. Instead of his white-shirt-and-black-slacks uniform, the young man wore a loose-fitting white sweatshirt with an orange Syracuse logo on the front, and new black jeans. In white tennis shoes, Dominguez did not venture into the snow, rather stayed on the shoveled sidewalk near the rear door.

The investigators were trading what-the-hell expressions when Cormier strode over and said, "You said you all were in a hurry—I thought you might need some help carrying the . . . uh . . . package inside."

"Thanks," Grissom said tightly, "but we can probably manage."

Cormier gestured toward the building. "You sure? We'll be going in through the delivery entrance down there. It's a long haul."

Maher said to Grissom, "I know it's not exactly what we had in mind, but why don't you and Herm and . . . what's your name, son?"

"Tony," the young man said, hands dug in his pants pockets.

"You should have a jacket, son."

"Mr. Cormier said this wouldn't take long."

"It doesn't have to. If you three will escort the . . . package inside, Ms. Sidle and I will get started out here. Snow's coming and the sooner we're at it, the better our chances of finding something useful."

Grissom, clearly not liking this a bit, nonetheless said, "All right."

Then Maher, Sara, and Grissom stripped the lawn tools and CSI equipment off the toboggan, and Sara and Maher—weighed down by their load—went off across the parking lot to where the tomato stakes barely peeked out of the snow.

While Sara worked with the constable, Gil Grissom took command of the corpse-hauling detail.

He said to Dominguez and Cormier, "You'll have to lead the way, gentlemen."

Cormier, who'd already shown himself to be squeamish around the remains, didn't make a move. And the young man just stood there staring at the sled.

"Is that the . . . body?" he asked.

Grissom shot an irritated look at Cormier, who shrugged and shook his head, his expression saying, *I didn't tell him!*

"So much for discretion," Grissom said to the hotel man. Then, with a tight smile, he said to the waiter, "This is a body, yes. It needs refrigeration. We're preserving evidence."

"Ohmigod . . ." The young man swallowed. "I thought it was just a rumor."

Grissom, whose patience had run out already, said, "Are you up to helping with this? I can get Ms. Sidle back here, if you two aren't capable."

Dominguez, his eyes still riveted to the space blanket lashed to the toboggan, said, "I . . . I'm up to it. Do we . . . undo this, unwrap it, or . . . are we moving the toboggan, too?"

"Toboggan and all," Grissom said. "There's other perishable evidence here, and it's all going into the cooler until the police arrive."

Grissom hated having another of the suspects this close to the remains, but at this point there was nothing to be done. It was almost as
if Cormier were trying to complicate matters.

He glanced over at the work going on in the parking lot, Maher with
the leaf blower, again dispersing snow, clearing the footprints near the
blue Grand Prix, Sara assisting. Already snowflakes were drifting to
earth all around, the wind picking up too, and Grissom knew that the
only way they had any chance of getting the prints from the parking lot
was to get the body inside with the help of the waiter—suspect or not.

"Can we do this, please?" Grissom asked.

Intimidated, the waiter took the front end and Grissom the rear,
facing each other as they lifted it between them.

"I'll get the doors and clear a path," Cormier said, moving out
ahead; but Dominguez was already backing toward the little receiving
dock at the far end of the parking lot.

They were off the shoveled area now, shuffling through high snow,
taking care to keep their balance. The sled and its charred cargo
seemed surprisingly heavy to Grissom. The victim hadn't been a particularly large man, but with the added weight of the toboggan, Grissom
might have been helping haul anvils. Having the corpse buried in snow
overnight, with the beginnings of the freezing process kicking in, had
cut the foul odor of the roasted flesh, at least.

"Who is this?" Dominguez asked suddenly, eyes on the space-blan-
ket-wrapped "package."

"No ID," Grissom said. "Don't look at it yet."

The two of them made eye contact then, the waiter backing toward
the loading dock, Grissom with the corpse before him, the pair working together, Cormier slogging through the snow to get ahead of them.

"Stairs," Grissom said, for the waiter's benefit, and they halted for
just a moment so Cormier could kick the snow off the four concrete
steps that led up to the dock. When the man had finished, the waiter
took a moment to get his bearings, then nodded at Grissom and
backed up the first step.

Starting up the steps put even more of the weight on Grissom, and
he let the young man set the pace—if Grissom pushed, they might
lose their grip and wind up dumping their cargo. But Dominguez—
slightly built though he was—was doing fine, taking the second and
third steps with no trouble. Cormier was unlocking and opening

a door on the loading dock when Dominguez reached the landing . . . and slipped.

The weight came forward, as if Grissom was on the down end of a seesaw, and Cormier—to his credit—quickly grabbed on to the waiter's abandoned end of the toboggan, bracing it.

In the meantime, Dominguez had sat down, rudely, on the loading dock, the baggy lefthand sleeve of his sweatshirt hiking up to reveal a white-gauze-bandaged arm. Quickly, obviously embarrassed, the young man got to his feet, tugging the sleeve down over his bandaged arm, and took his end of the sled back from the older man.

"You all right, Tony?" Grissom asked.

"Caught some ice—sorry."

Grissom, gritting his teeth and supporting most of the weight himself, asked, "Ready?"

"Sure."

Cormier had returned to his post, holding open the door, as they once again started moving.

"Just a littler further," Cormier said.

The complex arrangement of rope and bungee cords that bound the body to the toboggan had held tight all the way down the hill, but now—as Grissom and the waiter turned the sled on an angle, to fit it through the narrow door—a rigor-stiffened hand slipped free.

No one but Grissom had noticed this—yet—and the CSI wasn't about to call attention to it, not and risk winding up holding the heavy end of the load alone, again. Once they were through the door, the CSI and the waiter tipped the toboggan back upright, the hand sliding partway back under the space blanket.

The hall was concrete—floor, walls, ceiling. Lightbulbs encased above in wire cages, every fifteen feet or so, half-heartedly lit their passage down this damp, cold hallway, which had all the charm and ambience of a Tower of London dungeon. Slipping by on Grissom's right, on the side away from the exposed hand, Cormier moved on ahead of them, boots clomping like horse hooves.

Grissom heard the click as Cormier tripped the padlock, then the cooler door yawned open, the rubber seal at its base scraping along a floor already scoured to a high sheen.

"You almost expect the Crypt Keeper to step out," Dominguez said with a nervous laugh.

Grissom, having no idea what the kid was talking about, nodded noncommittally.

"All the way to the far wall, now," Cormier said from behind the open door. "I keep the meat on the left, and I don't want this thing near it. . . . Tony, you know where to stow it."

"You got it, Mr. C," Tony called.

The refrigerated room was about the size of a holding cell. Shelves on the left wall were stacked with boxes marked with the names of individual cuts and types of meat, fish, poultry, and pork. The wall at right was lined with wire baskets, small bins brimming with bags of lettuce, stalks of celery, bunches of radishes, bags of carrots, sacks of onions, and also some fruit—grapefruit, oranges, melons. Behind Grissom, on the wall the door opened from, were stacked cartons of ketchup and mustard bottles, jars of pickles and relish, gallon tubs of salad dressing and the like. The far wall was a blank metal slate, nothing even piled there, and that was where Cormier directed them to deposit this delivery.

Cormier was throwing together a basket of food—meat, vegetables, fruit, as if he'd been shopping. "I need to get tonight's food out of here—rest of this stuff is probably gonna be condemned."

"Fine," Grissom said.

The hotel manager was scurrying out as Grissom and the waiter set the sled down with great care on the concrete floor, parallel to the steel wall. They both stood and then Dominguez glanced down and saw the hand. Kneeling, he raised the edge of the blanket to tuck the hand back under.

"I'll get that," Grissom said.

But Dominguez had already seen more than any of them had bargained for; his expression was horror-struck.

Grissom said, "You know this man?"

Gasping, the waiter was backing away, then turned and ran, almost knocking Grissom down and bumping into Cormier, who was on his way back in.

The young man collapsed against the corridor wall, in a sprawled sitting position, heaving sobs, hugging himself.

Grissom exited the cooler. To Cormier he said, "Keep an eye on him."

"What the hell happened?"

"He recognized the victim."

While Cormier stayed with the waiter, Grissom went back inside and carefully repackaged the body under the blanket. When Grissom emerged, Dominguez was still sitting, leaning against the wall, his head in his hands, Cormier crouching next to him, a hand on the young man's shoulder.

"You have the keys?" Grissom asked Cormier.

The hotel man nodded.

Grissom snapped the padlock shut. At least the body was secure, now.

Still crouching by his employee, Cormier handed up a ring with three identical keys to Grissom. "This is all of them."

With a dismissive nod, pocketing the keys, Grissom turned his attention to the waiter. The CSI pulled off his stocking cap, stuffed it in a jacket pocket, removed the muffler, did the same with it; gloves came off, too. All the while he was watching Dominguez as he might an insect specimen, observing as the waiter seemed to implode there against the wall, his legs stretched out in front of him, face buried in his hands, sobs racking his body.

"If you can get ahold of yourself," Grissom said to the waiter, as gently as he could, "we should talk. All right?"

Dominguez didn't acknowledge Grissom's presence, much less his question.

Cormier remained at Dominguez's side, that supportive hand still on the boy's shoulder. Taking the other side, Grissom sat beside the boy, too.

"How did you recognize the victim?" Grissom asked. "Without seeing his face?"

Dominguez looked up at Grissom, finally; tears pearled the handsome boy's long eyelashes. The waiter's voice was a pitiful rasp. "I knew . . . know . . . the coat. I gave it to him. To James."

"James? Jim Moss?" Cormier interrupted.

Dominguez nodded.

"He's a waiter here," Cormier explained.

Grissom nodded, his attention on the boy.

"You gave that coat to James. You must have been good friends."

Dominguez shrugged. "We were lovers."

Cormier's eyes widened and he blew out breath, like Old Man

Winter; but whatever Old Man Cormier might have thought about such a relationship, his hand never left Dominguez' shoulder.

"He really loved that coat," Dominguez was saying.

A coat, Grissom knew, wasn't near good enough for an ID. "Does James have any distinguishing marks?"

"Well . . . a tattoo."

"Where? Could you describe it?"

"On his back." Dominguez touched a spot just over his own shoulder. "A rose. A tiny rose . . . for his mom. Her name was Rose. She died when he was in high school."

Suddenly Dominguez grabbed the front of Grissom's varsity jacket, startling the CSI. "That's the kind of person James was! Remember that! You tell people that! Be sure to!"

"I will," Grissom assured the boy, who released the CSI's jacket and sat back again, deflated after the outburst.

Cormier, whose hand had been jerked away when Dominguez sat forward, was sitting quietly, just watching his employee.

"Tony," Grissom said, each word emerging with care, "I'm going to need you to identify that tattoo."

The waiter's eyes went wide again and he shook his head rapidly. "Oh no, oh no! I can't go back in there!"

"You can," Grissom said. "You have to."

"I do not have to!"

"If you want to help James—"

"He can't be helped now!"

"We have to determine what happened to him. That's the only help we can give him, now. . . . All right?"

The boy thought about that.

Then he swallowed and nodded.

"Herm," Grissom said, "please sit here with Tony."

"No problem," Cormier said, and put his hand on the boy's shoulder again.

Grissom rose. "Now, Tony—just wait here. Stay calm. I have to go in and get things ready. Then all you have to do is identify the tattoo . . . if there is one."

Another swallow, another nod.

Grissom arched an eyebrow. "Remember, this could be someone wearing a coat like James's, or even wearing James's own coat. We have to be sure."

The boy's eyes brightened. "You mean, it might not be him!"

"That is possible."

"It could be someone else wearing his coat! Somebody he loaned it to, 'cause of the cold. He was always helping people . . ."

The CSI supervisor noticed that Dominguez had used the past tense. Did that mean anything, or was the boy's mind already accepting the inevitability that the corpse in the cooler was James?

Grissom unlocked the door. Inside the cooler, he uncovered the body, rolled it over to get at the victim's back, which hadn't been burned at all, and slowly peeled away layers until he got to the dead man's shoulder . . .

. . . where could be seen a small red-and-blue rose, a rather delicate tattoo.

After covering as much of the body as he could, leaving only the area with the tattoo exposed, Grissom called, "Mr. Cormier! Would you bring Tony in here, please."

Cormier's arm was around the boy, who entered on wobbly legs.

"Is this James?" Grissom asked. He was kneeling next to the body, gesturing to the red-and-blue rose. "Do you recognize the tattoo?"

Dominguez stepped away from Cormier's protective arm, staggered over and glanced down. Again he swallowed, nodded, and tears immediately began to flow again, sobs shaking his chest. Grissom covered the victim up, nodded to Cormier to lead Dominguez back to the corridor, which he did, and then Grissom exited and relocked the cooler door.

Cormier was standing beside the boy, who again sat slumped against the wall, staring hollowly, breathing hard, but the tears and sobs had ceased, for now anyway.

"Give us a few moments, Mr. Cormier," Grissom said.

The hotel man nodded, said, "You'll be fine, Tony—Dr. Grissom here is a good man. . . . I left my basket of food out on the dock. I'll cart it up to the kitchen."

"Do that," Grissom said.

And then Cormier left them alone, the inquisitive CSI and the heartbroken waiter.

"What was your friend's full name?" Grissom asked.

The reply was sharp, angry; that was bound to come. "He wasn't my friend. He was my lover . . . okay?"

"What was your lover's full name?"

"James R. Moss. The 'r' stood for Rosemont. It was a family name. Maybe that's why his mother was named Rose. . . . You're a doctor?"

"Not a medical doctor, Tony. Tell me about James."

Dominguez answered with his own question. "How did he get burned like that?"

Grissom wondered if the question was serious or calculated to keep him from suspecting Dominguez. He had no reason to doubt that this boy had loved James Moss; but love, like hate, was among the most common murder motives.

Grissom gave it to him straight: "He was shot and killed."

"Oh my God . . ."

"And whoever did that, for some reason, set fire to the body afterward."

"What? Why?"

"That's part of what I'm trying to determine. That's the kind of a doctor I am, Tony. Forensics."

" . . . for the conference this weekend."

"Right. Tell me about him."

Dominguez wiped his eyes with the back of a sweatshirt sleeve, the one belonging to the arm without the bandage. "James was sweet and funny and kind. Honest, too, very honest. Nobody would ever want to hurt him."

"Did the two of you have any problems?"

"Oh, no! We were happy. Very compatible."

Grissom gestured toward the boy's sleeve. "When we almost dropped the sled out there, I noticed you have a kind of nasty cut, there."

Unconsciously, the waiter touched his wounded arm. "How could you see that?"

"Well, I mean . . . I saw the bandage."

Dominguez pushed up the loose sleeve and exposed gauze running from his elbow nearly to his wrist. "Looks bad, huh? Hurts worse."

"How did that happen, Tony?"

The boy took a moment, then said, casually, "Working on my car."

"I need you to be more specific."

He shrugged. "Cut myself putting on a new exhaust system."

"Really?" Grissom said, with an insincere smile. "People still do that themselves?"

Dominguez found a small grin somewhere, relieved by the apparent subject change. "Well, I do. I've got an old car. I do it to save money, but I'm into it, maybe 'cause it's so . . . so . . ." He laughed a little. ". . . butch."

"Is your car in the hotel lot right now?"

His smile faded. "No. Why? Does that matter?"

"James was your lover."

"I told you that."

"The evidence indicates that James fought back. That his assailant was cut. That fact, along with your intimate relationship with the victim, makes you a suspect in James's murder."

Dominguez' eyes widened. "You think I killed James? That's bull-shit, man, I loved the dude! He was the only thing that kept me going in this hellhole!"

"I said you're a suspect . . . and you are. And so is everyone else in this place. Even me, and my assistant, because we found James, and the first people to discover a body . . . they're always the first suspects."

"What are you trying to say?"

"Just don't get bent out of shape. Try not to give in to this grief. Help me find who did this to James." Grissom paused, drew a breath, went on. "Tony, being a suspect doesn't make you guilty; but we should both recognize that the probability is . . . James was killed by someone he knows."

"Why? Everybody loved him!"

"Love can be a murder motive. And the statistics say that most murder victims know their murderers . . . often intimately. None of this makes you guilty or makes me believe that you're the killer . . . but, Tony, you're bright. You must see how this looks."

Calming down, Dominguez finally nodded. "I can see how it looks," he admitted. But then he bitterly added, "Two gay guys—one must be a homicidal maniac."

Grissom shook his head. "That's not the issue."

"The one you *should* be hounding is Amy."

"Amy Barlow? The waitress?"

"That's right," Dominguez said. "Amy Barlow, the waitress. She was with James before, you know . . . me."

Grissom's eyes tightened. "James was bisexual?"

"Whatever. I'm not into labels."

"What do you know about his relationship with Amy?"

Dominguez shrugged. "She latched on to him when he started here. Maybe a year and a half ago. They went together for, oh . . . six months, I guess. Then he and I got to be friends—we liked the same music, same movies. We were just made for each other. Really clicked."

"That's nice."

"It was nice, and Amy, she didn't like it at all. When James started seeing me, she really flipped. She just would not let it go."

"Even though James told her it was over?"

Dominguez shrugged again. "Truth is . . . he never did really break it off with her, not entirely. His dad is this retired master sergeant from the marines—Born Again, superstraight. And James just didn't think the old man could've understood his lifestyle—he would've died if his dad ever called him a faggot."

Grissom winced at the word.

"Anyway, I don't know, I guess James just couldn't let it go. He kinda did keep stringing Amy along."

"How did you feel about James living this double life?"

The waiter's face turned to stone. "What do you think? I hated it."

"It had to make you angry, that he hid your relationship."

Dominguez said, "I hated it, but I could never be angry with James. I knew he loved me, and that's all that mattered. I was his real love—Amy was the sham."

"All right, Tony." Grissom stood. "I appreciate your frankness."

The boy got to his feet, too. "You need to talk to Amy. You really do."

"Oh, I will. But I'll be talking to a lot of people. By the way," Grissom added, glancing down at the waiter's tennis shoes, "those surely aren't the shoes you wore to work, yesterday."

"These are strictly for the dining room. You don't live up here and not have good boots. I got a kick-ass pair of Doc Martens. . . . James gave them to me."

"Generous of him," Grissom said.

"He was a wonderful guy," Dominguez said.

"Honest, too," Grissom said.

"As the day is long."

Grissom did not point out that the days were getting shorter.

He merely walked the waiter out into the cold air of another gathering storm, anxious to report what he'd learned to Maher and
Sara.

He knew who the murder victim was, now; and, he felt confident,
soon would know who the murderer was, as well.

Honest.

10

After five grueling hours at the Charleston Boulevard garbage dump—wearing white Tyvek jumpsuits over their clothes, painter's masks, multiple pairs of latex gloves, and fireman boots—the graveyard CSIs dragged in to HQ for showers and to climb in their spare clothes and finish out their shift.

Warrick caught up with Nick in the Trace lab, hunkered over the MP4 camera, enlarging prints. Nick would feed these prints into the AFIS terminal on the desk, over against a side wall keeping company with a little family of filing cabinets.

The back wall was home to a refrigerator for chemicals, a work counter, and a paper-heating oven. Racks of chemicals owned the other side wall, and on a large central table sat the comparative microscope, which allowed the matching of parts of two different slides—an invaluable tool for bullet comparison.

"That was fun," Warrick said dryly, meaning their garbage-dump duty.

Nick smirked. "Vegas is one glamorous town."

"Who's the AFIS candidate?" Warrick asked, at Nick's side now.

"Suffocated naked woman, number two."

Catherine wandered in with a newspaper folded under her arm and that devilish half-smile and single-arched eyebrow expression of hers that told Warrick she was onto something.

"Either of you guys into the local avant-garde scene?"

Nick gave her half a smile back. "I have a buddy in the National Guard."

She dropped the folded newspaper onto the desk next to Nick—the Arts section of the *Las Vegas Sun*. "Lavien Rose mean anything to you, boys?"

Warrick, trying, said, "Edith Piaf song, isn't it?"

Nick looked up at his friend. "Woah . . . Mr. Music. You can name that tune in how many notes?"

"Actually," Catherine said, "he missed that question—it's not 'La Vie En Rose' . . . it's Lavien Rose."

She tapped a red-nailed finger next to a photograph on the folded-over Arts section. "Look familiar, fellas?"

An article on local performance artists included a sullen photograph of the spiky-haired blonde woman they had not long ago seen in the dead altogether out on Charleston Boulevard.

"Is that what that was," Warrick asked, "back at that trash pile? Performance art?"

Nick's eyes were large as he picked up the paper and stared at the punky blonde. "If so, it must've been closing night."

Catherine was grinning almost ferally. "I knew I'd seen that face somewhere before!"

Doc Robbins' voice came over the intercom. "Catherine, you in there?"

She stepped over to the intercom and touched the talk button. "Yeah, Doc—Trace lab, a CSI's home away from home. What have you got for us?"

"Cause of death on your blonde Jane Doe."

"Great," Catherine said, "only she's not a Jane Doe anymore—we got her IDed."

"Well, come on down and fill out the form. But just so you know, she suffocated with the help of a plastic bag. Same heightened CO_2 count in her blood as Missy Sherman."

They all traded meaningful looks.

Catherine said, "Thanks, Doc! Be down in a few, to fill out the ID."

"Paperwork rules us all, Catherine."

Warrick stood with hands on hips. "Another naked woman killed with a plastic bag? Tell me this isn't a serial."

"The similarity of MO suggests serial," Nick said. "But the victim profile is out of whack."

"I don't know," Warrick said, shaking his head. "Two attractive women, about the same age . . . ?"

"True. But otherwise, what do a brunette middle-class housewife and a blonde starving artist have in common?"

"I don't know if she was a starving artist, exactly," Catherine said. "Bulimic, maybe."

"She was a skinny thing," Nick said.

"Easily overpowered," Warrick said.

The computer chirped and Nick turned to see a match on the woman's prints. He tapped the keys and was soon looking at an arrest report.

"Her name was Sharon Pope," Nick said.

Archly, Catherine said, "You don't suppose 'Lavien Rose' was a stage name, by any chance?"

"Ms. Pope was arrested two years ago September," Nick continued, reading from the screen. "Part of a group protesting at Nellis."

Nellis Air Force Base—northeast of the city, out Las Vegas Boulevard—frequently drew protesters of one kind or another, so a Federal record like that popping up was not a shock.

Still, someone had to ask; and it was Catherine: "Arrested for?"

"Trespassing," Nick said, "failure to disperse, interfering with an officer."

Catherine lifted her eyebrows. "Well, she hit the trifecta."

"Touched all the bases at the base, yes," Nick said. "A fine but no jail time."

"Address?"

Nick read it aloud, then added, "But we better check it—this arrest is a couple of years old. She could've moved by now." His forehead furrowed. "You know, I've heard that name somewhere before."

"Lavien Rose?" Catherine asked.

"No. Sharon Pope. . . ."

Nick mulled that over as his fingers danced on the keyboard, checking out the Pope woman's address—and another red flag came up.

"Well," Nick said, "and the hits just keep on comin'. . . ."

"What song is Lavien Rose singing now?" Warrick asked.

Frowning suspiciously, Nick turned toward Warrick and Catherine and gestured to the monitor screen. "See for yourself—her current address is the same as two years ago, but when I typed in her performance-artist alias, a different address came up."

Catherine and Warrick leaned in on either side of Nick and read over his shoulder.

Nick asked, "Why is our bulimic artist keeping two cribs under two names?"

"We need to check them both," Catherine said.

Warrick's expression was doubtful as he pointed out, "It's almost end of shift."

"This is a fresh murder case." Catherine's features were firmly set. "We need to stay on it."

Nick said, "Brass sent a memo around saying the Missy Sherman case is on the approved-for-OT list . . . and the two murders may be connected. MO indicates it."

Warrick shrugged. "Good enough for me."

"All right!" Catherine said, eyes bright. "We'll split up. . . . I'll see if I can round up Brass and check the Pope address. O'Riley's back on graveyard rotation—you guys grab him and head over to Edith Piaf's."

"Don't forget to give that ID to Robbins," Nick reminded her.

"On my way out," Catherine assured him.

Twenty minutes later, Warrick and Nick stood outside apartment 217H in The Palms, a vaguely seedy two-story apartment complex on heavily traveled Paradise Road. Six-thirty in the morning was a little early to be bothering the super, but Sergeant O'Riley was off doing just that.

The morning had a tentative quality, dawn not quite finished with the sky, and the temperature still hung around the freezing mark. Warrick had thrown his good leather jacket over his running togs; hands in his jacket pockets, he bounced foot to foot, staying warm while they waited on the second-floor concrete walkway.

Finally, O'Riley appeared, coming up the steps. A stubby Hispanic man, the super presumably, trailed behind him in flip-flops, cut-off denim shorts, and a threadbare Santana T-shirt, and didn't seem to notice it was colder out than the inside of a Kenmore freezer.

As the detective and super drew closer, Warrick got a better look at the super—unruly black hair over a wide forehead, red-rimmed brown eyes, and a frequently broken nose that meant either an ex-boxer or street fighter.

"This couldn't wait till after my damn breakfast?" the man was saying.

"No," O'Riley said gruffly. "Just open the door, then we'll be out of your way in no time, and you can get back to your bacon and eggs."

"They're probably already cold," the super protested.

"Then it's a moot frickin' point," O'Riley said. To Warrick and Nick, he said, "Meet the super, Hector Ortiz."

Nods were exchanged as the super riffled through a ring of keys. "Miz Rose, she in trouble?"

Ignoring Ortiz' question, Warrick gestured toward the door with his chin. "What kind of tenant?"

"Best kind—quiet as a church mouse. Always pays the rent on time, pays in cash—what's not to like?"

"Pays in cash . . . Is that typical around here?"

Shrugging, the super asked, "Who knows what's typical these days. Who am I to argue with money? And hers is always on time."

"What's she pay?"

Ortiz gave Warrick a sideways look. "I'm not sure I have to answer that."

Warrick sighed. "You have any openings, here at the beautiful Palms?"

"Maybe. Why?"

"In case I wanna move. If I do, what kind of rent am I lookin' at?"

"One bedroom?"

"I guess. Something like Ms. Rose has."

"Five bills—five-fifty, you want a garage."

"Pretty reasonable, considering," Warrick admitted.

"I know, everybody else around here's twenty percent over that, easy. But the landlord's a nice guy, and 'cause of that, we tend to hang on to tenants."

"Ms. Rose have a garage?" asked Nick.

"No."

Finally the super opened the place up, and they peered in at an empty living room—not a stick of furniture, as if the renter had moved out in the night, or burglars had made a hell of a haul.

The super, astounded, blurted, "What the hell?"

As they stepped into the living room, O'Riley asked Ortiz, "When was the last time you were in here?"

"I guess, lemme think—not since Ms. Rose signed the lease. She never had any complaints, and nothin' went wrong, no plumbing trouble or nothing. She shows up at my door with the envelope of money. . . . What reason did I have to come in?"

Not even the impressions of furniture could be seen on the well-worn wall-to-wall carpet; no one had lived here for some time. Some cheap but heavy curtains blotted out the window. Warrick opened the front closet door—not even a wire hanger.

A doorless doorway at the right led to the kitchen, where several appliances waited—a stove, a refrigerator. Warrick followed Nick, who opened the fridge, checked the cupboards.

Nick looked back at Warrick, eyes tight. "Got a box of cinch-top bags and a roll of duct tape," he said.

Warrick grunted noncommittally, then wandered back into the living room, where the super stood in the middle, arms folded, rocking on his heels, bored to death. O'Riley was poised before two closed doors that faced each other in a tiny alcove at the rear of the living room.

Frowning in thought, Warrick said, "Why rent an empty apartment?"

Opening the alcove's right-hand door, O'Riley said, "Bathroom! . . . Not much, pretty stripped. Empty squirt bottle on the sink, is about all."

"What?" Warrick asked, coming over.

The big man shrugged. "You know—like to water plants."

"Shit," Warrick said.

O'Riley turned. "What?"

"I think I know why we're standin' in an empty apartment. . . . Do not touch anything else!"

O'Riley, eyes wide, held his hands up in surrender. "Okay, okay . . ."

"We're in a crime scene," Warrick said. "Nick!"

"What?" Nick asked, coming from the kitchen, a wary expression around his eyes.

Warrick said, "The only thing in this apartment is a squirt bottle, some duct tape, and tie-bags. . . . You wanna guess what's behind door number two?"

Nick paled. Somber, businesslike, he said, "Detective O'Riley, you escort Mr. Ortiz out, now—don't touch anything." Nick got latex gloves out of his jacket pocket, and started snugging them on. "I'll get the door for you. . . ."

The burly cop took Ortiz by the arm and said, "We need to leave."

"Well, don't get rough about it! Are you arresting me or what? I didn't do nothin'!"

Nick was already at the door; he carefully opened it with a gloved hand. "Sir, we've stumbled into a probable crime scene. Just our presence potentially contaminates evidence. Please step outside and we'll explain."

Once the four of them were back on the concrete walkway, O'Riley asked, "What did you see that I didn't see?"

While Nick went off to gather their equipment from the Tahoe, Warrick filled the detective in. "Didn't you read Doc Robbins's report? He said Missy Sherman was frozen, and had to be wetted down in order to avoid freezer burn."

O'Riley's eyes widened and he nodded, getting it. "I remember—the doc said it could have been accomplished with somethin' as simple as a . . . squirt bottle."

Ortiz stepped closer to Warrick. "What does all this mean?"

"We're going to be investigating in there."

Ortiz frowned, shaking his head as if warding off flying insects. "Don't you people need a warrant or something?"

"Not for a probable crime scene, sir."

"But . . . how long you gonna be around?"

"Long as it takes."

Nick came up the stairs with their field kits in his hands, and started by unpacking his camera.

The super looked stricken. "The landlord might not like this."

"I thought you said he was a nice guy."

"Oh, he is . . . but this is private property, and—"

"Sir," Nick said, his camera out, "we're going back inside. If we don't find what we expect in there, we'll be out in fifteen minutes. If we do find what we expect, we're going to be here for . . . a while. Let us go in and find out—if we need to stay longer, you can call the landlord, and we'll talk to him, personally."

"Maybe I should call him now."

With a boyish grin, Nick said, "That's your choice, sir. But be sure to mention that you've already given us access, voluntarily."

Ortiz' face took on a sick look; he hung his head and leaned heavily against the wrought-iron rail of the walkway.

Warrick nodded to O'Riley, who nodded back—an exchange that meant, *Stay with this guy and keep an eye on him.*

Nick and Warrick went back inside.

While Nick snapped some pictures of the squirt bottle in the bathroom, Warrick faced the closed door that might lead to a bedroom. Touching as little of the knob as possible, he turned it and allowed the door to swing open, mostly under its own power.

Like the living room, this room was empty. It too had old carpeting, and cheap heavy curtains; but stretching from an outlet on the wall opposite him, a long orange extension cord snaked away to slip under the closet door at right. The closet was formidable—three sliding doors, each almost thirty inches wide.

"Nick!" Warrick called. "Looks like we were right!"

Nick joined him in the bedroom as Warrick slid the far door to the left. Filling most of the closet was a large white Kenmore chest freezer, a padlock joining lid to chassis.

Warrick said, "That's the model Catherine came up with."

"Oh yeah."

Warrick inspected the lock, and said, "We're going to need a cutter and goggles. I left the tool bag on the walkway. I'll go get the stuff; you're the man with the camera."

"Go," Nick said.

Outside, Warrick found O'Riley and the super leaning against the rail.

"What's the verdict?" the detective asked.

" 'Guilty,' eventually—we have what appears to be the murder site."

"Holy mother of shit," blurted the super. "Should I call the landlord now?"

"I wish you would," Warrick said. "We're going to be here a while."

Warrick bent down, sorting through his bag to get out the electric cutter.

O'Riley, taking notes, was asking Ortiz, "What's your landlord's name?"

"Sherman," the super said, who had calmed down. "Nice guy. He won't give you any trouble."

On his feet now, cutter in hand, Warrick froze. "Sherman? Alex Sherman?"

"Yeah! You know him? Him and his wife bought this place, couple of years ago. She's the lady that disappeared. Since she vanished, he hasn't been around much. Leaves most of the maintenance work for me to do. . . . It's a little much for me, really. We're gettin' kinda run-down."

Warrick said, "Well, he needs to come around now—in person."

O'Riley said, "Where's your office, Mr. Ortiz? I'll help you call him."

Warrick's cell phone trilled. He pulled it off his belt and punched the button. "Warrick Brown."

"Catherine," the familiar voice said. "At the Sharon Pope residence. Nothing to write home about here."

"Well, you might want to stop by over here," Warrick said. "There's plenty of subject matter at the Rose crib."

He quickly filled her in.

"Blink and I'm there," she said and hung up.

With the cutter and two pairs of goggles in hand, Warrick went back where Nick was snapping pictures of the plug snaking across the carpet.

"You ready for this?" Warrick asked, hands on hips. "You want to take a flyin' stab at who owns this lavish apartment complex?"

Nick shrugged. "Alex Sherman?"

Warrick frowned. "Now how the hell did you figure that?"

"Catherine mentioned that Sherman and his wife had real estate and you just made it clear somebody tied to the case owns this place. Had to be Alex Sherman."

"You been reading Gris's Sherlock Holmes books?"

"No. But I was raised on Encyclopedia Brown."

Warrick smirked. "I was a kid strictly into John Shaft."

"Shut your mouth . . . and pop that freezer. And don't pout, Richard Roundtree—you were the one who figured out the Kenmore'd be in here."

"I was, wasn't I?"

Warrick tossed Nick one pair of the goggles while he put on the other, then plugged the cutter in and turned it on, small blade whizzing back and forth at 20,000 rpm. Leaning in, he touched the tool to the hasp and sparks flew. He was through the cheese-ball lock in less than a minute, the smell of burning metal leaving its industrial bouquet hanging in the air.

With the lock out of the way, they each carefully took a corner of the lid and raised it—the best way not to disturb any fingerprints where people might typically lift the lid.

The freezer was about a quarter full of water, with a short, slotted metal shelf at one end and a little blue nipple on the back wall that—when ice-covered—was a manufacturer's signal for time to defrost.

"Killer's trying to clean up after himself," Nick said, "with this defrosting. Get the water out, get the evidence out."

"Trouble is, we got the water first . . . which means we have the evidence."

"See, we do like it to be easy," Nick said.

Warrick pointed at the blue tip on the freezer's back wall. "That look like a match to the mark on Missy's cheek?"

Nick studied it for a second. "Sure does. Slots on the shelf should match up to the marks on her arm, too."

"I'll work the freezer, and find O'Riley and give him the good news that he's gotta get us a truck to haul this bad boy back to the lab."

"Sounds good. Then I'll take another look around—never hurts to look twice."

"Never hurts to look three times."

Warrick was just finishing lifting fingerprints off the lid when Nick returned holding a clear oversize plastic bag with two large shopping bags inside. The bags within the evidence bag—one white and one red—were from boutiques in Caesar's Palace. One of them looked to be stuffed with clothes.

"Where'd you find those?" Warrick asked.

"Under the sink in the bathroom. Nobody'd got to that yet, when we shooed O'Riley and Ortiz out." Nick hefted the bag. "When Brass and I talked to the Mortensons, Missy's friend Regan Mortenson said Missy bought some clothes at the Caesar's mall, day she disappeared."

Warrick shook his head, gave Nick a wry half-grin. "You may be right about this 'easy' theory."

Nick opened the evidence pouch and withdrew a pair of jeans from one of the shopping bags. Nick pointed to a silver stripe several inches wide, near the cuff. "Looks like the killer duct-taped the victim, while she was dressed."

"Which is why no duct tape residue was found on the body— Missy was stripped naked after the killing."

"And that's why there's no signs of struggle, even though the killer killed Missy by holding a plastic bag over her head."

Warrick sighed, sourly. "Trussed up like that, woman never had a chance. Killer ties a bag over the victim's head, sits back, and just watches while she dies."

"Smoke 'em if you got him," Nick said.

"We have one cold killer here, Nick. We been up against our share of evil ones, but this . . ."

"Let's see if we can't hold this to two kills. I don't want to do any more crime scenes where women die like this."

"Good plan."

Catherine and Brass arrived at the Palms apartment complex after a ride during which the detective had continually pissed and moaned about not being able to use the siren because it wasn't an "emergency."

"What's the point of being a cop if you can't use the siren once in a while?" he griped.

"Life just isn't fair," Catherine said, and he looked at her, searching for sarcasm, but apparently wasn't a good enough detective to find it.

Catherine, in latex gloves, her own silver field kit in hand, entered the apartment, took in the empty landscape, then went into the bedroom to help Nick and Warrick secure the freezer. They bagged and packed the squirt bottle, the cinch-top bags, the duct tape, the extension cord, the old padlock, and the boutique bags with the clothes, all of which Nick hauled down to the Tahoe.

Catherine slapped a new combination padlock onto the freezer, saying to Warrick, "We don't want this popping open on the ride back to HQ."

Waiting for the truck to arrive and haul the freezer away, the CSIs and the two detectives stood outside in the early morning sunshine. Bone-tired from the extended shift, they were nonetheless basking in the overtime they were squeezing out of Sheriff Mobley, as well as enjoying the thought of the progress they'd made on what had been until now a stubborn, frustrating investigation.

They were still waiting for the PD truck when Alex Sherman rolled in, in his Jaguar. Dressed business-casual, the dark-haired Sherman looked as though he'd taken his time getting ready.

"Captain Brass," Sherman said. "I'm surprised to see you—I spoke to a Detective O'Riley, on the phone. He said we had some kind of crime scene here. . . ."

"Mr. Sherman," Brass said, "we believe we've found the place where your wife may have been murdered."

Understandably, Sherman paled at the mention of his wife in those terms, but quickly he asked, "You did? Where?"

"Here." Brass pointed up toward the second-floor apartments.

"Oh, my God! Right in one of our own apartments?"

Brass nodded. "217H."

Sherman's eyes flicked to Ortiz, who shrugged. Then Sherman said, "I don't even know what to say. . . . Can I see . . . ?"

"No. It's a crime scene. I will tell you that the apartment was in the name of a woman named Lavien Rose."

"Never heard of her."

Brass arched an eyebrow. "She was your tenant."

"That's Mr. Ortiz' job. What does she have to say?"

"Nothing. The apartment is empty except for a chest freezer."

"Oh, Christ . . ."

"And as for Ms. Rose, she and your wife actually have something in common."

"What's that?"

"They're both murder victims."

"Oh . . . oh hell . . ."

"Both suffocated with a plastic bag over the head."

Sherman stumbled over to the cement steps and sat heavily. He looked dejected, haunted; but he did not cry.

"I didn't kill my wife," he said. "I didn't even know this . . . Rose person."

Brass went to him. "Mr. Sherman, we need to move this talk to the station."

" . . . police station?"

"Yes, sir."

Sherman took a long breath and let it out slowly. Then his face turned to stone, the color draining out of it. Was he going to throw up? Catherine wondered. Clearly the man was fighting hard to maintain control.

His voice hard, Sherman asked, "Do I need a lawyer?"

The detective shrugged. "That's your decision. You don't have to make it now. We'll provide you with a phone."

"Oh, is that right?" he asked bitterly. "My 'one phone call'?"

"You can make all the calls you want, Mr. Sherman. But you need to come with us."

"Should I . . . leave my car?"

"Why don't you? We'll give you a ride back."

Brass and Catherine accompanied Sherman, while Warrick and Nick piled their tools into the Tahoe. O'Riley and the super were left to wait for the truck that would carry the freezer back to CSI. O'Riley would bring Ortiz in, too, though the super was clearly not as strong a suspect as Sherman now seemed.

When they got back to HQ, the first thing the CSIs did was finger-print Sherman. The computer-whiz-cum-landlord had been reluctant to allow them to do it, but once Catherine assured him it was the fastest way to prove his innocence, and get them back on the trail of the real killer, he'd complied. Ortiz, on the other hand, allowed his prints to be taken without question, with the air of a man accepting his role in a system vastly larger than himself.

In the Trace lab, as Warrick and Catherine tested the prints of the men—she through AFIS, he using the comparison microscope on prints lifted from the apartment—Warrick said, "That was smooth in there with Sherman, Cath."

"Thanks."

"You really think he's innocent?"

She shrugged, laughed humorlessly. "I can't seem to tell, anymore. I used to think I had good instincts with people, and you'd think that would only sharpen and improve, after years on the job . . . but the longer I stay at this, the less I feel I know anything about people. They are always a surprise."

"And so seldom a good surprise." Warrick got back to his work, then added, "Ortiz seems like a dead end."

"I agree. A harmless nobody. And next thing you know, we'll find a freezer in every Palms apartment with a dead plastic-bagged-suffocated girl in it and his fingerprints all over."

Warrick let out a nasty laugh. "Gacy the Chamber of Commerce guy, Ed Gein the shy, quiet farmer, Bundy the nice helpful dude wantin' to give you a lift . . ."

Catherine grunted a sigh. "There's only one thing that keeps me going."

"Which is?"

"The victims."

They kept at it.

Finally, Catherine said, "Nothing from AFIS. Far as it goes, Sherman's clean." A minute later, she said, "Ortiz is clean too."

She pitched in to help Warrick as he went through every print they'd gathered in the apartment, doorknobs, appliances, toilet handle, and most significantly, the freezer. Not a single print matched Sherman and only the front doorknob had a print from Ortiz.

They were just sitting there, a long way away from the euphoria they'd felt a short time ago, and were just wondering if they should call it a shift, when Nick entered, bright-eyed as a puppy.

"Freezer's here," he said. "I'm going to work on it. Anybody want to give me a hand?"

"I'm in," Warrick said, sighing, standing. "Not doing any good in here, anyway."

Catherine rose. "I'm gonna go eavesdrop on Brass and Sherman."

And she did, watching through the two-way glass as the short detective managed to loom over a disheartened-looking Alex Sherman, his crisp business attire now looking as wilted as he did. Sherman sat at one of the four chairs at the table—the room's sole furnishings—feet flat on the floor, hands folded in front of him.

Brass was saying, "You told us before that you never owned a freezer."

"I don't. Didn't. Never have."

"What about the Kenmore in apartment 217H?"

"None of our apartments have freezers, unless you count the little built-in ones that come with the refrigerators."

"So, we just imagined that freezer in apartment 217H?"

"It must belong to the tenant."

"Lavien Rose."

"If you say so."

"A dead woman."

"Again, I only know that, Detective Brass, because you mentioned it."

"Your wife handled the business end of your real estate holdings."

"Mostly, yes."

"Would she have known Lavien Rose?"

"No. Hector dealt with all of that. The name may have been written down somewhere, but we don't deal directly with the tenants."

"Does the name Sharon Pope mean anything to you?"

Sherman shook his head. "Never heard of her, either."

Catherine was watching Sherman closely. Her gut told her the man was telling the truth; but then she recalled what she'd just told Warrick about trusting her instincts. . . . Maybe the guy was just a hell of an actor.

"Who is she?" Sherman asked, turning the tables on Brass. "I mean, who was she? My tenant?"

"Lavien Rose."

"No, I mean—who was she? That's an odd name. It sounds like . . . a stage name."

"It is," Brass said, obviously unnerved by the turnabout of the interrogation.

"Well, I never heard of her—what was she, an actress? A stripper?"

Catherine blinked.

"Performance artist," Brass said.

Sherman twitched a half-smirk. "I have to admit, that's a concept that eludes me . . . performance art. But Regan might know her."

Brass sat down. "Regan?"

"Missy's friend. She hangs out with half the artists in town, in her job. Particularly the pretentious ones."

Catherine felt an electric tingle.

Brass was saying to the suspect, "Remind me—what's Mrs. Mortenson do again?"

"She's a fund raiser for Las Vegas Arts—meets with not only patrons of the arts, but also the artists . . . the screwballs who apply for grants."

"Excuse me, Mr. Sherman," Brass said, getting up. "I'll be with you in a moment."

Sherman was giving him a quizzical look as Brass walked out. He instructed the uniformed officer on the door to stay put.

Catherine caught up with Brass in the next interview room, where he was gazing through the two-way glass at O'Riley interrogating Hector Ortiz. Nothing of import seemed to be going down.

"I caught most of that interrogation," Catherine said. "Come with me."

"You got something?"

"I will have."

They went to the break room, where Catherine had left that newspaper with the article on local performance art. Brass stood patiently while she quickly scanned it.

"Lavien Rose," she said, looking at the article, "has been awarded numerous grants by Las Vegas Arts. . . . Can you wait while I check something?"

"I can keep you company."

This time she led Brass to the computer terminal in the layout room. It took less than fifteen minutes to learn that Sharon Pope, aka Lavien Rose, had made about twelve thousand dollars last year as a performance artist.

"At least," Catherine said, Brass next to her as she gestured to the monitor, "those were the grants she got from Las Vegas Arts. And I can't find any other job for her. Now, we know her rent at The Palms was six thousand a year; we also know her real home across town cost her seventy-eight hundred a year. That's almost fourteen thousand in rent alone. How do you squeeze fourteen G's outa twelve thousand bucks?"

Brass said, "You don't."

"Exactly. But maybe the rent for The Palms wasn't coming out of her pocket."

Brass had a hollow-eyed look. "Oh, shit . . ."

"What?"

"I missed something."

"What?"

He was shaking his head, his expression self-recriminatory. "When I interviewed Regan Mortenson, and she said she worked for the Las Vegas Arts Council, she told me she'd had an appointment, a meeting with somebody, right after the lunch with Missy."

"And?"

"It was with an artist . . . a woman. I'd have to check the notes

I made from the interview tape . . . but I'm almost positive Regan said the woman's name was Sharon Pope."

Catherine's eyes widened. "That's who Regan claims she was spending her time with, while Missy was getting murdered?"

"I think so. . . . Maybe 'Lavien Rose' was supposed to be her alibi, and it went south on her? D'you think Regan ended up whacking her alibi?"

Catherine hadn't processed that fully when Greg Sanders knocked on the doorjamb. The DNA tech, working on a soul patch that was not making it, carried a sheaf of papers in one hand.

Rather irritably, she said, "What, Greg?"

"Woah! Chill—I'm just lookin' for Warrick and Nick. They brought me the hairs they found in that freezer. They told me it was a rush job, and now they're MIA."

"What did you find?"

"Hairs from Missy Sherman and an as-yet-unidentified person."

Sitting up, Brass asked, "What do you know about the other person?"

"Blonde, female," Sanders said. "All I know at this point is that her hair matches one Warrick brought me earlier."

Getting that electric tingle again, Catherine asked, "Where did he get it?"

"Not sure—if you can find Warrick, you can ask him."

Catherine looked at Brass, who said, "Regan Mortenson and Sharon Pope—both blonde."

Catherine nodded. "But only one of them is still alive. We have enough to call on Regan Mortenson, wouldn't you say?"

"Oh yeah," Brass said.

Nick appeared in the doorway next to Sanders, putting a hand on the lab rat's shoulder and smiling at him impatiently. "Tell me you have our results."

Jumpily, Sanders gave up the papers like a thief caught in the act.

"Thank you," Nick said.

"Don't go anywhere, Greg," Catherine said.

She convened the group in the layout room. Nick, Warrick, and Sanders sat, while an edgy Brass paced by the door.

"What good things have you been up to?" she asked the two CSIs.

"We were in the Trace lab," Warrick said, "running prints and matching evidence."

"I thought we were past that," Catherine said.

"Yeah," Warrick said, "but when prints from Sherman and Ortiz didn't match anything, I decided to go back to try to match our freezer prints against the one I lifted from Missy's visor mirror."

"And?"

"Perfect match . . . I'm good, by the way."

"I noticed," Catherine said with a smile.

Nick said, "I may not be as good as John Shaft here, but I matched the duct tape adhesive we found in the apartment to the adhesive on Missy Sherman's clothes. That do anything for you?"

"Nice," Catherine said. "Greg—your turn."

Sanders filled Warrick and Nick in on what he'd found; then Brass told them what he and Catherine had been discussing, including the Sharon Pope detail, an oversight he copped to.

"I missed it, too," Nick said, through clenched teeth. "Damn—it was in your notes, Jim! . . . That's why that name seemed familiar."

"We need to go see Regan Mortenson," Warrick said.

"Actually," Catherine said, "Jim and I'll handle that. You and Nick'll gather the rest of the evidence we need. . . . Nick?"

"Yes?"

"Talk to the people at Las Vegas Arts and see if we can track the money."

Nick was on his feet. "On it."

"Warrick—run down that freezer. The Sears stores are open by now. Kenmore's the house brand."

"Shopping on overtime," Warrick said, getting up. "Fine by me."

Then they were in the hall, walking together, except for Sanders, who made his getaway back to his lab cubbyhole.

"In the meantime," Catherine told her fellow CSIs, "Captain Brass and I will discuss the fine art of murder with Regan Mortenson."

"Maybe you'll get a grant," Warrick said.

11

Having just emerged onto the loading dock, in snow driven by a stiff wind, Gil Grissom and Tony Dominguez stood with hotel manager Herm Cormier, as snug in his parka as the waiter in his sweatshirt was not. Though it was barely 5 p.m., night was already conspiring with the storm, ready to cast the Mumford Mountain Hotel into darkness.

Grissom looked toward the parking lot, where Constable Maher and Sara Sidle had been working, and saw nothing but the snow-covered vehicles. "Where did they go?" he demanded of Cormier, having to work his voice over the wind.

Cormier shook his head. "They went off that way," he said, pointing toward the far end of the parking lot. Grissom could barely hear the man, but could read his lips.

"I'm going to join my associates," Grissom told the hotel manager. "You two need to get back inside!"

"No argument!" Cormier said.

But Dominguez—so underdressed in this bitter snowy weather—said nothing, his eyes staring but not seeing. The tears had stopped, but the grief was probably just starting. Grissom had no doubt this boy had loved James Moss; that just didn't mean Dominguez hadn't killed him.

And much as he hated losing custody of his best suspect, Grissom wanted to hook back up with Maher and Sara, and share what he'd learned, and see what they'd found. Anyway, where was there for Tony Dominguez to run?

The criminalist had nothing on the waiter, beyond the circumstantial evidence of a sexual relationship with the victim and a cut forearm. The most dangerous aspect of releasing the suspect—Grissom was half-forgetting his lack of authorization, here—was the possibility that Dominguez would get rid of his boots before Grissom could try to make a match. But he didn't think the boy knew that his Doc Martens were potential evidence.

Shouting over the wind, Grissom said to the pair, "You need to go in and act like you don't know anything about this!"

That riled the waiter out of his funk, momentarily anyway. "Don't know anything?" Dominguez exploded. "That's James in there! How can you expect me to—"

"Tony," Grissom said, cutting him off. "If you're as innocent as you say you are . . . there's likely a murderer in that hotel."

"Yeah, that bitch Amy!" he snarled.

"If that's so, I can't have you tipping her off that we suspect her." The wind howled. "Do . . . you . . . understand?"

The young man nodded. He was shivering now.

"Now get inside. You're freezing."

Through the haze of snow, Dominguez was studying Grissom. "You say you suspect Amy . . . but you really suspect me, don't you?"

"I told you, everyone here is a suspect, including Mr. Cormier and Constable Maher. The only people not on my list are Sara and myself."

"You suspect me?" Cormier blurted, eyes wild.

Calmly, Grissom said, "You and everyone at the hotel, Herm. But no innocent person need worry—the evidence doesn't lie. And re-member—the fewer people who know what we know, the easier it'll be to catch the killer."

Cormier nodded.

Dominguez said, "I'll do what you want . . . for James's sake."

"Good. Now go in and warm up and dry off!"

Cormier locked up the loading dock door and he and Dominguez went down the stairs and trudged through the deepen-ing snow to the hotel's rear door.

Grissom shuffled out onto the parking lot, going first to the blue Grand Prix. The tomato stakes were still visible, but Sara and the con-stable—and their equipment—were gone. Their tracks, however, weren't hard to follow.

The sky was a gunmetal gray, a darkening shroud over him, as Gris-som slogged on past the parking lot to the end of the building, where he still saw nothing but drifted snow. He turned the corner and, as he plodded on, slowly scanned the horizon. In the distance, through the slanting white, he could—finally!—make out two dark figures.

They were standing on the lake.

He had a tiny jarring moment before he realized the lake would be frozen over and safe—relatively safe—for human footsteps.

Soon, moving as fast as he could, Grissom had made his way around and to the front of the hotel; he began to tramp down the hill, almost losing his balance. He could now plainly see Maher and Sara up ahead. Shouting would be useless, he knew, over the ghostly shriek of the growing blizzard; his voice just wouldn't carry to them.

And then he had an odd, dread-inducing thought—what if Maher was the killer? What if all the help in the snow, the forensics magic, had been deception and cover-up, not straightforward detection? What if Maher had lured Sara out there, to where the man knew the ice was weak, to throw her to an icy death?

The thought of Sara thrashing in the glacial waters, her screams in the storm unheard by a world gone deaf, gave Grissom a ghastly chill; Sara, another victim for him to process . . .

He had closed half the distance between himself and them when he glanced left and saw the dock. He knew instantly that he was running across the lake and that Sara and Maher were almost in the middle of the thing. The ice would get thin, the farther out they went—but as he neared, he realized that his imagination had run away with itself; and he felt foolish.

Maher, his metal detector still tucked under his left arm, was leaning over and digging through the snow with his right hand. He seemed to be going very carefully. Nearby, in her parka, Sara—now a convert to the Canadian's ways—liberally sprayed gray primer into a footprint.

They both looked up at the sound of his approach.

"You're all right?" Grissom said to Sara.

Still kneeling, she gazed up at him curiously. "Of course . . . We're doing the best we can, in this snow."

"What happened to working the tomato stakes?" he asked the constable.

Maher said, "Somebody must have figured out what we were up to, and moved them to try to throw us off."

"But whoever moved the stakes left new prints," Sara said, "and they led down here."

Grissom smiled a little. "That confirms the presence of the murderer in the hotel."

"Yes it does," Maher said.

"And I know who the victim is," Grissom added.

Sara got to her feet, her eyes bright. "Who?"

"James Moss—a waiter."

Maher and Sara traded a look.

Grissom frowned. "What?"

"Amy Barlow's boyfriend, you mean?" Sara said.

"Well, yes and no," Grissom said, and he explained about the love triangle involving the two waiters and the one waitress.

"Amy told us that 'Jimmy' didn't make it in to work yesterday," Sara said. "They usually ride together, but he had an appointment with somebody."

Grissom shook his head. "She's lying."

Maher said, "Is she? What if that 'appointment' was with Dominguez?"

Sara arched an eyebrow. "Amy's got that cut on her hand, remember."

"And Dominguez has a cut on his forearm," Grissom said. "Claims it's from working on his car."

"We should go back and talk to Amy," Sara said.

Maher said, "Not just yet—I got a major hit on the metal detector. . . . Let me dig a minute."

And he was back on his hands and knees. Sara and Grissom exchanged shrugs and were about to join him, when Maher called, "Jackpot!"

The Canadian stood and displayed his find: a plastic ziplock bag that seemed to have some heft to it.

"It may not be Christmas yet," Grissom said, "but I'd go ahead and open that. . . ."

The Canadian did, carefully undoing the ziplock top, and they all looked in at the contents: a pair of bloody leather winter gloves, a rock about the size and shape of a softball, and—peeking out from under the gloves—the silver barrel of a small gun.

"Are we looking at the murder weapon?" Maher asked.

Sara, snow-flecked eyebrows high, said, "That a .32? Looks about right."

"Obvious, isn't it?" Grissom asked.

Feeling the noose tightening, the killer decides to lose the murder weapon. He or she packs the gun and the incriminating gloves in the plastic bag, adds a rock for weight, and walks out and buries the package in the snow atop frozen Lake Mumford. In the spring, the snow and ice will melt, the package will sink and the evidence will be gone forever.

Using a pen down its barrel, Maher lifted the .32 Smith and Wesson revolver out of the ziplock bag. He carefully opened the cylinder and allowed five spent cartridges and one bullet to drop out, down into the bag, then he closed the cylinder and slid the pistol back into the bag as well.

"Okay," Grissom said. "Sara, you have pictures of the footprints out here?"

She nodded.

"Good—can we still cast it?"

"I've got one block of sulfur left," Maher said.

The snow was hammering them now, the wind whistling its carefree tuneless tune—the storm had plenty of time. The criminalists didn't. They worked fast and accurately and made a cast of the print Sara had shot . . .

. . . and the team was back inside the hotel in less than an hour. The newfound evidence was dry and safe, locked inside Sara's field kit. Soaked and freezing, they paused in the underpopulated lobby and stripped off their coats.

Cormier had been waiting for them, and he carried over an armload of towels. The trio of detectives sat down in front of the roaring fireplace and began to dry off. Grissom and Sara, both in black, shared a sofa facing the fireplace, Maher in a nearby overstuffed chair perpendicular to the fire.

The hotel manager went over to the desk, used the phone, and came back and reported to Grissom, "Just called up to the restaurant—somebody'll bring some hot coffee right down for you folks."

Grissom glanced around the lobby—at the Christmas tree, the big picture window looking on a winter landscape that seemed far more picturesque from the indoors and the handful of guests seated reading and relaxing. Then he turned to the hotel man, who stood alongside the sofa, and said, "I don't see Tony Dominguez."

"He's locked himself in his room, Dr. Grissom."

"I was hoping you'd keep an eye on him."

"He's not going anywhere. He's a wreck."

Grissom curled a finger and the hotel man drew closer, as the CSI whispered, "Tony talk to anybody?"

Cormier shook his head. "No, sir. I took him up to his room, and neither one of us said not a damn word to nobody. . . . Just like you said. Listen, Dr. Grissom—you don't really consider me a suspect, do you?"

Grissom beamed at him. "Of course."

Cormier frowned, and moved off.

A moment later, Amy Barlow—in her white shirt, black bow tie, and black slacks outfit—appeared with a pot of coffee and a tray of cups. The bandage on her hand appeared fresh and Grissom made a show of studying it as the waitress placed a steaming green mug of coffee on the low-slung table in front of him.

"Is that any better?" Grissom said, nodding toward her bandage.

"I'll live," she said.

"Cutting onions in the kitchen, wasn't it?"

"That's right. . . . Maybe I'll sue ol' Herm and wind up ownin' this place. . . . Any of you folks need anything else?"

They all said no, she gave them a quick smile, then Grissom's eyes followed her as she walked back toward the stairs to the dining room.

When the waitress disappeared from his view, Grissom said to Sara, "Got a pen and notebook?"

"Sure." She scrounged them out of her coat pocket, on the floor, and handed them to him.

He turned to Maher and asked, "Don't suppose you brought any fingerprint powder along, for your demonstration?"

Shaking his head, the Canadian said, "Didn't bother—too basic. Sucks to travel with, eh? So easy to get that stuff all over everything."

Grissom nodded, having had similar experiences. He quickly scrawled a list and tore the page out of the notebook.

"What's that about?" Sara asked.

Grissom glanced over at the desk, behind which Cormier had retreated. "Herm! A moment?"

The hotel manager came right over and Grissom said, "I need a few things," and handed the man the paper.

Cormier took the list, read it over, and looked up in confusion. "What kind of scavenger hunt are you on, Dr. Grissom?"

"The best kind. Can you fill my grocery list?"

"Well, certainly."

"Good. And what room is Tony Dominguez in?"

Cormier told him.

"Thank you. Could you deliver those items to my room?"

"Sure—but I wouldn't mind knowin' what you have in mind with 'em."

"Show you when you get up there, Herm . . . but the quieter we keep this, the better."

"I know, I know. . . . You're kind of a Johnny One Note, ain't ya?"

Cormier wandered off, going over the list again as he went.

Then, turning to Sara, Grissom said, "Let's go up to my room."

She just looked at him.

He continued: "Or don't you want to solve this murder?"

"Am I invited, too?" Maher asked.

"Your attendance is required, Constable. I'm going to need your help. But, first, I need you and Sara to go up to Tony's room, to pick up a couple more items."

Maher frowned. "What items?"

Grissom told him.

"Will he cooperate?"

"I think so. But as he is still a suspect, I'd like both of you to go."

Sara's eyes tightened. "You think he's dangerous?"

"Whoever killed James Moss is definitely dangerous. And just because Tony seems devastated, that doesn't mean he isn't our man."

Sara nodded.

"You two be careful," he said. To Maher, he said, "Look after her."

"I can look . . ." Sara said, but then stopped. She was obviously going to say she could look after herself, but for some reason she didn't complete the thought. Instead, she smiled and said to Grissom, "Thanks."

What was that all about? he wondered.

Maher and Sara headed out of the lobby, while Grissom lagged. Gingerly, he picked up his coffee cup, careful to touch only the handle—the part Amy hadn't touched—and walked across the lobby. In the men's room, he dumped the coffee down the drain. Again carrying the cup by only the handle, he went to the elevator and waited for its return—Sara and Maher had already gone up.

Grissom's room was hardly designed to be a crime lab, but, this evening, it would just have to suffice.

The door and bathroom occupied the north wall; a window on the south wall overlooked the lake, in front of which squatted a round table and two chairs. The east wall was home to a fireplace, and to the left stood an armoire with three drawers and two doors that opened to reveal the small television. The single bed and a nightstand hugged the west wall.

He had just finished clearing the table of his books and hotel literature when a knock came at the door, which he opened to reveal a perplexed Herm Cormier, standing next to a galvanized steel garbage can.

"How'd you do, Herm?"

"Hope you been a good boy, Dr. Grissom, 'cause Santa brought you everything on your damn list . . . but I can't for the life of me figure why you wanted this bunch of stuff."

"You're welcome to stay, Herm—and see for yourself."

"I thought I was a damn suspect!"

"You are," Grissom said pleasantly. "This way I can keep an eye on you."

Shaking his head, Cormier picked up the garbage can and squeezed past Grissom into the room. "You know, Dr. Grissom, I can't tell when you're kiddin' or not."

"Good," Grissom said.

Before the CSI supervisor could close the door, Sara and Maher appeared as well, the constable holding a pair of stylishly clunky black boots, Sara holding a plastic bag with a drinking glass inside.

"Mr. Cormier, could you get me that pan now, please?"

"Sure."

"Make sure it's good and hot."

"Oh I will," he said, and stepped back out, pulling the door shut behind him.

"He'll be right back," Grissom assured his confused associates. Turning to Sara, he asked, "Any trouble with Dominguez?"

"No," Sara said, and her expression was compassionate. "He really is broken up. Just sitting there. Not even crying, just . . ."

Maher finished for her: "Kid says he'll help us any way he can, to catch James's killer."

Sara shrugged a little. "He seemed sincere."

"Well, let's see," Grissom said. "First, Sara, I want you to compare Tony's boots to the castings from both the crime scene and the lake. You can use the bed as a workstation."

She nodded and Maher handed her the boots.

"Set the glass on the table," Grissom said to her. "That's my finger-printing station."

She placed the plastic bag next to the coffee cup that Grissom had brought up from the lobby. "Amy's prints?" Sara asked, indicating the cup.

"That's right," Grissom said.

"What can I do to pitch in?" the constable asked.

"You can start with helping me unload that garbage can. Then we'll set you up in the bathroom."

Maher grinned. "That's my station, eh?"

They took the lid off the can and were greeted by a cornucopia of seemingly unrelated items. Grissom reached in for a battery-operated drill and handed it to Maher, who gave him a quizzical look. Next Grissom withdrew a five-pound sack of flour, a basting brush, a tube of Super Glue, two wire coat hangers, a magnifying glass, and an inkpad for rubber stamps.

"Not exactly a cutting-edge lab," Maher said.

"No, but they like it rustic here at Mumford Mountain Hotel, right? . . . Let's start by getting you going. Cormier'll be back soon, and we need to be ready."

Sara, already hard at work, called out, "Size is way off on the boot—not even close. Soles have way different markings too."

"Appears the Doc Martens are innocent, anyway," Grissom said. "Now, Sara, see what you can get from the gloves."

She went back to work.

In the bathroom, Maher put the garbage can in the tub, then sat on the toilet, drilling holes in the can's lid, while Grissom pulled down hard on the bottom of one wire coat hanger, thinning and elongating the hanger until it was hotdog-shaped with a hook on one end; then he pulled the tail end up into a U, forming a small rack.

"How's the trashcan?" asked Grissom.

Maher said, "She's ready."

A knock at the door told Grissom that Cormier was ready, too. Putting the hangers in the sink, the CSI left the bathroom and answered the door.

Herm Cormier stared at the nearly red-hot pan he clutched in a pot-holder-protected hand.

"Hot comin' through," the hotel man said.

Grissom stood aside and allowed Cormier to pass by, holding the orange-bottomed frying pan away from him, as if he had a skunk by the tail.

"Bathroom, Herm," Grissom said. "Put 'er right in the bottom of the garbage can."

Cormier did as he was told, then backed out of the bathroom.

"Good job," Grissom said to him.

But Cormier had the dazed expression of a small child forced to attend a long ballet.

In the bathroom, Grissom found that Maher was ahead of him, having already bent the hooks of the hangers through the holes in the lid of the garbage can. Grissom dripped drops of Super Glue onto the red-hot pan, as Maher carefully draped the folded ziplock bag from the lake over the normal hanger. On the bent hanger, the constable balanced the knife across the bars of the U, and said, "Ready."

After a dozen or so drops, Grissom stopped and waited; a few seconds crawled by and the glue began to smoke. "All right," Grissom said, timing it, "now."

Maher eased the lid down on top of the garbage can.

"Mind if I ask you boys what the hell you're up to?" Cormier asked.

Matter-of-factly, Grissom said, "Fingerprinting."

The old boy's eyebrows rose. "Fingerprinting . . . with Super Glue, coat hangers, and a garbage can?"

Grissom shrugged. "You use the tools at your disposal."

Rising from the toilet, Maher said, "If you don't mind, eh, I'll step out in the hall and have a smoke."

"It's a life choice," Grissom said.

Maher thought about that for just a moment, then went out.

It would be at least ten minutes, Grissom knew, before they could open the can. The process would have to be repeated with the gun, the casings, and the bullet. While he was waiting, he went in to check on Sara's progress.

Cormier was now leaning against the armoire, watching Sara work.

Sara smiled tightly at Grissom, holding up the gloves, and said, "Killer definitely wore these."

"The cut on the cloth mirrors the cut on Amy Barlow's hand."

Enthusiasm danced in the young woman's eyes, though her words were understated: "I would say so."

Grissom prized her love for the job.

The hotel manager stood away from the armoire; confronted with damning evidence regarding his waitress, he looked stricken. "I can't believe it—Amy? She's such a nice girl . . . such great people skills."

Sara arched an eyebrow. "You may wish to revise that opinion."

Grissom moved to the table by the window on the lake, and sat down with the flour and the basting brush. Carefully, he applied a little flour to the coffee mug that Amy had served him downstairs—that it was a dark green cup was a nice little break. Brushing away the excess flour, he saw a surprisingly well-defined partial.

Flour was maybe five percent as good as commercial fingerprint powder, but in a spot like this, five percent was a good number. When he finished, Grissom had three partials and a pretty good thumbprint. He dusted the glass from Tony's room and discovered a workable set of prints there as well. Of course, Sara had asked the waiter to pick up the glass specifically to provide his fingerprints—no trickery, as with the waitress—so Grissom wasn't terribly impressed.

Maher strolled back in and they opened the garbage can to reveal several smudged fingerprints, a couple of good ones and what appeared to be a partial off the glove. And they got three more prints from the ziplock.

Grissom called out for Cormier.

A few moments later, the hotel manager peeked into the bathroom; he still had a shell-shocked look, no doubt due to learning his waitress, a good and valued employee, was likely a murderer.

Without looking at the man, Grissom asked, "Could you heat the pan up again?"

"Yes, sir," Cormier said, and Maher handed him the pan and the potholder.

The hotel manager, his expression hollow, sleepwalked away, and Grissom followed him, stopping him at the hotel room door. "You do know you can't say anything to anyone about this."

"Yes, Dr. Grissom."

From across the room, Sara called, "That includes Pearl, Mr. Cormier!"

"Pearl," the hotel manager said numbly, " 'specially."

Grissom said, "Mr. Cormier?"

Seeming to snap out of it a little, Cormier looked at Grissom.

"If you give Amy a heads-up," Grissom said, smiling his pleasant smile that was not at all pleasant, "I'd have to construe that as aiding and abetting."

Cormier came fully awake. "Wouldn't do that, sir. Amy's just an employee. . . . I only . . . it's just . . ."

"People are a disappointment?"

Cormier swallowed. "Yes, sir."

Grissom made a clicking sound in his cheek. "I find insects are much more consistent. . . . Go."

"All right," said Cormier, then he walked out the door, a little of the zombie creeping back in.

While they waited for the hotel manager to come back, Grissom and Maher sat at the table by the window and, using the magnifying glass, compared the prints from the coffee cup and the ziplock bag.

"I think that's a match," Maher said, frowning.

"Tough to tell in conditions like this," Grissom said. "But it does look close—statistically, prints from such a small sample of people, appearing this similar, would just about have to be a match."

When Cormier returned with the heated pan in hand, he said, "I need to get back downstairs."

Still at the table, Grissom, not exactly suspicious—not exactly not suspicious—glanced over at Cormier, poised at the doorway, and asked, "Why is that, sir?"

"Pearl got through to the sheriff once," the hotel man said, "but got cut off. I'm gonna take another crack with my ham radio."

As the hotel manager was leaving, Sara got her cell phone out of her purse and punched in Catherine's number. This time she heard nothing, not even the robotic voice. She put the cell phone away and went back to work.

Grissom and Maher returned to their bathroom crime lab. Grissom attached the pistol to the hanger, placed the bullets into a glass wrapped in one of the hangers, dripped more Super Glue on the reheated pan, then placed the lid on top. Again they waited and again they were rewarded: good prints revealed themselves, from several of the casings and the bullet. The gun had been mostly wiped clean, but a glove print appeared on the barrel, and Grissom felt sure it would match the wear patterns on the gloves Sara was processing.

Grissom sighed in satisfaction, and gave Maher a businesslike smile.

"What say we go find Amy Barlow?" Grissom said.

"And her boots," Maher said.

The trio of criminalists went to the waitress's room, and Grissom knocked on the door, but got no response.

"We could pick the lock," Maher said.

"Not and have what we find hold up in court," Grissom said. "Not in this country."

Maher frowned. "What about getting Cormier to give us permission? I mean, he's the manager."

Sara said, "Supreme Court ruled in 1948 that, under the Fourth Amendment, a hotel room counts as a person's home."

Grissom added for the constable's benefit, "Even if our buddy Herm gave us his permission, whatever we found would still get thrown out."

The three tried the dining room, on the second floor, but the waitress was not there. They split up and looked around the main floor, but couldn't find her. They met at the front desk, to track down Cormier and see if he had any notion where Amy Barlow had gone.

Through an open doorway behind the desk, they could see the hotel man in a small office, seated at a desk, bending over a microphone, fiddling with knobs on his ham radio set.

"Tom," Cormier was saying into the mike, "can you hear me?"

Static was the only response.

Grissom slipped behind the desk, the others following him. He stood in the doorway and said, "Excuse me . . . Herm?"

The hotel manager jumped and swung around. "Judas H. Priest! You have to scare me like that, with a murderer on the loose?"

Grissom smiled. "Just the kind of discretion I was counting on, Herm."

". . . I'm sorry. Really, Dr. Grissom, I haven't told a soul. . . ."

"Have you seen Amy?"

He nodded. "Just a few minutes ago."

Grissom's eyes tightened. "Where?"

Cormier gestured vaguely. "Out in the lobby. Said she was wondering what was wrong with Tony. Said she hadn't seen him since he came draggin' in, looking all depressed, and since it was almost time for the dinner rush . . ."

Grissom turned to give Sara and Maher a concerned look, even as he said to Cormier, "And you didn't think maybe you should've called that to my attention?"

Sara was shaking her head, eyes wide with dread. "Oh, she wouldn't . . . would she? With us around?"

"With her people skills," Grissom said, already on the move, "she just might."

The trio sprinted across the lobby, eyes of the scattered guests popping up from books and magazines, responding to the unusual commotion in this quiet place. Grissom punched the UP button and they waited as the ancient car made its slow descent.

When the bell dinged and the doors groaned open, Grissom was about to rush in, when he found himself nose to nose with . . .

. . . Amy Barlow.

This gave the slender but bosomy waitress a start, and she jumped back, dark ponytail swinging, eyes wide in shock, her hands coming up in a defensive pose.

Recovering quickly, Grissom held the elevator door open and looked in at the woman, in the cell-like space, and said, "Amy Barlow, you're under arrest."

As he recited her rights, Amy made a face—part confusion, part disgust. "What the hell for? You're not a cop!"

"Call it a citizen's arrest . . . for the murder of James Moss."

Her eyes widened more. "What? . . . Is that who was killed out in the woods? Jimmy?"

Sara stepped up beside Grissom, further boxing the woman in. "This is where you try to summon up some tears. I'd save the indignant act for later."

The waitress just stood frozen for several long moments; then she said, "I'm shocked, that's all. He was my boyfriend. . . . Everybody deals with grief, different."

"I heard you two broke up," Grissom said.

"That's a lie! Who told you that? That queer?"

Grissom sighed, then stepped aside and gestured with mock gallantry for her to step out of the elevator. "Why don't you come with us . . . for a little grief counseling?"

She glared at him, slouching out into the lobby.

Grissom took her firmly by the arm, and turned to Maher. "Constable, go get a passkey from Cormier and get upstairs, and check on Tony Dominguez."

"I thought Cormier couldn't open a—"

"I'm not worried about evidence," the CSI said. "I'm concerned for that kid's life."

Amy sneered at them. "Why? He isn't!"

"Charming," Sara said.

But Cormier, to his credit, had anticipated this, and was right there with the passkey, which he handed to Maher, who got onto the elevator.

"Sara," Grissom said, "hold the door! . . . Herm, you need to accompany the constable."

Cormier joined Maher in the elevator and, before the doors closed, Grissom—still holding on to his sullen suspect's arm—said, "Mr. Cormier, could we use your office?"

The hotel manager nodded as he gazed at the waitress in disbelief. "I just can't fathom it, Amy, you doing this."

"I didn't do anything, you old fart," she said.

Cormier's eyes showed white all around, as the elevator doors shut over him.

Grissom and Sara each took an arm and guided Amy behind the front desk to the larger of the offices back there, which was still fairly small, just a wooden desk, a couple file cabinets, and a big calendar of Hawaiian scenery—people who ran resorts longed for vacations, too, Grissom figured.

He ushered the waitress to the desk chair, as Sara closed the door.

"I didn't do anything to anybody," Amy said. Superficially, she seemed calm, but a tiny tremor underlined her words. "You should be after that faggot, Tony—he's been, like . . . stalking Jimmy. What musta happened is, Jimmy spurned his pervert advances, and that sick creep went ballistic."

Grissom said, "That's your theory, is it?"

Sara, leaning against the door, arms folded, said, "Somehow you don't seem very upset, or surprised, for a woman who just lost the love of her life."

She shrugged. "I'm in, like . . . shock."

Sara smiled a pretend smile at the waitress and said, "You might want to, like . . . work on that before your trial."

Amy's eyes got huge. "I'm telling you people—it's Tony. He's a fag! Can you imagine? Trying to steal Jimmy away from me? . . . Guys are after me all the time. I can have my damn pick."

"Tony didn't just try to steal Jimmy away from you," Grissom said. "He succeeded. Didn't he?"

She shook her head, emphatically. "Jimmy didn't want anything to do with that deviant shit."

A knock at the door startled Sara; she opened it and Cormier—his face deathly pale—staggered in a step, then leaned against the door-jamb.

"We . . . we were too late," the hotel man said.

"For what?" Sara asked.

"Poor kid . . . he's dead."

The waitress did not react.

Grissom, not leaving his position by the suspect, said gently, "What happened, Herm?"

The old boy swallowed; his eyes were moist. "Found him in the tub . . . slashed his wrists." The hotel manager shook his head, his eyes haunted. "It . . . sprayed everyplace. Goddamn mess . . . never seen the like."

All eyes went to Amy.

Her expression went from bland to aggravated, as she realized what they were thinking. "Hey, I had nothing to do with that."

Grissom noted the inflection.

"Sounds like he killed himself," she said, with a shrug. "Fags do that every day."

His voice calm, Grissom said, "You told Mr. Cormier that you were going up to Tony's room to check on him."

Amy started to rise, but a firm-jawed Sara lurched forward and put a hand on the suspect's shoulder.

"If you're not growing," Sara said, "sit down."

And shoved her back in the chair.

Amy straightened herself and said, "Let's not all get our panties in a bunch. . . . Yes, I went up to his room. Just 'cause he's a swish don't mean he's not a co-worker who I gotta work with and, like . . . respect."

Sara rolled her eyes.

"But the asshole didn't even answer me," she said. "I know he was in there."

Grissom asked, "How?"

She shrugged. "I heard him bawlin'."

Silence draped the small room.

Then Amy plunged back in: "Anyway, when he wouldn't open the door, I tried the knob; but it was locked. I was worried about him."

Sara almost laughed. "Worried?"

"Yeah. We needed his help in the dining room. So I came downstairs to get Herm, to try to get Tony outa his room. That's why I was on the elevator—remember?"

Grissom had a sinking feeling: how close they'd come to preventing this . . . if she was lying, and if she wasn't lying.

The phone on the desk rang, and Cormier excused himself past Sara and picked up the receiver. His voice was shaky as he said, "Hello?"

Several moments later, the old man handed the phone to Grissom, saying, "The constable—wants you."

Grissom took the phone and heard the Canadian say, in a somberly professional manner, "I've locked myself in the room to protect the scene. We can work it whenever you're ready."

"We're interviewing Amy on that subject now," Grissom said. "She claims she went to the room and he wouldn't answer. Says she didn't do this."

"She have any blood on her?"

"No."

"What's she wearing?"

"Standard waitress uniform."

"Unless she dumped her clothes somewhere and switched into a spare uniform, she's probably telling the truth. The bathroom walls are red. Dripping from the damn ceiling. Hit an artery—incredible spray."

"I've seen it often," Grissom said grimly.

"If Amy Barlow was in that room, she'd have blood on her somewhere."

Grissom said, "Yeah. Okay. Thanks." He hung up. "Amy, we'd like to look in your room. You say you're innocent, and the only way we can help you prove that is—"

"Help me? Right."

"We need your permission."

"What, so you can try to find evidence to lock me up?" She thrust her middle finger at him.

"I'm going to take that as a 'no,' " Grissom said.

He picked the phone up, got an outside line, a dial tone, and—after punching the numbers—was pleasantly surprised to hear the voice of an operator.

"Nine-one-one," the crisp female voice said. "Please state your emergency."

"I need to speak to the sheriff—we have another suspicious death at the Mumford Mountain Hotel. At least one is a murder."

A long silence ensued and Grissom wondered if the woman had heard him. He was about to repeat himself when she intoned, "Transferring."

Covering the mouthpiece, Grissom asked Cormier, "Who will I be talking to?"

"Sheriff Tom Woods."

When Sheriff Woods came on the line, Grissom introduced himself and began to explain the situation. He wasn't very far along when the husky-voiced Woods asked to speak to Herm Cormier.

Grissom handed Cormier the receiver; the hotel man held it in a hand as shaky as his voice, saying, "Hello, Tom—this is Herm. . . . No, he's for real, a forensics man from Vegas who made it in for that conference 'fore the storm hit. . . . Yup, happened just like he was saying. You better hear the rest."

Cormier listened again, then handed the phone back to Grissom. "Wants you, Dr. Grissom."

"This is Grissom, Sheriff."

"Would you continue, please," Woods requested.

Grissom finished filling him in.

"We're damn lucky to have you there, Mr. Grissom. But the fact is, you're not a peace officer in New York State. You have no jurisdiction. What do you propose we do?"

"I would happily turn this over to you," Grissom said.

"Lord knows I'd love to help, but the roads won't be open today, for sure . . . and maybe not tomorrow. Record snowfall, y'know."

"Right now, I need a search warrant for our suspect's room."

Amy, sitting with her arms folded, sneered at a wall.

The line crackled while Woods thought about it. Then the deep voice said, "Here's how we're going to handle this, Mr. Grissom. Would you raise your right hand, please?"

". . . Are you deputizing me?"

"I'm appointing you a special deputy for Ulster County. That allows me to get a judge to grant you your search warrant—and allows you to serve it. Your hand in the air?"

Sara grinned as Grissom, feeling a little foolish, switched the receiver to his left hand and raised his right. Over the phone, Sheriff Woods read him the oath, at the end of which, Grissom said solemnly, "I do."

"Deputy Grissom, I'll fax that warrant to the hotel as soon as Judge Bell grants it. Put Herm on so I can get the number."

"Thanks, Sheriff Woods. I appreciate this." And he gave the receiver to Cormier.

Half an hour later, a fax warrant in hand, Grissom served it on Amy Barlow. Maher stayed behind in the manager's office, watching the prisoner, while Grissom and Sara searched the room. Sara found the boots in a closet; not only did they match the castings from both the crime scene and the lake, multiple dried drops of blood were visible on the upper portion of both boots.

They searched the room carefully but found no sign of bloody clothing that would tie the waitress to Tony Dominguez's death. The hotel would have to be searched, but the likelihood that the boy had taken his own life seemed strong.

Back in the office, Grissom confronted the young woman with the bloody boots. Amy remained adamant about her innocence. "I still say Tony did it, and a couple boots with a couple flecks of blood ain't gonna convince anybody otherwise." She gave him a satisfied smile, saying, "And looks like Tony won't be around to defend himself, either."

"He won't have to be," Grissom said. "We have your boots. We have matching footprints at the crime scene. We found James's . . . Jimmy's . . . knife, with blood on it, which I'm confident will match yours. Oh, and we found your bloody gloves and the gun you threw out on the lake. . . . Next time, Amy, when you throw evidence in a lake, better that it not be frozen over."

She paled.

But Grissom wasn't through: "We've got your fingerprints on a coffee cup you served me this afternoon . . . remember? . . . and they match the prints on the ziplock bag . . . the one you put the gun and gloves in, when you tried to hide them in the lake?"

The weight of the evidence seemed to sink her deeper and deeper into the chair.

"Anything you'd like to tell us, Amy?" he asked.

Her voice seemed small, childlike, and not as cruel. "I loved Jimmy. I gave him everything . . . I was a lover, a friend, a mother to him . . . and he throws me over for . . . a guy?" She shook her head, swallowed, and finally some tears came—no sobs, just crystal trails dribbling down her cheeks. She looked at Sara and said, bitterly, "Try that out on your self-esteem, honey."

Sara asked, "Was it self-defense?"

Now the usual Amy reasserted herself. "Fuck no! Jimmy was weak . . . weak in a lotta ways, I see that now. What I was gonna do was beat the shit out of him, for what he did to me. I only took the gun along to scare him, humiliate him like I was humiliated. . . ."

Sara said, "He hurt you."

The tears began their gentle trail again; her voice trembled. "He didn't hurt me . . . he killed me. He ripped the woman part of me out and stomped on it. He made me feel like a useless, worthless, unwanted skank."

Grissom asked, "What happened, Amy?"

She shrugged, taking the tissue Sara handed her. "I was yelling at him, beating on him. He couldn't feel the kind of . . . inside pain I felt, but I could at least hurt the outside of his sorry ass."

"Is that when he pulled the knife?" Grissom asked.

". . . He pulled that damned knife and I just looked at him. You know what I said? I said, Well, faggot—looks like you still wanna stick somethin' in me after all! . . . And he did. Got in a lucky one." She gestured with her wounded hand. "So I pulled out the gun and . . ." She laughed. "He ran . . . ran like the scared little girl that he was."

Sara asked, "When you hit him, was that a . . . miss? A mistake?"

"Knowing Jimmy, *that* was the mistake. No, honey, I meant to shoot the son of a bitch, and I did. He wasn't gonna hurt me no more."

Grissom asked, "Amy . . . why did you burn him?"

She wiped the tears off her face, drew breath in through her nose. "I turned him over and he was looking up at me. He was dead, and he was still fuckin' mocking me." She swallowed. "And I still hurt inside. So what else could I do? I went back to the toolshed and got the gasoline."

She folded her arms, as if trying to warm herself; she smiled—a terrible smile.

"When he was burning," she said, "finally . . . I felt better. I felt like I was a woman again."

Grissom glanced at Sara, who said, "Then you heard someone coming, right? Heard someone and ran?"

"Yeah." She looked from one CSI to the other. "What, was that you two?"

Grissom nodded. So did Sara.

Her eyes narrowed and she bared her teeth, a vicious animal. "Well, go to hell, both of you . . . go to hell for spoiling my fun. I wanted to see that prick turn to ashes."

Grissom looked at Sara and shrugged; she did the same—neither had any more questions for the suspect, who sat, eyes glazed, sinking into the chair, arms tight across her chest, her face as blank as a baby's.

"Herm," Grissom said. "Keep an eye on her for a second."

"Sure thing, Dr. Grissom."

Grissom and Sara stepped out of the little room, behind the front counter.

"What now?" Sara asked.

"We still have plenty to do. We should process that scene upstairs. Try to determine whether Tony committed suicide or Amy did it."

"I'm betting Amy."

"We'll wait for evidence. Oh, and another thing . . ." Grissom nodded toward the open doorway of the little office, where dead-eyed Amy sat. "We'll need to keep tabs on our perp till the police arrive."

Sara said, "I'll take first watch, if you don't mind. I'm not anxious to work that red room upstairs."

"I don't blame you. Could be another long night."

A pretty half-smile dug a dimple in the young woman's cheek. "Could be worse."

Grissom huffed a laugh. "How?"

She grinned. "Could be outdoors. . . ."

12

Jim Brass was in no hurry.

The Taurus was in a late-morning line of residential traffic consisting of churchgoers bound for home or maybe brunch, as opposed to salvation. Getting a judge to sign a warrant for DNA on a Sunday was never an easy assignment, and he'd delegated O'Riley to track down a magistrate who owed Brass a favor.

But cell phone reports from the crew-cut detective indicated the judge was proving elusive, and Brass had no intention of sitting outside the Mortenson home, waiting for a warrant. If Regan Mortenson proved to be guilty—which with the evidence the crime lab had amassed seemed a dead certainty—she was a cold-blooded murderer, possibly psychotic and capable of God knew what; so the homicide captain preferred not to announce his presence in advance by sitting in an unmarked car on Goldhill Road, about as inconspicuous as a Good Humor truck.

Next to him as he slogged through Sunday morning traffic, Catherine sat back, her eyes closed, her breath not heavy—not asleep, just relaxing. Brass felt fairly alert, though he, like Catherine, had been up forever. They both knew that Sheriff Mobley would be apoplectic over the OT, but graveyard was so close to breaking the Missy Sherman case, they couldn't bear to pass the ball to Ecklie's day-shift crew, who had screwed it up in the first place. The eventual media attention would salve any wounds the overtime created, anyway.

A cell phone ring gave him a rush—Brass was surprised by how eager he was for that warrant—but he settled back behind the wheel when he realized it was Catherine's phone. Her eyes opened slowly and she answered it on the third ring.

She identified herself, then listened for a long moment. "So they were already looking into it? . . . But they hadn't gone to the authorities yet?"

Brass took an exit ramp off 215, easing down to a stoplight. He took a quick right and pulled into a gas station. He'd worked up a thirst, waiting for O'Riley's call.

"Water?" he mouthed to her, as Catherine continued on the phone, and she nodded.

About five minutes later, when Brass returned with two bottles of Evian, Catherine was still on the phone. He got in, handed her a bottle, removed the cap from his, and took a long pull.

"All right, then," Catherine said, finally. "Keep me posted, Nick, will you? . . . Thanks." She clicked off.

"What did Nick have?"

"Plenty," she said, and unscrewed the cap on her water. "He got hold of Gloria Holcomb, the accountant for Las Vegas Arts. She agreed to meet with him in her office."

"On Sunday morning?"

She lifted both eyebrows and gave him a wry look—nobody did wry looks better, or prettier, than Catherine Willows. "Seems Ms. Holcomb needs the LVMPD as much as the LVMPD needs her. She has strong suspicions that the Arts council has an embezzler in its midst . . . more than suspicions, really."

"Why hasn't she gone to her boss?"

"She reports to the suspected embezzler—Regan Mortenson."

Brass grunted a laugh. "Versatile girl, our Regan. But I thought she was just a volunteer worker."

"Seems Regan started out that way. Made such a strong impression, she was offered more responsibility. But the council could only provide her a nominal salary, which she said was fine with her—she just wanted to help out."

"Or help herself."

"I should say—about six figures worth."

"Which, end of the day—not that nominal," Brass said. "Is that our murder motive?"

"You mean, friend Missy found out Regan was embezzling? Probably not—Regan only moved from volunteer status to 'nominal' salary maybe a month prior to Missy's disappearance."

"It's possible, then," Brass said. "It does predate Missy camping out in that Kenmore."

"But not by much—Regan would have to be knee-deep in pilfering during her first month on the job, and Missy would somehow have to stumble onto it. And I never heard that the Sherman woman was even active with the Arts council."

Soon they were headed back for the interstate. They were barely back on the expressway when another phone ring got Brass's hopes up— his own cell, this time.

And it was O'Riley, beautiful O'Riley, saying, "Signed, sealed, and 'bout to be delivered . . . on my way."

"What's the deal? Stop at Denny's for a couple Grand Slams?"

"Hey, I deserve better—Judge Hewitt was playing golf. I had to rent a cart."

"What the hell's he playing golf for?"

"I know, it's a dumb sport."

"No, I mean it's like forty-five degrees out."

"Temperature does not seem to be an issue for his honor. But getting interrupted when he's playing golf . . . that is. An issue, I mean."

"You did good. How long?"

"Ten minutes."

Brass thanked O'Riley and clicked off.

He hit the lights, but not the siren. They whizzed along 215 toward Eastern Avenue.

"I take it we've got the warrant," Catherine said.

"A calligraphy class couldn't've taken longer coming up with one." Then he laughed abruptly.

"What?" Catherine said, Brass's laughter infectious enough to put a smile on her face.

"Just thinkin' about the sight of O'Riley riding the golf course in a cart, chasin' that judge."

Less than five minutes later, they drew up in front of the Mortensons' mission-style house. As a precaution, Brass parked his Taurus at an angle blocking the driveway.

"Wait for O'Riley?" Catherine asked.

"No. He'll be here."

They strolled to the front door, keeping their manner as low-key as possible—Brass in front, Catherine a step behind and to his left, both conscious that in a matter like this, a detective never knew when he might have to draw his gun, the CSI knowing better than to be in the way. His badge was pinned to his sport-coat breast pocket; this would be all the credentials he'd need. He rang the doorbell.

Regan Mortenson, her blonde hair pulled back in a loose ponytail, peeked out the window next to the door, forehead crinkled, as she studied her callers.

Brass tapped his badge. He stopped short of yelling, but tried to make sure his voice would be heard through the glass: "We need to talk to you, Mrs. Mortenson!"

She nodded, and seemed about to leave her lookout to let them in, when a screeching sound froze her, and she—and Brass and Catherine, turning—watched as O'Riley's Taurus jerked to a stop in front of the house. Then the big detective jumped out and charged the house, warrant in hand, like a pro football tackle bearing down on a quarterback.

Brass and Catherine looked back at the window and Regan was gone.

Huffing, O'Riley was next to Brass now, proffering the warrant. "Got it!"

"You forgot the bullhorn," Brass said to him, and O'Riley just looked at him.

They gave it a few seconds, until it became obvious Regan Mortenson had not left the window to answer the door.

"She's ducked back inside," Brass said.

O'Riley said, "I've got the rear," and went hustling around the garage.

Catherine was shaking her head. "What does she think she's accomplishing with this?"

"Either she's making a break for it," Brass said, "or getting ready to hole up."

He tugged the nine millimeter from its hip holster, held it with barrel pointed down, per safety regs. With his left hand, he checked the door—double-locked . . . lock in the knob and a dead bolt. No kicking this sucker in; no shooting the lock, either—why risk a ricochet?

"Catherine," he said, his voice tranquil, eyes on the door, "battering ram in the trunk—go get it. Cover you."

She huffed out a little anxious breath. "Keys?"

Pistol still pointed downward, Brass—feeling that strange calm that came over him, in such potentially violent situations—reached into his sportcoat pocket, withdrew the Taurus keys, and tossed them toward the sound of her voice, eyes never leaving the door.

He could hear Catherine's low heels click on the concrete for a couple of steps, then she must have cut across the lawn. Standing staring at the door, he was wondering which way to play it when Catherine returned. The manual said he should call in SWAT, but hell with that— this wasn't a bunch of holed-up gangbangers or some heist crew, this was a suburban housewife with ice water in her homicidal veins, and moreover this was an important bust. His bust.

His immediate concerns were more concrete. Was Catherine strong enough to bust the lock with the ram? The Thor's Hammer battering ram resembled a giant croquet mallet, a nonsparking and nonconductive ram, perfect for entering, say, the meth labs that seemed to be springing up everywhere. But it was a heavy mother, and not equipment a CSI often handled.

If Catherine wasn't up to it, Brass would have to trust her to cover him while he broke the door. Not really a problem, though. Of the night-shift CSIs, Catherine was the most skilled with her weapon and had, in recent years, taken two perps down in clean kills that passed the Shooting Board with flying colors. She might be a scientist, but at heart she was all cop and there wasn't a man or woman on the LVMPD who wouldn't trust Catherine Willows with their lives.

Catherine appeared beside him, hefting the big, black hammer like a lumberjack, despite her fashion-model looks. She gazed at him with an admirably flinty-eyed expression—she was ready. He was about to give her the go-ahead, when the latch suddenly clicked.

The nine millimeter swung up automatically and, as the door opened, Brass pushed through, moving inside, pistol in the lead.

Regan Mortenson stood before him in the stucco entryway—small, blonde, and very pale. She looked like a teenage girl in a Dali-print black T-shirt and blood-red sweatpants, her feet bare, toenails painted red, fingernails, too.

"Las Vegas Police," Brass barked. "Show me your hands."

But her hands were empty, and so were her eyes, staring at the black hole of the barrel without fear or apparent interest. Behind

Brass, Catherine had set down the battering ram and filled her right hand with her automatic. She followed Brass in, as Regan backed up, her hands high, palms open, head bowed, the stairway to the second floor at her back.

Clipping the words, Brass said, "Hands behind your head—now."

She was doing that when a shattering noise shook them all—from the rear of the house!—the brittle music of breaking glass.

Regan flinched, her raised hands covering herself, as if that glass might be raining down on her.

"Easy," Brass told her, as he kept his pistol trained on the young woman. "Catherine, check that out."

But Brass had the sinking feeling he knew what it was already. And indeed, before Catherine could respond to Brass's request, O'Riley came barreling into the hallway.

"Police!" he shouted, as he leveled his pistol at Regan.

"Sliding glass doors?" Brass asked.

"Yeah," O'Riley said, breathing hard.

Brass was just thinking the city could afford the price of a little glass, considering, when another noise shook the house.

Brian Mortenson came tromping down the stairs, his eyes wide and indignant, the close-trimmed goatee looking smudgy on his chin, like he'd been eating chocolate cake by sticking his face in it.

About halfway down, he yelled, "What the hell is going on . . ."

His voice trailed off as he saw Catherine—in shooting stance at the bottom of the stairs—aiming her pistol up at him.

"Las Vegas Metro Police," she said, not yelling, but there was no mistaking the no-nonsense meaning.

He stopped with one foot on one step, the other on another, hands shooting skyward, a pose that vaguely recalled his college basketball background.

Brass said, "Walk slowly down the rest of the stairs, sir, and please keep your hands where we can see them."

Mortenson obeyed the command, and Catherine gave him a quick frisk. Then she told him he could lower his hands. The tableau consisted of Brass holding his nine millimeter on the woman of the house, just beyond the entryway, and Catherine training her automatic on the man of the house, at the bottom of the stairs. O'Riley stood in the archway of the living room as if on guard, his weapon in hand.

It only took Brian Mortenson a few moments to regain his composure. "What is going on here?" he demanded. "You better have a warrant or I'll build a parking lot where the police station used to be."

"We're here to serve a warrant," Catherine said. "Specifically, to serve your wife with a warrant for DNA and fingerprints . . . but she decided not to cooperate."

Mortenson frowned. "So you people decided to dismantle our house?"

"Your wife resisted," Brass said.

The childlike Regan finally found her voice. She turned on Brass with indignation: "You scared me! I was going to let you in until . . ." She turned toward O'Riley, who was standing on the periphery like an oversize garden gnome with a gun. "That big brute came running across our lawn, and I thought . . . I thought . . . I don't know what I thought! I was just scared."

"Mrs. Mortenson," Brass said, "we properly identified ourselves— and I'm sure you recognized me."

"How could I forget you?" she asked.

Mortenson gestured to Catherine's weapon, still trained on him. "Do you mind? . . . You searched me. Could I go to my wife?"

Catherine nodded; and she holstered her weapon.

Before she allowed the husband to stand at his wife's side, she quickly but thoroughly frisked the young woman, too.

She glanced at Brass—clean.

Mortenson slipped an arm around his wife and brought her to him; somehow, she didn't seem terribly interested.

He asked, "Regan, honey . . . are you all right?"

She nodded.

But Brass wasn't so sure—something didn't look quite right about the petite blonde, and he could tell Catherine was concerned, too, flicking little glances Regan's way. Missy Sherman's "best friend" had claimed to be scared, and maybe she was; but did that explain why she was sweating so profusely, and why her skin had lost its color?

One arm still looped around his wife's shoulders, Mortenson said, "Let's see your warrant. What's it all about, anyway?"

Finally Brass holstered his weapon, and nodded to O'Riley to do the same. Then the burly detective came over and handed the warrant to Brass, who, in turn, passed it on to Mortenson.

"This warrant," Brass said, "gives us the right to fingerprint your wife and for CSI Willows, here, to swab Mrs. Mortenson's mouth for DNA."

Mortenson, forehead taut as he quickly scanned the document, said, "That still doesn't tell me what this is about." He drew the blank-faced Regan even closer. "Now explain yourself, or I call my attorney, right now."

"That's your prerogative, Mr. Mortenson," Brass said. "But the purpose of our visit? Your wife is the primary suspect in the murder of Missy Sherman."

". . . What?" Mortenson was astounded; they might have told him Martians were on the rooftop. "What kinda ridiculous bullshit . . ."

Regan's eyes were huge; she seemed to be in shock, kind of weaving there, Stevie Wonder–style, under his wing.

Meanwhile, her husband was going strong. "Is that what my tax dollars go for? So you can come up with some wild-ass asinine theory that Regan killed her own best friend? Jesus!"

"Mr. Mortenson," Catherine said, "it's best you just comply."

He stepped forward, and Regan slipped out from his shielding grasp. "It's not enough she's lost her best friend . . . now you have to go and say she killed her? Shit!"

"Mr. Mortenson . . . ," Brass began.

But the husband was off and away on his rant. "This is how you treated Alex, isn't it? He cooperates, and then you accuse him! You put him through this same shit, I heard all about it. What, are you just going door to door, accusing people? Maybe it's a conspiracy! Maybe we all did it!"

Finally Mortenson paused to take a breath—Brass had decided to let him blow off some steam—but now the homicide captain waded in.

"Sir," Brass said, "let me explain why your wife is our primary suspect."

"Please! Enlighten me!"

"A blonde hair was found inside the freezer where Missy's body was hidden away; it matched a blonde hair we got from Missy's Lexus."

Mortenson's mouth was open, but no words came out; and confusion tightened his eyes.

Brass continued: "We also believe that fingerprints from the freezer and the SUV will match your wife's."

Mortenson turned to his wife. "You don't know anything about this, do you, baby? . . . They're fuckin' crazy. Tell them they're fucking crazy, baby."

She stared at him. He slipped his big arm around her again, drew her to him. "This'll go away, baby. We'll make it go away. This is just circumstantial bullshit they're misinterpreting. Don't you worry one little—"

"Let me go!" She wrenched away from him. Then she looked at Brass, her icy eyes huge, wild. "You have to protect me!"

Her husband winced, as if he were trying to see her through a haze. "Baby . . . honey?"

She pointed at him, shaking. "I won't lie for him any more! . . . He admitted it, months ago, and I've had to live with it! He did it!"

Mortenson's mouth hung open.

"Don't deny it, Brian. You did it, you know you did it!" She turned pleadingly toward Brass. "You have to believe me. . . . He and Missy were having an affair, and he tried to break it off—"

"What?" Mortenson said, apparently bewildered.

"And when Missy threatened to tell Alex, he killed her! That's his blonde hair!"

Her husband looked like an actor who'd walked into the wrong scene in some strange play. "My . . . ? What . . . ?"

Regan moved from Brass to O'Riley to Catherine, searching their eyes for support, coming up empty.

Finally, standing before Catherine, she said, "You have to protect me—he said if I ever told anybody, he'd kill me, too! Put a plastic bag over my head and suffocate me!"

"Regan," Mortenson said, "what are you saying? What is wrong with you? . . . She's sick, Officers. Something's wrong with her. . . ."

"She's sick, all right," Brass said.

Looking at the pretty blonde, blue eyes to blue eyes, Catherine said, "I'd call your husband's hair more a light brown, Mrs. Mortenson. And, anyway, the hairs we got from Missy's Lexus and the freezer belong to a blonde . . . woman. A long-haired blonde woman."

"No . . . it's not true!" Regan screamed. "He'll kill me if you don't—"

"Regan," Brian Mortenson said. He stared at his wife as though he didn't know whether to embrace her or slap her. This seemed to be moving way too fast for him. Finally he managed, "You're trying to blame me . . . for your friend's death?"

"She can try to blame you," Catherine said, "she can try to blame the Boston Strangler . . . it's not going to help. You see, your wife doesn't think we know about Sharon Pope." Catherine turned toward Regan with a tiny smile. "Lavien Rose?"

Regan's lovely features seemed to wilt. "No . . . I . . ." The woman teetered for a moment, losing her balance, as if the room had begun to spin . . .

. . . and then dropped to the floor.

"Regan!" Mortenson shrieked, and he dove to her side, and held her, tenderly, as if she had not, moments before, tried to fit him in a frame for murder.

Brass knelt. "What's wrong with her? Has she been ill? Does she have a medical problem, a condition?"

"Nothing . . . nothing serious. . . . What have you people done to her? . . . You saw her, she had some kind of mental breakdown. . . ."

Catherine ducked into the first-floor bathroom, then called, "Jim!"

Brass said to O'Riley, "Watch them," and joined Catherine in the bathroom, where she had found the answer on the counter: a small white bottle.

"Ambien," Catherine said, reading the label. "Dosage, ten milligrams. If Regan had a full month's supply, that means three hundred milligrams."

"She killed herself?"

"Maybe. But people've been brought back after taking as much as four hundred milligrams. Ambien's engineered to make it difficult to use for suicide." Catherine tucked the bottle in her slacks pocket, and they rushed back to the hallway.

"Overdose," she said, mostly for O'Riley's benefit, dropping to her knees and pushing the husband out of the way. "Sleeping pills."

"Oh my God," Mortenson moaned. "She has sinus headaches . . . can't sleep."

She was having no trouble sleeping now.

Catherine began CPR. "Let's take her in your car, Jim. Label says it was refilled yesterday, and if she took the whole thing, we don't want to wait for an ambulance—she could be gone."

But Brass was already halfway out the door.

O'Riley and Mortenson carried Regan, racing to the Taurus. Brass cranked the key as the men loaded the blonde in the back with Catherine. Mortenson tried to climb in back with them, but Catherine pushed him away.

"Hey, I'm her damn husband! I'm going with her."

"Ride in front, then!"

"I have a right—"

Catherine snapped, "Do you want to waste time?"

Mortenson climbed in front.

O'Riley gunned his Taurus and pulled up next to Brass. "I'll lead," he said. "That new hospital, St. Rose Dominican, Siena Campus? That's closest."

Before Brass could answer, O'Riley hit the lights and was off. Brass hit his lights and siren as well and tore off after O'Riley.

Mortenson leaned over the passenger seat, his eyes moist and focused on Regan. Catherine kept up with the compressions, but things did not look good. She gave Regan mouth-to-mouth—once, twice, three times. Then she resumed CPR.

The woman's skin was the color of an overcast sky. She was limp and lifeless, and when Catherine checked, Regan's pulse was weak. Though the young woman still took the occasional breath on her own, those seemed to be coming more and more infrequently.

O'Riley served as lead blocker as Brass twisted the Taurus through traffic. He sawed the wheel and turned onto St. Rose Parkway—former Lake Mead Boulevard—and slammed down the gas again.

The Siena Campus, the second St. Rose Dominican facility, was mission-style—like the Sherman and Mortenson homes—white stucco with a red tile roof. O'Riley slid to a stop in front of the emergency room entrance and was out of the car and through the doors before Brass even had his car stopped.

A crew dressed in scrubs came running out with a gurney, and Catherine handed Regan over into their care; they wheeled the woman inside, with Brass, O'Riley, and Brian Mortenson in hot pursuit. Catherine remained behind, sitting in the backseat for several long moments, letting the adrenaline rush subside.

She was quite sure Regan Mortenson had killed Missy Sherman and Sharon Pope—cold-bloodedly, for reasons as yet undetermined.

There could be little doubt that Regan was a sociopathic monster. And yet Catherine had just tried her best to save the woman's life.

If a cop asked her why, she might have said, to make sure that bitch didn't have an easy out, so that a murderer would live to face justice. But Catherine knew it was something else that had driven her. Let the sociopaths take life lightly. She would choose to save a life, if she could.

And if Regan Mortenson lived today, to die via lethal injection tomorrow, that would be another's judgment, not Catherine's.

She went inside to join her colleagues.

Better than an hour went by before a young doctor came out to tell Catherine and Mortenson that "it had been touch and go," but Regan would be fine. While the woman was still unconscious, Catherine got her DNA swab and she already had Regan's fingerprints on the Ambien bottle.

Catherine Willows went home to spend some of what remained of her Sunday with her daughter, and to sleep a few hours, before going in to CSI HQ to process her new evidence. And toward the end of shift, not long before sunup, Catherine found herself back at the hospital with Brass, Nick, and Warrick.

They stood at the foot of the bed where Regan Mortenson lay like a tiny broken doll; tubes ran in and out of her, and she looked frail, and had as yet said nothing. But she was not in a coma. The doctor assured them of that.

Brian Mortenson stood next to his wife, two hands holding her limp one. No explaining love, Catherine thought. This woman had killed two people, tried to frame her husband for the crimes, and still, several times he had mentioned that he was convinced his wife was suffering from a mental condition; that these things, if she did them, Regan could only have done if she were not in her right mind.

Brass said, "Mr. Mortenson, we've matched Regan's fingerprints to the freezer and Missy's Lexus. Her DNA was inside the freezer, in the car and on Missy's clothes."

"No way," Mortenson said.

The detective shrugged. "Believe what you like, but the facts tell us your wife killed her best friend."

"It's a lie," Regan said.

Her voice was small and cold. Her eyes, finally open, were big and cold.

Her husband beamed at her. "Baby . . . darling . . . you're going to be fine."

"Welcome back to the world, Mrs. Mortenson," Brass said, and read her her rights.

Regan stared at the ceiling, the icy blues unreadable; her husband, grasping her hand, might well have not been there, for all she seemed to care.

"Do you understand these rights, Mrs. Mortenson?"

"I understand."

"Would you like to tell us anything?"

She turned toward Brass. "I'd like you to tell me something, Detective."

"What?"

"When are visiting hours over?"

"Why did you do all this, Regan? Why did you kill a woman who was supposedly your best friend?"

"Is that Old Spice, Captain Brass? Tell me you don't wear Old Spice."

"Why Sharon Pope?"

"Have you ever seen a performance artist?"

"Why did you freeze Missy Sherman's body?"

"How do you like my responses so far?"

Brass looked toward Catherine, who shrugged. Mortenson, at his wife's side, continued to hold her hand; but he was looking at her oddly now, as if this were a person he'd never seen before, as if perhaps his wife had been replaced in the night by a pod person.

"Brian!"

Everyone looked at the man who'd just appeared in the doorway: Alex Sherman.

The late Missy Sherman's husband—unshaven, in slept-in-looking dark-green sweater and brown slacks—looked distraught. "Brian, I got here as soon as I could." He went to his friend, seated at Regan's bedside, and put a consoling hand on the man's shoulder.

"Thanks," Mortenson managed, but didn't look at his friend.

Regan, however, was staring at Alex Sherman. "You . . . you came."

"Of course I came," he said, and smiled, reassuringly. "Worried about you two."

Catherine went to Sherman and drew him away from Mortenson. She whispered harshly, "What in the hell are you doing here?"

Confused, perhaps even a little hurt by her question, Sherman said, "Well . . . Brian called and told me that Regan had overdosed on sleeping pills. . . . So of course I came right away."

Catherine's eyes flicked to Mortenson, then back to Sherman. "Well, that's sweet all around. . . . Did Brian tell you why Regan took those pills?"

"No . . . It's not like her—she's always so 'up.' I didn't even know she was depressed. What is going on?"

Catherine arched an eyebrow and gave it to him straight. "Regan OD'd because she knew we had evidence proving she killed your wife . . . as well as that woman, the performance artist—Sharon Pope?"

Sherman looked as if the switch on his brain had been shut off—nothing was processing, eyes open, mouth open, but no movement. Finally, the gears started to work again, and he looked toward Regan, searchingly, then accusingly . . . and she looked away.

"She did this?" Sherman asked. "Really did this?"

Catherine said, "We have her cold."

"But . . . why?" Sherman asked.

"She won't tell us."

"I'll tell you," a voice said.

Regan's voice.

Her eyes were on Alex Sherman.

"I didn't do it for myself," she said. "I did it for you . . . Alex."

Dumbfound, Sherman staggered to the bedside opposite the seated husband, who wore a similarly poleaxed expression. With the tension in the air, Warrick moved into position, nearby.

Sherman said, "What . . . what do you mean . . . ? For . . . you killed Missy for . . ."

"You. That's how much I care."

"You care? About me?"

Regan shook her head and looked lovingly up at him. "She wasn't good enough for you, Alex. She was never good enough for you. Not smart enough, not funny enough, not sexy enough, not pretty enough.

Don't you know who you should have been with, all along? . . . Me, of course. Because I love you, Alex—I've always loved you."

Brian Mortenson dropped his wife's hand.

Regan glanced at him. The loving expression she'd shown Sherman fell away. And she laughed.

Her husband's face reddened and he drew back a big fist.

Brass shouted, "No!"

Warrick threw himself over the woman as Mortenson's fist arced down, but at the last moment, the big man caught himself, punch glancing off Warrick's shoulder as Nick sprang around and grabbed Mortenson from behind, in weight-lifter's arms. The big man struggled for only a second, then settled down—all the air, all the fight, all the life, out of him—as Nick dragged him out of the room. Regan's husband didn't start crying till he got out in the hall, but it echoed in.

Regan was still laughing, lightly, but laughing.

Warrick pushed up off Regan, and she looked and blew him a kiss. "My hero."

Warrick twisted away from her and stood, appalled. "Been at this a long time, lady . . . and you win the prize."

Brass asked Warrick, "You all right, Brown?"

The CSI nodded, glared at the woman and walked out of the room, to join Nick and Mortenson in the hall.

Sherman staggered around into the chair Regan's husband had vacated. He didn't seem angry, exactly; more stunned, confused, just trying to understand.

"For me?" Sherman said. "You did this for me? But you knew I loved Missy. There was never a damn thing between us, Regan!"

"But there could have been, and there should have been." Regan shook her head again, her eyes wild. "You stupid, sad son of a bitch! I am the great missed opportunity of your life! Why do you think I came to Vegas—to be near my 'friend'? Missy was all right. But nothing special. I came out to Vegas to be near you. To be where you were. I wanted to be with you."

"But . . . Brian?"

A tiny shrug from a tiny woman. "To make ends meet . . . till you came to your senses."

Catherine knew she would never forget the look of horror on Alex's face. But he did not cry. Something inside of him kept him alert—he'd said he wanted to help them find his wife's killer.

And now he helped.

"Why did you hide her body away like that?" he asked.

Catherine glanced at Brass; they both knew the man would have liked to either strangle the woman, or run from the room in tears. But Sherman had the presence of mind to keep her talking.

"I kept the body as a sort of . . . back-up. A prop."

"A . . . prop?"

"I thought when Missy 'ran off,' you'd finally see, Alex . . . see that I was the one who really cared about you. And wasn't I there for you?"

"Oh yes," he said. "You came over all the time."

"Yes—trying to help you get past this . . . terrible tragedy . . . but you're such an idiot. All those times, me sitting next to you, alone in that house, you could have had me. . . . Instead, you just went softer and softer over that dumb dead little bitch. For a year I throw myself at you, and all I hear is Missy, Missy, Missy . . . and that's why it was so smart of me to hold onto her body.

"You see, I anticipated that you might need closure . . . that the disappearance might not be enough. That you might be holding out hope, longing for the missing Missy."

"Closure . . ."

"I had hoped that her disappearance would make you think she'd left you—that you'd fall into my arms, desolate, needing the solace only someone who really loved you could provide . . . but no. You needed further convincing. So Missy had to come out of cold storage."

Alex Sherman stood. He looked down at the beautiful young woman, who smiled up at him, adoringly, with ice-blue eyes that to Catherine, frighteningly, did not appear at all crazed.

Regan said, "Do you see now, Alex? Do you see who has really loved you, all these years?"

Alex nodded. He walked slowly to the door, paused, and looked back—not at Regan, but at Brass.

"It's lethal injection in this state, isn't it?" he asked.

"Yes," Brass said. "And family members of victims can attend."

Again Alex nodded. ". . . See you later, Regan."

He slipped out.

She frowned, staring at the empty space where he'd been.

Now that Regan was talking, Brass tossed in his own question. "Where does Sharon Pope fit in?"

She brought those cold eyes around and they landed on Brass like a pair of bugs. "Are you still here?"

Catherine stepped up beside Brass. "Figuring the Pope woman's part, Jim . . . it's not that hard."

A starving performance artist hits up the new Arts council fundraiser, and offers to make kickbacks, if grants come her way. Regan now knows that Sharon can be bought, can be used, and when she needs someone to rent an apartment for her, Regan finds the starving artist is the perfect front.

But when Missy Sherman's body brings the case back to life, Sharon becomes a loose end. Possibly "Lavien Rose" discovered what that apartment she's been renting has been used for—and has begun blackmailing the patron of the Las Vegas Arts, who in turn embezzles to pay off the performance artist . . . deciding, finally, to tie off the loose end as well as stop the extortion, all with one plastic bag over one spiky-haired head. . . .

"By the end of our next shift, Jim," Catherine assured the cop, "Warrick'll have matched the tracks from Charleston Boulevard with the casts from Lake Mead."

A jury might see the evidence as circumstantial, but they had a mountain of it. The actual murder weapons—two cinch-top plastic bags—were long gone; but the CSIs had everything else—the tire tracks, the fingerprints, the DNA, the motive, and now Regan's own lovestruck confession.

Back at HQ, with the shift winding down, Catherine sat in the break room with Nick. She'd had only occasional sleep over the past forty-eight hours, and there wasn't much left to do now except go home, get some rest, and come back tonight to start over.

Monday nights were sometimes slow, or as slow as Vegas ever got; so she hoped next shift she'd be able to take it easy. She gulped the last of her coffee and pushed her chair back, but before she could rise, Sara Sidle straggled in, also looking less than fresh.

"Didn't you used to work here?" Nick said, leaning back on two legs of his chair.

Before Sara could reply, Catherine tossed in her own question. "You're not due in till next shift—miss us that much?"

Sara staggered over to the counter where a mixture suspected to be coffee awaited. "Wanted to get rid of the equipment we took, so we didn't have to drag it all home and back again, tonight."

"So?" Nick said. "Give!"

"Yeah," Catherine said. "How was the vacation with pay?"

"Don't ask," Sara sighed, pouring herself a cup of coffee and dropping into a chair. "Murder and a suicide."

Nick looked skeptical. "You mean, one of the workshops was on murder, and another was on suicide."

"No," she said, "I mean, we were snowbound, no cops, and had a murder and a suicide to work."

Sara's story seemed to reenergize Catherine, who sat up. "That phone call—when we got cut off, that was about a homicide, there?"

Sara nodded, smirked humorlessly, and in a monotone rattled off the following: "In the woods behind the hotel. Waitress killed a waiter for having a gay affair. Then waiter number two, who was having the affair with waiter number one, killed himself, and it looked like the waitress had done him, too. Only it came up suicide. A Canadian CSI helped us—eh?"

Grissom stuck his head in the door. "I see the place didn't burn down while I was gone."

Catherine simply nodded. "Sheer boredom without you."

Grissom—leaning against the jamb—nodded back, as if that sounded like the most reasonable response.

"So, Gris," Nick said, grinning his boyish grin, "did you teach the yokels all about big-city high-tech crime scene investigation in the twenty-first century?"

Grissom lifted his eyebrows. "More like nineteenth century. Right, Sara?"

With a weary smile, she revealed, "Grissom is an Ulster County Deputy Sheriff now."

Their boss smirked. "And for that singular honor, I get to go back to New York, one of these days, and testify at the trial of a woman who you would not wish on your worst enemy."

"I know the kind," Catherine said.

"Did they give you a bullet to keep in your breast pocket, Deputy?" Nick asked.

Grissom frowned. "Is that a movie reference? Books, Nick. Stick with books."

Their supervisor gave them a little grin, then was gone.

"So the trip turned into one big crime scene?" Catherine asked. Struggling to keep the glee out of her voice, she added, "That's just terrible."

Sara shrugged and rose. "Most of it was pretty hard, actually. Snowed in for two days. Froze our butts off guarding, then working the crime scene, had gallons of blood at the suicide, had to find the killer and watch her till the local cops showed, and then catch a redeye to get back, so we could be home to work tonight."

Catherine said, "Tough," but couldn't repress the smile any longer. And Nick, arms folded, rocking back, was grinning openly.

Sara paused at the door. "Last day—Sunday? That was nice and cozy, though. We spent the day reading by the fire."

She slipped out, leaving behind two co-workers who were looking at each other with wide eyes and open mouths.

"No," Catherine said.

"No way," Nick said.

In the hallway, Sara was smiling to herself. Nick and Cath didn't know that she and Grissom had separate fireplaces in their separate rooms.

And they didn't need to know.

Let them wonder.

AUTHOR'S NOTE

I would like to acknowledge the contribution of Matthew V. Clemens.

Matt—who has collaborated with me on numerous published short stories—is an accomplished true-crime writer, as well as a knowledgeable fan of CSI. He helped me develop the plots of these novels, and worked up lengthy story treatments, which included all of his considerable forensic research, for me to expand my novels upon.

Criminalist Sergeant Chris Kaufman CLPE—the Gil Grissom of the Bettendorf Iowa Police Department—provided comments, insights and information that were invaluable to this project, including material from his own book on winter crime scenes. Thank you also to Jaimie Vitek of the Mississippi Valley Regional Blood Center for sharing her expertise.

Books consulted include two works by Vernon J. Gerberth: *Practical Homicide Investigation Checklist and Field Guide* (1997) and *Practical Homicide Investigation: Tactics, Procedures and Forensic Investigation* (1996). Also helpful was *Scene of the Crime: A Writer's Guide to Crime-Scene Investigations* (1992), Anne Wingate, Ph.D. Any inaccuracies, however, are my own.

Jessica McGivney at Pocket Books provided support, suggestions and guidance. The producers of CSI were gracious in providing scripts, background material and episode tapes, without which this novel would have been impossible.

Finally, the inventive Anthony E. Zuiker must be singled out as creator of this concept and these characters. Thank you to him and other CSI writers, whose lively and well-documented scripts inspired these novels and have done much toward making the series such a success both commercially and artistically.

ABOUT THE AUTHOR

MAX ALLAN COLLINS, a Mystery Writers of America Edgar Award nominee in both fiction and non-fiction categories, was hailed in 2004 by *Publishers Weekly* as "a new breed of writer." He has earned an unprecedented fifteen Private Eye Writers of America Shamus nominations for his historical thrillers, winning twice for his Nathan Heller novels *True Detective* (1983) and *Stolen Away* (1991).

His other credits include film criticism, short fiction, songwriting, trading-card sets, and movie/TV tie-in novels, including *Air Force One*, *In the Line of Fire*, and the *New York Times* bestseller *Saving Private Ryan*.

His graphic novel *Road to Perdition* is the basis of the Academy Award–winning DreamWorks 2002 feature film starring Tom Hanks, Paul Newman, and Jude Law, directed by Sam Mendes. His many comics credits include the *Dick Tracy* syndicated strip; his own *Ms. Tree*; *Batman*; and *CSI: Crime Scene Investigation*, based on the hit TV series for which he has also written video games, jigsaw puzzles, and a *USA Today* bestselling series of novels.

An independent filmmaker in his native Iowa, he wrote and directed *Mommy*, which premiered on Lifetime in 1996, as well as a 1997 sequel, *Mommy's Day*. The screenwriter of *The Expert*, a 1995 HBO world premiere, he also wrote and directed the innovative made-for-DVD feature *Real Time: Siege at Lucas Street Market* (2000). *Shades of Noir* (2004)—an anthology of his short films, including his award-winning documentary *Mike Hammer's Mickey Spillane*—is included in the recent DVD boxed set of Collins's indie films, *The Black Box*. He recently completed a documentary, *Caveman: V.T. Hamlin and Alley Oop*, and another feature, *Eliot Ness: An Untouchable Life*, based on his Edgar-nominated play.

Collins lives in Muscatine, Iowa, with his wife, writer Barbara Collins; their son, Nathan, is a recent graduate in computer science and Japanese at the University of Iowa and is currently pursuing post-grad studies in Japan.